The
DIVINE
COMEDY

The DIVINE COMEDY

of DANTE ALIGHIERI

THE CARLYLE-OKEY-WICKSTEED TRANSLATION

Introduction by the late C. H. GRANDGENT
Professor of Romance Languages, Harvard University

Bibliography by ERNEST H. WILKINS
President Emeritus, Oberlin College

VINTAGE BOOKS

A DIVISION OF RANDOM HOUSE

New York

VINTAGE BOOKS
are published by ALFRED A. KNOPF, INC.
and RANDOM HOUSE, INC.
Manufactured in the United States of America
50 49 48 47

CONTENTS

Introduction

By C. H. GRANDGENT

"THE COMEDY OF DANTE ALIGHIERI, a Florentine by birth but not in character" was the title given by the author to his work, if we are to believe the letter to Can Grande della Scala, written presumably by Dante and sent to his famous patron with the first canto of the *Commedia*. The epithet "divine" was not attached to it until centuries later, and was used to express the feeling of the reading public for Italy's great masterpiece. From its first appearance it was a "divine" poem, and so it has remained even to our day—"divine" for its sacred subject, for its wisdom, for its power, for its superhuman beauty. But what shall we make of the phrase "Comedy of Dante Alighieri"? Does it indicate Dante merely as the author, or does it designate him as the subject, the protagonist of the poem? It might mean either, with regard to language or to fact; and it probably means both; for Dante surely wrote the *Comedy*, and wrote it about himself. And the work is a "comedy," as the aforesaid letter states, because it begins in disaster and ends in happiness; if the first *cantica* is named "Hell," the third and last is entitled "Paradise." Furthermore, it is written, not in the sustained loftiness of tragedy, but in the middle style which lies between the highest and the lowest. It is, in fact, composed in the author's native Florentine, in which, as he says, "even females communicate." Elevated in many parts by exalted thought and abundance of Latinisms, it sinks at times into the plain vernacular. It must be remembered that the terms "tragedy" and "comedy" had in the Middle Ages no necessarily theatrical associations: the former meant the story of the downfall of a great personage; the latter is the narrative of a happy escape from misery.

"Florentine by birth" Dante certainly was. The Alighieri had for generations dwelt in the city by the Arno, people of some importance but not rich. Dante was born there in 1265, probably in the latter part of May. He associated with the best society, and was in early boyhood affianced to a daughter of the aristocratic Donati clan, whom he eventually married. His schooling must have been as good as could then be had; he was fond of music, addicted to art, and participated in the sports of gentility. While still very young, he took part in two military campaigns. We find him mixing in municipal politics by the time he was thirty and in the summer of 1300 he was for two months a member of the council of six which had the highest administrative authority.

But to the epithet "Florentine by birth" Dante adds the bitter modifier "not in character." In a passage of the *Inferno* the inhabitants of the Arno Valley are compared to various beasts: in the upper Casentino they are "pigs"; in Arezzo, "curs"; in Pisa, "foxes"; in Florence, "wolves." Not wolflike, as his countrymen are, Dante declares himself in his dedication. In a notable phrase of the *Paradiso* he calls himself a "lamb" whom wolves attack. A victim, then, an innocent victim, of wolflike fierceness and rapacity: such was the author of our poem. His repudiation of Florence, and the hatred upon which it is based, can hardly be a result of his closer personal relations. We know really nothing of his matrimonial experience; but his references to children and to family life, rather numerous in the *Comedy*, are singularly sweet and tender. Although he was reputed haughty, he seems to have been on good terms with his neighbors. The rich, talented, and proud Guido Cavalcanti he calls his "first friend." His early poetic efforts were evidently well appreciated. He was appointed ambassador, for an important mission, to the neighboring hill-town of San Gimignano, the city of towers, whose proudest possession today is the town hall, where Dante once appeared to present his case (successfully) before the council; the hall being now restored to its 13th century aspect, so that one can almost imagine Dante standing there.

His subsequent experience, however, was not so happy. Political strife, the bane of Italian city life, embittered his career, cut short his activity, made him an exile, a wanderer, a dependent. The more than nation-wide quarrel of Guelfs and Ghibellines did not rage long in Florence, where the Guelf party, defeated by the Sienese and the Ghibelline exiles in 1260, five years before Dante's birth, at Montaperti, was victorious six years later at Benevento, and Florence was thenceforth a Guelf city. Theoretically, the Guelfs were Pope's men, the Ghibellines Emperor's men; but cities adopted one side or the other according to their own immediate advantage, and individuals followed the party of their family, with little more discrimination in principle than exists here between the Republicans and Democrats. The Alighieri were Guelfs, although for some reason Dante's father was not banished during the Ghibelline supremacy of 1260-66. A new cause of strife soon arose in the unified Guelf community. Florence had under her control the city of Pistoia, which came to be rent by a bloody feud between two branches of the Cancellieri clan; and, to break up the enmity, Florence took out of the rent town the leaders of both branches and made them dwell in her own midst. The result of this well-meant action was a division in the new home, where the leading families took sides with the two branches of the Cancellieri, who had come to be known as Blacks and Whites. Although the grounds of partisanship are confused, one may say, in general, that the Black party in Florence came to represent the old feudal aristocracy, largely of Germanic origin, while the Whites stood for the industrial and new-rich class. Doubtless the principal cause of antagonism was social rivalry. The Blacks, who, in their pride, were relatively poor, drew closer and closer to the Pope, hoping to be restored to their ancient leadership; the Whites, on the other hand, cultivated a spirit of municipal independence.

The Pope, Boniface VIII, had a certain ancient claim on Tuscany, and wished to bring it under his power. He made on Florence certain demands, which the Whites rejected; we hear that Dante took part in the objection. Finally, on a May Day, open hostility broke out between the two social parties in the city, and blood was shed. It was in that summer that Dante, in accordance with the custom of rotation in office, was elected one of the six Priors. This council opposed the claims of the Pope and, to stop the scandal in the city, voted to banish the leaders of both the Blacks and the Whites.

Dante's one desire was to keep the peace. His sympathies must have been divided. The Donati family, to which he had become allied, was foremost among the Blacks, while Guido Cavalcanti, his "first friend," was prominent among the Whites and was among those sentenced to banishment. Furthermore, Dante was a strong supporter of independence for Florence; he was naturally inclined to aristocracy; but he belonged to a Guelf family and had much in common with the Whites. With one or two others, he was sent to Boniface, to attempt a reconciliation. During his absence, the Pope induced Florence to accept a "mediator," no other than that royal adventurer, Charles of Valois, brother of Philip IV, King of France. No sooner were the gates opened to him and his troops, than he turned over the city to the Blacks, who set up a Black government and proceeded to persecute their former opponents. Against many of these, including the absent Dante, suits were brought, charging malfeasance in office and various specific offenses; and they were summoned to appear for trial. Knowing what the outcome would be, they refused to go, and Dante was condemned in contumacy. His property was confiscated, and he was condemned to death by fire if he ever should be caught in Florentine territory. That was in 1302. From that time on, he never saw his city. His family—his wife and four children—remained behind; but he became a wanderer, lonely and poor. For a while he consorted with his fellow-exiles, Guelf and Ghibelline, who were straining every effort to regain admission. In a couple of years he fell out with them, and stood alone. At some time—we do not know exactly when—he inhabited the great university town of Bologna. Verona, under the rule of the della Scala family, was an early refuge. Henceforth his doings are little known to us. He was with the Malaspina house in Lunigiana, in northwestern Italy, in 1306. We hear of him in the Casentino, in Padua, in Lucca, but we have no details. His last years he spent in Ravenna with Guido Novello da Polenta, a nephew of the Francesca da Rimini he had immortalized. There he was joined by his two sons, Pietro and Jacopo, and by a daughter; his wife remained in Florence. He died in 1321, on September 14.

One great hope and great excitement Dante experienced during his exile. He had adopted the idea (rather Ghibelline than Guelf) that the Emperor should be independent of the Pope, the two being coördinate powers, both ordained by God and both answerable only to Him. The evil condition of the world is due mainly to neglect of Italy by the Emperors and the usurpation of Imperial authority by the Popes. Now, when Henry of Luxembourg, an idealistic reformer, holding these same views, was elected Emperor with the title of Henry VII, and descended into Italy to restore the balance, establish justice, and win over the rebellious cities, Dante's spirits rose to a high pitch of exaltation shown in several letters he wrote at that period. One was a letter of bitter rebuke to the Florentines, who stubbornly resisted Henry VII. At some time of his life, Dante wrote a Latin treatise, *Monarchia*, in which he clearly exposed his political views Unsuccessful in his enterprise, Henry died in 1313, thus apparently quenching all expectation of reformation and of Dante's restoration. Crushing as this failure must have been, Dante did not lose courage. In God's own time and in God's own way, justice must eventually be restored; that serene belief permeates the *Paradiso*.

It is easy to understand, however, that Dante cherished his indignation against his fellow-townsmen. A modest hope he had had, almost to the end: that the glory of his great poem might induce them to restore and honor him. But their recognition came too late. Wolves they were and wolves they remained, until his death.

Quickly, however, the masterpiece imposed itself. Boccaccio was invited to expound it publicly to the Florentines, and the city vainly implored Ravenna for the transfer of his remains to his home. The *Commedia* was, and has always remained, the world's great poem of sin, reparation, redemption, and beatitude. It is in the form of an autobiographical narrative. The poet comes to himself, in the midst of a dark, wild wood, on the night before Good

Friday, 1300. Beyond the trees he catches sight of a mountain whose summit is already gilded by the rising sun. This height he determines to scale; but when the ascent is scarcely begun, his way is barred by three beasts, who, one after another, come to block his way: a leopard, a lion, a wolf. Reduced to despair by the persistence of the last, he is about to turn back, when a mysterious figure comes to his rescue. This turns out to be the ghost of Virgil, the great sage of antiquity, who has been sent to help him by three heavenly ladies,—the Blessed Virgin, St. Lucia, and a certain Beatrice whom Dante has loved and celebrated in her lifetime. She was probably Beatrice Portinari, married to a banker, Simone de' Bardi. For her Dante had written many beautiful lyrics and a little autobiographical work, in verse and prose, the *Vita Nuova*, which had won him renown. A later and much bigger book, autobiographical and philosophical, the *Convivio* or *Banquet*, in prose with bits of verse, the author had never finished. Neither had he carried to completion a great Latin treatise on versification, *De Vulgari Eloquentia*, or *On Vernacular Composition*, which contains an interesting preliminary discussion of dialects and their possible use in literature. Even before the *Comedy*, then, Dante was a man of note, and in some way a disciple of Virgil.

His ghostly rescuer explains to him that he cannot escape by climbing the mountain; his only way lies through the earth, from side to side, traversing the whole of Hell, after which he is to ascend the mountain of Purgatory, which lies in the middle of the great ocean, on the side of the earth just opposite Jerusalem. Thence he is to be lifted up to Heaven. Under the wise Virgil's guidance, after some trepidation Dante starts on his fearful journey, which takes him through all the punishments of the damned. These pains are distributed over the nine circles of the inverted cone of Hell, eight of them on circular shelves which surround the pit; the ninth, on the bottom of the pit itself, at the center of the earth. Each penalty is appropriate to its sin, and all are grouped according to a philosophical plan. The nine circles fall into three great groups: first, the sins of "incontinence," or lack of self-control;

second, the sins of violence, or beastliness; third, the sins of malice, or fraud. Guardians or tormentors, in the various regions, are the demons, or fallen angels, some of them taken out of classical mythology. At the center of all is Satan, imbedded in a round plain of ice—a three-faced, six-winged, hideous monster, whose three mouths are crunching the three arch-traitors. After inspecting the various inmates of Hell, and conversing with some of them, Dante is carried by Virgil down the shaggy side of Satan into a cavern beyond the earth's center; after which the two travelers climb in some fashion out to the other side, where they emerge, on the early morning of Easter Sunday, on the shore of the island, which contains the huge mountain of Purgatory. The upper part of its conical surface is cut into seven terraces, where repentant souls are doing penance, or discipline, for the seven cardinal vices from which all sins spring. Below the terraces, on the lower slopes, are held those who, on account of some negligence or insubordination, are not yet admitted to the disciplines which they are eager to begin. At the very top of the mountain is the Garden of Eden, with its woods, birds, flowers, and streams. There Dante, having accomplished his ascent still under tutorship of his guide, is met by an imposing procession—a pageant of the Church, or Triumph of Revelation, the central figure of which is the same Beatrice who has come to his rescue before. She it is who leads Dante up through the revolving heavens of the Ptolemaic skies into the real, eternally motionless heaven of God, the angels, and the blest. On the way up, he has encountered, in appropriate skies, the variously happy souls of the elect. The climax of all is the vision of God himself.

As may be readily guessed, the whole story is an allegory, representing "mankind, as, by its merits or demerits, it exposes itself to the rewards or the punishments of Justice." One might have guessed it, even if the allegorical intention and its purport had not been expressly stated in the letter to Can Grande. The punishments in Hell represent the sinful life on earth, each penalty being a symbol of the sin itself. The pains in Purgatory stand for the disciplines undergone by the penitent sinner, on his way to reformation and salvation. The heavens with their inhabitants are the life of contemplation and righteousness. The narrative shows the progress from sin (the dark wood), the vain attempt to escape by mere human effort, barred by the opposition of wicked habits (portrayed in the three beasts). The long climb from the center to the island is the laborious and uneventful process of breaking away from sinfulness; the ascent of the mountain shows the disciplines needed to rid the soul of all evil inclinations, every one of the sufferings representing a cure of one of the capital vices. The Garden of Eden is the state of innocence, regained by the faithful. "Blessed are the pure in heart, for they shall see God." The sundry types of virtue appear in the several heavens. The final vision is the consummation of the pure heart's desire. Virgil, the guide through the first two stages, is human reason, which reveals the true nature of sin, in all its hideousness and folly and hatefulness, and shows also the real meaning of reformation. Matilda, the lovely guardian of Eden, is the perfect life of innocent activity. Beatrice, or Revelation, makes clear the truth. St. Bernard, who takes her place when the presence of God is reached, is intuition, higher than reason, higher even than revelation. Each of these characters is a real person, called from his or her immortal seat to perform an appropriate function; the poet himself is in his symbolic experiences the real Dante, representative of mankind but at the same time a distinct individual personality.

Such symbolic representation is not an arbitrary and artificial device; it is a part of the medieval conception of life and the world. For, to the Middle Ages, all things, without ceasing to be literal realities, are symbols of other things. The qualities of stones and beasts have a moral meaning, intended by their Creator. The events of history, likewise, in addition to their actual happening, serve as prophecies of things to come. Virgil, the great poet and sage of antiquity, is, to his understanding disciple, an inspirer of wisdom. Beatrice, from her first appearance to Dante at the age of eight, in the home city, had always impressed him as a revelation of the heavenly on earth. So she appears even in the youthful *Vita Nuova*. The two significances, literal and allegorical, are so perfectly adjusted that the one seems a necessary and inevitable complement of the other. A modern reader, uninformed, could peruse the whole *Commedia*, satisfied with the mere literal story, and entranced by its unparalled beauty of language and imagery; but he would miss the inspiration of that higher message which so clearly merits the name of "divine."

Perhaps no other work of pure literature has aroused so much admiration in so many countries and so many readers as *The Divine Comedy*. And it is quite likely that the majority of all these readers—at least, of those foreign to Italy—have derived their enjoyment and admiration from translations. In a version in another tongue one of course misses the magic of Dante's verse; but one may find, if the work is well done, Dante's thought, his emotion, and his imagery. This consideration has moved the publishers of [Vintage Books] to make easily available an English version of the poem.

After careful consideration of all the English translations of Dante, the work of John Aitken Carlyle, Thomas Okey, and P. H. Wicksteed was chosen. It is a translation that is clear, dignified, and accurate, in simple, idiomatic prose. It can be readily followed without any reference to the original Italian text. Its scholarly notes cover all obscure points more than adequately.

This [Vintage] edition of *The Divine Comedy* is destined to reveal the full scope of Dante's work to thousands of readers who are ignorant of Italian.

Bibliography

J. S. Carroll, *Exiles of eternity: an exposition of Dante's Inferno*, 2d ed., 1904; *Prisoners of hope: an exposition of Dante's Purgatorio*, 1906; and *In patria: an exposition of Dante's Paradiso*, 1911: all London, Hodder and Stoughton.

C. A. Dinsmore, *The teachings of Dante*, 1902; and *Aids to the study of Dante*, 1903: both Boston and New York, Houghton Mifflin.

E. G. Gardner, *Dante*, New York, Dutton, 1923; and *Dante's ten heavens*, 2d ed., London, Constable, 1904.

Etienne Gilson, *Dante the philosopher*, trans. from the French by David Moore, New York, Sheed & Ward, 1949.

C. H. Grandgent, *Dante*, New York, Duffield, 1921; *The power of Dante*, Boston, Jones, 1918; and *Discourses on Dante*, Cambridge, Harvard University Press, 1924.

H. D. Sedgwick, *Italy in the thirteenth century*, 2 vols., Boston and New York, Houghton Mifflin, 1912.

H. O. Taylor, *The mediaeval mind*, 2 vols., 4th ed., Cambridge, Harvard University Press, 1949.

Paget Toynbee, *Dante in English literature from Chaucer to Cary*, 2 vols., New York, Macmillan, 1919; *Dante Alighieri: his life and works*, 4th ed., London, Methuen, 1910; and *Concise dictionary of proper names and other notable matters in the works of Dante*, Oxford, Clarendon Press, 1914.

Karl Vossler, *Mediaeval culture*, trans. from the German by W. C. Lawton, 2 vols., New York, Harcourt, Brace and Co., 1929.

E.H.W

Publisher's Note

For this Modern Library edition of Dante's Divine Comedy the best translations have been followed: Inferno, *by John Aitken Carlyle*; Purgatorio, *by Thomas Okey*; Paradiso, *by Philip H. Wicksteed. The Notes (edited for this edition by Julie Eidesheim) follow, in the main, the excellent notes for the* Inferno *and the* Purgatorio *by Dr. H. Oelsner, and those prepared jointly by Dr. Oelsner and Philip H. Wicksteed for the* Paradiso.

THE TRANSLATORS have attempted to satisfy them-selves first as to the author's exact meaning, and then to express it (1) precisely, (2) with lucidity, (3) worthily, (4) with as close adherence to the vocabulary and syntax of the original as English idiom allows. They have con-sciously adopted a happy turn of expression in one passage from Mr. Norton's translation of the *Paradiso*, and in two cases borrowed words from Mr. Butler. The many other coincidences with these (and doubtless other) translations arose, to the best of their belief, independently.

The skill of a translator is shown in his power of so pur-suing any one of the objects he has in view as to make it at the same time advance, or at any rate not obstruct the others; but wherever he fails in this, his principles of trans-lation will declare themselves in the conscious or uncon-scious scale of equivalence whereby he adjusts their rival claims. What gain in one direction will he consider the equivalent of a given loss in another? Such a scale cannot be drawn out in words, and therefore no translator can accurately define his own principles of translation; but the order in which the objects aimed at have been enumerated above will indicate the translator's general conception of his task.

That translator of Dante, and particularly of the *Para-diso*, is not to be envied who can issue his work without a grieved sense of something near akin to profanation, in that he has striven, counter to Dante's own protest (see *Conu*

i. 7), to "expound the sense of his poems where they themselves cannot take it together with their beauty"; and, moreover, in the *Paradiso*, if anywhere, the beauty is itself at once an integral and an untransferable part of the sense. The translators' hope is that all who read the translation may find their eye turning from time to time to Dante's words, till they are insensibly taught to understand and love them; and that, in the great majority of cases, the work from the first may be taken only as a help to the understanding of Dante's words, not as a substitute for them.

The Arguments have been prepared with special care, in the hope that they may be helpful to the beginner, and of interest to the more advanced student, as an attempt to facilitate the perception of the perspective, the articulation, and the wider significance of the several portions of the poem.

The notes at the end of each Canto are to be taken in close connection with the Arguments, which, when carefully read, will be found to contain, directly or by implication, many explanations that the reader may perhaps have looked for in vain in the notes.

In the notes an effort has been made to give all possible help to the reader unacquainted with the classics, both by marking quantities and by explaining, as far as space allowed, even the more obvious classical allusions, but by no means so uniformly or fully as to supersede the constant use of a classical dictionary.

References are given throughout to the most important illustrative passages from the Bible, but have seldom given the words. We have also assumed that the reader who is desirous of further information has access to all Dante's works, to Gardner's *Dante Primer*, to Wallace's *Outlines of the Philosophy of Aristotle*, and to Selfe and Wicksteed's *Selections from Villani's Chronicle*. In references to other writers, their own words are generally given, merely adding the author's name without more specific reference. The references to Dante's works will be found in Dr. Moore's *Oxford Dante*.

Obligations cannot be acknowledged in detail. They include the generally accessible commentaries and other sources of information. Mr. Paget Toynbee's *Dante Dictionary*[1] has been specially useful. Many dates and some historical and biographical details have been taken direct from it.

Questions of disputed readings have not been dealt with in any systematic or consistent way; and controversial matter and æsthetic points or allegorical refinements, have seldom or never been touched upon but in addition to explaining references, an effort has been made to deal, however concisely, with the more serious difficulties of the thought and teaching of the poem, so as to make the Commentary, within its limits, as complete as possible. But in these weightier matters the reader must, after all, be his own commentator; for, as one of the earliest and best of Dante scholars (Benvenuto da Imola) has remarked: "It is rather great wit than great learning that is needed for the understanding of this book."

[1] *A Dictionary of Proper Names and Notable Matters in the Works of Dante*, by Paget Toynbee, M.A. Oxford.

INFERNO

Inferna tetigit possit ut supera assequi. Seneca.

Note on Dante's Hell

THE ARRANGEMENT of the sins in Dante's Hell has been the subject of protracted and sometimes heated controversy. The reader who wishes to know something of the different views that have been taken, and the arguments brought to their support, may consult Dr. Witte's essay on "The Ethical Systems of the Inferno and the Purgatory," together with the Appendix in the English translation.[1] The present note simply aims at stating the view which seems to the writer the most satisfactory.

All three portions of the poem are built upon the number scheme of 3, 7, 9, 10. The primary division into 3 being raised by subdivision to 7, then by two somewhat unlike additions to 9, and lastly, by a member of a markedly different kind, to 10. This scheme is carried out in all the three Cantiche, though it is not so clearly and symmetrically developed in the *Inferno* as in the other two.

In Dante's Hell the primary division of reprehensible actions into three classes is based upon Aristotle; but some ambiguity is introduced by the adoption in the first instance of a nomenclature for a portion of the subject matter derived from Cicero. The Aristotelian division is into—

I. Incontinence, which includes all wrong action due to the inadequate control of natural appetites or desires.

II. Brutishness, or Bestiality, which is characteristic of morbid states in which what is naturally repulsive becomes attractive; and

III. Malice or Vice, which consists of those evil actions which involve the abuse of the specifically human attribute of reason.

Aristotle distinctly asserts that brutishness is a "different kind of thing" from vice or malice; but owing to a very natural misunderstanding of the Greek text, the Latin translators, followed by the Schoolmen, understood him to say

[1] "Essays on Dante," by Dr. Karl Witte, selected, translated and edited with introduction, notes and appendices by C. Mabel Lawrence, B.A., and Philip H. Wicksteed, M.A.

3

that brutishness was "another kind of malice"; so that to them malice became a generic term including brutish malice and malice proper. Hence, when Cicero declares that all injurious conduct acts either by violence or by fraud, it was easy to identify his "injuriousness" with Aristotle's supposed generic "malice," his violence with Aristotle's brutish "malice," and his fraud with Aristotle's "malice" proper or specific "malice." The primary division then yields—

    I. Incontinence.
    II. Violence or Brutishness.
    III. Fraud or Malice.

By subdivision of the first of these categories into 4, and the last into 2, we obtain the total of 7. Add to these unbelief (heathen and unbaptized) and misbelief (heretics) as standing outside the Aristotelian classification, but demanding a place in Hell as conceived by the medieval Catholic, and we have the nine circles of Hell. Add again the circle outside the river of Acheron, where are the Trimmers, rejected alike by Heaven and Hell, and we then have a tenfold division (9+1) corresponding to those of Purgatory and Paradise. There is, however, a further subdivision peculiar to the Inferno; for the three last circles, 7, 8, 9, are subdivided respectively into 3, 10, and 4 divisions, so that the locally distinct abiding-places of unblest souls mount in all to twenty-four. These divisions are set forth in the appended table.

Trimmers		0	1
	Heathen	1	2
I. Incontinence {	i. carnality	2	3
	ii. gluttony	3	4
	iii. avarice	4	5
	vi. anger	5	6
	Heretics	6	7

II. Violence or brutishness } v. violent 7 {
- i. against neighbour — 8
- ii. " self — 9
- iii. " God — 10

III. Fraud or malice {

vi. simple 3 {
- i. seducers and panders — 11
- ii. flatterers — 12
- iii. simonists — 13
- iv. diviners — 14
- v. peculators — 15
- vi. hypocrites — 16
- vii. thieves — 17
- viii. evil counsellors — 18
- ix. sowers of dissension — 19
- x. forgers — 20

vii. treacherous 9 {
- i. against kin — 21
- ii. " country — 22
- iii. " hospitality — 23
- iv. " lords and benefactors — 24

The Chronology of the "Inferno"

THE CHRONOLOGY of the Divine Comedy has been discussed still more elaborately than the topography and the division of sins; and here again all that this note attempts is to set forth in plain terms the view which approves itself to the writer. References are given to the passages which support the statements made; but there is no attempt to defend the interpretation adopted against other views.

The year of the Vision is 1300; *Inf.* i and xxi; *Purg.* ii; *Par.* ix. The Sun is exactly in the equinoctial point at Spring, the change of his position during the action of the poem being ignored; *Inf.* i; *Par.* x; and less precisely *Par.* i. The night on which Dante loses himself in the forest is the night preceding the anniversary of the death of Christ; *Inf.* xxi. At some period during that night the moon is at the full; *Inf.* xx; and (as will presently appear) a comparison of *Inf.* xx with xxi, together with a reference to *Purg.* ix, indicates that the precise moment of full moon coincided with the sunrise at the end of the night in question. We have then the following data: the Sun is in the equinox; the moon is at the full; and it is the night preceding the anniversary of the crucifixion. There is no day in the year 1300 which meets all these conditions. We are therefore in the presence of an ideal date, combining all the phenomena which we are accustomed to associate with Easter, but not corresponding to any actual day in the calendar. All discussions as to whether we are to call the day that Dante spent in the attempt to climb the mountain March 25 or April 8 (both of which, in the year 1300, were Fridays), are therefore otiose.

The Sun is rising, on Friday morning, when Dante begins his attempt to scale the mountain, *Inf.* i; it is Friday evening when he starts with Virgil on his journey, ii; all the stars which were mounting as the poets entered the gate of Hell, are descending as they pass from the 4th to the 5th circle, vii; that is to say, it is midnight between

6

Friday and Saturday. As they descend from the 6th to the 7th circle the constellation of Pisces (which at the spring equinox immediately precedes the Sun) is on the horizon, xi; that is to say, it is somewhere between 4 and 6 A.M. on the Saturday morning. They are on the centre of the bridge over the 4th chasm of the 8th circle as the moon sets (Jerusalem time), xx. Now according to the rule given by Brunetto Latini, we are to allow fifty-two minutes' retardation for the moon in every twenty-four hours; that is to say, if the moon sets at sunrise one day, she will set fifty-two minutes after sunrise the next. If then (see above) we suppose the moon to have been full at the moment of sunrise on Friday morning, we shall have six o'clock on Friday morning and 6.52 on Saturday morning for moonset. This will give us eight minutes to seven as the moment at which the two poets stood on the middle of the bridge over the 4th chasm. The next eight minutes are crowded; so crowded, indeed, as to constitute a serious difficulty in the system of interpretation here adopted; for the poets are already in conference with the demons on the inner side of chasm 5 by seven o'clock, xxi (compared with *Conv.* iv. 23). In mitigation of the difficulty, however, it may be noted that the 5th chasm, like some at least of the others, appears to be very narrow, xxii. The moon is under their feet as they stand over the middle of the 9th chasm, xxix, which, allowing for the further retardation of the moon, will give the time as a little past one o'clock on Saturday afternoon. They have come close to Satan at nightfall, six o'clock on Saturday evening, xxxiv; and they spend an hour and a half first in clambering down Satan's sides, to the dead centre of the universe, then turning round and clambering up again towards the antipodes of Jerusalem. It is therefore 7.30 *in the morning* in the hemisphere under which they now are (7.30 in the evening in the hemisphere which they have left), when they begin their ascent of the tunnel that leads from the central regions to the foot of Mount Purgatory, xxxiv. This ascent occupies them till nearly dawn of the next day. The period of this ascent therefore corresponds to the greater part of the night between Saturday and Sunday and of the day of Easter Sunday by Jerusalem time. By Purgatory time it is day and night, not night and day. It is simplest to regard the period as Easter Sunday and Sunday night; but some prefer to regard it as Saturday (over again) and Saturday night. It depends on whether we regard the Sunday, or other day, as beginning with sunrise at Purgatory and going all round the world with the sun till he rises in Purgatory again; or as running in like manner from sunrise to sunrise at Jerusalem, rather than Purgatory. In the former case it will be found that after spending three days and three nights on the Mount of Purgatory and six hours in the Earthly Paradise Dante rises to Heaven at midday on Thursday and goes round the world with Thursday till he is about over Italy as the sun sets in Jerusalem, *Par.* xxvii, on Thursday evening. If the other view be taken we shall say that it is noonday on Wednesday (not Thursday) when Dante rises to Heaven, and that he goes round with Wednesday till he is over the meridian of Jerusalem, when the day changes to Thursday.

In any case the action of the Divine Comedy lasts just a week, and ends on the Thursday evening.

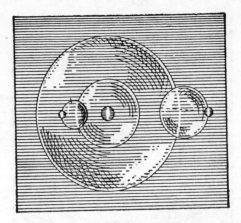

Fig. I

*Plan of concentric spheres, showing Earth enclosed in the sphere
(bearing the epicycle) of the Moon, and these again enclosed in the
sphere (bearing the epicycle) of Mercury. The scale approximately
conforms to the estimated magnitudes as given by Alfraganus (fl.
early 9th cent. A.D.; translated into Latin mid. 12th cent.): but for
simplicity the magnitudes of the epicycles have been exaggerated
by the amounts (notable in the case of the Moon) of the eccen-
tricities, so as to include all the magnitudes which affect the maxi-
mum and minimum distances of the heavenly bodies from the earth.*

*The bulks of Earth, Moon, and Mercury are arbitrarily exag-
gerated, the scale being too small to show them in proportion to
each other or to the spheres. Their diameters should be (very
roughly) as 18 (Earth), 6 (Moon), and 1 (Mercury).*

*Section of a portion of the eight revolving heavens (Fig. II)
that bear the Moon (☾), Mercury (☿), Venus (♀), the Sun (☉),
Mars (♂), Jupiter (♃), Saturn (♄), and the fixed stars (* * * *);
all except ☉ and * * * * carrying epicycles. The diameters of the
spheres and the epicycles (cf. explanation of Fig. I) are represented
approximately on the scale of the logarithms of their dimensions,
as estimated by Alfraganus.*

*The centres of all the epicycles are represented in the figure as
being in the same longitude as the Sun. This was supposed always
to be the case with respect to the epicycles of Mercury and Venus;
but the centres of the other epicycles assumed every position from
that of opposition to that of conjunction in the course of their
periodic movements. Note that the maximum distance of one heav-
enly body coincides with the minimum distance of the next (the
variation in the Sun's distance being due to eccentricity alone).*

*The sphere of the Primum Mobile, and the Empyrean, are not
represented.*

9

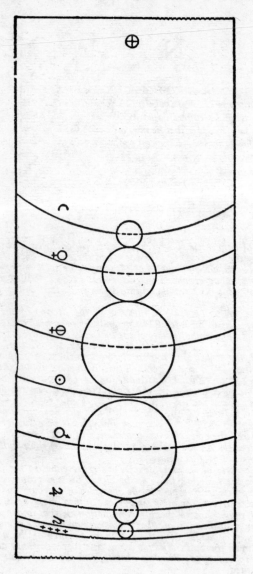

ÇANTO I

Dante finds himself astray in a dark Wood, where he spends a night of great misery. He says that death is hardly more bitter, than it is to recall what he suffered there; but that he will tell the fearful things he saw, in order that he may also tell how he found guidance, and first began to discern the real causes of all misery. He comes to a Hill; and seeing its summit already bright with the rays of the Sun, he begins to ascend it. The way to it looks quite deserted. He is met by a beautiful Leopard, which keeps distracting his attention from the Hill, and makes him turn back several times. The hour of the morning, the season, and the gay outward aspect of that animal, give him good hopes at first; but he is driven down and terrified by a Lion and a She-wolf. Virgil comes to his aid, and tells him that the Wolf lets none pass her way, but entangles and slays every one that tries to get up the mountain by the road on which she stands. He says a time will come when a swift and strong Greyhound shall clear the earth of her, and chase her into Hell. And he offers to conduct Dante by another road; to show him the eternal roots of misery and of joy, and leave him with a higher guide that will lead him up to Heaven.

IN THE middle of the journey of our life[1] I came to myself in a dark wood[2] where the straight way was lost.

Ah! how hard a thing it is to tell what a wild, and rough, and stubborn wood this was, which in my thought renews the fear!

So bitter is it, that scarcely more is death: but to treat of the good that I there found, I will relate the other things that I discerned.

I cannot rightly tell how I entered it, so full of sleep was I about the moment that I left the true way.

But after I had reached the foot of a Hill[3] there, where that valley ended, which had pierced my heart with fear,

I looked up and saw its shoulders already clothed with the rays of the Planet[4] that leads men straight on every road.

11

Then the fear was somewhat calmed, which had continued in the lake of my heart the night that I passed so piteously.

And as he, who with panting breath has escaped from the deep sea to the shore, turns to the dangerous water and gazes:

so my mind, which still was fleeing, turned back to see the pass that no one ever left alive.

After I had rested my wearied body a short while, I took the way again along the desert strand, so that the right foot always was the lower.[5]

And behold, almost at the commencement of the steep, a Leopard,[6] light and very nimble, which was covered with spotted hair.

And it went not from before my face; nay, so impeded my way, that I had often turned to go back.

The time was at the beginning of the morning; and the sun was mounting up with those stars,[7] which were with him when Divine Love

first moved those fair things: so that the hour of time and the sweet season caused me to have good hope

of that animal with the gay skin; yet not so, but that I feared at the sight, which appeared to me, of a Lion.[8]

He seemed coming upon me with head erect, and furious hunger; so that the air seemed to have fear thereat;

and a She-wolf,[9] that looked full of all cravings in her leanness; and has ere now made many live in sorrow.

She brought such heaviness upon me with the terror of her aspect, that I lost the hope of ascending.

And as one who is eager in gaining, and, when the time arrives that makes him lose, weeps and afflicts himself in all his thoughts:

such that restless beast made me, which coming against me, by little and little drove me back to where the Sun is silent.

Whilst I was rushing downwards, there appeared before my eyes one[10] who seemed hoarse from long silence.

When I saw him in the great desert, I cried: "Have pity on me, whate'er thou be, whether shade or veritable man!"

He answered me: "Not man, a man I once was; and my

parents were Lombards, and both of Mantua by country.

I was born *sub Julio*,[11] though it was late; and lived at Rome under the good Augustus, in the time of the false and lying Gods.

A poet I was; and sang of that just son of Anchises, who came from Troy after proud Ilium was burnt.[12]

But thou, why returnest thou to such disquiet? why ascendest not the delectable mountain, which is the beginning and the cause of all gladness?"

"Art thou then that Virgil, and that fountain which pours abroad so rich a stream of speech?" I answered him, with bashful front.

"O glory, and light of other poets! May the long zeal avail me, and the great love, that made me search thy volume.

Thou art my master and my author; thou alone art he from whom I took the good style that hath done me honour.

See the beast from which I turned back; help me from her, thou famous sage; for she makes my veins and pulses tremble."

"Thou must take another road," he answered, when he saw me weeping, "if thou desirest to escape from this wild place:

because this beast, for which thou criest, lets not men pass her way; but so entangles that she slays them;

and has a nature so perverse and vicious, that she never satiates her craving appetite; and after feeding, she is hungrier than before.

The animals to which she weds herself are many;[13] and will yet be more, until the Greyhound[14] comes, that will make her die with pain.

He will not feed on land or pelf, but on wisdom, and love, and manfulness; and his nation shall be between Feltro and Feltro.

He shall be the salvation of that low[15] Italy, for which Camilla the virgin, Euryalus, and Turnus, and Nisus, died of wounds;[16]

he shall chase her through every city, till he have put her into Hell again; from which envy first set her loose

13

Wherefore I think and discern this for thy best, that thou follow me; and I will be thy guide, and lead thee hence through an eternal place,[17]

where thou shalt hear the hopeless shrieks, shalt see the ancient spirits in pain, so that each calls for a second death;[18]

and then thou shalt see those who are contented in the fire:[19] for they hope to come, whensoever it be, amongst the blessed;

then to these, if thou desirest to ascend, there shall be a spirit[20] worthier than I to guide thee; with her will I leave thee at my parting:

for that Emperor who reigns above, because I was rebellious to his law, wills not that I come into his city.[21]

In all parts he rules and there holds sway; there is his city, and his high seat: O happy whom he chooses for it!"

And I to him: "Poet, I beseech thee by that God whom thou knowest not: in order that I may escape this ill and worse,

lead me where thou now hast said, so that I may see the Gate of St. Peter,[22] and those whom thou makest so sad." Then he moved; and I kept on behind him.

* See "Note on Dante's Hell" and "The Chronology of the *Inferno*," at pp. 3 and 6.

1. The Vision takes place at Eastertide of the year 1300, that is to say, when Dante was thirty-five years old. Cf. *Psalms* xc. 10: "The days of our years are threescore years and ten." See also *Convito* iv: "Where the top of this arch of life may be, it is difficult to know. . . . I believe that in the perfectly natural man, it is at the thirty-fifth year."

2. Cf. *Convito* iv: " . . . the adolescent who enters into the Wood of Error of this life would not know how to keep to the good path if it were not pointed out to him by his elders." *Politically:* the *wood* stands for the troubled state of Italy in Dante's time.

3. The "holy Hill" of the Bible; Bunyan's "Delectable Mountains."

4. *Planet*, the sun, which was a planet according to the Ptolemaic system. Dante speaks elsewhere (*Conv.* iv) of the "spiritual Sun, which is God."

5. Any one who is ascending a hill, and whose left foot is always the lower, must be bearing to the *right*.

6. Worldly Pleasure; *politically:* Florence.

7. According to tradition, the sun was in Aries at the time of the Creation.

8. Ambition; *politically:* the Royal House of France.

9. *Avarice; politically:* the Papal See. The three beasts are obviously taken from *Jeremiah* v. 6.

10. Virgil, who stands for Wordly Wisdom, and is Dante's guide through Hell and Purgatory (see Gardner, pp. 87, 88).

hoarse, perhaps because the study of Virgil had been long neglected.

11. Virgil was born at Andes, near Mantua, in the year 70 B.C. When Cæsar was murdered (44 B.C.), Virgil had not yet written his great poem, so that he did not enjoy Cæsar's patronage.

12. In the *Æneid.*

13. An allusion to the Papal alliances.

14. The *Greyhound* is usually explained as Can Grande della Scala (1290–1329), whose "nation" (or, perhaps better, "birthplace") was Verona, between Feltre in Venetia and Montefeltro in Romagna, and who became a great Ghibelline leader. Cf. *Par.* xvii. This is, on the whole, the most satisfactory interpretation, though the claims of several other personages (notably Uguccione della Faggiuola and Pope Benedict XI) have been advanced. In any case it is as well to bear in mind that Dante rested his hopes of Italy's deliverance on various persons in the course of his life.

15. Either "low-lying" or "humble." If the latter be correct, the epithet is, of course, applied sarcastically.

16. All these personages occur in the *Æneid.*

17. Hell.

18. Cf. *Revelation* xx. 14.

19. The souls in Purgatory.

20. Beatrice, or Heavenly Wisdom, will guide Dante through Paradise. No student of Dante should omit to read the *Vita Nuova*, in which the poet tells the story of his youthful love (see also Gardner, pp. 8, 9, and 87, 88).

21. Virgil's position is among the virtuous pagans in Limbo (see Canto iv).

22. The gate of Purgatory (*Purg.* ix). The Angel at this gate has charge of the two keys of St. Peter.

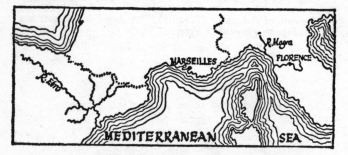

*In illustration of Dante's method of geographical description
(see "Inferno," i; "Paradiso," ix).*

ÇANTO II

End of the first day. Brief Invocation. Dante is discouraged at the outset, when he begins seriously to reflect upon what he has undertaken. That very day, his own strength had miserably failed before the Lion and the She-wolf. He bids Virgil consider well whether there be sufficient virtue in him, before committing him to so dreadful a passage. He recalls the great errands of Æneas and of Paul, and the great results of their going to the immortal world; and comparing himself with them, he feels his heart quail, and is ready to turn back. Virgil discerns the fear that has come over him; and in order to remove it, tells him how a blessed Spirit has descended from Heaven expressly to command the journey. On hearing this, Dante immediately casts off pusillanimity, and at once accepts the Freedom and the Mission that are given him.

THE DAY was departing, and the brown air taking the animals, that are on earth, from their toils; and I, one alone,

was preparing myself to bear the war both of the journey and the pity, which memory, that errs not, shall relate.

O Muses, O high Genius, now help me! O Memory, that hast inscribed what I saw, here will be shown thy nobleness.

I began: "Poet, who guidest me, look if there be worth in me sufficient, before thou trust me to the arduous passage.

Thou sayest that the father of Syivius,[1] while subject to corruption, went to the immortal world, and was there in body.

But if the Adversary of all evil was propitious to him, considering the high effect, and who and what should come from him,

it seems not unfitting to an understanding mind: for in the empyreal heaven, he was chosen to be the father of generous Rome, and of her Empire;[2]

both these, to say the truth, were established for the holy place, where the Successor of the greatest Peter sits.[3]

17

By this journey, for which thou honourest him, he learned things[4] that were the causes of his victory, and of the Papal Mantle.

Afterwards, the Chosen Vessel[5] went thither, to bring confirmation of that Faith which is the entrance of the way of salvation.

But I, why go? or who permits it? I am not Æneas, am not Paul; neither myself nor others deem me worthy of it.

Wherefore, if I resign myself to go, I fear my going may prove foolish; thou art wise, and understandest better than I speak."

And as one who unwills what he willed, and with new thoughts changes his purpose, so that he wholly quits the thing commenced,

such I made myself on that dim coast: for with thinking I wasted the enterprise, that had been so quick in its commencement.

"If I have rightly understood thy words," replied that shade of the Magnanimous, "thy soul is smit with coward fear,

which oftentimes encumbers men, so that it turns them back from honoured enterprise; as false seeing does a startled beast.

To free thee from this dread, I will tell thee why I came, and what I heard in the first moment when I took pity of thee.

I was amongst them who are in suspense;[6] and a Lady, so fair and blessed that I prayed her to command, called me.

Her eyes shone brighter than the stars; and she began soft and gentle to tell me with angelic voice, in her language:

'O courteous Mantuan Spirit, whose fame still lasts in the world, and will last as long as Time!

my friend, and not the friend of fortune, is so impeded in his way upon the desert shore, that he has turned back for terror;

and I fear he may already be so far astray, that I have risen too late for his relief, from what I heard of him in Heaven.

Now go, and with thy ornate speech, and with what is

necessary for his escape, help him so, that I may be consoled thereby.

I am Beatrice who send thee; I come from a place where I desire to return; love moved me, that makes me speak.

When I shall be before my Lord, I oft will praise thee to him.' She was silent then, and I began:

'O Lady of virtue, through whom alone mankind excels all that is contained within the heaven which has the smallest circles![7]

so grateful to me is thy command, that my obeying, were it done already, seems tardy; it needs not that thou more explain to me thy wish.

But tell me the cause, why thou forbearest not to descend into this centre here below from the spacious place, to which thou burnest to return.'

'Since thou desirest to know thus far, I will tell thee briefly,' she replied, 'why I fear not to come within this place.

Those things alone are to be feared that have the power of hurting; the others not, which are not fearful.

I am made such by God, in his grace, that your misery does not touch me; nor the flame of this burning assail me.

There is a noble Lady in Heaven[8] who has such pity of this hindrance, for which I send thee, that she breaks the sharp judgment there on high.

She called Lucia,[9] in her request, and said: "Now thy faithful one has need of thee; and I commend him to thee."

Lucia, enemy of all cruelty,[10] arose and came to the place where I was sitting with the ancient Rachel.[11]

She said: "Beatrice, true praise of God; why helpest thou not him who loved thee so, that for thee he left the vulgar crowd?

Hearest not thou the misery of his plaint? Seest thou not the death which combats him upon the river over which the sea has no boast?"[12]

None on earth were ever swift to seek their good, or flee their hurt, as I, after these words were uttered,

to come down from my blessed seat; confiding in thy noble speech, which honours thee, and them who have heard it.'

After saying this to me, she turned away her bright eyes weeping; by which she made me hasten more to come;

and thus I came to thee, as she desired; took thee from before that savage beast, which bereft thee of the short way to the beautiful mountain.

What is it then? why, why haltest thou? why lodgest in thy heart such coward fear? why art thou not bold and free,

when three such blessed Ladies care for thee in the court of Heaven, and my words promise thee so much good?"

As flowerets, by the nightly chillness bended down and closed, erect themselves all open on their stems when the sun whitens them:

thus I did, with my fainting courage; and so much good daring ran into my heart, that I began as one set free:

"O compassionate she, who succoured me! and courteous thou, who quickly didst obey the true words that she gave thee!

Thou hast disposed my heart with such desire to go, by what thou sayest, that I have returned to my first purpose.

Now go, for both have one will; thou guide, thou lord and master." Thus I spake to him; and he moving, I entered on the arduous and savage way.

1. Virgil relates the descent of Æneas (Sylvius' father) to Hell in a passage that served Dante as a model in many respects (*Æneid* vi).
2. Æneas regarded as the ancestor of the founder of Rome, which became the seat of the Empire.
3. The intimate relations between the Empire and Papacy, which, according to Dante's view (see *De Mon.*), supplemented each other, are well brought out in these lines.
4. Æneas learns from Anchises the greatness of the stock that is to spring from him (c. *Æn.* vi).
5. The reference is obviously not to 2 *Cor.* xii. 2, but to the medieval Vision of St. Paul in which is described the saint's descent to Hell. St. Paul is called "chosen vessel" in *Acts* ix. 15.
6. The souls in Limbo that "without hope live in desire (Canto iv).
7. Divine Wisdom (Beatrice) raises mankind higher than aught else on earth. The sphere of the moon is the one nearest to the earth, and has, therefore, the smallest circumference.
8. The Virgin Mary: Divine Grace.
9. Lucia: Illuminating Grace. She is probably identical with the Syracusan saint (3rd century) who became the special patroness of those afflicted with weak sight. This would explain her symbolical

position, and the expression *thy faithful one:* for Dante suffered with his eyes (*cf. Vita Nuova,* § 40; *Conv.* iii. 9). For Lucy, see *Purg.* ix, and *Par.* xxxii.

10. Illuminating Grace affects only gentle souls.

11. Rachel stands for the Contemplative Life. For Beatrice and Rachel see *Par.* xxxii.

12. Spiritual death is identical with the *dark wood* of Canto i, and the stormy river of life with the three beasts. The second verse appears to mean that life can be as tempestuous as the sea itself.

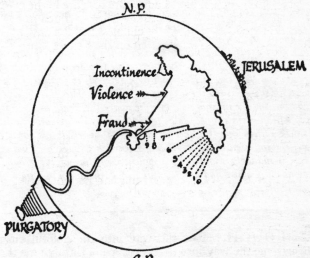

Section of the Earth, showing Hell, Purgatory, and the passage by which the poets ascend

ÇANTO III

Inscription over the Gate of Hell, and the impression it produces upon Dante. Virgil takes him by the hand, and leads him in. The dismal sounds make him burst into tears. His head is quite bewildered. Upon a Dark Plain, which goes round the confines, he sees a vast multitude of spirits running behind a flag in great haste and confusion, urged on by furious wasps and hornets. These are the unhappy people, who never were alive—never awakened to take any part in either good or evil, to care for anything but themselves. They are mixed with a similar class of fallen angels. After passing through the crowd of them, the Poets come to a great River, which flows round the brim of Hell; and then descends to form the other rivers, the marshes, and the ice that we shall meet with. It is the river Acheron; and on its Shore all that die under the wrath of God assemble from every country to be ferried over by the demon Charon. He makes them enter his boat by glaring on them with his burning eyes. Having seen these, and being refused a passage by Charon, Dante is suddenly stunned by a violent trembling of the ground, accompanied with wind and lightning, and falls down in a state of insensibility.

"THROUGH ME is the way into the doleful city; through me the way into the eternal pain; through me the way among the people lost.

Justice moved my High Maker; Divine Power made me, Wisdom Supreme, and Primal Love.[1]

Before me were no things created, but eternal;[2] and eternal I endure: leave all hope, ye that enter."

These words, of colour obscure, saw I written above a gate; whereat I: "Master, their meaning to me is hard."

And he to me, as one experienced: "Here must all distrust be left; all cowardice must here be dead.

We are come to the place where I told thee thou shouldst see the wretched people, who have lost the good of the intellect."

And placing his hand on mine, with a cheerful counte-

22

nance that comforted me, he led me into the secret things.

Here sighs, plaints, and deep wailings resounded through the starless air: it made me weep at first.

Strange tongues, horrible outcries, words of pain, tones of anger, voices deep and hoarse, and sounds of hands amongst them,

made a tumult, which turns itself unceasing in that air for ever dyed, as sand when it eddies in a whirlwind.

And I, my head begirt with horror, said: "Master, what is this that I hear? and who are these that seem so overcome with pain?"

And he to me: "This miserable mode the dreary souls of those sustain, who lived without blame, and without praise.

They are mixed with that caitiff choir of the angels, who were not rebellious, nor were faithful to God; but were for themselves.[3]

Heaven chased them forth to keep its beauty from impair; and the deep Hell receives them not, for the wicked would have some glory over them."[4]

And I: "Master, what is so grievous to them, that makes them lament thus bitterly?" He answered: "I will tell it to thee very briefly.

These have no hope of death; and their blind life is so mean, that they are envious of every other lot.

Report of them the world permits not to exist; Mercy and Justice disdains them: let us not speak of them; but look, and pass."

And I, who looked, saw an ensign,[5] which whirling ran so quickly that it seemed to scorn all pause;

and behind it came so long a train of people, that I should never have believed death had undone so many.

After I had recognized some amongst them, I saw and knew the shadow of him[6] who from cowardice made the great refusal.

Forthwith I understood and felt assured, that this was the crew of caitiffs, hateful to God and to his enemies.

These unfortunates, who never were alive, were naked, and sorely goaded by hornets and by wasps that were there.

These made their faces stream with blood, which mixed with tears was gathered at their feet by loathsome worms.

And then, as I looked onwards, I saw people on the Shore of a great River: whereat I said: "Master, now grant

that I may know who these are; and what usage makes them seem so ready to pass over, as I discern by the faint light."

And he to me: "The things shall be known to thee, when we stay our steps upon the joyless strand of Acheron."

Then, with eyes ashamed and downcast, fearing my words might have offended him, I kept myself from speaking till we reached the stream.

And lo! an old man, white with ancient hair, comes towards us in a bark, shouting: "Woe to you, depraved spirits!

hope not ever to see Heaven: I come to lead you to the other shore; into the eternal darkness; into fire and into ice.

And thou who art there, alive, depart thee from these who are dead." But when he saw that I departed not,

he said: "By other ways, by other ferries, not here, shalt thou pass over: a lighter boat must carry thee."

And my guide to him: "Charon, vex not thyself: thus it is willed there, where what is willed can be done; and ask no more."

Then the woolly cheeks were quiet of the steersman on the livid marsh, who round his eyes had wheels of flame.

But those spirits, who were foreworn and naked, changed colour and chattered with their teeth, soon as they heard the bitter words.

They blasphemed God and their parents; the human kind; the place, the time, and origin of their seed, and of their birth.

Then all of them together, sorely weeping, drew to the accursed shore, which awaits every man that fears not God.

Charon the demon, with eyes of glowing coal, beckoning them, collects them all; smites with his oar whoever lingers.

As the leaves of autumn fall off one after the other, till the branch sees all its spoils upon the ground:

so one by one the evil seed of Adam cast themselves from that shore at signals, as the bird at its call.

Thus they depart on the brown water; and ere they have

landed on the other shore, again a fresh crowd collects on this.

"My son," said the courteous Master, "those who die under God's wrath, all assemble here from every country;

and they are prompt to pass the river, for Divine Justice spurs them so, that fear is changed into desire.

By this way no good spirit ever passes; and hence, if Charon complains of thee, thou easily now mayest know the import of his words."

When he had ended, the dusky champaign trembled so violently, that the remembrance of my terror bathes me still with sweat.

The tearful ground gave out wind, which flashed forth a crimson light that conquered all my senses; and I fell, like one who is seized with sleep.

1. Power, Wisdom and Love—the Holy Trinity.
2. The "eternal things" are first matter, the angels and the heavens (see *Par.* vii).
3. There is no mention of these angels in the Bible. Dante evidently followed a popular tradition, traces of which may be found in the medieval Voyage of St. Brandan.
4. The other sinners were at least able to make up their mind.
5. The shifting flag is symbolical of the wavering spirit of these souls.
6. Probably Celestine V, who was elected Pope in 1294, at the age of eighty, and resigned five months later in favour of Boniface VIII: this latter circumstance is in itself sufficient to account for Dante's wrath. Objections may be raised against this interpretation; but the other names suggested (such as Esau, or Vieri de' Cerchi, chief of the Florentine Whites) are even less satisfactory.

ÇANTO IV

Dante is roused by a heavy thunder, and finds himself on the brink of the Abyss. Not in his own strength has he crossed the dismal river. Virgil conducts him into Limbo, which is the First Circle of Hell, and contains the spirits of those who lived without Baptism or Christianity. The only pain they suffer is, that they live in the desire and without the hope of seeing God. Their sighs cause the eternal air to tremble, and there is no other audible lamentation amongst them. As Dante and Virgil go on, they reach a hemisphere of light amid the darkness, and are met by Homer and other Poets, and conducted into a Noble Castle, in which they see the most distinguished of the Heathen women, statesmen, sages, and warriors. Homer and the other Poets quit them; and they go on to a place of total darkness.

A HEAVY thunder broke the deep sleep in my head; so that I started like one who is awaked by force;

and, having risen erect, I moved my rested eyes around, and looked steadfastly to know the place in which I was.

True is it, that I found myself upon the brink of the dolorous Valley of the Abyss, which gathers thunder of endless wailings.

It was so dark, profound, and cloudy, that, with fixing my look upon the bottom, I there discerned nothing.

"Now let us descend into the blind world here below," began the Poet all pale; "I will be first, and thou shalt be second."

And I, who had remarked his colour, said: "How shall I come, when thou fearest, who are wont to be my strength in doubt?"

And he to me: "The anguish of the people who are here below, on my face depaints that pity, which thou takest for fear.

Let us go; for the length of way impels us." Thus he entered, and made me enter, into the first circle that girds the abyss.

Here there was no plaint, that could be heard, except of sighs, which caused the eternal air to tremble;

and this arose from the sadness, without torment, of the crowds that were many and great, both of children, and of women and men.

The good Master to me: "Thou askest not what spirits are these thou seest? I wish thee to know, before thou goest farther,

that they sinned not; and though they have merit, it suffices not: for they had not Baptism, which is the portal of the faith that thou believest;

and seeing they were before Christianity, they worshipped not God aright; and of these am I myself.

For such defects, and for no other fault, are we lost; and only in so far afflicted, that without hope we live in desire."

Great sadness took me at the heart on hearing this; because I knew men of much worth, who in that Limbo were suspense.

"Tell me, Master; tell me, Sir," I began, desiring to be assured of that Faith which conquers every error;

"did ever any, by his own merit, or by others', go out from hence, that afterwards was blessed?" And he, understanding my covert speech,

replied: "I was new in this condition, when I saw a Mighty One[1] come to us, crowned with sign of victory.

He took away from us the shade of our First Parent, of Abel his son, and that of Noah; of Moses the Legislator and obedient;

Abraham the Patriarch; David the King; Israel with his father and his children, and with Rachel, for whom he did so much;

and many others, and made them blessed; and I wish thee to know, that, before these, no human souls were saved."

We ceased not to go, though he was speaking; but passed the wood meanwhile, the wood, I say, of crowded spirits.

Our way was not yet far since my slumber, when I saw a fire,[2] which conquered a hemisphere of the darkness.

We were still a little distant from it; yet not so distant, that I did not in part discern what honourable people occupied that place.

"O thou, that honourest every science and art; who are these, who have such honour, that it separates them from the manner of the rest?"

And he to me: "The honoured name, which sounds of them, up in that life of thine, gains favours in heaven which thus advances them."

Meanwhile a voice was heard by me: "Honour the great Poet! His shade returns that was departed."

After the voice had paused, and was silent, I saw four great shadows come to us; they had an aspect neither sad nor joyful.

The good Master began to speak: "Mark him with that sword in hand, who comes before the three as their lord:

that is Homer, the sovereign Poet; the next who comes is Horace the satirist; Ovid is the third, and the last is Lucan.

Because each agrees with me in the name, which the one voice sounded, they do me honour: and therein they do well."

Thus I saw assembled the goodly school of those lords of highest song, which, like an eagle, soars above the rest.

After they had talked a space together, they turned to me with a sign of salutation; and my Master smiled thereat.

And greatly more besides they honoured me for they made me of their number, so that I was a sixth amid such intelligences.

Thus we went onwards to the light, speaking things which it is well to pass in silence, as it was well to speak there where I was.[3]

We came to the foot of a Noble Castle,[4] seven times circled with lofty Walls, defended round by a fair Rivulet.

This we passed as solid land; through seven gates I entered with those sages; we reached a meadow of fresh verdure.

On it were people with eyes slow and grave, of great authority in their appearance; they spoke seldom, with mild voices.

Thus we retired on one of the sides, into a place open, luminous, and high, so that they could all be seen.

There direct, upon the green enamel, were shown to me

the great spirits, so that I glory within myself for having seen them.

I saw Electra with many companions: amongst whom I knew both Hector and Æneas; Cæsar armed, with the falcon eyes.[5]

I saw Camilla and Penthesilea on the other hand, and saw the Latian King, sitting with Lavinia his daughter.

I saw that Brutus who expelled the Tarquin; Lucretia, Julia, Marcia, and Cornelia;[6] and by himself apart, I saw the Saladin.[7]

When I raised my eyelids a little higher, I saw the Master of those that know,[8] sitting amid a philosophic family.

All regard him; all do him honour; here I saw Socrates and Plato, who before the rest stand nearest to him;[9]

Democritus, who ascribes the world to chance: Diogenes, Anaxagoras, and Thales; Empedocles, Heraclitus, and Zeno;[10]

and I saw the good collector of the qualities, Discorides I mean; and saw Orpheus, Tully, Linus, and Seneca the moralist;

Euclid the geometer, and Ptolemæus; Hippocrates, Avicenna, and Galen; Averroës,[11] who made the great comment.

I may not paint them all in full: for the long theme so chases me, that many times the word comes short of the reality.

The company of six diminishes to two; by another road the sage guide leads me, out of the quiet, into the trembling air; and I come to a part where there is naught that shines.

1. Dante follows the legend, probably based on 1 *Peter* iii. 19, according to which Christ descended to Hell in the year 33 (that is to say, fifty-two years after Virgil's death) and liberated certain souls.
2. The genius of the inhabitants of the castle in a measure atones for their unbaptized state.
3. It is difficult to believe that these lines should be accepted as a testimony of Dante's modesty: our poet was distinctly not a modest man. The passage has not yet been satisfactorily explained.
4. The symbolism here is not very obvious. Perhaps the castle stands for Philosophy; the seven walls: the liberal virtues (*i.e.*, Prudence, Justice, Fortitude and Temperance, Wisdom, Knowledge and Understanding); the stream: Eloquence; the seven gates: the liberal

arts (Grammar, Logic, Rhetoric, Music, Arithmetic, Geometry and Astronomy).

5. Electra: the daughter of Atlas and mother of Dardanus, the founder of Troy (cf. Æn. viii, and De Mon, ii, 3) Hector and Æneas: the Trojan heroes; Penthesilea, Queen of the Amazons, assisted the Trojans after Hector's death; Camilla died while opposing the Trojans in Italy (cf. Canto i); Latinus and Lavinia: the father-in-law and wife of Æneas; Cæsar is introduced here as a descendant of Æneas (the mythical founder of the Roman Empire).

6. Lucius Junius Brutus brought about the overthrow of Tarquinius Superbus, whose son had dishonoured Collatine's wife Lucretia (510 B.C.); Julia: the daughter of Julius Cæsar and wife of Pompey; Marcia: the wife of Cato of Utica (cf. Purg. i); Cornelia: daughter of Publius Cornelius Scipio Africanus Major, and wife of Tiberius Sempronius Gracchus, whom she bore two sons, Tiberius and Caius, the famous tribunes (cf. Par. xv).

7. The famous Saladin (1137-1193), who was known throughout Europe during the Middle Ages for his munificence and who became the type of the Eastern potentate. He opposed the Crusaders and was defeated by Richard Cœur de Lion.

8. Aristotle.

9. Plato's influence in the Middle Ages was not nearly so great as that of Aristotle.

10. Early Greek Philosophers (7th-4th centuries B.C.).

11. Dioscorides (author of a medical work, treating of the qualities of plants), Hippocrates and Galen were Greek physicians; Orpheus and Linus: mythical Greek singers and poets; Tullius is, of course, Cicero, and Seneca, the writer whose ethical works were much read in the Middle Ages; Ptolemy's astronomical system was generally accepted throughout the Middle Ages and adopted by Dante; Avicenna (980-1037) and Averroës (12th century): Arabian physicians and philosophers, both of whom wrote commentaries on Aristotle (the former one on Galen, too). Averroës' work was translated into Latin ca. 1250, and enjoyed a great vogue in Europe, where it was largely instrumental in bringing about the revival of Aristotle's philosophy. For other occupants of this circle see Purgatorio, xxii.

ÇANTO V

The Second Circle, or proper commencement of Hell; and Minos, the Infernal Judge, at its entrance. It contains the souls of Carnal sinners; and their punishment consists in being driven about incessantly, in total darkness, by fierce winds. First amongst them comes Semiramis, the Babylonian queen. Dido, Cleopatra, Helena, Achilles, Paris, and a great multitude of others, pass in succession. Dante is overcome and bewildered with pity at the sight of them, when his attention is suddenly attracted to two Spirits that keep together, and seem strangely light upon the wind. He is unable to speak for some time, after finding that it is Francesca of Rimini, with her lover Paolo; and falls to the ground, as if dead, when he has heard their painful story.

THUS I descended from the first circle down into the second, which encompasses less space, and so much greater pain, that it stings to wailing.

There Minos sits horrific, and grins: examines the crimes upon the entrance; judges, and sends according as he girds himself.

I say, that when the ill-born spirit comes before him, it confesses all; and that sin-discerner

sees what place in hell is for it, and with his tail makes as many circles round himself as the degrees he will have it to descend.

Always before him stands a crowd of them; they go each in its turn to judgment; they tell, and hear; and then are whirled down.

"O thou who comest to the abode of pain!" said Minos to me, when he saw me leaving the act of that great office;

"look how thou enterest, and in whom thou trustest; let not the wideness of the entrancy deceive thee." And my guide to him: "Why criest thou too?

Hinder not his fated going; thus it is willed there where what is willed can be done: and ask no more."

Now begin the doleful notes to reach me; now am I come where much lamenting strikes me.

I came into a place void of all light, which bellows like the sea in tempest, when it is combated by warring winds.

The hellish storm, which never rests, leads the spirits with its sweep; whirling, and smiting it vexes them.

When they arrive before the ruin, there the shrieks, the moanings, and the lamentation; there they blaspheme the divine power.

I learnt that to such torment are doomed the carnal sinners, who subject reason to lust.

And as their wings bear along the starlings, at the cold season, in large and crowded troop: so that blast, the evil spirits;

hither, thither, down, up, it leads them. No hope ever comforts them, not of rest but even of less pain.

And as the cranes go chanting their lays, making a long streak of themselves in the air: so I saw the shadows come, uttering wails,

borne by that strife of winds; whereat I said: "Master, who are those people, whom the black air thus lashes?"

"The first of these concerning whom thou seekest to know," he then replied, "was Empress[1] of many tongues.

With the vice of luxury she was so broken, that she made lust and law alike in her decree, to take away the blame she had incurred.

She is Semiramis, of whom we read that she succeeded Ninus, and was his spouse; she held the land which the Soldan rules.

That other is she who slew herself in love,[2] and broke faith to the ashes of Sichæus; next comes luxurious Cleopatra.[3]

Helena[4] see, for whom so long a time of ill revolved; and see the great Achilles,[5] who fought at last with love;

see Paris, Tristan";[6] and more than a thousand shades he showed to me, and pointing with his finger, named to me those whom love had parted from our life.

After I had heard my teacher name the olden dames and cavaliers, pity came over me, and I was as if bewildered.

INFERNO

I began: "Poet, willingly would I speak with those two⁷ that go together, and seem so light upon the wind."

And he to me: "Thou shalt see when they are nearer to us; and do thou then entreat them by that love, which leads them; and they will come."

Soon as the wind bends them to us, I raised my voice: "O wearied souls! come to speak with us, if none denies it."

As doves called by desire, with raised and steady wings come through the air to their loved nest, borne by their will:

so those spirits issued from the band where Dido is, coming to us through the malignant air; such was the force of my affectuous cry.

"O living creature, gracious and benign; that goest through the black air, visiting us who stained the earth with blood:

if the King of the Universe were our friend, we would pray him for thy peace; seeing that thou hast pity of our perverse misfortune.

Of that which it pleases thee to hear and to speak, we will hear and speak with you, whilst the wind, as now, is silent for us.

The town,⁸ where I was born, sits on the shore, where Po descends to rest with his attendant streams.

Love, which is quickly caught in gentle heart, took him with the fair body of which I was bereft; and the manner still afflicts me.

Love, which to no loved one permits excuse for loving, took me so strongly with delight in him, that, as thou seest, even now it leaves me not.

Love led us to one death; Caïna⁹ waits for him who quenched our life." These words from them were offered to us.

After I had heard those wounded souls, I bowed my face, and held it low until the Poet said to me: "What are thou thinking of?"

When I answered, I began: "Ah me! what sweet thoughts, what longing led them to the woeful pass!"

Then I turned again to them; and I spoke, and began:

33

"Francesca, thy torments make me weep with grief and pity.

But tell me: in the time of the sweet sighs, by what and how love granted you to know the dubious desires?"

And she to me: "There is no greater pain than to recall a happy time in wretchedness; and this thy teacher knows.[10]

But if thou hast such desire to learn the first root of our love, I will do like one who weeps and tells.

One day, for pastime, we read of Lancelot,[11] how love constrained him; we were alone, and without all suspicion.

Several times that reading urged our eyes to meet, and changed the colour of our faces; but one moment alone it was that overcame us.

When we read how the fond smile was kissed by such a lover, he, who shall never be divided from me,

kissed my mouth all trembling: the book, and he who wrote it, was a Galeotto.[12] that day we read in it no farther."

Whilst the one spirit thus spake, the other wept so, that I fainted with pity, as if I had been dying; and fell, as a dead body falls.

1. According to Orosius, Semiramis succeeded her husband Ninus as ruler of Assyria. She was known for her licentious character. Dante appears to have confused the ancient kingdoms of Assyria or Babylonia in Asia with the Babylon in Egypt, for only the latter was ruled by the Sultan. Or perhaps he followed a tradition according to which Ninus conquered Egypt. The mention of the *many tongues* is probably due to the fact that Babylon and Babel were commonly held to be identical.

2. Dido, Queen of Carthage, fell in love with Æneas, after the death of her husband Sichæus, to whose memory she had sworn eternal fidelity. When Æneas left her to go to Italy, she slew herself on a funeral pyre.

3. Cleopatra, Queen of Egypt, the mistress of Cæsar and Antony.

4. Helen, the wife of Menelaus, King of Sparta, was carried off by Paris of Troy, and was thus the cause of the Trojan war.

5. According to medieval legend, Achilles was slain by Paris in a Trojan temple, whither he had gone with the intention of marrying Paris' sister Polyxena, who had been promised him as a reward if he would join the Trojans.

6. Tristan of Lyonesse, one of King Arthur's knights, who loved Yseult, the wife of his uncle, King Mark of Cornwall, and was killed by the outraged husband.

7. Francesca, daughter of Guido Vecchio da Polenta (and aunt of the Guido Novello at whose court in Ravenna Dante found his last refuge), was, for political reasons, married to Gianciotto, the deformed son of Malatesta da Verrucchio, Lord of Rimini (*ca.* 1275). About ten years later Gianciotto, having surprised his wife with his younger brother Paolo, stabbed the guilty pair. These are the bald historical facts, to which legend early began to add romantic details, tampering not only with the dates of the events and the ages of the persons concerned, but with the actual facts. Thus, it is quite possible that Paolo took part in the preliminary negotiations connected with his brother's marriage; but this circumstance was utilized in such a way as to make it appear as though Francesca actually went through the ceremony of marriage with the handsome Paolo, and did not discover the trick till it was too late. Dante followed this tradition.

8. Ravenna, situated close by the shore of the Adriatic Sea, at the mouth of the Po.

9. The region of Hell reserved for those who had slain a relative (see Canto xxxii).

10. Although these words are translated literally from Boethius, and although we know that Dante had made a special study of Boethius, yet we cannot well identify the *teacher* with this philosopher: for how can we be expected to assume that Francesca was acquainted with these two facts? The reference is probably to Virgil, and to his position in Limbo.

11. The passage in the Old French version of the Lancelot Romance which alone contains all the details given by Dante, here and in *Par.* xv, is now known, thanks to Mr. Paget Toynbee. That Dante was acquainted with the old French poems dealing with the *matière de Bretagne* is proved by *De Vulg. El.* i. 10.

12. *Galeotto* synonymous with "pander": for, in the Old French poem, Gallehault renders Lancelot and Guinivere the same service that Pandarus rendered Troilus and Cressida, according to the Trojan legend.

ÇANTO VI

On recovering his senses, Dante gazes round, and finds himself in the midst of new torments, and a new kind of sinners. During his swoon (as at the river Acheron), he has been transported, from the tempests and precipices of the Second, into the Third Circle. It is the place appointed for Epicures and Gluttons, who set their hearts upon the lowest species of sensual gratification. An unvarying, eternal storm of heavy hail, foul water, and snow, pours down upon them. They are all lying prostrate on the ground; and the three-headed monster Cerberus keeps barking over them and rending them. The shade of a citizen of Florence, who had been nicknamed Ciacco (Pig), eagerly sits up as the Poets pass; and from him Dante hears of various events, that await the two parties by which the city is divided and distracted. After leaving Ciacco, the Poets have still some way to go in the disgusting circle, but notice nothing more in it. They wade on slowly in the mixture of the Shadows and the rain, talking of the great Judgment and Eternity, till they find Plutus at the next descent.

ON SENSE returning, which closed itself before the pity of the two kinsfolk that stunned me all with sadness,

I discern new torments, and new tormented souls, whithersoever I move, and turn, and gaze.

I am in the Third Circle, that of the eternal, accursed, cold, and heavy rain; its law and quality is never new.

Large hail, and turbid water, and snow, pour down through the darksome air; the ground, on which it falls, emits a putrid smell.

Cerberus, a monster fierce and strange, with three throats, barks dog-like over those that are immersed in it.

His eyes are red, his beard greasy and black, his belly wide, and clawed his hands; he clutches the spirits, flays, and piecemeal rends them.

The rain makes them howl like dogs; with one side they screen the other; they often turn themselves, the impious wretches.

36

When Cerberus, the great Worm, perceived us, he opened his mouths and showed his tusks: no limb of him kept still.

My Guide, spreading his palms, took up earth; and, with full fists, cast it into his ravening gullets.

As the dog, that barking craves, and grows quiet when he bites his food, for he strains and battles only to devour it:

so did those squalid visages of Cerberus, the Demon, who thunders on the spirits so, that they would fain be deaf.

We passed over the shadows whom the heavy rain subdues; and placed our soles upon their emptiness, which seems a body.

They all were lying on the ground save one,[1] who sat up forthwith when he saw us pass before him.

"O thou, who through this Hell art led," he said to me, "recognize me if thou mavest; thou wast made before I was unmade."

And I to him: "The anguish which thou hast, perhaps withdraws thee from my memory, so that it seems not as if I ever saw thee.

But tell me who art thou, that art put in such a doleful place, and in such punishment; that, though other may be greater, none is so displeasing."

And he to me: "Thy city, which is so full of envy that the sack already overflows, contained me in the clear life.

"You, citizens, called me Ciacco; for the baneful crime of gluttony, as thou seest, I languish in the rain;

and I, wretched spirit, am not alone, since all these for like crime are in like punishment"; and more he said not.

I answered him: "Ciacco, thy sore distress weighs upon me so, that it bids me weep; but tell me if thou canst,

what the citizens of the divided city shall come to?[2] if any one in it be just; and tell me the reason why such discord has assailed it."

And he to me: "After long contention, they shall come to blood, and the party of the woods shall expel the other with much offence [3]

Then it behoves this to fall within three suns, and the other to prevail through the force of one who now keeps tacking.

It shall carry its front high for a long time,[4] keeping the other under heavy burdens, however it may weep thereat and be ashamed.

Two[5] are just; but are not listened to there; Pride, Envy, and Avarice are the three sparks which have set the hearts of all on fire."

Here he ended the lamentable sound. And I to him: "Still I wish thee to instruct me, and to bestow a little further speech on me.

Farinata and Tegghiaio, who were so worthy; Jacopo Rusticucci, Arrigo and Mosca, and the rest who set their minds on doing good;[6]

tell me where they are, and give me to know them: for great desire urges me to learn whether Heaven soothes or Hell empoisons them."

And he to me: "They are amongst the blackest spirits; a different crime weighs them downwards to the bottom; shouldst thou descend so far, thou mayest see them.

But when thou shalt be in the sweet world, I pray thee recall me to the memory of men; more I tell thee not, and more I answer not."

Therewith he writhed his straight eyes asquint; looked at me a little; then bent his head, and fell down with it like his blind companions.

And my Guide said to me: "He wakes no more until the angel's trumpet sounds; when the adverse Power shall come,

each shall revisit his sad grave; shall resume his flesh and form; shall hear that which resounds to all eternity."[7]

Thus passed we through the filthy mixture of the shadows and the rain, with paces slow, touching a little on the future life.

Wherefore I said: "Master, shall these torments increase after the great Sentence, or grow less, or remain as burning?"

And he to me: "Return to thy science,[8] which has it, that the more a thing is perfect, the more it feels pleasure and likewise pain.

Though these accursed people never attain to true perfection, yet they look to be nearer it after than before."

We went round along that road, speaking much more than I repeat; we reached the point where the descent begins; here found we Plutus,[9] the great enemy.

1. This person, nicknamed Ciacco (Hog), was noted for his gluttony; his redeeming feature appears to have been a ready wit. He is said to have died in 1286.

2. It is not till later in his journey (see Canto x) that Dante learns to what extent the souls in Hell are able to foresee future events.

3. These verses contain, in brief, the political history of Florence from 1300-1302 (see Gardner, pp. 18-23). The Black and White Guelfs, headed by Corso Donati and Vieri de' Cerchi, respectively, came to blows on May 1, 1300. In May, 1301, the Whites (that is, either ."party of the woods": because the Cerchi came from the wooded district of Val di Sieve, in the Mugello; or "wild" party: as opposed to the more aristocratic faction of the Donati) expelled the Blacks. But, with the covert aid of Boniface VIII, the Blacks soon gained the upper hand, and drove their rivals from the city. The last important decrees of exile against the Whites were signed in the latter half of 1302; and their decisive defeat took place in the first quarter of 1303; both of which dates fall within the third year from the time at which Ciacco is speaking (cf. Purg. xx).

4. Dante did not live to see his party triumph.

5. Probably Dante himself, and his friend Guido Cavalcanti (for whom see Canto x, *note* 8).

6. For Farinata, see Canto x; for Tegghiaio and Rusticucci: Canto xvi; and for Mosca: Canto xxviii. Arrigo is not mentioned again; but, according to the old commentators, he was one of Mosca's fellow-conspirators, and is therefore presumably punished in the same circle.

7. The Last Judgment (see *Matthew* xxv. 31-46). The *adverse Power* is, of course, Christ, the enemy of the wicked.

8. These lines are clear when taken in conjunction with *Par.* xiv, *note* 2. *Thy science* is the doctrine of Aristotle (as incorporated in Thomas Aquinas).

9. It seems probable that Dante, following the general medieval tradition (traces of which appear even in classical times), did not distinguish clearly between Pluto, the God of the lower regions, and Plutus, the God of riches.

ÇANTO VII

Plutus, the ancient god of riches, whom the Poets find on the brink of the Fourth Circle, swells with rage and astonishment when he sees them about to enter it; and succeeds in uttering some strange words. Virgil, with brief and sharp reproof, makes him collapse and fall to the ground. In this circle—divided into two halves—the Poets find two separate classes of spirits, that are coming in opposite directions, rolling large dead Weights, smiting these against one another; and then, with bitter mutual reproaches, each turning round his Weight, and rolling it backwards, till all meet and smite again, "at the other joust," or other end of the two Half-circles. It is the souls of the Prodigal and Avaricious that have this punishment. In the left semicircle, which is occupied by the avaricious, Dante notices many that are tonsured; and is told that they were once High Dignitaries of his Church, but have now grown so dim, that it would be vain to think of recognizing any of them. After speaking of Fortune and the things committed to her charge, the Poets hasten across the circle to the next descent. Upon its brink they find a stream of dark water, gushing down through a cleft, which it has worn out for itself; and they accompany this water till it forms a marsh called Scyx, which occupies the Fifth Circle. In this Marsh they see spirits, all muddy and naked, assailing and tearing each other. These are the souls of the Wrathful. Beneath them, and covered with the black mud, are the souls of the Gloomy-sluggish, gurgling in their throats a dismal chant. The Poets, after going a long way round the edge of the loathsome pool, come at last to the foot of a high tower.

"PAPE SATAN! pape Satan, aleppe!" began Plutus, with clucking voice; and that gentle Sage, who knew all,[1]

said, comforting me: "Let not thy fear hurt thee: for, whatever power he have, he shall not hinder thee from descending this rock."

Then he turned himself to that inflated visage, and said: "Peace, cursed Wolf! consume thyself internally with thy greedy rage.

Not without cause is our journey to the deep: it is willed

on high, there where Michael took vengeance of the proud adultery." [2]

As sails, swelled by the wind, fall entangled when the mast breaks: so fell that cruel monster to the ground.

Thus we descended into the fourth concavity, taking in more of the dismal bank, which shuts up all the evil of the universe.

Ah, Justice Divine! who shall tell in few the many fresh pains and travails that I saw? and why does guilt of ours thus waste us?

As does the surge, there above Charybdis,[3] that breaks itself against the surge wherewith it meets: so have the people here to counter-dance.

Here saw I too many more than elsewhere, both on the one side and on the other, with loud howlings, rolling weights by force of chests;

they smote against each other, and then each wheeled round just there, rolling aback, shouting "Why holdest thou?" and "Why throwest thou away?"

Thus they returned along the gloomy circle, on either hand, to the opposite point, again shouting at each other their reproachful measure.

Then every one, when he had reached it, turned through his half-circle towards the other joust. And I, who felt my heart as it were stung,

said: "My Master, now show me what people these are, and whether all those tonsured on our left were of the clergy."[4]

And he to me: "In their first life, all were so squint-eyed in mind, that they made no expenditure in it with moderation.

Most clearly do their voices bark out this, when they come to the two points of the circle, where contrary guilt divides them.

These were Priests, that have not hairy covering on their heads, and Popes and Cardinals, in whom avarice does its utmost."

And I: "Master, among this set, I surely ought to recognize some that were defiled by these evils."

And he to me: "Vain thoughts combinest thou: their

undiscerning life, which made them sordid, now makes
them too obscure for any recognition.

To all eternity they shall continue butting one another;
these shall arise from their graves with closed fists; and
these with hair shorn off.

Ill-giving, and ill-keeping, has deprived them of the
bright world, and put them to this conflict; what a conflict
it is, I adorn no words to tell.

But thou, my Son, mayest now see the brief mockery of
the goods that are committed unto Fortune, for which the
human kind contend with one another.

For all the gold that is beneath the moon, or ever was,
could not give rest to a single one of these weary souls."

"Master," I said to him, "now tell me also: this Fortune,[5]
of which thou hintest to me; what is she, that has the good
things of the world thus within her clutches?"

And he to me: O foolish creatures, how great is this
ignorance that falls upon ye! Now I wish thee to receive
my judgment of her.

He whose wisdom is transcendent over all, made the
heavens and gave them guides, so that every part shines to
every part,

equally distributing the light; in like manner, for
worldly splendours, he ordained a general minister and
guide,[6]

to change betimes the vain possession, from people to
people, and from one kindred to another, beyond the
hindrance of human wisdom:

hence one people commands, another languishes; obey-
ing her sentence, which is hidden like the serpent in the
grass.

Your knowledge cannot understand her: she provides,
judges, and maintains her kingdom, as the other Gods do
theirs.

Her permutations have no truce; necessity makes her be
swift; thus he comes oft who doth a change obtain.

This is she, who is so much reviled, even by those who
ought to praise her, when blaming her wrongfully, and
with evil words.[7]

But she is in bliss, and hears it not: with the other Primal

Creatures[8] joyful, she wheels her sphere, and tastes her blessedness.

But let us now descend to greater misery; already every star is falling,[9] that was ascending when I set out, and to stay too long is not permitted."

We crossed the circle, to the other bank, near a fount, that boils and pours down through a cleft, which it has formed.

The water was darker far than perse; and we, accompanying the dusky waves, entered down by a strange path.

This dreary streamlet makes a Marsh, that is named Styx, when it has descended to the foot of the grey malignant shores.

And I, who stood intent on looking, saw muddy people in that bog, all naked and with a look of anger.

They were smiting each other, not with hands only, but with head, and with chest, and with feet; maiming one another with their teeth, piece by piece.

The kind Master said: "Son, now see the souls of those whom anger overcame; and also I would have thee to believe for certain,

that there are people underneath the water, who sob, and make it bubble at the surface; as thy eye may tell thee, whichever way it turns.

Fixed in the slime, they say: 'Sullen were we in the sweet air, that is gladdened by the Sun, carrying lazy smoke within our hearts;

now lie we sullen here in the black mire.' This hymn they gurgle in their throats, for they cannot speak it in full words."

Thus, between the dry bank and the putrid fen, we compassed a large arc of that loathly slough, with eyes turned towards those that swallow of its filth; we came to the foot of a tower at last.

1. Virgil understood these words; but as for us, it seems best to admit that we do not even know to which language they belong, though various attempts have been made to connect them with Hebrew, Greek, and French.
2. See *Rev.* xii 7-9. "Adultery" in the Biblical sense (*Ezek.* xxiii. 37).
3. The whirlpool of Charybdis (in the straits of Messina) which

43

was specially dangerous by reason of its proximity to the rock Scylla, is frequently alluded to in classical literature.

4. The avarice of the clergy was held in special aversion by Dante (cf. Cantos i, note 9, and xix).

5. At the time of the composition of the *Convito* (iv) Dante himself did not yet connect Fortune in any way with the Deity.

6. Even as the Intelligences were created by God to regulate the Heavens (cf. *Par.* xxviii), so a power was ordained by Him to guide the destinies of man on earth; and this power is Fortune.

7. These lines may mean that Fortune should not be blamed seeing that, on the one hand, she acts under God's direction, while, on the other, man has the power of free will and a conscience, altogether beyond the pale of her influence (see Canto xv). They may also be taken to imply that the man who has experienced the blows of Fortune should rejoice: for the turn of her wheel may soon bring him happiness.

8. The Angels, created together with the Heavens (cf. *Purg.* xi and xxxi).

9. At the beginning of Canto ii the Poet describes the evening of the first day of the journey; it is now past midnight.

CANTO VIII

Before reaching the high tower, the Poets have observed two flame-signals rise from its summit, and another make answer at a great distance; and now they see Phlegyas, coming with angry rapidity to ferry them over. They enter his bark; and sail across the broad marsh, or Fifth Circle. On the passage, a spirit, all covered with mud, addresses Dante, and is recognized by him. It is Filippo Argenti, of the old Adimari family; who had been much noted for his ostentation, arrogance, and brutal anger. After leaving him, Dante begins to hear a sound of lamentation; and Virgil tells him that the City of Dis (Satan, Lucifer) is getting near. He looks forward, through the grim vapour; and discerns its pinnacles, red, as if they had come out of fire. Phlegyas lands them at the gates. These they find occupied by a host of fallen angels, who deny them admittance.

I SAY continuing,[1] that, long before we reached the foot of the high tower, our eyes went upwards to its summit,

Because of two flamelets, that we saw put there, and another from far give signal back, so far that the eye could scarcely catch it.

And I turned to the Sea of all intelligence; I said: "What says this? and what replies yon other fire? And who are they that made it?"

And he to me: "Over the squalid waves, already thou mayest discern what is expected, if the vapour of the fen conceal it not from thee."

Never did cord impel from itself an arrow, that ran through the air so quickly, as a little bark which I saw

come towards us then through the water, under the guidance of a single steersman, who cried: "Now art thou arrived, fell spirit?"

"Phlegyas, Phlegyas," said my Lord, "this time thou criest in vain; thou shalt not have us longer than while we pass the wash."

As one who listens to some great deceit which has been

done to him, and then sore resents it: such grew Phlegyas in his gathered rage.

My Guide descended into the skiff, and then made me enter after him; and not till I was in, did it seem laden.

Soon as my Guide and I were in the boat, its ancient prow went on, cutting more of the water than it is wont with others.[2]

Whilst we were running through the dead channel, there rose before me one[3] full of mud, and said: "Who art thou, that comest before thy time?"

And I to him: "If I come, I remain not; but thou, who art thou, that hast become so foul?" He answered: "Thou seest that I am one who weep."

And I to him: "With weeping, and with sorrow, accursed spirit, remain thou! for I know thee, all filthy as thou art."

Then he stretched both hands to the boat, whereat the wary Master thrust him off, saying: "Away there with the other dogs!"

And he put his arms about my neck, kissed my face, and said: "Indignant soul! blessed be she that bore thee.

In your world, that was an arrogant personage; good there is none to ornament the memory of him: so is his shadow here in fury.

How many up there now think themselves great kings, that shall lie here like swine in mire, leaving behind them horrible reproaches!"

And I: "Master, I should be glad to see him dipped in this swill, ere we quit the lake."

And he to me: "Before the shore comes to thy view, thou shalt be satisfied; it is fitting that thou shouldst be gratified in such a wish."

A little after this, I saw the muddy pople make such rending of him, that even now I praise and thank God for it.

All cried: "At Filippo Argenti!" The passionate Florentine spirit turned with his teeth upon himself.

Here we left him, so that of him I tell no more; but in my ears a wailing smote me, whereat I bent my eyes intently forward.

The kind Master said: "Now, Son, the city that is named

of Dis draws nigh, with its grave citizens, with its great company." [4]

And I: "Master, already I discern its mosques, distinctly there within the valley, red as if they had come out of fire."

And to me he said: "The eternal fire, which causes them to glow within, shows them red, as thou seest, in this low Hell."

We now arrived in the deep fosses, which moat that joyless city; the walls seemed to me as if they were of iron.

Not before making a long circuit, did we come to a place where the boatman loudly cried to us: "Go out: here is the entrance."

Above the gates I saw more than a thousand spirits, rained from the Heavens,[5] who angrily exclaimed: "Who is that, who, without death,

goes through the kingdom of the dead?" And my sage Master made a sign of wishing to speak with them in secret.

Then they somewhat shut up their great disdain, and said: "Come thou alone; and let that one go, who has entered so daringly into this kingdom.

Let him return alone his foolish way; try, if he can: for thou shalt stay here, that hast escorted him through so dark a country."

Judge, Reader, if I was discouraged at the sound of the accursed words: for I believed not that I ever should return hither.

"O my loved Guide, who more than seven[6] times hast restored me to safety, and rescued from deep peril that stood before me,

leave me not so undone," I said, "and if to go farther be denied us, let us retrace our steps together rapidly."

And that Lord, who had led me thither, said to me: "Fear not, for our passage none can take from us: by Such has it been given to us.

But thou, wait here for me; and comfort and feed thy wearied spirit with good hope: for I will not forsake thee in the low world."

Thus the gentle Father goes, and leaves me here, and I remain in doubt: for yes and no contend within my head.

I could not hear that which was offered to them; but he

had not long stood with them, when they all, vying with one another, rushed in again.

These our adversaries closed the gates on the breast of my Lord who remained without; and turned to me with slow steps.

He had his eyes upon the ground, and his eyebrows shorn of all boldness, and said with sighs: "Who hath denied me the doleful houses?"

And to me he said: "Thou, be not dismayed, though I get angry: for I will master the trial, whatever be contrived for hindrance.

This indolence of theirs is nothing new:[7] for they showed it once at a less secret gate, which still is found unbarred.

Over it thou sawest the dead inscription; and already, on this side of it, comes down the steep, passing the circles without escort, one[8] by whom the city shall be opened to us."

1. No importance need be attached to the tradition based on this word, according to which the first seven cantos were written by Dante before his exile, and the composition of the work was resumed after a considerable interval.
2. The others being spirits.
3. Filippo Argenti's disagreeable character is not sufficient to account for Dante's special hatred. There is evidence to show that members of the Adimari family, to which Filippo belonged, were hostile to the poet himself. In *Par.* xvi Cacciaguida's reference to them is anything but flattering.
4. So far, only sins of *incontinence* have been punished. Within the City of Dis (or Pluto) are punished the graver sins of *malice* and *bestiality* (cf. Canto xi).
5. The angels that fell with Satan (cf. *Rev.* xii. 9).
6. *Seven* is not to be taken literally: cf. *Psalms* cxix. 164; *Proverbs* xxiv. 16.
7. These same demons had opposed Christ at the gate of Hell (cf. *Inf.* iii), when he descended to Limbo (cf. *Inf.* iv).
8. The angel whose coming is described in the next canto.

ÇANTO IX

Dante grows pale with fear when he sees his Guide come back from the gate, repulsed by the Demons, and disturbed in countenance. Virgil endeavours to encourage him, but in perplexed and broken words which only increase his fear. They cannot enter the City of Lucifer in their own strength. The three Furies suddenly appear, and threaten Dante with the head of Medusa. Virgil bids him turn round; and screens him from the sight of it. The Angel, whom Virgil has been expecting, comes across the angry marsh; puts all the Demons to flight, and opens the gates. The Poets then go in, without any opposition; and they find a wide plain, all covered with burning sepulchres. It is the Sixth Circle; and in the sepulchres are punished the Heretics, with all their followers, of every sect. The Poets turn to the right hand, and go on between the flaming tombs and the high walls of the city.

THAT COLOUR which cowardice painted on my face, when I saw my Guide turn back, repressed in him more quickly his new colour.[1]

He stopped attentive, like one who listens: for his eye could not lead him far, through the black air and the dense fog.

"Yet it behoves us to gain this battle," he began; "if not . . . such help was offered to us. Oh! how long to me it seems till some one come!"

I saw well how he covered the beginning with the other that came after, which were words differing from the first.

But not the less his language gave me fear: for perhaps I drew his broken speech to a worse meaning than he held.

"Into this bottom of the dreary shell, does any ever descend from the first degree, whose only punishment is hope cut off?"[2]

This question I made, and he replied to me: "Rarely it occurs that any of us makes this journey on which I go.

It is true, that once before I was down here, conjured

49

by that fell Erichtho,[3] who recalled the shadows to their bodies.

My flesh had been but short time divested of me, when she made me enter within that wall, to draw out a spirit from the Circle of Judas.

That is the lowest place, and the most dark, and farthest from the Heaven, which encircles all; well do I know the way: so reassure thyself.

This marsh, which breathes the mighty stench, all round begirds the doleful city, where we cannot now enter without anger."

And more he said, but I have it not in memory: for my eye had drawn me wholly to the high tower with glowing summit,

where all at once had risen up three Hellish Furies, stained with blood; who had the limbs and attitude of women,

and were girt with greenest hydras; for hair, they had little serpents and cerastes, wherewith their horrid temples were bound.

And he, knowing well the handmaids of the Queen[4] of everlasting lamentation, said to me: "Mark the fierce Erinnyes! [5]

This is Megæra on the left hand; she, that weeps upon the right, is Alecto; Tisiphone is in the middle"; and therewith he was silent.

With her claws each was rending her breast; they were smiting themselves with their palms, and crying so loudly, that I pressed close to the Poet for fear.

"Let Medusa come, that we may change him into stone," [6] they all said, looking downwards; "badly did we avenge the assault of Theseus." [7]

"Turn thee backwards, and keep thy eyes closed: for if the Gorgon show herself, and thou shouldst see her, there would be no returning up again."

Thus said the Master, and he himself turned me, and trusted not to my hands, but closed me also with his own.

O ye, who have sane intellects, mark the doctrine, which conceals itself beneath the veil of the strange verses! [8]

And now there came, upon the turbid waves, a crash of fearful sound, at which the shores both trembled;

a sound as of a wind, impetuous for the adverse heats, which smites the forest without any stay;

shatters off the boughs, beats down, and sweeps away; dusty in front, it goes superb, and makes the wild beasts and the shepherds flee.

He loosed my eyes, and said: "Now turn thy nerve of vision on that ancient foam, there where the smoke is harshest."

As frogs, before their enemy the serpent, run all asunder through the water, till each squats upon the bottom:

so I saw more than a thousand ruined spirits flee before one, who passed the Stygian ferry with soles unwet.

He waved that gross air from his countenance, often moving his left hand before him; and only of that trouble seemed he weary.

Well did I perceive that he was a Messenger of Heaven; and I turned to the Master; and he made a sign that I should stand quiet, and bow down to him.

Ah, how full he seemed to me of indignation! He reached the gate, and with a wand opened it: for there was no resistance.

"O outcasts of Heaven! race despised!" began he, upon the horrid threshold, "why dwells this insolence in you?

Why spurn ye at that Will, whose object never can be frustrated, and which often has increased your pain?

What profits it to butt against the Fates? Your Cerberus, if ye remember, still bears his chin and his throat peeled for doing so." [9]

Then he returned by the filthy way, and spake no word to us; but looked like one whom other care urges and incites

than that of those who stand before him. And we moved our feet towards the city, secure after the sacred words.

We entered into it without any strife; and I, who was desirous to behold the condition which such a fortress encloses,

as soon as I was in, sent my eyes around; and saw, on

either hand, a spacious plain full of sorrow and of evil torment.

As at Arles, where the Rhone stagnates, as at Pola near the Quarnaro gulf,[10] which shuts up Italy and bathes its confines,

the sepulchres make all the place uneven: so did they here on every side, only the manner here was bitterer:

for amongst the tombs were scattered flames, whereby they were made all over so glowing-hot, that iron more hot no craft requires.

Their covers were all raised up; and out of them proceeded moans so grievous, that they seemed indeed the moans of spirits sad and wounded.

And I: "Master, what are these people who, buried within those chests, make themselves heard by their painful sighs?"

And he to me: "Here are the Arch-heretics with their followers of every sect; and much more, than thou thinkest, the tombs are laden.

Like with like is buried here; and the monuments are more and less hot." Then, after turning to the right hand, we passed between the tortures and the high battlements.

1. Virgil forces himself to appear composed, so as not to alarm Dante still more.

2. Dante wishes to find out whether Virgil is really able to aid him in the present difficulty. There is much ingenuity in the question, which is framed in such a way as not to wound Virgil's susceptibilities.

3. Before the battle of Pharsalia, Sextus Pompeius bids the sorceress Erichtho summon the spirit of one of his dead soldiers, so as to learn the issue of his campaign against Cæsar. The passage in which this episode is related by Lucan (*Pharsalia* vi) probably accounts for the appearance of Erichtho here as a sorceress. But the tradition referring to the spirit in Giudecca (for which circle see Canto xxxiv) has not come down to us. Dante probably found it in one of the numerous medieval legends relating to Virgil.

4. Proserpine was carried off by Pluto and became queen of the lower world.

5. The Furies.

6. The head of the Gorgon Medusa was so terrible as to turn any one that beheld it into stone.

7. Theseus, King of Athens, made an unsuccessful attempt to carry off Proserpine from the lower regions. According to the more com-

mon form of the legend, he is punished by being forced to remain in Hell to all eternity; but Dante follows the other version, which tells how he was eventually rescued by Hercules.

8. A bad conscience (the Furies) and stern obduracy which turns the heart to stone (Medusa) are impediments that obstruct the path of every sinner intent on salvation. Reason (Virgil) may do much to obviate these evil influences; but Divine aid is necessary to dissipate them altogether.

9. The last of Hercules' twelve labours was to bring Cerberus to the upper world; in the course of which operation the brute sustained the injuries here alluded to.

10. Aleschans, near Arles, was noted for the tombs of Christians slain in battle against the infidels. The soldiers of Charlemagne were said to have been buried there after the rout of Roncesvalles; and the battle of Aleschans (see the Old French *chanson de geste* of that name), in which William of Orange was defeated by the Saracens, must have added considerably to the number of the tombs.—Pola, a seaport near the southern extremity of the Istrian peninsula, on the Gulf of Quarnero, is still famous for its antiquities, though rather for a Roman amphitheatre than for the tombs mentioned by Dante.

ÇANTO X

The Poets go on, close by the wall of the city, with the fiery tombs on their left; and Dante, observing that the lids of these are all open, inquires if it would be possible to see the spirits contained in them. Virgil, understanding the full import and object of his question, tells him that the Epicurean Heretics are all buried in the part through which they are then passing; and that he will therefore soon have his wish gratified. Whilst they are speaking, the soul of Farinata, the great Ghibelline chief, of whom Dante has been thinking, addresses him from one of the sepulchres. Farinata was the father-in-law of Guido Cavalcanti, Dante's most intimate friend; and Cavalcante de' Cavalcanti, the father of Guido, rises up in the same sepulchre, when he hears the living voice, and looks round to see if his son is there. Amongst other things, Farinata foretells the duration of Dante's exile; and explains to him how the spirits in Hell have of themselves no knowledge concerning events that are actually passing on earth, but only of things distant, either in the past or in the future.

NOW BY a secret path, between the city-wall and the torments, my Master goes on, and I behind him.

"O Virtue supreme! who through the impious circles thus wheelest me, as it pleases thee," I began; "speak to me, and satisfy my wishes.

Might these people, who lie within the sepulchres, be seen? the covers are all raised, and none keeps guard."

And he to me: "All shall be closed up, when, from Jehosaphat, they return here with the bodies which they have left above.

In this part are entombed with Epicurus all his followers, who make the soul die with the body.[1]

Therefore to the question, which thou asketh me, thou shalt soon have satisfaction here within; and also to the wish which thou holdest from me."[2]

And I: "Kind Guide, I do not keep my heart concealed

from thee, except for brevity of speech, to which thou hast ere now disposed me." [3]

"O Tuscan! who through the city of fire goest alive, speaking thus decorously; may it please thee to stop in this place.

Thy speech clearly shows thee a native of that noble country, which perhaps I vexed too much."

Suddenly this sound issued from one of the chests; whereat in fear I drew a little closer to my Guide.

And he said to me: "Turn thee round; what art thou doing? lo there Farinata! [4] who has raised himself erect; from the girdle upwards thou shalt see him all."

Already I had fixed my look on his; and he rose upright with breast and countenance, as if he entertained great scorn of Hell;

and the bold and ready hands of my Guide pushed me amongst the sepultures to him, saying: "Let thy words be numbered."

When I was at the foot of his tomb, he looked at me a little; and then, almost contemptuously, he asked me: "Who were thy ancestors?"

I, being desirous to obey, concealed it not; but opened the whole to him: [5] whereupon he raised his brows a little;

then he said: "Fiercely adverse were they to me, and to my progenitors, and to my party; so that twice I scattered them." [6]

"If they were driven forth, they returned from every quarter, both times," I answered him; "but yours have not rightly learnt that art."

Then, beside him, there rose a shadow, [7] visible to the chin; it had raised itself, I think, upon its knees.

It looked around me, as if it had a wish to see whether some one were with me; but when all its expectation was quenched,

it said, weeping: "If through this blind prison thou goest by height of genius, where is my son [8] and why is he not with thee?"

And I to him: "Of myself I come not: he, that waits yonder, leads me through this place; whom perhaps thy Guido held in disdain." [9]

55

Already his words and the manner of his punishment had read his name to me: hence my answer was so full.

Rising instantly erect, he cried: "How saidst thou: he had? lives he not still? does not the sweet light strike his eyes?"

When he perceived that I made some delay in answering, supine he fell again, and showed himself no more.

But that other, magnanimous, at whose desire I had stopped, changed not his aspect, nor moved his neck, nor bent his side.

"And if," continuing his former words, he said, "they have learnt that art badly, it more torments me than this bed.

But the face of the Queen, who reigns here, shall not be fifty times[10] rekindled ere thou shalt know the hardness of that art.

And so mayest thou once return to the sweet world, tell me why that people is so fierce against my kindred in all its laws?"

Whereat I to him: "The havoc, and the great slaughter, which dyed the Arbia red, causes such orations in our temple."[11]

And sighing, he shook his head; then said: "In that I was not single; nor without cause, assuredly, should I have stirred with the others;

but I was single there, where all consented to extirpate Florence,[12] I alone with open face defended her."

"Ah! so may thy seed sometime have rest," I prayed him, "solve the knot which has here involved my judgment.

It seems that you see beforehand what time brings with it, if I rightly hear; and have a different manner with the present."

"Like one who has imperfect vision, we see the things," he said, "which are remote from us; so much light the Supreme Ruler still gives to us;

when they draw nigh, or are, our intellect is altogether void; and except what others bring us, we know nothing of your human state.

Therefore thou mayest understand that all our knowledge shall be dead, from that moment when the portal of the Future shall be closed."[13]

Then, as compunctious for my fault, I said: "Now will you therefore tell that fallen one, that his child is still joined to the living.

And if I was mute before, at the response, let him know, it was because my thoughts already were in that error which you have resolved for me."

And now my Master was recalling me: wherefore I, in more haste, besought the spirit to tell me who was with him.

He said to me: "With more than a thousand lie I here; the second Frederick[14] is here within, and the Cardinal;[15] and of the rest I speak not."

Therewith he hid himself; and I towards the ancient Poet turned my steps, revolving that saying which seemed hostile to me.

He moved on; and then, as we were going, he said to me: "Why art thou so bewildered?" And I satisfied him in his question.

"Let thy memory retain what thou hast heard against thee," that Sage exhorted me; "and now mark here"; and he raised his finger.

"When thou shalt stand before the sweet ray of that Lady, whose bright eye seeth all, from her shalt thou know the journey of thy life."[16]

Then to the sinister hand he turned his feet; we left the wall, and went towards the middle, by a path that strikes into a valley, which even up there annoyed us with its fetor.

1. The essential doctrine of Epicurus' philosophy is that the highest happiness is of a negative nature, consisting in absence of pain. This is how Dante himself expounds the philosophy in *Conv.* iv. 6. The present passage contains rather a corollary of Epicurus' teaching. Epicurus' *summum bonum* is conceivable on earth, whereas the Catholic Church teaches that life on earth is but "a running unto death," and that true happiness is to be found only in the life beyond.—Note that heresy, as defined in this verse, is elsewhere designated by Dante as the worst form of bestiality (*Conv.* ii. 9). This accounts for the position of the heretics in the City of Dis (*cf.* Canto xi).

2. Perhaps the wish to see some more of his fellow-citizens.

3. See Canto iii.

4. The Uberti family were leaders of the Ghibelline faction in Florence (see *Par.* xvi, *note* 25). Farinata, the present speaker, was born at the beginning of the thirteenth century and became head of his house in 1239.

5. Cf. *Par.* xvi.

6. The Guelfs were overthrown by the Ghibellines in 1248 and in 1260; but each time they managed to regain the upper hand (in 1251 and 1266, respectively). The Uberti were held in special aversion, for even after a general pacification between the two factions had taken place, in 1280, they were among the families who were forbidden to return.

7. Cavalcante Cavalcanti is mentioned in the Decameron, sixth day, ninth story.

8. Guido Cavalcanti (born between 1250 and 1259) was the son of Cavalcante and the son-in-law of Farinata, whose daughter he married at a time when marriages between Guelfs and Ghibellines were frequently resorted to as a means of reconciling the two factions. He and Dante are the chief representatives of the Florentine school of lyrical poetry, which superseded the Bolognese school of Guido Guinicelli (see *Purg.* xi). The friendship of the two poets began with the publication of Dante's first sonnet (*A ciascun' alma presa e gentil core*), to which Guido, among others, replied (1283). The *Vita Nuova* is dedicated to Guido and contains several references to him as the author's best friend. In politics Guido was a White Guelf, and a violent opponent of Corso Donati. Things came to such a pass during Dante's Priorate that it was decided to banish the heads of the two factions. The Whites were sent to Sarzana in the Lunigiana, the climate of which place proved fatal to Guido, who died at the end of August, 1306; so that he was still among the living at the date of the vision.

9. Why Guido should disdain Virgil has been a sore puzzle to the commentators. Some hold that Guido, as a student of philosophy, despised a mere poet; others, that, as an ardent Guelf, he could not admire Virgil—the representative of the Imperial Roman idea; others, quoting *Vita Nuova* xxxi, maintain that he advocated vulgar poetry as opposed to Latin; others, finally, lay stress on his Epicurean principles, as contrasted with Virgil, who represents Reason *illuminated by Divine Grace* (Beatrice having sent him to Dante's aid).

10. Dante was banished in 1302, and the efforts of Pope Benedict XI to bring about the return of the exiles were finally frustrated in June of the year 1304. As Dante is so precise, we must take it that this was less (though it could not have been very much less) than fifty months (Proserpina = Luna) from the time at which Farinata is speaking.

11. At the battle of Montaperti (a village near Siena, situated on a hill close to the Arbia), which was fought on September 4, 1260, the

Sienese and exiled Ghibellines utterly routed the Florentine Guelfs. The last phrase may be taken to mean either that this battle caused The Guelfs to pray for the downfall of the Ghibellines; or that it roused the hatred of the Guelfs to such a degree as to make them sign the decrees of exile against their enemies—a formality which was in those days actually carried out in churches, when they were again in power.

12. After the battle of Montaperti all the Ghibelline leaders, save Farinata, recommended that Florence should be razed to the ground, and this would doubtless have been done, but for Farinata's eloquent appeal on behalf of his native city.

13. That is, after the Last Judgment, when the conception of time is merged in that of eternity.

14. Frederick II (1194-1250) became King of Sicily and Naples in 1197 and Emperor in 1212. Villani says of him that "he was addicted to all sensual delights, and led an Epicurean life, taking no account of any other."

15. Cardinal Ottaviano degli Ubaldini (ca. 1210-1273), an ardent Ghibelline, is said by Villani to have been the only one of the Papal Court who rejoiced at the issue of Montaperti; and, according to Benvenuto, he is reported to have uttered the words: "If I have a soul, I have lost it a thousand times over for the Ghibellines."

In view of the fact that three of Dante's heretics are Ghibellines, it may be worth mentioning that there is contemporary evidence to prove that adherents of this party were frequently suspected of unorthodox opinions merely because they were opposed to the Pope. Dante's judgment, however, was not swayed by any such considerations, as is shown by his condemnation of the Guelf Cavalcanti.

16. As a matter of fact Beatrice does not herself actually relate Dante's future to him; but it is owing to her words that the poet is induced to ask Cacciaguida to enlighten him as to coming events (see *Par.* xvii).

CANTO XI

After crossing the Sixth Circle, the Poets come to a rocky precipice which separates it from the circles beneath. They find a large monument, standing on the very edge of the precipice, with an inscription indicating that it contains a heretical Pope; and are forced to take shelter behind it, on account of the fetid exhalation that is rising from the abyss. Virgil explains what kind of sinners are punished in the three circles which they have still to see; and why the Carnal, the Gluttonous, the Avaricious and Prodigal, the Wrathful and Gloomy-sluggish, are not punished within the city of Dis. Dante then inquires how Usury offends God; and Virgil having answered him, they go on, towards the place at which a passage leads down to the Seventh Circle.

UPON THE edge of a high bank, formed by large broken stones in a circle, we came above a still more cruel throng;

and here, because of the horrible excess of stench which the deep abyss throws out, we approached it under cover

of a great monument, whereon I saw a writing that said: "I hold Pope Anastasius,[1] whom Photinus drew from the straight way."

"Our descent we must delay, till sense be somewhat used to the dismal blast, and then we shall not heed it."

Thus the Master; and I said to him: "Find some compensation, that the time may not be lost." And he: "Thou seest that I intend it.

My Son, within these stones," he then began to say, "are three circlets in gradation,[2] like those thou leavest.

They are all filled with spirits accurst; but, that the sight of these hereafter may of itself suffice thee, hearken how and wherefore they are pent up.

Of all malice,[3] which gains hatred in Heaven, the end is injury; and every such end, either by force or by fraud, aggrieveth others.

But because fraud is a vice peculiar to man, it more displeases God; and therefore the fraudulent are placed beneath, and more pain assails them.

All the first circle is for the violent; but as violence may be done to three persons, it is formed and distinguished into three rounds.

To God, to one's self, and to one's neighbour, may violence be done; I say in them and in their things, as thou shalt hear with evident discourse.

By force, death and painful wounds may be inflicted upon one's neighbour; and upon his substance, devastations, burnings, and injurious extortions:

wherefore the first round torments all homicides and every one who strikes maliciously, all plunderers and robbers, in different bands.

A man may lay violent hand upon himself, and upon his property: and therefore in the second round must every one repent in vain

who deprives himself of your world, gambles away and dissipates his wealth, and weeps there where he should be joyous.

Violence may be done against the Deity, in the heart denying and blaspheming Him; and disdaining Nature and her bounty:

and hence the smallest round seals with its mark both Sodom and Cahors,[4] and all who speak with disparagement of God in their hearts.

Fraud, which gnaws every conscience, a man may practise upon one who confides in him; and upon him who reposes no confidence.

This latter mode seems only to cut off the bond of love which Nature makes: hence in the second circle nests

hypocrisy, flattery, sorcerers, cheating, theft and simony, panders, barrators,[5] and like filth.

In the other mode is forgotten that love which Nature makes, and also that which afterwards is added, giving birth to special trust:

hence in the smallest circle, at the centre of the universe and seat of Dis, every traitor is eternally consumed."

And I: "Master, thy discourse proceeds most clearly, and

excellently distinguishes this gulf,[6] and the people that possess it.

But tell me: Those of the fat marsh; those whom the wind leads, and whom the rain beats; and those who meet with tongues so sharp,—

why are they not punished in the red city,[6] if God's anger be upon them? and if not, why are they in such a plight?"

And he said to me: "Wherefore errs thy mind so much beyond its wont? or are thy thoughts turned somewhere else?

Rememberest thou not the words wherewith thy Ethics treat of the three dispositions[7] which Heaven wills not,

incontinence, malice, and mad bestiality? and how incontinence less offends God,[8] and receives less blame?

If thou rightly considerest this doctrine, and recallest to thy memory who they are that suffer punishment above, without,

thou easily wilt see who they are separated from these fell spirits, and why, with less anger, Divine Justice strikes them."

"O Sun! who healest all troubled vision, thou makest so glad when thou resolvest me, that to doubt is not less grateful than to know.

Turn thee yet a little back," I said, "to where thou sayest that usury offends the Divine Goodness, and unravel the knot."

He said to me: "Philosophy, to him who hears it, points out, not in one place alone, how Nature takes her course

from the Divine Intellect, and from its art; and if thou note well thy Physics,[9] thou wilt find, not many pages from the first,

that your art, as far as it can, follows her, as the scholar does his master; so that your art is, as it were, the grandchild of the Deity.[10]

By these two, if thou recallest to thy memory Genesis at the beginning, it behoves man to gain his bread and to prosper.[11]

And because the usurer takes another way, he contemns

Nature in herself and in her follower, placing elsewhere his hope.

But follow me now, as it pleases me to go: for the Fishes are quivering on the horizon, and all the Wain lies over Caurus,[12] and yonder far onwards we go down the cliff."

1. There is a confusion here between Pope Anastasius II (469-498) and his contemporary the Emperor Anastasius (491-518). It is the latter who was induced by Photinus, a deacon of Thessalonica, to adopt the Acacian heresy, which denied the divine birth of Christ.
2. The reader is referred to the note on "Dante's Hell" on p. 9.
3. It should be noted that later in the present canto, Dante classifies the sins under the heads of incontinence, bestiality and malice. Here, however, the word includes both bestiality and malice.
4. For Sodom, see *Genesis* xix. Cahors, in the South of France, was so notorious for its usurers in the Middle Ages, that "Caorsinus" was frequently employed as a synonym for "usurer."
5. Barratry means traffic in public offices; it is, in fact, the secular equivalent for simony.
6. The "gulf" and "red city" (*cf.* Canto viii) are, of course, the city of Dis.
7. See the *Nicomachean Ethics* of Aristotle, vii: ". . . there are three species of moral character to be avoided, viz., vice, incontinence and bestiality."
8. See the *Ethics*, vii: "It is more pardonable to follow natural desires. . . . The more treacherous men are the wickeder. . . . Bestiality is a lesser thing than vice."
9. Possibly in allusion to Aristotle's phrase: ". . . if Art mimics Nature," in the *Physics* ii.
10. Nature being the connecting link.
11. See *Genesis* i. 28: ". . . replenish the earth and subdue it"; and iii. 19: "In the sweat of thy face shalt thou eat bread." If these really are the verses Dante had in mind, he possibly selected the former (for which ii. 15 may be substituted) to represent Nature, and the latter to represent Art, conceiving the one to be adressed to the agriculturist, the other to the artisan.
12. The sun was in Aries at the time of the Vision (see Canto i, *note* 1). As the constellation of Pisces which immediately precedes that of Aries is now on the horizon, the time indicated is about two hours before sunrise (of the second day). At the same hour the position of Charles' Wain, or Boötes, is in the north-west (Caurus=the north-west wind).

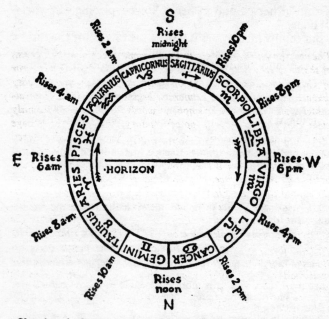

Showing the hours at which the several signs of the Zodiac begin to rise at the spring equinox. Each sign begins to set twelve hours after it begins to rise. The spectator is looking South.

CANTO XII

The way down to the Seventh Circle commences in a wild chasm of shattered rocks. Its entrance is occupied by the Minotaur, horror of Crete, and emblem of the bloodthirsty violence and brutality that are punished below. The monster begins to gnaw himself threateningly; but Virgil directs emphatic words to him, which instantly make him plunge about in powerless fury, and leave the passage free for some time. Dante is then led down amongst loose stones, which are lying so steep, that they give way under the weight of his feet. The river of Blood comes to view as they approach the bottom of the precipice. It goes round the whole of the Seventh Circle, and forms the First of its three divisions. All who have committed Violence against others are tormented in it; some being immersed to the eyebrows, some to the throat, &c., according to the different degrees of guilt; and troops of Centaurs are running along its outer bank, keeping each sinner at his proper depth. Nessus is appointed by Chiron, chief of the Centaurs, to guide Dante to the shallowest part of the river, and carry him across it. He names several of the tyrants, murderers, assassins, &c., that appear as they go along; and then repasses the river by himself to rejoin his companions.

THE PLACE to which we came, in order to descend the bank, was alpine, and such, from what was there besides, that every eye would shun it.

As is the ruin, which struck the Adige in its flank, on this side Trent,[1] caused by earthquake or by defective prop,—

for from the summit of the mountain, whence it moved, to the plain, the rock is shattered so, that it might give some passage to one that were above:

such of that rocky steep was the descent; and on the top of the broken cleft lay spread the infamy of Crete,[2]

which was conceived in the false cow; and when he saw us he gnawed himself, like one whom anger inwardly consumes.

My Sage cried towards him: "Perhaps thou thinkest the

55

Duke of Athens may be here, who, in the world above, gave thee thy death?

Get thee gone, Monster! for this one comes not, instructed by thy sister; but passes on to see your punishments."

As a bull, that breaks loose, in the moment when he has received the fatal stroke, and cannot go, but plunges hither and thither:

so I saw the Minotaur do. And my wary Guide cried: "Run to the passage; whilst he is in fury, it is good that thou descend."

Thus we took our way downwards on the ruin of those stones, which often moved beneath my feet, from the unusual weight.

I went musing, and he said: "Perhaps thou art thinking of this fallen mass, guarded by that bestial rage, which I quelled just now.

I would have thee know, that, when I went the other time, down here to the deep Hell,[3] this rock had not yet fallen.

But certainly, if I distinguish rightly, short while before He[4] came, who took from Dis the great prey of the upmost circle,

on all sides the deep loathsome valley trembled so, that I thought the universe felt love,[5] whereby, as some believe,

the world has oft-times been converted into chaos; and in that moment, here, and elsewhere, this ancient rock made such downfall.[6]

But fix thy eyes upon the valley: for the river of blood draws nigh, in which boils every one who by violence injures others."

O blind cupidity both wicked and foolish, which so incites us in the short life, and then, in the eternal, steeps us so bitterly!

I saw a wide fosse bent arcwise, as embracing all the plain, according to what my Guide had told me;

and between it and the foot of the bank were Centaurs,[7] running one behind the other, armed with arrows, as they were wont on earth to go in hunting.

Perceiving us descend, they all stood still; and from the band three came forth with bows and javelins chosen first.

And one of them cried from far: "To what torment come ye, ye that descend the coast? Tell from thence; if not, I draw the bow."

My Master said: "Our answer we will make to Chiron,[9] there near at hand; unhappily thy will was always thus rash."

Then he touched me and said: "This is Nessus, who died for the fair Dejanira, and of himself took vengeance for himself;

he in the middle, who is looking down upon his breast, is the great Chiron, he who nursed Achilles; that other is Pholus, who was so full of rage.

Around the foss they go by thousands, piercing with their arrows whatever spirit wrenches itself out of the blood farther than its guilt has allotted for it."

We drew near those rapid beasts; Chiron took an arrow, and with the notch put back his beard upon his jaws.

When he had uncovered his great mouth, he said to his companions: "Have ye perceived that the one behind moves what he touches?

The feet of the dead are not wont to do so." And my good Guide, who was already at the breast of him, where the two natures are consorted,

replied: "Indeed he is alive, and solitary thus have I to show him the dark valley; necessity brings him to it, and not sport.

From singing Alleluiah, came She who gave me this new office; he is no robber, nor I a thievish spirit.

But by that virtue through which I move my steps on such a wild way, give us some one of thine whom we may follow,

that he may show us where the ford is, and carry over him upon his back, for he is not a spirit to go through the air."

Chiron bent round on his right breast, and said to Nessus: "Turn, and guide them then; and if another troop encounter you, keep it off."

We moved onwards with our trusty guide, along the

border of the purple boiling, wherein the boiled were making loud shrieks.

I saw people down in it even to the eyebrows; and the great Centaur said: "These are tyrants who took to blood and plunder.

Here they lament their merciless offences; here is Alexander;[9] and fierce Dionysius,[10] who made Sicily have years of woe;

and that brow which has the hair so black is Azzolino;[11] and that other, who is blonde, is Obizzo of Este,[12] who in verity

was quenched by his stepson up in the world." Then I turned me to the Poet, and he said: "Let him be chief guide to thee now, and me second."

A little farther on, the Centaur paused beside a people which, as far as the throat, seemed to issue from that boiling stream.

He showed us a spirit by itself apart, saying: "That one, in God's bosom, pierced the heart which still is venerated on the Thames."[13]

Then some I saw, who kept the head and likewise all the chest out of the river; and of these I recognized many.

Thus more and more that blood grew shallow, until it cooked the feet only; and here was our passage through the fosse.

"As thou seest the boiling stream, on this side, continually diminish," said the Centaur, "so I would have thee to believe

that, on this other, it lowers its bottom more and more, till it comes again to where tyranny is doomed to mourn.[14]

Divine Justice here torments that Attila,[15] who was a scourge on earth; and Pyrrhus and Sextus;[16] and to eternity milks

tears, which by the boiling it unlocks, from Rinier of Corneto, from Rinier Pazzo,[17] who on the highways made so much war." Then he turned back, and repassed the ford.

1. It is best to take this as the landslip known as the Slavini di Marco, on the left bank of the Adige, near Roveredo, between Verona and Trento.

2. Pasiphaë, the wife of Minos, King of Crete, became enamoured

of a bull, and gave birth to the Minotaur, half-man, half-bull. Minos, whose son Androgeos had been killed by the Athenians, exacted from them an annual tribute of seven youths and seven maidens who were devoured by the brute. It was eventually slain by Theseus, King of Athens, with the aid of Minos' daughter Ariadne who gave him a sword and the clue wherewith to unravel the labyrinth in which the monster lived.

3. See Canto ix.

4. For the descent of Christ to Hell see Canto iv. The earthquake at the moment of Christ's death is mentioned in *Matthew* xxvii. 51.

5. Empedocles taught that the universe exists by reason of the discord of the elements and that if harmony (*amor*) were to take the place of this discord a state of chaos would ensue.

6. See Canto xxi.

7. Mythological creatures, half-men, half-horses.

8. Chiron the teacher of Achilles, Hercules and other renowned Greeks (*cf. Purg.* ix). For Nessus see *Par.* ix, *note* 17. Of Pholus we know nothing save that he is often mentioned by the classical poets; Dante's *full of rage* is probably a reminiscence of Virgil's *furentem Centaurum ... Pholum* (*Georg* ii).

9. Probably Alexander the Great is meant, although Dante elsewhere (*Conv.* iv. 11 and *De Mon.* ii. 9) eulogizes this hero. There are several instances of such inconsistency in our poet's works. Some try to avoid the difficulty by identifying *Alessandro* with the Thessalian tyrant of that name (Alexander of Pheræ).

10. Dionysius the Elder, tyrant of Syracuse (405-367 B.C.).

11. Ezzelino III da Romano (1194-1259), the chief of the Ghibelline party in Northern Italy.

12. Obizzo II da Este, Marquis of Ferrara and of the March of Ancona (1264-1293), was an ardent Guelf. It is doubtful whether his son Azzo VIII (1293-1308) really murdered him: possibly Dante is only following a popular tradition. Azzo (who is again mentioned in *Purg.* v, and perhaps in *Inf.* xviii, *note* 4) is evidently called *stepson* with reference to his unnatural crime.

13. Simon de Montfort, who led the English barons against their king, Henry III, was defeated and slain by Henry's son, Edward, at the battle of Evesham (1265). The reference here is to Simon's son, Guy, who avenged his father's death in 1271, while Vicar-General of Tuscany, by openly murdering the English king's nephew, Henry, in a church at Viterbo. Henry's heart was enclosed in a casket, which was placed on a pillar over London Bridge, or, according to another account, in the hand of his statue in Westminster Abbey.

14. Note that the tyrants are punished more severely than even the murderers.

15. Attila, King of the Huns (433-453), known as the *flagellum Dei* (see Canto xiii, *note* 10).

16. This may be Pyrrhus, the son of Achilles, who took part in the

Trojan War, killed Priam and his son Polites and sacrificed his daughter Polyxena to the shade of Achilles; Virgil lays special stress on his cruelty (*Æn.* ii). Or perhaps the reference is to the fabled descendant of this Pyrrhus, the King of Epirus (318-272 B.C.), who was eventually defeated by the Romans (*cf. Par.* vi); the fact that Dante (in the *De Mon.* ii. 10) speaks of Pyrrhus' contempt for gold does not affect the validity of this interpretation: in the first place for the reason given before in *note 9*, and secondly because contempt for gold is not incompatible with great violence and cruelty.

Sextus Pompeius, the son of Pompey the Great, was defeated by Cæsar at Munda, 45 B.C. (*cf. Par.* vi). Lucan and Orosius give him a very bad character.

17. These notorious highwaymen were contemporaries of Dante.

ÇANTO XIII

The Second Round, or ring, of the Seventh Circle; the dismal mystic Wood of Self-murderers. The souls of these have taken root in the ground, and become stunted trees, with withered leaves and branches; instead of fruit, producing poison. The obscene Harpies, insatiable foreboders of misery and despair, sit wailing upon them and devouring them. Pietro delle Vigne is one of the suicides; and he tells Dante what had made him destroy himself, and also in what manner the souls are converted into those uncouth trees. Their discourse is interrupted by the noise of two spirits all naked and torn, who come rushing through the dense wood, pursued by eager female hell-hounds. The first of them is Lano; the second, Jacomo da Sant' Andrea. Both had violently wasted their substance, and thereby brought themselves to an untimely end, and to this punishment. Dante finds a countryman, who, after squandering all his substance, had hanged himself; and hears him speak superstitiously about the calamities of Florence.

NESSUS HAD not yet reached the other side, when we moved into a wood, which by no path was marked.

Not green the foilage, but of colour dusky; not smooth the branches, but gnarled and warped; apples none were there, but withered sticks with poison.

No holts so rough or dense have those wild beasts, that hat the cultivated tracts, between Cecina and Corneto.[1]

Here the unseemly Harpies make their nests, who chased the Trojans from the Strophades[2] with dismal note of future woe.

Wide wings they have, and necks and faces human, feet with claws. and their large belly feathered; they make rueful cries on the strange trees.

The kind Master began to say to me: "Before thou goest farther, know that thou art in the second round; and shalt be, until

thou comest to the horrid sand. Therefore look well,

and thou shalt see things which would take away belief from my speech."

Already I heard wailings uttered on every side, and saw no one to make them: wherefore I, all bewildered, stood still.

I think he thought that I was thinking so many voices came, amongst those stumps, from people who hid themselves on our account.

Therefore the Master said: "If thou breakest off any little shoot from one of these plants, the thoughts, which thou hast, will all become defective."

Then I stretched my hand a little forward, and plucked a branchlet from a great thorn; and the trunk of it cried, "Why dost thou rend me?"[3]

And when it had grown dark with blood, it again began to cry: "Why dost thou tear me? hast thou no breath of pity?

Men we were, and now are turned to trees: truly thy hand should be more merciful, had we been souls of serpents."

As a green brand, that is burning at one end, at the other drops, and hisses with the wind which is escaping:

so from that broken splint, words and blood came forth together: whereat I let fall the top, and stood like one who is afraid.

"If he, O wounded Spirit!" my Sage replied, "could have believed before, what he has seen only in my verse,[4]

he would not have stretched forth his hand against thee; but the incredibility of the thing made me prompt him to do what grieves myself.

But tell him who thou wast; so that, to make thee some amends, he may refresh thy fame up in the world, to which he is permitted to return."

And the trunk: "Thou so allurest me with thy sweet words, that I cannot keep silent; and let it not seem burdensome to you, if I enlarge a little in discourse.

I am he, who held both keys[5] of Frederick's heart, and turned them, locking and unlocking so softly,

that from his secrets I excluded almost every other man;

so great fidelity I bore to the glorious office, that I lost thereby both sleep and life.

The harlot,[6] that never from Cæsar's dwelling turned her adulterous eyes, common bane, and vice of courts,

inflamed all minds against me; and these, being inflamed, so inflamed Augustus, that my joyous honours were changed to dismal sorrows.

My soul, in its disdainful mood, thinking to escape disdain by death, made me, though just, unjust against myself.

By the new roots of this tree, I swear to you, never did I break faith to my lord, who was so worthy of honour.

And if any of you return to the world, strengthen the memory of me, which still lies prostrate from the blow that envy gave it."

The Poet listened awhile, and then said to me: "Since he is silent, lose not the hour; but speak, and ask him, if thou wouldst know more."

Whereat I to him: "Do thou ask him farther, respecting what thou thinkest will satisfy me; for I could not, such pity is upon my heart."

He therefore resumed: "So may the man do freely for thee what thy words entreat him, O imprisoned spirit, please thee

tell us farther, how the soul gets bound up in these knots; and tell us, if thou mayest. whether any ever frees itself from such members."

Then the trunk blew strongly, and soon that wind was changed into these words: "Briefly shall you be answered.

When the fierce spirit quits the body, from which it has torn itself, Minos sends it to the seventh gulf.

It falls into the wood, and no place is chosen for it; but wherever fortune flings it, there it sprouts, like grain of spelt;

shoots up to a sapling, and to a savage plant; the Harpies, feeding then upon its leaves, give pain, and to the pain an outlet.

Like the others, we shall go for our spoils, but not to the end that any may be clothed with them again: for it is not just that a man have what he takes from himself.[7]

Hither shall we drag them, and through the mournful

wood our bodies shall be suspended, each on the thorny tree of its tormented shade."

We still were listening to the trunk, thinking it would tell us more, when by a noise we were surprised;

like one who feels the boar and chase approaching to his stand, who hears the beasts and the branches crashing.

And, lo! on the left hand, two spirits,[8] naked and torn, fleeing so violently that they broke every fan of the wood.

The foremost: "Come now, come, O death!" And the other, who thought himself too slow, cried· "Lano, thy legs were not so ready

at the jousts of Toppo." And since his breath perhaps was failing him, of himself and of a bush he made one group.

Behind them, the wood was filled with black braches, eager and fleet, as greyhounds that have escaped the leash.

Into him, who squatted, they thrust their teeth, and rent him piece by piece; then carried off his miserable limbs.

My Guide now took me by the hand, and led me to the bush, which was lamenting through its bleeding fractures, in vain.

"O Jacomo da Sant' Andrea!" it cried,[9] "what hast thou gained by making me thy screen? what blame have I of thy sinful life?"

When the Master had stopped beside it, he said: "Who wast thou, who, through so many wounds, blowest forth with blood thy dolorous speech?"

And he to us: "Ye spirits, who are come to see the ignominious mangling which has thus disjoined my leaves from me,

O gather them to the foot of the dismal shrub! I was of the city that changed its first patron for the Baptist,[10] on which account he

with his art will always make it sorrowful; and were it not that at the passage of the Arno there yet remains some semblance of him,

those citizens, who afterwards rebuilt it on the ashes left by Attila, would have laboured in vain. I made a gibbet for myself of my own dwelling."

1. The river Cecina and the Marte, on whose banks stands the town of Corneto, indicate the northern and southern boundaries of the marshy coast district of the Maremma in Tuscany.

2. In the third book of the *Æneid*, Virgil narrates how, on the islands of the Strophades, the Harpies defile the viands of the Trojans, who attack the hideous birds. One of these, Celæno (*infelix vates*), prophesies the misfortunes that will befall the Trojans and how they will endure the famine before attaining their goal.

3. The speaker is Pier delle Vigne (*ca.* 1190-1249) minister of the Emperor Frederick II and Chancellor of the two Sicilies. In the latter capacity he rearranged all the laws of the kingdom. Till the year 1247 he enjoyed the utmost confidence of his master. But suddenly he fell into disgrace (the reason usually given being that he plotted with Pope Innocent IV against Frederick); he was blinded and imprisoned and eventually committed suicide. Pier's Latin letters are of great interest and his Italian poems neither better nor worse than the rest of the poetry of the Sicilian school.

4. See *Æn.* iii. The episode of Æneas and Polydorus evidently served Dante as a model for the present passage.

5. When at the height of his power, Pier was often compared to his namesake, the Apostle Peter. This explains the reminiscence of *Matthew* xvi. 19 in these verses, the *keys* being, of course, the keys of punishment and mercy.

6. The *harlot* is Envy.

7. See Canto vi.

8. Jacomo da Sant' Andrea, of Padua, was notorious for the extraordinary way in which he wasted his own and other people's substance, one of the favourite methods he employed being arson. He appears to have been put to death by Ezzelino da Romano in 1239.

Lano, a Sienese, was another spendthrift (*cf.* Canto xxix, *note* 7). Having squandered his fortune, he courted death at a ford called Pieve del Toppo (near Arezzo), where the Sienese were defeated by the Aretines in 1288.

9. This speaker has not been identified, though Benvenuto gives the names of some Florentines who hanged themselves about this time.

10. In Pagan times the patron of Florence was Mars, but when the Florentines were converted to Christianity they built a church in the place of the temple that had been raised in his honour, and dedicated it to St. John the Baptist. The statue of Mars was first stowed away in a tower near the Arno, into which river it fell when the city was destroyed by Attila (whom Dante, following a common error of the time, confounds with Totila). It was subsequently re-erected on the Ponte Vecchio, though in a mutilated state; but for this circumstance, so the superstition ran, the Florentines would never have succeeded in rebuilding the city. As it was, they attributed the unceasing strife within their walls to the offended dignity of the heathen God (see *Par.* xvi).

ÇANTO XIV

Dante cannot go on till he has collected the scattered leaves, and restored them to that wretched shrub in which the soul of his countryman is imprisoned. He is then led by Virgil, across the remainder of the wood, to the edge of the Third Round, or ring, of the Seventh Circle. It is a naked plain of burning Sand; the place appointed for the punishment of those who have done Violence against God, against Nature, and against Nature and Art. (Canto xi.) The Violent against God, the least numerous class, are lying supine upon the sand, and in greater torment than the rest. The Violent against Nature and Art are sitting all crouched up; and the Violent against Nature are moving about, in large troops, with a speed proportioned to their guilt. A slow eternal Shower of Fire is falling upon them all. Capaneus is amongst the supine, unsubdued by the flames, blaspheming with his old decisiveness and fury. After speaking with him, the Poets go on, between the burning sand and the wood of Self-murderers, and soon come to a crimson streamlet that gushes forth from the wood and crosses the sandy plain. Virgil here explains the origin of all the rivers and marshes of Hell.

THE LOVE of my native place constraining me, I gathered up the scattered leaves; and gave them back to him, who was already hoarse.

Then we came to the limit, where the second round is separated from the third, and where is seen a fearful device of justice.

To make the new things clear, I say we reached a plain which from its bed repels all plants.

The dolorous wood is a garland to it round about, as to the wood the dismal fosse; here we stayed our steps close to its very edge.

The ground was a sand, dry and thick, not different in its fashion from that which once was trodden by the feet of Cato.[1]

O vengeance of God! how shouldst thou be feared by every one who reads what was revealed to my eyes!

76

I saw many herds of naked souls, who were all lamenting very miserably; and there seemed imposed upon them a diverse law.

Some were lying supine upon the ground; some sitting all crouched up; and others roaming incessantly.[2]

Those that moved about were much more numerous; and those that were lying in the torment were fewer, but uttered louder cries of pain.

Over all the great sand, falling slowly, rained dilated flakes of fire, like those of snow in Alps without a wind.

As the flames which Alexander, in those hot regions of India, saw fall upon his host,[3] entire to the ground;

whereat he with his legions took care to tramp the soil, for the fire was more easily extinguished while alone:

so fell the eternal heat, by which the sand was kindled, like tinder under flint and steel, redoubling the pain.

Ever restless was the dance of miserable hands, now here, now there, shaking off the fresh burning.

I began: "Master, thou who conquerest all things, save the hard Demons, that came forth against us at the entrance of the gate,

who is that great spirit,[4] who seems to care not for the fire, and lies disdainful and contorted, so that the rain seems not to ripen him?"

And he himself, remarking that I asked my Guide concerning him, exclaimed: "What I was living, that am I dead.

Though Jove weary out his smith, from whom in anger he took the sharp bolt[5] with which on my last day I was transfixed;

and though he weary out the others, one by one, at the black forge in Mongibello, crying: 'Help, help, good Vulcan!'

as he did at the strife of Phlegra; and hurl at me with all his might, yet should he not thereby have joyful vengeance."

Then my Guide spake with a force such as I had not heard before: "O Capaneus! in that thy pride remains unquenched,

thou art punished more: no torture, except thy own raving, would be pain proportioned to thy fury."

Then to me he turned with gentler lip, saying: "That was the one of the seven kings who laid siege to Thebes; and he held, and seems to hold,

God in defiance and prize him lightly; but, as I told him, his revilings are ornaments that well befit his breast.

Now follow me, and see thou place not yet thy feet upon the burning sand; but always keep them back close to the wood."

In silence we came to where there gushes forth from the wood a little rivulet,[6] the redness of which still makes me shudder.

As from the Bulicame[7] issues a streamlet, which the sinful women share amongst themselves: so this ran down across the sand.

Its bottom and both its shelving banks were petrified, and also the margins near it: whereby I discerned that our passage lay there.

"Amidst all the rest that I have shown thee, since we entered by the gate whose threshold is denied to none,

thy eyes have discerned nothing so notable as the present stream, which quenches all the flames above it."

These were words of my Guide: wherefore I prayed him to bestow on me the food, for which he had bestowed the appetite.

"In the middle of the sea lies a waste country," he then said, "which is named Crete, under whose King the world once was chaste.[8]

A mountain is there, called Ida, which once was glad with waters and with foliage; now it is deserted like an antiquated thing.

Rhea of old chose it for the faithful cradle of her son;[9] and the better to conceal him, when he wept, caused cries to be made on it.

Within the mountain stands erect a great Old Man,[10] who keeps his shoulders turned towards Damietta, and looks at Rome as if it were his mirror.

His head is shapen of fine gold, his arms and his breast are pure silver; then he is of brass to the cleft;

from thence downwards he is all of chosen iron, save

that the right foot is of baked clay; and he rests more on this than on the other.

Every part, except the gold, is broken with a fissure that drops tears, which collected perforate that grotto.

Their course descends from rock to rock into this valley; they form Acheron, Styx, and Phlegethon, then, by this narrow conduit, go down

to where there is no more descent; they form Cocytus,[11] and thou shalt see what kind of lake that is: here therefore I describe it not."

And I to him: "If the present rill thus flows down from our world, why does it appear to us only on this bank?"

And he to me: "Thou knowest that the place is round, and though thou hast come far, always to the left, descending towards the bottom,

thou has not yet turned through the entire circle: wherefore if aught new appears to us, it ought not to bring wonder on thy contenance."

And I again: "Master, where is Phlegethon and Lethe found: for thou speakest not of the one, and sayest the other is formed by this rain?"

"In all thy questions truly thou pleasest me," he answered; "but the boiling of the red water might well resolve one of those thou askest.

Lethe thou shalt see, but out of this abyss,[12] there where the spirits go to wash themselves, when their guilt is taken off by penitence."

Then he said: "Now it is time to quit the wood; see that thou follow me; the margins which are not burning, form a path and over them all fire is quenched."

1. The Libyan desert traversed by Cato of Utica, when he led the Pompeian army to effect a junction with Juba, King of Numidia, in the year 47 B.C. The march is described by Lucan, *Phars.* ix.

2. The blasphemers, usurers, and Sodomites respectively.

3. These details are taken from an apocryphal letter, very popular in the Middle Ages, in which Alexander is supposed to send an account of the marvels of India to Aristotle. The original narrative says that the soldiers trampled on the snow, and that they warded off the flames, which subsequently descended from the sky, by means of their garments. The discrepancy we note in Dante occurs already in a version of the episode given by Albertus Magnus in his

De Meteoris, which must, accordingly, have been Dante's imme-diate source.

4. Capaneus, whose defiance of the gods, especially of Jupiter, at the siege of Thebes, is narrated by Statius in a passage (*Thebaid* x) from which Dante borrowed several details.

5. When Jupiter hurled a thunderbolt at Capaneus, before the walls of Thebes, the king did not fall, but met his death standing. Mongi-bello = Mount Etna, in which Vulcan and the Cyclopes forged Jove's thunderbolts. At the battle of Phlegra the giants who at-tempted to storm Olympus were defeated and slain by Jupiter.

6. This is a kind of tributary of the Phlegethon (*cf.* Canto xii).

7. The Bulicame was a noted spring near Viterbo. The fact that its waters were sulphurous and of a reddish colour makes the compari-son specially appropriate. An edict has been unearthed which shows that a portion of the waters was reserved in the manner indicated by Dante as late as the year 1469.

8. The Golden Age, under Saturn, the mythical King of Crete.

9. It having been prophesied to Saturn, Rhea's husband, that he would be dethroned by one of his children, he devoured each one as soon as it was born. To save Jupiter from this fate, Rhea retired to Mount Ida, duped Saturn with a stone wrapped up in swaddling clothes, which he duly swallowed, and as a further precaution, bade the Corybantes make such an uproar that the child's cries could not be heard.

10. This figure, the primary conception of which is based on *Daniel* ii. 32-35, is an allegory of the history of the human race. The four metals are the four ages of man, as then reckoned (*cf.* Ovid, *Metam.* i). The iron foot and that of clay are generally explained as the secular and spiritual authority, respectively; the latter, according to Dante's view, having, since the "donation of Constantine" (see *Par.* xx, *note* 6), always been the more powerful. The old man stands in Crete, partly, perhaps, on account of the central position of this island, situated midway between Asia, Africa, and Europe; but principally because of Virgil's verses (*Æn.* iii): *Creta Jovis magni medio jacet insula ponto, Mons Idæus ubi, et gentis cunabula nostræ*—"our race" being, of course, the Trojans, who were re-garded by Dante as the ancestors of the Romans (*cf.* Canto ii, *note* 4). Damietta, in Egypt, stands for the Eastern civilization, which was superseded by that of Rome (*cf. Par.* vi). The Golden Age alone gave no cause for tears.

11. For Cocytus see Cantos xxxii to xxxiv.

12. That is, in the Terrestrial Paradise, see *Purg.* xxviii.

ÇANTO XV

The crimson stream—whose course is straight across the ring of burning sand, towards the ring of Hell—sends forth a dark exhalation that quenches all the flames over itself and its elevated margins. Upon one of these Dante continues to follow his Guide, in silence, till they have got far from the wood, when they meet a troop of spirits coming along the sand by the side of the bank. Dante is recognized by one of them, who takes him by the skirt; and, on fixing his eyes over the baked and withered figure, he finds it is Brunetto Latini. They speak to each other with great respect and affection, recalling the past, and looking forward to the future under the pressure of separate eternities. Their colloquy has a dark background, which could not be altered; and it stands there in deep perennial warmth and beauty.

NOW ONE of the hard margins bears us on, and the smoke of the rivulet makes shade above, so that from the fire it shelters the water and the banks.

As the Flemings between Wissant and Bruges,[1] dreading the flood that rushes towards them, make their bulwark to repel the sea;

and as the Paduans, along the Brenta, to defend their villages and castles ere Chiarentana[2] feels the heat:

in like fashion those banks were formed, though not so high nor so large, the master, whoever it might be, made them.

Already we were so far removed from the wood, that I should not have seen where it was, had I turned back,

when we met a troop of spirits, who were coming alongside the bank; and each looked at us, as in the evening men are wont

to look at one another under a new moon; and towards us sharpened their vision, as an aged tailor does at the eye of his needle.

Thus eyed by that family, I was recognized by one[3] who took me by the skirt, and said: "What a wonder!"

And I, when he stretched out his arm to me, fixed my eyes on his baked aspect, so that the scorching of his visage hindered not

my mind from knowing him; and bending my face to his, I answered: "Are you here, Ser Brunetto?"

And he: "O my son! let it not displease thee, if Brunetto Latini turn back with thee a little, and let go his train."

I said: "With all my power I do beseech it of you; and if you wish me to sit down with you, I will do so, if it pleases him there, for I go with him."

"O my son," he said, "whoever of this flock stops one instant, lies a hundred years thereafter without fanning himself when the fires strikes him.

Therefore go on; I will follow at thy skirts; and then will I rejoin my band, that go lamenting their eternal losses."

I durst not descend from the road to go level with him; but kept my head bent down, like one who walks in reverence.

He began: "What chance, or destiny, brings thee, ere thy last day, down here? and who is this that shows the way?"

"There above, up in the clear life, I lost myself," replied I, "in a valley, before my age was full."

Only yester morn I turned my back to it; he appeared to me, as I was returning into it, and guides me home again by this path."

And he to me: "If thou follow thy star, thou canst not fail of glorious haven, if I discerned rightly in the fair life;

and if I had not died so early, seeing Heaven so kind to thee, I would have cheered thee in the work.

But that ungrateful, malignant people, who of old came down from Fiesole,[4] and still savours of the mountain and the rock,

will make itself an enemy to thee for thy good deeds; and there is cause: for amongst the tart sorbtrees, it befits not the sweet fig to fructify.

Old report on earth proclaims them blind, a people avaricious, envious, and proud: look that thou cleanse thyself of their customs.

Thy fortune reserves such honour for thee, that both

parties will have a hunger of thee; but far from the goat shall be the grass.

Let the beasts of Fiesole make litter of themselves and not touch the plant, if any yet springs up amid their rankness,

in which the holy seed revives of those Romans who remained there, when the nest of so much malice was made."

"Were my desire all fulfilled," I answered him, "you had not yet been banished from human nature:

for in my memory is fixed, and now goes to my heart, the dear and kind, paternal image of you, when in the world, hour by hour,

you taught me how man makes himself eternal; and whilst I live, beseems my tongue should show what gratitude I have for it.

That which you relate about my course, I write; and keep it, with another text, for a Lady to comment, who will be able if I get to her.

Thus much I would have you know; so conscience chide me not, I am prepared for Fortune as she wills.

Not new to my ears is such earnest: therefore, let Fortune turn her wheel as pleases her, and the boor his mattock."[5]

Thereupon my Master turned backward on his right, and looked at me, then said: "He listens well who notes it."

Not the less I go on speaking with Ser Brunetto, and ask who are the most noted and highest of his companions.

And he to me: "It is good to know of some; of the rest it will be laudable that we keep silence, as the time would be too short for so much talk.

In brief, know that all were clerks, and great scholars, and of great renown; by one same crime on earth defiled.

Priscian[6] goes with that wretched crowd, and Francesco d'Accorso;[7] also, if thou hadst had any longing for such scurf, thou mightest have seen

him[8] there, who by the Servant of servants was translated from the Arno to the Bacchiglione, where he left his ill-strained nerves.

I would say more, but my going and my speech must

not be longer: for there I see new smoke arising from the great sand.

People are coming with whom I may not be; let my 'Treasure,' in which I still live, be commended to thee; and more I ask not."

Then he turned back, and seemed like one of those who run for the green cloth at Verona[9] through the open field; and of them seemed he who gains, not he who loses.

1. Bruges, about ten miles from the sea, and Wissant, between Calais and Cape Grisnez, roughly indicate the western and eastern limits of the coast-line of Flanders (as then constituted).

2. In the Middle Ages the Duchy of Chiarentana, or Carinthia, extended as far as the Paduan district, the inhabitants of which built dykes to protect themselves against the waters of the Brenta, when swollen by the melted snows of the Carnic Alps.

3. Brunetto Latini or Latino (*ca.* 1210-1294), a Florentine Guelf and one of the leading figures in the political life of his native town. As an author, his fame rests on two works written between 1262 and 1266, the *Livre dou Tresor*, a prose encyclopædia composed in French, and the *Tesoretto*, a popular didactic poem in Italian, which contains in a condensed form much of the matter of the larger work. Dante was well acquainted with both these compilations, but was specially indebted to the latter, which is in the form of an allegorical journey. It is absurd to regard Latini as a kind of schoolmaster: he was far too busy a man in other walks of life. The words should obviously be taken in the widest sense; and there can be no doubt that Dante's thought was largely moulded and directed by his illustrious friend.

4. According to tradition, Catiline was besieged by Cæsar in Fiesole, the Roman Fæsulæ, situated on a hill three miles north-west of the future site of Florence. When the town fell, a new city was founded on the Arno, Florence, to wit. The inhabitants were composed partly of the Fiesolans, and partly of the remnants of the Roman army. The Florentine commons (Whites) were commonly held to be descended from the former stock, the nobles (Blacks) from the latter. These two strains were always at variance: hence there was unceasing internal strife at Florence. Dante ingeniously utilizes the *mountain* on which Fiesole stood, and the *rock* of the Fiesolan quarries, with which a great part of Florence was built, to indicate the rough and hard nature of his fellow-citizens. The reference to Dante's fortune has usually been taken to mean that both the Blacks and the Whites would be eager to win over to their side a man of Dante's calibre; but in view of the actual historical facts, which are summarized by Dante in *Par.* xvii, it is perhaps better to adopt Casini's interpretation, that both parties would vie with each other in persecuting the poet—the Blacks with their decrees of exile (after

be opposed the entry of Charles of Valois, which is probably the act specially referred to—see Gardner, pp. 21, 22), and the Whites with their hatred, caused by his defection from their party. The Florentines are called "blind" either because they thoughtlessly opened their gates to Attila, or because, in the year 1117, they lost some booty that was due to them, owing to an ingenious trick played them by the Pisans.

5. Dame Fortune's varying moods affect him as little as the act of the peasant.

6. It is an insult to Dante to assume that he condemns Priscian merely because, as a grammarian and teacher of youth, he was specially liable to fall into the vice here condemned. There must have been some medieval tradition to account for Priscian's position in this circle.

7. Francesco d'Accorso (1225-1293) the son of a great jurist, and himself a lawyer of distinction, lectured at Bologna and at Oxford.

8. Andrea dei Mozzi belonged to a wealthy and influential Florentine family, who were White Guelfs. He was Bishop of Florence from 1287 till the year 1295, when he was translated to the See of Vicenza (on the Bacchiglione) by Boniface VIII (*servus servorum Dei* being one of the official styles of the Popes, from the time of Gregory I).

9. This race was run on the first Sunday in Lent, the prize being a piece of green cloth.

ÇANTO XVI

Dante keeps following his Guide on the same path, and has already got so far as to hear the crimson stream falling into the next circle, when another troop of spirits presents itself under the burning rain. They are the souls of men distinguished in war and council, suffering punishment for the same crime as Brunetto and his companions. Three of them, seeing Dante to be their countryman by his dress, quit the troop and run towards him, entreating him to stop. They allude to their wretched condition, as if under a sense of shame; and make their names known in order to induce him to listen to their eager inquiries. Two of them, Tegghiaio and Rusticucci, are mentioned before (Canto vi); all three were noted for their talents and patriotism; and the zeal they still have for Florence suspends "their ancient wail" of torment. He answers them with great respect; and, in brief emphatic words, declares the condition of the "perverse city." Virgil then leads him to the place where the water descends; makes him unloose a cord wherewith he had girded himself; and casts it down into the abyss, on which a strange and monstrous shape comes swimming up through the dark air.

ALREADY I was in a place where the resounding of the water, that fell into the other circle, was heard like the hum which bee-hives make;

when three shades together, running, quitted a troop that passed beneath the rain of the sharp torment.

They came towards us, and each cried: "Stay thee, thou who by thy dress to us appearest to be some one from our perverse country."

Ah me! what wounds I saw upon their limbs, recent and old, by the flames burnt in. It pains me yet, when I but think thereof.

To their cries my Teacher listened; turned his face toward me, and said: "Now wait: to these courtesy is due;

and were there not the fire, which the nature of the place darts, I should say the haste[1] befitted thee more than them."

They recommenced, as we stood still, their ancient wail;

86

and when they had reached us, all the three made of themselves a wheel.

As champions, naked and anointed, were wont to do, spying their grasp and vantage, ere they came to blows and thrusts at one another:

thus, wheeling, each directed his visage toward me, so that the neck kept travelling in a direction contrary to the feet.

And one of them began: "If the misery of this loose[2] place, and our stained and scorched aspect, bring us and our prayers into contempt,

let our fame incline thy mind to tell us who thou art, that thus securely movest thy living feet through Hell.

He in whose footsteps thou seest me tread, all naked and peeled though he be, was higher in degree than thou believest.

Grandson of the good Gualdrada, his name was Guido Guerra;[3] and in his lifetime he did much with counsel and with sword.

The other, that treads the sand behind me, is Tegghiaio Aldobrandi, whose fame should be grateful up in the world.

And I, who am placed with them in torment, was Jacopo Rusticucci;[4] and certainly, more than aught else, my savage wife injures me."

Had I been sheltered from the fire, I should have thrown myself amid them below, and I believe my Teacher would have permitted it.

But as I should have burnt and baked myself, fear overcame the good will which made me greedy to embrace them.

Then I began: "Not contempt, but sorrow, your condition fixed within me, so deeply that it will not leave me soon,

when this my Lord spake words to me, by which I felt that such men as you are might be coming.

Of your city am I, and always with affection have I rehearsed and heard your deeds and honoured names.

I leave the gall, and go for the sweet apples promised me

by my veracious Guide; but to the centre it behoves me first to fall."

"So may the soul long animate thy members," he then replied, "and so thy fame shine after thee;

tell, if courtesy and valour abide within our city as they were wont, or have gone quite out of it?

for Guglielmo Borsiere[5]—who has been short time in pain with us, and yonder goes with our companions—greatly torments us with his words.'

"The upstart people and the sudden gains, O Florence, have engendered in thee pride and excess, so that thou already weepest thereat."

Thus I cried with face uplifted; and the three, who understood this as an answer, looked at one another as men look when truth is told.

"If otherwhile it costs thee so little to satisfy others," they all replied, "happy thou, if thus thou speakest at thy will!

Therefore, if thou escape out of these gloomy regions, and return to see again the beauteous stars; when thou shalt rejoice to say, 'I was,'[6]

see that thou speak of us to men." Then they broke their wheel; and, as they fled, their nimble legs seemed wings.

An "Amen" could not have been said so quickly as they vanished: wherefore it please my Master to depart.

I followed him; and we had gone but little, when the sound of the water was so near us, that in speaking we should scarce have heard each other.

As that river[7]—which first has a path of its own from Monte Veso toward the east, on the left skirt of the Apennine;

which is called Acquacheta above, ere it descends to its low bed, and is vacant of that name at Forlì—

resounds from the mountain, there above San Benedetto, in falling at a descent, where for a thousand there should be refuge:

thus down from a steep bank we found that tainted water re-echoing, so that in little time it would have stunned the ear.

I had a cord girt round me; and with it I thought some time to catch the Leopard of the painted skin.[8]

After I had quite unloosed it from me, as my Guide commanded me, I held it out to him coiled and wound up.

Then he bent himself toward the right side, and threw it, some distance from the edge, down into that steep abyss.

"Surely," said I within myself, "something new must answer this new signal, which my Master thus follows with his eye."

Ah! how cautious ought men to be with those who see not only the deed, but with their sense look through into the thoughts!

He said to me: "What I expect will soon come up; and what thy thought dreams of, soon must be discovered to thy view."

Always to that truth which has an air of falsehood, a man should close his lips, so far as he is able, for, though blameless, he incurs reproach;

but here keep silent I cannot; and, Reader, I swear to thee, by the notes of this my Comedy—so may they not be void of lasting favour—

that I saw, through that air gross and dark, come swimming upwards, a figure[9] marvellous to every steadfast heart;

like as he returns, who on a time goes down to loose the anchor, which grapples a rock or other thing that in the sea is hid, who spreads the arms and gathers up the feet.

1. The haste to do them reverence.
2. Because of the sand.
3. According to a romantic story, Guido Guerra IV married Gualdrada at the instigation of the Emperor Otto IV, whom she had given a striking proof of her chaste disposition. Their grandson was, contrary to the family tradition, a zealous Guelf, who, having served his party faithfully from 1250 to 1266, was appointed Vicar of Tuscany by Charles of Anjou, and held this post till his death (1272). In one of the most notable events of his career he was associated with Tegghiaio Aldobrandi (a powerful Guelf of the Adimari family, for which see Canto viii). Before the expedition against the Sienese, which resulted in the disastrous defeat of the Guelfs at Montaperti (1260), Tegghiaio acted as the spokesman of the Guelf nobles (headed by Guido Guerra) who voted against the expedition, knowing that the enemy had been reinforced by German mer-

cenaries (see Villani, vi).—The reference to Aldobrandi should perhaps be rendered: ". . . whose words of advice should have been accepted in the world above."

4. Jacopo Rusticucci, a Florentine of lowly origin whose savage-tempered wife appears to have been partly responsible for his present position.

5. Little is known of this personage, save that he appears to have been a purse-maker, who exchanged his trade for a life of social pleasure.

6. "I was," namely—in the world below.

7. The Montone, which (under the name of Acquacheta) rises in the Etruscan Alps, and flows past Forlì and Ravenna into the Adriatic, was, in Dante's time, the first river, rising in those parts, that did not flow into the Po. (Now the Lamone would answer this description.)—Monte Viso is a peak of the Cottian Alps in Piedmont where the Po rises. If the *where* refers to the monastery known as San Benedetto in Alpe and standing on a hill bearing the same name, Dante would mean that the foundation was able to support many more monks than actually were supported by it. But the monastery appears always to have been in want of money; so it is better to refer *where* to *descent*, and to adopt Boccaccio's explanation that the allusion is to a castle and settlement which the Conti Guidi contemplated building for their vassals on this spot.

8. The symbolism here would be quite clear, if we could credit Buti's statement that Dante joined the Franciscans in his youth; but unfortunately the story has every appearance of having been fabricated for the purpose of elucidating this passage. References to *Isaiah* xi. 5 and 6 do not help us much. On the other hand, there can be no doubt that the leopard of Canto i stands for Luxury, that the cord was the symbol of an order noted for the severity of its rule, and that Dante, having just witnessed the tortures inflicted on the luxurious, might be expected henceforth to lead a life of purity without any further reminder. It is not necessary to carry the symbolism further. Virgil, having need of something to attract Geryon's attention, uses the cord merely because it has now become superfluous, and because he has nothing else at hand.

9. This is Geryon, in classical mythology a King of Spain, who was slain by Hercules for the sake of his oxen. His position as guardian of the fraudulent is accounted for by the medieval tradition, according to which he enticed strangers into his power and stealthily killed them. Virgil and other classical poets speak of Geryon as a monster with three bodies; but Dante's description is based rather on *Rev.* ix, 7, 10, 19.

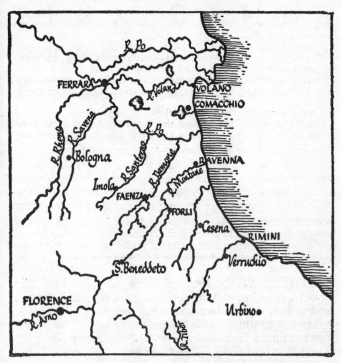

The Rivers of Romagna and the Mouth of the Po in Dante's time ("Inferno," xvi and xxvii).

CANTO XVII

The monster Geryon is described; and the Poets leave the rocky margin of the streamlet, and go down, on the right hand, to the place where he has landed himself. Virgil remains with him, and sends Dante, by himself alone (not without significance), to see the last class of sinners that are punished on the burning sand,—the Usurers who have done Violence to Nature and Art. (Canto xi.) They are sitting all crouched up, tears gushing from their eyes; and each of them has a Purse, stamped with armorial bearings, hanging from his neck. Dante looks into the faces of some; but finds it quite impossible to recognize any one of them. He briefly examines their condition, in the way of duty; listens to a few words that make him understand it completely; and then turns away without speaking at all to them. He goes back to his Guide; and Geryon conveys them down to the Eighth Circle.

"BEHOLD THE savage beast with the pointed tail, that passes mountains, and breaks through walls and weapons; behold him that pollutes the whole world."

Thus began my Guide to speak to me; and beckoned him to come ashore, near the end of our rocky path;

and that uncleanly image of Fraud came onward, and landed his head and bust, but drew not his tail upon the bank.

His face was the face of a just man, so mild an aspect had it outwardly; and the rest was all a reptile's body.

He had two paws, hairy to the armpits; the back and the breast, and both the flanks, were painted with knots and circlets:

never did Tartars or Turks make cloth with more colours, groundwork and broidery; nor by Arachne[1] were such webs laid on her loom.

As at times the wherries lie on shore, that are part in water and part on land; and as there amongst the guzzling Germans,

the beaver[2] adjusts himself to wage his war: so lay that

worst of savage beasts upon the brim which closes the great sand with stone.

In the void glanced all his tail, twisting upwards the venomed fork, which, as in scorpions, armed the point.

My Guide said: "Now must we bend our way a little, to that wicked brute which couches there."

Then we descended on the right, and made ten paces towards the edge, that we might quite avoid the sand and flames;

and when we came to him, I saw upon the sand, a little farther onwards, people sitting near the empty space.

Here my Master said to me: "That thou mayest carry full experience of this round, go and see the state of these.

Let thy talk with them be brief; till thou returnest, I will speak with this beast, that he may lend us his strong shoulders."

Thus also, on the utmost limit of that seventh circle, all alone I went to where the woeful folk were seated.

Through the eyes their grief was bursting forth; on this side, on that, they with their hands kept warding off, sometimes the flames, sometimes the burning soil.

Not otherwise the dogs in summer do, now with snout, now with paw, when they are bitten by fleas, or flies, or breezes.

After I had set my eyes upon the visages of several on whom the dolorous fire falls, I knew not any of them; but I observed

that from the neck of each there hung a pouch, which had a certain colour and a certain impress, and thereon it seems their eye is feasting.

And as I came amongst them looking, on a yellow purse I saw azure, that had the semblance and gesture of a lion.[3]

Then, my look continuing its course, I saw another of them, red as blood, display a goose more white than butter.[4]

And one[5] who, with a sow azure and pregnant, had his argent sacklet stamped, said to me: "What art thou doing in this pit?

Get thee gone; and, as thou art still alive, know that my neighbour Vitaliano[6] shall sit here at my left side.

With these Florentines am I, a Paduan; many a time they

din my ears, shouting: 'Let the sovereign cavalier[7] come, who will bring the pouch with three goats!'" Then he writhed his mouth, and thrust his tongue out, like an ox that licks his nose.

And I, dreading lest longer stay might anger him who had admonished me to stay short time, turned back from those forwearied souls.

I found my Guide, who had already mounted on the haunch of the dreadful animal; and he said to me: "Now be stout and bold!

Now by such stairs must we descend; mount thou in front: for I wish to be in the middle, that the tail may not do hurt to thee."

As one who has the shivering of the quartan so near, that he has his nails already pale and trembles all, still keeping the shade,

such I became when these words were uttered; but his threats excited in me shame, which makes a servant brave in presence of a worthy master.

I placed myself on those huge shoulders; I wished to say, only the voice came not as I thought: "See that thou embrace me."

But he, who at other times assisted me in other difficulties, soon as I mounted, clasped me with his arms, and held me up;

then he said: "Geryon, now move thee! be thy circles large, and gradual thy descent: think of the unusual burden that thou hast."

As the bark goes from its station backwards, backwards, so the monster took himself from thence; and when he felt himself quite loose,

there where his breast had been he turned his tail, and stretching moved it, like an eel, and with his paws gathered the air to him.

Greater fear there was not, I believe, when Phaëton[8] let loose the reins, whereby the sky, as yet appears, was burnt;—

nor when poor Icarus[9] felt his loins unfeathering by the heating of the wax, his father crying to him, "An ill way thou goest!"—

than was mine, when I saw myself in the air on all sides, and saw extinguished every sight, save of the beast.

He goes on swimming slowly, slowly; wheels and descends; but I perceive it not, otherwise than by a wind upon my face and from below.

Already, on the right hand, I heard the whirlpool make a hideous roaring under us; whereat, with eyes downwards, my head I stretched.

Then was I more timorous as regards dismounting: for I saw fires and heard lamentings, so that I cower all trembling.

And then I saw—for I had not seen it before—the sinking and the wheeling, through the great evils which drew near on diverse sides.

As the falcon, that has been long upon his wings—that, without seeing bird or lure, makes the falconer cry, "Ah, ah! thou stoopest"—

Descends weary; then swiftly moves himself with many a circle, and far from his master sets himself disdainful and sullen:

so at the bottom Geryon set us, close to the foot of the ragged rock; and, from our weight relieved, he bounded off like an arrow from the string.

1. For Arachne see *Purg.* xii.
2. The beaver is gradually being driven northward: in Dante's time it appears to have been found principally in Germany, and now it is more common in Sweden and Norway. Natural histories teach us that the beaver is a vegetable feeder; so that the idea implied in these lines, and probably taken from some medieval Bestiary, that it uses its tail for catching fish, is a fallacy.
3. The arms of the Florentine Gianfigliazzi, who belonged to the faction of the Black Guelfs.
4. The arms of the Florentine Ubbriachi, a Ghibelline family.
5. Rinaldo de' Scrovigni of Padua.
6. Another Paduan, Vitaliano de' Vitaliani.
7. The Florentine Messer Giovanni Buiamonte de' Bicci.
8. Phaëton, the son of Phœbus Apollo, in order to prove his parentage, which had been doubted, asked his father to let him drive the chariot of the sun for one day. The request was granted, but Phaëton was too weak to hold in the chargers, scorched a portion of the Heavens and almost set the Earth on fire. To save the latter from destruction, Jupiter put a stop to Phaëton's erratic course by killing him with a thunderbolt (*cf. Par.* xvii). The Pythagoreans

explained the Milky Way as being due to Phaëton's misadventure (*cf. Conv.* ii. 15).

9. Icarus attempted to fly with the help of a pair of wings supplied him by his father Dædalus, but was drowned owing to his approaching too near the sun, which melted the wax with which the wings were fastened (*cf. Par.* viii).

ÇANTO XVIII

During the "circling and sinking," on the back of Geryon, Dante has observed the outlines of the lowest Hell, and here briefly describes them. He is now far beneath the circles of Violence, &c.; and has to see the punishment of far graver sins. Everything around him is made of dark solid rock. The high wall of the great circular shaft, in which he has descended with Geryon, forms the outer barrier of the Eighth Circle, where he and his Guide have just been landed. The circle itself occupies the whole of a shelving space, which lies between the foot of the high wall and the brim of another (lower) shaft or "well" that is exactly in the centre; and it is divided (in successive rings) into ten deep fosses or chasms, resembling the trenches which begird a fortress, and each containing a different class of sinners. Across these chasms, and the banks which separate them from one another, run cliffs from the outer border of the circle down to the central well, forming lines of roads and bridges that also resemble those by which a fortress is entered from different sides. The well contains the Traitors and Satan, "Emperor of the dolorous kingdom," in the middle of them. Virgil turns to the left, and conducts Dante along the outer edge of the first chasm, till they come to one of the cliffs. This they ascend; and, turning to the right, pass two of the bridges, and examine the chasms beneath them. In the First are Panders (Ruffiani) and lying Seducers, hurrying along in two separate crowds—meeting one another—all naked and scourged by Horned Demons. In the Second, Flatterers immersed in filth.

THERE IS a place in Hell called Malebolge,[1] all of stone, and of an iron colour, like the barrier which winds round it.

Right in the middle of the malignant field yawns a well exceeding wide and deep, whose structure I shall tell in its own place.[2]

The border therefore that remains, between the well and the foot of the high rocky bank, is round; and it has its bottom divided into ten valleys.

As is the form that ground presents, where to defend the walls successive ditches begird a castle:

such image these made here; and as, from the thresholds of the fortress, there are bridges to the outward bank:

so from the basis of the rock proceeded cliffs that crossed the embankments and the ditches, down to the well which truncates and collects them.

In this place; shaken from the back of Geryon, we found ourselves; and the Poet kept to the left, and I moved behind.

On the right hand I saw new misery, new torments, and new tormentors, wherewith the first chasm was filled.

In its bottom the sinners were naked; on our side of the middle they came facing us; and, on the other side, along with us, but with larger steps:

thus the Romans, because of the great throng, in the year of Jubilee,[3] upon the bridge have taken means to pass the people over;

so that, on the one side, all have their faces towards the Castle, and go to St. Peter's; at the other ledge, they go towards the Mount.

On this side, on that, along the hideous stone, I saw horned Demons with large scourges, who smote them fiercely from behind.

Ah! how they made them lift their legs at the first strokes! truly none waited for the second or the third.

As I went on, my eyes were met by one,[4] and instantly I said: "This one I have seen before."

I therefore stayed my feet to recognize him; and the kind Guide stood still with me, and allowed me to go back a little.

And that scourged spirit thought to hide himself, lowering his face; but little it availed him, for I said: "Thou, that dost cast thy eye upon the ground,

if the features which thou wearest be not false, thou art Venedico Caccianimico; but what brings thee to such a biting pickle?"

And he to me, "Unwillingly I tell it; but thy clear speech, that makes me recollect the former world, compels me.

It was I who led the fair Ghisola to do the Marquis' will, however the unseemly tale may sound.

And I am not the only Bolognese that weeps here: nay, this place is so filled with us, that as many tongues are not now taught

to say *sipa* between Savena and Reno; and if thou desirest assurance and testimony thereof, recall to thy memory our avaricious heart."

And as he thus spake, a Demon smote him with his lash, and said: "Away! pander, there are no women here to coin."

I rejoined my Escort; then, with a few steps, we came to where a cliff proceeded from the bank.

This we very easily ascended; and, turning to the right upon its jagged ridge, we quitted those eternal circles.

When we reached the part where it yawns beneath to leave a passage for the scourged, my Guide said: "Stay, and let the look

strike on thee of these other ill-born spirits, whose faces thou hast not yet seen, for they have gone along with us."

From the ancient bridge we viewed the train, who were coming towards us, on the other side, chased likewise by the scourge.

The kind Master, without my asking, said to me: "Look at that great soul who comes, and seems to shed no tear for pain:

what a regal aspect he yet retains! That is Jason,[5] who, by courage and by counsel, bereft the Colchians of the ram.

He passed, by the isle of Lemnos, after the bold merciless women had given all their males to death.

There, with tokens and fair words, did he deceive the young Hypsipyle, who had before deceived all the rest.

He left her there pregnant and forlorn: such guilt condemns him to such torment; and also for Medea vengeance is taken.

With him go all who practise the like deceit; and let this suffice to know respecting the first valley, and those whom it devours."

We had already come to where the narrow pathway

crosses the second bank, and makes of it a buttress for another arch.

Here we heard people whining in the other chasm, and puffing with mouth and nostrils, and knocking on themselves with their palms.

The banks were crusted over with a mould from the vapour below, which concretes upon them, which did battle with the eyes and with the nose.

The bottom is so deep, that we could see it nowhere without mounting to the ridge of the arch, where the cliff stands highest.

We got upon it; and thence in the ditch beneath, I saw a people dipped in excrement, that seemed as it had flowed from human privies.

And whilst I was searching with my eyes, down amongst it, I beheld one with a head so smeared in filth, that it did not appear whether he was layman or clerk.

He bawled to me: "Why are thou so eager in gazing at me, more than the others in their nastiness?" And I to him: "Because, if I rightly recollect,

I have seen thee before with thy hair dry; and thou art Alessio Interminei[6] of Lucca: therefore do I eye thee more than all the rest."

And he then, beating his pate: "Down to this, the flatteries wherewith my tongue was never weary have sunk me!"

Thereupon my Guide said to me: "Stretch thy face a little forwards, that thy eyes may fully reach the visage

of that unclean and dishevelled strumpet, who yonder with her filthy nails scratches herself, now cowering low, now standing on her feet.

It is Thais, the harlot, who answered her paramour, when he said: 'Dost thou thank me much?' 'Nay, wondrously.'[7] And herewith let our view rest sated."

1. Literally, Evil Pouches.
2. See Canto xxxii.
3. The first Jubilee of the Roman Church was instituted by Boniface VIII in the year 1300. The bridge is that of Castello Sant' Angelo, so called from the castle that stood at one end of it, while the *mount* is either Mount Janiculum, or, more probably, the Monte Giordano.

4. Venedico de' Caccianemici, whose father, Alberto, was head or the Guelfs of Bologna. In politics he adhered to the family tradition and was a follower of the Marquis of Este, being finally exiled from his native city (1289). His sister's seducer was either Obizzo II or Azzo VIII of Este (see Canto xii, *note* 12); probably the former, as Ghisola eventually married a certain Niccolò da Fontana in 1270, and Azzo did not succeed to the Marquisate till 1293. Dante alludes to the fact that several versions of the story had got abroad, according to one of which Venedico was innocent.

There are two local touches in this passage. The word *pickle* is evidently selected with reference to the Salse, a ravine near Bologna into which the bodies of criminals were thrown; and *sipa = sia* is the Bolognese equivalent for the affirmative particle *sì*. The Savena flows two miles to the west, and the Reno two miles to the east of Bologna.

5. Jason is in this circle first, for having, on his way to Colchis, seduced Hypsipyle, the daughter of King Thoas of Lemnos, whose life she had managed to save, when the Lemnian women put all their males to death; and secondly, for having abandoned Medea, the daughter of King Æëtes of Colchis, whom he married as a reward for having enabled him to carry off the Golden Fleece, but whom he subsequently deserted for Creusa.

6. Little is known of Alessio de' Intermine (ll) i, save that his family were prominent Whites of Lucca, and that he was still alive in the year 1295.

7. At the beginning of the third act of Terence's *Eunuchus*, Thraso asks his servant Gnatho, with reference to a slave he had sent to Thais: *Magnas vero agere gratias Thais mihi?*—whereupon Gnatho answers: *Ingentes*. It should be noted that Dante holds Thais responsible for the messenger's reply, and that his knowledge of the passage is evidently derived from the *De Amicitia* (§38) of Cicero, who quotes it as a typical instance of flattery, with the remark that the proper answer would have been *magnas*, rather than *ingentes*

CANTO XIX

In the Third chasm are the Simonists. The heart of Dante seems almost too full for utterance when he comes in sight of them. To him they are, as it were, a more hateful species of panders and seducers than those he has just left; and they lie beneath the vile flatterers "that call evil good, and good evil; that put darkness for light, and light for darkness." It is they who have prostituted the things of God for gold and silver, and made "His house a den of thieves." They are all fixed one by one in narrow round holes along the sides and bottom of the rock, with the head downwards, so that nothing more than the feet and part of the legs stands out. The soles of them are tormented with flames, which keep flickering from the heels to the toes, and burn with a brightness and intensity proportioned to the different degrees of guilt. Dante is carried down by his Guide to the bottom of the chasm; and there finds Pope Nicholas III, who, with a weeping voice, declares his own evil ways, and those of his successors Boniface VIII and Clement V. The Poet answers with a sorrow and indignation proportionate to his reverence for the Mystic Keys, speaking as if under the pressure of it. Virgil then lifts him up again, and lightly carries him to the rough summit of the arch which forms a passage over the next chasm.

O SIMON MAGUS![1] O wretched followers of his and robbers ye, who prostitute the things of God, that should be wedded unto righteousness,

for gold and silver! now must the trump sound for you: for ye are in the third chasm.

Already we had mounted to the following grave, on that part of the cliff which hangs right over the middle of the fosse.

O Wisdom Supreme, what art thou showest in heaven, on earth and in the evil world, and how justly thy Goodness dispenses!

I saw the livid stone, on the sides and on the bottom, full of holes, all of one breadth; and each was round.

Not less wide they seemed to me, nor larger, than those
that are in my beauteous San Giovanni made for stands to
the baptizers;[2]

one of which, not many years ago, I broke to save one
that was drowning in it: and be this a seal to undeceive all
men.

From the mouth of each emerged a sinner's feet, and
legs up to the calf; and the rest remained within.

The soles of all were both on fire: wherefore the joints
quivered so strongly, that they would have snapped in
pieces withes and grass-ropes.

As the flaming of things oiled moves only on their outer
surface: so was it there, from the heels to the points.

"Master! who is that who writhes himself,[3] quivering
more than all his fellows," I said, "and sucked by ruddier
flame?"

And he to me: "If thou wilt have me carry thee down
there, by that lower bank, thou shalt learn from him about
himself and about his wrongs."

And I: "Whatever pleases thee, to me is grateful: thou
art my lord, and knowest that I depart not from thy will;
also thou knowest what is not spoken."

Then we came upon the fourth bulwark; we turned
and descended, on the left hand, down there into the per-
forated and narrow bottom.

The kind Master did not yet depose me from his side,
till he brought me to the cleft of him who so lamented with
his legs.

"O whoe'er thou be that hast thy upper part beneath,
unhappy spirit, planted like a stake!" I began to say; "if
thou art able, speak."

I stood, like the friar who is confessing a treacherous
assassin that, after being fixed,[4] recalls him and thus delays
the death;

and he cried: "Art thou there already standing, Boni-
face?[5] art thou there already standing? By several years the
writ has lied to me.

Art thou so quickly sated with that wealth, for which
thou didst not fear to seize the comely Lady[6] by deceit,
and then make havoc of her?"

I became like those who stand as if bemocked, not comprehending what is answered to them, and unable to reply.

Then Virgil said: "Say to him quickly, 'I am not he, I am not he whom thou thinkest.'" And I replied as was enjoined me.

Whereat the spirit quite wrenched his feet; thereafter, sighing and with voice of weeping, he said to me: "Then what askest thou of me?

If to know who I am concerneth thee so much, that thou hast therefore passed the bank, learn that I was clothed with the Great Mantle;

and verily I was a son of the She-bear, so eager to advance the Whelps, that I pursed wealth above, and here myself.

Beneath my head are dragged the others who preceded me in simony, cowering within the fissures of the stone.

I too shall fall down thither, when he comes for whom I took thee when I put the sudden question.

But longer is the time already, that I have baked my feet and stood inverted thus, than he[7] shall stand planted with glowing feet:

for after him, from westward, there shall come a lawless Shepherd, of uglier deeds, fit to cover him and me.

A new Jason[8] will it be, of whom we read in Maccabees; and as to that high priest his king was pliant, so to this shall be he who governs France."

I know not if here I was too hardy, for I answered him in this strain: "Ah! now tell me how much treasure

Our Lord required of St. Peter, before he put the keys into his keeping? Surely he demanded nought but 'Follow me!'[9]

Nor did Peter, nor the others, ask of Matthias gold or silver, when he was chosen for the office which the guilty soul had lost.[10]

Therefore stay thou here, for thou art justly punished; and keep well the ill-got money, which against Charles made thee be bold.[11]

And were it not that reverence for the Great Keys thou heldest in the glad life yet hinders me,

I should use still heavier words: for your avarice grieves

the world, trampling on the good, and raising up the wicked.

Shepherds such as ye the Evangelist perceived, when she, that sitteth on the waters,[12] was seen by him committing fornication with the kings;

she that was born with seven heads, and in her ten horns had a witness so long as virtue pleased her spouse.

Ye have made you a god of gold and silver; and wherein do ye differ from the idolater, save that he worships one, and ye a hundred?

Ah Constantine! to how much ill gave birth, not thy conversion, but that dower which the first rich Father took from thee!"[13]

And whilst I sung these notes to him, whether it was rage or conscience gnawed him, he violently sprawled with both his feet.

And indeed I think it pleased my Guide, with so satisfied a look did he keep listening to the sound of the true words uttered.

Therefore with both his arms he took me; and, when he had me quite upon his breast, remounted by the path where he had descended.

Nor did he weary in holding me clasped to him, till he bore me away to the summit of the arch which is a crossway from the fourth to the fifth rampart.

Here he placidly set down the burden, pleasing to him on the rough steep cliff, which to the goats would be a painful passage; thence another valley was discovered to me.

1. Simon of Samaria who was rebuked by St. Peter for thinking that the "gift of God may be purchased with money" (see *Acts* viii. 9-24). The Simonists or Simoniacs—those guilty of trafficking in spiritual offices—derive their name from him.
2. The font in the Baptistery of Florence was surrounded by holes in which the officiating priest stood, so as to be free from the pressure of the crowd. Dante once broke the marble round one of these holes, to save the life of a boy who had got wedged into it; and he uses the present opportunity to free himself from certain charges (probably of sacrilege) that were levied against him at the time.
3. This is Nicholas III of the Orsini family who occupied the Papal See from 1277 till 1280.

4. According to Florentine law, hired assassins were executed by being planted, nead downwards, in a hole in the earth which was then filled up again.

5. Note the ingenuity with which Dante assigns Boniface VIII (born *ca.* 1227, Pope 1294–1303) his place in Hell, though he survived the date of the Vision by three and a half years (see *Purg.* xx, *note* 16).

6. The Church, according to the allegory of the *Song of Solomon.*

7. Nicholas had held the uppermost position among the simoniacal Popes in Hell for twenty years (1280–1300), but Boniface will occupy it for a period of eleven years only—from his death in 1303, till the death of Clement V in 1314. The latter, Bertrand de Got, Archbishop of Bordeaux, was elected Pope in 1305, through the influence of Philip the Fair of France. It was he who transferred the Papal See to Avignon, where it remained till 1377 (*cf. Par.* xxx).

8. Jason induced Antiochus Epiphanes, by means of bribes, to make him high priest and to permit the introduction of pagan customs (see *2 Maccabees* iv. 7); similarly, Clement abused his high office in return for the good services Philip had done him.

9. See *Matthew* iv. 19, *John* xxi. 19.

10. See *Acts* i. 13–26; the *guilty soul* is, of course, Judas.

11. Charles of Anjou, having refused to let his nephew marry a niece of Nicholas, the latter turned against him, and, having been bribed by the Emperor Palælogus (who feared Charles's designs on the Eastern Empire), assisted John of Procida in his conspiracy against the House of Anjou, which culminated in the Sicilian Vespers (1282). Some modern historians, regarding all this as legend, and pointing to the fact that Nicholas died two years before the Vespers, prefer to take the *ill-got money* as the tithes which Nicholas employed to carry out his plans against Charles. But the former seems the more satisfactory interpretation.

12. For "the great whore that sitteth upon many waters," see *Revelation* xvii. The "seven heads" are explained as the seven virtues or the seven sacraments, and the "ten hours" as the ten commandments, which were kept while the occupants of the Holy See were virtuous.

13. See *Par.* xx, *note* 6.

CANTO XX

From the arch of the bridge, to which his Guide has carried him, Dante now sees the Diviners, Augurs, Sorcerers, &c., coming slowly along the bottom of the Fourth Chasm. By help of their incantations and evil agents, they had endeavoured to pry into the Future which belongs to the Almighty alone, interfering with His secret decrees; and now their faces are painfully twisted the contrary way; and, being unable to look before them, they are forced to walk backwards. The first that Virgil names is Amphiaräus; then Tiresias the Theban prophet, Aruns the Tuscan. Next comes Manto, daughter of Tiresias; on seeing whom, Virgil relates the origin of Mantua his native city. Afterwards he rapidly points out Eurypylus, the Grecian augur; Michael Scott, the great magician, with slender loins (possibly from his northern dress); Guido Bonatti of Forlì; Asdente, shoemaker of Parma, who left his leather and his awls to practise divination; and the wretched women who wrought malicious witchcraft with their herbs and waxen images. And now the Moon is setting in the western sea; time presses, and the Poets hasten to the next chasm.

OF NEW punishment behoves me to make verses, and give matter for the twentieth canto of the first canzone, which concerns the sunken.

I now was all prepared to look into the depth discovered to me, which was bathed with tears of anguish;

and through the circular valley I saw a people coming silent and weeping, at the pace which the Litanies[1] make in this world.

When my sight descended lower on them, each seemed wondrously distorted, between the chin and the commencement of the chest:

for the face was turned towards the loins; and they had to come backward, for to look before them was denied.

Perhaps by force of palsy some have been thus quite distorted; but I have not seen, nor do believe it to be so.

Reader, so God grant thee to take profit of thy reading, now think for thyself how I could keep my visage dry,

when near at hand I saw our image so contorted, that the weeping of the eyes bathed the hinder parts at their division?

Certainly I wept, leaning on one of the rocks of the hard cliff, so that my Escort said to me: "Art thou, too, like the other fools?

Here pity lives when it is altogether dead. Who more impious than he that sorrows at God's judgment?

Raise up thy head, raise up, and see him for whom the earth opened herself before the eyes of the Thebans, whereat they all cried, 'Whither rushest thou,

Amphiaräus?[2] Why leavest thou the war?' And he ceased not rushing headlong down to Minos, who lays hold on every sinner.

Mark how he has made a breast of his shoulders: because he wished to see too far before him, he now looks behind and goes backward.

Behold Tiresias[3] who changed his aspect, when of male he was made woman, all his limbs transforming;

and afterwards he had again to strike the two involved serpents with his rod, before he could resume his manly plumes.

That is Aruns, who to the belly of him (Tiresias) has his back, he who in the mountains of Luni,[4] where hoes the Cararese that dwells beneath,

amongst the white marbles had the cave for his abode; from which he could observe the stars and the sea with unobstructed view.

And she that covers her bosom, which thou seest not, with her flowing tresses, and has all her hairy skin on the other side,

was Manto,[5] who searched through many lands, then settled there where I was born: whence it pleases me a little to have thee listen to me.

After her father went out of life, and the city of Bacchus came to be enslaved,[6] she for a long time roamed the world.

Up in beautiful Italy there lies a lake, at the foot of the

Alps which shut in Germany above the Tyrol, which is called Benacus.[7]

Through a thousand fountains, I believe, and more, the Apennine, between Garda and Val Camonica, is irrigated by the water which stagnates in that lake.

At the middle there is a place where the Trentine pastor, and he of Brescia, and the Veronese might bless, if they went that way.

Peschiera, a fortress beautiful and strong to front the Brescians and the Bergamese, sits where the shore around is lowest.

There all that in the bosom of Benacus cannot stay, has to descend and make itself a river, down through green pastures.

Soon as the water sets head to run, it is no longer named Benacus, but Mincio,—to Governo where it falls into the Po.

Not far has it flowed, when it finds a level, on which it spreads and makes a marsh thereof, and is wont in summer to be at times unwholesome.

The cruel virgin, passing that way, saw land amidst the fen, uncultivated and naked of inhabitants.

There, to shun all human intercourse, she halted with her ministers to do her arts; and there she lived and left her body vacant.

Afterwards the men, that were scattered round, gathered together on that spot which was strong by reason of the marsh it had on every side.

They built the city over those dead bones; and for her who first chose the place, they called it Mantua without other augury.

Once the inhabitants were denser in it, ere the folly of Casalodi was cheated by Pinamonte.[8]

Therefore I charge thee, if thou ever hearest other origin given to my city, let no falsehood defraud the truth."

And I: "Master, thy words are to me so certain, and so take hold of my belief, that all others would be to me extinguished coals.

But tell me of the people that are passing, if thou seest

any of them worthy of note: for to that alone my mind recurs."9

Then he said to me: "That one, who from the cheek stretches forth his beard upon his dusky shoulders, was an augur, when Greece was so empty of males,10

that hardly they remained even in the cradles; and in Aulis he, with Calchas, gave the time for cutting the first cable. Eurypylus his name; and my high Tragedy thus sings him in some place: well knowest it thou, who knowest the whole.

That other who is so small about the flanks was Michael Scott;11 and of a truth he knew the play of magic frauds.

See Guido Bonatti; see Asdente,12 who now would wish he had attended to his leather and his cord, but too late repents.

See the wretched women who left the needle, the shuttle, and the spindle, and made themselves divineresses; they wrought witchcraft with herbs and images.

But now come! for Cain and his thorns already holds the confine of both hemispheres, and under Seville touches the wave;

and already yesternight the Moon was round; well must thou remember: for she did not hurt thee any time in the deep wood." Thus he spake to me, and we went on meanwhile.

1. The processions in which the litanies are chanted.
2. For Amphiaräus, the prophet of Argos, see *Par.* iv. *note* 15.
3. This story of the Theban soothsayer Tiresias (the father of Manto) is told by Ovid, *Metam.* iii.
4. Aruns, the Etruscan soothsayer (his face is reversed over his back), prophesied the civil war which ended in the victory of Cæsar and the death of Pompey (Lucan, *Phars.* i).—For Luni, see *Par.* xvi, *note* 17.
5. Dante makes Virgil in this passage give an account of the foundation of Mantua that differs considerably from the version given in *Æn.* x. This is no slip, as is shown by Virgil's last words. On the other hand, it certainly is a slip (and one which it is futile to attempt to account for) that Manto should here be placed among the soothsayers, while in *Purg.* xxii she is referred to as being in Limbo.
6. Referring either to the tyrannous rule which Thebes (the birthplace of Bacchus) had to endure under Cleon, or to the capture of that city by the Epigoni.

7. Now known as Lago di Garda; the Val Camonica is a valley some fifty miles long in North-East Lombardy; Mount Apennino is probably a spur of the Rhætian Alps, above Gargnano; Gardia is a town on the east side of the lake; the *place* is either the little island dei Frati, some miles south of Sali, or the mouth of the river Tignalga, near Campione; the fortress of Peschiera, at the south-east extremity of the lake, was raised by the Veronese, as a defence against the people of Brescia and Bergamo; Governo is the modern Governolo, on the right bank of the Mincio, about 12 miles from Mantua.

8. In 1272, the Brescian Counts of Casalodi made themselves masters of Mantua, but were very unpopular and threatened with expulsion. Pinamonte de Buonaccorsi, who was anxious to become lord of Mantua himself, advised Albert of Casalodi to banish all the nobles of importance, representing to him that they were the chief source of danger. Then he put himself at the head of the populace, massacred all the families of note that remained, and expelled the Count, retaining the lordship of the city till 1291.

9. *Cf. Par.* xvii.

10. At the time of the Trojan war, all the Greeks were absent from their country, taking part in the siege of Troy. Before the Greeks left Aulis, Calchas advised Agamemnon to sacrifice Iphigenia. But Eurypylus had nothing to do with this incident, which Dante appears to have confused with the passage in which Virgil tells how both Eurypylus and Calchas are consulted with reference to the departure of the Greeks from Troy (*Æn.* ii).—For the use of the word *Tragedy* see *de Vulg. El.* ii. 4—*Per tragediam superiorem stilum inducimus; per comediam inferiorem*, etc.; see also *Epist. ad Can. Grand.* x.

11. Michael Scott of Balwearie (*ca.* 1190–1250) studied at Oxford, Paris and Toledo; he followed the Emperor Frederick II to his court, but died in Scotland. In philosophy proper he appears to have figured only as a translator, *e. g.*, of Aristotle; his original work deals with the occult sciences. For further particulars see Scotts Note O to the *Lay of the Last Minstrel.*

12. Guido Bonatti, of Forlì, tiler and astrologer, author of a *Liber introductorius ad Judicia Stellarum* (written *ca.* 1170). He acted as the private astrologer of Guido da Montefeltro (see Canto xxvii) and is credited with a share in his victory over the French Papal forces at Forlì in 1282.

Asdente, a shoemaker of Parma, who was noted as a soothsayer in the second half of the 13th century. In *Conv.* iv. 16, Dante says that Asdente would be noble, if notoriety were tantamount to nobility.

13. *Cain and his thorns*—the moon (see *Par.* ii, *note* 4). The "Pillars of Hercules" were regarded by Dante and his contemporaries as the extreme western limit of the world, and he designates this boundary variously as Spain, Gades, the Iberus, Morocco, or Seville, as here (see *Par.* xxvii, *note* 11). During the night preceding Good Friday,

the moon (which guided Dante's steps in the dark wood, see Canto 1) was at full. The poet is now describing the setting of the moon (or rising of the sun) on the Saturday morning, which, for reasons given in the chronological note on page 6, may be timed as having taken place at 6.52.

ÇANTO XXI

The Poets come to the arch of the Fifth Chasm or Budget which holds the Barterers or Barrators, the malefactors who made secret and vile traffic of their Public offices and authority, in order to gain money. And as the Tyrants and Assassins (Canto xii) are steeped in boiling Blood, and have the Centaurs (emblems of Violence) watching them with arrows, and keeping each at his proper depth; so here the Barterers lie covered with filthy Pitch which clings to them, and get themselves rent in pieces by horrid Demons —Shadows of their sins—whenever they appear above its surface. The chasm is very dark, and at first Dante can see nothing but the pitch boiling in it. A Demon arrives with one of the Senators of Lucca on his shoulders, throws him down from the bridge, tells what a harvest of Barrators there is in that city, and hastens away for more. Other Demons, hitherto concealed beneath the bridge (like secret sins), rush out and fiercely teach the poor sneaking senator under what conditions he has to swim in the pitch. After some parley with Malacoda, chief of the Fiends, the Poets are sent on, along the edge of the chasm with an ugly and questionable escort of Ten.

THUS FROM bridge to bridge we came, with other talk which my Comedy cares not to recite; and held the summit, when

we stood still to see the other cleft of Malebolge and the other vain lamentings; and I found it marvellously dark.

As in the arsenal of the Venetians boils the clammy pitch in winter, to caulk their damaged ships,

which they cannot navigate; and, instead thereof, one builds his ship anew, one plugs the ribs of that which hath made many voyages;

some hammer at the prow, some at the stern; some make oars, and some twist ropes; one mends the jib, and one the mainsail:

so, not by fire but by art Divine, a dense pitch boiled down there, and overglued the banks on every side.

113

It I saw; but saw naught therein, except the bubbles which the boiling raised, and the heaving and compressed subsiding of the whole.

Whilst I was gazing fixedly down on it, my Guide, saying, "Take care, take care!" drew me to him from the place where I was standing.

Then I turned round, like one who longs to see what he must shun, and who is dashed with sudden fear,

so that he puts not off his flight to look; and behind us I saw a black Demon come running up the cliff.

Ah, how ferocious was his aspect! and how bitter he seemed to me in gesture, with his wings outspread, and light of foot!

His shoulders that were sharp and high, a sinner with both haunches laded; and of each foot he held the sinew grasped.

"Ye Malebranche[1] of our bridge!" he said, "lo! one of Santa Zita's[2] Elders; thrust him under, while I return for others

to that city which I have provided well with them: every one there is a barrator, except Bonturo;[3] there they make 'Ay' of 'No' for money."

Down he threw him, then wheeled along the flinty cliff; and never was mastiff loosed with such a haste to follow thief.

The sinner plunged in, and came up again writhing convolved; but the Demons, who were under cover of the bridge, cried: "Here the Sacred Face[4] besteads not;

here swim ye otherwise than in the Serchio:[5] therefore, unless thou wishest to make trial of our drags, come not out above the pitch."

Then they struck him with more than a hundred prongs, and said: "Covered thou must dance thee here; so that, if thou canst, thou mayest pilfer privately."

Not otherwise do the cooks make their vassals dip the flesh into the middle of the boiler with their hooks, to hinder it from floating.

The kind Master said to me: "That it may not be seen that thou art here, cower down behind a jag, so that thou mayest have some screen for thyself;[6]

and whatever outrage may be done to me, fear not thou: for I know these matters, having once before been in the like affray."

Then he passed beyond the head of the bridge; and when he arrived on the sixth bank, it was needful for him to have a steadfast front.

With that fury and that storm, wherewith the dogs rush forth upon the poor man who where he stops suddenly seeks alms,

rushed those Demons from beneath the bridge, and turned against him all their crooks; but he cried: "Be none of ye outrageous!

Before ye touch me with your forks, let one of you come forth to hear me, and then take counsel about hooking me."

All cried: "Let Malacoda go"; thereat one moved himself, the other standing firm, and came to him, saying: "What will this avail him?"

"Dost thou expect, Malacoda," said my Master, "to find I have come here, secure already against all your hindrances,

without will Divine and fate propitious? Let me pass on: for it is willed in Heaven that I show another this savage way."

Then was his pride so fallen, that he let the hook drop at his feet, and said to the others: "Now strike him not!"

And my Guide to me: "O thou that sittest cowering, cowering amongst the great splinters of the bridge, securely now return to me!"

Whereat I moved, and quickly came to him; and the Devils all pressed forward, so that I feared they might not hold the compact.

And thus once I saw the footmen, who marched out under treaty from Caprona,[7] fear at seeing themselves among so many enemies.

I drew near my Guide with my whole body, and turned not away my eyes from the look of them, which was not good.

They lowered their drag-hooks, and kept saying to one another: "Shall I touch him on the rump?" and answering: "Yes, see thou nick it for him."

But that Demon, who was speaking with my Guide, turned instant round, and said: "Quiet, quiet, Scarmiglione!"

Then he said to us: "To go farther by this cliff will not be possible: for the sixth arch lies all in fragments at the bottom;

and if it please you still to go onward, go along this ridge: near at hand is another cliff which forms a path.

Yesterday, five hours later than this hour,[8] completed a thousand two hundred and sixty-six years since the way here was broken.

Thitherward I send some of these my men, to look if anyone be out airing himself; go with them, for they will not be treacherous."

"Draw forward, Alichino and Calcabrina," he then began to say, "and thou, Cagnazzo; and let Barbariccia lead the ten.

Let Libicocco come besides, and Draghignazzo, tusked Ciriatto, and Graffiacane, and Farfarello, and furious Rubicante.

Search around the boiling glue; be these two safe as far as the other crag, which all unbroken goes across the dens."

"Oh me! Master, what is this that I see?" said I; "ah, without escort let us go alone, if thou knowest the way; for as to me, I seek it not!

If thou beest so wary, as thou art wont, dost thou not see how they grind their teeth, and with their brows threaten mischief to us?"

And he to me: "I would not have thee be afraid; let them grind on at their will: for they do it at the boiled wretches."

By the sinister bank they turned; but first each of them had pressed his tongue between the teeth toward their Captain, as a signal; and he of his rump had made a trumpet.

1. Evil Claws.
2. Lucca, of which city Zita (who died *ca.* 1275 and was canonized by Nicholas III) was the patron saint. Buti says this alderman was a certain Martino Bottaio, and that he died in 1300.
3. Bonturo Dati was head of the popular party of Lucca at this time, and surpassed all his fellow-townsmen in barratry.
4. An ancient wooden image of Christ, preserved in the Church of San Martino, and invoked by the inhabitants in their hour of need.

5. The Serchio flows a few miles north of Lucca.

6. Note that Dante is more terrified in this circle of the barrators, and has more cause for alarm than anywhere else in the Inferno. It would almost seem as though the demons are intended by the poet to recall his Florentine enemies, who persecuted and exiled him on the strength of false charges of barratry. The names afford no clue; unless, indeed, we may connect the *frog* of Canto xxiii with Ranieri di Zaccaria, who signed the decree of November 6, 1315.

7. In August, 1289, the Tuscan Guelfs captured the Pisan fortress of Caprona. We may assume that Dante actually took part in this operation: for the opening lines of the following canto point conclusively to his having been present at the continuation of the same campaign in the Aretine territory; and from Bruni we learn that he fought at the battle of Campaldino (*Purg.* v) earlier in the same year.

8. In *Conv.* iv. 23 Dante says that Jesus died at noon. It is, therefore, now seven o'clock of the morning following Good Friday. For the earthquake, see Canto xii, and *note* 4.

CANTO XXII

The Demons, under their "great Marshal" Barbariccia, lead the way, along the edge of the boiling Pitch; and Dante, who keeps looking sharply, relates how he saw the Barrators lying in it, like frogs in ditch-water, with nothing but their "muzzles" out, and instantly vanishing at sight of Barbariccia; and how Graffiacane booked one of them and hauled him up like a fresh-speared otter, all the other Demons gathering round and provoking Rubicante to mangle the unlucky wretch. At Dante's request, Virgil goes forward, and asks him who he is; and no sooner does the pitchy thief mention how he took to barratry in the service of worthy King Thibault of Navarre, than he is made to feel the bitter force of Ciriatto's tusks. Barbariccia now clasps him with both arms, and orders the rest to be quiet, till Virgil has done with questioning. But "Scarletmoor" loses patience; "Dragon-face" too will have a clutch at the legs; Farfarello, "wicked Hell-bird" that he is, glares ready to strike; and their "Decurion" has difficulty in keeping them off. At last the cunning barrator, though Cagnazzo raises his dog-face in scornful opposition, plays off a trick by which he contrives to escape. Thereupon Calcabrina and Alichino fall to quarrelling, seize each other like two mad vultures, and drop into the burning pitch; and the whole troop is left in fitting disorder.

I HAVE ere now seen horsemen moving camp, and commencing the assault, and holding their muster, and at times retiring to escape;

coursers have I seen upon your land, O Aretines! and seen the march of foragers, the shock of tournaments and race of jousts,

now with trumpets, and now with bells,[1] with drums and castle-signals, and with native things and foreign:

but never yet to so uncouth a cornet saw I cavaliers nor footmen move, nor ship by mark of land or star.

We went with the ten Demons: ah, hideous company! but, "In church with saints, and with guzzlers in the tavern."

Yet my intent was on the pitch, to see each habit of the chasm and of the people that were burning in it.

As dolphins, when with the arch of the back they make sign to mariners that they may prepare to save their ship:[2]

so now and then, to ease the punishment, some sinner showed his back and hid in less time than it lightens.

And as at the edge of the water of a ditch, the frogs stand only with their muzzles out, so that they hide their feet and other bulk:

thus stood on every hand the sinners; but as Barbariccia approached, they instantly retired beneath the seething.

I saw, and my heart still shudders thereat, one[3] linger so, as it will happen that one frog remains while the other spouts away;

And Graffiacane, who was nearest to him, hooked his pitchy locks and hauled him up, so that to me he seemed an otter.

I already knew the name of everyone, so well I noted them as they were chosen, and when they called each other, listened how.

"O Rubicante, see thou plant thy clutches on him, and flay him!" shouted together all the accursed crew.

And I: "Master, learn if thou canst, who is that piteous wight, fallen into the hand of his adversaries."

My Guide drew close to his side and asked him whence he came; and he replied: "I was born in the kingdom of Navarre.

My mother placed me as a servant of a lord; for she had borne me to a ribald waster of himself and of his substance.

Then I was domestic with the good king Thibault; here I set myself to doing barratry, of which I render reckoning in this heat."

And Ciriatto, from whose mouth on either side came forth a tusk as from a hog, made him feel how one of them did rip.

Amongst evil cats the mouse had come; but Barbariccia locked him in his arms, and said: "Stand off whilst I enfork him!"

And turning his face to my Master: "Ask on," he said,

"if thou wouldst learn more from him, before some other undo him."

The Guide therefore: "Now say, of the other sinners knowest thou any that is a Latian, beneath the pitch?" And he: "I parted

just now from one[4] who was a neighbour of theirs on the other side; would I still were covered with him, for I should not fear claw nor hook!"

And Libicocco cried: "Too much have we endured!" and with the hook seized his arm, and mangling carried off a part of brawn.

Draghignazzo, he too, wished to have a catch at the legs below; whereat their Decurion wheeled around with evil aspect.

When they were somewhat pacified, my Guide without delay asked him that still kept gazing on his wound:

"Who was he, from whom thou sayest that thou madest an ill departure to come ashore?" And he answered: "It was Friar Gomita,

he of Gallura, vessel of every fraud, who had his master's enemies in hand, and did so to them that they all praise him for it:

money took he for himself, and dismissed them smoothly, as he says; and in his other offices besides, he was no petty but a sovereign barrator.

With him keeps company Don Michel Zanche of Logodoro;[5] and in speaking of Sardinia the tongues of them do not feel weary.

Oh me! see that other grinning; I would say more; but fear he is preparing to claw my scurf."

And their great Marshal, turning to Farfarello, who rolled his eyes to strike, said: "Off with thee, villainous bird!"

"If you wish to see or hear Tuscans or Lombards," the frightened sinner then resumed, "I will make them come.

But let the evil claws hold back a little, that they may not fear their vengeance; and I, sitting in this same place,

for one that I am, will make seven come, on whistling as is our wont to do when any of us gets out."

Cagnazzo at these words raised his snout, shaking his

head, and said: "Hear the malice he has contrived, to throw himself down!"

Whereat he, who had artifices in great store, replied: "Too malicious indeed! when I contrive for my companions greater sorrow."

Alichino held in no longer, and in opposition to the others said to him: "If thou stoop, I will not follow thee at gallop,

but beat my wings above the pitch; let the height be left and be the bank a screen, to see if thou alone prevailest over us."

O Reader, thou shalt hear new sport! All turned their eyes toward the other side, he first who had been most unripe for doing it.

The Navarrese chose well his time; planted his soles upon the ground, and in an instant leapt and from their purpose freed himself.

Thereat each was stung with guilt; but he most who had been cause of the mistake; he therefore started forth, and shouted: "Thou'rt caught!"

But little it availed him; for wings could not outspeed the terror the sinner went under; and he, flying, raised up his breast:

not otherwise the duck suddenly dives down, when the falcon approaches, and he returns up angry and defeated.

Calcabrina, furious at the trick, kept flying after him, desirous that the sinner might escape, to have a quarrel.

And, when the barrator had disappeared, he turned his talons on his fellow, and was clutched with him above the ditch.

But the other was indeed a sparrowhawk to claw him well; and both dropt down into the middle of the boiling pond.

The heat at once unclutched them; but rise they could not, their wings were so beglued.

Barbariccia with the rest lamenting, made four of them fly over to the other coast with all their drags; and most rapidly

on this side, on that, they descended to the stand; they stretched their hooks towards the limed pair, who were already scalded within the crust; and we left them thus embroiled.

1. See *note* 7 of the preceding canto. Each Italian city had its car which was used as a kind of rallying-point in battle, and provided with a bell.

2. This is evidently a popular belief of Dante's time, and is referred to, for example, in Giamboni's Italian version of Latini's *Tresor*.

3. This is a certain Ciampolo, so the early commentators say, without adding anything to the facts given by Dante. The King Tebaldo is Teobaldo II (Thibault V, Count of Champagne), King of Navarre (1253–1270).

4. Gomita was a Sardinian friar in the service of Nino Visconti of Pisa (see *Purg* viii), judge of Gallura. The Pisans, to whom Sardinia belonged at this time, divided the island into four judicial districts: Gallura is in the north-east. His acts of barratry were overlooked, till Nino discovered that the friar was favouring the escape of certain prisoners; whereupon he had him hanged.—*on the other side*, *i.e.* in Sardinia.

5. Enzio, the natural son of Frederick II, who made him King of Sardinia, married Adelasia di Torres, mistress of Logodoro (northwest of Sardinia) and Gallura. Being called to Italy by the wars of his house, he appointed Michel Zanche his Vicar in Logodoro. Enzio was captured by the Bolognese in 1249, and remained their prisoner till his death (1271). In the meantime, Adelasia obtained a divorce and married Michel, who governed the provinces till he was murdered by his son-in-law, Branca d'Oria, about the year 1290 (see Canto xxxiii).

ÇANTO XXIII

Dante keeps following his Guide in silence, with head bent down, meditating on the things he has had to witness in that chasm of the pitch. The fable of the Frog and the Mouse comes into his mind; then fear that the ugly Demons may seek vengeance for their misfortune. He sees them coming with outstretched wings, when Virgil takes him in his arms, and rapidly glides down with him into the next chasm. Here they find the Hypocrites walking along the narrow bottom in slow procession, heavy-laden with cloaks of lead, which are gilded and of dazzling brightness on the outside. Dante speaks with Catalano and Loderingo, two Friars of Bologna; and has just begun to tell them what he thinks of their evil deeds, when he observes Caiaphas stretched across the narrow road, and fixed to it, in such a way that all the other Hypocrites have to trample on him as they pass. The sight of that High Priest and His ignominious punishment is enough. Hypocrisy did its very utmost in him and "the others of that Council," for which the Jews still suffer. The Poets hasten away to another class of sinners.

SILENT, apart, and without escort we went on, the one before and the other after; as Minor Friars go their way.

My thought was turned, by the present strife, to Æsop's fable where he spoke of the frog and mouse: [1]

for Ay and Yea pair not better, than does the one case with the other, if with attentive mind the beginning and end of each be well accoupled.

And as one thought from the other springs, so arose from that another then, which made my first fear double.

I thus bethought me: "These through us are put to scorn, and with damage and mockery of such sort, as I believe must greatly vex them.

If rage be added to their malice, they will pursue us, fiercer than the dog that leveret which he snaps."

Already I felt my hair all rise with fear; and was looking back intently, as I said: "Master, if thou do not hide

thyself and me speedily, I dread the Malebranche: they

123

are already after us; I so imagine them that I hear them now."

And he: "If I were of leaded glass, I should not draw thy outward image more quickly to me, than I impress that (image) from within.

Even now thy thoughts were entering among mine, with similar act and similar face; so that of both I have made one resolve.

In case the right coast so slopes, that we may descend into the other chasm, we shall escape the imagined chase."

He had not ended giving this resolve, when I saw them come with wings extended, not far off, in will to seize us.

My Guide suddenly took me, as a mother—that is awakened by the noise, and near her sees the kindled flames—

who takes her child and flies, and caring more for him than for herself, pauses not so long as even to cast a shift about her;

and down from the ridge of the hard bank, supine he gave himself to the pendent rock, which dams up one side of the other chasm.

Never did water run so fast through spout to turn a landmill's wheel, when it approaches nearest to the ladles,

as my Master down that bank, carrying me away upon his breast, as his son and not as his companion.

Scarcely had his feet reached the bed of the depth below, when they were on the height above us; but no fear it gave him:

for the high Providence, that willed to place them ministers of the fifth ditch, takes the power of leaving it from all.

There beneath we found a painted people, who were going round with steps exceeding slow, weeping, and in their look tired and overcome.

They had cloaks on, with deep hoods before their eyes, made in the shape that they make for the monks in Cologne.

Outward they are gilded, so that it dazzles; but within all lead, and so heavy, that Frederick's compared to them were straw.[2]

O weary mantle for eternity! We turned again to the left hand, along with them, intent upon their dreary weeping;

but that people, tired by their burden, came so slowly that our company was new at every movement of the hip.

Wherefore I to my Guide: "See that thou find someone who may by deed or name be known; and move thy eyes around as we go on."

And one, who understood the Tuscan speech, cried after us: "Stay your feet, ye who run so fast through the brown air;

perhaps thou shalt obtain from me that which thou askest." Whereat my Guide turned round and said: "Wait, and then at his pace proceed."

I stood still, and saw two, showing by their look great haste of mind to be with me; but the load and the narrow way retarded them.

When they came up, long with eye askance they viewed me, without uttering a word; then they turned to one another, and said between them:

"This one seems alive by the action of his throat; and if they are dead, by what privilege go they divested of the heavy stole?"

Then they said to me: "O Tuscan, that are come to the college of the sad hypocrites! to tell us who thou art disdain not."

And I to them: "On Arno's beauteous river, in the great city I was born and grew and I am with the body that I have always had.

But you, who are ye from whom distils such sorrow as I see, down your cheeks? and what punishment is on ye that glitters so?"

And one of them replied to me: "Our orange mantles are of lead so thick, that the weights thus cause their scales to creak.

We were Jovial Friars, and Bolognese: I named Catalano, and Loderingo he; and by thy city chosen together,[3]

as usually one solitary man is chosen, to maintain its peace; and we were such, that it yet appears round the Gardingo."

I began: "O Friars, your evil"—but said no more, for to my eyes came one, cross-fixed in the ground with three stakes.

When he saw me, he writhed all over, blowing into his beard with sighs; and Friar Catalano, who perceived this,

said to me: "That confixed one, on whom thou gazest, counselled the Pharisees that it was expedient to put one man to tortures for the people.[4]

Traverse and naked he is upon the road, as thou seest; and his to feel the weight of every one that passes;

And after the like fashion his father-in-law is racked in this ditch, and the others of that Council, which was a seed of evil for the Jews."

Then I saw Virgil wonder over him that was distended on the cross so ignominiously in the external exile.

Afterwards he to the Friar addressed these words: "Let it not displease you, so it be lawful for you, to tell us if on the right hand lies any gap

by which we both may go out hence, without constraining any of the Black Angels to come and extricate us from this bottom."

So he answered: "Nearer than thou dost hope, there is a stone that moves from the great circular wall, and bridges all the cruel valleys,

save that in this 'tis broken and covers it not: you will be able to mount up by its ruins, which slope down the side, and on the bottom make a heap."

The Guide stood still awhile with head bent down, then said: "Falsely did he tell the way, who hooks the sinners yonder."[5]

And the Friar: "I heard once at Bologna many of the Devil's vices told; amongst which, I heard that he is a liar and the father of lies."

Then with large steps my Guide went on, somewhat disturbed with anger in his look whereat I from the laden spirits parted, following the prints of his beloved feet.

1. A frog having offered to carry a mouse across a piece of water tied it to its leg; but when they got half-way, the frog treacherously dived and the mouse was drowned. Suddenly a kite swooped down and devoured both of them. This fable is not to be found in the original Æsop, but is contained, with slight variations, in most of the medieval collections of fables that went under his name. In one of these versions, as Mr. Paget Toynbee points out, the mouse escapes, and this may have been the form of the story known to

Dante, whose *mouse* escapes, too, though of course, only for a time.

2. Frederick II punished those guilty of treason by having them fastened in cloaks of lead which were then melted over a fire.

3. Catalano de' Catalani, or de' Malavolti (*ca.* 1210–1285), a Guelf of Bologna, and Loderingo degli Andolò, a Ghibelline of the same city, were in 1266 jointly appointed to the office of *Podestà* of Florence, as it was thought that two outsiders, belonging to different factions, would be likely to rule impartially. The *Gardingo*, that portion of Florence now occupied by the Piazza di Firenze, was the site of the palace of the Uberti, which was destroyed in 1266 during a popular rising against the Ghibellines.—*Frati Gaudenti* was the nickname given to the *Ordo militiæ beatæ Mariæ*, founded at Bologna in 1261, with the approval of Urban IV. The objects of the Order were praiseworthy (reconciliation of enemies, protection of the weak, etc.), but the rules were so lax that it soon had to be disbanded.

4. The words of the high priest Caiaphas at the Council were: "Ye know nothing at all, nor consider that it is expedient for us, that one man should die for the people, and that the whole nation perish not" (*John* xi. 49, 50). For the father-in-law of Caiaphas see *John* xviii. 13.

5. For Malacoda's falsehood see Canto xxi.

ÇANTÓ XXIV

In this canto, the vehement despair of the poor Italian peasant, who has no food for his sheep, and thinks he is going to lose them, gives a lively image of Dante's dependence on his mystic Guide; while the Sun with freshened hair points to the real Virgil. Here too on the shattered bridge, as at the foot of the Hill in Canto First, help in many senses is necessary; and Dante, put quite out of breath by climbing from the den of the Hypocrites, sits down exhausted. Virgil reminds him of their Errand—of the great things which lie beyond this painful journey through Hell—and he rises instantly; and "keeps speaking," as they go on, "that he may not seem faint." In the Seventh Chasm, which is very dark and filled with hideous serpents, they find the Thieves; and get speech of Vanni Fucci. He is ashamed at being found amongst the Thieves, and recognized by Dante, who had "seen him a man of blood and brutal passions"; and he foretells the disasters that will lead to the Poet's exile.

IN THAT PART of the youthful year, when the Sun tempers his locks beneath Aquarius, and the nights already wane towards half the day,[1]

when the hoar-frost[2] copies his white sister's image on the ground, but short while lasts the temper of his pen,

the peasant, whose fodder fails, rises, and looks and sees the fields all white; whereat he smites his thigh,

goes back into the house, and to and fro laments like a poor wight who knows not what to do; then comes out again, and recovers hope,

observing how the world has changed its face in little time; and takes his staff, and chases forth his lambs to feed:

thus the Master made me despond, when I saw his brow so troubled; and thus quickly to the sore the plaster came.

For when we reached the shattered bridge, my Guide turned to me with that sweet aspect which I saw first at the foot of the mountain.

He opened his arms after having chosen some plan within himself, first looking well at the ruin, and took hold of me.

128

And as one who works, and calculates, always seeming to provide beforehand: so, lifting me up towards the top

of one big block, he looked out another splinter, saying: "Now clamber over that, but try first if it will carry thee."

It was no way for one clad with cloak of lead: for scarcely we, he light and I pushed on, could mount up from jag to jag.

And were it not on that precinct the ascent was shorter than on the other, I know not about him, but I certainly had been defeated.

But as Malebolge all hangs towards the entrance of the lowest well, the site of every valley imports

that one side rises and the other descends; we, however, came at length to the point from which the last stone breaks off.

The breath was so exhausted from my lungs, when I was up, that I could no farther; nay, seated me at my first arrival.

"Now it behoves thee thus to free thyself from sloth," said the Master: "for sitting on down, or under coverlet, men come not into fame;

without which whoso consumes his life, leaves such vestige of himself on earth, as smoke in air or foam in water;

and therefore rise! conquer thy panting with the soul, that conquers every battle, if with its heavy body it sinks not down.

A longer ladder must be climbed: to have quitted these is not enough; if thou understandest me, now act so that it may profit thee."

I then rose, showing myself better furnished with breath than I felt, and said: "Go on; for I am strong and confident."

We took our way up the cliff, which was rugged, narrow, and difficult, and greatly steeper than the former.

Speaking I went, that I might not seem faint; whereat a voice came from the other fosse, unsuitable for forming words.

I know not what it said, though I already was on the ridge of the arch which crosses there; but he who spake seemed moved to anger.

I had turned myself downwards; but my living eyes could not reach the bottom for the darkness; wherefore I: "Master, see that thou get

to the other belt, and let us dismount the wall: for as I hear from hence and do not understand, so I see down and distinguish nothing."

"Other answer I give thee not," he said, "than the deed: for a fit request should be followed with the work in silence."

We went down the bridge, at the head where it joins with the eighth bank; and then the chasm was manifest to me:

and I saw within it a fearful throng of serpents, and of so strange a look, that even now the recollection scares my blood.

Let Libya boast no longer with its sand; for, though it engenders chelydri, jaculi and pareæ, and cenchres with amphisbæna,

plagues so numerous or so dire it never showed, with all Ethiopia, nor with the land that lies by the Red Sea.[8]

Amid this cruel and most dismal swarm were people running, naked and terrified, without hope of lurking hole or heliotrope.[4]

They had their hands tied behind with serpents; these through their loins fixed the tail and the head, and were coiled in knots before.

And lo! at one, who was near our shore, sprang up a serpent, which transfixed him there where the neck is bound upon the shoulders.

Neither "O" nor "I" was ever written so quickly as he took fire, and burnt, and dropt down all changed to ashes;

and after he was thus dissolved upon the ground, the powder reunited of itself and at once resumed the former shape:

thus by great sages 'tis confest the Phœnix[5] dies, and then is born again, when it approaches the five-hundredth year;

in its life it eats no herb or grain, but only tears of incense and amomum; and nard and myrrh are its last swathings.

And as one who falls, and knows not how, through force

ot Demon which drags him to the ground, or of other obstruction that fetters men;

who, when he rises, looks fixedly round him, all bewildered by the great anguish he has undergone, and looking sighs: [6]

such was the sinner when he rose. Power of God! O how severe, that showers such blows in vengeance!

The Guide then asked him who he was; whereupon he answered: "I rained from Tuscany, short while ago, into this fierce gullet.

Bestial life, not human, pleased me, mule that I was; I am Vanni Fucci,[7] savage beast; and Pistoia was a fitting den for me."

And I to the Guide: "Tell him not to budge; and ask what crime thrust him down here, for I saw him once a man of blood and rage."

And the sinner who heard, feigned not; but directed towards me his mind and face, with a look of dismal shame;

then he said: "It pains me more that thou hast caught me in the misery wherein thou seest me, than when I was taken from the other life.

I cannot deny thee what thou askest: I am put down so far, because I robbed the sacristy of its goodly furniture;

and falsely once it was imputed to others. But that thou mayest not joy in this sight, if ever thou escape the dark abodes,

open thy ears and hear what I announce: Pistoia first is thinned of Neri; then Florence renovates her people and her laws.

Mars brings from Valdimagra a fiery vapour, which is wrapt in turbid clouds, and with impetuous and angry storm

a battle shall be fought on Piceno's field; whence it suddenly shall rend the mist, so that every Bianco shall be wounded by it.[8] And I have said this so that it may grieve thee."

1. When the sun is in Aquarius, i.e. between January 21 and February 21, he is more in evidence in proportion as the days and nights become more and more equal. This is the usual explanation of these verses. But there is much to be said for Butler's interpretation (based

on the *Ottimo*): when "the nights are already passing away to the south," the sun is, of course, proceeding northwards.

2. Hoar-frost melts sooner than snow.

3. The serpents in these verses were suggested by Lucan (*Phars. ix*). The country *by the Red Sea* is Arabia.

4. The heliotrope (a stone) was credited with the power of making its wearer invisible.

5. The peculiarities of the phœnix are alluded to by many classical and medieval writers; Dante's immediate source was evidently Ovid, *Metam.* xv.

6. Dante would appear to be describing an epileptic fit.

7. In 1293 Vanni Fucci, a Black of Pistoia, robbed the treasure of San Jacopo in the Church of San Zeno, together with two accomplices. The real culprits remained undetected for a year; but in the meantime, a certain Rampino de' Foresi was suspected of the theft and detained in prison.

8. The Bianchi, having assisted in the expulsion of the Neri from Pistoia (May, 1301), were themselves driven from Florence in November, 1301, when Charles of Valois entered the city. For some time Pistoia remained the stronghold of the Whites. The last lines probably refer to the capture, in 1302, of Serravalle (near Pistoia. Campo Piceno is the tract between Serravalle and Montecatini) by the Florentine and Lucchese Guelfs, under Moroello Malaspina, Marquis of Giovagallo in Valdimagra (the extremity of Lunigiana). For Moroello, see *Purg.* viii, *note* 5.

CANTO XXV

At the end of his angry prophecy, Fucci rises into a boundless pale rage, such as is hardly known in northern countries; and like the sacrilegious thief and brute that he is, gives vent to it in the wildest blasphemy. The serpents instantly set upon him, and inflict such punishment, that Dante regards them as friends ever after. Cacus too, with a load of serpents on his haunch and a fiery dragon on his shoulders, comes shouting in pursuit of him. Dante afterwards finds five of his own countrymen—first three in human shape, then two changed into reptiles—and by dint of great attention learns the names of them all, and very accurately sees the unheard-of transformations they have to undergo. The reptiles are Cianfa de' Donati and Guercio de' Cavalcanti; the three in human shape are Agnello de' Brunelleschi, Buoso degli Abati, and Puccio de' Galigai—all five of very noble kindred, "all from Florence, and great thieves in their time" (omnes de Florentina, et magni fures suo tempore. Pietro).

AT THE conclusion of his words, the thief raised up his hands with both the figs,[1] shouting: "Take them, God, for at thee I aim them!"

From this time forth the serpents were my friends; for one of them then coiled itself about his neck, as if saying: "Thou shalt speak no further!"

and another about his arms; and it tied him again, riveting itself in front so firmly, that he could not give a jog with them.

Ah, Pistoia! Pistoia! why dost thou not decree to turn thyself to ashes, that thou mayest endure no longer since thou outgoest thy seed[2] in evil-doing?

Through all the dark circles of Hell, I saw no spirit against God so proud, not even him who fell at Thebes down from the walls.[3]

He fled, speaking not another word; and I saw a Centaur, full of rage, come crying: "Where is, where is the surly one?"

Maremma, I do believe, has not so many snakes as he had on his haunch, to where our human form begins.

Over his shoulders, behind the head, a dragon lay with outstretched wings; and it sets on fire every one he meets.

My Master said: "That is Cacus,[4] who, beneath the rock of Mount Aventine, full often made a lake of blood.

He goes not with his brethren on one same road, because of the cunning theft he made of the great herd that lay near him:

whence his crooked actions ceased beneath the club of Hercules, who gave him perhaps a hundred blows with it; and he felt not the first ten."

Whilst he thus spake, the Centaur ran past, and also under us there came three spirits, whom neither I nor my Guide perceived,

until they cried: "Who are ye?" Our story therefore paused and we then gave heed to them alone.[5]

I knew them not; but it happened, as usually it happens by some chance, that one had to name another,

saying: "Where has Cianfa stopt?" Whereat I, in order that my Guide might stand attentive, placed my finger upwards from the chin to the nose.

If thou art now, O Reader, slow to credit what I have to tell, it will be no wonder: for I who saw it, scarce allow it to myself.

Whilst I kept gazing on them, lo! a serpent with six feet darts up in front of one, and fastens itself all upon him.

With its middle feet it clasped his belly, with the anterior it seized his arms; then fixed its teeth in both his cheeks.

The hinder feet it stretched along his thighs; and put its tail between the two, and bent it upwards on his loins behind.

Ivy was never so rooted to a tree, as round the other's limbs the hideous monster entwined its own;

then they stuck together, as if they had been of heated wax, and mingled their colours; neither the one, nor the other, now seemed what it was at first:

as up before the flame on paper, goes a brown colour which is not yet black, and the white dies away.

The other two looked on, and each cried: "O me!

Agnello, how thou changest! lo, thou art already neither two nor one!"

The two heads had now become one, when two shapes appeared to us mixed in one face, where both were lost.

Two arms were made of the four lists; the thighs with the legs, the belly, and the chest, became such members as were never seen.

The former shape was all extinct in them: both, and neither the peverse image seemed; and such it went away with languid step.

As the lizard, beneath the mighty scourge of the canicular days, going from hedge to hedge, appears a flash of lightning, if it cross the way:

so, coming towards the bowels of the other two, appeared a little reptile burning with rage, livid and black as peppercorn.

And it pierced that part, in one of them, at which we first receive our nourishment; then fell down stretched out before him.

The pierced thief gazed on it but said nothing; nay, with his feet motionless, yawned only as if sleep or fever had come upon him.

He eyed the reptile, the reptile him; the one from his wound, the other from its mouth, smoked violently, and their smoke met.

Let Lucan now be silent, where he tells of poor Sabellus and Nasidius;[6] and wait to hear that which is now sent forth.

Of Cadmus and of Arethusa be Ovid silent: for if he, poetizing, converts the one into a serpent and the other into a fount, I envy him not:

for never did he so transmute two natures front to front, that both forms were ready to exchange their substance.

They mutually responded in such a way, that the reptile cleft its tail into a fork, and the wounded spirit drew his steps together.

The legs and the thighs along with them so stuck to one another, that soon their juncture left no mark that was discernible.

The cloven tail assumed the figure that was lost in the other; and its skin grew soft, the other's hard.

I saw the arms enter at the armpits, and the two feet of the brute, which were short, lengthen themselves as much as those arms were shortened.

Then the two hinder feet, twisted together, became the member which man conceals; and the wretch from his had two thrust forth.

Whilst the smoke with a new colour veils them both, and generates on one part hair, and strips it from another,

the one rose upright, and prostrate the other fell, not therefore turning the impious lights, under which they mutually exchanged visages.

He that was erect, drew his towards the temples; and from the too much matter that went thither, ears came out of the smooth cheeks;

that which went not back, but was retained, of its superfluity formed a nose, and enlarged the lips to a fit size.

He that lay prone, thrusts forward his sharpened visage, and draws back his ears into the head, as the snail does its horns;

and his tongue, which was before united and apt for speech, cleaves itself; and in the other the forked tongue recloses; and the smoke now rests.

The soul that had become a brute, fled hissing along the valley, and after it the other talking and sputtering.

Then he turned his novel shoulder towards it, and said to the other: "Buoso shall run crawling, as I have done, along this road!"

Thus I beheld the seventh ballast change and rechange; and here let the novelty excuse me, if my pen goes aught astray.

And though my eyes were somewhat perplexed, and my mind dismayed, those could not flee so covertly,

But that I well distinguished Puccio Sciancato: and it was he alone, of the three companions that first came, who was not changed; the other was he whom thou, Gaville, lamentest.

---

1. This obscene and insulting gesture, the origin of which has been

variously explained, was made by inserting the thumb between the index and middle finger.

2. Pistoia was said to have been founded by the remnants of Catiline's army.

3. Referring to Capaneus, for whom see Canto xiv.

4. Cacus was a monster inhabiting a cave in Mount Aventine and noted for his thefts. He dragged into his cave, by their tails, some of the oxen that Hercules had stolen from Geryon, and was slain by that hero. In the mode of his death Dante follows Livy's account, but in other respects Virgil served as his model. Cacus was not really a Centaur: Dante was evidently led astray by Virgil. (See Canto xii.)

5. The five noble Florentines punished in this circle are (a) three spirits: Agnello of the Brunelleschi, a Ghibelline family; Buoso degli Abati, or, perhaps, de' Donati (if the latter is intended, he is identical with the Buoso mentioned in Canto xxx); and Puccio Sciancato ("The Lame") de' Galigai; (b) Cianfa de' Donati, who is merged with Agnello; (c) Francesco de' Cavalcanti who assumes Buoso's human shape, while Buoso becomes a serpent. He was slain by the people of Gaville (a village in the upper Val d' Arno), the murderers being summarily dealt with by his kinsmen.

6. Sabellus and Nasidius, two soldiers of Cato's army, who, in their march across the Libyan desert, were stung by serpents, with the result that the former was reduced to a kind of puddle, while the latter swelled to such a size that his coat of mail gave way (Lucan, *Pharsalia*, ix). The transformations of Cadmus and Arethusa are narrated by Ovid in *Metam.* iv and v.

CANTO XXVI

Dante, after having seen and recognized the five Noble Thieves, addresses his native city in bitter concentrated sorrow and shame, mingled with heartfelt longings and affection. The calamities which misgovernment, faction, and crime had been preparing for many years before the date of his mystic Vision, and which he himself as Chief Magistrate in 1300 had done his utmost to prevent, are notified in form of prophecy. His own exile, though not directly alluded to, and his hopes of "morning"—of deliverance for Florence and himself, and of justice on their enemies—were nearly connected with those calamities. And when he sees the fate of Evil Counsellors in the Eighth Chasm, to which his Guide now leads him, he "curbs his genius," and deeply feels he has not to seek that deliverance and justice by fraud. The arts of the fox, on however great a scale, are extremely hateful to him. To employ that superior wisdom, which is the good gift of the Almighty, in deceiving others, for any purpose, is a Spiritual Theft of the most fearful kind; and the sinners, who have been guilty of it, are running along the narrow chasm, each "stolen" from view, wrapt in the Flame of his own Consciousness, and tormented by its burning. Ulysses and Diomed are also here united in punishment. The former, speaking through the Flame, relates the manner and place of his death.

JOY, FLORENCE, since thou art so great that over sea and land thou beatest thy wings, and thy name through Hell expands itself!

Among the thieves I found five such, thy citizens; whereat shame comes on me, and thou to great honour mountest not thereby.

But if the truth is dreamed of near the morning, thou shalt feel ere long what Prato,[1] not to speak of others, craves for thee.

And if it were already come, it would not be too early; so were it! since indeed it must be: for it will weigh the heavier on me as I grow older.

138

We departed thence; and, by the stairs which the curb-stones had made for us to descend before, my Guide remounted and drew me up;

and pursuing our solitary way among the jags and branches of the cliff, the foot without the hand sped not.

I sorrowed then, and sorrow now again when I direct my memory to what I saw; and curb my genius more than I am wont,

lest it run where Virtue guides it not; so that, if kindly star or something better have given to me the good, I may not grudge myself that gift.

As many fireflies as the peasant who is resting on the hill—at the time that he who lights the world least hides his face from us,[2]

when the fly yields to the gnat—sees down along the valley, there perchance where he gathers grapes and tills:

with flames thus numerous the eighth chasm was all gleaming, as I perceived, so soon as I came to where the bottom showed itself.

And as he,[3] who was avenged by the bears, saw Elijah's chariot at its departure, when the horses rose erect to heaven,—

for he could not so follow it with his eyes as to see other than the flame alone, like a little cloud, ascending up:

thus moved each of those flames along the gullet of the fosse, for none of them shows the theft, and every flame steals a sinner.

I stood upon the bridge, having risen so to look, that if I had not caught a rock, I should have fallen down without being pushed.

And the Guide, who saw me thus attent, said: "Within those fires are the spirits; each swathes himself with that which burns him."

"Master," I replied, "from hearing thee I feel more certain; but had already discerned it to be so, and already wished to say to thee:

who is in that fire, which comes so parted at the top, as if it rose from the pyre where Eteocles with his brother was placed?"[4]

He answered me: "Within it there Ulysses is tortured, and Diomed;[5] and thus they run together in punishment, as erst in wrath;

and in their flame they groan for the ambush of the horse, that made the door by which the noble seed of the Romans came forth;

within it they lament the artifice, whereby Deidamia in death still sorrows for Achilles; and there for the Palladium they suffer punishment."

"If they within those sparks can speak," said I, "Master! I pray thee much, and repray that my prayer may equal a thousand,

deny me not to wait until the horned flame comes hither; thou seest how with desire I bend me towards it."

And he to me: "Thy request is worthy of much praise, and therefore I accept it; but do thou refrain thy tongue.

Let me speak: for I have conceived what thou wishest; and they, perhaps, because they were Greeks, might disdain thy words."[6]

After the flame had come where time and place seemed fitting to my Guide, I heard him speak in this manner:

"O ye, two in one fire! if I merited of you whilst I lived, if I merited of you much or little,

when on earth I wrote the High Verses, move ye not; but let the one of you tell where he, having lost himself, went to die."

The greater horn of the ancient flame began to shake itself, murmuring, just like a flame that struggles with the wind.

Then carrying to and fro the top, as if it were the tongue that spake, threw forth a voice, and said: "When

I departed from Circe, who beyond a year detained me there near Gaeta,[7] ere Æneas thus had named it,

neither fondness for my son, nor reverence for my aged father, nor the due love that should have cheered Penelope,[8]

could conquer in me the ardour that I had to gain experience of the world, and of human vice and worth;

I put forth on the deep open sea,[9] with but one ship, and with that small company, which had not deserted me.

Both the shores I saw as far as Spain, far as Morocco, and saw Sardinia and the other isles which that sea bathes round.

I and my companions were old and tardy, when we came to that narrow pass, where Hercules assigned his landmarks

to hinder man from venturing farther; on the right hand, I left Seville; on the other, had already left Ceuta.

'O brothers!' I said, 'who through a hundred thousand dangers have reached the West, deny not, to this the brief vigil

of your senses that remains, experience of the unpeopled world behind the Sun.

Consider your origin: ye were not formed to live like brutes, but to follow virtue and knowledge.'

With this brief speech I made my companions so eager for the voyage, that I could hardly then have checked them;

and, turning the poop towards morning, we of our oars made wings for the foolish flight, always gaining on the left.

Night already saw the other pole, with all its stars; and ours so low, that it rose not from the ocean floor.

Five times the light beneath the Moon had been rekindled and quenched as oft, since we had entered on the arduous passage,

when there appeared to us a Mountain, dim with distance; and to me it seemed the highest I had ever seen.

We joyed, and soon our joy was turned to grief: for a tempest rose from the new land, and struck the forepart of our ship.

Three times it made her whirl round with all the waters; at the fourth, made the poop rise up and prow go down, as pleased Another, till the sea was closed above us."

1. Probably the Cardinal Nicholas of Prato, who was, in 1304, sent to Florence by Benedict XI to endeavour to reconcile the hostile factions. His efforts proving futile, he laid the city under an interdict; and several local disasters that occurred shortly after, such as the fall of a bridge and a great conflagration, were attributed to the curse of the Church. This interpretation is better than taking Prato

as the town ten miles north-west of Florence: for this place appears to have been on friendly terms with Florence.

2. In the summer-time, when the days are longest.

3. Elisha, having seen Elijah carried up to heaven in a chariot of fire, was mocked by little children, who were devoured by bears, as a punishment for having scoffed at him (2 *Kings* ii. 11, 12, 23, 24).

4. Eteocles and Polynices, sons of Œdipus, King of Thebes, quarrelled over the succession to the throne. This dispute gave rise to the war of the Seven against Thebes, in the course of which the brothers slew each other in single combat. Their hatred continued after death, for, according to Statius (*Thebaid* xii), the very flame of their funeral pyre was divided.

5. The Wooden Horse, in which were concealed the Greeks who opened the gates of Troy to their countrymen, thus raising the siege and causing Æneas and his followers to leave the city.—Deidamia, daughter of Lycomedes, King of Scyros, at whose court Thetis had left her son Achilles in female disguise, to prevent his taking part in the expedition against Troy (see *Purg.* ix). After Deidamia had become enamoured of Achilles and borne him a son, Ulysses discovered the hero's secret and induced him to sail for Troy, whereupon Deidamia died of grief.—The Palladium, a statue of Pallas, was stolen by Ulysses because the fortunes of Troy were supposed to depend on it.

6. There can be no doubt that Dante was ignorant of Greek and that his knowledge of everything relating to Greece was derived from intermediate Latin sources, principally Virgil. Perhaps this is the meaning intended.

7. Gaeta, a town in southern Italy, north of Campania, thus named by Æneas after his nurse, Caïeta. For Circe, see *Purg.* xiv, *note* 3.

8. The name of Ulysses' father was Laertes, that of his wife Penelope, and that of his son Telemachus.

9. This account of Ulysses' voyage is entirely of Dante's invention. The "columns of Hercules" (*i.e.* Mount Abyla in North Africa and Mount Calpe=Gibraltar) were regarded as the western limit of the habitable world. The *other pole* would indicate that the ship had crossed the equator. The *Mountain* can be no other than the Mount of Purgatory.

ÇANTO XXVII

The Flame of Ulysses, having told its story, departs with permission of Virgil; and is immediately followed by another, which contains the spirit of Count Guido da Montefeltro, a Ghibelline of high fame in war and counsel. It comes moaning at the top, and sends forth eager inquiries about the people of Romagna, Guido's countrymen. Dante describes their condition under various petty tyrants, in 1300. His words are brief, precise, and beautiful; and have a tone of large and deep sadness. Guido, at his request, relates who he is, and why condemned to such torment; after which, the Poets pass onwards to the bridge of the Ninth Chasm.

THE FLAME was now erect and quiet, having ceased to speak, and now went away from us with license of the sweet Poet;

when another,[1] that came behind it, made us turn our eyes to its top, for a confused sound that issued therefrom.

As the Sicilian bull[2] (which bellowed first with the lament of him—and that was right—who had tuned it with his file)

kept bellowing with the sufferer's voice; so that, although it was of brass, it seemed transfixed with pain:

thus, having at their commencement no way or outlet from the fire, the dismal words were changed into its language.

But after they had found their road up through the point, giving to it the vibration which the tongue had given in their passage,

we heard it say: "O thou, at whom I aim my voice! and who just now wast speaking Lombard, saying, 'Now go, no more I urge thee';

though I have come perhaps a little late, let it not irk thee to pause and speak with me; thou seest it irks not me, although I burn.

If thou art but now fallen into this blind world from that sweet Latian land, whence I bring all my guilt,

143

tell me if the Romagnuols have peace or war: for I was of the mountains there, between Urbino and the yoke from which the Tiber springs."[3]

I still was eager downwards and bent, when my Leader touched me on the side, saying: "Speak thou; this is a Latian."

And I, who had my answer ready then, began without delay to speak: "O soul, that there below art hidden!

thy Romagna is not, and never was, without war in the hearts of her tyrants; but openly just now I there left none.

Ravenna stands, as it has stood for many years: the Eagle of Polenta[4] broods over it, so that he covers Cervia with his pinions.

The city, which made erewhile the long probation, and sanguinary heap of the Frenchmen, finds itself again under the Green Clutches.[5]

The old Mastiff of Verrucchio and the young,[6] who of Montagna made evil governance, there, where they are wont, ply their teeth.

The cities of Lamone and Santerno guide the Lioncel of the white lair, who changes faction from the summer to the winter;[7]

and that city whose flank the Savio bathes, as it lies between the plain and mount, so lives it between tyranny and freedom.[8]

Now I pray thee, tell us who thou art; be not more hard than one has been to thee, so may thy name on earth maintain its front."

After the flame had roared awhile as usual, it moved the sharp point to and fro, and then gave forth this breath:

"If I thought my answer were to one who ever could return to the world, this flame should shake no more;

but since none ever did return alive from this depth, if what I hear be true, without fear of infamy I answer thee.

I was a man of arms; and then became a Cordelier,[9] hoping, thus girt, to make amends; and certainly my hope were come in full,

but for the Great Priest, may ill befall him! who brought me back to my first sins; and how and why, I wish thee to hear from me.

Whilst I was the form of bones and pulp, which my mother gave me, my deeds were not those of the lion, but of the fox.

All wiles and covert ways I knew; and used the art of them so well, that to the ends of the earth the sound went forth.

When I saw myself come to that period of my age at which everyone should lower sails and gather in his ropes,

that which before had pleased me, grieved me then; and with repentance and confession I became a monk; ah woe alas! and it would have availed me.

The Prince of the new Pharisees[10]—waging war near to the Lateran, and not with Saracens or Jews;

for every enemy of his was Christian, and none had been to conquer Acre, nor been a merchant in the Soldan's land—

regarded not the Highest Office nor Holy Orders in himself, nor in me that Cord which used to make those whom it girded leaner.

But as Constantine sought Silvestro within Soracte to cure his leprosy, so this man called me as an adept

to cure the fever of his pride; he demanded counsel of me; and I kept silent, for his words seemed drunken.

And then he said to me: 'Let not thy heart misdoubt; even now I do absolve thee, and do thou teach me so to act, that I may cast Penestrino to the ground.

Heaven I can shut and open, as thou knowest; for two are the keys that my predecessor held not dear.'

Then the weighty arguments impelled me to think silence worst; and I said: 'Father! since thou cleansest me

from that guilt into which I now must fall, large promise, with small observance of it, will make thee triumph in thy High Seat.'

Saint Francis afterwards, when I was dead, came for me;[11] but one of the Black Cherubim said to him: 'Do not take him; wrong me not.

He must come down amongst my menials; because he give the fraudulent counsel, since which I have kept fast by his hair:

for he who repents not, cannot be absolved; nor is it possible to repent and will a thing at the same time, the contradiction not permitting it.'

O wretched me! how I started when he seized me, saying to me: 'May be thou didst not think that I was a logician!'

To Minos he bore me, who twined his tail eight times round his fearful back, and then biting it in great rage,

said: 'This is a sinner for the thievish fire'; therefore, I, where thou seest, am lost; and going thus clothed, in heart I grieve."

When he his words had ended thus, the flame, sorrowing, departed, writhing and tossing its sharp horn.

We passed on, I and my Guide, along the cliff up to the other arch that covers the fosse, in which their fee is paid to those who, sowing discord, gather guilt.

1. This is Guido, Count of Montefeltro (1223–1298) who became head of the Ghibellines of Romagna in 1274, and worked untiringly for the cause.
2. The brazen bull was designed by Perillus for Phalaris, the Sicilian tyrant. The shrieks of those being roasted inside it were intended to remind the bystanders of the roaring of a bull. Perillus was the first on whom the machine was tested.
3. Montefeltro is between Urbino and Mount Coronaro.
4. Ravenna was in 1300 ruled by Guido Minore, or Vecchio. The family arms contained an eagle. Cervia is about twelve miles south of Ravenna.
5. In 1282, Forlì was successfully defended by the Guido who is now being addressed against the French troops led by John of Appia, Count of Romagna, and sent at the instigation of Pope Martin IV. In 1300 the city was under the rule of Sinibaldo degli Ordelaffi, whose arms consisted of a green lion.
6. Malatesta and his son Malatestino of Rimini (Verrucchio=the castle inhabited by the lords of Rimini) are called hounds on account of their cruelty. Montagna de' Parcitati, head of the Ghibellines of Rimini, was taken prisoner by the father (1295) and put to death by the son.
7. Mainardo Pagano, Lord of Faenza (on the Lamone), of Imola (near the Santerno) and of Forlì, whose arms were "on a field argent a lion azure," was a Ghibelline in the north but supported the Guelfs in Florence. He died in 1302 (see *Purg.* xiv).
8. Cesena (between Forlì and Rimini at the foot of the Apennines) was ruled by Captains or *Podestà* about this time; but in 1314 Malatestino of Rimini became lord of the town.
9. About the year 1292, Guido became reconciled to the Pope, and in 1296 he entered the Franciscan order. This accounts for St. Francis's intercession on his behalf.

10. The long-standing feud between Boniface VIII and the Colonna family, came to a head in 1297. The latter retired to the stronghold of Penestrino, now Palestrina, some twenty-five miles east of Rome; cf. Par. xxxi, note 5. Guido, who was the Pope's adviser in this campaign, counselled that an amnesty should be offered them; but when the Colonnesi surrendered on these conditions (Sept., 1298) their stronghold was razed to the ground. Reference is to the legend that Pope Sylvester (314–335) was summoned from his hiding-place in Mount Soracte by the Emperor Constantine, whom he converted to Christianity and then cured of his leprosy. The *predecessor* is Pope Celestine V, for whom see Canto iii, *note 6.*—Acre, which had belonged to the Christians for a hundred years, was retaken by the Saracens in 1291.

11. Compare the very similar passage, *Purg.* v, relating to Guido's son Buonconte.

CANTO XXVIII

*Our Pilgrim—more and more heavy-laden, yet rapid and uncon-
querable—is now with his Guide looking down into the Ninth
Chasm; and briefly describes the hideous condition of the "sowers
of Scandal and Schism" that are punished in it. First comes Ma-
homet: in Dante's view, a mere Sectarian who had taken up Chris-
tianity and perverted its meaning. The shadow of him, rent asunder
from the chin downwards, displays the conscious vileness and cor-
ruption of his doctrines. He tells how Ali his nephew "goes weep-
ing before him, cleft from chin to forelock." He then asks what
Dante is doing there; and on learning his errand and the likelihood
of his return to earth, bids him give due warning to "Brother Dol-
cino," a Schismatic and Communist, who is stirring up strife in
Piedmont and Lombardy. Next come Pier da Medicina, Curio,
Mosca de' Lamberti of Florence, and lastly, Bertrand de Born. All
of them have punishments representing their crimes.*

WHO, even with words set free, could ever fully tell, by
oft relating, the blood and the wounds that I now saw?

Every tongue assuredly would fail, because of our
speech and our memory that have small capacity to com-
prehend so much.

If all the people too were gathered, who of old upon
Apulia's fateful land wailed for their blood,[1]

by reason of the Trojans, and of that long war which
made so vast a spoil of rings, as Livy writes, who errs not;

with those who, by withstanding Robert Guiscard, felt
the pains of blows; and the rest whose bones are gathered
still

at Ceperano, where each Apulian proved false; and there
at Tagliacozzo, where old Alardo conquered without
weapons;

and one should show his limbs transpierced, and another
his cut off: it were naught to equal the hideous mode of the
ninth chasm.

Even a cask, through loss of middle-piece or cant, yawns

148

not so wide as one[2] I saw, ripped from the chin down to the part that utters vilest sound:

between his legs the entrails hung; the pluck appeared, and the wretched sack that makes excrement of what is swallowed.

Whilst I stood all occupied in seeing him, he looked at me, and with his hands opened his breast, saying: "Now see how I dilacerate myself!

See how Mahomet is mangled! Before me Ali weeping goes, cleft in the face from chin to forelock;

and all the others, whom thou seest here, were in their lifetime sowers of scandal and of schism; and therefore are they thus cleft.

A Devil is here behind, who splits us thus cruelly, reapplying each of this class to his sword's edge,

when we have wandered round the doleful road; for the wounds heal up ere any goes again before him.

But who art thou, that musest on the cliff, perhaps in order to delay thy going to the punishment, adjudged upon thy accusations?"

"Not yet has death come to him; nor does guilt lead him," replied my Master, "to torment him; but to give him full experience,

it behoves me, who am dead, to lead him through the Hell down here, from round to round; and this is true as that I speak to thee."

More than a hundred, when they heard him, stopped in the fosse to look at me, through wonder forgetting their torment.

"Well, then, thou who perhaps shalt see the sun ere long, tell Fra Dolcino,[3] if he wish not speedily to follow me down here,

so to arm himself with victuals, that stress of snow may not bring victory to the Novarese, which otherwise would not be easy to attain."

After lifting up one foot to go away, Mahomet said this to me; then on the ground he stretched it to depart.

Another, who had his throat pierced through, and nose cut off up to the eyebrows, and had but one single ear,

standing to gaze in wonder with the rest, before the rest

opened his weasand, which outwardly was red on every part,

and said: "Thou! whom guilt condemns not, and whom I have seen above on Latian ground, unless too much resemblance deceive me;

remember Pier da Medicina,[4] if ever thou return to see the gentle plain that from Vercelli slopes to Marcabò.

And make known to the worthiest two of Fano,[5] to Messer Guido and to Angiolello likewise, that, unless our foresight here be vain,

they shall be cast out of their ship, and drowned near the Cattolica, by a fell tyrant's treachery.

Between the isles of Cyprus and Majorca, Neptune never saw so great a crime—not even with pirates, not even with Argives.

That traitor who sees with but one eye, and holds the land which one who is here with me would wish that he had never seen.

will make them come to parley with him; then act so, that they shall need no vow nor prayer for Focara's wind."

And I to him: "Show me and explain, if thou wouldst have me carry tidings up of thee, who he is that rues that sight."

Then he laid his hand upon the jaw of one of his companions; and opened the mouth of him, saying: "This is he, and he speaks not;

this outcast quenched the doubt in Cæsar, affirming that to men prepared delay is always hurtful."

Oh, how dejected, with tongue slit in his gorge, seemed Curio[6] to me, who was so daring in his speech!

And one who had both hands cut off, raising the stumps through the dim air so that their blood defiled his face,

said: "Thou wilt recollect the Mosca,[7] too, ah me! who said, 'A thing done has an end!' which was the seed of evil to the Tuscan people."

"And death to thy kindred!" I added thereto, wherefore he, accumulating pain on pain, went away as one distressed and mad.

But I remained to view the troop, and saw a thing which I should be afraid even to relate, without more proof;

but that conscience reassures me, that good companion which fortifies a man beneath the hauberk of his self-felt purity.

Certainly I saw, and still seem to see it, a trunk going without a head, as the others of that dismal herd were going.

And it was holding by the hair the severed head, swinging in his hand like a lantern; and that looked at us and said: "O me!"

Of itself it made for itself a lamp, and they were two in one, and one in two; how this can be, He knows who so ordains.

When it was just at the foot of our bridge, it raised its arm high up, with all the head, to bring near to us its words,

which were: "Now see the grievous penalty, thou, who breathing goest to view the dead; see if any be as great as this!

And that thou mayest carry tidings of me, know, that I am Bertram de Born,[8] he who to the Young King gave evil counsels.

I made the father and the son rebels to each other, Ahithophel did not do more with Absalom and David by his malicious instigations.

Because I parted persons thus united, I carry my brain, ah me! parted from its source which is in this trunk. Thus the law of retribution is observed in me."

1. The following wars and battles, all of which took place in Apulia, are alluded to: (a) The wars of the Romans (descended from the Trojans) against the Samnites, 343–290 B.C. (b) The Punic wars (264–146 B.C.), in the second of which was decided the battle of Cannæ (216 B.C.), where so many Romans fell that, as Livy tells (xxiii), Hannibal was able to produce before the senate at Carthage three bushels of gold rings taken from their bodies (cf. Conv. iv. 5). (c) From 1059 till 1080 Robert Guiscard (cf. Par. xviii) opposed the Greeks and Saracens in southern Italy and in Sicily. (d) The Apulian barons, to whom Manfred had entrusted the pass of Ceperano (on the Liris), turned traitors, and allowed Charles of Anjou to advance, thus paving the way for Manfred's defeat at Benevento (1266). (e) At the battle of Tagliacozzo (1268), Charles overthrew Manfred's nephew, Conradin, by a stratagem. The latter was gaining the day and engaged in pursuing the enemy, when Charles turned the tables

on him, with the aid of a number of troops whom he had, following the advice of Erard de Valéry, held in reserve for this purpose.

2. When Mohammed (*ca.* 570–632) died, his son-in-law Ali (born *ca.* 597) did not immediately succeed him, but allowed three of the other disciples of the prophet to take precedence. He himself occupied the Caliphate from 656 till his assassination in 661.

3. Fra Dolcino became head of the sect of the Apostolic Brothers on the death of its founder Segarelli in 1300. These people appear to have merely desired to restore the Church to the purity of Apostolic times, but they were accused of holding various heretical doctrines, such as the community of goods and women. In 1305 Clement V ordered the extirpation of the sect, and a crusade was preached against them. They retired to the hills between Novara and Vercelli, but were eventually forced to surrender. Dolcino and the beautiful Margaret of Trent, who was generally held to be his mistress, were burnt at Vercelli in June, 1307.

4. Pier della Medicina, belonged to the Biancucci family, who were lords of Medicina (about 20 miles east of Bologna). He was deprived by Frederick II of a prætorship he held, and his family were driven from Romagna in 1287. He then turned his attention to intriguing among the rulers of Romagna and was chiefly successful in setting the houses of Polenta and Malatesta against each other; his method being to make each of them suspicious of the other's designs. The towns of Vercelli and Marcabò are used to designate the west and east extremities of the old Romagna.

5. Malatestino of Rimini, desiring to add Fano to his dominions, invited Angiolello da Carignano and Guido del Cassero, two of the principal men of the town, to a conference at La Cattolica (on the Adriatic, between Fano and Rimini) and had them treacherously drowned off the headland of Focara (between Fano and La Cattolica). The latter was so notorious for the strong winds sweeping round it, that the sailors used to offer up prayers to ensure a safe passage. The *Argives* are mentioned perhaps with reference to the Argonauts.

6. According to Lucan it was Curio who advised Cæsar to cross the Rubicon (near Rimini), by which act the latter declared war against the republic (49 B.C.). At that time the stream formed the boundary between Italy and Cisalpine Gaul.

7. For Mosca, see *Par.* xvi, *note* 35. The murder of Buondelmonte was the origin of the Guelf and Ghibelline factions in Florence.

8. Bertrand de Born (*ca.* 1140–1215) Lord of Hautefort, near Périgord (see the following canto), the greater part of whose life was spent in feudal warfare, and who ended his days in the Cistercian monastery of Dalon, near Hautefort. He was one of the most individual of the Provençal troubadours, his finest poem being a song of lamentation on the death of the "Young King" (the name given to Prince Henry, son of Henry II of England, because he was twice crowned during his father's lifetime). The King's refusal to yield the sovereignty of England or Normandy to his son caused the out-

break of hostilities, which lasted till the latter's death in 1183. Dante's idea of the part played by Bertrand in this strife was apparently derived from the early Provençal biographies of the poet.—Reference is, course, to Absalom's conspiracy against his father David and to the counsel he received from Ahithophel (see 2 *Sam.* xv-xvii).

CANTO XXIX

The numberless Shadows of discord and bloody strife have filled the Poet's eyes with tears; and he still keeps gazing down, expecting to find his own father's cousin, Geri del Bello, among them. Virgil makes him quit the miserable spectacle; and tells, as they go on, how he had seen Geri, at the foot of the bridge, pointing with angry gesture, and then departing in the crowd. From the arch of the Tenth Chasm, Dante now hears the wailings of a new class of sinners, the last in Malebolge. They are the Falsifiers of every sort: punished with innumerable diseases, in impure air and darkness. Pietro di Dante enumerates three classes of Falsifiers: in things, in deeds, and in words. Of the first class are the Alchemists, Forgers, &c., such as Griffolino of Arezzo, and Capocchio of Siena, in the present canto, and Adamo da Brescia in the next, where we shall also find the other two classes.

THE MANY PEOPLE and the diverse wounds had made my eyes so drunken that they longed to stay and weep;

but Virgil said to me: "Why art thou gazing still? wherefore does thy sight still rest, down there, among the dismal mutilated shadows?

Thou hast not done so at the other chasms; consider, if thou thinkest to number them, that the valley goes round two-and-twenty miles;[1]

and the Moon already is beneath our feet;[2] the time is now short, that is conceded to us; and other things are to be seen than thou dost see."

"Hadst thou," I thereupon replied, "attended to the cause for which I looked, perhaps thou mightest have vouchsafed me yet to stay."

Meantime the Guide was going on; and I went behind him, now making my reply, and adding: "Within that cavern,

where I kept my eyes so fixed, I believe that a spirit of

my own blood laments the guilt which costs so much down there."

Then the Master said: "Let not thy thought henceforth distract itself on him; attend to somewhat else, and let him stay there:

for I saw him, at the foot of the little bridge, point to thee, and vehemently threaten with his finger; and heard them call him Geri del Bello.[3]

Thou wast then so totally entangled upon him who once held Altaforte, that thou didst not look that way; so he departed."

"O my Guide! his violent death, which is not yet avenged for him," said I, "by any that is a partner of his shame,

made him indignant: therefore, as I suppose, he went away without speaking to me; and in that has made me pity him the more."

Thus we spake, up to the first place of the cliff, which shows the other valley, if more light were there, quite to the bottom.

When we were above the last cloister of Malebolge, so that its lay-brethren could appear to our view,

lamentations pierced me, manifold, which had their arrows barbed with pity; whereat I covered my ears with my hands.

Such pain as there would be, if the diseases in the hospitals of Valdichiana, between July and September, and of Maremma and Sardinia,[4]

were all together in one ditch: such was there here; and such stench issued thence, as is wont to issue from putrid limbs.

We descended on the last bank of the long cliff, again to the left hand; and then my sight was more vivid,

down towards the depth in which the ministress of the Great Sire, infallible Justice, punishes the falsifiers that she here registers.

I do not think it was a greater sorrow to see the people in Ægina all infirm; when the air was so malignant,

that every animal, even to the little worm, dropt down; and afterwards, as Poets hold for sure, the ancient peoples

155

were restored from seed of ants:[5] than it was to see, through that dim valley, the spirits languishing in diverse heaps.

This upon the belly, and that upon the shoulders of the other lay; and some were crawling on along the dismal path.

Step by step we went, without speech, looking at and listening to the sick who could not raise their bodies.

I saw two sit leaning on each other, as pan is leant on pan to warm, from head to foot spotted with scabs;

and never did I see currycomb plied by stableboy for whom his master waits, nor by one who stays unwillingly awake,

as each of these plied thick the clawing of his nails upon himself, for the great fury of their itch which has no other succour.

And so the nails drew down the scurf, as does a knife the scales from bream or other fish that has them larger.

"O thou!" began my Guide to one of them, "who with thy fingers dismailest thyself, and sometimes makest pincers of them;

tell us if there be any Latian among these who are here within; so may thy nails eternally suffice thee for that work."

"Latians are we, whom thou seest so disfigured here, both of us," replied the one weeping; "but who art thou that hast inquired of us?"

And the Guide said: "I am one, who with this living man descend from steep to steep, and mean to show him Hell."

Then the mutual propping broke, and each turned trembling towards me, with others that by echo heard him.

The kind Master to me directed himself wholly, saying: "Tell them what thou wishest." And I began, as he desired:

"So may your memory not fade away from human minds in the first world, but may it live under many suns,

tell us who ye are, and of what people; let not your ugly and disgusting punishment frighten you from revealing yourselves to me."

"I was of Arezzo,"[6] replied the one, "and Albert of Siena had me burned; but what I died for does not bring me here.

'Tis true, I said to him, speaking in jest: 'I could raise myself through the air in flight'; and he, who had a fond desire and little wit,

willed that I should show him the art; and only because I made him not a Dædalus, he made me be burned by one who had him for a son.

But to the last budget of the ten, for the alchemy that I practised in the world, Minos, who may not err, condemned me."

And I said to the Poet: "Now was there ever people so vain as the Sienese? certainly the French not so by far."

Whereat the other leper, who heard me, responded to my words: "Except Stricca who contrived to spend so moderately;

and Niccolò, who first discovered the costly usage of the clove, in the garden where such seed takes root;

and except the company in which Caccia of Asciano squandered his vineyard and his great forest, and the Abbagliato showed his wit.[7]

But that thou mayest know who thus seconds thee against the Sienese, sharpen thine eye towards me, that my face may give thee right response;

so shalt thou see I am the shadow of Capocchio,[8] who falsified the metals by alchemy; and thou must recollect, if I rightly eye thee, how good an ape I was of Nature."

1. See *note* 5 of the following canto.
2. It is now about one o'clock on the Saturday afternoon.
3. For Geri del Bello, the cousin of Dante's father, see the table on p. 625. According to one account, he caused discord among the Sacchetti and was slain by a member of that family in consequence, his death not being avenged till thirty years later, when his nephews killed one of the Sacchetti. Buti says that the murder of Geri's father was the origin of the feud.
4. Valdichiana and Maremma are selected as two of the most unhealthy districts of Tuscany, Sardinia being notorious for the same reason.
5. The inhabitants of the island of Ægina having died of a pestilence sent by Juno, Jupiter restored the population by transforming the ants into men, who were called Myrmidons (*cf.* Ovid, *Metam.* vii).
6. Griffolino of Arezzo obtained money from Albero of Siena by pretending that he could teach him the art of flying. On discovering

that he had been tricked, Albero induced his father or patron, who was Bishop of Siena, to have Griffolino burned as an alchemist.
7. These four men were members of the *Brigata Spendereccia,* a club founded in the second half of the thirteenth century by twelve wealthy Sienese youths, who vied with each other in squandering their money on riotous living. The reference is to some expensive dish prepared with cloves, as to the nature of which the old commentators are not agreed. The *garden* is probably Siena. The Lano mentioned in Canto xiii also belonged to this "Spendthrift Brigade."
8. Capocchio was probably a Florentine and a friend of Dante's. The early commentators give anecdotes vouching for his skill as a draughtsman and his powers of mimicry. He was burnt at Siena in 1293, for practising alchemy.

CANTO XXX

Still on the brim of the Tenth Chasm, in which new horrors await us. "Here," says the Ottimo Com., "all the senses are assailed: the sight, by murky air; the ear, by lamentations that 'have arrows shod with pity'; the smell, by stench of 'putrid limbs'; the touch, by hideous scurf, and by the sinners lying on one another; and the taste, by thirst that 'craves one little drop of water.'" Here Gianni Schicchi of Florence, and Myrrha, who counterfeited the persons of others for wicked purposes, represent the Falsifiers "in deeds"; Sinon and Potiphar's wife, the Falsifiers "in words." The canto ends with a dialogue between Master Adam of Brescia and Sinon, who strike and abuse each other with a grim scorn and zeal. Dante gets a sharp and memorable reproof from Virgil, for listening too eagerly to their base conversation.

AT THE TIME that Juno was incensed for Semele[1] against the Theban blood, as she already more than once had shown,

Athamas grew so insane, that he, seeing his wife, with two sons, go laden on either hand,

cried: "Spread we the nets, that I may take the lioness and her young lions at the pass"; and then stretched out his pitiless talons,

grasping the one who had the name Learchus; and whirled him, and dashed him on a rock; and she with her other burden drowned herself.

And when Fortune brought low the all-daring pride of the Trojans, so that the King together with his kingdom was blotted out;

Hecuba,[2] sad, miserable, and captive, after she had seen Polyxena slain, and forlorn, discerned her Polydorus,

on the sea-strand, she, out of her senses, barked like a dog; to such a degree had the sorrow wrung her soul.

But neither Theban Furies nor Trojan were ever seen in aught so cruel—not in stinging brutes, and much less human limbs;

as I saw in two shadows, pale and naked, which ran biting in the manner that a hungry swine does when he is thrust out from his sty.

The one came to Capocchio, and fixed its tusks on his neckjoint, so that, dragging him, it made the solid bottom claw his belly.

And the Aretine, who remained trembling, said to me: "That goblin is Gianni Schicchi;[3] and, rabid, he goes thus mangling others."

"Oh!" said I to him, "so may the other not plant its teeth on thee, be pleased to tell us who it is, ere it snatch itself away."

And he to me: "That is the ancient spirit of flagitious Myrrha, who loved her father with more than rightful love.

She came to sin with him disguised in alien form; even as the other who there is going away, undertook,

that he might gain the Lady of the troop, to disguise himself as Buoso Donati, making a testament and giving to it a legal form."

And when the furious two, on whom I had kept my eye, were passed, I turned it to observe the other ill-born spirits.

I saw one shapen like a lute,[4] if he had only had his groin cut short at the part where man is forked.

The heavy dropsy, which with its ill-digested humor so disproportions the limbs, that the visage corresponds not to the paunch,

made him hold his lips apart, as does the hectic patient, who for thirst curls the one lip towards the chin, and the other upwards.

"O ye! who are exempt from every punishment (and why I know not), in this grim world," said he to us, "look and attend

to the misery of Master Adam: when alive, I had enough of what I wished; and now, alas! I crave one little drop of water.

The rivulets that from the verdant hills of Casentino descend into the Arno, making their channels cool and moist,

stand constantly before me, and not in vain: for the image of them dries me up far more than the disease which from my visage wears the flesh.

The rigid Justice, which searches me, takes occasion from the place at which I sinned, to give my sighs a quicker flight.

There is Romena where I falsified the alloy, sealed with the Baptist's image: for which on earth I left my body burnt.

But if I could see the miserable soul of Guido here, or of Alessandro, or their brother, for Branda's fount I would not give the sight.

One is in already, if the mad shadows that are going round speak true; but what avails it me whose limbs are tied?

Were I only still so light, that I could move one inch in a hundred years, I had already put myself upon the road,

to seek him among this disfigured people, though it winds round eleven miles, and is not less than half a mile across.[5]

Through them am I in such a crew: they induced me to stamp the florins that had three carats of alloy."

And I to him: "Who are the abject two, lying close to thy right confines, and smoking like a hand bathed in wintertime?"

"Here I found them, when I rained into this pinfold," he answered; "and since then they have not given a turn, and may not give, I think, to all eternity.

One is the false wife who accused Joseph; the other is false Sinon,[6] the Greek from Troy; burning fever makes them reek so strongly."

And one of them, who took offence perhaps at being named thus darkly, smote the rigid belly of him with his fist;

it sounded like a drum, and Master Adam smote him in the face with his arm, that did not seem less hard,

saying to him: "Though I am kept from moving by my weighty limbs, I have an arm free for such necessity."

Thereat he answered: "When thou wast going to the fire, thou hadst it not so ready; but as ready, and more, when thou wast coining."

And he of the dropsy: "In this thou sayest true; but thou wast not so true a witness there, when questioned of the truth at Troy."

"If I spoke false, thou too didst falsify the coin," said Sinon; "and I am here for one crime, and thou for more than any other Demon."

"Bethink thee, perjurer, of the horse," answered he who had the inflated paunch; "and be it a torture to thee that all the world knows thereof."

"To thee be torture the thirst that cracks thy tongue," replied the Greek, "and the foul water which makes that belly such a hedge before thy eyes."

Then the coiner: "Thus thy jaw gapes wide, as usual, to speak ill: for if I have thirst, and moisture stuffs me,

thou hast the burning, and the head that pains thee; and to make thee lap the mirror of Narcissus[7] thou wouldst not require many words of invitation."

I was standing all intent to hear them, when the Master said to me: "Now keep looking, a little longer and I quarrel with thee!"

When I heard him speak to me in anger, I turned towards him with such shame, that it comes over me again as I but think of it.

And as one who dreams of something hurtful to him, and dreaming wishes it a dream, so that he longs for that which is, as if it were not:

such grew I, who, without power to speak, wished to excuse myself and all the while excused, and did not think that I was doing it.

"Less shame washes off a greater fault than thine has been," said the Master: "therefore unload thee of all sorrow;

and count that I am always at thy side, should it again fall out that Fortune brings thee where people are in similar contests: for the wish to hear it is a vulgar wish."

1. Semele, the daughter of Cadmus, King of Thebes, was beloved by Jupiter, to whom she bore a son, Bacchus; whereupon Juno wreaked her vengeanc. 1 the Theban royal house in several ways. Two of these are recor d by Ovid in the *Metam*, iii; while the madness of

Athamas, the husband of Semele's sister Ino, is narrated in the fourth book.

2. After the fall of Troy, Hecuba, the wife of King Priam, was carried off as a slave to Greece. On the way thither, the sacrifice of her daughter and the sight of her son's murdered body drove her mad (*Metam.* xiii).

3. Gianni Schicchi, a Florentine of the Cavalcanti family, well known for his mimicry. On the death of Buoso Donati (see Canto xxv), his son Cimone induced Gianni to personate the dead man and dictate a will in his favour. In doing this, Gianni added several clauses by which he himself benefited, and thus obtained, among other things, a beautiful mare, known as the *Lady of the troop*. The story of Myrrha is told by Ovid, *Metam.* x.

4. Master Adam of Brescia was induced by the Conti Guidi of Romena to counterfeit the Florentine golden florin, for which crime he was burnt in the year 1281.—*Branda's fount* is either a well-known fountain at Siena, or a more obscure one near Romena.

5. Attempts have been made to obtain the exact measurement of Dante's Hell, by calculations based on this passage, and on the reference in the preceding canto; but it is evident that Dante did not aim at any uniformity of design. The bank leading down to the tenth chasm must have been of considerable depth; but those leading to the second and sixth chasms were evidently quite short descents (see Cantos xviii and xxiii). In the same way, we have here, in the tenth chasm, a half-mile bottom, while in the fifth chasm, the fiends on either bank can, apparently, touch hooks with one another (Canto xxii). See *Purg.* xiii, *note* 1.

6. For Potiphar's wife, see *Genesis* xxxix. 6–23. Sinon is the Greek who allowed the Trojans to take him prisoner, and then persuaded them to admit the Wooden Horse within their city walls (*cf. Aen.* ii, and see Canto xxvi, *note* 5).

7. Water.

CANTO XXXI

The Poets now mount up, and cross the bank, which separates the
last chasm of the Malebolge from the Central Pit, or Ninth Circle,
wherein Satan himself is placed. The air is thick and gloomy (Zech.
xiv. 6, 7; Rev. ix. 2); so that Dante can see but little way before
him. The sound of a horn, louder than any thunder, suddenly at-
tracts all his attention; and, looking in the direction from which it
comes, he dimly discerns the figures of huge Giants standing round
the edge of the Pit. These are the proud rebellious Nephilim and
"mighty men which were of old" (Gen. vi. 4); "giants groaning
under the water" (Job xxvi. 5, Vulg.); "sons of earth" who made
open war against Heaven. The first of them is Nimrod of Babel, who
shouts in perplexed unintelligible speech, and is himself a mass
of stupidity and confusion: for Dante elsewhere (Vulg. Eloq. i)
tells how "man, under persuasion of the Giant, took upon him to
surpass Nature and the Author of Nature" on the plain of Shinar,
and was baffled and confounded. After seeing him, the Poets turn
to the left hand, and go along the brim of the Pit till they come
to Ephialtes; and then to Antæus, who takes them in his arms and
sets them down "into the bottom of all guilt," or lowest part of
Hell, where external cold freezes and locks up Cocytus, the marsh
(Canto xiv) that receives all its rivers.

ONE AND THE SAME tongue first wounded me so
that it tinged with blushes both my cheeks, and then held
forth the medicine to me.

Thus I have heard that the lance of Achilles, and of his
father, used to be occasion first of sad and then of healing
gift.

We turned our back to the wretched valley, up by the
bank that girds it round, crossing without any speech.

Here was less than night and less than day, so that my
sight went little way before me; but I heard a high horn
sound

so loudly, that it would have made any thunder weak;

which directed my eyes, that followed its course against itself, all to one place:

after the dolorous rout, when Charlemain had lost the holy emprise, Roland did not sound with his so terribly.[1]

Short while had I kept my head turned in that direction, when I seemed to see many lofty towers; whereat I: "Master! say, what town is this?"

And he to me: "Because thou traversest the darkness too far off, it follows that thou errest in thy imagining.

Thou shalt see right well, if thou arrivest there, how much the sense at distance is deceived: therefore spur thee somewhat more."

Then lovingly he took me by the hand, and said: "Ere we go farther, that the reality may seem less strange to thee,

know, they are not towers, but Giants; and are in the well, around its bank, from the navel downwards all of them."

As when a mist is vanishing, the eye by little and little reshapes that which the air-crowding vapour hides;

so whilst piercing through that gross and darksome air, more and more approaching towards the brink, error fled from me, and my fear increased.

For as on its round wall Montereggione[2] crowns itself with towers: so with half their bodies, the horrible giants,

whom Jove from heaven still threatens when he thunders, turreted the bank which compasses the pit.

And already I discerned the face of one,[3] the shoulders and the breast, and great part of the belly, and down along his sides both arms.

Nature certainly, when she left off the art of making animals like these, did very well, in taking away such executioners from Mars;

and if she repents her not of Elephants and Whales,[4] whoso subtly looks, therein regards her as more just and prudent:

for where the instrument of the mind is joined to evil will and potency, men can make no defence against it.

His face seemed to me as long and large as the pine of

St. Peter's at Rome,[5] and his other bones were in proportion to it;

so that the bank, which was an apron from his middle downwards, showed us certainly so much of him above, that three Frieslanders had vainly boasted

to have reached his hair: for downwards from the place where a man buckles on his mantle, I saw thirty large spans of him.

"Rafel mai amech zabi almi,"[6] began to shout the savage mouth, for which no sweeter psalmody was fit.

And towards him my Guide: "Stupid soul! keep to thy horn; and vent thyself with that, when rage or other passion touches thee.

Search on thy neck, and thou wilt find the belt that holds it tied, O soul confused, and see the horn itself that girdles thy huge breast."

Then he said to me: "He accuses himself; this is Nimrod, through whose ill thought one language is not still used in the world.

Let us leave him standing, and not speak in vain: for every language is to him as to others his which no one understands."

We therefore journeyed on, turning to the left; and, a crossbow-shot off, we found the next far more fierce and large.

Who and what the master could be that girt him thus, I cannot tell; but he had his right arm pinioned down behind, and the other before,

with a chain which held him clasped from the neck downwards, and on the uncovered part went round to the fifth turn.

"This proud spirit willed to try his power against high Jove," said my Guide: "whence he has such reward.

Ephialtes[7] is his name; and he made the great endeavours, when the giants made the Gods afraid; the arms he agitated then, he never moves."

And I to him: "If it were possible, I should wish my eyes might have experience of the immense Briareus."[8]

Whereat he answered: "Thou shalt see Antæus[9] near at

hand, who speaks, and is unfettered. who will put us into the bottom of all guilt.

He whom thou desirest to see is far beyond; and is tied and shaped like this one, save that he seems in aspect more ferocious."

No mighty earthquake ever shook a tower so violently, as Ephialtes forthwith shook himself.

Then more than ever I dreaded death; and nothing else was wanted for it but the fear, had I not seen his bands.

We then proceeded farther on, and reached Antæus, who full five ells, besides the head, forth issued from the cavern.

"O thou! who in the fateful valley, which made Scipio heir of glory when Hannibal retreated with his hosts,

didst take of old a thousand lions for thy prey; and through whom, hadst thou been at the high war of thy brethren, it seem yet to be believed.

that the sons of earth had conquered; set us down—and be not shy to do it—where the cold locks up Cocytus.

Do not make us go to Tityos nor Typhon; this man can give of that which here is longed for: therefore bend thee, and curl not thy lip in scorn.

He can yet restore thy fame on earth: for he lives, and still awaits long life, so Grace before the time call him not unto herself."

Thus spake the Master; and he in haste stretched forth the hands, whence Hercules of old did feel great stress, and took my Guide.

Virgil, when he felt their grasp, said to me: "Come here, that I may take thee"; then of himself and me he made one bundle.

Such as the Carisenda[10] seems to one's view, beneath the leaning side, when a cloud is going over it so, that it hangs in the contrary direction:

such Antæus seemed to me who stood watching to see him bend; and it was so terrible a moment, that I should have wished to go by other road;

but gently on the deep, which swallows Lucifer with Judas, he set us down; nor lingered there thus bent, but raised himself as in a ship the mast.

1. In the course of the battle of Roncesvalles, when the Saracens were gaining the day, Roland sounded his horn, so as to induce Charlemagne, who was eight miles away, to return to the aid of the Christians; and he sounded it with such violence, that, as the Old French *Chanson de Roland* says, *Parmi la buche en salt fors li clers sancs, De sun cervel la temple en est rumpant.* The Emperor heard it, but was misled by the advice of the traitor Ganelon, and gave no heed to his nephew's call.

2. Montereggioni is a castle that belonged to the Sienese, and is situated about eight miles north-west of their city; the wall surrounding it is surmounted by twelve turrets.

3. Nimrod, the reputed builder of the Tower of Babel (*Genesis* x and xi). There is, of course, no Biblical tradition as to his having been a giant.

4. Elephants and whales are less dangerous, not being endowed with reason.

5. The bronze cone-pine, which, in Dante's time, stood in front of St. Peter's, is about seven and a half feet high.

6. In view of Dante's express statement, it is absurd to attempt the interpretation of this line.

7. Ephialtes and his brother Otus, the sons of Neptune, warred against the Olympian Gods, and attempted to pile Ossa on Olympus and Pelion on Ossa, but were slain by Apollo.

8. Briareus was another of the giants who defied the Gods of Olympus. Virgil (*Æn.* x) describes him as having a hundred arms and fifty heads, and Statius (*Theb.* ii) speaks of him as *immensus*.

9. Antæus is unfettered because he held aloof from the strife against the Gods. Dante has borrowed the details concerning him from Lucan's *Phars.* iv. Hercules, having discovered that Antæus lost his strength when his body did not touch the earth, lifted him in the air and crushed him. The exploit of the lions took place near Zama, where Scipio defeated Hannibal.—Tityos and Typhon were two giants, who, having incurred the wrath of Jupiter, were hurled into Tartarus (which was held to be beneath Mount Ætna, *cf. Par.* viii).

10. The Carisenda is a leaning tower at Bologna.

CANTO XXXII

This Ninth and Last, or frozen Circle, lowest part of the Universe, and farthest remote from the Source of all light and heat, divides itself into four concentric Rings. The First or outermost is the Caina, which has its name from Cain who slew his brother Abel, and contains the sinners who have done violence to their own kindred. The Second or Antenora, so called "from Antenor the Trojan, betrayer of his country" (Pietro di Dante, &c.), is filled with those who have been guilty of treachery against their native land. Dante finds many of his own countrymen, both Guelfs and Ghibellines, in these two rings; and learns the names of those in the First from Camicion de' Pazzi, and of those in the Second from Bocca degli Abati. He has a very special detestation of Bocca, through whose treachery so many of the Guelfs were slaughtered, and "every family in Florence thrown into mourning"; and, as the Ottimo remarks, "falls into a very rude method, that he has used to no other spirit." The canto leaves him in the Antenora beside two sinners that are frozen close together in the same hole.

IF I HAD rhymes rough and hoarse, as would befit the dismal hole, on which all the other rocky steeps converge and weigh,

I should press out the juice of my conception more fully; but since I have them not, not without fear I bring myself to tell thereof:

for to describe the bottom of all the universe is not an enterprise for being taken up in sport, nor for a tongue that cries mamma and papa.

But may those Ladies help my verse, who helped Amphion with walls to close in Thebes;[1] so that my words may not be diverse from the fact.

O ye beyond all others, miscreated rabble, who are in the place, to speak of which is hard, better had ye here on earth been sheep or goats!

When we were down in the dark pit, under the Giant's feet, much lower, and I still was gazing at the high wall,

I heard a voice say to me: "Look how thou passest: take care that with thy soles thou tread not on the heads of thy weary wretched brothers."

Whereat I turned myself, and saw before me and beneath my feet a lake, which through frost had the semblance of glass and not of water.

Never did the Danube of Austria make so thick a veil for his course in winter, nor the Don afar beneath the frigid sky,

as there was here: for if Tambernic had fallen on it, or Pietrapana,[2] it would not even at the edge have given a creak.

And as the frog to croak, sits with his muzzle out of the water, when the peasant-woman oft dreams that she is gleaning:[3]

so, livid, up to where the hue of shame appears, the doleful shades were in the ice, sounding with their teeth like storks.

Each held his face turned downwards; by the mouth their cold, and by the eyes the sorrow of their hearts is testified amongst them.

When I had looked round awhile, I turned towards my feet; and saw two so pressed against each other, that they had the hair of their heads intermixed.

"Tell me, ye who thus together press your bosoms," said I, "who you are." And they bended their necks; and when they had raised their faces towards me,

their eyes, which only inwardly were moist before, gushed at the lids, and the frost bound fast the tears between them, and closed them up again.

Wood with wood no cramp did ever gird so strongly: wherefore they, like two he-goats, butted one another; such rage came over them.

And one, who had lost both ears by the cold, with his face still downwards said: "Why art thou looking so much at us?

If thou desirest to know who are these two,[4] the valley whence the Bisenzio descends was theirs, and their father Albert's.

They issued from one body; and thou mayest search the
170

whole Caina, and shalt not find a shade more worthy to be fixed in gelatine:

not him, whose breast and shadow at one blow were pierced by Arthur's hand;[5] not Focaccia;[6] not this one, who so obstructs me

with his head that I see no farther, and who was named Sassol Mascheroni:[7] if thou beest a Tuscan, well knowest thou now who he was.

And that thou mayest not put me to further speech, know that I was Camicion de' Pazzi,[8] and am waiting for Carlino to excuse me."

Afterwards I saw a thousand visages, made doggish by the cold: whence shuddering comes over me, and always will come, when I think of the frozen fords.

And as we were going towards the middle at which all weight unites, and I was shivering in the eternal shade,

whether it was will, or destiny or chance, I know not; but, walking amid the heads, I hit my foot violently against the face of one.

Weeping it cried out to me: "Why tramplest thou on me? If thou comest not to increase the vengeance for Montaperti,[9] why dost thou molest me?"

And I: "My Master! now wait me here, that I may rid me of a doubt respecting him; then shalt thou, however much thou pleasest, make me haste."

The Master stood; and to that shade, which still kept bitterly reviling, I said: "What art thou, who thus reproachest others?"

"Nay, who art thou," he answered, "that through the Antenora[10] goest, smiting the cheeks of others; so that, if thou wert alive, it were too much?"

"I am alive," was my reply; "and if thou seekest fame, it may be precious to thee, that I put thy name among the other notes."

And he to me: "The contrary is what I long for; take thyself away! and pester me no more: for thou ill knowest how to flatter on this icy slope."

Then I seized him by the afterscalp, and said: "It will be necessary that thou name thyself, or that not a hair remain upon thee here!"

Whence he to me: "Even if thou unhair me, I will not tell thee who I am; nor show it thee, though thou fall foul upon my head a thousand times."

I already had his hair coiled on my hand, and had plucked off more than one tuft of it, he barking and keeping down his eyes,

when another cried: "What ails thee, Bocca? is it not enough for thee to chatter with thy jaws, but thou must bark too? what Devil is upon thee?"

"Now," said I, "accursed traitor! I do not want thee to speak; for to thy shame I will bear true tidings of thee."

"Go away!" he answered; "and tell what pleases thee; but be not silent, if thou gettest out from hence, respecting him, who now had his tongue so ready.

Here he laments the Frenchman's silver. 'Him of Duera,'[11] thou canst say, 'I saw there, where the sinners stand pinched in ice.'

Shouldst thou be asked who else was there, thou hast beside thee the Beccheria[12] whose gorge was slit by Florence.

Gianni de' Soldanier,[13] I think, is farther on, with Ganellone, and Tribaldello[14] who unbarred Faenza when it slept."

We had already left him, when I saw two frozen in one hole so closely, that the one head was a cap to the other;

and as bread is chewed for hunger, so the uppermost put his teeth into the other there where the brain joins with the nape.

Not otherwise did Tydeus gnaw the temples of Menalippus for rage,[15] than he the skull and the other parts.

"O thou! who by such brutal token showest thy hate on him whom thou devourest, tell me why," I said; "on this condition,

that if thou with reason complainest of him, I, knowing who ye are and his offence, may yet repay thee in the world above, if that, wherewith I speak, be not dried up."

1. Amphion, aided by the Muses, played the lyre with such charm that he drew from Mount Cithæron the stone which, placing themselves of their own accord, formed the walls of Thebes.
2. Tambernic is apparently a mountain in the east of Slavonia, while

Pietrapana is a peak probably identical with the ancient Pietra Apuana in north-west Tuscany.

3. That is to say, in summer-time.

4. Alessandro and Napoleone, the sons of Count Alberto degli Alberti (whose possessions included Vernia and Cerbaia in the Val di Bisenzio), quarrelled over their inheritance and killed each other.

5. Mordred having done his utmost to usurp the dominion of his father, King Arthur, the latter determined to kill him. He pierced his body with a lance, and, in the words of the Old French romance, "after the withdrawal of the lance there passed through the wound a ray of sun so manifest that Girflet saw it." Thereupon Mordred, feeling that he had received his death wound, slew his father.

6. Focaccia, one of the Cancellieri of Pistoia, appears to have been largely responsible for the feud which broke out in that family, in the course of which many of the kinsmen, who were divided into Neri and Bianchi, slew each other. The aid of Florence was invoked, with the result that the Black and White factions were introduced into that city, too.

7. Sassol Mascheroni, one of the Florentine Toschi, killed his nephew (or, according to other accounts, his brother) so as to obtain the inheritance.

8. Camicion de' Pazzi slew his kinsman Ubertino, with whom he had certain interests in common.

In 1302 Carlino de' Pazzi was holding the castle of Piantravigne in the Valdarno for the Whites of Florence against the Blacks of that city and the Lucchese; but, having been bribed, he treacherously surrendered it to the enemy.

9. The defeat of the Florentine Guelfs at Montaperti (see Canto x, *note* 11) was largely due to the fact that Bocca degli Abati, who, though a Ghibelline, was fighting on the Guelf side, at a critical moment cut off the hand of the Florentine standard-bearer.

10. According to medieval tradition (as preserved for example in the *Dictys Cretensis*, the *Dares Phrygius* and the later *Roman de Troie*) it was the Trojan Antenor who betrayed his city to the Greeks.

11. When Charles of Anjou began his campaign against Manfred in 1266, he entered Parma without any opposition, although Manfred had made arrangements for his force to be resisted. This omission was generally held to be due to the treachery of the leader of the Cremonese, Buoso da Duera, who was accused of having been bribed by the French.

12. Tesauro de' Beccheria of Pavia, Abbot of Vallombrosa and Legate of Alexander IV in Florence, was put to death for plotting against the Guelfs, after the Ghibellines had been expelled from the city in 1258.

13. Gianni de' Soldanier, though a Ghibelline, became the leader of the Guelf commons of Florence, when, after the defeat of Manfred at Benevento (1265), they rebelled against the government of Guido Novello and the Ghibelline nobles.

14. For Ganelon see *note* 1 of the preceding canto.—The Ghibelline Lambertazzi, a Bolognese family that had taken refuge in Faenza, were, in 1280, put to the sword by their enemies the Geremei, a Guelf family of Bologna. This was brought about by the treachery of a certain Tribaldello (or Tebaldello), one of the Zambrasi of Faenza, who had a spite against the Lambertazzi, and opened the city gates to their enemies.

15. Though Tydeus had been mortally wounded by Menalippus, in the war of the Seven against Thebes, he still managed to kill his opponent; whose head having been brought to him, he set to gnawing the skull, in a frenzy of rage. The incident is related by Statius in the eighth book of the *Thebaid*.

CANTO XXXIII

*"Wherewithal a man sinneth, by the same also shall he be punished"
is the unalterable law which Dante sees written—not only in the
ancient Hebrew records, but in every part of the Universe. The
sinners whom he here finds frozen together in one hole are Count
Ugolino and Archbishop Ruggieri (Roger) of Pisa, traitors both;
and Ruggieri has the Shadow of Ugolino's hunger gnawing upon
him in the eternal ice, while Ugolino has the image of his own base
treachery and hideous death continually before him. He lifts up
his head from the horrid meal, and pauses, when Dante recalls to
him his early life, in the same way as the storm paused for Fran-
cesca; and the Archbishop is silent as Paolo. After leaving Ugolino,
the Poets go on to the Third Ring or Ptolomæa, which takes its
name from the Ptolomæus (1 Maccab. xvi. 11) who "had abundance
of silver and gold," and "made a great banquet" for his father-in-
law Simon the high priest and his two sons; and, "when Simon and
his sons had drunk largely," treacherously slew them "in the ban-
queting place." Friar Alberigo and Branca d'Oria are found in it.*

FROM THE FELL repast that sinner raised his mouth,
wiping it upon the hair of the head he had laid waste be-
hind.

Then he began: "Thou willest that I renew desperate
grief, which wrings my heart, even at the very thought,
before I tell thereof.

But if my words are to be a seed, that may bear fruit of
infamy to the traitor whom I gnaw, thou shalt see me speak
and weep at the same time.

I know not who thou mayest be, nor by what mode thou
hast come down here; but, when I hear thee, in truth thou
seemest to me a Florentine.

Thou hast to know that I was Count Ugolino, and this
the Archbishop Ruggieri;[1] now I will tell thee why I am
such a neighbour to him.

That by the effect of his ill devices I, confiding in him,

175

was taken and thereafter put to death, it is not necessary to say.

But that which thou canst not have learnt, that is, how cruel was my death, thou shalt hear and know if he has offended me.

A narrow hole within the mew, which from me has the title of Famine, and in which others yet must be shut up,

had through its opening already shown me several moons, when I slept the evil sleep that rent for me the curtain of the future.

This man seemed to me lord and master, chasing the wolf and his whelps, upon the mountain[2] for which the Pisans cannot see Lucca.

With hounds meagre, keen, and dexterous, he had put in front of him Gualandi with Sismondi, and with Lanfranchi.[3]

After short course, the father and his sons seemed to me weary; and methought I saw their flanks torn by the sharp teeth.

When I awoke before the dawn, I heard my sons[4] who were with me, weeping in their sleep, and asking for bread.

Thou art right cruel, if thou dost not grieve already at the thought of what my heart foreboded; and if thou weepest not, at what art thou used to weep?

They were now awake, and the hour approaching at which our food used to be brought us, and each was anxious from his dream,

and below I heard the outlet of the horrible tower locked up: whereat I looked into the faces of my sons, without uttering a word.

I did not weep: so stony grew I within; they wept; and my little Anselm said: 'Thou lookest so, father, what ails thee?'

But I shed no tear, nor answered all that day, nor the next night, till another sun came forth upon the world.

When a small ray was sent into the doleful prison, and I discerned in their four faces the aspect of my own,

I bit on both my hands for grief. And they, thinking that I did it from desire of eating, of a sudden rose up,

and said: 'Father, it will give us much less pain, if thou

wilt eat of us: thou didst put upon us this miserable flesh, and do thou strip it off.'

Then I calmed myself, in order not to make them more unhappy; that day and the next we all were mute. Ah, hard earth! why didst thou not open?

When we had come to the fourth day, Gaddo threw himself stretched out at my feet, saying: 'My father! why don't you help me?'

There he died; and even as thou seest me, saw I the three fall one by one, between the fifth day and the sixth: whence I betook me,

already blind, to groping over each, and for three days called them, after they were dead; then fasting had more power than grief."[5]

When he had spoken this, with eyes distorted he seized the miserable skull again with his teeth, which as a dog's were strong upon the bone.

Ah, Pisa; scandal to the people of the beauteous land where "sì" is heard, since thy neighbours are slow to punish thee,

let the Caprara and Gorgona[6] move, and hedge up the Arno at its mouth, that it may drown in thee every living soul.

For if Count Ugolino had the fame of having betrayed thee of thy castles,[7] thou oughtest not to have put his sons into such torture:

their youthful age, thou modern Thebes![8] made innocent Uguccione and Brigata, and the other two whom my song above has named.

We went farther on, where the frost[9] ruggedly inwraps another people, not bent downwards, but all reversed.

The very weeping there allows them not to weep; and the grief, which finds impediment upon their eyes, turns inward to increase the agony:

for their first tears form a knot, and, like crystal vizors, fill up all the cavity beneath their eyebrows.

And although, as from a callus, through the cold all feeling had departed from my face,

it now seemed to me as if I felt some wind; whereat I:

"Master, who moves this? Is not all heat extinguished here below?"

Whence he to me: "Soon shalt thou be where thine eye itself, seeing the cause which rains the blast,[10] shall answer thee in this."

And one of the wretched shadows of the icy crust cried out to us: "O souls, so cruel that the last post of all is given to you!

Remove the hard veils from my face, that I may vent the grief, which stuffs my heart, a little, ere the weeping freeze again."

Wherefore I to him: "If thou wouldst have me aid thee, tell me who thou art; and if I do not extricate thee, may I have to go to the bottom of the ice."

He answered therefore: "I am Friar Alberigo,[11] I am he of the fruits from the ill garden, who here receive dates for my figs."

"Hah!" said I to him, "then art thou dead already?" And he to me: "How my body stands in the world above, I have no knowledge.

Such privilege has this Ptolomæa, that oftentimes the soul falls down hither, ere Atropos[12] impels it.

And that thou more willingly mayest rid the glazen tears from off my face, know that forthwith, when the soul betrays,

as I did, her body is taken from her by a Demon who thereafter rules it, till its time has all revolved.

She falls rushing to this cistern; and perhaps the body of this other shade, which winters here behind me, is stlll apparent on the earth above.

Thou must know it, if thou art but now come down: it is Ser Branca d'Oria;[13] and many years have passed since he was thus shut up."

"I believe," said I to him, "that thou deceivest me: for Branca d'Oria never died; and eats, and drinks, and sleeps, and puts on clothes."

"In the ditch above, of the Malebranche," said he, "there where the tenacious pitch is boiling, Michel Zanche had not yet arrived,

when this man left a Devil in his stead in the body of

178

himself, and of one of his kindred who did the treachery along with him.

But reach hither thy hand: open my eyes"; and I opened them not for him: and to be rude to him was courtesy.

Ah, Genoese! men estranged from all morality, and full of all corruption, why are ye not scattered from the earth?

For with the worst spirit of Romagna, found I one of ye, who for his deeds even now in soul bathes in Cocytus, and above on earth still seems alive in body.

1. In 1288 the Guelfs were paramount in Pisa, but they were divided into two parties, led by Ugolino della Gherardesca and by his grandson, Nino de' Visconti (for whom see *Purg.* viii), respectively. The head of the Ghibellines was the Archbishop of the city, Ruggieri degli Ubaldini. In order to obtain supreme authority, Ugolino intrigued with Ruggieri, and succeeded in expelling Nino. He was, however, in his turn betrayed by the Archbishop who, seeing that the Guelfs were weakened, had Ugolino and four of his sons and grandsons imprisoned. When Guido of Montefeltro took command of the Pisan forces in March of the following year, 1289, the keys of the prison were thrown into the river and the captives left to starve.
2. The Monte di S. Giuliano.
3. Leading Ghibelline families of Pisa.
4. *Sons.* Of Ugolino's four companions, only two were actually his sons—Gaddo and Uguccione; Nino and Anselmuccio being his grandsons.
5. This verse has given rise to much controversy. The meaning obviously is, not that Ugolino was forced by the pangs of hunger to feed on the bodies, but that hunger brought about his death.
6. The islands of Caprara and Gorgona, north-west of Elba and south-west of Livorno, respectively, were at that time under the dominion of Pisa.
7. In 1284, after the defeat of the Pisans by the Genoese at Meloria, Ugolino yielded certain castles to the Florentines and Lucchese. Some hold that his motives were loyal, and that his only object was to pacify these enemies of Pisa. But Dante evidently knew more of the circumstances. Besides, if the Count is atoning his treachery against Nino rather than this action, how does he come to be in Antenora?
8. Dante often alludes to the stories of bloodshed, hate and vengeance for which Thebes was notorious (see Cantos xxvi and xxx).
9. The name of this division is almost certainly derived from Ptolemy, the captain of Jericho, who "inviteth Simon and two of his sons into his castle, and there treacherously murdereth them" (1 *Maccabees* xvi).
10. See the following canto.
11. In a dispute relating to the lordship of Faenza, Alberigo, a mem-

ber of the Manfredi family and one of the *Frati Gaudenti*, was struck by his younger brother, Manfred (1284). Alberigo pretended to forget all about this, but in the following year he invited Manfred and his son to a banquet, and, at a given signal (the words "Bring the fruit"), they were both murdered. *The evil fruit of Friar Alberigo* passed into a proverb.

12. Atropos—the Fate that severs the thread of life.

13. Branca d'Oria, member of a famous Ghibelline family of Genoa, aided by a nephew, murdered his father-in-law, Michel Zanche (for whom see Canto xxii), at a banquet to which he had invited him.

ÇANTO XXXIV

The Judecca, or Last Circlet of Cocytus, takes its name from Judas Iscariot, and contains the souls of those "who betrayed their masters and benefactors." The Arch Traitor Satan, "Emperor of the Realm of Sorrow," stands fixed in the Centre of it; and he too is punished by his own Sin. All the streams of Guilt keep flowing back to him, as their source; and from beneath his three Faces (Shadows of his consciousness) issue forth the mighty wings with which he struggles, as it were, to raise himself; and sends out winds that freeze him only the more firmly in his ever-swelling Marsh. Dante has to take a full view of him too; and then is carried through the Centre by his Mystic Guide—"grappling on the hair of Satan," not without significance; and set down on "the other face of the Judecca." And now the bitter journey of our Pilgrim is over; and a tone of gladness goes through the remaining verses. Hell is now behind him, and the Stars of Heaven above: he has got beyond the 'Everlasting No,' and is "sore travailled," and the "way is long and difficult," but it leads from Darkness to the "bright world." After some brief inquiries, "without caring for any repose," by aid of the heaven-sent Wisdom he "plucks himself from the Abyss"; and follows climbing, till they see the Stars in the opposite hemisphere.

"VEXILLA REGIS prodeunt inferni[1] towards us: therefore look in front of thee," my Master said, "if thou discernest him."

As, when a thick mist breathes, or when the night comes on our hemisphere, a mill, which the wind turns, appears at distance:

such an edifice did I now seem to see; and, for the wind, shrunk back behind my Guide, because no other shed was there.

Already I had come (and with fear I put it into verse) where the souls were wholly covered, and shone through like straw in glass.

Some are lying; some stand upright, this on its head, and

that upon its soles; another, like a bow, bends face to feet.

When we had proceeded on so far, that it pleased my Guide to show to me the Creature which was once so fair,

he took himself from before me, and made me stop, saying: "Lo Dis! and lo the place where it behoves thee arm thyself with fortitude."

How icy chill and hoarse I then became, ask not, O Reader! for I write it not, because all speech would fail to tell.

I did not die, and did not remain alive; now think for thyself, if thou hast any grain of ingenuity, what I became, deprived of both death and life.

The Emperor of the dolorous realm, from mid breast stood forth out of the ice; and I in size am liker to a giant,

than the giants are to his arms: mark now how great that whole must be, which corresponds to such a part.

If he was once as beautiful as he is ugly now, and lifted up his brows against his Maker, well may all affliction come from him.

Oh how great a marvel seemed it to me, when I saw three faces on his head! The one in front, and it was fiery red;

the others were two, that were adjoined to this, above the very middle of each shoulder; and they were joined at his crest;

and the right seemed between white aud yellow; the left was such to look on, as they who come from where the Nile descends.[2]

Under each there issued forth two mighty wings, of size befitting such a bird: sea-sails I never saw so broad.

No plumes had they; but were in form and texture like a bat's: and he was flapping them, so that three winds went forth from him.

Thereby Cocytus all was frozen; with six eyes he wept, and down three chins gushed tears and bloody foam.

In every mouth he champed a sinner with his teeth, like a brake; so that he thus kept three of them in torment.

To the one in front, the biting was nought, compared with the tearing: for at times the back of him remained quite stript of skin.

"That soul up there, which suffers greatest punishment,"

said the Master, "is Judas Iscariot, he who has his head within, and outside plies his legs.

Of the other two, who have their heads beneath, that one, who hangs from the black visage, is Brutus: see how he writhes himself, and utters not a word;

and the other is Cassius,[3] who seems so stark of limb. But night is reascending;[4] and now must we depart: for we have seen the whole."

As he desired, I clasped his neck; and he took opportunity of time and place; and when the wings were opened far,

applied him to the shaggy sides, and then from shag to shag descended down, between the tangled hair and frozen crusts.

When we had come to where the thigh revolves just on the swelling of the haunch, my Guide with labour and with difficulty

turned his head where he had had his feet before, and grappled on the hair, as one who mounts; so that I thought we were returning into Hell again.

"Hold thee fast! for by such stairs," said my Guide, panting like a man forspent, "must we depart from so much ill."

Thereafter through the opening of a rock he issued forth, and put me on its brim to sit; then towards me he stretched his wary step.

I raised my eyes, and thought to see Lucifer as I had left him; and saw him with the legs turned upwards;

and the gross people who see not what that point is which I had passed, let them judge if I grew perplexed then.

"Rise up!" said the Master, "upon thy feet: the way is long, and difficult the road; and already to middle tierce the Sun returns."[5]

It was no palace-hall, there where we stood, but natural dungeon with an evil floor and want of light.

"Before I pluck myself from the Abyss," said I when risen up, "O Master! speak to me a little, to draw me out of error.

Where is the ice? and this, how is he fixed thus upside

down? and how, in so short a time, has the Sun from eve to morn made transit?"

And he to me: "Thou imaginest that thou art still upon the other side of the centre, where I caught hold on the hair of the evil Worm which pierces through the world.

Thou wast on that side, so long as I descended; when I turned myself, thou then didst pass the point to which all gravities from every part are drawn;

and now thou art arrived beneath the hemisphere opposed to that which canopies the great dry land,[6] and underneath whose summit was consumed

the Man, who without sin was born and lived; thou hast thy feet upon a little sphere, which forms the other face of the Judecca.

Here it is morn, when it is evening there; and this Fiend, who made a ladder for us with his hair, is still fixed as he was before.

On this side fell he down from Heaven; and the land, which erst stood out here, through fear of him veiled itself with sea,

and came to our hemisphere; and perhaps, in order to escape from him, that which on this side appears left here the empty space, and upwards rushed."[7]

Down there, from Beelzebub as far removed as his tomb extends, is a space. not known by sight but by the sound

of a rivulet[8] descending in it, along the hollow of a rock which it has eaten out with tortuous course and slow declivity.

The Guide and I entered by that hidden road, to return into the bright world; and, without caring for any rest,

we mounted up, he first and I second, so far that I distinguished through a round opening the beauteous things which Heaven bears; and thence we issued out, again to see the Stars.[9]

1. This is a parody of the first line of a Latin hymn by Fortunatus (6th century)—*Vexilla regis prodeunt*. The advancing standards are the wings of Lucifer.
2. The red, yellow and black faces have been variously explained. The best interpretation seems to be the one which makes them rep-

resentative of hatred, impotence and ignorance—the qualities opposed to those of the Holy Trinity.

3. These three arch-sinners betrayed, in the persons of their lords and benefactors, the two most august representatives of Church and State—the founder of Christianity and the founder of the Roman Empire. The other sinners in Giudecca are not specified save in a general way.

4. It is now about six o'clock on the Saturday evening.

5. See the chronological note on page 12. *Tierce* was the first of the four canonical divisions of the day, and would, at the equinox, last from six till nine; *middle tierce* is therefore equivalent to half-past seven.

6. The northern hemisphere was held to be covered with land, the southern with water.

7. This passage has generally been taken to establish a connection between the cone of the Mount of Purgatory and the funnel of Hell. It is obvious, however, that Hell was in existence ready to receive Satan, and that the *empty space* and the *tomb* refer not to Hell, but to the cavern into which the nether bulk of Satan is thrust.

8. The *rivulet* is Lethe (see *Purg.* xxviii), which bears the memory of sin from Purgatory down to the place of sin in Hell.

9. The word *stars*, with which each of the three *canticles* closes, indicates the constant aspiration of the poem, and of the soul whose journey it depicts towards the highest things.

PURGATORIO

Ordina quest' Amore, O tu che m'ami.
JACOPONE DA TODI.

Note on Dante's Purgatory

THE KEY to the comprehension of Dante's representation of Purgatory is to be found in the connection of the mountain with the Earthly Paradise, or Garden of Eden, situated at its summit. We learn from careful reading of the last lines of the *Inferno* that the mountain of Purgatory was thrown up (like a mole-hill, if one may use such an illustration) when Satan was hurled down from heaven to the centre of the earth. His upper bulk was thrust into Hell, which was already there to receive him, and beneath the Mount of Purgatory the earth closed up behind him, leaving a huge cavern, into which his nether limbs stretched up.

So the fall of Satan was the occasion for a portion of the substance of the earth to leap up heavenward above all the elemental perturbations of the lower atmosphere, thus making itself worthy to become the seat of that human race which was to replace the fallen angels.

Now the life of Eden, had man persevered, was to have been an earthly life, including what may be thought of as natural religion,—a consciousness of the love and nearness of God, a perfect spontaneity of human joy and goodness, and a knowledge of all earthly wisdom. But the higher revelations which would complete the life of man, not as an earthly but as a heavenly being, were to have been subsequently added. Therefore, when man fell he forfeited immediately the perfect earthly life, and ultimately the perfect heavenly life. His first task, then, must be to recover the life of the Earthly Paradise; and as purgation, or recovery from the fall, consists primarily in regaining Eden, the mountain pedestal of the Garden of Eden becomes by a necessity of symbolic logic the scene of purgation. Physically and spiritually man must climb back to the "uplifted garden." Hence the key-note of the *Purgatorio* is primarily ethical, and only by implication spiritual. Cato, the type of the moral virtues, is the guardian of the place; Virgil, the type of human philosophy, is the guide; and the Earthly Paradise, the type of the "blessedness of this life" (*De Mon.* iii. 16), is the immediate goal. Beatrice is only realized by Dante as he had known her in the Eden-like "new life" of his youth, and by no means as the august impersonation of revealed truth. She appears to him in due course, surrounded by her escort, when he has reached the state of earthly perfection; and the vacancy of that region of earthly bliss is explained to him by the Vision of false and confused government, wherein is portrayed the failure of Church and State to bring man back to the life of Eden. To the Church as an earthly organization, or regimen, the grace of God has committed by anticipation such revealed truth as is necessary to help the enfeebled will of man to recover the state of Eden. But the Church, as a regimen, is not to be confounded with Revelation (Beatrice) herself. The proper office of the Church, as a regimen, ends when the proper office of Beatrice begins. See *De Monarchia*, iii. 4.

§2. THE DIVISIONS OF THE PURGATORY

The details of the second cantica follow the general schemes; based on three, sub-divided into seven, raised by unlike additions to nine, and by a final member on a totally different plane, to ten.

The threefold division, which is expounded at length in Canto xvii, rests on the distinction between (i) perverse, (ii) defective, and (iii) excessive love. By perverse love is meant a delight in things which ought to grieve us, and of the three natural objects of love, God, self, and neighbour, the two first are secured (except in case of such monstrous perversion as is punished in Circle 7 of Hell) from hate. (I) Perverse love, then, must consist in taking a delight in evils that befall others. The proud man desires to excel, and therefore rejoices in defeating the attempt of others (i). The envious man hates being over-shadowed and made to think meanly of himself and his belongings and therefore rejoices in the misfortunes of others (ii). The angry man wishes in his indignation to make those who have offended him smart, and so finds a satisfaction in their sufferings (iii). (II) They who are spiritually and intellectually sluggish in the contemplation of divine goodness, or sluggish in the will to pursue it, are alike guilty of sloth, or inadequate love (iv). (III) And those who pursue wealth (v), or the pleasures of the table (vi), or carnal appetite (vii), without observing due limitations, are guilty of excessive and ill-regulated love for things which should only take a secondary place in their affections. Hence the threefold division, by sub-division of its extreme members, has given us a sevenfold division which coincides with the seven deadly sins of the Catholic Church. Besides this we have on the island at the base of the mountain those who have died in contumacy against the Church; and on the slopes of the mount below the gate we have the late-repentant. These two classes raise seven to nine; and at the top of the mountain we have the Earthly Paradise, not part of Purgatory at all, but the goal to which the purified souls are led.

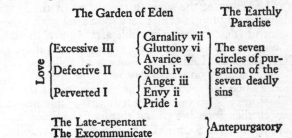

10	The Garden of Eden		The Earthly Paradise
9 8 7 6 5 4 3	Love { Excessive III · Defective II · Perverted I	{ Carnality vii · Gluttony vi · Avarice v · Sloth iv · Anger iii · Envy ii · Pride i }	The seven circles of purgation of the seven deadly sins
	The Late-repentant · The Excommunicate		} Antepurgatory

The Chronology of the "Purgatorio"

IT IS NEAR SUNRISE when the Poets issue at the eastern
base of the Mount of Purgatory (i), and close upon sunrise,
6 A.M., as they leave Cato. The stars in mid-heaven have
disappeared when the souls are discharged from the angel's
boat (ii), though shadows are not yet distinctly visible
since the souls recognize Dante as a living man only by his
breathing. The sun is up and the hour of Vespers 3 P.M.,
has already arrived in Italy, as the Poets turn westward
again towards the mountain (iii). The conversation with
Manfred is over about 9.20 A.M. (iv). It is noonday when
Dante has finished his conversation with Belaqua; that is to
say, the sun is in the north; and since the poets are almost
on the due east portion of the mountain, it is not long
ere the sun disappears behind the hill (vi). So Dante casts
no shadow, and is not recognized as a living man by Sor-
dello, with whom Virgil converses till day is declining
(vii). At sunset the souls in the valley of the kings sing
their evening hymn (viii); very soon after which the poets
descend (descent being possible after sunset, though they
could not have ascended, cf. vii) into the valley, as twi-
light deepens. Taking the moment of full moon to have
been at sunrise on the Friday morning, it is now 3 × 24
hours since full moon, and the retardation of the moon is
therefore 3 × 52 minutes = 2 hours 36 minutes; and the
moon, therefore, has passed through the Scales and is 36
minutes deep in Scorpion. The first stars of Scorpion, then,
and the glow of the lunar aurora are on the horizon, and it
is just over 8.30 P.M. on what (with the reservations indi-
cated in the chronological note on the *Inferno*) we may
call Monday evening, when Dante falls asleep (ix). Before
dawn on the next morning Dante has a vision of the eagle,
and is in point of fact carried up by Lucia near to the gate
of Purgatory, where he awakes at about 8 A.M. The re-
tardation of the moon is now 3 hours and 2 minutes, and
when they issue upon the first terrace she has already
set (x). It is therefore about 9 A.M. About 12 o'clock noon

they reach the stair to the second circle (xii). When the Poets pass from the second to the third terrace they are walking westward and have therefore reached the northern quarter of the mount, and it is 3 o'clock in the afternoon (xv); and their direction has not sensibly changed when they meet the wrathful. The sun has already set at the base of the mountain (xvii) when the final visions of the circle of the wrathful come upon Dante, and he sets to the Poets, high up on the mountain, just as they have completed the ascent of the stair to the fourth circle. By comparing these data, it will be seen that the Poets traverse portions of the first three circles, constituting altogether a quadrant or a little more, during this day. They start on the eastern side of the mountain, and end at the north, or a little west of it, and have spent about three hours in each circle. About three hours more are occupied by Virgil's discourse, which ends towards midnight, when the moon, which rose at 9.28, a good way south of east, now first appears due east, or a trifle north of due east, from behind the mountain (xviii). Before dawn (xix) on what we may call Wednesday, Dante has his vision of the Siren, and it is full daylight when he wakes. They still travel due, or nearly due, west, with the newly risen sun at their backs. They swiftly pass the fourth circle and reach the fifth, in which they stay so long that it is after ten when they reach the sixth circle (xxii). Though they are now well to the west of the mountain, the sun has travelled with them, so that Dante casts a shadow (xxiii). Indeed it is after two o'clock when they reach the stair which leads to the seventh circle (xxv), so that by this time shadows are visible on the mountain from near the north-east to near the south-west of its surface. As Dante converses with the shades on the seventh terrace the sun is almost due west; the Poet is walking nearly due south, the sun on his right and the flame growing redder under his shadow at the left (xxvi). And the position is not perceptibly changed when the angel of the circle appears to them as the sun sets at the base of the mountain (xxvii); nor have they mounted many stairs after passing through the flame, before the sun, exactly behind them, sets on the higher regions of the mount where they

193

now are. Before sunrise on the day we may call Thursday, Dante sees Leah in his vision, and wakes at dawn of day. The sun shines full upon their faces as they enter the Earthly Paradise from the western point, facing east; and it is noonday (xxxiii) as they reach the source of Lethe and Eunoë.

For the time references in the *Paradiso*, see *Par. xxvii* and *Argument*.

ÇANTO I

Prologue. *The Poets issue on the low-lying shore east of the Mount of Purgatory, and Dante's eyes, which in Hell have shared the misery of his heart, becomes once more the instruments of delight, as he looks into the clear blue sky and sees Venus near the eastern horizon. The South Pole of the Heavens is well above the southern horizon, and all is bathed in the light of the glorious constellation never seen since man, at the Fall, was banished to the Northern Hemisphere. Turning north, the Poet perceives the venerable figure of Cato, his face illuminated by the four stars, typifying the four moral virtues. He challenges the Poets as though fugitives from Hell; but Virgil pleads the command of a Lady of Heaven, and explains that Dante still lives, and is seeking that liberty for love of which Cato himself had renounced his life. He further appeals to him, by his love of Marcia, to further their journey through his realm. Cato is untouched by the thought of Marcia, from whom he is now inwardly severed; but in reverence for the heavenly mandate he bids Virgil gird Dante with the rush of humility and cleanse his face with dew from the stains of Hell, that he may be ready to meet the ministers of Heaven. The sun, now rising, will teach them the ascent. The Poets seek the shore, as the sea ripples under the morning breeze; and Virgil follows Cato's behest, cleansing Dante's face with dew, and plucking the rush, which instantly springs up again miraculously renewed.*

TO COURSE o'er better waters now hoists sail the little bark of my wit, leaving behind her a sea so cruel.

And I will sing of that second realm, where the human spirit is purged and becomes worthy to ascend to Heaven.

But here let dead poesy rise up again, O holy Muses, since yours am I, and here let Calliope[1] rise somewhat,

accompanying my song with that strain whose stroke the wretched Pies felt so that they despaired of pardon.

Sweet hue of orient sapphire which was gathering on the clear forehead of the sky, pure even to the first circle, to mine eyes restored delight, soon as I issued forth from the dead air which had afflicted eyes and heart.

The fair planet which hearteneth to love[2] was making the whole East to laugh, veiling the Fishes that were in her train.

I turned me to the right hand, and set my mind on the other pole, and saw four stars[3] never yet seen save by the first people.

The heavens seemed to rejoice in their flames. O Northern widowed clime, since thou art bereft of beholding them!

When I was parted from gazing at them, turning me a little to the other pole, there whence the Wain had already disappeared,[4]

I saw near me an old man[5] solitary, worthy of such great reverence in his mien, that no son owes more to a father.

Long he wore his beard and mingled with white hair, like unto his locks of which a double list fell on his breast.

The rays of the four holy lights adorned his face so with brightness, that I beheld him as were the sun before him.

"Who are ye that against the dark stream[6] have fled the eternal prison?" said he, moving those venerable plumes.

"Who hath guided you? or who was a lamp unto you issuing forth from the deep night that ever maketh black the infernal vale?

Are the laws of the pit thus broken, or is there some new counsel changed in Heaven that being damned ye come to my rocks?"

Then did my Leader lay hold on me, and with words, and with hand, and with signs, made reverent my knees and brow.

Then answered him: "Of myself I came not. A lady came down from Heaven through whose prayers I succoured this man with my company.

But since it is thy will that more be unfolded of our state, how it truly is, my will it cannot be that thou be denied.

He hath ne'er seen the last hour,[7] but by his madness was so near to it, that very short time there was to turn.

Even as I said, I was sent to him to rescue him, and no other way there was but this along which I have set me.

I have shown him all the guilty people, and now do purpose showing those spirits that purge them under thy charge.

How I have brought him, 'twere long to tell thee: Virtue descends from on high which aids me to guide him to see thee and to hear thee.

Now may it please thee to be gracious unto his coming: he seeketh freedom, which is so precious, as he knows who giveth up life for her.

Thou knowest it; since for her sake death was not bitter to thee in Utica, where thou leftest the raiment which at the great day shall be so bright.

The eternal laws by us are not violated, for he doth live and Minos[8] binds me not; but I am of the circle where are the chaste eyes

of thy Marcia,[9] who visibly yet doth pray thee, O holy breast, that thou hold her for thine own: for love of her then incline thee unto us.

Let us go through thy seven kingdoms: thanks of thee I will bear back to her, if thou deign to be mentioned there below."

"Marcia was so pleasing to mine eyes while I was yonder,"[10] said he then, "that every grace she willed of me I did.

Now that she dwells beyond the evil stream,[11] no more may she move me, by that law which was made when I thence came forth.

But if a heavenly lady moves and directs thee, as thou sayest, no need is there for flattery: let it suffice thee that in her name thou askest me.

Go then, and look that thou gird this man with a smooth rush, and that thou bathe his face so that all filth may thence be wiped away:

for 'twere not meet with eye obscured by any mist to go before the first minister of those that are of Paradise.

This little isle all round about the very base, there, where the wave beats it, bears rushes on the soft mud.

No other plant that would put forth leaf or harden can live there, because it yields not to the buffetings.

Then be not this way your return; the sun, which now

is rising, will show you how to take the mount at an easier ascent."

So he vanished; and I uplifted me without speaking, and drew me all back to my Leader, and directed mine eyes to him.

He began: "Son, follow thou my steps: turn we back, for this way the plain slopes down to its low bounds."

The dawn was vanquishing the breath of morn which fled before her, so that from afar I recognized the trembling of the sea.

We paced along the lonely plain, as one who returns to his lost road, and, till he reach it, seems to go in vain.

When we came there where the dew is striving with the sun, being at a place where, in the cool air, slowly it is scattered;

both hands outspread, gently my Master laid upon the sweet grass; wherefore I who was ware of his purpose,

raised towards him my tear-stained cheeks: there made he all revealed my hue which Hell had hidden.

We came then on to the desert shore, that never saw man navigate its waters who thereafter knew return.

There he girded me even as it pleased Another: O marvel! that such as he plucked the lowly plant, even such did it forthwith spring up again, there whence he tore it.

1. Calliope—the Muse of Epic Poetry.—The Pierides, the nine daughters of Pierus, King of Emathia, having challenged the Muses to a contest of song and suffered defeat, were changed by them into magpies (see Ovid's *Metam.* v).

2. Venus was not actually in Pisces in the spring of 1300, but Dante is probably following a tradition as to the position of all the planets at the moment of Creation (*cf. Inf.* i). In the representation of the Creation in the Collegiate Church at San Gemignano, Venus is depicted as being in Pisces. See diagram on p. 222.

3. We must assume either that Dante invented these four stars, which he identifies with the four cardinal virtues—Prudence, Justice, Fortitude and Temperance (*cf.* Cantos xxix and xxxi; or that he had learnt the existence of the Southern Cross from some traveller.—The *first people* are probably Adam and Eve. When these were driven from the Earthly Paradise (situated on the summit of the

*See "Note on Dante's Purgatory" and "The Chronology of the *Purgatorio*" at pp. 189 and 192.

Mount of Purgatory), the southern hemisphere was held to be un-inhabited (*cf. Inf.* xxvi): for according to medieval geography the whole of Asia and Africa were north of the equator.

4. Only a portion of the Wain would at any time be visible in the supposed latitude of Purgatory, and it was now completely below the horizon.

5. Cato of Utica (born 95 B.C.), one of the chief opponents of Cæsar's measures. After the battle of Thapsus, he committed suicide rather than fall into his enemy's hands (B.C. 46). This was regarded as the supreme act of devotion to liberty (*Conv.* iii. 5; *De Mon.* ii 5), and partly accounts for his position here; though Virgil's line—*secretosque pios, his dantem jura Catonem (Æn.* viii), which refers to the good set apart from the wicked in the world beyond, prob-ably weighed more heavily with Dante. Our poet's general concep-tion of Cato is derived from Lucan (*Pharsalia,* ii); and his intense admiration of the man and of his character finds expression in several passages of the *Convito* (iv. 5, 6, 27, 28). Cato's position as warder of the Christian Purgatory is probably to be explained in a similar way as the position of Ripheus in Paradise (see *Par.* xx, *notes* 8 and 12); note especially the allegorical significance of the stars, and the fact that *sun* is often synonymous with God.

6. See *Inf.* xxxiv.

7. *last hour,* here used in the double sense of bodily and spiritual death (*cf. Conv.* iv. 7). The verses refer, of course, to the allegory of *Inf.* i.

8. For Minos, see *Inf.* v.

9. Marcia (for whom see *Inf.* iv) was the second wife of Cato, who yielded her to his friend Q. Hortensius. On the death of the latter, she was again married to Cato. The *Convito* (iv. 28) contains an elaborate allegory, in which the return of Marcia to Cato signifies the return of the noble soul to God.

10. *yonder* when used by itself in the *Purgatorio* always means "in the other hemisphere."

11. The *evil stream* is the Acheron (see *Inf.* iii).

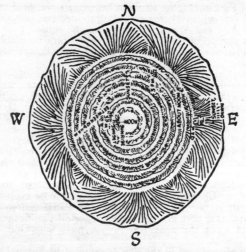

The course of the Poets round and up the northern half of the Mount of Purgatory, from East to West. Seen from above.

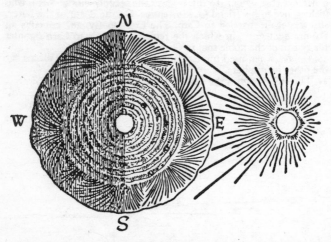

Showing the portions of the mountain under light and shade at 6 o'clock a.m. Cf. Purg. ii, ix (two hours later), xix. xxvii

ÇANTO II

At Jerusalem day is setting and night rising, and in Purgatory day rising and night setting; and as the Poets, pondering on their course, are delaying their journey against their will, they see glowing red in the east a light swiftly approaching them; which Virgil soon recognizes as Charon's angelic counterpart, who with stroke of wing guides a light bark with its charge of happy souls to the mountain of purification. As they land the souls chant the psalm of the Exodus, and with the sign of the cross their angelic guard departs, to renew his mission. The risen sun now shoots full daylight into the sky, obliterating Capricorn from the zenith; the new-come folk inquire the way and Virgil answers that he and his companion are strangers like themselves, whereon the shades observe that Dante breathes and is still in the first life, and in their eagerness almost forget the cleansing for which they have come to the mount. One especially, the musician Casella, presses forward with a look of such affection that the Poet opens his arms to embrace him, but he only clasps an empty shade. Dante must now explain the mystery of his own presence in that place while still in the flesh, and Casella in his turn must explain the delay of many months between his death and his admission into the boat of the redeemed that gathers its happy charge at the mouth of Tiber. Dante's heart and senses are still aching from the anguish of Hell; and the loveliness of earth, sea and sky has re-awakened his perception of the healing power of beauty. So a great longing comes over him once more to hear the sweet singer's voice that has so often soothed him and banished all his cares. Does that power of song which on earth seems akin to the spirit world, survive the great change? Casella's answer is to sing, in tones the sweetness whereof can never die, a song that Dante himself had written to the praise of Wisdom; whereon Virgil and all the other souls gather eagerly around, till rebuked for this premature indulgence and repose by the stern Cato, who bids them to press forward the cleansing work of the mountain. Whereon they scud along the plain like startled doves.

ALREADY HAD the sun reached the horizon, whose meridian circle covers Jerusalem with its highest point,

and night which opposite to him revolves, from Ganges forth was issuing with the Scales, that fall from her hand when she prevails;

so that fair Aurora's white and rubby cheeks, there where I was, through too great age were turning orange.[1]

We were alongside the ocean yet, like folk who ponder o'er their road, who in heart do go and in body stay;

and lo, as on the approach of morn, through the dense mists Mars burns red, low in the West o'er the ocean-floor;

such to me appeared—so may I see it again!—a light coming o'er the sea so swiftly, that no flight is equal to its motion;

from which, when I had a while withdrawn mine eyes to question my Leader, I saw it brighter and bigger grown.

Then on each side of it appeared to me a something white; and from beneath it, little by little, another whiteness came forth.

My Master yet did speak no word, until the first whitenesses appeared as wings; then, when well he knew the pilot,

he cried: "Bend, bend thy knees; behold the Angel of God: fold thy hands: henceforth shalt thou see such ministers.

Look how he scorns all human instruments, so that oar he wills not, nor other sail than his wings, between shores so distant.

See how he has them heavenward turned, plying the air with eternal plumes, that are not mewed like mortal hair."

Then as more and more towards us came the bird divine, brighter yet he appeared, wherefore mine eye endured him not near:

but I bent it down, and he came on to the shore with a vessel so swift and light that the waters nowise drew it in.

On the stern stood the celestial pilot, such, that blessedness seemed writ upon him, and more than a hundred spirits sat within.

"*in exitu Israel de Ægypto*," sang they all together with one voice, with what of that psalm[2] is thereafter written.

Then made he to them the sign of Holy Cross, whereat they all flung them on the strand and quick even as he came he went his way.

The throng that remained there seemed strange to the place, gazing around like one who assayeth new things.

On every side the sun, who with his arrows bright had chased the Goat from midst of heaven, was shooting forth the day,[3]

when the new people lifted up their faces towards us, saying to us: "If ye know show us the way to go to the mount."

And Virgil answered: "Ye think perchance that we have experience of this place, but we are strangers even as ye are.

We came but now, a little while before you, by other way which was so rough and hard, that the climbing now will seem but play to us."

The souls who had observed me by my breathing that I was yet alive, marvelling grew pale;

and as to a messenger, who bears the olive, the folk draw nigh to hear the news, and none shows himself shy at trampling;

so on my face those souls did fix their gaze, fortunate every one, well nigh forgetting to go and make them fair.

I saw one of them draw forward to embrace me with such great affection, that he moved me to do the like.

O shades empty save in outward show! thrice behind it my hands I clasped, and as often returned with them to my breast.

With wonder methinks I coloured me, whereat the shade smiled and drew back, and I, following it, flung me forward.

Gently it bade me pause: then knew I who it was, and did pray him that he would stay a while to speak to me.

He answered me: "Even as I loved thee in the mortal body so do I love thee freed; therefore I stay: but wherefore goest thou?"

"Casella[4] mine, to return here once again where I am, make I this journey," said I, "but how hath so much time been taken from thee?"

And he to me: "No wrong is done me, if he who bears away when and whom he pleases hath many times denied me this passage;

for of a just will his will is made. Truly for three months[5] past he hath taken, in all peace, whoso hath wished to enter.

Wherefore I, who now was turned to the seashore where Tiber's wave grows salt,[6] kindly by him was garnered in.

To that mouth now he hath set his wings, because evermore are gathered there, they who to Acheron sink not down."

And I: "If a new law take not from thee memory or skill in that song of love which was wont to calm my every desire,

may it please thee therewith to solace awhile my soul, that, with its mortal form journeying here, is sore distressed."

"*Love that in my mind discourseth to me,*" began he then so sweetly, that the sweetness yet within me sounds.

My Master and I and that people who were with him, seemed so glad as if to aught else the mind of no one of them gave heed.

We were all fixed and intent upon his notes; and lo the old man venerable, crying: "What is this, ye laggard spirits?

what negligence, what tarrying is this? Haste to the mount and strip you of the slough, that lets not God be manifest to you."

As doves when gathering wheat or tares, all assembled at their repast, quiet and showing not their wonted pride,

if aught be seen whereof they have fear, straightway let stay their food, because they are assailed by greater care;

so saw I that new company leave the singing, and go towards the hillside, like one who goes, but knoweth not where he may come forth; nor was our parting less quick.

1. It is sunset at Jerusalem; and midnight on the Ganges, *i.e.*, in India [when the sun is in Aries, the night is in the opposite sign of

Libra, or the Scales; and Libra falls from the hand of night at the time of the autumn equinox, when the sun enters the constellation, and the nights become longer than the days]: it is therefore sunrise in Purgatory (see the diagram on p. 200).

2. According to Dante (*Ep. ad Can. Grand* § 7) the anagogical meaning of this Psalm (cxiv) is "the exit of the sanctified soul from the slavery of this corruption to the liberty of eternal glory." Cf. *Conv.* ii. 1; and see *Par.* xxv, *note* 7.

3. See the chronological note, p. 192. The light of the rising sun (which was in Aries) had blotted Capricorn out of mid-heaven (Capricorn touching the meridian at the moment when Aries touches the horizon). See diagram on p. 222.

4. Casella, a musician of Florence or of Pistoia, and a personal friend of Dante's, some of whose verses he is said to have set to music, including perhaps the ballad *Love that in my mind discourseth to me*, which was subsequently annotated by the poet in the third book of his *Convito*.

5. *for three months, i.e.*, since the beginning of the Jubilee (*cf. Inf.* xviii).

6. Salvation is to be attained only in the true Church, which has its seat at Rome: hence the souls of those that are not damned assemble at the mouth of the Tiber, the port of Rome.

ÇANTO III

When Dante has recovered from his confusion, and Virgil from the self-reproach caused by his momentary neglect of his charge, the Poets look west toward the mountain. The sun shines behind them and throws Dante's shadow right before him. Now for the first time he misses Virgil's shadow, and thinks that he has lost his companionship; but Virgil reassures him. It is nine hour agone since the sun rose in the place where lies that part of him which once cast a shadow. The nature of the aerial bodies in the spirit world is unfathomable by human philosophy, which yearns in vain for solutions of the mysteries of faith. When they arrive at the foot of the mountain, the Poets are at a loss how to scale its precipices; but at their left Dante perceives a group of souls slowly moving toward them from the south. With Virgil's sanction they go to meet them, and by thus reversing the usual direction which the souls take, following the sun, they excite the amazement of the elect spirits from whom they inquire their way. These sheep without a shepherd—for they are the souls of such as died in contumacy against the Church, and they must dree their rebellion against the chief Shepherd by thirty times as long a space of shepherdless wandering—are yet more amazed than before when they see Dante's shadow and hear from Virgil that he is still in the first life. They make sign to them to reverse their course; and one of them, King Manfred, when Dante has failed to recognize him, tells the story of his death at the battle of Benevento; of the pitiless persecution even of his lifeless body by the Bishop of Cosenza and Pope Clement. He declares that the Infinite Goodness hath so wide an embrace that it enfolds all who turn to it; explains the limitations of the power of the Church's malediction, and implores the prayers of his daughter Constance.

ALTHOUGH THEIR sudden flight was scattering them o'er the plain, turned to the mount where justice probes us,

I drew me close to my faithful comrade; and how should I have sped without him? who would have brought me up the mountain?

206

Gnawed he seemed to me by self-reproach. O noble con-
science and clear, how sharp a sting is a little fault to thee!

When his feet had lost that haste which mars the dignity
of every act, my mind, that erewhile was centred within,

widened its scope as in eager search, and I set my face
to the hillside which rises highest heavenward from the
waters.

The sun, that behind us was flaming red, was broken in
front of me in the figure in which it had its beams stayed
by me.

I turned me aside from fear of being forsaken, when I
saw only before me the earth darkened.

And my Comfort began to say to me, turning full round:
"Why dost thou again distrust? believest thou not me
with thee and that I do guide thee?

It is already evening[1] there, where the body buried lies
within which I made shadow: Naples possesses it, and from
Brindisi 'tis taken.[2]

Now, if before me no shadow falls, marvel not more
than at the heavenly spheres, that one doth not obstruct
the light from the other.

To suffer torments, heat and frost, bodies such as these
that power disposes, which wills not that its workings be
revealed to us.

Mad is he who hopes that our reason may compass that
infinitude which one substances in three persons fills.

Be ye content, O human race, with the *quia!*[3] For if ye
had been able to see the whole, no need was there for Mary
to give birth;[4]

and ye have seen such *sages* desire fruitlessly, whose
desire had else been satisfied, which is given them for
eternal grief.

I speak of Aristotle and of Plato, and of many others."
And here he bent his brow, and said no more, and re-
mained troubled.

We reached meanwhile the mountain's foot: there found
we the cliff so steep that vainly there would legs be nimble.

'Twixt Lerici and Turbia,[5] the way most desolate, most
solitary, is a stairway easy and free, compared with that.

"Now who knows on which hand the scarp doth slope,"

said my Master, halting his steps, "so that he may climb who wingless goes?"

And while he held his visage low, searching in thought anent the way, and I was looking up about the rocks,

on the left hand appeared to me a throng of souls, who moved their feet towards us, and yet seemed not *to advance*, so slow they came.

"Master," said I, "lift up thine eyes, behold there one who will give us counsel; if of thyself thou mayest have it not."

He looked at them, and with gladsome mien answered: "Go we thither, for slowly they come, and do thou confirm thy hope, sweet son."

As yet that people were so far off (I mean after a thousand paces of ours) as a good slinger would carry with his hand,

when they all pressed close to the hard rocks of the steep cliff, and stood motionless and close, as he halts to gaze around who goes in dread.

"O ye whose end was happy, O spirits already chosen," Virgil began, "by that same peace which I believe by you all is awaited,

tell us where the mountain slopes, so that it may be possible to go upward; for time lost irks him most who knoweth most."

As sheep come forth from the pen, in ones, in twos, in threes, and the others stand all timid, casting eye and nose to earth,

and what the first one doeth, the others do also, huddling up to her if she stand still, silly and quiet, and know not why,

so saw I then the head of that happy flock move to come on, modest in countenance, in movement dignified.

When those in front saw the light broken on the ground on my right side, so that the shadow was from me to the rock,[8]

they halted, and drew them back somewhat; and all the others that came after, knowing not why, did the like.

"Without your question I confess to you, that this is a
208

human body ye see, by which the sun's light on the ground is cleft.

Marvel ye not, but believe that not without virtue which cometh from heaven, he seeks to surmount this wall."

So my Master; and that worthy people said: "Turn ye, enter then before us," with the backs of their hands making sign.

And one of them began: "Whoever thou art, thus while going turn thy face, give heed if e'er thou sawest me yonder."

I turned me to him, and steadfastly did look: golden-haired was he, and fair, and of noble mien; but one of his eyebrows a cut had cleft.

When I humbly had disclaimed ever to have seen him, he said: "Now look"; and he showed me a wound above his breast.

Then smiling said: "I am Manfred,[7] grandson of Empress Constance; wherefore I pray thee, that when thou returnest,

thou go to my fair daughter, parent of the glory of Sicily and of Aragon, and tell her sooth, if other tale be told.

After I had my body pierced by two mortal stabs, I gave me up weeping to him who willingly doth pardon.

Horrible were my transgressions; but infinite goodness hath such wide arms that it accepteth all that turn to it.

If Cosenza's Pastor, who to chase of me was set by Clement, then had well read that page in God,

the bones of my body would yet be at the bridgehead near Benevento, under the guard of the heavy cairn.

Now the rain washes them, and the wind stirs them, beyond the Realm, hard by the Verde, whither he translated them with tapers quenched.

By curse of theirs man is not so lost, that eternal love may not return, so long as hope retaineth aught of green.

True is it, that he who dies in contumacy of Holy Church, even though at the last he repent, needs must stay outside this bank

thirtyfold for all the time that he hath lived in his presumption, if such decree be not shortened by holy prayers,

Look now, if thou canst make me glad, by revealing to

209

my good Constance how thou hast seen me, and also this ban: for here, through those yonder, much advancement comes."

1. *evening* is the last of the four divisions of the day, from 3 to 6 P.M. (*cf. Conv.* iii. 6; iv. 23). When it is 3 P.M. in Italy, it is 6 P.M. at Jerusalem and 6 A.M. in Purgatory.

2. This tradition is recorded by Virgil's biographers, Donatus and Suetonius. The body was transferred by order of Augustus (*cf.* Canto vii).

3. Be satisfied *that it is*, without asking the reason *why*. "Demonstration is two-fold: the one demonstrates by means of the cause, and is called *propter quid* ... the other by means of the effect, and is called the demonstration *quia*" (Thomas Aquinas).

4. Had human reason been capable of penetrating these mysteries, there would have been no need for the revelation of the Word of God.

5. Lerici and Turbia are at the eastern and western extremities of Liguria, respectively.

6. The mountain was on their right, and the sun on their left.

7. This is Manfred (*ca.* 1231–1266), grandson of the Emperor Henry VI and of his wife Constance (for whom see *Par.* iii), and natural son of the Emperor Frederick II. Manfred's wife, Beatrice of Savoy, bore him a daughter who (in 1262) married Peter III of Aragon (for whom and for whose sons see Canto vii; *cf.* also *Par.* xix). Manfred became King of Sicily in 1258, usurping the rights of his nephew Conradin. The Popes naturally opposed him, as a Ghibelline, and excommunicated him; and in 1265, Charles of Anjou came to Italy with a large army, on the invitation of Clement IV, and was crowned as counter King of Sicily. On February 26, 1266, Manfred was defeated by Charles at Benevento (some thirty miles north-east of Naples), and slain. He was buried near the battlefield, beneath a huge cairn (each soldier of the army contributing a stone); but his body was disinterred by order of the Pope, and deposited on the banks of the Verde (now the Garigliano, *cf. Par.* viii), outside the boundaries of the Kingdom of Naples and of the Church States, and with the rites usual at the burial of those who died excommunicated.

In the eagerness of his attention to Manfred's tale, Dante takes no note of the passing time, and thereby furnishes a practical refutation of the Platonic doctrine of the plurality of souls; for if the soul that presides over hearing were one, and the soul that notes the passage of time another, then the completest absorption of the former could not so involve the latter as to prevent it from exercising its own special function. It is three and a half hours from sunrise when the souls point out the narrow cleft by which the pilgrims are to ascend the mountain; after which they take their leave of them. It is only the wings of longing and hope that enable Dante to overcome the impediments of the ascent, and bring him through the cleft to the open slope of the mountain, which he breasts at Virgil's direction though it lies at an angle of more than forty-five degrees. In answer to his weary plea for a pause, Virgil urges him to gain a terrace that circles the mount a little above them. There they rest, and, looking east, survey their ascent, after the complacent fashion of mountain-climbers; but Dante is amazed to find that the sun is north of the equator and strikes on his left shoulder. Virgil explains that this is because they are in the southern hemisphere, at the antipodes of Jerusalem. Were the sun in Gemini instead of Aries, he would be further to the north yet. Dante rehearses and expands the lesson Virgil has taught him, and then (having meanwhile apparently turned west, facing the slope) makes inquiry as to the height of the mountain. Virgil, without making any direct answer, cheers his weary companion by assuring him that as they mount higher, the ascent becomes ever less arduous, till mounting up becomes as spontaneous as the movement of a ship dropping down stream; and then comes rest. Whereat a voice suddenly rising from behind a great stone lying south of them, intimates to Dante that he will probably experience a keen desire for rest before that consummation. Whereon the Poets move to the shady or southern side of the rock where they see souls whose repentance had been deferred to the moment of death, stretched in attitudes of indolence. And in particular Belacqua, an old friend of Dante's, sits hugging his knees like Sloth's own brother. It is he who had given Dante his mocking warning, and who now in the same vein taunts him with his readi-

*ness to reproach others for their sloth the moment after he himself
had implored Virgil to wait for him; and also with his slowness to
understand the astronomical phenomena of the southern heavens. A
smile of relief and amusement lightens Dante's face as he finds his
friend among the saved, and still his old self. Cannot even the spirit
life check his nimble wit or stir his sluggish members? But Belacqua
answers sadly that unless aided by the prayer of some soul in grace,
he must live as long excluded from purgation as he had lived in the
self-exclusion of impenitence upon earth. It is now noonday in Pur-
gatory; night reigns from Ganges to Morocco; and Virgil urges his
charge to continue the ascent.*

WHEN THROUGH impression of pleasure, or of
pain, which some one of our faculties receives, the soul is
wholly centred on that faculty,

it seems that it gives heed to no other of its powers; and
this is contrary to that error, which believes that one soul
above another is kindled within us.[1]

And therefore, when aught is heard or seen which holds
the soul strongly bent to it, the time passes away and we
perceive it not;

for one faculty is that which notes it, and another that
which possesses the undivided soul; the former is as 'twere
bound, the latter free.[2]

Of this I had true experience, while hearing that spirit
and marvelling; for full fifty degrees had climbed

the sun,[3] and I had not perceived it, when we came to
where those souls with one voice cried out to us: "Here
is what you ask."

A bigger opening many a time the peasant hedges up
with a little forkful of his thorns, when the grape is
darkening,

than was the gap by which my leader mounted, and I
after him, we two alone, when the troop parted from us.

One can walk at Sanleo and get down to Noli; one can
mount Bismantova[4] to its summit, with feet alone; but
here a man must fly,

I mean with the swift wings and with the plumes of

great desire, behind that Leader, who gave me hope, and was a light to me.

We were climbing within the cleft rock, and on either side the surface pressed against us, and the ground beneath required both feet and hands.

After we were on the upper edge of the high cliff, out on the open hillside, "Master mine," said I, "what way shall we take?"

And he to me: "Let no step of thine descend; ever up the mount behind me win thy way, until some wise escort appear to us."

So high was the top that it surpassed my sight, and the slope steeper far than a line from mid-quadrant to centre.[5]

Weary was I when I began: "O sweet father, turn thee and look how I remain alone, if thou stay not."

"My son," said he, "so far as there drag thee," pointing out to me a terrace a little higher up, which on that side circles the whole mountain.

So did his words spur me on, that I forced me, creeping after him, so far that the ledge was under my feet.

There we both did sit us down, turned towards the East, whence we had ascended; for to look back is wont to cheer men.

First mine eyes I directed to the shores below; then did raise them to the sun, and marvelled that we were smitten by it on the left side.[6]

Right well the Poet perceived that I was all astonished at the chariot of the light, where 'twas entering between us and the North.

Whereupon he to me: "If Castor and Pollux were in company of that mirror, which purveys of his light upward and downward,[7]

thou wouldst see the glowing Zodiac revolve yet closer to the Bears, unless it strayed from its ancient path.

If thou wouldst have power to conceive how that may be, rapt within thyself, imagine Zion and this mount to be placed on the earth

so that both have one sole horizon and different hemispheres; wherefore the way, which, to his hurt, Phaëton knew not how to drive,[8]

213

thou shalt see must needs pass this on the one side when it passes Zion on the other, if thy mind right clearly apprehends."

"Of a surety, Master mine," said I, "never saw I so clearly as I discern, there where my wit seemed at fault,

that the median circle of the heavenly motion, which is called Equator in one of the sciences, and which ever remains 'twixt the sun and winter,"

for the reason that thou tellest, departs here towards the North, as far as the Hebrews used to see it towards the hot climes.[9]

But if it please thee, willingly would I know how far we have to go, for the hillside rises higher than mine eyes can reach."

And he to me: "This mountain is such, that ever at the beginning below 'tis toilsome, and the more a man ascends the less it wearies.

Therefore when it shall seem to thee so pleasant that the ascending becomes to thee easy, even as in a boat to descend with the stream,

then shalt thou be at the end of this path: there hope to rest thy weariness. No more I answer, and this I know for truth."

And when he had said his word, a voice[10] hard by sounded: "Perchance ere that thou wilt have need to sit."

At sound of it each of us turned him round, and we saw on the left a great mass of stone, which neither I nor he perceived before.

Thither drew we on; and there were persons, lounging in the shade behind the rock, even as a man settles him to rest for laziness.

And one of them, who seemed to me weary, was sitting and clasping his knees, holding his face low down between them.

"O sweet my Lord," said I, "set thine eye on that one who shows himself lazier than if Sloth were his very sister."

Then turned he to us and gave heed, moving his face only over his thigh, and said: "Now go thou up who art valiant."

Then knew I who he was, and that toil which still oppressed a little my breath, did not hinder my going to him; and after

I had got to him, his head he scarce did lift, saying: "Hast thou truly seen how the sun drives his chariot on thy left side?"

His lazy actions and the brief words moved my lips to smile a little; then I began: "Belacqua, it grieves me not[11]

for thee now; but tell me, why art thou seated here? dost thou await escort, or hast thou but resumed thy wonted habit?"

And he: "Brother, what avails it to ascend? For God's winged angel that sits at the gate, would not let me pass to the torments.

First must the heavens revolve around me outside it, so long as they did during my life, because I delayed my healing sighs to the end:

unless before, a prayer aids me, which may rise up from a heart that lives in grace: what profits another that in heaven is not heard?"

And already the poet was mounting before me, and saying: "Come on now, thou seest the meridian is touched by the sun, and Night already with her foot covers from Ganges' banks to Morocco."[12]

1. "Plato asserted that there were divers souls with distinct organs in one and the same body" (Thomas Aquinas). On the Aristotelian doctrine of the three kinds of soul—vegetative, animal, and rational, see Canto xxv.

2. For this use of *former* and *latter*, cf. Canto xxv.

3. The sun traverses fifteen degrees every hour: it is therefore now 9.20 A.M.

4. Sanleo: in the territory of Urbino; Noli: on the coast of Liguria, between Savona and Albenga; Bismantova: a hill in the Emilia, about twenty miles south of Reggio.

5. The angle of the quadrant (quarter of a circle) is 90°; that of a half quadrant is therefore 45°.

6. They were looking east, and therefore had the north to their left and the south to their right. South of the equator the equinoctial sun is north of the zenith at midday, for the same reason that north of the equator he is south of it.

7. See *Argument*. Castor and Pollux = the Twins (*cf. Par*. xxvii and *note* 12), which sign is further north of the equator than Aries. The sun is called *mirror* (like Saturn in *Par*. xxi), because, in common with the other planets [for the sun = a planet, cf. *Inf*. i, *note* 4], he

receives the divine light from above, the spheres intervening, and reflects it downwards (*cf. Par.* xxviii); and this is probably the attribute of the sun referred to as *upward and downward*, though some commentators take the line to mean that he illuminates the northern and southern hemisphere alternately. The *glowing Zodiac* = that part of the Zodiac in which the sun is. The *Bears* indicate the North Pole.

8. Consider that Purgatory is at the exact antipodes of Jerusalem.— The *way* = the path of the sun, the ecliptic. For Phaëton, see *Inf.* xvii, *note* 8.

9. The equator is equi-distant from Jerusalem and from the Mount of Purgatory.

10. The Florentine Belacqua, a friend of Dante's, was a maker of musical instruments, notorious for his sloth.

11. Seeing that thou art on the road to salvation.

12. It is noon in Purgatory, sunrise on the Ganges, and sunset in Morocco = Spain (see the diagram below).

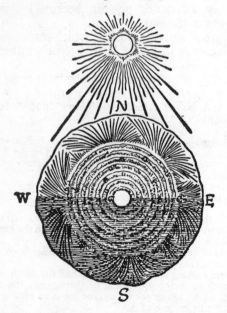

Showing the portion of the mountain under light and shade at noonday. Cf. Purg. iv, xii (compare xxii with xxv), xxiii.

216

CANTO V

As they pass up the mountain, Dante's shadow still excites the amazement of the souls; but Virgil bids him pay no heed to their exclamations. A group of souls chanting the Miserere *breaks into a cry of wonder, and when two of them, sent out as messengers, have received Virgil's statement that Dante is still in the first life, the whole group crowd around him. They tell him that they are souls of the violently slain, who repented and made their peace with God at the last moment. Virgil bids Dante pursue his path, but suffers him to promise to bear news of these souls to their friends on earth and implore their prayers. Dante hears the tale of Jacopo del Cassero. Then Buonconte da Montefeltro tells the story of his death at Campaldino, the struggle of the angel and the devil for his soul, and the fate of his deserted body. And lastly Pia rehearses, in brief pathetic words, the tragedy of her wedded life, and implores the Poet when he is rested from his long journey to bethink him of her.*

I WAS ALREADY parted from those shades, and was following my leader's footsteps, when behind me, pointing his finger,

one cried: "See, it seemeth not that the light shines on the left of him below, and he appears to demean himself like one alive."

Mine eyes I turned at sound of these words, and saw them gazing in astonishment at me alone, me alone, and at the light that was broken.

"Why is thy mind so entangled," said the Master, "that thou slackenest thy pace? what matters it to thee what they whisper here?

Follow me and let the people talk; stand thou as a firm tower which never shakes its summit for blast of winds:

for ever the man in whom thought wells up on thought, sets back his mark, because the one saps the force of the other."

What could I answer, save: "I come"? This I said, suffused somewhat with that colour which ofttimes makes a man worthy of pardon.

And meanwhile across the mountain slope came people a little in front of us, chanting the *Miserere*[1] verse by verse alterne.

When they perceived that I gave no place, because of my body, to the passage of the rays, they changed their chant to an Oh! long and hoarse;

and two of them in the guise of messengers ran to meet us, and asked of us: "Make us to know of your condition."

And my Master: "Ye may go hence and bear back to those who sent you that the body of this man is very flesh.

If they stayed for seeing his shadow, as I opine, enough is answered: let them do him honour and he may be precious to them."

Ne'er saw I flaming vapours[2] so swiftly cleave the bright sky at early night, or August clouds at setting sun,

but that they returned upward in less, and, arrived there, with the others wheeled round to us, like a troop that hastes with loosened rein.

"This people that presses on to us is many, and they come to entreat thee," said the poet; "but go thou ever on and, while going, listen."

"O soul, that goest to be glad with those members which thou wast born with," they came crying, "arrest a while thy step.

Look if e'er thou sawest any one of us, so that thou mayst bear tidings of him yonder: ah, wherefore goest thou? ah, wherefore stayest thou not?

We were all slain by violence and sinners up to the last hour: then light from heaven made us ware

so that, repenting and pardoning, we came forth from life reconciled with God, who penetrates us with desire to behold him."

And I: "How much soever I gaze in your faces, I recognize none; but if aught I can do may please you, ye spirits born for bliss,

speak ye; and I will do it for the sake of that peace, which, following the steps of such a guide, makes me pursue it from world to world."

And one[3] began: "Each of us trusts in thy good offices without thine oath, if only want of power cut not off the will.

Wherefore I, who merely speak before the others, pray thee, if e'er thou see that country which lies between Romagna and that of Charles,

that thou be gracious to me of thy prayers in Fano, so that holy orison be made for me, that I may purge away my heavy offences.

Thence sprang I; but the deep wounds whence flowed the blood wherein my life was set, were dealt me in the bosom of the Antenori,

there where I thought to be most secure. He of Este had it done, who held me in wrath far beyond what justice would.

But if I had fled towards La Mira, when I was surprised at Oriaco, I should yet be yonder where men breathe.

I ran to the marshes, and the reeds and the mire entangled me so, that I fell; and there saw I a pool growing on the ground from my veins."

Then said another: "Prithee,—and so be that desire satisfied which draws thee up the lofty mount—with kindly pity help my desire.

I was of Montefeltro, I am Buonconte;[4] Giovanna, or any other hath no care for me; wherefore I go among these, with downcast brow."

And I to him: "What violence or what chance made thee stray so far from Campaldino, that thy burial place ne'er was known?"

"Oh," answered he, "at Casentino's foot a stream crosses, which is named Archiano, and rises in the Apennines above the Hermitage.

There where its name is lost, did I arrive, pierced in the throat, flying on foot, and bloodying the plain.

There lost I vision, and ended my words upon the name of Mary; and there fell I, and my flesh alone was left.

I will speak sooth, and do thou respeak it among the living; the angel of God took me, and one from Hell cried: 'O thou from Heaven, wherefore robbest thou me?

Thou hearest hence the eternal part of this man, for one

little tear that snatches him from me; but with the other will I deal in other fashion.'

Thou knowest how in the air that damp vapour gathers, which turns again to water soon as it ascends where the cold condenses it.

He united that evil will, which seeks ill only, with intellect, and stirred the mist and wind by the power which his nature gave.

Then when day was spent, he covered the valley from Pratomagno to the great mountain chain with mist, and the sky above made lowering

so that the saturated air was turned to water: the rain fell, and to the water-rills came what of it the earth endured not;

and as it united into great torrents, so swiftly it rushed towards the royal stream, that naught held it back.

My frozen body at its mouth the raging Archian found, and swept it into the Arno, and loosed the cross on my breast,

which I made of me when pain o'ercame me: it rolled me along its banks and over its bed, then covered and wrapped me with its spoils."

"Pray, when thou shalt return to the world, and art rested from thy long journey," followed the third spirit after the second,

"Remember me, who am La Pia:[5] Siena made me, Maremma unmade me: 'tis known to him who, first plighting troth, had wedded me with his gem."

---

1. The *Miserere*—Psalm li.
2. Medieval science held falling stars and weather lightning to be due to "flaming vapours."
3. Jacopo del Cassero (probably related to the Guido of *Inf.* xxviii), a Guelf of Fano (situated in the mark of Ancona, between Romagna and the kingdom of Naples, which was ruled by Charles II of Anjou) was Podestà of Bologna in 1296. Having incurred the wrath of Azzo VIII of Este (for whom see *Inf.* xii; *cf.* also *Purg* xx), whose designs on the city he had frustrated, he hoped to escape his vengeance by exchanging the office at Bologna for a similar one at Milan (1298). He was, however, murdered by Azzo's orders [among the assassins being Riccardo da Cammino, for whom see *Par.* ix] while on his way thither, at Oriaco, between Venice and Padua [the Paduans are called Antenori, from their reputed founder Antenor, for whom see

Inf. xxxii, *note* 10; his escape to Italy after the fall of Troy, and his building of Padua are recorded by Virgil, *Æn.* i]. Oriaco is situated in a marshy country, while La Mira would have been easier of access to Jacopo in his flight.

4. Buonconte of Montefeltro, son of the Guido whose death forms the subject of a very similar episode in *Inf.* xxvii, and, like his father, a Ghibelline leader. He was in command of the Aretines when they were defeated by the Florentine Guelfs at Campaldino, on June 11, 1289, and was himself among the slain. [According to Bruni's testimony, Dante took part in this battle on the Guelf side; see *Inf.* xxi, *note* 7]. Giovanna was Buonconte's wife. Campaldino is in the Upper Val d'Arno, or District of Casentino (bounded by the mountains of Pratomagno on the west and by the principal chain of the Apennines on the east; *cf. Inf.* xxv and *Purg.* xiv) between Poppi and Bibbiena. At the latter place the Archiano which rises in the Apennines at the monastery of Camaldoli (*cf. Par.* xxii *note* 4), falls into the Arno.—*Cf. Purg.* xxviii.

5. Until recently the story of La Pia, as given by the various commentators, was as follows:—The unfortunate lady belonged to the Sienese family of the Tolomei, and married Nello d'Inghiramo dei Pannocchieschi (Podestà of Volterra in 1277, and of Lucca in 1314; captain of the Tuscan Guelfs in 1284; still living in 1322). She was put to death by her husband in 1295 at the Castello della Pietra, in the Sienese Maremma: some say that she was thrown out of a window, by Nello's orders, others that she died in some mysterious way (which probably gave rise to the tradition that the unhealthy marshes of the district were intended to, and actually did, kill her). Nello's motives are variously given; according to some accounts he was jealous (with or without cause); according to others he wished to get rid of his wife in order to be able to marry the Countess Margherita degli Aldobrandeschi, the widow of Guy of Montfort.— In the year 1886 this identification of La Pia was proved (by Banchi) to be impossible; and it is difficult to say how much truth there may be in the legends clustering round her name, till fresh documents concerning her are unearthed.

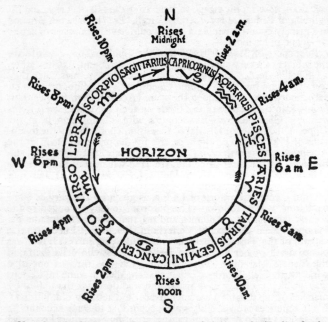

*Showing the hours at which the several signs of the Zodiac begin
to rise at the spring equinox. Each sign begins to set twelve hours
after it begins to rise. The spectator is looking North.*

ÇANTO VI

Like a successful gamester who must cleave his way by payments
through the host whose quickened sense of friendship overflows in
obstructive congratulations and reminiscences, so Dante must pay his
way by promises through the crowd of souls to whom he has power
of granting such precious boons. Of some of these souls he tells us
news, not without side thrusts of warning or reproach at the living
When again free to converse with his guide, Dante asks him to ex-
plain the seeming contradiction between the anxiety of these souls
for the prayers of others, and his (Virgil's) declaration that the
divine Fates cannot be bent by prayer. Virgil explains, firstly, that
no bending of the divine will is involved in the granting of prayer;
secondly, that his rebuke was uttered to souls not in grace; and,
finally, that the complete solution of such questions is not for him
(Virgil), but for Beatrice; at the mention of whose name Dante
wishes to make greater speed in ascending the mountain, whereto
Virgil answers that the journey is of more days than one. The Poets,
now in the shade of the mountain (since they are on its eastern slope
and the sun is already west of north) so that Dante no longer casts
a shadow, and is therefore not instantly to be recognized as a living
man, perceive the soul of Sordello gazing upon them like a couching
lion; but on hearing that Virgil is a Mantuan, he breaks through all
reserve and embraces him as his fellow-countryman. The love of
these two fellow-citizens calls back to Dante's heart the miserable
dissensions that rend the cities of Italy, and the callousness with
which the Emperors leave them to their fate. But from the re-
proaches thus launched against the Italians, Florence is sarcastically
excepted, till the sarcasm breaks down in a wail of reproachful pity.

WHEN THE GAME of dice breaks up, he who loses
stays sorrowing, repeating the throws, and sadly learns:

with the other all the folk go away: one goes in front,
another plucks him from behind, and another at his side
recalls him to his mind.

He halts not and attends to this one and to that: those

to whom he stretches forth his hand press no more; and so he saves him from the crowd.

Such was I in that dense throng, turning my face to them, now here, now there, and by promising freed me from them.

There was the Aretine[1] who by the savage arms of Ghin di Tacco met his death; and the other[2] who was drowned as he ran in chase.

There was praying with outstretched hands Federigo Novello, and he of Pisa who made the good Marzucco[3] show fortitude.

I saw Count Orso,[4] and the soul severed from its body through hatred and envy, so it said, and not for any sin committed—

Pierre de la Brosse[5] I mean: and here let the Lady of Bradant take heed, while she is on earth, so that for this she be not of a worser herd.

When I was free from all those shades whose one prayer was that others should pray, so that their way to blessedness be sped,

I began: "It seemeth that thou, O my Light, deniest expressly in a certain passage, that prayer may bend heaven's decree;[6]

and these people pray but for this. Can then their hope be vain? or are not thy words right clear to me?"

And he to me: "My writing is plain and the hope of them is not deceived if well thou considerest with mind whole.

For the height of justice is not abased because fire of love fulfils in one moment the satisfaction which he owes who here is lodged:

and there where I affirmed that point, default could not be amended by prayer, because the prayer was severed from God.

But do not rest in so profound a doubt except she tell it thee, who shall be a light between truth and intellect.

I know not if thou understand: I speak of Beatrice; thou shalt see her above, on the summit of this mount, smiling and blessed."

And I: "My Lord, go we with greater haste; for already

I grow not weary as before, and look, the hillside doth now a shadow cast."

"We with this day will onward go," answered he, "so far as yet we may; but the fact is other than thou deemest.

Ere thou art above, him shalt thou see return that now is being hidden by the slope, so that thou makest not his rays to break.

But see there a soul which, placed alone, solitary, looketh towards us; it will point out to us the quickest way."

We came to it: O Lombard soul, how wast thou haughty and disdainful, and in the movement of thine eyes majestic and slow!

Naught it said to us, but allowed us to go on, watching only after the fashion of a lion when he couches.

Yet did Virgil draw on towards it, praying that it would show to us the best ascent; and that spirit answered not his demand,

but of our country and of our life did ask us. And the sweet Leader began: "Mantua," . . . and the shade, all rapt in self,

leapt towards him from the place where first it was, saying: "O Mantuan, I am Sordello[7] of thy city." And one embraced the other.

Ah Italy, thou slave, hostel of woe, vessel without pilot in a mighty storm, no mistress of provinces, but a brothel!

That gentle spirit was thus quick, merely at the sweet name of his city, to give greeting there to his fellow-citizen;

and now in thee thy living abide not without war, and one doth rend the other of those that one wall and one fosse shuts in.

Search, wretched one, around thy seacoasts by the shores, and then gaze in thy bosom, if any part of thee enjoy peace.

What avails it that Justinian should refit thy bridle if the saddle is empty?[8] But for that the shame were less.

Ah people, that shouldst be obedient, and let Cæsar sit in the saddle, if well thou understandest what God writeth to thee!

See how this beast hath grown vicious, for not being

corrected by the spurs, since thou hast put thy hand to the bridle.[9]

O German Albert,[10] that dost forsake her who is become wanton and savage, and that oughtest to bestride her saddlebow,

may just judgment fall from the stars upon thy blood, and be it strange and manifest, so that thy successor may have fear thereof:

for thou and thy father, held back yonder by covetousness, have suffered that the garden of the empire be laid waste.

Come and see Montagues and Capulets, Monaldi and Filippeschi,[11] thou man without care: those already sad, and these in dread.

Come, cruel one, come, and see the oppression of thy nobles and tend their sores, and thou shalt see Santafior[12] how secure it is.

Come and see thy Rome that weepeth widowed and alone, and day and night doth cry: "Cæsar mine, wherefore dost thou not companion me?"

Come and see how thy people love one another; and if no pity for us move thee, come and shame thee for thy fame.

And if it be permitted me, O highest Jove, who on earth for us wast crucified, are thy just eyes turned elsewhither;

or is it preparation which thou art making in the depths of thy counsel, for some good end wholly cut off from our vision?

For the cities of Italy are all full of tyrants, and every clown that comes to play the partisan becomes a Marcellus.[13]

O my Florence, thou indeed mayst rejoice at this digression which touches thee not, thanks to thy people that reasons so well.

Many have justice in their hearts, but slowly it is let fly, for it comes not without counsel to the bow; but thy people hath it ever on its lips.

Many refuse the public burdens; but thy people answers eagerly without call, and cries out: "I bend me to the charge."

Now make thee glad, for thou hast good reason: thou rich, thou at peace, thou so wise. If I speak sooth, the facts do not conceal it.

Athens and Lacedemon, that framed the laws of old and were so grown in civil arts, gave a mere hint at well living

beside thee, who dost make such subtle provision, that to mid-November reaches not what thou in October spinnest.

How often in the time which thou rememberest, laws, coinage, offices, and customs hast thou changed, and renewed thy members!

And if thou well bethink thee, and see clear, thou shalt behold thee like unto that sick one, who can find no rest upon the down, but by turning about shuns her pain.

1. "The Aretine" is Benincasa da Laterina, who, as judge to the Podestà of Siena, condemned to death a relative of Ghir. di Tacco, a notorious highwayman. The latter subsequently revenged himself by murdering Benincasa, while he was sitting as a magistrate at Rome.

2. "The other Aretine" is Guccio of the Tarlati, which family was at the head of the Ghibellines of Arezzo. He was drowned in the Arno; according to some accounts, while engaged in pursuing the Bostoli (a family of exiled Aretine Guelfs, who had taken refuge in the Castel di Rondine), according to others, while being pursued by them after the battle of Campaldino (for which see preceding canto).—Federico Novello, a member of the great Conti Guidi family, was slain by one of the Bostoli at Campaldino, while assisting the Tarlati.

3. It seems probable that Marzucco, of the Pisan Scornigiani family, "showed his fortitude" by pardoning the murderer of his son (the *he of Pisa*); though other authorities declared that he slew the assassin.

4. This murder points to a continuation of the feud between the brothers Alessandro and Napoleone degli Alberti, alluded to in *Inf.* xxxii: for Count Orso was the son of Napoleone, and his murderer Alberto the son of Alessandro.

5. Pierre de la Brosse was surgeon and afterwards chamberlain of King Philip III of France. On the sudden death, in 1276, of Louis, Philip's son by his first wife, and heir to the throne, his second wife, Mary of Brabant, was suspected of having poisoned him, so that her own son might succeed. Among her accusers was Pierre de la Brosse. She determined to poison all minds against him and bring about his downfall. According to popular tradition she accused him of having made an attempt on her honour; but as Pierre was eventually (in 1278) hanged on a charge of treasonable correspondence with

Philip's enemy, Alfonso X, of Castile, it seems more probable that she attained her end by causing these letters to be forged.

6. Among the persons Æneas meets in hell is his former pilot, Palinurus, who, having been drowned at sea, is not allowed to cross the Acheron for a hundred years: that being the penalty imposed on the souls of those who have not been duly interred. He entreats Æneas to take him across the river, whereupon the Sibyl rebukes him with the words: "Cease to hope that the decrees of the Gods are to be altered by prayers" (*Æn.* vi). These words are addressed to a heathen and to a spirit in hell. Note that Æneas, whose aid is invoked by Palinurus, is a heathen, too, and does not fulfil the conditions of *Purg.* iv and xi.

7. Sordello, one of the most distinguished among the Italian poets who elected to write in Provençal rather than in their mother-tongue, was born at Goito, some ten miles from Mantua, about the year 1200. He led a chequered and wandering life, the latter portion of which was devoted to the service of Charles of Anjou, by whom he was well rewarded. The latest record of him that has come down to us is dated 1269. To the Dante student one episode of Sordello's life and one of his poems are of special interest. Between the years 1227–1229, while staying at Treviso with Ezzelino III of Romano, he had a liaison with the latter's sister Cunizza (see *Par.* ix) who was the wife of Count Ricciardo di San Bonifazio, but whom Sordello had abducted (for political reasons) at the request of her brother. When the latter discovered the intrigue Sordello was forced to flee to Provence. About the year 1240 he wrote a very fine *planch* (or song of lamentation) on the death of Blacatz, himself a poet and one of the barons of Count Raymond Berengar IV. In this poem the leading sovereigns and princes of Europe are exhorted to eat of the dead man's heart, so that their courage may increase, and they be fired on to noble deeds. These verses may have indirectly inspired the patriotic outburst for which the appearance of Sordello is made the pretext; and they certainly induced Dante to assign to Sordello the task of pointing out the princes in the following canto.—There is a reference to Sordello in the *Vulg. Eloq.* i. 15.

8. One of the many passages to be found throughout Dante's works, which show that what was really in his mind when he spoke of the Roman Empire was an executive power adequate to enforce Roman law. (For Justinian in this connection, *cf. Par.* vi, *Argument*). Much confusion in medieval thought, and much difficulty in understanding Dante's position arises from the fact that the King of the Germans was the feudal head of the territorial nobility who represented the invaders and conquerors of Italy, whereas the Emperor of Rome was the traditional champion of Roman law and civilization which represents the native Italian aspirations; and since the King of Germany and the Emperor of Rome were one and the same person, it was possible to regard him as the representative of either of the two conflicting tendencies and ideals, on the clash of which the whole medieval history of Italy turns.

9. These lines are addressed to the priests, who should leave all secular rule to the Emperor.

10. Both Rudolf (for whom see following canto) and his son Albert I (Emperor from 1298-1308) neglected Italy: the former devoted his attention to Austria and Suabia, while a specimen of the latter's activity is given in *Par.* xix. Reference is made, by anticipation, to Albert's violent death, at the hands of his nephew, John. Albert was succeeded by Henry VII of Luxemburg, on whom Dante rested all his hopes (see Gardner; *cf.*, too, the following canto, and *Par.* xvii and xxx).

11. Shakespeare has so familiarized us with the feud of the Veronese Montagues and Capulets, that a hint from the old commentators to the effect that the Monaldi and Filippeschi were hostile families of Orvieto is sufficient to assure us that Dante is here giving us two examples of the internal strife so common in the Italian cities of those days. The reference appears to be to party strife in general, not to the factions of the Guelfs and Ghibellines in particular. A more recent interpretation, according to which all the four names are those of Ghibelline families belonging to different towns and requiring the aid of the Emperor, falls to the ground, because at least one of the families (the Monaldi) was certainly Guelf.

12. Santafiora—a county in the Sienese Maremma, held for almost five centuries by the great Ghibelline family of the Aldobrandeschi (see Canto xi). These were constantly at war with the commune of Siena, till the year 1300 when an agreement was arrived at.

13. An opponent of the empire [Marcellus, the Roman consul, was one of Cæsar's most violent opponents].

ÇANTO VII

*After repeatedly embracing Virgil, only because he is a Mantuan,
Sordello questions him further; and on hearing who he is, after a
moment's pause, amazed and half-incredulous, falls at his feet to
embrace his knees. In answer to Sordello, Virgil rehearses in words
of deepest pathos the nature of his mission and the state of the souls
in Limbo who practised the moral, but were never clad with the
theological, virtues. In answer to Virgil's questioning concerning
the way, Sordello expounds the law of the mount which suffers no
soul to ascend while the sun is below the horizon; and he offers to
lead the pilgrims, ere the now approaching sunset, to a fitting place
of rest, where they shall find noteworthy souls. In a little lap or dell
of the mountain they find the pensive souls of kings and rulers who
had neglected their higher functions for selfish ease or selfish war.
Now they are surrounded by every soothing beauty of nature; but
relief from the serious cares of life, which erst they sought unduly,
is now an anguish to them, and their yearning goes forth to the ac-
tive purgation of the seven terraces of torment above them. With
the enumeration of the kings—old enemies singing in harmony, and
fathers mourning over the sins of their still living sons—are mingled
tributes to the worth, or gibes at the degeneracy of the reigning
monarchs, and reflections on the unlikeness of sons and fathers.*

AFTER THE GREETINGS dignified and glad had
been repeated three and four times, Sordello drew him
back, and said: "Who art thou?"

"Ere to this mount were turned those spirits worthy to
ascend to God, my bones by Octavian[1] had been buried.

I am Virgil; and for no other sin did I lose heaven than
for not having faith":[2] thus answered then my Leader.

As one who seeth suddenly a thing before him whereat
he marvels, who believes, and believes not, saying: "It is,
it is not";

such seemed he, and forthwith bent his brow, and
humbly turned back towards my Leader, and embraced
him where the inferior clasps.

230

"O glory of the Latins," said he, "by whom our tongue showed forth all its power, O eternal praise of the place whence I sprang,

what merit or what favour showeth thee to me? If I am worthy to hear thy words, tell me if thou comest from Hell, and from what cloister."

"Through all the circles of the woeful realm," answered he him, "came I here. A virtue from heaven moved me, and with it I come.

Not for doing, but for not doing,[2] have I lost the vision of the high Sun, whom thou desirest, and who too late by me was known.

Down there is a place not sad with torments, but with darkness alone, where the lamentations sound not as wailings, but as sighs.

There do I abide with the innocent babes, bitten by the fangs of death, ere they were exempt from human sin.

There dwell I with those who clad them not with the three holy virtues, and without offence knew the others and followed them all.

But if thou knowest and canst, give us some sign whereby we may most quickly come there where Purgatory has right beginning."

He answered: "No fixed place is set for us: 'tis permitted to me to go up and around; so far as I may go, as guide I place me beside thee.

But see now how the day is declining, and ascend by night we cannot; therefore 'tis well to think of some fair resting-place.

Here are souls on the right apart; if thou allow it I will lead thee to them, and not without joy will they be known to thee."

"How is that?" was answered; "he who wished to ascend by night, would he be hindered by others, or would he not ascend because he could not?"

And the good Sordello drew his finger across the ground, saying: "Look, even this line thou wouldst not cross after the sun is set;

not for that aught else than the darkness of night gave

231

hindrance to going upward: that hampers the will with lack of power.[3]

Truly by night one might return downwards, and walk, wandering around the mountain side, while the horizon holds the day closed."

Then my Lord, as tho' marvelling, said: "Lead us therefore where thou sayest we may have delight in tarrying."

Short way had we thence advanced, when I perceived that the mount was scooped out, after the fashion that valleys scoop them out here.

"There," said the shade, "we will go where the mountain-side makes of itself a bosom, and there will await the new day."

Neither steep nor level was a winding path, that led us to the side of that hollow, there where the valley's edge more than half dies away.

Gold and fine silver, cramoisy and white, Indian wood bright and clear, fresh emerald at the moment it is split,

would each be surpassed in colour by the grass and by the flowers placed within that fold, as the less is surpassed by the greater.

Not only had Nature painted there, but of the sweetness of a thousand scents made there one, unknown and indefinable.

There, seated on the grass and on the flowers, singing *Salve Regina*,[4] saw I souls who because of the valley were not seen from without.

"Ere the little sun now sinks to his nest," began the Mantuan who had led us aside, "desire not that I guide you among them.

From this terrace ye will better know the acts and faces of them all, than if received among them down in the hollow.

He who sits highest, and hath semblance of having left undone what he ought to have done, and who moves not his lips with the others' songs,

was Rudolph the Emperor,[5] who might have healed the wounds that were the death of Italy, so that too late through another she is succoured.

The other, who looks to be comforting him, ruled the land where the water rises which the Moldau carries away into the Elbe, and the Elbe into the sea:

Ottocar for name had he, and in swaddling clothes was better far than bearded Wenceslas his son, whom lust and sloth consume.

And that snub-nosed one,[6] who seems close in counsel with him that hath so kindly a mien, died in flight and deflowering the lily:

look there how he is beating his breast. The other see, who sighing, hath made a bed for his cheek with the palm of his hand.

Father and father-in-law are they of the plague of France: they know his wicked and foul life, and hence comes the grief that pierceth them so.

He who seems so stout of limb,[7] and accords his singing with him of the virile nose, was begirt with the cord of every worth.

And if the lad who sits behind him had remained king after him, the worth would in truth have passed from vessel to vessel;

which may not be said of the other heirs. James and Frederick have the realms: of the better heritage none hath possession.[8]

Rarely doth human probity rise through the branches: and this he wills who giveth it, so that it may be prayed for from him.[9]

Also to the big-nosed one my words do go, not less than to the other, Peter, who is singing with him, wherefore Apulia and Provence now moan.

So much is the plant degenerate from its seed as, more than Beatrice and Margaret, Constance yet boasts of her husband.[10]

See the king of the simple life, sitting there alone, Henry of England:[11] he in his branches hath better issue.

That one who lower down humbleth himself among them, gazing upward, is William the Marquis,[12] through whom Alessandria and its war make Montferrato and the Canavese to weep."

1. *Octavian,* the Emperor Augustus (*cf.* Canto iii, *note* 2).

2. See *Inf.* iv.

3. The symbolism is clear if we bear in mind the analogy between the sun and God.

4. *Salve Regina,* the famous antiphon invoking the aid of the Virgin Mary. It is sung after vespers.

5. The Emperor Rudolf I (1218-1272-1292; see the preceding canto) began by serving under Ottocar II, King of Bohemia (1253-1278); but on his election as Emperor he asserted his supremacy. Ottocar's refusal to acknowledge it gave rise to hostilities which ended in his defeat and death in a battle near Vienna (1278). Ottocar's son, Wenceslas IV (1278-1305), was permitted to retain Bohemia, but had to yield Austria, Styria, Carinthia and Carniola to Rudolf, who placed them under the rule of his own sons, Albert and Rudolf.

6. Philip III, the Bold, of France (1245-1270-1285), the *snub-nosed,* was in 1285 defeated by Roger di Loria, the admiral of Peter III of Aragon (see the following note), whose crown he was attempting to seize on behalf of his son, Charles of Valois, and with the connivance of Pope Martin IV. Philip's son, Philip IV, the Fair (1268-1285-1314; one of Dante's pet aversions: see *Inf.* xix; *Purg.* xx, xxxii; *Par.* xix), married Joan, the daughter of Henry, the Fat, of Navarre (1270-1274); and it is the young man's wickedness that is here uniting his father and his father-in-law in a common sorrow.

7. Peter III of Aragon (1276-1285) and his former enemy, Charles I of Anjou (1220-1285; King of Naples and Sicily, 1266-1282), respectively. When Charles was driven from the throne of Sicily after the terrible outbreak known as the "Sicilian Vespers," he was succeeded by Peter, whose claim to the crown was based on his marriage with Constance, the daughter of Manfred, King of Sicily. In spite of strenuous efforts, Charles was never able to regain the kingdom.—Note that Peter III and both his French foes, Charles I of Anjou and Philip III (uncle and nephew), all died in the same year, 1285.

8. Peter III of Aragon had three sons, Alfonso III (King of Aragon, 1285-1291), the *lad;* James II (King of Sicily, 1285-1296, King of Aragon, 1291-1397); and Frederick II (King of Sicily, 1296-1337). In the present passage Alfonso is praised, while the other two are termed degenerate. The blame is repeated in *Par.* xix, xx; *Conv.* iv; *De Vulg. El.* i. But *Purg* iii raises a difficulty. The verse cannot apply to Alfonso, who was never King of Sicily. The *glory* of Sicily is generally taken to be Frederick, and the *glory* of Aragon, James. There is no inconsistency here if we consider that Manfred is speaking of his grandsons, and assume that the view expressed is his rather than Dante's. Some scholars reject the theory on the ground that it is inadmissible to regard the repentant Manfred as displaying a mere national pride, and hold that, at a certain period of his life, Dante lapsed into an unprejudiced and just estimate of James and Frederick. To those who cannot conscientiously subscribe to either of these two theories, it may be pointed out that, in any case, there

is no definite historical inaccuracy. For it was Frederick's very devotion to Sicily that led him to neglect the wider imperial interests of Italy, an omission which probably accounts for Dante's adverse judgment in the other passages (*cf. Par.* xix, *note* 11). With regard to James, it is true that his conduct in Sicilian affairs was dishonourable; but he must have ruled well in Spain, else his subjects would not have called him "the Just." So that it is, at a stretch, possible to explain the words *glory of Sicily and of Aragon,* even if we take them to represent Dante's own consistent view.

9. On the subject of heredity see *Par.* viii.

10. Charles II (1243–1309), King of Naples (=Apulia) and Count of Anjou and Provence, is as inferior to his father, Charles I of Anjou (the *big-nosed*), as this Charles I (the husband first of Beatrice of Provence and then of Margaret of Burgundy) is inferior to Peter III of Aragon (the husband of Constance). Dante frequently inveighs against Charles II (see *Purg.* xx. *Par.* xix, xx; *Conv.* iv. 6; *De Vulg El.* i. 12); in return for which he once gives him a word of praise (*Par.* viii).

11. Henry III, the pious King of England (1216–1226–1272), who formed so strong a contrast to his active and warlike son, Edward I (1239–1272–1307). It is worth noting that Henry's wife, Eleanor of Provence, was a sister of the Beatrice mentioned above.

12. William, Marquis of Montferrat and Canavese (1254–1292), at one time favoured Charles I of Anjou, but subsequently became the chief of a formidable league against him, which was joined by several important towns, including Alessandria (in Piedmont). Some of these towns at times rebelled, and in 1290 Alessandria rose against him. While attempting to quell this disturbance, he was captured by the citizens, and exhibited by them in an iron cage for seventeen months (till his death in 1292). William's son, John I, tried to avenge his father; but his efforts ended in failure, for the Alessandrians invaded Montferrat and captured several places.

CANTO VIII

At the pensive hour of sunset the souls devoutly join in their eve-
ning hymn, with eyes uplifted to heaven. As though to remind them
that while outside the gate of the true Purgatory their wills are not
intrinsically above the reach of temptation, but are guarded only by
the express intervention and protection of divine grace, two angels
descend and stand on either bank of the dell to guard them against
the serpent who would enter this counterpart of Eden. At the men-
tion of the serpent Dante shrinks close up to Virgil; but Sordello in-
vites them to descend, as the twilight deepens, into the little vale,
where Dante meets his friend Nino, Judge of Gallura, and in answer
to his question tells him that he is still in the first life; whereon
both he and Sordello start back in amazement. Nino summons Con-
rad Malaspina to witness this wonder of God's grace, and then turn-
ing to Dante again, implores him to obtain the prayers of his
daughter; for his wife, betrothed to a Visconte, has surely forgotten
him. Dante, looking to heaven, notes that in this season of repose the
four stars that represent the moral virtues have vanished behind the
mountain, and the three that represent the theological virtues shine
in the sky. This is one of the many indications that the proper busi-
ness of Purgatory is ethical, the recovery of the sound moral will.
The season in which the souls may actually ascend is the one over
which the four stars preside. Meanwhile the dreaded serpent ap-
proaches, but the angels swoop like celestial hawks upon it, and
having put it to flight return to their posts. During the whole assault
Conrad has not ceased to gaze on Dante; and he now asks him for
news of his country of Valdemagra, and of his kinsfolk there; to
which Dante replies that he has never visited those parts, but the
noble character of the Malaspini rings through all Europe; whereon
he receives the significant comment that ere six years are gone he
shall know the worth of the Malaspini better than reportingly.

'TWAS NOW the hour[1] that turns back the desire of
those who sail the seas and melts their heart, that day when
they have said to their sweet friends adieu,

and that pierces the new pilgrim with love, if from afar
236

he hears the chimes which seem to mourn for the dying day;

when I began to annul my sense of hearing, and to gaze on one of the spirits, uprisen, that craved a listening with its hand.

It joined and lifted up both its palms, fixing its eyes towards the east, as though 'twere saying to God: "For aught else I care not."

"*Te lucis ante*"[2] so devoutly proceeded from its mouth, and with such sweet music, that it rapt me from my very sense of self.

And the others then sweetly and devoutly accompanied it through the entire hymn, having their eyes fixed on the supernal wheels.

Reader, here sharpen well thine eyes to the truth, for the veil now is indeed so thin, that of a surety to pass within is easy.

I saw that noble army thereafter silently gaze upward, as if in expectancy, pale and lowly;

and I saw two angels come forth from on high and descend below with two flaming swords, broken short and deprived of their points.

Green, as tender leaves just born, was their raiment, which they trailed behind, fanned and smitten by green wings.[3]

One came and alighted a little above us, and the other descended on the opposite bank, so that the people was contained in the middle.

Clearly I discerned the fair hair of them; but in their faces the eye was dazed, like a faculty which by excess is confounded.

"Both come from Mary's bosom," said Sordello, "as guard of the vale, because of the serpent that straightway will come."

Whereat i, who knew not by what way, turned me around, and placed me all icy cold close to the trusty shoulders.

And Sordello again : "Now go we into the vale among the mighty shades, and we will speak to them: great joy will it be to them to see you."

Only three steps methinks I descended, and was below, and saw one who was gazing only at me, as tho' he would recognize me.

'Twas now the time when the air was darkening, yet not so dark but that what between his eyes and mine before was hidden, now grew clear.

He advanced towards me, and I to him: Noble judge Nino,[4] how did I rejoice when I saw thee, and not among the damned!

No fair greeting was left unsaid between us; then he asked: "How long is it since thou camest to the foot of the mount over the far waters?"

"Oh," said I to him, "from within the places of woe came I this morn, and am in my first life, albeit by this my journeying I gain the other."

And when my answer was heard, Sordello and he shrank back like folk suddenly bewildered.

The one turned to Virgil, and the other to one who was seated there, crying: "Up, Conrad,[5] come and see what God by his grace hath willed."

Then turning to me: "By that especial grace which thou owest to him who so hideth his first purpose that there is no ford to it,

when thou art beyond the wide waters, tell my Giovanna that she pray for me there where the innocent are heard.

I do not think her mother loves me more, since she hath changed her white wimples, which hapless she must long for once again.

By her right easily may be known, how long the fire of love doth last in woman, if eye and touch do not oft re-kindle it.

The viper that the Milanese blazons on his shield will not make her so fair a tomb as Gallura's cock would have done."

Thus spake he, his countenance stamped with the mark of that righteous zeal which in due measure glows in the breast.

My yearning eyes were again turned towards heaven, even there where the stars are slowest, like a wheel nearest the axle.

And my leader: "Son, what gazest thou at up there?"
And I to him: "At those three torches, wherewith the
whole pole here is flaming."

And he to me: "The four bright stars which thou sawest
this morn are low on the other side, and these are risen
where they were."[6]

As he was speaking, lo Sordello drew him to himself,
saying: "See there our adversary," and pointed his finger
so that he should look thither.

On that side where the little vale hath no rampart, was a
snake, perchance such as gave to Eve the bitter food.

Through the grass and the flowers came the evil reptile,
turning round now and again its head to its back, licking
like a beast that sleeks itself.

I saw not, and therefore cannot tell, how the celestial
falcons moved; but full well I saw both in motion.

Hearing the green wings cleave through the air, the ser-
pent fled, and the angels wheeled around, flying in equal
measure back to their posts.

The shade[5] that had drawn close to the judge when he
called, through all that assault was not loosed a moment
from gazing at me.

"So may that light which guideth thee on high, find in
thy will as much wax as is needful to reach the enamelled
summit,"

it began, "if thou know true tidings of Valdimacra, or of
neighbouring parts, tell it me who once was mighty there.

I was called Conrad Malaspina: not the elder am I, but
descended from him: to mine own I bore that love which
here is purified."

"Oh," said I to him, "through your lands I ne'er have
been, but where do men dwell throughout Europe to
whom they are not renowned?

The fame which honours your house proclaims abroad
its lords and proclaims the country, so that he knows of it
who there hath never been.

And I swear to you, so may I go on high, that your hon-
oured race strips not itself of the glory of the purse and of
the sword.

Custom and nature so do privilege it, that for all that

the guilty head sets the world awry, it alone goeth straight and scorns the path of evil."

And he: "Now depart, for the sun goeth not to rest seven times in the bed which the Ram covers and bestrides with all four feet.

ere this courteous opinion shall be nailed in the midst of thy head, with bigger nails than other men's swords, if course of judgment be not stayed."

1. For this and other references to the time of day, see diagram on p. 241.
2. The Ambrosian hymn, *Te lucis ante terminum*, sung at Compline (the last office of the day).
3. In addition to the general explanation given in the *Argument*, the following points should be noted. The green robes and wings of the angels speak of hope. The pointless swords are usually taken to indicate justice tempered with mercy (*cf.* Canto xxxi, *note* 3); but perhaps they mean that the battle is in truth already decided, the deadly thrust no longer needed, and that the sword-edge alone is adequate (see Canto xxxi).
4. Nino de' Visconti of Pisa (for whom see *Inf.* xxii, *note* 4, and xxxiii, *note* 4) was appointed by the Pisans to the judgeship of Gallura in Sardinia, in the last decade of the 13th century. He married Beatrice of Este (see the table on p. 611; and those on pp. 616, 617), by whom he had a daughter, Giovanna [it is interesting to note that in 1328 the Commune of Florence voted a pension of 100 *piccoli fiorini* to this Giovanna, on account of her father's faith and devotion to Florence and the Guelf party, for the injuries and vexations he had suffered from the Ghibellines, and as compensation for the spoliation of all her goods by the Ghibellines]. After his death, Beatrice married Galeazzo Visconti, of Milan; the formalities were probably completed by Easter, 1300, but the ceremony did not actually take place till June of that year. *Changed her white whimples* refers to casting off the garb of widowhood (black robe and white veil), and the next line to the misfortunes of the Milanese Visconti, which date from 1302. The viper and the cock indicate the arms of the Milanese and Pisan Visconti, respectively. These two families appear to have been in no way connected with each other; the former were Ghibelline, the latter Guelf.
5. Currado I of the Malaspina family (the *elder* named) was grandfather of the three cousins, Currado II (d. *ca.* 1294), the present speaker; Morello III (d. *ca.* 1315), to whom Dante's third epistle, accompanied by Canzone xi, is probably addressed, and for whom see *Inf.* xxiv, *note* 7; and Franceschino (d. between 1313 and 1321), who was Dante's host at Sarzana, in Lunigiana, in the autumn of 1306 (less than seven years—the sun now being in Aries—from the moment at which Currado is speaking). The Malaspini were for the

most part Ghibellines; but Moroello III formed a notable exception. *Valdimacra:* the Macra flows through Lunigiana (north-west of Tuscany), which formed part of the territory of the Malaspini (*cf. Inf.* xxiv). A table of the Malaspina family will be found on p. 620; see, too, the table on p. 617.

Wax material to feed the flame (*light*) of God's grave; the *enamelled summit* being either the summit of the Mount of Purgatory or the Empyrean. With *the guilty head sets the world awry* compare xvi; though some refer the words specifically to Boniface VIII.

6. It must be steadily borne in mind that only half the heavens are visible to Dante at this point of the journey. The steep wall of Purgatory cuts off the whole portion of them west of the meridian. The four bright stars are near the south pole; but in the latitude of Purgatory the pole itself is only about 32° above the horizon, and the stars are now behind the mountain and beneath the pole.

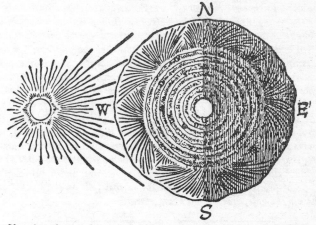

Showing the portions of the Mountain under light and shade at 6 o'clock p.m. Cf. "Purgatorio," viii, xvii, xxvii.

CANTO IX

*It is now about two and a half hours since sunset. The Scorpion has
begun to pass the horizon, and the lunar aurora is already whiten-
ing in the east, when Dante, reclining in the bosom of the valley,
resting from his four-night watch and the toil and anguish of his
journey, drops into a deep sleep. In the morning hour when dreams
are true, he seems to be clasped in the talons of an eagle—the symbol
at once of justice and of baptismal regeneration—and to be borne
up into the sphere of fire, the burning of which awakens him; and he
starts to find himself alone with Virgil, higher on the mount, nigh
to the gate of Purgatory proper. He learns from his guide that, as
he slept, Lucia bore him away from Sordello and the other denizens
of the valley, and placed him here. His dismay is thus turned into
delight as he follows his guide to the narrow portal with its three
steps and its angel guard, who first challenges the pilgrims, but on
learning their divine authority gives them courteous welcome. On
the steps of sincerity, contrition and love, the Poet mounts to the
gate and throws himself at the feet of its guardian to implore admis-
sion. The angel carves on Dante's brow seven P's, the symbol of
the seven deadly sins (peccata), which are purged on the terraces
above, and then turning the golden and the silver key which he
holds in charge from Peter, he admits Dante; with the solemn warn-
ing that he is not to look behind him, when once past the gate. The
seldom-turned hinges grate as the portal swings, and a half-heard
song of praise to God is the first sound that falls on the Poet's ear
within the gate, drawing his heart upward.*

NOW WAS THE concubine of ancient Tithonus at
eastern terrace growing white, forth from her sweet lover's
arms;

with gems her forehead was glittering, set in the form of
the cold animal that strikes folk with its tail;

and Night, in the place where we were, had made two of
the steps wherewith she climbs, and the third was already
down-stooping its wings;[1]

when I, who with me had somewhat of Adam, vanquished by sleep, sank down on the grass where already all we five were seated.

At the hour when the swallow begins her sad lays nigh unto the morn, perchance in memory of her former woes,[2]

and when our mind, more of a wanderer from the flesh and less prisoned by thoughts, in its visions is almost prophetic;

in a dream methought I saw an eagle[3] poised in the sky, with plumes of gold, with wings outspread, and intent to swoop.

And meseemed to be there where his own people were abandoned by Ganymede, when he was snatched to the high consistory.

I thought within me: "Haply he strikes only here through custom, and perchance scorneth to bear aught upward from other place in his talons."

Then meseemed that, having wheeled awhile, terrible as lightning, he descended and snatched me up far as the fiery sphere.

There it seemed that he and I did burn, and the visionary flame so scorched that needs was my slumber broken.

Not otherwise Achilles[4] startled, turning his awakened eyes around, and knowing not where he might be,

when his mother carried him away sleeping in her arms from Chiron to Scyros, there whence the Greeks afterwards made him depart,

than I startled, soon as sleep fled from my face, and I grew pale even as a man who freezes with terror.

Alone beside me was my Comfort, and the sun was already more than two hours high,[5] and mine eyes were turned to the sea.

"Have no fear," said my Lord, "make thee secure, for we are at a good spot: hold not back, but put out all thy strength.

Thou art now arrived at Purgatory; see there the rampart that compasseth it around; see the entrance there where it seems cleft.

Erewhile, in the dawn which precedes the day, when thy soul was sleeping within thee upon the flowers wherewith down below is adorned,

243

came a lady and said: 'I am Lucy,[6] let me take this man who sleepeth, so will I prosper him on his way.'

Sordello remained and the other noble forms. She took thee, and as day was bright, came on upward, and I followed in her track.

Here she placed thee, and first her fair eyes did show to me that open entrance; then she and sleep together went away."

As doth a man who in dread is reassured, and who changes his fear to comfort after the truth is revealed to him,

I changed me; and when my Leader saw me freed from care, he moved up by the rampart, and I following, towards the height.

Reader, well thou seest how I exalt my subject, therefore marvel thou not if with greater art I sustain it.

We drew nigh, and were at a place, whence there where first appeared to me a break just like a fissure which divides a wall,

I espied a gate, and three steps beneath to go to it, of divers colours, and a warder[7] who as yet spake no word.

And as more I opened mine eyes there, I saw him seated upon the topmost step, such in his countenance that I endured him not;

and in his hand he held a naked sword which reflected the rays so towards us, that I directed mine eyes to it oft in vain.[8]

"Tell, there where ye stand, what would ye?" he began to say; "where is the escort? Beware lest coming upward be to your hurt!"

"A heavenly lady who well knows these things," my Master answered him, "even now did say to us: 'Go ye thither, there is the gate.'"

"And may she speed your steps to good," again began the courteous door-keeper; "come then forward to our stairs."

There where we came, at the first step, was white marble so polished and smooth that I mirrored me therein as I appear.

The second darker was than perse, of a stone, rugged and calcined, cracked[9] in its length and in its breadth.

The third, which is massy above, seemed to me of porphyry so flaming red as blood that spurts from a vein.

Upon this God's angel held both his feet, sitting upon the threshold, which seemed to me adamantine stone.[10]

Up by the three steps, with my good will, my Leader brought me, saying: "Humbly ask that the bolt be loosed."

Devoutly I flung me at the holy feet; for mercy I craved that he would open to me; but first on my breast thrice I smote me.

Seven P's[11] upon my forehead he described with the point of his sword and: "Do thou wash these wounds when thou art within," he said.

Ashes, or earth which is dug out dry, would be of one colour with his vesture,[12] and from beneath it he drew forth two keys.[13]

One was of gold and the other was of silver; first with the white and then with the yellow he did so to the gate that I was satisfied.

"Whensoever one of these keys fails so that it turns not aright in the lock," said he to us, "this passage opens not.

More precious is one, but the other requires exceeding art and wit ere it unlocks, because it is the one which unties the knot.

From Peter I hold them; and he told me to err rather in opening, than in keeping it locked, if only the people fell prostrate at my feet."

Then he pushed the door of the sacred portal, saying: "Enter, but I make you ware that he who looketh behind returns outside again."

And when in their sockets were turned the pivots of that sacred portal, which are of metal ringing and strong,

Tarpeia roared not so, nor showed her so harsh, when good Metellus was taken from her, whereby she after remained poor.[14]

I turned me intent for the first sound, and *Te Deum laudamus*[15] meseemed to hear in a voice mingled with sweet music.

Just such impression gave me that which I heard, as we

are wont to receive when people are singing with an organ,
and now the words are clear, and now are not.

1. Dante never distinguishes between the signs and the constellations of the Zodiac; that is to say, he disregards the phenomena which he held to be the proper motion of the sphere of the stars (*cf. Vita Nuova*, § ii, and *Conv.* ii. 3 and 15). It is the phenomenon known in modern astronomy as the precession of the equinoxes. Perhaps the reason why Dante did not make this correction was that he regarded it as counterbalanced by the error of the Julian calendar (see *Par.* xxvii, *note* 15), in the other direction. Thus, he would regard the day on which, by the uncorrected calendar, the sun enters the *constellation* of Aries as coinciding with the day on which, by the corrected calendar, he would be in the real equinox, *i.e.* the first point of the *sign* of Aries. He chose, therefore, to take his ideal equinox rather by calendar and constellation than by the strict astronomical equinoctial point. This seems to be the meaning of *Inf.* i, and may account for his treating the statement that the sun was at the equinoctial point at the time of his journey now as an exact statement (*Par.* x) and now as an approximation (*Par.* i). This premised, a reference to the chronological note on page 192 will show that the retardation of the moon now amounted to two hours and thirty-six minutes, and that she was therefore in the constellation of Scorpio. Of the six hours in which the night rises, two were gone, and the third had just passed the summit of its course. The lunar aurora was therefore on the horizon. By a somewhat odd analogy she is called the "mistress" of Tithonus because she is a spurious aurora, and the genuine Aurora was the "wife" of Tithonus.

2. See Canto xvii, *note* 3.

3. The eagle, in the "Bestiaries," is said to fly up in his old age into the circle of fire, where he burns off all his feathers and falls blinded into a fountain of water, whence he issues with his youth renewed. This is a symbol of baptismal regeneration. And here Dante, true to the ethical note which pervades the Purgatory, connects him with moral rather than with ceremonial purification by connecting him with Troy, *i.e.* Rome, *i.e.* the Empire, law and justice: for Ganymede (whose beauty had attracted Jupiter, and who, having been borne aloft by an eagle while hunting with his friends on Mount Ida in Mysia, became the cup-bearer of the Gods) was the son of Tros, an ancestor of Æneas.

This is the first of three dreams or visions (for the other see Cantos xix and xxvii), each of which takes place shortly before dawn (the time being indicated in a verse beginning with the words *At* [or *In*] *the hour*) and is a forecast of the events immediately following.

4. See *Inf.* xxvi, *note* 5. The amazement of Achilles is recorded by Statius (*Achill.* i).

5. See the diagram on p. 200.

6. For Lucy, who must be more or less closely identified with the eagle of Dante's dream, see *Inf.* ii, *note* 9.

7. *warder*—this angel represents the priest confessor.

8. The sword of Divine Justice, whose ways are inscrutable to men.

9. *cracked*, perhaps because contrition breaks the stubbornness of the heart.

10. The stone of adamant possibly indicates the firmness and constancy of the confessor.

11. Kraus connects the seven P's not only with the seven sins (*peccata*), but with the seven scrutinies as well, which figured in the Roman Liturgy till the end of the 12th century, and formed part of the service on the seven Sundays from the first in Lent to Easter Sunday.

12. This hue appears to be a token of the humility with which the confessor should exercise his function.

13. Cf. *Par.* v, *note* 5.

14. Metellus, a follower of Pompey, made a futile effort to protect the Roman treasury (kept in the temple of Saturn on Mons Tarpeius) against Cæsar (B.C. 29). Lucan (*Phars.* iii) lays special stress on the noise made by the opening of the temple gates on this occasion.

15. The famous Ambrosian hymn, sung at matins and on solemn occasions. Some commentators refer to *Luke* xv. 10, and connect the present singing of the hymn with the entry of a soul into Purgatory.

ÇANTO X

The closing door rings, behind the Poets, but Dante, mindful of the warning, looks not back. The cleft through which the pilgrims mount is as tumultuous as the heaving sea, and it is three hours after sunrise ere they issue upon the first terrace, some eighteen feet in breadth, stretching uniformly as far as the eye may reach in either direction. The outer rim of the terrace verges unprotected upon the precipitous downward slope of the mount. The inner side is of marble, cut vertically out of the mountain, and carved with scenes from sacred and pagan history, illustrative of humility, seeming to live and speak in their beautiful and compelling reality. As Dante is gazing unsatiated upon the intaglios, Virgil bids him look to the left, where he beholds strange objects approaching him, which his eyes cannot at first disentangle, but which presently reveal themselves as human forms bent under huge burdens of stone, crumpled up in postures of agonized discomfort. These are the forms of the proud, mere larvæ not yet developed into the angelic imago, who had none the less exalted themselves on earth in unseasonable pride, and now wail only that the limits of their strength enable them to bear no more and bend no lower in their humility.

WHEN WE WERE within the threshold of the gate, which the evil love[1] of souls disuses, because it makes the crooked way seem straight,

by the ringing sound I heard it was shut again; and had I turned mine eyes to it what would have been a fitting excuse for the fault?

We climbed through a cleft rock, which was moving on one side and on the other, even as a wave that recedes and approaches.

"Here we must use a little skill," began my Leader, "in keeping close, now hither now thither, to the side that is receding."

And this made our steps so scant, that the waning orb of the moon regained its bed to sink again to rest

ere we were forth from that needle's eye. But when we

were free and on the open above, where the mount is set back,

I wearied and both uncertain of our way, we stood still on a level place more solitary than roads through deserts.

From its edge where it borders on the void, to the foot of the high bank which sheer ascends, a human body would measure in thrice;

and so far as mine eye could wing its flight, now on the left now on the right side, such this cornice appeared to me.

Thereon our feet had not yet moved, when I discerned that circling bank (which, being upright, lacked means of ascent)

to be of pure white marble, and adorned with sculptures so that not only Polycletus,[2] but Nature there would be put to shame.

The angel that came to earth with the decree of peace wept for since many a year, which opened heaven from its long ban,

before us appeared so vividly graven there in gentle mien, that it seemed not an image which is dumb.

One would have sworn that he was saying: *Ave*, for there she was fashioned who turned the key to open the supreme love.[3]

And in her attitude were imprinted these words, *Ecce ancilla Dei*, as expressly as a figure is stamped on wax.

"Keep not thy mind only on one place," said the sweet Master, who had me on that side where folk have the heart;

wherefore I moved my face about, and saw behind Mary, on that side of me where he was who was urging me on,

another story set in the rock, wherefore I crossed by Virgil and drew me nigh, that it might be displayed to mine eyes.

There was graven on the very marble the cart and the oxen drawing the sacred ark, whereby we fear an office not committed to us.

In front appeared people; and the whole divided into seven choirs, to two of my senses, made the one say "no," the other, "yes, they do sing."

In the like wise, at the smoke of the incense which there

249

was imaged, eyes and nose were made discordant with yes and no.

There went before the blessed vessel the lowly Psalmist, dancing, girt up;[4] and more and less than king was he in that case.

Figured opposite at a window of a great palace was Michal, looking on even as a woman scornful and sad.

I moved my feet from the place where I stood, to scan closely another story which behind Michal shone white before me.

There was storied the high glory of the Roman prince whose worth moved Gregory to his great victory;

of Trajan the emperor I speak;[5] and a poor widow was at his bridle in the attitude of tears and of grief.

Round about him appeared a trampling and throng of horsemen and the eagles in gold above him moved visibly to the wind.

The poor creature among all these seemed to say: "Lord, do me vengeance for my son who is slain, whereby my heart is pierced."

And he to answer her: "Now wait until I return." And she, like a person in whom grief is urgent: "My Lord, if thou do not return?" And he: "One who shall be in my place will do it for thee." And she: "What to thee will be another's good deed if thou forget thine own?"

Wherefore he: "Now comfort thee, for needs must I fulfill my duty ere I stir; justice wills and pity holds me back."

He, who ne'er beheld a new thing, wrought this visible speech, new to us because here it is not found.

While I was rejoicing to look on the images of humilities so great and for their Craftsman's sake precious to see,

"Lo here," murmured the Poet, "much people, but few they make their steps; these will send us on to the high stairs."

Mine eyes, that were intent on gazing to see new things whereof they are fain, were not slow in turning towards him.

I would not, reader, that thou be scared from a good purpose through hearing how God wills that the debt be paid.

Heed not the form of the pain; think what followeth, think that at worst beyond the great judgment it cannot go.

I began: "Master, that which I see moving towards us seems not persons to me, yet I know not what, so wanders my sight."

And he to me: "The grievous state of their torment doubles them down to earth so that mine eyes at first thereat were at strife.

But look steadily there and disentwine with thy sight what is coming beneath those stones; already thou canst discern how each one beats his breast."

O ye proud Christians, wretched and weary, who, sick in mental vision, put trust in backward steps,

perceive ye not that we are worms, born to form the angelic butterfly that flieth to judgment without defence?

Why doth your mind soar on high, since ye are as 'twere imperfect insects, even as the grub in which full form is wanting?

As to support ceiling or roof is sometimes seen for corbel a figure joining knees to breast,

which of unreality begetteth real discomfort in him who beholds it; in such wise saw I these when I gave good heed.

True it is that more and less were they contracted, according as they had more or less upon them, and he who had most patience in his bearing, weeping seemed to say: "I can no more."

1. *the evil love*—see Canto xvii.
2. The Greek sculptor Polycletus (*ca.* 452–412 B.C.) is lauded by a number of classical writers known in the Middle Ages, and his art is extolled by Italian poets prior to Dante.
3. The Annunciation (see *Luke* i). Note that the first example of the virtue opposed to the vice punished on the seven terraces (here, humility as opposed to pride) is, in each case, an episode drawn from the life of the Virgin Mary.
4. For David dancing before the Ark, see 2 *Sam.* vi.
5. This version of the popular Trajan story is apparently derived from the *Fiore di Filosofi*, which used to be erroneously attributed to Brunetto Latini. The incident is again alluded to in *Par.* xx. The ethical bearings of the legend that Pope Gregory's intercession brought about Trajan's recall from Hell, so that the Emperor might have a respite for repentance, are discussed in *Par.* xx (see *notes*). The reference is to the metal (gold-bronze) eagle, the outspread wings of which might seem to be fluttering in the wind.

ÇANTO XI

The humbled souls approach, with a paraphrase of the Lord's Prayer upon their lips, the petition for protection against temptation being uttered for the sake of those they have left behind, whether on earth or, perhaps, in the Antepurgatory, since souls inside the gate are beyond its reach; which loving offices of prayer the living should surely reciprocate for those who are now purging themselves. In answer to Virgil's inquiry, one of the souls directs the pilgrims to turn to the right, circling the mount with the sun. It is the Sienese Omberto, whose insolence had made him little better than a brigand, and had involved all his race in ruin. As the Poet bends down to hearken, another soul, painfully turning beneath his burden, gazes upon Dante who recognizes him as the miniature painter, Oderisi, now willing to admit the superior excellence of his rival Franco, and fully sensible of the empty and transitory nature of human glory. Cimabue's school of painting is superseded by Giotto's; the older poetic school of Guittone, or Guido, of Arezzo and his companions has been superseded by that of Guido Guinicelli, to which Guido Cavalcanti and Dante himself belong; and who knows whether the founder of yet another school that shall relegate them all to obscurity, may not already be born! Worldly reputation is always of the same empty quality, though the momentary object to which it attaches itself changes, one empty reputation differing from another only in name, and all of them swallowed up in the course of years, what matter whether few or many! One of the heroes of Montaperti and victims of Colle de Valdelsa, who is pacing before them, is already all but forgotten on the very scene of his triumphs and defeats. What are his reputation and his pride to him now, where the only act of his life that avails him is his self-humiliation in begging ransom for his friend, in the market place of Siena? an act which Dante himself shall learn better to appreciate in the days of his own anguish of humiliation.

"O OUR FATHER who art in heaven, not circum-
scribed, but through the greatest love thou hast for thy
first works on high,

252

praised be thy name and thy worth by every creature, as 'tis meet to give thanks to thy sweet effluence.

May the peace of thy kingdom come upon us, for we cannot of ourselves attain to it with all our wit, if it come not.

As of their will thine angels make sacrifice to thee, singing *Hosanna*, so many men make of theirs.

Give us this day our daily manna, without which he backward goes through this rough desert, who most toileth to advance.

And as we forgive every one the evil we have suffered, do thou forgive in loving-kindness and regard not our desert.

Put not our virtue, which lightly is subdued, to trial with the old adversary, but deliver us from him who so pricks it.[1]

This last prayer, dear Lord, is not made for us, for need is not, but for those who have remained behind us."

Thus those shades, praying good speed for them and for us, were going under their burden, like that whereof we sometimes dream,

unequal all in anguish around and weary, along the first cornice, purging away the foul mists of the world.

If there ever a good word for us is said, what can be said and done for them here, by those who have their will rooted in good?

Truly we ought to help them to wash away their stains, which they have borne hence, so that pure and light they may go forth to the starry spheres.

"Pray!—so may justice and pity soon unload you, that ye may spread the wing which may uplift you according to your desire,—

show us on which hand we go quickest towards the stairway; and if more than one passage there be, tell us that which least steeply ascends;

for he who cometh with me, because of the weight of Adam's flesh wherewith he is clad, at climbing up is slow against his will."

From whom came the words which were returned to those which he whom I was following had said, was not manifest,

but it was said: "To the right hand along the bank come

with us, and ye shall find the pass possible for a living person to ascend.

And if I were not impeded by the stone which subdues my proud neck, wherefore needs must I carry my visage low,

him who is yet alive, and names not himself, would I look at, to see if I know him, and to make him pitiful to this burden.

I was Italian and son of a great Tuscan: Guglielmo Aldobrandesco was my father; I know not if his name was ever with you.

The ancient blood and gallant deeds of my ancestors made me so insolent that, thinking not of our common mother,

all men I held in such exceeding scorn that it was the death of me, as the Sienese know, and every child knows in Campagnatico.

I am Humbert;[2] and not to me alone pride works ill, for all my fellows hath it dragged with it to mishap.

And here must I therefore bear this load among the dead, until God be satisfied, since I did it not among the living."

Listening, I bent down my face; and one of them,[3] not he who was speaking, twisted himself beneath the weight which encumbers him;

and saw me and knew me and was calling out keeping his eyes with difficulty fixed upon me, who all bent was going with them.

"Oh," said I to him, "art thou not Oderisi, the honour of Gubbio, and the honour of that art which in Paris is called 'illuminating'?"

"Brother," said he, "more pleasing are the leaves which Franco Bolognese paints; the honour now is all his and mine in part.

Truly I should not have been so courteous while I lived, because of the great desire of excelling whereon my heart was bent.

For such pride here the fine is paid; and I should not yet be here, were it not that having power to sin, I turned me to God.

O empty glory of human powers! How short the time

its green endures upon the top, if it be not overtaken by rude ages![4]

Cimabue thought to hold the field in painting, and now Giotto hath the cry, so that the fame of the other is obscured.[5]

Even so one Guido hath taken from the other the glory of our tongue; and perchance one is born who shall chase both from the nest.[6]

Earthly fame is naught but a breath of wind, which now cometh hence and now thence, and changes name because it changes direction.

What greater fame shalt thou have, if thou strip thee of thy flesh when old, than if thou hadst died ere thou wert done with pap and chink,[7]

before a thousand years are passed? which is shorter space to eternity than the twinkling of an eye to the circle which slowest is turned in heaven.

All Tuscany rang with the sound of him[8] who moves so slowly along the way in front of me, and now hardly is a whisper of him in Siena,

whereof he was lord, when the rage of Florence was destroyed who at that time was proud even as now she is degraded.

Your repute is as the hue of grass which cometh and goeth, and he[9] discolours it through whom it springeth green from the ground."

And I to him: "Thy true saying fills my heart with holy humility, and lowers my swollen pride, but who is he of whom but now thou wast speaking?"

"That," he answered, "is Provenzan Salvani; and he is here because in his presumption he thought to bring all Siena in his grasp.

Thus he hath gone and goes without rest since he died; such coin he pays back in satisfaction who yonder is too daring."

And I: "If that spirit who awaits the brink of life, ere he repents, abides there below, and mounts not up hither,

unless holy prayers aid him, until so much time be passed as he hath lived,[10] how has the coming here been vouchsafed to him?"

"When he lived in highest glory," said he, "in the market-place of Siena he stationed himself of his free will and put away all shame;

and there, to deliver his friend from the pains he was suffering in Charles's prison, he bought himself to tremble in every vein.

No more will I tell, and darkly I know that I speak, but short time will pass ere thy neighbours will act so, that thou shalt be able to interpret it.[11] This deed released him from those confines."

1. A paraphrase of the Lord's Prayer (*Matt.* vi. 9–13; *Luke* xi. 2–4). —The *first works* are the heavens and the angels. For *circumscribed* see Canto xxv.

2. Omberto, Count of Santafiora, in the Sienese Maremma, was a member of the Aldobrandeschi family for which see Canto vi, *note* 12. He was put to death at Campagnatico in 1259 by the Sienese, who had long been at warfare with the family and were anxious to be rid of their authority. The mode of Omberto's death is variously given.

3. Oderisi (of Gubbio in Umbria), an illuminator and miniature painter. He appears to have been at Rome in 1295, for the purpose (so says Vasari) of illuminating some MSS. in the Papal Library for Boniface VIII. According to the same authority, the work on that occasion was shared by Franco of Bologna.

4. A reputation does not survive the generation in which it was built up, unless a gross and unenlightened age happens to follow.

5. The works of the Florentine painter Cimabue (*ca.* 1240–*ca.* 1302) are instinct with genius, and mark a considerable advance on the stiff Byzantine school; but it was reserved for his pupil, Giotto (1266–1336), to draw his inspiration at the fount of Nature herself, and to become the father of modern painting.—Giotto is said to have been a friend of Dante's, and the well-known Bargello portrait of the poet is doubtfully attributed to him.

6. The interpretation of these verses given in the *Argument* is not the one usually adopted; the view generally held being that the two Guidos are Guido Guinicelli (see Canto xxvi) and Guido Cavalcanti (see *Inf.* x, *note* 8), and that Dante himself is the poet destined to eclipse the latter. Against this more obvious interpretation, it may be urged that it would be out of keeping with the general tone of the passage: and specifically with xii. Moreover, there is no indication in Dante's works of his regarding Guido Guinicelli as a superseded worthy, or distinguishing between the schools of these two Guidos; although he repeatedly contrasts the school of Guido (or Guittone) of Arezzo with the new school of which he regarded Guido Guinicelli as the chief, and Guido Cavalcanti and himself as disciples (xxvi; see, further, xxiv and xxvi: *De vulg. El.* i. 13; ii.

6). On the other hand, it may be advanced in favour of the more popular theory, that, whatever Dante may say in other passages, Guido Cavalcanti and the other Florentines actually did write poetry superior to that of Guido Guinicelli; that a pupil may surpass his teacher and yet regard him with affection and admiration; that Dante would probably have used the form *Guittone* in this passage, so as to make his meaning clear; and that the prophecy may well refer to our poet himself, who, though in the circle of the Proud, is probably as conscious of his literary greatness now as he was in Limbo (see *Inf.* iv).

7. Before you left off your child's prattle: *pap* = bread, and *chink* = money (*cf. Inf.* xxxii).

8. Provenzan Salvani, a Ghibelline, was chief in authority among the Sienese at the time of the battle of Montaperti; and after the defeat of the Florentines he was the strongest advocate in favour of the destruction of their city (see *Inf.* x, *notes* 11 and 12). He once humbled himself by affecting the garb and manner of a beggar in the market-place of Siena, so as to procure the money wherewith to ransom a friend, who was the prisoner of Charles of Anjou. Provenzan was eventually defeated and slain (June, 1269) in an engagement with the Florentines at Colle, in Valdelsa (see Canto xiii).

9. *he* = the sun.

10. See Canto iv.

11. A prophecy of Dante's exile from Florence (1302). The poet will know from bitter experience what it is to live on the charity of others (*cf. Par.* xvii).

ÇANTO XII

Dante has bent down in a sympathetic attitude of humility to converse with Oderisi, and when Virgil bids him make better speed he straightens his person so far as needful to comply, but still remains bowed down in heart, shorn of his presumptuous thoughts. As he steps forward with a good will, Virgil bids him once more look down at the pavement which he is treading, and there he sees as it were the lineaments of the defeated proud, from Lucifer and Briareus to Cyrus and Holofernes and Troy. The proud are laid low upon the pavement as the humble were exalted to the upspringing mountainside. A wide stretch of the mountain is circled ere they come to the gentle angel of this terrace of the proud, whose glory is tempered as a morning star, and who promises them an easier ascent henceforth. A stroke of his wing touches the Poet's brow, who then approaches such a stair as was made to ease the ascent to San Miniato in the good old days when weights and measures were true and public records ungarbled. As they mount the stair the blessing of the poor in spirit falls on their ears, with sound how different from the wild laments of Hell! And Dante notes how the steep ascent seems far more easy than the level terrace of a moment back. It is because the P of pride was erased by the stroke of the angel's wing, and thereon all the other six became shallower. This Dante, at a hint from Virgil, ascertains by feeling his brow with outspread fingers, and in innocent delight at the discovery of the cause of his lightened steps, he looks into Virgil's face which answers with a smile of sympathy and encouragement.

EVEN IN step, like oxen which go in the yoke, I went beside that burdened spirit, so long as the sweet pedagogue suffered it.

But when he said: "Leave him, and press on, for here 'tis well that with sail and with oars, each one urge his bark along with all his might";

erect, even as is required for walking I made me again with my body, albeit my thoughts remained bowed down and shrunken.

1 had moved me, and willingly was following my master's steps, and both of us already were showing how light of foot we were,

when he said to me: "Turn thine eyes downward: good will it be, for solace of thy way, to see the bed of the soles of thy feet."

As in order that there be memory of them, the tombs on the ground over the buried bear figured what they were before;

wherefore there, many a time men weep for them, because of the prick of remembrance which only to the pitiful gives spur;

so saw I sculptured there, but of better similitude according to the craftsmanship, all that which for road projects from the mount.

I saw him who was created nobler far than other creature, on one side descending like lightning from heaven.[1]

I saw Briareus,[2] transfixed by the celestial bolt, on the other side, lying on the earth heavy with the death chill.

I saw Thymbræus, I saw Pallas and Mars, armed yet, around their father, gazing on the scattered limbs of the giants.[3]

I saw Nimrod[4] at the foot of his great labour, as though bewildered, and looking at the people who were proud with him in Shinar.

O Niobe,[5] with what sorrowing eyes I saw thee graven upon the road between seven and seven thy children slain!

O Saul,[6] how upon thine own sword there didst thou appear dead on Gilboa, which thereafter felt nor rain nor dew!

O mad Arachne,[7] so saw I thee already half spider, sad upon the shreds of the work which to thy hurt was wrought by thee!

O Rehoboam, now thine image there seems no more to threaten; but full of terror a chariot beareth it away ere chase be given![8]

It showed—the hard pavement—again how Alcmæon made the luckless ornament seem costly to his mother.[9]

It showed how his sons flung themselves upon Sennacherib within the temple, and how, him slain, there they left him.[10]

It showed the destruction and the cruel slaughter which Tomyris wrought when she said to Cyrus: "For blood thou didst thirst and with blood I fill thee!"[11]

It showed how in a rout the Assyrians fled, after Holofernes was slain,[12] and also the relics of the assassination.

I saw Troy in ashes and in ruins: O Ilion, thee how base and vile it showed—the sculpture which there is discerned![13]

What master were he of brush or of graver, who drew the shades and the lineaments, which there would make every subtle wit stare?

Dead seemed the dead, and the living, living. He saw not better than I who saw the reality of all that I trod upon while I was going bent down.

Now wax proud and on with haughty visage, ye children of Eve, and bow not down your faces, so that ye may see your evil path!

Already more of the mount was circled by us, and of the sun's path much more spent, than the mind, not set free, esteemed;

when he, who ever in front of me alert was going, began; "Lift up thy head, this is no time to go thus engrossed.

See there an angel who is making ready to come towards us; look how the sixth handmaiden is returning from the days' service.[14]

Adorn with reverence thy bearing and thy face, so that it may delight him to send us upward; think that this day never dawns again."

Right well was I used to his monitions never to lose time, so that in that matter he could not speak to me darkly.

To us came the beauteous creature, robed in white, and in his countenance, such as a tremulous star at morn[15] appears.

His arms he opened and then outspread his wings; he said: "Come; here nigh are the steps, and easily now is ascent made."

To this announcement few be they who come. O human

folk, born to fly upward, why at a breath of wind thus **fall** ye down?

He led us where the rock was cut; there he beat **his** wings upon my forehead, then did promise me my journey secure.

As on the right hand, to ascend the mount where stands the church which, over Rubaconte, dominates the well-guided city,[16]

the bold scarp of the ascent is broken by the steps, which were made in the times when the records and the measure were safe.[17]

Even so is the bank made easier, which here right steeply falls from the other cornice, but on this side and on that the high rock grazes.

While we were turning there our persons, *"Beati pauperes spiritu"*[18] voices so sweetly sang, that no speech would tell it.

Ah! how different are these openings from those in Hell! for here we enter through songs, and down there through fierce wailings.

Now were we mounting up by the sacred steps, and meseemed I was exceeding lighter, than meseemed before on the flat;

wherefore I: "Master, say, what heavy thing has been lifted from me, that scarce any toil is perceived by me in journeying?"

He answered: "When the P's which have remained still nearly extinguished on thy face, shall, like the one, be wholly rased out,

thy feet shall be so vanquished by good will, that not only will they feel it no toil, but it shall be a delight to them to be urged upward."

Then did I. like those who go with something on their head unknown to them, save that another's signs make them suspect;

wherefore the hand lends its aid to make certain, and searches, and finds, and fulfils that office which cannot be furnished by the sight;

and with the fingers of my right hand outspread, I found

261

but six the letters, which he with the keys had cut upon me
over the temples: whereat my Leader looking did smile.

1. Satan (*cf. Luke* x. 18).—Not only are the examples of the vices
drawn alternately from sacred and profane history like those of the
virtues; but, within certain limits, the two sets of examples on each
terrace correspond numerically. On the first, third, fourth, and
seventh terraces, the correspondence is exact; on the second and
fifth it becomes so, if we divide the second set into groups; while
on the sixth there is apparently no attempt at carrying out the
design.
2. Briareus (for whom, see *Inf.* xxxi, *note* 8) must be separated from
the other giants. The parallels are, Lucifer: Briareus; the Giants:
Nimrod.
3. Jupiter, Apollo (called Thymbræus, from his temple at Thymbra
in the Troad), Minerva and Mars, having defeated and slain the
giants, are gazing upon their scattered limbs.
4. For Nimrod, see *Inf.* xxxi, *note* 3.
5. Niobe, the wife of Amphion, King of Thebes, was so proud of
her fourteen children that she offended Latona, who had only two—
Apollo and Diana. These latter, in revenge, shot all the fourteen
with their arrows, and Niobe herself was changed by Jupiter into a
stone statue, lifeless save for the tears it shed (see Ovid, *Metam.* vi).
6. Saul, after his defeat by the Philistines at Mount Gilboa, "took a
sword and fell upon it" (1 *Sam.* xxxi. 1–4). Reference is to the
words of David's lament on the death of Saul: "Ye mountains of
Gilboa, let there be no dew, neither let there be rain, upon you, nor
fields of offerings" (2 *Sam.* i. 21).
7. Arachne of Lydia, having boasted of her skill in weaving (*cf.
Inf.* xvii) and challenged Minerva to a contest, was eventually
changed by the goddess into a spider for her presumption (see
Ovid, *Metam.* vi).
8. The ten tribes revolted against Rehoboam, King of Israel, be-
cause he refused to lighten their taxes. "Then King Rehoboam sent
Adoram, who was over the tribute; and all Israel stoned him with
stones, that he died. Therefore King Rehoboam made speed to get
him up to his chariot, to flee to Jerusalem" (1 *Kings* xii. 1–18).
9. See *Par.* iv, *note* 15.
10. Sennacherib, King of Assyria, was defeated by Hezekiah, King
of Judah, and subsequently slain by his own sons (2 *Kings* xix. 37).
11. Cyrus, founder of the Persian Empire (560–529 B.C.), treacher-
ously murdered the son of Tomyris, the Scythian queen, whereupon
he was himself defeated and slain by the outraged mother. She had
his head cast into a vessel filled with blood, and scoffed at it, saying:
*Satia te sanguine quem sitisti cujus per annos triginta insatiabilis
persevarasti* (Orosius, ii. 7 § 6). Cf. *De Mon.* ii. 9.
12. When Holofernes, one of Nebuchadnezzar's captains, was be-
sieging Bethulia, the Jewish widow Judith obtained access to his tent

and cut off his head. This she had displayed on the walls of the city; whereupon the Assyrian host took to flight, pursued by the Jews (*Judith* x-xiv).

13. Cf. *Inf.* i and xxx; see, too, *Æn.* iii. 2: *Ceciditque superbum Ilium.*

14. It is therefore just past noon. The conception of the hours as handmaidens serving the day is repeated in Canto xxii. See the diagram on p. 217

15. *a star at morn* is used, rather than the "the morning star," because the latter, being a planet, does not twinkle.

16. The church of San Miniato commands Florence *across* the Rubaconte bridge [*i.e.* Miniato is not *above* the bridge].—*the well-guided,* as applied to Florence, is, of course, ironical.

17. See *Par.* xvi, *notes* 12 and 23.

18. "Blessed are the poor in spirit; for theirs is the kingdom of heaven" (*Matt.* v. 3). Towards the end of Dante's sojourn on each terrace, he hears one of the Beatitudes from the Sermon on the Mount. In each case, except the present, the angel of the respective circle is specially named as uttering the words. It has therefore been suggested that the angel is speaking here, too. But the word *voices* constitutes a considerable difficulty, nor is this difficulty removed by a reference to the *words* in second stanza of Canto xxii (Dante uses *voci* in both cases).

ÇANTO XIII

The Poets mount to the second terrace; of dark rock, tenantless so far as the eye can stretch, and without mark or indication of any kind. Virgil apostrophizes the sun, and in lack of any counter reason, determines to follow him from east to west. After a time voices ring through the air in praise of generosity, the virtue counter to envy; and Virgil anticipates the direct warning against that vice ere they leave this the circle of its purification. Meanwhile they encounter the once envious spirits, appealing with full confidence to the ungrudging love of Mary, of the angels, and of the saints. The envious eyes that once found food for bitterness in all sights of beauty and joy, must now in penance refrain from drinking in the gladness of sea and sky and human love, for their lids are drawn together with such a suture of wire as is used to tame the wildness of the untrained hawk; and their inward darkness is matched by their sober raiment. They lean one against another in mutual love and for mutual support, and upturn their sightless countenances like the blind beggars that gather round church portals. Dante is shamed, as though he were taking ungenerous advantage of those whom he sees, but who cannot know his presence; and, having gained Virgil's leave, addresses the souls in words of soothing beauty and aspiration. In answer to his question whether any of them are of Latium, Sapia the Sienese tells that they are all citizens of one true city; but that she, amongst others, had lived in her earthly pilgrimage in Latium. She tells the story of her evil joy at the defeat of the Sienese by the Florentines at Colle in Valdelsa, and utters her thanks to the humble saint whose prayers have secured her admission to expiatory suffering earlier than the else appointed time. In her turn Sapia questions Dante as to his journey,—with open eyes as she judges, and with breath-formed speech,—around this circle; and he answers that he too shall one day have his eyes closed there, but not for long, since he has sinned far less through envy than through pride. He further reveals to her the wonder of his pilgrimage and receives her petition for his own prayers, and her commission to bear news of her to her kinsfolk among the vain and light-minded Sienese.

WE WERE at the top of the stairway where a second time the mount is cut away which, by our ascent, frees us from evil.

There a cornice binds the hill around like unto the first, save that its curve more sharply bends.

No shade is there, nor figure which may be seen; so naked the bank appears and even so the way, with the livid hue of the stone.

"If here we await people to ask of," the poet was saying, "I fear perchance that our choice may have too great delay."

Then fixedly on the sun his eyes he set; he made of his right side a centre of movement, and the left part of him did turn.

"O sweet light, in whose trust I enter on the new way, do thou lead us," said he, "as we would be led here within;

thou givest warmth to the world, thou shinest upon it; if other reason urges not to the contrary, thy beams must ever be our guide."

As far as here counts for a mile,[1] so far there had we already gone, in short time, by reason of our ready will;

and, flying towards us were heard, but not seen, spirits, speaking courteous invitations to the table of love.

The first voice which passed by in its flight loudly said, "*Vinum non habent*,"[2] and went on repeating it behind us.

And ere it had wholly passed out of hearing through distance, another passed crying: "I am Orestes,"[3] and also stayed not.

"O Father," said I, "what voices are these?" and as I was asking, lo the third saying: "Love them from whom ye have suffered evil."[4]

And the good Master: "This circle doth scourge the sin of envy, and therefore the cords of the whip are drawn from love.

The bit must be of contrary sound; I think thou wilt hear it, as I opine, ere thou reachest the Pass of Pardon.[5]

But fix thine eyes through the air full steadily, and thou shalt see people sitting down in front of us, and each one along the cliff is seated."

Then wider than before mine eyes I opened; I looked before me, and saw shades with cloaks not different from the hue of the stone.

And after we were a little further forward, I heard a cry: "Mary, pray for us"; a cry: "Michael, and Peter, and all Saints."[6]

I believe not that on earth there goeth this day a man so hardened, who were not pierced with compassion at what I then saw;

for when I had reached so nigh to them that their features came distinctly to me, heavy grief was running from mine eyes.

With coarse haircloth they seemed to me covered, and one was supporting the other with the shoulder, and all were supported by the bank.

Even so the blind, to whom means are lacking, sit at Pardons begging for their needs; and one sinks his head upon the other,

so that pity may quickly be awakened in others, not only by the sound of their words, but by their appearance which pleads not less.

And as to the blind the sun profits not, so to the shades there where I was now speaking, heaven's light will not be bounteous of itself;

for all their eyelids an iron wire pierces and stitches up, even as is done to a wild hawk because it abideth not still.

I seemed to do them wrong as I went my way seeing others, not being seen; wherefore I turned me to my wise Counsel.

Well knew he what the dumb would say, and therefore awaited not my questioning, but said: "Speak and be brief and to the point."

Virgil was coming with me on that side of the cornice whence one may fall because it is surrounded by no parapet;

on the other side of me were the devout shades, who, through the horrible seam, were pressing forth tears so that they bathed their cheeks.

I turned me to them and began: "O people assured of seeing the Light above, which alone your desire hath in its care;

so may grace quickly clear away the scum of your con-
science, that the stream of memory may descend clearly
through it,

tell me (for to me 'twill be gracious and dear) if any soul
be among you that is Italian, and perchance it will be good
for him if I know of it."

"O brother mine, each one is a citizen of a true city; but
thou wouldest say, that lived a pilgrim in Italy."

This meseemed to hear for answer somewhat farther on
than there where I was; wherefore I made me heard yet
more that way.

Among the others I saw a shade[7] that was expectant in
look, and if one would ask, "how so?" its chin it lifted up
after the manner of the blind.

"Spirit," said I, "that dost subdue thee to mount up; if
thou art that one who answered me, make thyself known
to me by place or by name."

"I was a Sienese," it answered, "and with these others
here do cleanse my sinful life, weeping unto Him that he
lend himself to us.[8]

Sapient was I not albeit Sapia I was named, and of others
hurt I was far more glad than of mine own good fortune.

And that thou mayst not think I deceive thee, hear if I
was mad as I tell thee. Already when the arc of my years
was descending,[9]

my townsmen, hard by Colle, were joined in battle with
their foes, and I prayed God for that which he had willed.

There were they routed, and rolled back in the bitter
steps of flight, and seeing the case I took joy exceeding all
other;

so much, that I lifted up my impudent face, crying to
God: 'Now I fear thee no more,' as the blackbird doth for
a little fair weather.[10]

I would have peace with God on the brink of my life;
and my debts were not yet reduced by penitence,

had it not been that Peter the Combseller[11] remembered
me in his holy prayers, who in his charity did grieve for me.

But who art thou that goest asking of our state, and bear-
est thine eyes unsewn, as I believe, and breathing dost
speak?"

"Mine eyes," said I, "from me here shall yet be taken; but for short time, for small is the offence they did through being turned in envy.

Greater far is the fear wherewith my soul is suspended, of the torment below, for even now the burden down there weighs upon me."[12]

And she to me: "Who then hath led thee up here among us, if thou thinkest to return below?" And I: "He who is with me and saith no word;

and I am living, and therefore do thou ask of me, spirit elect, if thou wouldst that yonder I lift yet for thee my mortal feet."

"Oh this is so new a thing to hear," she answered, "that 'tis a great token that God loveth thee; therefore profit me sometimes with thy prayers.

And I beseech thee by all thou most desirest, if e'er thou tread the land of Tuscany, that thou restore my fame among my kinsfolk.

Thou wilt see them among that vain people who put their trust in Talamone, and will lose there more hopes than in finding the Diana; but the admirals shall lose most there."[13]

1. The expression "so far as here counts for a mile" (that is to say, "if you think of walking a mile, you will get the right impression"), is an indication which should be carefully noted, that we must not expect to be able to arrive at any consistent representation by exact matter-of-fact measurements in Hell and Purgatory. Dante was well acquainted with the approximate size of the earth (*Conv.* iii. 5 and elsewhere), and cannot represent himself, for example, as having literally climbed from the centre to the circumference in something under 24 hours. He is content to avoid all glaring errors of principle, and to make the several scenes realizable (cf. *Inf.* xxx, *note* 5).

2. At the marriage in Cana. "And when they wanted wine, the mother of Jesus said unto him, They have no wine" (*John* ii. 3).

3. Orestes, the son of Agamemnon, renowned for his friendship with Pylades. When Orestes was condemned to death, Pylades wished to take his place, saying that he was Orestes. Cicero alludes to this incident in a passage of the *De Amicitia* (§ 7), which was certainly known to Dante.

4. "But I say unto you, Love your enemies, bless them that curse you, do good to them that hate you, and pray for them which despitefully use you, and persecute you" (*Matt.* v. 44).

5. The examples of charity are the "whip," the examples of envy,

the "bit" (*cf.* Canto xiv); and for the "Pass of Pardon" (of which there is, of course, one on each terrace), see, in the present case, Canto xv.

6. The Litany of the Saints, in which, after the Trinity, are invoked the Virgin Mary, the archangel Michael with the other angels, St. Peter with the other apostles, and finally the other saints.

7. Sapia, a noble lady of Siena, the wife of Viviano dei Saracini, lord of Castiglioncello. She was filled with envy of her fellow-citizens, and rejoiced at their defeat under Provenzan Salvani at Colle (see Canto ix, *note* 8). In 1265 she assisted her husband in founding a hospice for wayfarers, and after his death (1269) she made a grant of his castle to the commune of Siena. These acts of generosity supply a gloss to her reference to penitence; and the latter of the two also proves that she must have become reconciled to the Sienese shortly after their route (1269).

8. *Cf. Par.* i.

9. *Cf. Inf.* i, *note* 1.

10. According to a popular Italian tradition and proverb, the black-bird, at the close of January, cries out: "I fear thee no more, O Lord, now that the winter is behind me." Sapia meant to imply that, now she had obtained the dearest wish of her heart, she had no more need or fear of God.

11. Pier, a native of Chianti, was a Franciscan who had settled at Siena, where he died in 1289. He was renowned for his piety, and long venerated as a saint, his festival being officially recognized in 1328.

12. Scartazzini, ever anxious to whitewash his hero, ingeniously quotes *Psalms* lxxiii. 3, to account for Dante's self-accusation of envy: "For I was envious at the foolish, when I saw the prosperity of the wicked."—With regard to our Poet's pride, his life and works afford ample proof thereof. Villani, among others, says of him: "On account of his learning, he was somewhat presumptuous, and harsh, and disdainful."

13. Siena still preserves two documents, dated 1295 and 1303 respectively; the former of which refers to a resolution to search for the stream of Diana, which was supposed to flow beneath the city; and the latter, to the purchase (for 8000 gold florins, from the Abbot of San Salvatore) of the small port of Talamone (on the Tyrrhenian Sea, south-west of the Sienese Maremma), which would have been a useful outlet to the sea, if only the creek could have been kept clear of sand and mud. Both projects failed (at any rate in Dante's time); and in the latter enterprise a number of admirals [perhaps = contractors, as some early commentators think], directing the dredging operations, lost their lives owing to the unhealthiness of the place.

ÇANTO XIV

As Dante converses with Sapia, revealing the wondrous conditions of his own pilgrimage and the mysterious presence of his guide, he is overheard by two spirits who are leaning for support one against another at his right. Nearest to him is Guido del Duca of Bertinoro, who is the chief speaker, the other being Rinieri da Calboli of Forlì. They speak chiefly to each other, but draw Dante into their conversation, questioning him as to his origin; and when he indicates by a circumlocution that his birthplace lies upon the Arno, Rinieri asks Guido why Dante conceals the name under dark hints as though it were a shameful thing; whereon Guido approves of Dante's shrinking from expressly naming this accursed ditch which rises in the midst of brutishness, and as it swirls through deeper pools, finds ever fiercer or more degraded neighbours, till it reaches the crowning infamy of Pisa. There follows a prediction of the woes which Rinieri's relative Fulcieri shall wreak on Florence in 1303. Deeply stirred by their discourse, Dante questions the spirits as to their own past, and Guido accompanies his answer by a lamentation over the degeneracy of the Romandiola from which they both spring; and implores Dante to pass upon his way and leave him to weep undisturbed. Assured that they are pursuing the right way, since the generosity of these once envious souls would else have notified them of their mistake, the two Poets pursue their way as the warning voices against envy, anticipated by Virgil, ring in their ears; to which Virgil adds his sad reflections on the things which human choice relinquishes and the things it grasps.

"WHO IS THIS that circles our mount ere death have given him flight, and opens and shuts his eyes at his will?"[1]

"I know not who he may be, but I know that he is not alone; do thou question him who are nearer to him, and gently greet him that he may speak."

Thus two spirits, one leaning against the other, were discoursing of me there on the right hand; then held up their faces to speak to me;

270

and one said: "O soul, that fixed yet in thy body dost journey towards heaven, for charity console us, and tell us whence thou comest, and who thou art; for thou dost make us marvel so greatly at thy grace, as needs must a thing that never was."

And I: "Through the midst of Tuscany there spreads a stream which rises in Falterona and a course of a hundred miles satiates it not.[2]

From its banks I bring this body; to tell you who I may be were to speak in vain, for my name as yet sounds not for much."

"If I penetrate truly thy meaning with my understanding," then answered me he who first spake, "thou art talking of the Arno."

And the other said to him: "Why did he conceal the name of that river, even as one does of horrible things?"

And the shade who was asked this question, acquitted him thus: "I know not, but verily 'tis meet that the name of such a vale perish;

for from its beginning (where the rugged mountain-chain, whence Pelorus is cut off, is so fruitful that in few places it exceeds that mark)

as far as there where it yields itself to restore that which the sky soaks up from the sea, whence rivers have that which flows with them,

virtue is driven forth as an enemy by all, even as a snake, either because of the ill-favoured place or of evil habit which incites them;

wherefore the dwellers in the wretched vale have so changed their nature that it seems as if Circe had them in her pasturing.[3]

Among filthy hogs, more worthy of acorns than of other food made for use of man, it first directs its feeble course.

Then, coming downward it finds curs snarling more than their power warrants, and from them scornfully turns aside its snout.

On it goes in its descent, and, the greater its increase, the more it finds the dogs growing to wolves, this accurst and ill-fated ditch.

Having then descended through many deep gorges, it finds the foxes, so full of fraud that they fear no wit that may trap them.

Nor will I cease speaking, for all that another may hear me; and it will be well for him if he mind him again of what true prophecy unfolds to me.

I see thy grandson,[4] who is becoming a hunter of those wolves on the bank of the fierce river, and strikes them all with terror.

He sells their flesh while yet alive; then slaughters them like worn-out cattle: many he deprives of life and himself of honour.

He cometh forth bloody from the sad wood; he leaves it such, that hence a thousand years it re-woods not itself to its primal state."

As at the announcement of grievous ills the face of him who listens is troubled, from whatever side the peril may assault him,

so saw I the other soul, that had turned round to hear, grow troubled and sad, after it had gathered these words to itself.

The speech of the one and the other's countenance made me long to know their names, and question I made of them mingled with prayers:

wherefore the spirit that first spake to me, began again: "Thou wouldst that I condescen in doing that for thee which thou wilt not do for me;

but since God wills that so much of his grace shine forth in thee, I will not be chary with thee; therefore know that I am Guido del Duca.

My blood was so inflamed with envy, that if I had seen a man make him glad, thou wouldst have seen me suffused with lividness.

Of my sowing such straw I reap. O human folk, why set the heart there where exclusion of partnership is necessary?[5]

This is Rinier; this is the glory and the honour of the House of Calboli, where none since hath made himself heir of his worth.[6]

And not only his blood between the Po and the mountains, and the seashore and the Reno, is stripped of the good required of truth and chivalry,

for inside these boundaries is choked with poisonous growths, so that tardily now would they be rooted out by cultivation.

Where is the good Lizio, and Arrigo Mainardi, Pier Traversaro and Guido di Carpigna? O ye Romagnols turned to bastards!

When in Bologna shall a Fabbro take root again? when in Faenza a Bernardin di Fosco, noble scion of a lowly plant?

Marvel thou not, Tuscan, if I weep, when I remember with Guido da Prata, Ugolin d' Azzo who lived among us,

Federico Tignoso and his fellowship, the House of Traversaro, and the Anastagi (the one race and the other now without heirs),

the ladies and the knights, the toils and the sports of which love and courtesy enamoured us, there where hearts are grown so wicked.

O Brettinoro, why dost thou not flee away, since thy household is gone forth, and much people in order not to be guilty?

Well doth Bagnacaval that beareth no more sons, and ill doth Castrocaro, and Conio worse, that yet troubleth to beget such Counts;

the Pagani will do well when their Demon shall go away; but not indeed that unsullied witness may ever remain of them.

O Ugolin de' Fantolin, thy name is safe, since no more expectation is there of one who may blacken it by degenerating.

But now go thy way, Tuscan, for now it delights me far more to weep than to talk, so hath our discourse wrung my spirit."

We knew that those dear souls heard us going; therefore by their silence they made us confident of the way.

After we were left alone journeying on, a voice, that seemed like lightning when it cleaves the air, smote against us, saying:

"Everyone that findeth me shall slay me";[7] and fled like

a thunderclap which peals away if suddenly the cloud bursts.

When from it our hearing had truce, lo the second, with such loud crash that 'twas like thunder that follows quickly:

"I am Aglauros who was turned to stone";[8] and then to press me close to the Poet, I made a step back, and not forward.

Now was the air quiet on every side, and he said to me: "That was the hard bit which ought to hold man within his bounds.

But ye take the bait, so that the old adversary's hook draws you to him, and therefore little avails bridle or lure.

The heavens call to you, and circle around you, displaying unto you their eternal splendours, and your eye gazes only to earth; wherefore he who discerns all things doth buffet you."

1. These words are spoken by Guido del Duca (who bears the brunt of the speaking throughout the canto) and Rinier da Calboli (who does most of the listening), respectively.

Guido del Duca, a Ghibelline of Bertinoro, belonged to the Onesti family of Ravenna (other members of which were Pietro and Romualdo; see *Par.* xxi and xxii). In 1199 he was judge to the Podestà of Rimini. For years (from 1202, or even earlier) he was an adherent of the Ghibelline leader, Pier Traversaro. In 1218, Pier, aided principally by the Mainardi of Bertinoro, obtained the chief power at Ravenna, and drove out the Guelfs; whereupon the latter attacked Bertinoro, destroyed the houses of the Mainardi, and expelled Pier's adherents. Among these was Guido, who followed his chief to Ravenna, and the last preserved record of whom is a deed signed by him in that city in 1229.

Rinier, belonging to the Guelf family of da Calboli, of Forlì, was Podestà of Faenza (1247), of Parma (1252) and of Ravenna (1265; and again in 1292). In 1276 he attacked Forlì (assisted by other Guelfs, among them Lizio da Valbona); but the force had to retire to Rinier's castle of Calboli (in the valley of Montone), where they surrendered to Guido of Montefeltro, the Captain of Forlì, who destroyed the stronghold. When Rinier was re-elected Podestà of Faenza in 1292, the captain of the city was Mainardo Pagano. The citizens, supported by their leaders, opposed a tax levied on them by the Count of Romagna. The expedition against him and the Ghibellines on his side (including the Count of Castrocaro) was entirely successful. In 1294 the da Calboli, who were becoming too powerful in Forlì, were expelled by the Ghibellines; but they returned, together with other exiled Guelfs, in 1296, when the bulk of their enemies were absent on an expedition against Bologna. Shortly afterwards, however, the Guelfs were again routed and expelled by the Ghibellines, led among others by one of the Ordelaffi On this occasion the aged Rinier was slain.

Guido's invective against Romagna should be compared with *Inf.* xxvii.

2. Falterona is a summit of the Tuscan Apennines (north-east of Florence), where the Arno has its source. *Fruitful*, as applied to the secondary mountain chains, springing from it; taken in conjunction with *in few places it exceeds that mark*, the latter is, geographically, the more correct interpretation. Peloro (the modern Cape Faro; *cf. Par.* viii) is at the north-east extremity of Sicily, being separated from the end of the Apennines only by the Strait of Messina; geologically, the Sicilian mountains are, of course, only a continuation of the Apennines.—After a course of about 150 miles, the Arno flows into the Mediterranean Sea (for the vapours exhaled by the sea through the heat of the sun come down again as rain, swell the rivers and are thus eventually restored to the sea).

3. Dante conceives the inhabitants of the Val d'Arno to have been, as it were, transformed into beasts by the enchantress Circe, who was endowed with this power. Thus the people of Casentino (see Canto v, *note* 4) have become hogs, the Aretines—curs, the Florentines—wolves, and the Pisans—foxes.

4. Rinier's grandson, Fulcieri da Calboli, was Podestà of various cities—Milan, Parma and Modena, but is chiefly notorious for his tenure of that office at Florence (1303), where he proved himself a bitter foe of the Whites and Ghibellines (see Villani, viii).—*Wood = Florence; cf. Inf.* i, *note* 2.

5. See the following canto.

6. The people mentioned in the following lines were all inhabitants of the Romagna (the limits of which are defined as the Po and the Apennines, the Adriatic and the Reno; for the latter *cf. Inf.* xviii). For some of the names see above, *note* 1.

Lizio da Valbona, a Guelf nobleman of Bertinoro and follower of Rinier da Calboli; he died between 1279 and 1300.—Arrigo Mainardi, a Ghibelline of Bertinoro and adherent of Pier Traversaro, together with whom he was captured by the people of Faenza in 1170; he was still alive in 1228.—Pier Traversaro (*ca.* 1145–1225), the most distinguished member of the Ghibelline family of the *casa Traversara;* he was repeatedly Podestà of his native city, and played a leading part in the politics of Romagna for many years.—Guido of the Carpegna (a noted family settled in the district of Montefeltro) was renowned for his liberality.—Fabbro, one of the Ghibelline Lambertazzi of Bologna, was Podestà of several cities. After his death, in 1259, his sons had a bitter feud with the Geremei (see *Inf.* xxxii, *note* 14).—Bernardin di Fosco distinguished himself in the siege of Faenza against the Emperor Frederick II (1240); his father was a field labourer.—Guido da Prata (d. *ca.* 1245), a native of

Ravenna, near which city he appears to have owned considerable property.—Ugolin d'Azzo, a wealthy inhabitant of Faenza, one of the Ubaldini (cf. Canto xxiv, note 5). He married Beatrice Lancia, the daughter of Provenzan Salvani (see Canto xi) and died at a great age in 1293.—Federico Tignoso: a nobleman of Rimini, noted for his generosity, who appears to have lived in the first half of the 13th century.—The Traversari and Anastagi were noble Ghibelline families of Ravenna. On the death of Pier Traversaro, his son Paolo turned Guelf—a *volte-face* that soon undermined the influence of the family. About the middle of the 13th century, the Anastagi were very much to the fore, owing to their strife with the Polentani and other Guelfs of Ravenna. A reconciliation was effected *ca.* 1258, and after this date there is no mention of them in the records.—Brettinoro (now Bertinoro), a little town between Forlì and Cesena; its inhabitants, several of whom figure in this canto, had a great reputation for hospitality. Dante is apparently alluding here to the compulsory exodus of the Ghibellines from the town (see above, *note* 1, on Guido del Duca), and rejoicing that they were spared the spectacle of the place in its present condition.—The Malavicini, Counts of Bagnacavallo (between Imola and Ravenna), were Ghibellines. In 1249 they drove Guido da Polenta and his fellow Guelfs from Ravenna. Subsequently they were notorious for their frequent change of party.—Castrocaro and Conio: strongholds near Forlì; the counts of the former place were Ghibellines, those of the latter Guelfs.—The Pagani were Ghibellines of Faenza (or Imola). For Mainardo see *Inf.* xxvii, *note* 7 (*cf.* Villani, vii). According to Benvenuto, he was called "devil" because of his cunning.—Ugolino de' Fantolini (d. 1278) did not take part in public affairs, but led an honourable retired life. One of his sons was killed at Forlì (1282) in the engagement with Guido of Montefeltro (see *Inf.* xxvii), and the other died before 1291.

7. The words of Cain, after he had slain his brother Abel (*Gen.* iv. 14).

8. Aglauros, the daughter of Cecrops, King of Athens, being jealous of Mercury's love for her sister, Hersë, was changed by the God into stone (see Ovid, *Metam.* xiv).

ÇANTO XV

It is three o'clock in the afternoon, and the Poets, (having circled nigh a fourth part of the mountain and reached its northern slope) are facing the westering sun, when the dazzling light of the angel guardian of the circle warns them that they have approached the next ascent. They are welcomed to a stair far less steep than those they have already surmounted, and hear the blessing of the merciful, together with songs of lofty encouragement, chanted behind them as they mount. Dante's mind goes back to words in which Guido del Duca, while confessing his own envious disposition on earth, had reproached mankind for fixing their hearts on the things which exclude partnership; and now he questions Virgil as to the meaning of this saying. Virgil answers first briefly, and then in full detail, that the more of any material thing one man has, the less of it there is for others; whereas the more peace or knowledge or love one man has, the more there is for all the others. Hence envy disturbs men's hearts only because they are fixed on material instead of spiritual things. If this exposition does not satisfy him, let him await further light from Beatrice, and meanwhile let him make all speed upon his journey. On this they reach the third terrace—that of the wrathful— whereon Dante in ecstatic vision beholds examples of meekness and patience. Waking, half-bewildered, from his trance, he is called to himself by Virgil, and the two walk toward the evening sun, till a dark cloud of smoke rolling towards them, plunges them into the blackness of more than night.

AS MUCH as between the end of the third hour and the beginning of the day appears of the sphere which ever sports after the fashion of a child,

so much appeared now to be left of the sun's course towards evening; it was vespers there, and here midnight.[1]

And the rays were smiting on the middle of our noses, for the mount was so far circled by us, that we now were going straight to the west,[2]

when I felt my brow weighed down by the splendour

far more than before, and amazement to me were the un-
known things;

wherefore I raised my hands towards the top of my eyes,
and made me the shade which dulls the excess of light.

As when a ray of light leaps from the water or from the
mirror to the opposite direction, ascending at an angle
similar

to that at which it descends, and departs as far from the
line of the falling stone in an equal space, even as experi-
ment and science shows,

so I seemed to be smitten by reflected light in front of
me, wherefore mine eyes were swift to flee.

"What is that, sweet Father, from which I cannot screen
my sight so that it may avail me," said I, "and seems to be
moving towards us?"

"Marvel thou not if the heavenly household yet dazes
thee," he answered me, "'tis a messenger that cometh to
invite us to ascend.

Soon will it be that to behold these things shall not be
grievous to thee, but shall be a joy to thee, as great as
nature hath fitted thee to feel."

When we had reached the blessed angel, with gladsome
voice, he said: "Enter here to a stairway far less steep than
the others."

We were mounting, already departed thence, and "*Beati
misericordes*" was sung behind, and "Rejoice thou that
overcomest."[3]

My Master and I, alone we two, were mounting up, and
I thought while journeying to gain profit from his words;

and I directed me to him thus asking: "What meant the
spirit from Romagna by mentioning 'exclusion' and 'part-
nership'?"[4]

Whereupon he to me: "He knoweth the hurt of his
greatest defect, and therefore let none marvel if he reprove
it, that it be less mourned for.

Forasmuch as your desires are centered where the por-
tion is lessened by partnership, envy moves the bellows to
your sighs.

But if the love of the highest sphere wrested your desire
upwards, that fear would not be at your heart;

for by so many more there are who say 'ours,' so much the more of good doth each possess, and the more of love burneth in that cloister."

"I am more fasting from being satisfied," said I, "than if I had kept silent at first, and more perplexity I amass in my mind.

How can it be that a good, when shared, shall make the greater number of possessors richer in it, than if it is possessed by a few?"

And he to me: "Because thou dost again fix thy mind merely on things of earth, thou drawest darkness from true light.

That infinite and ineffable Good, that is on high, speedeth so to love as a ray of light comes to a bright body.

As much of ardour as it finds, so much of itself doth it give, so that how far soever love extends, eternal goodness giveth increase upon it;

and the more people on high who comprehend each other, the more there are to love well, and the more love is there, and like a mirror one giveth back to the other.

And if my discourse stays not thy hunger, thou shalt see Beatrice, and she will free thee wholly from this and every other longing.

Strive only that soon, even as the other two are, the five wounds may be rased out, which are healed by our sorrowing."

As I was about to say: "Thou dost satisfy me," I saw me arrived on the next circuit, so that my eager eyes made me silent.

There meseemed to be suddenly caught up in a dream of ecstasy, and to see many persons in a temple,

and a woman about to enter, with the tender attitude of a mother, saying: "My son, why hast thou thus dealt with us?

Behold thy father and I sought thee sorrowing";[5] and as here she was silent, that which first appeared, disappeared.

Then appeared to me another woman,[6] with those waters adown her cheeks which grief distils when it rises in one by reason of great anger, and saying: "If thou art lord of the city for whose name was so great strife among the gods, and whence all knowledge sparkles,

avenge thee of those daring arms which embraced our daughter, O Pisistratus." And the lord seemed to me kindly and gently

to answer her with placid mien: "What shall we do to him who desires ill to us, if he who loveth us is condemned by us?"

Then saw I people, kindled with the fire of anger, slaying a youth with stones,[7] and ever crying out loudly to each other: "Kill, kill!"

And him saw I sinking towards the ground, because of death, which already was weighing him down, but of his eyes ever made he gates unto heaven,

praying to the high Lord in such torture, with that look which unlocks pity, that he would forgive his persecutors.

When my soul returned outwardly to the things which are true outside it, I recognized my not false errors.[8]

My Leader, who could see me acting like a man who frees himself from sleep, said: "What aileth thee that thou canst not control thyself,

but art come more than half a league, veiling thine eyes, and with staggering legs, after the manner of him whom wine or sleep overcomes?"

"O sweet Father mine, if thou listen to me, I will tell thee," said I, "what appeared to me when my legs were thus taken from me."

And he: "If thou hadst a hundred masks upon thy face, thy thoughts, however slight, would not be hidden from me.

What thou sawest was in order that thou have no excuse from opening thy heart to the waters of peace, which are poured from the eternal fount.

I asked not: 'What aileth thee,' for that reason which he asks who looks but with the eye that seeth not when senseless the body lies,

but I asked to give strength to thy feet; so must the slothful be goaded who are slow to use their waking hour when it returns."

We were journeying on through the evening, straining our eyes forward, as far as we could, against the evening and shining rays;

and lo, little by little, a smoke, dark as night, rolling towards us, nor any room was there to escape from it. This reft us of sight and the pure air.

1. The Zodiac, which is improperly described as a sphere (instead of a zone or great circle on the sphere), is compared to a skipping child, because in the course of the day its extremities on the horizon play up and down, and the semi-circle above the horizon is now all north of the equator, now all south, and now crossing it from north to south, or from south to north. At the equinox a quarter of it crosses the eastern horizon between sunrise and nine o'clock. Dante tells us, therefore, that, at the moment of which he is speaking, a quarter of it had to cross the western horizon before sunset, *i.e.* it was three o'clock in the afternoon (here, in Italy, it was midnight, for Roman time is nine hours later than Purgatory time, and there it was Vespers, or 3 P.M.; see Canto iii, note 1).

2. The representations of the Mount of Purgatory given in the editions of the *Commedia* usually depict the poets as having circled the whole mountain in the course of their journey. But this is erroneous. They circle only the northern or sunny side, from east to west. Here, towards the close of the day, they are travelling almost due west, and are almost at the northern point of the mountain.

3. "Blessed are the merciful, for they shall obtain mercy" (*Matt.* v. 7).—The words *Rejoice thou that overcomest* are variously referred to *Matt.* v. 12; *Rom.* xii, 21; or *Rev.* ii. 7.

4. See the preceding canto.

5. Mary's words to the child Jesus, after he had "tarried behind in Jerusalem, and Joseph and his mother knew not of it." See *Luke* ii. 43-50.

6. *Pisistratus Atheniensium tyrannus* [*ca.* 605-527 B.C.], *cum adolescens quidam, amore filiæ ejus virginis accensus, in publico obviam sibi factam osculatus esset, hortante uxore, ut ab eo capitale supplicium sumeret, respondit: "Si eos, qui nos amant, interficimus, quid his faciemus, quibus odio sumus?"* (Valerius Maximus, *Fact. et dict. mem.* vi). Allusion is made to the strife between Minerva and Neptune, as to which of them should name the city of Athens (see Ovid, *Metam.* vi).

7. The stoning of Stephen (*Acts* vii. 54-60).

8. Dante recognized that the scenes which had passed before him were merely visions (*errors*), though visions of events that had actually occurred in times gone by (therefore, *not false*).

ÇANTO XVI

Closing his eyes against the gross and bitter fog, led by Virgil like a blind man, Dante hears the harmonious and tender chant of the "Lamb of God" arise from the lips of the once wrathful spirits. One of them, who has heard Dante's conversation with Virgil, questions him and turns back with him to hear his wondrous tale. The spirits in other circles have recognized the special grace shown to Dante in his anticipated vision of unseen things; and to this grace Dante himself now appeals to win from his new companion an account of himself, and directions as to the journey; for meeting these souls circling from west to east raises a doubt in his mind whether he and Virgil have been right in still following the sun. The spirit reveals himself as Marco Lombardo, refers, as other spirits had done, to the degeneracy of the times, reassures Dante as to the course he is taking and implores his prayers. Dante, while giving him the required pledge, catches at this renewed insistence on the evil times, and asks whether it is due to unfavourable conjunctions in the heavens or to inherent degeneracy of earth. Marco heaves a deep sigh at the blindness implied in such a question; as if man were handed over helplessly to planetary influences! As if he had no free will and no direct dependence upon God, which may make him superior to all material influences! The causes of degeneracy must be sought on earth and will be found in the absence of any true governor who perceives at least the turrets of the true city, and so can lead the guileless and impressionable souls of men on the right path. And this evil springs not from corruptness of human nature in general, but from the worldliness and ambition of the clergy who have grafted the sword upon the crook, so that the two lights of the world that once shone in Rome have quenched each other; and the temporal and spiritual powers, confounded together, have ceased to guide and check each other. Hence the world is so degenerate that only three good old men remain as a rebuke to the living generation. Dante accepts the sad wisdom of Marco's discourse, only requesting a word of personal explanation as to one of the three still surviving types of antique virtues; and thereon he begins to see the light struggle through the enveloping darkness, and is told that the angel guardian of the next stair is at hand.

282

GLOOM OF HELL and of a night bereft of every planet under a meagre sky, darkened by cloud as much as it can be,

made not to my sight so thick a veil, nor of a pile so harsh to the feel, as that smoke which there covered us;

for it suffered not the eye to stay open: wherefore my wise and trusty Escort closed up to me, and offered me his shoulder.

Even as a blind man goeth behind his guide in órder not to stray, and not to butt against aught that may do him hurt, or perchance kill him,

so went I through the bitter and foul air, listening to my Leader who was saying ever: "Look that thou be not cut off from me."

I heard voices, and each one seemed to pray for peace and for mercy, to the Lamb of God that taketh away sins.

Only *"Agnus Dei"* were their beginnings;[1] one word was with them all, and one measure; so that full concord seemed to be among them.

"Are those spirits, Master, that I hear?" said I. And he to me: "Thou apprehendest truly, and they are untying the knot of anger."

"Now who art thou that cleavest our smoke, and speak-est of us even as if thou didst still measure time by calends?"[2]

Thus by a voice was said; wherefore my Master said: "Answer thou and ask if by this way we go upward."

And I: "O creature that art cleansing thee to return fair unto him who made thee, a marvel shalt thou hear if thou follow me."

"I will follow thee so far as is permitted me," it answered, "and if the smoke lets us not see, hearing shall keep us in touch in its stead."

Then began I: "With those swathings[3] which death dis-solves I am journeying upward and here did come through the anguish of Hell;

and if God hath received me so far into his grace that he wills that I may behold his court in a manner quite outside modern use,[4]

hide not from me who thou wast before death, but tell it

me, and tell me if I am going aright for the pass; and thy words shall be our escort."

"A Lombard was I and was called Mark; I had knowledge of the world, and loved that worth at which now every one hath unbent his bow;

for mounting up thou goest aright." Thus answered he, and added: "I pray thee that thou pray for me, when thou art above."

And I to him: "By my faith I bind me to thee to do that which thou askest of me, but I am bursting within at a doubt, if I free me not from it.

First 'twas simple, and now is made double by thy discourse, which makes certain to me, both here and elsewhere, that whereto I couple it.

The world is indeed so wholly desert of every virtue, even as thy words sound to me, and heavy and covered with sin;

but I pray that thou point the cause out to me, so that I may see it, and that I may show it to others; for one places it in the heavens and another here below."

A deep sigh, which grief compressed to "Alas!" he first gave forth, and then began: "Brother, the world is blind, and verily thou comest from it.

Ye who are living refer every cause up to the heavens alone, even as if they swept all with them of necessity.

Were it thus, Free Will in you would be destroyed, and it were not just to have joy for good and mourning for evil.

The heavens set your impulses in motion; I say not all, but suppose I said it, a light is given you to know good and evil,

and Free Will, which, if it endure the strain in its first battlings with the heavens, at length gains the whole victory, if it be well nurtured.

Ye lie subject, in your freedom, to a greater power and to a better nature;[5] and that creates in you mind which the heavens have not in their charge.

Therefore, if the world to-day goeth astray, in you is the cause, in you be it sought, and I now will be a true scout to thee therein.

From his hands who fondly loves her ere she is in being,

there issues, after the fashion of a little child that sports, now weeping, now laughing,

the simple, tender soul, who knoweth naught save that, sprung from a joyous maker, willingly she turneth to that which delights her.

First she tastes the savour of a trifling good; there she is beguiled and runneth after it, if guide or curb turn not her love aside.

Wherefore 'twas needful to put law as a curb, needful to have a ruler who might discern at least the tower of the true city.

Laws[6] there are, but who putteth his hand to them? None; because the shepherd that leads may chew the cud, but hath not the hoofs divided.[7]

Wherefore the people, that see their guide aiming only at that good whereof he is greedy, feed on that and ask no further.

Clearly canst thou see that evil leadership is the cause which hath made the world sinful, and not nature that may be corrupted within you.

Rome, that made the good world, was wont to have two suns, which made plain to sight the one road and the other; that of the world, and that of God.

One hath quenched the other; and the sword is joined to the crook; and the one together with the other must perforce go ill;

because, being joined, one feareth not the other. If thou believest me not, look well at the ear, for every plant is known by the seed.

Over the land which the Adige and the Po water, worth and courtesy were wont to be found, ere Frederick met opposition;[8]

now, safely may it be traversed by whomsoever had, through shame, ceased to hold converse with good men, or to draw near them.

Truly three elders yet are there in whom the olden times rebuke the new, and it seems to them long ere God removes them to the better life:

Corrado da Palazzo, and the good Gerard, and Guido

da Castel, who is better named in French fashion the guileless Lombard.[9]

Say henceforth, that the Church of Rome, by confounding two powers in herself, falls into the mire, and fouls herself and her burden."

"O my Mark," said I, "well thou reasonest, and now I perceive why Levi's sons were exempt from inheriting;[10]

but what Gerard is that, who thou sayest is left behind for ensample of the extinct people, in reproof of the barbarous age?"

"Either thy speech beguiles me, or it tempts me," he answered me, "for thou, speaking to me in Tuscan, seemest to know naught of the good Gerard.

By other surname I know him not, except I take it from his daughter Gaia. God be with you, for no further I come with you.

See the light, that beams through the smoke, now waxing bright; the angel is there, and it behooves me to depart ere I am seen of him." So turned he back and no more would hear me.

1. See *John* i. 29; though the reference here is rather to the prayer in the Mass—*Agnus Dei qui tollis peccata mundi, miserere nobis, dona nobis pacem.*

2. The speaker is Marco Lombardo, of Venice, a learned and honourable courtier, noted for his liberality, who flourished in the latter half of the 13th century.

measure time by calends = as though thou wert still alive. In the eternal regions human measurements of time do not apply.

3. *With those swathings, i.e.* with my body.

4. *quite outside modern use.* See *Inf.* ii.

5. The free will by its nature seeks good (*Par.* xxxiii), and since God is the supreme good, the free agent is subject to him in the sense that the whole course of his action is determined by him as its goal. But this determination of the will to good is the fulfilment, not the restriction of liberty. The idea is familiar to us from the words of the Prayer Book: . . . " whose service is perfect freedom."

6. See Canto vi, *note* 8.

7. "Nevertheless these shall ye not eat of them that chew the cud, or of them that divide the hoof: as the camel, because he cheweth the cud, but divideth not the hoof; he is unclean unto you" (*Lev.* xi. 4). According to Thomas Aquinas the "chewing of the cud" signifies meditation and understanding of the Scriptures; while the "cloven hoof" stands for the power to discern and distinguish be-

tween certain sacred things—here used apparently of the spiritual and temporal power (which are, of course, not mentioned by Aquinas).

8. Lombardy, or, in the wider sense, Upper Italy—a veritable hotbed of dissension, by reason of the struggle between the Emperor Frederick II and the Pope.

9. Currado da Palazzo, a Guelf of Brescia, Vicar for Charles of Anjou at Florence (1276), Podestà of Siena(1279) and of Piacenza (1288).

Gherardo da Cammino, Captain-General of Treviso from 1283 till his death in 1306 (when he was succeeded by his son Riccardo; see *Par.* ix). The commentators differ as to whether his daughter Gaia, who died in 1311, was renowned for her virtue or notorious for her loose morals; probably the latter is the correct interpretation. Dante once again takes Gherardo as a type of nobility in the *Conv.* iv. 14.

Guido da Castel was a gentleman of Treviso, famed for his bounty and hospitality. Some think that reference is to the fact that the French called all Italians *Lombart;* but Guido *was* a Lombard, so that there would be no point in this unless we lay the stress on the *guileless,* and assume that he was known to them as "the *simple* Italian." Mr. Toynbee's theory that *guileless Lombard* = "honest usurer," is ingenious; the French often used the appellation *Lombart* for "usurer," and so this nickname might have been playfully given to Guido, with reference to his generosity. Guido is alluded to in the *Conv.* iv. 16, by way of contrast with the Asdente of *Inf.*, xx.

10. So that they might confine themselves to spiritual affairs. See *Num.* xviii. 20, *Deut.* xviii. 2, *Josh.* xiii. 14; and cf. *De Mon.* iii. 13.

ÇANTO XVII

As the mists cleave on a mountain side and reveal the prospect, so
the cloud that swathed the wrathful opened, and the Poets looked
on the setting sun, as the shadow of night was already creeping up
the slope. Visions of the wrathful, corresponding to the visions of
the placable and peaceful already seen, come upon Dante; from
which he is awakened by the shining light and the glad summons of
the angel of the stair, to whose spontaneous invitation the Poets
gladly respond. On the first step Dante feels again the stroke of the
angel's wing and hears the blessing of the peace-makers. But already,
when they reach the summit of the stair, the shadow has passed be-
yond them, the rays of the sun fall only on the higher reaches of the
mount, and in accordance with the law of the place they can rise
no higher while night reigns. After listening in vain for any sound
in the new circle, Dante questions his guide as to the nature of the
offence purged there. Virgil answers that it is sloth, and takes occa-
sion to expound the general system of Purgatory. Not only the
Creator, but every creature also, is moved by love. Natural love, as
that of heavy bodies for the centre, of fire for the circumference, or
of plants for their natural habitat, is unerring; but rational love may
err by being misdirected; or by being disproportionate, by defect or
excess. Love directed to primal and essential good, or to secondary
good in due measure, cannot lead to sin; but perverse and dispro-
portioned love is the seed of all sin, just as much as rightly directed
and measured love is the seed of all virtue. A human being who has
not become a monster cannot love (that is, cannot be drawn to-
wards and take delight in) evil to himself or evil to the God on
whom his very being depends. All perverse rejoicing, then, must be
rejoicing in the ill of our neighbour, and this may be caused by
pride, envy, or anger, which are purged on the three circles already
passed. Apart from these evil gratifications, every one has at least
some confused apprehension of a supreme good wherein the soul can
rest, and every one therefore seeks to gain it. But this supreme love,
which is no other than the love of God, may err by defect, either
speculative or practical; and the slothful who have thus erred re-
cover their lost tone in the circle the pilgrims have now reached.
The innocent or needful enjoyment of which the bodily frame is the

*reat, cannot confer true bliss and may be pursued with dispropor-
tionate keenness, or in neglect of the divinely imposed restraints.
Such sins are purged in the three uppermost circles.*

READER, if ever in the mountains a mist hath caught
thee, through which thou sawest not otherwise than moles
do through the skin,[1] remember

how, when the damp and dense vapours begin to melt
away, the sphere of the sun enters feebly through them:

and thy fancy will lightly come to see how first I beheld
the sun again, that now was at the setting.

So, measuring mine with the trusty steps of my Master,
I issued forth from such a cloud, to the rays already dead
on the low shores.

O fantasy, that at times dost so snatch us out of ourselves
that we are conscious of naught, even though a thousand
trumpets sound about us,

who moves thee, if the senses set naught before thee? A
light moves thee which takes its form in heaven, of itself,
or by a will that sendeth it down.[2]

The traces of her impiety, who changed her form into
the bird that most delights to sing,[3] appeared in my fancy;

and here my mind was so restrained within itself, that
from outside came naught which was then received by it.

Then fell within my lofty fantasy one crucified, scorn-
ful and fierce in mien, and even so was he dying.

Round about him were the great Ahasuerus, Esther his
wife, and the just Mordecai, who in speech and deed was
so sincere.[4]

And as this fancy broke of itself, after the fashion of a
bubble to which the water fails wherein it was made,

there arose in my vision a maiden weeping sorely, and
she was saying: "O Queen, wherefore through wrath hast
thou willed to be naught?

Thou hast slain thee not to lose Lavinia;[5] now me hast
thou lost; I am she that mourns, mother, for thy ruin rather
than for another's."

As sleep is broken when on a sudden new light strikes on

the closed eyes, and being broken, quivers ere it wholly dies away;

so my imagination fell down soon as a light smote on my face, greater far than that which is in our use.

I turned me to see where I was, when a voice which removed me from every other intent, said: "Here one ascends";

and it gave my desire to behold who it was that spake, such eagerness as never rests until it sees face to face.

But, as at the sun which oppresses our sight, and veils his form by excess, so my virtue there was failing me.

"This is a divine spirit, that directs us to the way of ascent without our prayer, and conceals itself with its own light.

It doeth unto us as a man doth unto himself; for he who awaits the prayer and sees the need, already sets him unkindly towards denial.

Now accord we our feet to such an invitation; strive we to ascend ere the night cometh, for then we could not until the day return."[6]

Thus spake my Leader, and I with him did turn our footsteps to a stairway; and soon as I was at the first step,

near me I felt as 'twere the stroke of a wing, and my face fanned, and heard one say: "*Beati pacifici* who are without evil wrath."[7]

Now were the last rays whereafter night followeth so far risen above us that the stars were appearing on many sides.

"O my virtue, wherefore dost thou pass away from me thus?" I said within me, for I felt the power of my legs put in truce.

We stood where the stairway ascended no higher, and were fixed even as a ship which arrives on the shore:

and I gave heed awhile if I might hear aught in the new circle; then did turn me to my Master and said:

"Sweet my Father, tell, what offence is purged here in the circle where we are? If our feet are stayed, stay not thy discourse."

And he to me: "The love of good, scant of its duty, just here restores itself; here is plied again the ill-slackened oar.

But that thou mayest understand yet more plainly, turn thy mind to me, and thou shalt take some good fruit from our tarrying."

He began:[8] "Nor Creator, nor creature, my son, was ever without love, either natural or rational; and this thou knowest.

The natural is always without error; but the other may err through an evil object, or through too little or too much vigour.

While it is directed to the primal goods, and in the secondary, moderates itself, it cannot be the cause of sinful delight;

but when it is turned awry to evil, or speeds towards the good with more or less care than it ought, against the Creator his creature works.

Hence thou mayst understand that love must be the seed of every virtue in you, and of every deed that deserves punishment.

Now inasmuch as love can never turn its face from the weal of its subject, all things are safe from self-hatred;

and because no being can be conceived as existing alone in isolation from the Prime Being, every affection is cut off from hate of him.

It follows, if I judge well in my division, that the evil we love is our neighbours', and this love arises in three ways in your clay.

There is he who through his neighbour's abasement hopes to excel, and solely for this desires that he be cast down from his greatness;

there is he who fears to lose power, favour, honour and fame because another is exalted, wherefore he groweth sad so that he loves the contrary;

and there is he who seems to be so shamed through being wronged, that he becomes greedy of vengeance, and such must needs seek another's hurt.

This threefold love down below is mourned for: now I desire that thou understand of the other, which hastes toward good in faulty degree.

Each one apprehends vaguely a good wherein the mind

may find rest, and desires it; wherefore each one strives to attain thereto.

If lukewarm love draws you towards the vision of it or the gaining of it, this cornice, after due penitence, torments you for it.

Another good there is, which maketh not men happy; 'tis not happiness, 'tis not the good essence, the fruit and root of all good.

The love that abandons itself too much to this, is mourned for above us in three circles: but how it is distinguished in three divisions, I do not say, in order that thou search for it of thyself."

1. See diagram on p. 241
2. Through the influence of the stars, or by Divine will.
3. Procne's husband, Tereus, dishonoured her sister Philomela, and cut out her tongue, so as to ensure her silence. The injured girl, however, imparted to her sister the knowledge of what had happened by means of a piece of tapestry; whereupon Procne, in a frenzy, slew her son Itys, and made Tereus unwittingly partake of his flesh at table. On discovering the truth he pursued the sisters with an axe, bent on slaying them; but at their prayer all three were changed into birds. According to Ovid (*Met.* vi), whom Dante follows, Procne became a nightingale, and Philomela a swallow (see Canto ix).
4. See *Esther* iii-vii. Ahasuerus, King of the Persians, advanced Haman to high honours, till the latter was accused by Esther of having designs on the life of Mordecai. "So they hanged Haman on the gallows that he had prepared for Mordecai. Then was the king's wrath pacified."
5. Lavinia, daughter of Latinus and Amata, was first betrothed to Turnus, and then promised to Æneas; whereupon hostilities broke out between the two heroes. In the course of these, Amata (who was opposed to the marriage with Æneas), thinking that Turnus was killed (though, in point of fact, he was not yet slain) hanged herself in a frenzy of despair (*Æn.* xii).
6. See Canto vii.
7. "Blessed are the peace-makers: for they shall be called the children of God" (*Matt.* v. 9).
8. A careful study of the *Argument*, and of the second paragraph in the "Note on Dante's Purgatory" on page 189, will make this important passage clear. See, too, Gardner.

rational love = conscious desire, as distinguished from the unconscious trend of inanimate beings [both of which impulses are regarded as "love"]; with these lines *cf. Conv.* iii and *Par.* i.—*the primal goods*, towards God and virtue; *the secondary*, towards worldly goods.

ÇANTO XVIII

Virgil's discourse has suggested to Dante's mind the question as to the nature of love which the group of poets to which he belonged were incessantly discussing. Would Virgil resent as irrelevant or flippant a question on this subject? Or might he (Dante) take this unique opportunity of learning the true answer? Virgil encourages his question, and then proceeds to answer. Love implies a potential attraction to the loved object. When first it is presented to the mind, the mind sways towards it, and then the experience of delight in communion with it confirms the original attraction; and the desire thus waked can only be stilled by fruition. Thus, while the capacity for love, that is to say, sensitiveness in general, is the sign of a higher organism, and therefore good, it is a profound misconception to regard every specific affection as itself good, since love of some sort is the root of all evil as of all good conduct. Dante follows keenly; but this universality of love as a motive power, this necessity of the presentation from without of its object, and this spontaneous response of the corresponding and pre-existing latent impulse within, seem to obliterate all merit or demerit. Virgil refers to Beatrice for the final answer, but declares meanwhile that every human soul has a certain intellectual and emotional constitution (for which it deserves neither praise nor blame) in virtue of which it cannot help believing the supreme truths (the axioms) and loving the supreme good (God). Intellectual merit begins when we refuse to believe things that present themselves to us with a specious appearance of truth but cannot really be affiliated to the axioms. And so moral merit begins when we refuse to love and follow things that are speciously attractive but cannot be affiliated to the love of God. It is not in loving God, then (which is natural to man), but in rejecting all impulses which do not harmonize with that love that man's moral freedom vindicates itself; and it is therein that his merit consists. It is now near midnight; the moon has been some hours above the horizon, but being well advanced in Scorpio, she has risen south of east, and has therefore not yet been visible to the Poets who are facing due north, and who command no portion of the southern semicircle of the horizon; now she emerges from behind the mountain. Dante is dropping into a contented slumber, when he is re-awakened

293

by the rush of the once slothful souls; who will not suspend their act of penance even in order to secure the prayers of the living which would hasten the fruits of their penitence; so they shout their directions and their answers to the questions they have been asked, together with the rehearsal of encouraging and warning examples, as they hurry past. Then Dante sinks through a succession of changing thoughts into dream and sleep.

———————————————

THE LOFTY Teacher had put an end to his argument, and was looking intent in my face, if I seemed satisfied;

and I, whom a new thirst was yet tormenting, was silent outwardly, and within said; "Perchance the too great questioning which I make irks him."

But that true Father, who perceived the shrinking desire which disclosed not itself, by speaking put courage in me to speak.

Wherefore I: "Master, my vision is so quickened in thy light, that I discern clearly all that thy discourse imports or describes;

therefore, I pray thee, sweet Father dear, that thou define love to me, to which thou dost reduce every good work and its opposite."

"Direct," said he, "towards me the keen eyes of the understanding, and the error of the blind who make them guides shall be manifest to thee.

The mind which is created quick to love, is responsive to everything that is pleasing, soon as by pleasure it is awakened into activity.

Your apprehensive faculty draws an impression[1] from a real object, and unfolds it within you, so that it makes the mind turn thereto.

And if, being turned, it inclines towards it, that inclination is love; that is nature, which through pleasure is bound anew within you.

Then, even as fire moves upward by reason of its form,[2] whose nature it is to ascend, there where it endures longest in its material;[3]

so the enamoured mind falls to desire, which is a spiritual

294

movement,[4] and never rests until the object of its love makes it rejoice.

Now may be apparent to thee, how deeply the truth is hidden from the folk who aver that every act of love is in itself a laudable thing,

because, forsooth, its material may seem always to be good; but not every imprint is good, albeit the wax may be good."

"Thy words and my attendant wit," I answered him, "have made love plain to me, but that has made me more teeming with doubt;

for if love is offered to us from without, and the soul walks with no other foot, it is no merit of hers whether she go straight or crooked."

And he to me: "So far as reason sees here, I can tell thee; from beyond that point, ever await Beatrice, for 'tis a matter of faith.

Every substantial form, which is distinct from matter and is in union with it,[5] has a specific virtue contained within itself[6]

which is not perceived save in operation, nor is manifested except by its effects, just as life in a plant by the green leaves.

Therefore man knows not whence the understanding of the first cognitions may come, nor the inclination to the prime objects of appetite,[7]

which are in you, even as the instinct in bees to make honey; and this prime will admits no desert of praise or of blame.

Now in order that to this will every other may be related, innate with you is the virtue which giveth counsel, and ought to guard the threshold of assent.[8]

This is the principle whence is derived the reason of desert in you, according as it garners and winnows good and evil loves.

Those who in their reasoning went to the foundation, perceived this innate freedom, therefore they left ethics to the world.

Wherefore suppose that every love which is kindled

within you arise of necessity, the power to arrest it is within you.

By the noble virtue Beatrice understands Freewill, and therefore, look that thou have this in mind,[9] if she betake her to speak with thee thereof."[10]

The moon, almost retarded to midnight, made the stars appear more thin to us, fashioned like a bucket all burning;

and her course against the heavens was on those paths which the sun inflames, when they in Rome see him between the Sardinians and the Corsicans at his setting.[11]

And that noble shade through whom Pietola[12] is more renowned than any Mantuan town, had put off the burden I had laid upon him;

wherefore I, who had garnered clear and plain reasons to my questionings, stood like one who is rambling drowsily.

But this drowsiness was taken from me on a sudden, by people who behind our backs had already come round to us.

And even as Ismenus and Asopus saw of old a fury and a rout along their banks by night, if but the Thebans had need of Bacchus,[13]

suchwise, along that circle, quickening their pace, were coming, by what I saw of them, those whom good will and just love bestride.

Soon were they upon us, because all that great throng was moving at a run; and two in front were shouting in tears:

"Mary ran with haste to the hill country,"[14] and "Cæsar to subdue Ilerda, stabbed Marseilles and then raced to Spain."[15]

"Haste! Haste! let no time be lost through little love," cried the others afterwards, "that striving to do well may renew grace."

"O people in whom keen fervour now perchance doth make good negligence and delay used by you through lukewarmness in well-doing,

this one who lives, and surely I lie not to you, desires to ascend, if but the sun shine to us again; therefore tell us where the opening is near."

These were my Leader's words; and one of those spirits said: "Come behind us, and thou shalt find the cleft.

We are so filled with desire to speed us, that stay we cannot; therefore forgive, if thou hold our penance for rudeness.

I was Abbot of San Zeno at Verona,[16] under the rule of the good Barbarossa, of whom Milan yet discourses with sorrow.

And one I know has already a foot in the grave, who soon shall mourn because of that monastery, and sad will be for having had power there;

because his son, deformed in his whole body and worse in mind, and who was born in shame, he has put there in place of its true shepherd."

If more he said, or if he was silent, I know not, so far already had he raced beyond us; but this I heard and was pleased to retain.

And he who was my succour in every need, said: "Turn thee hither, see two of them that come biting at sloth."

Last of them all they said: "The people for whom the sea opened, were dead ere Jordan saw its heirs";[17]

and: "That folk who endured not the toil to the end with Anchises' son, gave them up to a life inglorious."[18]

Then, when those shades were so far parted from us, that they could be seen no more, a new thought was set within me,

wherefrom many and divers others sprang; and so from one to another I rambled, that I closed mine eyes for very wandering, and thought I transmuted into dream.

1. The apprehensive faculty receives the impression (*intenzione*) of the concrete thing, form and material alike (see *intention, Par.* xxiv, *note* 8, for this word with a different sense). According to Albertus Magnus, "the intention is not part of the thing like the form, but rather the appearance of the whole thing as apprehended." [Thus, the form of a statue would not be affected by the nature of the material—marble, bronze, &c., but the intention would].—Cf. *Par.* iv, *note* 4.

2. *form*, i.e. its essential principle.

3. The circle of fire.

4. All chance or action is regarded in the Aristotelian philosophy as motion. The act of love is a spiritual as distinct from a local movement.

5. These lines contain a definition of the human soul. Thomas
Aquinus says that "rational souls" are "forms which are in a certain
sense separated, but yet have to abide in material"; which he explains
by adding that the intellect is separated inasmuch as it is not "the
act of any bodily organ, as the visual power is of the eye" (see
Canto xxv, note 6), but is nevertheless the vital principle of a
(human) body. Cf., further, Bonaventura: "Spiritual substances
[i.e., beings] are either completely joined to bodies, as is the case
with brute souls, or joined separately to them, as are rational souls,
or completely separated from them, as are celestial spirits which the
philosophers call intelligence, and we call angels."
6. A power specific to it as a human soul, i.e. belonging to all human
souls and to them only. This specific power is that of the "possible
intellect," better known to students of English literature as the
"discursive" intellect, that is, the intellect which proceeds con-
structively from the known to the unknown, develops itself and
passes from one object to another; as distinct from the "intuitive"
intellect of angels, which understands without process of thought
and embraces all objects of contemplation at once (cf. Par. xxix,
note 6; De Mon. i. 3; Conv. iii. 3; Paradise Lost, v; and see below,
Canto xxv, note 6).
7. The primal or supreme conceptions or notions = the axioms; the
primal or supreme objects of desire = God. The plural form is
doubtless used because the supreme good may present itself in many
forms (goodness, perfect and noble things, blessedness, truth, su-
preme existence, supreme unity, etc.), but all of these "supreme ob-
jects of desire" are not rivals but rays meeting and coinciding in
the focus, God.
8. Ought to be absolute master, whether the will assent or dissent.
9. The Italian idiom reverses our own. Cf. Vita Nuova, § 39: il
cuore intendo per l'appetito, "by the heart I mean the appetite."
10. See Par. v.
11. The setting of the sun between Sardinia and Corsica cannot be
actually seen from Rome, so that the accuracy of this datum would
depend on a rather elaborate calculation, and would be limited by
the accuracy of Dante's knowledge of the exact latitude and longi-
tude of the places in question. The modern astronomers give Sagit-
tarius, but Benvenuto da Imola, who perhaps better reflects the state
of knowledge in Dante's time, gives Scorpio as the position of the
moon indicated. The latter agrees with our other data.
12. Pietola is identical with the classical Andes, Virgil's birthplace.
13. The Thebans, when invoking the aid of Bacchus for their vine-
yards, were wont to crowd to the banks of the Ismenus and Asopus,
rivers of Bœotia, near Thebes (cf. Statius, Theb. ix).
14. After the Annunciation. "And Mary arose in those days, and
went into the hill country with haste, into a city of Juda" (Luke
i. 39).
15. In order to save time, Cæsar left the siege of Marseilles, on which
he had been engaged, in the hands of Brutus, and rushed off to Ilerda

(the modern Lerida) in Catalonia, where he defeated Afranius and Petreius, the lieutenants of Pompey (49 B.C.). Lucan (*Phars.* i) speaks of Cæsar as a thunderbolt.

16. The speaker is a certain Abbot of San Zeno (a church and monastery at Verona), probably Gherardo II, who died in 1187 (during the reign of Frederick Barbarossa, 1152–1190; Milan was destroyed by the Emperor in 1162, and rebuilt in 1169). He upbraids Alberto della Scala (d. 1301), for appointing his illegitimate and depraved son, Giuseppe, to the abbacy of San Zeno. Giuseppe held the office from 1291 till 1314, so that Dante may have known him during his first sojourn at Verona (1303–1304). For the Della Scala family, see the table on page 613.

17. The Israelites who, after being delivered from Pharaoh in the Red Sea, still murmured and refused to follow Moses, whereupon they perished in the desert, before reaching the Promised Land (the Jordan = Palestine). See *Ex.* xiv. 10–20; *Num.* xiv. 1–39; *Deut.* i. 26–36.

18. The Trojans, whom Æneas left behind in Sicily with Acestes—"as many of the people as were willing, souls that had no desire of high renown" (*Æn.* v. cf. *Conv.* iv. 26, where the incident is quoted in proof of Æneas' solicitude for old age).

CANTO XIX

As morning approaches Dante has a vision of the Siren, whose filthiness Virgil, at the exhortation of a lady from heaven, exposes. Dante
is roused by Virgil's repeated summons. The sun is fully up, and the
pilgrim, deep in thought, advances to the next stair, where once
again he feels the breath of the angel's wing, and hears the blessing
of them that mourn. Dante is still plunged in his reverie, from which
Virgil rouses him by question, explanation, and admonition. They
who have yielded to the Siren,—foul but seeming fair,—must expiate their offences in the three remaining circles. Let Dante tread
the earth like a man and raise his eyes to the heavens above. And so
they reach the fifth circle. There the souls of the avaricious and
prodigal cleave to the pavement, no longer in sordid love, but in the
anguished sense that they are unworthy to look upon aught more
fair; and the limbs which had bound themselves on earth are now
held in helpless captivity. Virgil inquires the way, and from the form
in which the answer is given Dante gathers the law of Purgatory,
hereafter to be more fully confirmed, which permits souls to pass
without delay or scathe through any circles of the mount wherein
sins are purged by which they themselves are unstained. He silently
asks Virgil's leave to stay and question the soul that has spoken. It
is Pope Adrian V who for little over a month bore the weight of
the papal mantle, scarce tolerable to him who would keep it from
defilement; and in answer to Dante's tender entreaty he expounds
the nature of the penalties of this circle. He himself had been given
over to avarice till he reached the summit of human greatness, saw
its emptiness and turned in penitence to God. When Dante speaks
again, Adrian perceives that he has knelt down, in reverence to
Peter's successor; whereon he bluntly bids him straighten his legs,
and explains that no formal or official position or relation, however
close or however august, has place in the spirit world, where personality is stripped of office. Then he urges Dante to pass on and leave
his penitence undisturbed, making a reference to his niece who had
married one of Dante's future friends the Malaspini; which reference the pilgrim may, if he so choose, interpret as a request for prayers for the departed soul.

IN THE HOUR when the day's heat, overcome by Earth or at times by Saturn, can no more warm the cold of the moon;

when the geomancers see their Fortuna Major, rising in the East, before the dawn, by a way which short time remains dark to it,[1]

there came to me in a dream,[2] a stuttering woman, with eyes asquint, and crooked on her feet, with maimed hands, and of sallow hue.

I gazed upon her; and as the sun comforteth the cold limbs which night weighs down, so my look made ready her tongue, and then set her full straight in short time, and her pallid face even as love wills did colour.

When she had her tongue thus loosed, she began to sing, so that with difficulty should I have turned my attention from her.

"I am," she sang, "I am the sweet Siren, who leads mariners astray in mid-sea, so full am I of pleasantness to hear.

I turned Ulysses from his wandering way with my song, and whoso liveth with me rarely departs, so wholly do I satisfy him."

Her mouth was not yet shut, when a lady appeared holy and alert alongside me, to put her to confusion.

"O Virgil, Virgil, who is this?" angrily she said; and he came with eyes ever fixed on that honest one.

He seized the other, and, rending her clothes, laid her open in front and showed me her belly; that awakened me with the stench which issued therefrom.

I turned my eyes, and the good Virgil said: "At least three calls have I uttered to thee; arise and come, find we the opening by which thou mayst enter."

Up I lifted me, and all the circles of the holy mount were now filled with the high day, and we journeyed with the new sun at our backs.[3]

Following him, I was bearing my brow like one that hath it burdened with thought, who makes of himself half an arch of a bridge,

when I heard: "Come, here is the pass," spoken in a tone so gentle and kind as is not heard in this mortal confine.

With outspread wings which swanlike seemed, he who thus spoke to us did turn us upward, between the two walls of the hard stone.

He stirred his pinions then, and fanned us, affirming *qui lugent* to be blessed, for they shall have their souls rich in consolation.[4]

"What aileth thee, that thou gazest ever to the ground?" my Guide began to say to me; both of us having mounted a little above the angel.

And I: "In such dread I am made to go by a strange vision,[2] which bends me to itself, so that I cannot keep me from thinking thereon."

"Sawest thou," he said, "that ancient witch because of whom alone above us now they weep? Sawest thou how man frees him from her?

Let that suffice thee, and spurn the earth with thy heels, turn thine eyes to the lure which the eternal King spinneth round with the mighty spheres."

Like the falcon, that first gazes at his feet, then turns at the call, and spreads his wings with desire of the repast which draws him there,

such I became; and, far as the rock is cleft to give passage to him who mounts, such I went, up to where the circling is begun.

When I was in the open, on the fifth circle, I saw people about it who wept, lying on the ground all turned downwards.

"*Adhæsit pavimento anima mea*,"[5] I heard them say with such deep sighs that hardly were the words understood.

"O chosen of God, whose sufferings both justice and hope make less hard, direct us towards the high ascents."

"If ye come secure from lying prostrate, and desire to find the way most quickly, let your right hands be ever to the outside."[6]

Thus prayed the poet, and thus a little in front of us was answer made; wherefore I noted what else was concealed in the words,[7]

and turned mine eyes then to my Lord; whereat he gave assent with glad sign to what the look of my desire was craving.

When I could do with me according to my own mind, I drew forward above that creature whose words before made me take note,

saying: "Spirit, in whom weeping matures that without which one cannot turn to God, stay a while for me thy greater care.

Who thou wast, and why ye have your backs turned upward, tell me, and if thou wouldst that I obtain aught for thee yonder, whence living I set forth."

And he[8] to me: "Wherefore heaven turneth our backs to itself shalt thou know; but first, *scias quod ego fui successor Petri*.

Between Sestri and Chiaveri flows down a fair river, and from its name the title of my race takes origin.

One month, and little more, I learned how the great mantle weighs on him who keeps it from the mire, so that all other burdens seem feathers.

My conversion, ah me! was late; but when I was made Pastor of Rome, so I discovered the life which is false.

I saw that there the heart was not at rest, nor could one mount higher in that life; wherefore love of this was kindled within me.

Up to that moment, I was a soul wretched and parted from God, wholly avaricious; now, as thou seest, here am I punished for it.

What avarice works, here is declared in the purgation of the down-turned souls, and no more bitter penalty hath the mount.

Even as our eye, fixed on earthly things, did not lift itself on high, so here justice hath sunk it to earth.

As avarice quenched our love for every good, wherefore our works were lost, so justice here doth hold us fast,

bound and seized by feet and hands; and so long as it shall be the pleasure of the just Lord, so long shall we lie here motionless and outstretched."

I had kneeled down, and was about to speak; but as I began, and he perceived my reverence merely by listening,

"What reason," he said, "thus bent thee down?" And I to him: "Because of your dignity my conscience smote me for standing."

"Make straight thy legs, uplift thee, brother," he answered; "err not, a fellow-servant am I with thee and with the others unto one Power.

If ever thou didst understand that hallowed gospel sound which saith, *'Neque nubent,'* well canst thou see why thus I speak.[9]

Now get thee hence; I desire not that thou stay longer, for thy tarrying disturbs my weeping, whereby I mature that which thou didst say.[10]

A niece have I yonder, by name Alagia, good in herself, if but our house make her not evil by ensample; and she alone is left me yonder."

1. An hour before dawn when the last stars of Aquarius and the first of Pisces would have risen. The portions of the constellations indicated may be conceived in the form : : : · · this being the figure termed *Fortuna Major* in geomancy (an occult science by which events are predicted according to points placed in certain positions). Reference is to the coldness of the earth before dawn, and of the frigid Saturn (Virgil's *Frigida Saturni . . . stella, Georg.* i; *cf. Par.* xviii, *note* 4, and xxii, *note* 13); *at times, i.e.,* when this planet is on the horizon.

2. Dante's second dream, that of the Siren (Sensual Pleasure) has reference to the three sins that remain to be purged: avarice, gluttony, and lust being conceived as due to the wiles of the Siren. The *lady* probably stands for the light of reason, which unites with human wisdom (Virgil; *cf. Inf.* i, *note* 10) in showing Dante the emptiness of sensual delights. There is a difficulty here: for, according to Homer, Ulysses, of course, withstood the Sirens. Dr. Moore suggests that Dante's knowledge of the episode is derived from a passage in which Cicero, commenting on Homer's Song of the Sirens, implies that Ulysses was ensnared by them (*De Finibus,* v). For the rest, *cf. Inf.* xxvi, *notes* 6 and 9.

3. See diagram on p. 200.

4. "Blessed are they that mourn: for they shall be comforted" (*Matt.* v. 4).

5. "My soul cleaveth unto the dust" (*Ps.* cxix. 25).

6. The speaker is Pope Adrian V (see *note* 8).

7. This line has been much discussed. We take the "concealed" or "implied" thing, which was involved in the direct answer to the question, to be a revelation of the fact that souls are purged in as many circles as may be necessary, but that some may pass free through certain circles, if they have not been guilty of the sins purified in them. This is the first indication in the poem of this fact; but it is illustrated later on by Statius rising from the circle of the Avaricious and making his way straight through the two that are

left, perhaps delaying his course somewhat for the sake of Virgil's company (Canto xxiv), but not retarded to endure the penalties of the circles. Dante has already indicated (Canto xiii) his anticipation of the necessity of sinful souls being purged severally in the successive terraces, and Statius' confession (Cantos xxi and xxii) subsequently confirms it. But this is the first passage which indicates the possibility of souls passing through any circle without enduring its penalties.

8. Ottobuono de' Fieschi (of Genoa), who had, while Cardinal, been sent to England as Papal legate (1268), was elected Pope, as Adrian V, on July 12, 1276, and died on August 18 of the same year. The Fieschi were Counts of Lavagna, and derived their title from a little river of that name, which flows into the Gulf of Genoa between Sestri Levante and Chiavari. The words ("Know that I was a successor of Peter") are spoken in Latin, as the official language of the Church and Popes.

Adrian's niece, Alagia, was the wife of Moroello III Malaspina (for whom see Canto viii, *note 5*). One of her sisters, Fiesca, married Alberto, belonging to a different branch of the Malaspina family; and the other, Jacopina, was the wife of Obizzo II of Este (see the tables on pp. 611, 617, 619 and 620).

9. The Sadducees, having told Jesus of a woman who had married seven brothers in succession, and asked him: "Therefore in the resurrection whose wife shall be of the seven? for they all had her." Jesus answered and said unto them, "Ye do err, not knowing the scriptures, nor the power of God. For in the resurrection they neither marry, nor are given in marriage, but are as the angels of God in heaven" (*Matt.* xxii. 23–30; *Mark* xii. 18–25; *Luke* xx. 27–35). The passage is usually taken to refer specifically to the Pope as the spouse of the Church (*cf. Inf.* xix; *Purg.* xxiv). But surely it may be taken with a wider reference. Marriage is regarded as the closest instance of special relations which have some legal or official sanction over and above the purely personal relations on which they are based, or which spring out of them. All such relations are abolished in the spirit world (*cf. Par.* vi and other passages).

10. The fruit of repentance.

ÇANTO XX

Unwilling to break short his conference, but more unwilling yet further to trespass on the courteous forbearance of his interlocutor, Dante passes among the weeping souls, through whose eyes that curse of all the world is distilling itself away! When will He come who shall chase the wolf of avarice from earth? Dante hears one of the prostrate souls rehearse examples of generous poverty, and learns that he is the ancestor of the royal line of France, the root of that evil tree that darkens all the Christian lands with its shadow. Comparatively harmless in its earlier generations, this house had gathered evil as it gathered strength; hero and saint alike have been its victims; it couched the lance of Judas against Florence; its own flesh and blood and the sacred orders of chivalry are alike regarded by it as things to coin; and the very person of the Vicar of Christ has been crucified by it while thieves were left alive. At such deeds wrath would torture the divine peace itself were it not soothed by the prospect of vengeance. Warning examples of avarice uttered at night balance the daily recitation of the virtuous counterparts. The mountain now shakes as with an earthquake, and a mighty cry of "Glory to God in the highest" rises from all its terraces; startled and perplexed by which, though bidden by Virgil not to fear, Dante swiftly pursues his path.

AGAINST A BETTER will fights ill, wherefore, against my pleasure, to please him, I drew the sponge from the water unfilled.

I moved on, and my Leader moved on by the free spaces, ever along the rock, as one goes by a wall close to the battlements;

for the people who distil through their eyes, drop by drop, the evil that fills the whole world, on the other side approach too near the edge.

Accurst be thou, she-wolf of old, that hast more prey than all the other beasts, for thy hunger endlessly deep!

O heaven, in whose revolution it seems that conditions

here below are thought to be changed, when will he come through whom she shall depart?[1]

We went on, with steps slow and scant, and I intent on the shades that I heard piteously weeping and complaining;

and by chance I heard one in front of us calling with tears: "Sweet Mary," even as a woman who is in travail;

and continuing: "So poor wast thou, as may be seen by that hostelry where thou didst lay down thy holy burden."[2]

Following I heard: "O good Fabricius, thou didst desire to possess virtue with poverty, rather than great riches with iniquity."[3]

These words were so pleasing to me, that I drew me forward to have knowledge of that spirit, from whom they seemed to have come.

It went on to speak of the bounty which Nicholas gave to the maidens, to lead their youth to honour.[4]

"O spirit, that discoursest so much of good, tell me who thou wast," said I, "and wherefore thou alone renewest these worthy lauds?

Thy words shall not be without reward, if I return to complete the short way of that life which is flying to its end."

And he:[5] "I will tell it thee, not for any solace that I expect from yonder, but because so much grace shineth in thee ere thou art dead.

I was the root of the evil tree which o'ershadows all Christian lands, so that rarely is good fruit plucked therefrom.

But if Douay, Lille, Ghent and Bruges had power, soon were vengeance taken for it,[6] and I beseech this from him who judgeth all.

Hugh Capet was I called yonder; of me are born the Philips and the Lewises by whom of late France is ruled.[7]

Son was I of a butcher of Paris. When the ancient kings came to an end, all save one given over to grey garments,[8]

I found tight in my hands the reins of the government of the realm, and so much power from new possessions, and so rich in friends, that to my son's head the widowed crown was promoted from whom began the consecrated bones of those.

So long as the great dowry of Provence[9] had not taken shame from my race, it was of little worth, but yet it did no evil.

There by force and fraud its rapine began; and then, for amends,[10] Ponthieu and Normandy it seized, and Gascony.[11]

Charles came to Italy, and, for amends, made a victim of Conradin;[12] and then thrust Thomas back to heaven,[13] for amends.

A time I see, not long after this day, that brings another Charles forth from France,[14] to make both him and his better known.

Forth he comes, alone, without an army, and with the lance wherewith Judas jousted; and that he couches so, that he makes the paunch of Florence to burst.

Thence shall he win, not land, but sin and shame, for himself so much the more grievous, as he the more lightly counts such wrong.

The other,[15] who once came forth a captive from a ship, I see selling his daughter, and haggling over her, as pirates do with other bondwomen.

O avarice, what more canst thou do to us, since thou hast so drawn my race to thee, that it hath no care of its own flesh?

In order that the ill to come and past, may seem less, I see the fleur-de-lys enter Alagna, and in his vicar Christ made captive.[16]

A second time I see him mocked; I see the vinegar and the gall renewed, and him slain between living thieves.

I see the new Pilate so cruel, that this sateth him not, but, lawlessly, he bears his greedy sails into the temple.[17]

O my Lord, when shall I rejoice to see the vengeance, which, being hidden, maketh sweet thine anger in thy secret counsel?[18]

What I was saying of that only Bride of the Holy Ghost, and which made thee turn toward me for some gloss,[19]

so much is the answer to all our prayers, as long as the

day last; but when the night cometh, a contrary sound we take up instead of that.

Then we rehearse Pygmalion,[20] whom insatiate lust of gold made traitor, thief, and parricide,

and the misery of the avaricious Midas,[21] which followed his greedy request, because of which 'tis right we forever laugh.

The mad Achan then each one recalls, how he stole the spoils, so that Joshua's wrath seems here yet to bite him.[22]

Then we accuse Sapphira and her husband;[23] we praise the kicks which Heliodorus[24] had; and all the mount doth circle in infamy

Polymnestor who slew Polydorus.[25] Last of all here we cry: 'Crassus, tell us, for thou knowest, of what savour is gold?'[26]

Sometimes we discourse, the one loud the other low, according to the impulse which spurs us to speak, now with greater, now with lesser force;

therefore at the good we tell of here by day, I was not alone before, but here, near by, no other person was raising his voice."

We were already parted from him, and striving to surmount the way so far as was permitted to our power,

when I felt the mountain quake, like a thing which is falling;[27] whereupon a chill gripped me, as is wont to grip him who is going to death.

Of a surety, Delos was not shaken so violently, ere Latona made her nest therein to give birth to heaven's two eyes.[28]

Then began on all sides a shout, such that the Master drew toward me, saying: "Fear not while I do guide thee."

"*Gloria in excelsis Deo,*"[29] all were saying, by what I understood from those near by, whose cry could be heard.

Motionless we stood, and in suspense, like the shepherds who first heard that hymn, until the quaking ceased and it was ended.

Then we took up again our holy way, looking at the shades, that lay on the ground already returned to their wonted plaint.

No ignorance, if my memory err not in this, did ever
with so great assault give me yearning for knowledge

as I then seemed to have, while pondering; nor by reason
of our haste was I bold to ask; nor of myself could I see
aught there: thus I went on timid and pensive.

1. The *evil* and the *she-wolf of old* are, of course, Avarice (see *Inf.*
i); while the deliverer anxiously alluded to corresponds to the *Grey-
hound* of *Inf.* i, though the indication here is less definite than in
the earlier passage—perhaps because Dante was beginning to lose
hope at the time of the composition of the present canto? See also
Canto xvi.
2. "And she brought forth her first-born son, and wrapped him in
swaddling clothes, and laid him in a manger; because there was no
room for them in the inn" (*Luke* ii. 7).—*Cf. Par.* xv and *note* 14.
3. Caius Fabricius, the Roman Consul (282 B.C.) and Censor (275
B.C.), refused the gifts of the Samnites on settling terms of peace
with them, and, subsequently, the bribes of Pyrrhus, King of Epirus,
when negotiating with him concerning an exchange of friends.
Virgil's words in this connection—*parvoque potentem Fabricium*
(*Æn.* vi) are quoted in the *De Mon.* ii. 5; and in the *Conv.* iv. 5,
there is a further allusion to Fabricius' refusal of the bribes (here he
is mentioned together with Curius Dentatus; as by Lucan, *Phars.* x,
who quotes the pair for their simplicity of manners and contempt
of luxury—*et nomina pauperis ævi Fabricios Curiosque graves*).
4. Nicholas (4th century), Bishop of Myra in Lycia) saved the three
daughters of a fellow-townsman, who was in dire straits of poverty,
from leading lives of shame, by secretly throwing into their window
at night bags of gold, which served them as dowries and enabled
them to marry (see the *Legenda Aurea* and *Brev. Rom.* ad 6
Decemb.).
5. The speaker is Hugh Capet, King of France (987–996); but as
some of the details given by Dante can apply only to his father,
Hugh the Great (Duke of the Franks, etc., and Count of Paris, d.
956), it is plain that the Poet has confused these two personages. We
find here a legend very generally accredited in those days, but
always referred to the father, never to the son. It is stated that when
the Carlovingian dynasty came to an end (with Louis V, d. 987),
the speaker's son succeeded, whereas in reality it was Hugh Capet
himself who succeeded. And it was Hugh Capet who founded the
Capetian dynasty, not his son and successor, Robert I.
6. The treachery of Philip the Fair and his brother Charles of Valois
towards the Count of Flanders in 1299 (Villani, viii) was avenged
three years later at the battle of Courtrai, in which the French were
completely routed by the Flemish (Villani, viii).
7. Between the years 1060 and 1300, the French throne was occupied
exclusively by four Philips (I–IV) and four Louis' (VI–IX).
8. When Louis V died in 987 without children there was only one

formidable Carlovingian left—Charles, Duke of Lorraine, the son of Louis IV. Hugh Capet, seeing the danger, promptly had him put into prison, where he died in 991. Dante is wrong in saying that Charles was a monk; there is probably a confusion with Childeric III, the last of the Merovingians, who was deposed in 752 and ended his days in a convent.

9. After the death of Count Raymond Berengar of Provence, Charles I of Anjou married, in 1246, his daughter, Beatrice, who had inherited the county (see Canto vii, note 10, and Par. vi, note 13).

10. Note the irony of the for amends, thrice repeated.

11. A reference to the English chronicles and histories will show that Dante does not adhere strictly to the correct chronology in this line, and that the origin of the differences between the French and English Kings alluded to goes back to a date earlier than that of the great dowry of Provence. However, he is right in all the essential facts, which held good, as stated by him, for many years. Thus, Villani says that Edward III, when on the point of invading France in 1346, told his barons that the French King "was wrongfully occupying Gascony, and the county of Ponthieu, which came to him [Edward] with the dowry of his mother, and that he was holding Normandy by fraud" (xii).

12. For Charles of Anjou's expedition to Italy, see Canto iii, note 7; and for the battle of Tagliacozzo, in which he defeated Conradin, the last of the Swabians, see Inf. xxviii, note 1. On October 29, 1268 two months after his defeat, Conradin, who was in his seventeenth year, was beheaded by Charles' orders.

13. Dante here follows a popular but erroneous tradition (see Villani, ix), according to which Thomas Aquinas, while proceeding to the Council of Lyons in 1274, was poisoned in the Abbey of Fossanuova, at the instigation of Charles of Anjou.

14. Charles of Valois, the brother of Philip the Fair, entered Florence, with some nobles and 500 horsemen, on November 1, 1301, and left the city on April 4 of the following year. For the success of the Blacks over the Whites, which was solely due to the favour he treacherously showed to the former party (at the instigation of Boniface VIII, who had sent him to Florence ostensibly as "peacemaker"), see Inf. vi. note 3, and Gardner, pp. 21–23. Charles was nicknamed "Lack-land," perhaps because of the ignominious failure of his expedition to Sicily in 1302, or because he was a younger son.

15. While Charles the Lame (see Canto vii, note 10; Par. vi, note 11) was assisting his father, Charles I of Anjou, in his futile attempt to recover Sicily, he was defeated by Roger di Loria, the admiral of Peter III of Aragon, and taken prisoner (June, 1284). In 1305 he married his youngest daughter, Beatrice, to Azzo VIII of Este, who was her senior by many years. We have no record of the monetary transaction which excited Dante's wrath.

16. For Boniface VIII (the cause of most of Dante's troubles, whom the Poet invariably condemns, but whose death is in the present

passage treated as an outrage on the Holy See) see *Inf.* vi, xix, xxvii; *Purg.* viii (?), xxxii, xxxiii; *Par.* xii, xvii, xxvii, xxx.

"Sciarra Colonna and William de Nogaret, [the *living thieves*] in the name of Philip the Fair [the *fleur-de-lys*] seized Boniface VIII at Anagni [the Pope's birthplace, about forty miles south-east of Rome] and treated the old Pontiff with such barbarity that he died at Rome in a few days, October 11th, 1303" (Gardner, p. 26; see Villani, viii).

17. Philip the Fair (who is called *new Pilate* because he delivered Boniface to his enemies, the Colonnesi, even as Pilate delivered Jesus to the will of the Jews) caused the Order of the Templars to be persecuted, from the year 1307. According to Villani (viii), many people held that the accusations levied against them were unjust, and prompted only by the desire to obtain their treasure.

18. *Cf. Par.* xxii.

19. Hugh is answering Dante's earlier question and relating the example drawn from the life of Mary among others.

20. According to Canto xii, *note* 1, the groups of the examples of vice are, on this fifth terrace, marked off by "putting *together* two or more instances from Profane and Sacred History respectively, instead of making the instances alternate" (E. Moore).

Pygmalion, the brother of Dido, and murderer of her husband (their uncle), Sichæus. "He, impious, and blinded with the love of gold, having taken Sichæus by surprise, secretly assassinates him before the altar, regardless of his sister's great affection" (*Æn.* i).

21. Bacchus was so grateful to Midas, King of Phrygia, for the kindness he had shown to his friend Silenus, that he promised to grant him any request. Midas wished everything he touched to be turned to gold, but soon begged Bacchus to relieve him of this privilege, when he found that even his food changed into the precious metal. It is somewhat strange that Dante should consider this incident laughable; the only really funny thing about Midas (which however, has nothing to do with greed of gold) being the asses' ears, that were bestowed on him by Apollo, for presuming to decide against him and in favour of Pan after a singing contest. (See Ovid, *Met.* xi.)

22. At the capture of Jericho, Joshua ordered all the treasure to be consecrated to the Lord; which decree having been disregarded by Achan, he and his family were stoned and burned (*Josh.* vi and vii).

23. After the Apostles had preached to the people, "the multitude of them that believed were of one heart and of one soul: neither said any of them that ought of the things which he possessed was his own; but they had all things common ... and great grace was upon them all. Neither was there any among them that lacked: for as many as were possessors of lands or houses sold them, and brought the prices of the things that were sold, and laid them down at the apostles' feet: and distribution was made unto every man according as he had need. And Joses ... having land, sold it, and brought the money, and laid it at the apostles' feet. But a certain man named

Ananias, with Sapphira his wife, sold a possession, and kept back part of the price, his wife also being privy to it, and brought a certain part, and laid it at the apostles' feet." Ananias and his wife were rebuked by Peter for their hypocrisy, and fell down dead. (See *Acts* iv. 32-37; v. 1-11.)

24. Heliodorus, the treasurer of King Seleucus, having gone with his guard to the Temple of Jerusalem, to remove the treasure, "there appeared unto them an horse with a terrible rider upon him, and adorned with a very fair covering, and he ran fiercely, and smote at Heliodorus with his forefeet, and it seemed that he that sat upon the horse had complete harness of gold" (2 *Macc.* iii. 25).

25. "This Polydore unhappy Priam had formerly sent in secrecy, with a great weight of gold, to be brought up by the King of Thrace [Polymnestor], when he now began to distrust the arms of Troy, and saw the city with close siege blocked up. He, as soon as the power of the Trojans was crushed, and their fortune gone, espousing Agamemnon's interest and victorious arms, breaks every sacred bond, assassinates Polydore, and by violence possesses his gold. Cursed thirst of gold, to what dost thou not drive the hearts of men!" (*Æn.* iii.)

26. Marcus Licinius Crassus, surnamed *Dives*, the Wealthy, was triumvir with Cæsar and Pompey, 60 B.C. He was so notorious for his love of gold, that when he had been slain in a battle with the Parthians, their King, Hyrodes, had molten gold poured down his throat. Florus (*Epitome*, iii) says that his head . . . *ludibrio fuit, neque indigno. Aurum enim liquidum in rictum oris infusum est, ut cujus animus arserat auri cupiditate, ejus etiam mortuum et exsangue corpus auro ureretur.*

27. See the following canto.

28. Juno, being jealous of Jupiter's love for Latona, drove the latter from place to place, till she reached Delos, which had been a floating island, tossing about in the sea, till Jupiter made it fast in order to receive her. Here she bore him two children—Apollo and Diana—the sun and the moon (*cf. Par.* x, xxii, xxix). See Ovid, *Met.* vi.

29. "Glory to God in the highest, and on earth peace, good will toward men" (see *Luke* ii. 8-14).

ÇANTO XXI

With the thirst for knowledge, which God only can slake, keen within him, hastening along the impeded path to keep pace with his leader, and pierced with sympathetic grief for the souls at his feet, Dante pursues his way, till a shade coming behind them gives them the salutation of peace, to which Virgil answers. They are on the western side of the mountain, and the sun still neighbours the east, so that Dante casts no shadow, and the new-come soul does not recognize him as one still living in the first life; and so he gathers from the words of Virgil's benediction that he and his companion alike are souls excluded from bliss. In answer to the question that hereon arises, Virgil explains his own state and Dante's; and to the keen satisfaction of the latter, asks in his turn for an explanation of the earthquake and the shout. The shade answers that no material or casual thing can affect the sacred ways of the mount. It trembles only when some soul rises from lying prone with the avaricious, or starts from any other point of the mount to ascend to the earthly Paradise. The repentant souls, though they wish to gain the term and gather the fruit of their penance, are meanwhile as keen to suffer as once they were to sin; and when their present impulse unites with their ultimate desire and creates the instant will to rise, this in itself is a token and assurance that their purgation is complete, and the whole mountain rings with the praises of the spirits. May they, too, soon be sped upon their way! Virgil now asks the shade to reveal himself, and learns that he is the poet Statius. He combines with an enumeration of his own works a glowing tribute to the Æneid and its author; to have lived on earth with whom he would accept another year of exile. Virgil's glance checks the smile that rises on Dante's face at these words, but not till Statius has caught its flash upon his features. Pressed on either side, the Poet is finally released from Virgil's prohibition, and informs Statius that he is indeed in the presence of that very one who strengthened him to sing of men and gods; whereon Statius, forgetting that he and Virgil are empty shades, drops at his dear master's feet to kiss them.

THE NATURAL thirst which never is sated,[1] save with the water whereof the poor Samaritan woman asked the grace,[2]

was burning within me, and haste was goading me along the encumbered way behind my Leader, and I was grieving at the just penance;

and lo, even as Luke writes to us that Christ appeared to the two who were on the way,[3] already risen from the mouth of the tomb,

a shade[4] appeared to us, and came on behind us, gazing at its feet on the prostrate crowd, nor did we perceive it until it first spake,

saying: "My brothers, God give you peace." Quickly we turned us, and Virgil gave back to him the sign that is fitting thereto.[5]

Then began: "May the true court, which binds me in eternal exile, bring thee in peace to the council of the blest."

"How," said he, and meantime we went sturdily, "if ye are shades that God deigns not above, who hath escorted you so far by his stairs?"

And my Teacher: "If thou lookest at the marks which this man bears, and which the angel outlines, clearly wilt thou see 'tis meet he reign with the good.

But since she who spins day and night, had not yet drawn for him the fibre which Clotho charges and packs on the distaff for each one,[6]

his spirit, which is thy sister and mine, coming up, could not come along, because it sees not after our fashion:[7]

wherefore I was brought forth from Hell's wide jaws to guide him, and I will guide him onward, so far as my school can lead him.[8]

But tell us, if thou knowest, why the mount gave before such shakings, and wherefore all seemed to shout with one voice down to its soft base."

Thus, by asking, did he thread the very needle's eye of my desire, and with the hope alone my thirst was made less fasting.

That spirit began: "The holy rule of the mount suffereth naught that is arbitrary, or that is outside custom.

315

Here it is free from all terrestrial change; that which Heaven receives into itself from itself[9] may here operate as cause, and naught else:

since neither rain, nor hail, nor snow, nor dew, nor hoarfrost, falls any higher than the short little stairway of the three steps.

Clouds, dense or thin, appear not, nor lightning flash, nor Thaumas' daughter,[10] who yonder oft changes her region.

Dry vapour rises not higher than the top of the three steps which I spake of, where Peter's vicar hath his feet.

It quakes perchance lower down little or much, but by reason of wind which is hidden in the earth, I know not how, it has never quaked up here.

It quakes here when some soul feeleth herself cleansed, so that she may rise up, or set forth, to mount on high, and such a shout follows her.

Of the cleansing the will alone gives proof, which fills the soul, all free to change her cloister, and avails her to will.

She wills indeed before,[11] but that desire permits it not which divine justice sets, counter to will, toward the penalty, even as it was toward the sin.

And I who have lain under this torment five hundred years and more, only now felt free will for a better threshold.

Therefore didst thou feel the earthquake, and hear the pious spirits about the mount give praises to that Lord—soon may he send them above."

Thus he spake to us; and since we enjoy most the draught in proportion as our thirst is great, I could not tell how much he profited me.

And the wise Leader: "Now I see the net that catches you here, and how one breaks through, wherefore it quakes here. and whereat ye make glad together.

Now may it please thee that I know who thou wast; and why thou hast lain here so many ages, let me learn from thy words."

"What time the good Titus with help of the Highest

King avenged the wounds whence issued the blood by
Judas sold,

with the name which most endures, and honours most,'
answered that spirit, "I was yonder, great in fame, but not
yet with faith.

So sweet was the music of my words, that me, a Tou-
lousian, Rome drew to herself, where I did merit a crown
of myrtle for my brow.

Statius folk yonder still do name me; I sang of Thebes,
and then of the great Achilles; but I fell by the way with
the second burden.

The sparks, which warmed me, from the divine flame
whence more than a thousand have been kindled, were the
seeds of my poetic fire:

of the Æneid I speak, which was a mother to me, and
was to me a nurse in poesy; without it I had not stayed the
weight of a drachm.

And to have lived yonder, when Virgil was alive, I
would consent to one sun more than I owe to my coming
forth from exile."

These words turned Virgil to me with a look that si-
lently said: "Be silent." But the virtue which wills is not all
powerful;

for laughter and tears follow so closely the passion from
which each springs, that they least obey the will in the
most truthful.

I did but smile, like one who makes a sign: whereat the
shade was silent and looked at me in the eyes, where most
the soul is fixed.

And he said: "So may such great toil achieve its end;
wherefore did thy face but now display to me a flash of
laughter?"

Now am I caught on either side; one makes me keep
silence, the other conjures me to speak; wherefore I sigh
and am understood

by my Master, and he said to me, "Have no fear of speak-
ing, but speak, and tell him that which he asketh with so
great desire."

Wherefore I: "Perchance thou dost marvel, O ancient

spirit, at the laugh I gave, but I desire that yet greater wonder seize thee.

He who guideth mine eyes on high, is that Virgil from whom thou drewest power to sing of men and gods.

If thou didst believe other cause for my laughter, set it aside as untrue, and believe it was those words which thou spakest of him."

Already was he stooping to embrace my Teacher's feet; but he said: "Brother, do not so, for thou art a shade and a shade thou seest."

And he, rising: "Now canst thou comprehend the measure of the love which warms me toward thee, when I forget our nothingness, and treat shades as a solid thing."

1. Dante begins his *Convito* by quoting Aristotle's words (*Metaphysics*, i), that "all men naturally desire knowledge."
2. See *John* iv. 7–15: "Whosover drinketh of the water that I shall give him shall never thirst; . . . The woman saith unto him, Sir, give me this water, that I thirst not. . . ."
3. *Luke* xxiv. 13–15: "And, behold, two of them went that same day to a village called Emmaus, which was from Jerusalem about threescore furlongs. And they talked together of all these things which had happened. And it came to pass, that, while they communed together and reasoned, Jesus himself drew near, and went with them."
4. This is the poet Statius, who remains with Dante till the end of the *Cantica* (see Canto xxxiii). He was born at Naples about the year 50, and died there *ca.* 96. In making Statius a native of Toulouse, Dante follows a common medieval error, probably due to a confusion with the poet's contemporary. Lucius Statius, the rhetorician, who really was born at Toulouse. The poet lived mostly at Rome during the reign of Vespasian (69–79), whose son, Titus, captured Jerusalem in the year 70 (*cf. Par.* vi and vii). The *name* is, of course, that of poet. Statius was author of the *Thebaid* and of the fragmentary *Achilleid*, which deal with the expedition of the Seven against Thebes and the Trojan war, respectively, and with which Dante was well acquainted. [The MS of the *Silvæ* was not discovered till the beginning of the 15th century.]
5. The early commentators, who probably knew best, say that the regular "countersign" consisted of the words—"And with thy spirit."
6. Clotho prepared the thread of life, which was spun by Lachesis and cut by Atropos (*cf. Inf.* xxxiii; *Purg.* xxv).
7. Being still chained to its body.
8. *Cf.* Canto xviii.

9. A human soul (see Canto xvi).

10. Iris, the daughter of Thaumas and Electra. In classical mythology she personified the rainbow, and was represented as the messenger of the gods (*cf. Par.* xii, xxviii, xxxiii).

11. Compare the distinction made between the absolute and the practical will, in *Par.* iv.

ÇANTO XXII

The pilgrims have already begun to mount the stair that leads to the sixth circle. Another P has been struck by an angel-wing from Dante's brow, and the blessing pronounced on those that thirst after righteousness. Virgil, with friendly insistence, presses to know how so great a soul as that of Statius could have harboured so puny a vice as avarice; whereon the other acknowledges with a smile the tender friendliness which this very perplexity implies, but answers that the keen scent of friendship is this time following a false track, for it is prodigality, not avarice, that has kept him more than five hundred years a prisoner in the fifth circle, where the two opposing sins are punished together. Nor had he escaped the pains of Hell for his offence, though committed in ignorance, had he not read a hidden warning in lines of Virgil's own. Virgil goes on to ask how Statius became a Christian, for there is no indication in his poems of his conversion; and Statius answers that it was Virgil's self who, like one passing through the night, bearing a lantern behind him, had lightened the path for the feet of others, though not for his own. It was that prophetic Eclogue which had revealed the truth to him, and won his sympathy for the persecuted saints; but he concealed his faith, and had atoned for his laggard love in the circle of the slothful for over four hundred years. Statius in his turn now questions Virgil as to the fate of other Latin poets, and Virgil tells him of the sad and noble life in Limbo, of the Greek and Latin poets there, and of the heroic souls whose story Statius himself had told. It is past ten o'clock in the morning when the pilgrims issue upon the sixth terrace, and, with the tacit approval of Statius, follow their usual course with the sun counter-clockwise, Dante eagerly hearkening to the converse of the two Latin poets. This is the circle of the gluttons; and the pilgrims encounter a wondrous tree, fruit-laden, and bedewed with clear water from a neighbouring fall, from the midst of the foliage of which a voice recites examples of abstinence.

ALREADY was the angel left behind us, the angel that had turned us to the sixth circle, having erased a scar from my face.

and had said to us that those who have their desire to righteousness were blessed, and his words accomplished that with *sitiunt*, and naught else.[1]

And I, lighter than by the other passages, went on so that without any toil I was following the fleet spirits upward,

when Virgil began: "Love, kindled by virtue, hath ever kindled other love, if but its flame were shown forth:

wherefore from that hour when Juvenal,[2] who made thy affection manifest to me, descended among us in the limbo of Hell

my good will towards thee hath been such as never yet did bind to an unseen person, so that now these stairs will seem short to me.

But tell me, and as a friend forgive me if too great confidence slacken my rein, and talk with me now as with a friend:

how could avarice find place in thy breast, amid so much wisdom as by thy diligence thou wast filled with?"

These words first moved Statius a little to laughter; then he answered: "Every word of thine is a precious token of love to me.

Truly many times things appear that give false matter for doubting, because of the true reasons which are hidden.

Thy question proves to me thy belief to be, that I was avaricious in the other life, perchance because of that circle where I was.

Now know that avarice was too far parted from me, and this excess thousands of moons have punished;

and were it not that I set straight my inclination, when I gave heed to the lines where thou exclaimest, angered as 'twere against human nature:

'Wherefore dost thou not regulate the lust of mortals, O hallowed hunger of gold?'—at the rolling I should feel the grievous jousts.[3]

Then I perceived that our hands could open their wings too wide in spending, and I repented of that as well as of other sins.

How many will rise again with shorn locks,[4] through

ignorance, which taketh away repentance of this sin during life and at the last hour!

And know that the offence which repels any sin by its direct opposite, here, together with it, dries up its luxuriance.[5]

Therefore if I, to purge me, have been among that people who bewail avarice, this hath befallen me because of its contrary."

"Now when thou didst sing of the savage strife of Jocasta's twofold sorrow," said the singer of the Bucolic lays,

"by that which Clio touches with thee there, it seems not that faith had yet made thee faithful, without which good works are not enough.[6]

If this be so, what sun or what candles dispelled the darkness for thee, so that thou didst thereafter set thy sails to follow the Fisherman?"[7]

And he to him: "Thou first didst send me towards Parnassus to drink in its caves, and then didst light me on to God.

Thou didst like one who goes by night, and carries the light behind him, and profits not himself, but maketh persons wise that follow him,

when thou saidst: 'The world is renewed, justice returns and the first age of man, and a new progeny descends from heaven.'[8]

Through thee I was a poet, through thee a Christian, but that thou mayest see better what I outline I will put forth my hand to fill in colour.

Already the whole world was big with the true belief, sown by the apostles of the everlasting kingdom;

and thy words, touched on above, harmonized so with the new preachers, that the habit took me of visiting them.

They then became so holy in my sight, that when Domitian persecuted them,[9] their wailings were not without tears of mine.

And while by me yon world was trod, I succoured them, and their righteous lives made me despise all other sects;

and ere in my poem I had brought the Greeks to Thebes'

rivers,[10] I received baptism, but through fear I was a secret Christian,

long time pretending paganism; and this lukewarmness made me speed round the fourth circle more than four times a hundred years.

Thou therefore, who hast lifted the covering which hid from me the great good I tell of, while we have time to spare on the ascent,

tell me, where is our ancient Terence, Cæcilius, Plautus, and Varro if thou knowest; tell me if they are dammed, and in what ward."

"They, and Persius, and I, and many others," my Leader answered, "are with that Greek to whom the Muses gave suck more than to any other,

in the first circle of the dark prison. Ofttimes we talk of the mount which hath our fostermothers ever with it.

Euripides is there with us, and Antiphon, Simonides, Agathon, and many other Greeks, who once decked their brows with laurel.[11]

There are seen of thy people Antigone, Deiphyle and Argia, and Ismene so sad as she was.

There is seen she who showed Langia; there is Tiresias' daughter, and Thetis, and Deidamia with her sisters."[12]

Now were both poets silent, intent anew on gazing around, freed from the ascent and from the walls;

and already four handmaids of the day were left behind, and the fifth was at the chariot pole, directing yet upward its flaming horn,[13]

when my Leader: "I think it behoves us to turn our right shoulders to the edge and circle the mount as we are wont to do."

Thus custom there was our guide, and we took up our way with less doubt because of the assent of that worthy spirit.

They journeyed on in front, and I, solitary, behind; and I hearkened to their discourse which gave me understanding in poesy.

But soon the sweet converse was broken by a tree[14] which we found in the midst of the way, with fruit wholesome and pleasant to smell.

And even as a pine tree grows gradually less from bough to bough upwards, so did that downwards; I think so that none may go up.

On the side where our path was blocked, a clear spring fell from the high rock and spread itself above the leaves.

The two poets drew near the tree; and a voice from within the foliage cried: "Of this food ye shall have scarcity."

Then it said: "Mary thought more how the wedding-feast might be honourable and complete, than of her own mouth, which now answers for you.[15]

And the Roman women of old were content with water for their drink,[16] and Daniel despised food and gained wisdom.[17]

The first age was fair as gold; it made acorns savoury with hunger, and every stream nectar with thirst.[18]

Honey and locusts were the meat which nourished the Baptist in the wilderness; therefore he is glorious, and so great as in the Gospel is revealed to you."[19]

1. *Matt.* v. 6: *Beati qui [esuriunt et] sitiunt justitiam;* "Blessed are they which do [hunger and] thirst after righteousness." The words of this Beatitude that have been placed in square brackets are reserved for the Angel of the sixth terrace (see Canto xxiv).

2. Juvenal, the satirist, lived *ca.* A.D. 47–130; he praises Statius in the seventh Satire.

3. Dante frequently misunderstood the classical Latin writers. He evidently read them with the same ease and security and the same keen appreciation but frequent misconception with which an Englishman, who has made no special study of Elizabethan English, reads Shakespeare. But if he really took Virgil's *quid non mortalia pectora cogis Auri sacra fames* (*Æn.* iii) to mean that a moderate, and therefore hallowed, desire for wealth ought to moderate extravagance, it constitutes a more portentous blunder in Latinity than any other that can be brought home to him. Many ingenious attempts have been made to escape this; but the only legitimate one is to suppose that Dante, while understanding the sense in which Virgil uttered the words, considered himself justified in supposing that his writings, like the Scripture, had many senses, and that for purposes of edification we must look into all the possible meanings that any passage might have apart from the context in which it occurs. [For the context of the passage in question, see Canto xx, *note* 25.] And, as a matter of fact, this was the generally received theory in Dante's day.—The last phrase alludes to the punishment of the Avaricious and Prodigal in Hell (see *Inf.* vii)

4. *Cf. Inf.* vii.

5. The idea of virtue being the mean between two extremes is, of course, the guiding principle of Aristotle's *Ethics*, but it does not harmonize well with the Christian scheme, which regarded many extremes that Aristotle actually or hypothetically condemned, as virtues. In the Christian scheme, for instance, there could be no excess of self-denial or of humility. In his abstract ethical sympathies, if not in his concrete instincts, Dante is far more Christian than Aristotelian, and can therefore find no room for the consistent application of the Aristotelian doctrine, which is indeed conspicuous by its absence from the *Commedia*. But here, where he finds a concrete instance which appeals to him, he takes the opportunity of expressing it as a general principle.

6. Jocasta, the mother, and afterwards the wife, of Œdipus, by whom she had the two sons alluded to in *Inf.* xxvi, *note* 4. Virgil (here called *singer of the bucolic lays,* probably in anticipation of the verses from his fourth Eclogue quoted below) is not referring to the invocation of Clio, the Muse of History, with which the *Thebaid* begins, but to the pagan theme and entirely pagan treatment of the whole poem.

7. St. Peter.

8. *Magnus ab integro sæculorum nascitur ordo Jam redit et virgo, redunt Saturnia regna; Jam nova progenies cæla demittitur alto* (Virgil, Eclogue iv). No one who reads Virgil's fourth Eclogue can fail to be impressed by its similarity to "Messianic" passages of the Old Testament, particularly Isaiah. It is easy to understand that it was universally accepted as a divinely inspired prophetic utterance in the Middle Ages. It seems probable that, as a matter of fact, the poem is an indirect imitation of Isaiah, for the Jews of Alexandria wrote a number of Sibylline verses; that is to say, Greek hexameters embodying their religious ideas, and largely based on Scripture, which they put into the mouths of the Sibyls. Some of these date from pre-Christian times, and Virgil may well have come across them, have been struck by them, and have combined them with features of the pagan tradition in this remarkable poem.

9. The Emperor Domitian (81–96) is accused by Eusebius and Tertullian of having cruelly persecuted the Christians; but there is no contemporary evidence of this.

10. With these words Statius is generally supposed to indicate the entire *Thebaid*, not any particular episode in the poem. We have no record of Statius' conversion.

11. All these writers, divided into two groups, Roman and Greek respectively, are in Limbo, together with Homer. Reference is, of course, to Mount Parnassus and the Muses.

Terence (195–159 B.C.), Cæcilius Statius (d. 168 B.C.), Plautus (254–184 B.C.): comic poets; Varro (born 82 B.C.): author of epics and satires [perhaps the reading should be *Vario;* in which case the reference is to Lucius Varius Rufus, author of a tragedy and epics, who lived in the Augustan Age and is mentioned by Horace, *Ars*

Poet., together with Cæcilius and Plautus]; Persius (A.D. 34–62); the satirist.—Euripides (480–441 B.C.), Antiphon and Agathon (*ca.* 448–400 B.C.): tragic poets; Simonides (*ca.* 556–467 B.C.): lyric poet.

12. The *people* of Statius are those he celebrates in the *Thebaid* and *Achilleid*:—

Antigone and Ismene: daughter of Œdipus, by his mother, Jocasta, and sisters of Eteocles and Polynices (see *note* 6); Deiphile (the mother of Diomed) and Argia (the wife of Polynices): daughters of Andrastus, King of Argos; Hypsipyle (*cf. Inf.* xviii) to whom Lycurgus had entrusted his son, Archemorus, directed the seven heroes who fought against Thebes to a fountain called Langia, and, the child having been killed by a serpent in her absence, Lycurgus would have slain her, had not her sons come to the rescue (see Canto xxvi, and *cf. Conv.* iii, 11) for Tiresias and his daughter Manto, see *Inf.* xx, *notes* 3 and 5; for Thetis and Deidamia, see *Inf.* xxvi, *note* 5.

13. It is past 10 A.M. *Cf.* Canto xii.

14. Some commentators hold that because the companion tree, situated at the end of the terrace, was raised from the tree of knowledge of good and evil (see Canto xxiv), the present tree must have some connection with the tree of life (*Gen.* ii. 9). But this appears somewhat doubtful.

15. Dante has already used this incident once, as an example of generosity (see Canto xiii).

16. Thomas Aquinas, in a passage recommending sobriety to women and young people, quotes the words of Valerius Maximus (II, i): *Vini usus olim romanis fœminis ignotus fuit.*

17. See *Dan.* i. 8, 17: "But Daniel purposed in his heart that he would not defile himself with the portion of the king's meat, nor with the wine which he drank: . . . and Daniel had understanding in all visions and dreams."

18. For the Golden Age, *cf. Inf.* xiv and *Purg.* xxviii. See, too, Ovid, *Met.* i, whose description Dante may have had in mind.

19. For the locusts and honey eaten by John the Baptist, see *Matt.* iii. 4, *Mark* i. 6; and for his glory and greatness, see *Matt.* xi. 11. *Luke* vii. 28.

CANTO XXIII

Dante's eyes search the foliage of the tree till he is summoned to advance by Virgil. Then he hears the cry, at once grievous and soothing, of the souls who presently overtake the travellers and turn to look upon them as they pass, though without pausing. These are the once gluttonous souls, with faces now drawn by thirst and hunger, so emaciated that the extremest examples of famine in sacred or profane records rush to Dante's mind. Their eye-sockets are like rings that have lost their gems; and he who reads omo (homo) 👁️ on the face of man would find the three strokes of the m writ plain enough in the gaunt bones of cheek and nose. How can the fruit and trickling water work in such fashion on the shadowy forms? One of them turns his eyes from deep down in the sockets upon Dante, who, when he speaks, recognizes his old companion Forese; and each of the astonished friends demands priority of satisfaction for his own amazed curiosity. Forese explains that there are other trees like to this, and that each renews the pain of the purging souls; nay, rather their solace; for they exult in crucifying with Christ the old Adam in them. Forese further shows how he owes to his widowed Nella his speedy promotion to the sweet bitterness of torment. She is all the dearer to God in proportion to the loneliness of her virtue in the place of infamy in which she lives. Forese proceeds to denounce the dissolute fashions of the women of Florence. Dante must now in his turn unfold the story of how he had been rescued from the worldly life which he and Forese had once lived together, of the strange journey on which Virgil has conducted him, of the promise that he shall meet Beatrice, and of the manner in which they have encountered Statius.

WHILE I WAS thus fixing mine eyes through the green leaves, even as he is wont to do who throws away his life after birds,

my more than father said to me: "Son, come now onward, for the time which is allotted to us must be more usefully apportioned."

I turned my face, and my step not less quickly, towarde

the sages, who were discoursing so that they made the going of no cost to me.

And lo, in tears and song was heard: "*Labia mea Domine*,"[1] in such manner that it gave birth to joy and grief.

"O sweet Father, what is that which I hear?" began I; and he: "Shades that perchance go loosening the knot of their debt."

Even as musing wayfarers do, who on overtaking strange folk by the way, turn round to them and stay not,

so behind us, moving more quickly, coming, and passing by, a throng of spirits, silent and devout, was gazing upon us in wonder.

Dark and hollow-eyed was each one, pallid of face, and so wasted away that the skin took form from the bones.

I do not believe that Erysichthon became thus withered to the very skin by hunger, when greatest fear he had thereof.[2]

I said in thought within me: "Behold the people that lost Jerusalem when Mary fed on her child."[3]

Their eye-sockets seemed gemless rings: he who reads "omo" in the face of man would clearly have recognized there the "m."[4]

Who, not knowing the reason, would believe that the scent of fruit and that of water had thus wrought, by begetting desire?

Already I was in astonishment at what thus famishes them, because of the reason not yet manifest, of their leanness, and of their sad scurf,

when lo, from the hollow of the head a shade[5] turned its eyes to me and fixedly did gaze; then cried aloud: "What grace is this to me?"

Never had I recognized him by the face, but in his voice, was revealed to me, that which was blotted out in his countenance.

This spark rekindled within me all my knowledge of the changed features, and I recognized the face of Forese.

"Ah stare not," he prayed, "at the dry leprosy which discolours my skin, nor at any default of flesh that I may have,

but tell me sooth of thyself, and who those two spirits

are that there make thy escort; abide thou not without speaking to me."

"Thy face," answered I him, "which in death I wept for once, gives me now not less grief, even unto tears, seeing it so disfigured.

Therefore tell me, in God's name, what strips you so; make me not talk while I am marvelling, for ill can he speak who is full of other desire."

And he to me: "From the eternal counsel virtue descends into the water, and into the tree left behind, whereby I thus do waste away.

All this people, who weeping sing, sanctify themselves again in hunger and thirst, for having followed appetite to excess.

The scent which issues from the fruit, and from the spray that is diffused over the green, kindles within us a desire to eat and to drink.

And not once only, while circling this road, is our pain renewed, I say pain and ought to say solace;

for that desire leads us to the tree, which led glad Christ to say: 'Eli' when he made us free with his blood."[6]

And I to him: "Forese, from that day on which thou didst change the world for a better life, not five years have revolved till now.

If power to sin more came to an end in thee ere the hour supervened of the holy sorrow which weds us anew to God,

how art thou come up here? I thought to find thee yet down below, where time for time is repaid."[7]

And he to me: "Thus soon hath led me to drink the sweet wormwood of the torments, my Nella by her flood of tears;

by her prayers devout and by sighs she hath brought me from the borders where they wait, and set me free from the other circles.

So much more precious and beloved of God is my dear widow, whom I loved so well, as she is the more lonely in good works;[8]

for the Barbagia of Sardinia is far more modest in its women than the Barbagia where I left her.

329

O sweet brother, what wouldst thou have me say? Already in my vision is a time to come to which this hour shall not be very old,

when the brazen-faced women of Florence shall be forbidden from the pulpit to go abroad showing their breasts with the paps.[9]

What Barbary, what Saracen women ever lived, to whom either spiritual or other discipline were necessary, to make them go covered?

But if the shameless creatures were assured of what swift heaven is preparing for them, already would they have their mouths open to howl:

for if prevision here beguile me not, they shall be sorrowing ere he shall clothe his cheeks with down, who now is soothed with lullaby.

Pray, brother, look that thou hide thee no longer from me; thou seest that not only I, but all this people are gazing where thou veilest the sun."

Wherefore I to him: "If thou bring back to mind what thou hast been with me and what I have been with thee, the present memory will still be grievous.

From that life he who goeth before me did turn me, the other day,[10] when full was shown to you the sister of him"[11]

(And I pointed to the sun). "This one through the deep night hath led me from the truly dead, in this solid flesh which follows him.

Thence his comforts have brought me up, ascending and circling the mount, which makes you straight whom the world made crooked.

So long he talks of making me his comrade, until I shall be there where Beatrice will be; there must I remain bereft of him.[12]

Virgil is he who thus speaks to me (and I pointed to him) and this other is that shade for whom before in every scarp your realm did shake which now discharges him from itself."

1. "O Lord, open thou my lips; and my mouth shall shew forth thy praise" (Ps. li. 15). [All the offices begin with the invocation *Domine labia mea aperies*.]

330

2. The Thessalian, Erysichthon, cut down an oak in the sacred grove of Ceres, whereupon the goddess punished him by making him endure such hunger that he was reduced to gnawing his own flesh; of which, by that time, there was so little left that his hunger opened the yet more terrible prospect of death by starvation (Ovid. *Met.* viii).

3. During the siege of Jerusalem by Titus, the famine became so terrible, that a Jewess, named Mary, killed her child and devoured it (see Josephus, *De Bello Jud.* vi).

4. Longfellow quotes an interesting passage from a sermon of Brother Berthold (a Franciscan friar who lived at Regensburg in the 13th century), which proves, what is indeed implied in Dante's words, that this conception was current at the time.

5. This is Dante's friend, Forese Donati, the brother of Corso (see the following canto) and of Piccarda (see the following canto and *Par.* iii, especially *note* 4). Forese, who bore the nickname of Bicci Novello, died on July 28, 1296. For his relations with Dante, which throw considerable light on the somewhat unedifying but highly interesting and important period of our poet's life that followed the death of Beatrice, also *cf.* Gardner, p. 14.

6. "And about the ninth hour Jesus cried with a loud voice, saying, Eli, Eli, lama sabachthani? that is to say, My God, my God, why hast thou forsaken me?" (*Matt.* xxviii. 46, *Mark* xv. 34).—*that desire* —the desire to conform our will to the will of God.

7. "If you delayed repentance till the last moment, how is it that you are not still in the Antepurgatorio?"

8. In one of the sonnets referred to in *note* 10, Dante describes Forese's neglect of his wife, Nella, but with a coarseness that is well-nigh incredible. The present passage may have been intended by the Poet to atone in a measure for that poem, and to offer the widow some consolation by representing Forese, in his new condition, as one of the tenderest of husbands.

9. Dante compares the shamelessness of the Florentine women with that of the women in Barbagia (a mountainous district in the south of Sardinia), who are said to have been descended either from the Vandals or the Saracens. We have no contemporary record of sermons or decrees relating to this subject. A law dealing with a kindred matter—the luxury of the women—is mentioned by Villani (ix) as having been passed in 1324. See *Par.* xv.

10. These verses afford a clear proof that the life from which Virgil rescued Dante was not merely one of philosophical or religious error, as has been contended, but of moral unworthiness. There is still extant a poetical correspondence between Dante and Forese (consisting of three sonnets by the former and two by the latter) on a level quite beneath anything else that we possess of Dante's. The two friends rail at each other in a vein which may have been meant playfully, but is extremely stinging and anything but refined.

11. See *Inf.* xx.

12. See *Inf.* i.

ÇÄNTO XXIV

The souls gather in amazement round the living man; who utters a surmise to his friend that Statius is perchance lingering on his way for the sake of Virgil's companionship; and then questions him concerning his sister Piccarda, and learns that she is already in heaven. The souls are so emaciated as to be barely recognizable, and Forese names a number of them as he points them out to Dante; an office which they accept with complacency, for recognition can bring no added shame, but may bring sympathy or aid to souls in Purgatory. Amongst them is Bonagiunta da Lucca, a poet of the old school of Guittone of Arezzo, who mutters a prophecy concerning a child of the name of Gentucca, whose gracious offices to Dante when she comes to woman's state, shall give him tender associations with that city of Lucca which he and others have so fiercely denounced. Then he questions Dante as to the secret of the new school of Tuscan poetry which has superseded the one to which he belonged, and learns that it lies in the principle of trying not to say things beautifully, but to say beautiful things truly; a cricitism in which he acquiesces with full content and satisfaction. Then all the other souls sweep forward, while Forese, like a straggler from a caravan, remains behind to question Dante as to his expected term of life, to hear his lamentations over the state of Florence, to utter a prophecy of the death of his relative Corso Donati, and then to speed forward to rejoin his companions, leaving Dante to follow the two great poets. The pilgrims now pass another tree like the one already encountered. They hear that it is a shoot from the one whereof Eve tasted the fruit; and from amongst its foliage warning examples of gluttonous excess are rehearsed. After a lengthened march in silent thought, they are startled by the blinding glory of the angel guardian, whose wing wafts a breath laden as with perfume of flowers on a May morning upon Dante's brow; and the pilgrims hear the blessing pronounced on those whose hunger is measured by righteousness.

NEITHER DID our speech make the going, nor the going, more slow; but, talking we went bravely on, even as a ship driven by a fair wind.

And the shades, that seemed things twice dead, drew in wonderment at me through the pits of their eyes, aware of my being alive.

And I, continuing my discourse, said: "Perchance he goeth upward more slowly than he would do, for another's sake.

But tell me, if thou knowest, where Piccarda[1] is; tell me if I see any person to be noted among this people who gaze so at me."

"My sister, who, whether she were more fair or more good I know not, now triumphs, rejoicing in her crown on high Olympus."

Thus spake he at first, and then: "Here 'tis not forbidden to name each one, since our features are so wrung by abstinence.

This (and he showed with his finger) is Bonagiunta, Bonagiunta of Lucca;[2] and that visage, beyond him, shrivelled more than the others,

held Holy Church within its arms: from Tours sprang he, and by fasting purges the eels of Bolsena and the sweet wine."[3]

Many others he named to me, one by one, and all did seem glad at the naming, so that I saw therefore not one black look.

I saw Ubaldino della Pila[4] using his teeth for very hunger on the void; and Boniface[5] who pastured many peoples with the rook.

I saw Messer Marchese,[6] who once had leisure to drink at Forlì with less thirst, and yet was so craving that he never felt sated.

But as he doth who looks, and then esteems one more than another, so did I to him of Lucca who seemed to have most knowledge of me.

He was muttering, and something like "Gentucca," I heard there where he was feeling the wounds of Justice, which so doth pluck them.

"O soul," said I, "that seemeth yearning so to talk with me, speak so that I may understand thee, and satisfy me and thee with thy speech."

"A woman is born and wears not yet the wimple," he

333

began, "who will make my city pleasing to thee, however man may rebuke it.

Thou shalt go hence with this prophecy; if thou hast taken my muttering in error, the real facts will make it yet clear to thee.[7]

But tell if I see here him who invented the new rhymes beginning: *'Ladies that have intelligence of Love.'*"[8]

And I to him: "I am one who, when Love inspires me take note, and go setting it forth after the fashion which he dictates within me."

"O brother," said he, "now I see the knot which kept back the Notary, and Guittone, and me, short of the sweet new style that I hear.[9]

Truly I see how your pens follow close after him who dictates, which certainly befell not with ours.

And he who sets himself to search farther, has lost all sense of difference between the one style and the other"; and, as if satisfied, he was silent.

As birds that winter along the Nile sometimes make of themselves an aerial squadron, then fly in greater haste and go in file;

so all the people that were there, facing round, quickened their pace, fleet through leanness and desire.

And as one who is weary of running lets his comrades go by, and walks until the panting of his chest be eased;

so Forese let the holy flock pass by, and came on behind with me, saying: "When shall it be that I see thee again?"

"I know not," answered I him, "how long I may live, yet my return will not be so soon but that I be not before with my desire at the bank:

for the place where I was put to live, is day by day more stripped of good, and seems doomed to woeful ruin."

"Now go," said he, "for him[10] who is most in fault I see dragged at the tail of a beast, towards the vale where sin is never cleansed.

Faster goes the beast at every step, increasing ever till it dashes him, and leaves his body hideously disfigured.

Yon wheels (and he lifted his eyes up to the heavens) have not long to revolve ere that shall be clear to thee which my words may no further declare.

Now remain thou behind, for time is precious in this realm, so that I lose too much coming with thee thus at equal pace."

As a horseman sometimes comes forth at a gallop from a troop that is riding, and goes to win the honour of the first encounter,

so parted he from us with greater strides; and I was left by the way with the two who were such great marshals of the world.

And when he had advanced so far ahead of us, that mine eyes made such pursuit of him, as my mind did of his words,

the laden and green boughs of another tree[11] appeared to me, and not very far away, for I was but then come round thither.

I saw people beneath it lifting up their hands, and crying out something towards the foliage, like spoilt and greedy children,

who beg, and he of whom they beg, answers not, but to make their longing full keen, holds what they desire on high, and hides it not.

Then they departed as though undeceived; and now we came to the great tree which mocks so many prayers and tears.

"Pass onward without drawing nigh to it; higher up is a tree which was eaten of by Eve, and this plant was raised from it."

Thus amid the branches some one spake; wherefore Virgil and Statius and I, close together, went forward by the side which rises.

"Remember," he said, "the accursed ones[12] formed in the clouds, who when gorged, fought Theseus with their double breasts;

and the Hebrews who showed themselves soft at the drinking, wherefore Gideon would have them not for comrades when he came down the hills to Midian."[13]

Thus we passed close against one of the two margins, hearing sins of gluttony, once followed by woeful gains.

Then, spread out along the solitary way, full a thousand paces and more bore us onward, each in contemplation without a word.

"What go ye thus pondering on, ye lone three," a sudden voice did say; wherefore I startled as frightened and timid beasts do.

I raised my head to see who it was, and never in a furnace were glasses or metals seen so glowing and red,

as I saw one who said: "If it please you to mount upward, here must a turn be given; hence goeth he who desires to go for peace."

His countenance had bereft me of sight; wherefore I turned me back to my Teachers, like one who goeth according as he listens.

And as the May breeze, herald of the dawn, stirs and breathes forth sweetness, all impregnate with grass and with flowers,

such a wind felt I give on the middle of my brow, and right well I felt the pinions move which wafted ambrosial fragrance to my senses;

and I heard say: "Blessed are they who are illumined by so much grace, that the love of taste kindleth not too great desire in their breasts, and who hunger always so far as is just."[14]

1. For Piccarda, see *Par.* iii.
2. Bonagiunta Orbicciani degli Overardi, a Lucchese poet, who was still living in 1296. See *note 9*.
3. Simon de Brie was Pope, as Martin IV, from 1281 till 1285. See Villani, vii; we learn that "he was a good man and very favourable to Holy Church and to those of the house of France, because he was from Tours." Martin died of eating too many eels from the Lake of Bolsena stewed in Vernaccia wine. His epitaph ran: *Gaudent anguillæ, quia mortuus hic jacet ille Qui quasi morte reas excoriabat eas.*
4. Of Ubaldin della Pila, a member of the Tuscan Ghibelline family of the Ubaldini, we know that he was a glutton, and that he was brother of the Cardinal Ottaviano (*Inf.* x), father of the Archbishop Roger of Pisa (*Inf.* xxxiii), and uncle of Ugolino d'Azzo (see Canto xiv).
5. This is probably Bonifazio dei Fieschi, who was Archbishop of Ravenna (1274–1295). We have no record of his greediness.—*rook* refers to the ornament, shaped like a rook at chess, at the top of the ancient pastoral staff of the Archbishops of Ravenna.
6. Messer Marchese, of Forlì, who belonged either to the Argogliosi or to the Ordelaffi family, was Podestà of Faenza in 1296. When told

that he was always drinking he retorted by saying that he was always thirsty.

7. A much discussed passage. A few of the early commentators, somewhat absurdly, took *Gentucca* as a substantive, the pejorative of *people*. It seems probable that Minutoli's identification is correct, and that the lady in question was Gentucca Morla, the beautiful wife of Cosciorino Fondora, of Lucca, in whose will (1317) she is mentioned. The friendship, for such it assuredly was, may be placed between the years 1314-1316, when Dante is most likely to have been at Lucca (see Gardner, p. 35). In 1300 Gentucca was still quite young and unmarried, and therefore did not yet wear the *wimple*, which was reserved for married women (and, when white, for widows, see Canto viii).

8. The first line of a canzone contained in the *Vita Nuova*, § xix.

9. Italian lyrical poetry before 1300 may be roughly divided into three schools. (*a*) The Sicilian school (continued in Central Italy), which was based on Provençal traditions; to this belongs Jacopo da Lentino, commonly called *il Notaio*, Bonagiunta, and Guittone of Arezzo in his first period. (*b*) The philosophical school, which may be represented by the later poems of Guittone and which reached its climax in the works of Guido Guinicelli of Bologna. (*c*) The Florentine school of the *dolce stil nuovo*, the most distinguished representatives of which are Guido Cavalcanti and Dante. Their poetry is strongly influenced by that of Guido Guinicelli, but shows more genuine inspiration than any that had gone before in Italy. See Canto xi, note 6. [Bonagiunta wrote a poem in derision of Guido Guinicelli; and if, as seems probable, this poem induced Dante to select Bonagiunta for the purpose of making him eat humble pie in the present canto, we have another piece of evidence in favour of the theory that the two Guidos are Guittone of Arezzo and Guido Guinicelli.]

10. Corso Donati, Podestà of Bologna (1283, 1288) and of Pistoia (1289), and head of the Florentine Blacks, was from all accounts a very distinguished man; but he ruined himself and wrought incalculable harm to others through his ambition. When the disturbances of Florence became so unbearable, in 1300, that the heads of both factions were exiled, he went to Rome and induced Boniface to send Charles of Valois to the city as peacemaker. The latter favoured the Blacks, who exiled their enemies and acted relentlessly towards them for many years. Corso finally tried to obtain supreme authority, and being suspected of a treacherous intrigue with his father-in-law, the Ghibelline captain Uguccione della Faggiuola, he was condemned to death. He attempted to escape but was captured on the way; whereupon, rather than meet so ignominious an end, he let himself slip from his horse and was killed (Oct. 6. 1308). See Villani. viii; *cf. Inf.* vi and *Purg.* xx.

11. See Canto xxii, *note* 14.

12. The Centaurs (born of Ixion and a cloud in the shape of Hera), were present at the wedding of their half-brother, Pirithoüs, King of

the Lapithæ, and Hippodame. One of their number, Eurytus, heated with wine, attempted to carry off the bride, and the rest followed his example with the other women. Theseus, the friend of Pirithoüs, having rescued Hippodame, a general fight ensued between the Lapithæ and the Centaurs, in which the latter were vanquished (see Ovid. *Met.* xii).

13. See *Judges* vii. 1–7: ... "and the Lord said unto Gideon, Every one that lappeth of the water with his tongue, as a dog lappeth, him shalt thou set by himself; likewise every one that boweth down upon his knees to drink. And the number of them that lapped, putting their hands to their mouths, were three hundred men: but all the rest of the people bowed down upon their knees to drink water. And the Lord said unto Gideon, By the three hundred men that lapped will I save you, and deliver the Midianites into thine hand: and let all the other people go every man unto his place."

14. "Blessed are they which do hunger [and thirst] after righteousness: for they shall be filled" (*Matt.* v. 6). See Canto xxii, *note* 1.

ÇANTO XXV

The pilgrims pursue their way up the stair in single file. As the little stork longs but ventures not to try its wings, so Dante feels the question as to the meaning of what he has seen ever kindled by longing and quenched by diffidence on his lips; till, encouraged by Virgil, he seeks for instructions as to how the shadowy forms which need no sustenance can present the appearance and experience the sensations of gnawing hunger. Virgil hints by analogies from pagan story and from natural philosophy that our own experiences and sensations may well reflect themselves in unsubstantial appearances; or may be connected with physical changes in matter other than that of our bodies of flesh and blood; but refers to Statius, his Christian counterpart, for fuller exposition; for in truth this matter, though no part of Christian revelation, yet verges on those mysterious and intricate portions of Aristotle's doctrine which none save Christian philosophers have had vision clear enough truly to expound. Statius, after a polite disclaimer, proceeds to expound the Aristotelian doctrines of generation and embryology, showing how the human fœtus passes through every stage, differing only from the lower forms of plant, polype, or animal, in that it possesses the potentiality of further development; whereas they have reached their goal. At the critical point now reached, Averroës himself went wrong, for finding no organ in the human body appropriated to the immaterial principle of intelligence, he conceived it to be no part of the individual life of man, but a universal all-pervading principle; whereas in truth the human soul or life is inbreathed direct by God into the perfect animal form of the man that is to be; and thereon it draws into itself all the lower vital functions already active there. Therefore when the body dies, the gates of sense are indeed closed; but the soul itself which came from without remains with the purely immaterial powers of memory, intelligence, and will, isolated indeed from intercourse with outward things, but in themselves more vivid than ever. Then the soul drops at once to the bank of Acheron or the mouth of Tiber, becomes aware of its destination, and reflects itself upon an aerial body, flame- or rainbow-like, and through the instrumentality of this aerial body renews its intercourse with the outer world and the experiences of sense. They have now reached

339

the topmost circle, which is filled with flames, save a narrow out-
ward margin on which the Poets march, single file, and whereon
Dante must take good heed to his steps; so that he can give but
broken attention to the souls who commemorate examples of chas-
tity from the midst of the glowing heat.

'TWAS AN HOUR when the ascent brooked no im-
pediment, for the sun to the Bull, and night to the Scorpion,
had left the meridian circle.[1]

Wherefore as does a man who halts not, but goes on his
way whatever may appear to him, if the spur of necessity
prick him,

so we entered by the gap, one in front of the other,
mounting the stairway, which by its straitness parts the
climbers.

And like the little stork that lifts its wing through desire
to fly, and, venturing not to abandon the nest, drops it
down,[2]

even so was I with desire to ask kindled and quenched,
going so far as the movement which he makes who is pre-
paring to speak.

My sweet Father did not cease, even though the pace was
swift, but said: "Discharge the bow of thy speech which
thou hast drawn to the iron."

Then securely I opened my mouth, and began: "How
can one grow lean there where the need of food is not felt?"

"If thou wouldst call to mind how Meleager[3] was con-
sumed at the consuming of a firebrand," said he, "this
would not be so difficult to thee;

and if thou wouldst think how, to your every movement
your image flits about in the mirror, that which seems
hard would seem easy to thee.

But in order that thou mayst find rest in thy desire, lo
here Statius, and him I call and pray, that he now be the
healer of thy wounds."

"If," answered Statius, "I unfold to him in thy presence
the eternal things he has seen, let my excuse be that I may
not deny thee."

340

Then he began: "Son, if thy mind heed and receive my words, they shall be a light unto thee on the how which thou utterest.

Perfect blood, which never is drunk by the thirsty veins, and is left behind,[4] as 'twere food which thou removest from the table,

acquires in the heart a virtue potent to inform all human members, like that blood which flows through the veins to become those.

Refined yet again, it descends there whereof to be silent is more seemly than to speak, and thence afterwards distils upon other's blood, in natural vessel.

There the one is mingled with the other; one designed to be passive, the other to be active, by reason of the perfect place whence it springs;

and, joined thereto, it begins to operate, first coagulating, and then giving life to that which it had solidified for its own material.

The active virtue having become a soul, like that of a plant,[5] in so far different that the former is on the way, and the latter is already at the goal,

then effects so much that now it moves and feels, like a sea-fungus;[5] and then sets about developing organs for the powers whereof it is the germ.

Now, son, expands, now distends, the virtue which proceeds from the heart of the begetter, where nature intends all human members;

but how from an animal it becomes a human being[5] thou seest not yet; this is that point which made one wiser than thou to err;

so that by his teaching he made the intellectual faculty separate from the soul, because he saw no organ occupied by it.[6]

Open thy breast to the truth which is coming, and know that so soon as the organization of the brain is perfect in the embyro,

the First Mover turns him to it, rejoicing over such handiwork of nature, and breathes into it a new spirit with virtue filled,

which draws into its substance that which it finds active

there, and becomes one single soul, that lives, and feels, and turns round upon itself.[7]

And that thou mayst marvel less at my words, look at the sun's heat, that is made wine when combined with the juice which flows from the vine.

And when Lachesis has no more thread,[8] it frees itself from the flesh, and bears away in potency both the human and the divine;

the other powers, the whole of them mute; memory, intelligence and will,[9] keener far in action than they were before.

Staying not, it falls of itself in wondrous wise to one of the shores; there it first learns its ways.[10]

Soon as it is circumscribed[11] in place there, the formative virtue radiates around, in form and quantity as in the living members;

and as the air, when it is full saturate, becomes decked with divers colours through another's rays which are reflected in it,

so the neighbouring air sets itself into that form which the soul that is there fixed impresses upon it by means of its virtue;

and then, like the flame which follows the fire wheresoever it moves, the spirit is followed by its new form.

Inasmuch as therefrom it afterwards has it semblance, it is called a shade; and therefrom it forms the organs of every sense even to sight.

By this we speak, and by this we laugh, by this we make the tears and the sighs which thou mayst have heard about the mount.

The shade takes its form according as the desires and the other affections prick us, and this is the cause of that whereof thou marvellest."

And now had we come to the last turning, and had wheeled round to the right hand, and were intent on other care.

There the bank flashes forth flames, and the cornice breathes a blast upward, which bends them back, and keeps them away from it;

wherefore it behoved us to go on the side which was

free one by one; and on this side I feared the fire, and on that I feared to fall downward.

My Leader said: "Along this place the rein must be kept tight on the eyes, because lightly a false step might be taken."

"*Summæ Deus clementiæ*"[12] I then heard sung in the heart of the great burning, which made me no less eager to turn aside;

and I saw spirits going through the flames; wherefore I looked at them and at my steps, with divided gaze from time to time.

After the end which is made to that hymn, they cried aloud: "*Virum non cognosco*";[13] then softly began the hymn again.

It being finished, they further cried: "Diana kept in the wood, and chased Helice forth who had felt the poison of Venus."[14]

Then turned they to their chanting; then cried they women and husbands who were chaste, as virtue and marriage require of us.

And this fashion I think suffices them for all the time the fire burns them: with such treatment, and with such diet, must the last wound be healed.

1. In Purgatory it is two o'clock P.M., or later. Aries being on the Purgatory meridian at noon, the succeeding sign of Taurus holds that position at 2 P.M.; while at the same time Scorpio (the sign opposite Taurus) is on the meridian of Jerusalem, where it is consequently 2 A.M.
2. The stork, in the "Bestiaries," is the type of obedience. It does not attempt to fly out of its nest till its mother gives it leave.
3. At the birth of Meleager, son of Œneus, King of Calydon, and Althæa, the Fates predicted that he would live as long as a certain log of wood was not consumed by fire. Subsequently he slew the Calydonian boar, and gave the skin to his mistress, Atalanta. His uncles (Althæa's brothers) having taken it from her, he killed them, too; whereupon Althæa in a rage threw the log on the fire, and brought about her son's death (Ovid. *Met.* viii).
4. With this passage, compare *Conv.* iv. 21.
5. The three souls, vegetative, animal and rational (*cf.* Canto iv).
6. Brutes have no *intellectus.* Man's intellect is "possible," *i.e.*, has powers undeveloped or not in action; whereas the angelic intellect is continuously and perfectly "actualized" (*cf. Par.* v and xxix). Hence "no creature save man, either above or below him, apprehends by

possible intellect" (*De mon.* i. 3). It follows that none of the corporal organs which are common to men and animals can be the seat of intellect. Whence "the possible intellect is called separate because it is not the act of a corporal organ" (Aquinas). For the erroneous inferences (adverse to the doctrine of personal immortality) which Averroës drew from this fact, see *Argument. Cf.*, too, Canto xviii, *note* 6.

7. On the subject of self-consciousness there is some confusion in the writings of the schoolmen. Dante with sound insight follows Averroës in making it the special characteristic of the rational or intellectual soul, as life is of the vegetable, and sensation of the animal soul. "The action of the intellect is likened to a circle, because it turns round upon itself and understands itself" (Averroës).

8. See Canto xxi, *note* 6.

9. *Cf. Par.* xxix.

10. See *Inf.* iii and *Purg.* ii.—It has been pointed out that in dealing with the two Montefeltros (*Inf.* xxvii, *Purg.* v) Dante follows the popular ideas rendered familiar by representations in art, but not strictly reconcilable with the doctrine here laid down.

11. *circumscribed.* "A thing is said to be in space by *circumscription,* when a beginning, middle and end can be assigned to it in space, or if its parts are measured by the parts of space; and in this sense the *body* is in space. A thing is said to be in space by *definition,* when it is here in such a sense as not to be elsewhere; and in this sense Angels are in space, for an Angel is where he is operative. And, according to Damascenus, this is the case also with disembodied souls. I say disembodied because the soul when united with the body is in the same place as the person in his totality. A thing is said to be in space *repletively,* because it fills space; and thus God is said to be in every place because he fills every place" (Albertus Magnus). *Cf. Purg.* xi and *Par.* xiv.

12. The hymn sung by the lustful began with the verse quoted by Dante in his day, and for some three hundred years after his time (till the Breviary was revised by Pope Urban VIII in 1631). This may be seen by a reference to the ancient "uses." The hymn is entirely appropriate to the occupants of this terrace, the third verse running—*Lumbos jecurque morbidum Flammis adure congruis, Accincti ut artus excubent Luxu remoto pessimo.*

13. "And, behold, thou shalt conceive in thy womb, and bring forth a son, and shalt call his name Jesus. . . . Then said Mary unto the angel, How shall this be, seeing I know not a man?" (*Luke* i. 31–34).

14. Helice or Callisto, one of Diana's nymphs, having borne Jupiter a son (named Arcas), was dismissed by Diana and changed into a bear by Juno, who was jealous of her. In that form she was being pursued by Arcas, when Jupiter set both the mother and the son in the sky as constellations (see Ovid, *Met.* ii, and *cf. Par.* xxxi).

CANTO XXVI

The flames redden under Dante's shadow and the amazed souls gather to him, careful, however, not to issue from the flame. One of them has barely questioned Dante, when a group, circling the mountain in the opposite direction, meets them with a brief salutation, and each group alike proclaims a warning example of lust; after which they sweep past each other like flocks of birds, and continue to utter the wail and song suited to their state. But this does not prevent their drawing again to Dante, who tells them his tale and questions them as to their state. When the souls have somewhat recovered from their amazement, one of them explains that the group accompanying the Poet failed to restrain their carnal appetites within the limits prescribed by the social institutions of humanity, whereas the other group had not even observed the laws laid down by nature. Dante's interlocutor is Guido Guinicelli, the founder (or precursor) of the new style of Tuscan poetry, the father of Dante and of his betters; to whom Dante renders his passionate homage of affection and loyalty. But he points to the shade of the Troubadour Arnaut Daniel as superior to himself and superior to all Provençal rivals by as much as the new Tuscan school excels the old school of Guittone of Arezzo. Then, with a petition for Dante's prayers, he yields his place to Arnaut himself; who tells of his state, in his own Provençal tongue; and in his turn implores Dante's prayers.

WHILE WE WERE thus advancing, one in front of the other, along the brink, often the good Master said: "Give heed, let my skill avail thee."

On my right shoulder the sun was beating, that already with his rays was changing the whole face of the west from azure to white;

and with my shadow, ruddier I made the flames appear, and even at so slight a sign many shades I saw, as they passed, give heed.

This was the cause which gave them an opening to speak

345

of me; and one to the other they began to say: "He doth not seem a shadowy body."

Then certain of them made towards me, so far as they could, ever on their guard not to come forth where they would not be burned.

"O thou that goest behind the others,[1] not for being slacker but perchance for reverence, make answer unto me who in thirst and fire do burn;

nor alone to me is thine answer needful, for all these have greater thirst for it than Indian or Ethiop for cold water.

Tell us how it is that thou makest of thee a wall against the sun, as if thou wert not yet caught within death's net."

Thus spake one of them to me, and already would I have revealed myself, had I not been intent on another strange thing which then appeared;

for through the midst of the fiery path, people were coming with their faces opposite to these, who made me pause in wonderment.

There I see on either side each shade make haste, and one kiss the other without staying, satisfied with short greeting:

even so within their dark battalions one ant rubs muzzle with another, perchance to spy out their way and their fortune.

Soon as they break off the friendly greeting, ere the first step there speeds onward, each one strives to shout loudest,

the new people, "Sodom and Gomorrah,"[2] and the other: "Pasiphaë[3] enters the cow that the young bull may haste to her lust."

Then like cranes that should fly, some to the Rhipean mountains,[4] others towards the sands; these shy of the frost, those of the sun,

the one people passes on, the other comes away, and weeping they return to their former chants, and to the cry which most befits them;

and those very same who had entreated me, drew close to me as before, intent on listening in their appearance.

I, who twice had seen their desire, began: "O souls, certain of having, whenever it may be, a state of peace, my members have not remained yonder, green or ripe, but here are with me, with their blood and with their joints.

Hence upward I go to be blind no longer; there is a lady above who winneth grace for us,[5] wherefore I bring my mortal body through your world.

But—so may your greater desire soon be satisfied, so that the heaven may house you which is filled with love and broadest spreads—[6]

tell me that I may yet trace it on paper, who are ye and what is that throng which is going away behind your backs?"

Not otherwise the dazed highlander grows troubled and stares about speechless, when rough and savage he enters the city,

than each shade did in its appearance; but after they were unladen of their bewilderment, which in lofty hearts soon is calmed,

"Blessed thou," began again the shade that first did ask of me, "who, for a holier life, art embarking knowledge of our borders!

The people who come not with us offended in that for which Cæsar of old in his triumph heard 'Regina' called out against him;[7]

therefore they part from us crying out 'Sodom' reproving themselves as thou hast heard, and aid the burning by their shame.

Our sin was hermaphrodite; but because we observed not human law,[8] and followed our lusts like brute beasts,

to our infamy by us is read, when we part us, the name of her who imbruted herself in the brute-like framework.

Now knowest thou our deeds and what we were guilty of; if haply thou wouldst know who we are by name, there is no time to tell, nor could I.

Thy desire of me, I will indeed make to wane: Guido Guinicelli am I, and already purge me, because I full repentance made before the end."

As in the sorrow of Lycurgus two sons became on beholding again their mother,[9] so became I, but not to such height do I rise,

when I hear name himself the father of me, and of others

my betters, who ever used sweet and graceful rhymes of love;

and without hearing and speaking, pondering I went, long time gazing at him, nor because of the fire drew I nigher thither.

When I was filled with beholding, I offered me all ready to his service, with the oath which compels another's belief.

And he to me: "Thou leavest, by that which I hear, traces so deep and so clear, that Lethe[10] cannot take them away, nor make them dim.

But if thy words just now sware truth, tell me, what is the cause wherefore thou showest in speech and look that thou holdest me so dear."

And I to him: "Your sweet ditties, which so long as modern use shall last, will make their very ink precious."

"O brother," said he, "this one[11] whom I distinguish to thee with my finger" (and he pointed to a spirit in front) "was a better craftsman of the mother tongue.

In verses of love, and prose tales of romance, all he surpassed, and let fools talk, who think that he of Limoges excels.

To rumour rather than to truth they turn their faces, and thus do fix their opinion ere art or reason is listened to by them.

So did many of our fathers with Guittone, shouting in turn and praising him alone; but truth has prevailed at length with most persons.

Now if thou hast such ample privilege, that 'tis permitted thee to go to the cloister wherein Christ is abbot of the college,

do me there the saying of a Pater Noster so far as is needful to us of this world, where power to sin is no more ours."

Then perchance to give place to another following close, he vanished through the flames, like a fish going through the water to the bottom.

A little forward I drew me towards the one he had pointed out, and said that my desire was preparing a grateful place for his name.

Willingly he began to say: "So doth your courteous request please me that I cannot, nor will I, hide me from you.

I am Arnault that weep and go a-singing; in thought I see my past madness, and I see with joy the day which I await before me.

Now I pray you, by that Goodness which guideth you to the summit of the stairway, be mindful in due time of my pain." Then he hid him in the fire which refines them.

1. The speaker is Guido Guinicelli (*ca.* 1230–*ca.* 1276; see Cantos xi, *note* 6, and xxiv, *note* 9), a member of the Ghibelline Principi family, of Bologna. Little is known of his life, save that he was Podestà of Castelfranco in 1270, and that he was exiled in 1274, together with the Lambertazzi (*cf. Inf.* xxxii, *note* 14; *Purg.* xiv, *note* 6); the city of his refuge and death may have been Verona. As a poet, Guido began as an imitator of the later method of Guittone d'Arezzo, but he soon outshone his model, and his best works (notably the famous canzone *Al cor gentil ripara sempre Amore*, which may be said to mark an epoch in Italian literature), inspired much of the poetry of the Florentine school. For Guido see, in addition to the references given above, *De Vulg. El.* i. and ii; *Conv.* iv; *Vita Nuova*, Sonnet x.

2. For Sodom and Gomorrah, see *Gen. xix.*

3. For Pasiphaë, who attained her end by entering an artificial cow, made by Dædalus, see *Inf.* xii, *note* 2.

4. "The Rhipean mountains"–a general term with medieval geographers and writers, to express mountains in the north of Europe and Asia; "the sands," *i.e.* those of the African desert.

5. Some hold that Dante is alluding to Beatrice (*Inf.* ii); others, that the reference is to the Virgin Mary (*ib.*).

6. The Empyrean; see *Par.* xxx.

7. This opprobrious epithet was given to Cæsar on account of his relations with Nicomedes, King of Bithynia. See Suetonius' *Cæsar* [49]; though Dante's immediate source was probably rather the *Magnæ Derivationes* of Uguccione da Pisa.

8. Their sin was indeed bi-sexual [*hermaphrodite:* Hermaphroditus, having excited the love of a nymph to which he remained indifferent, she prayed that their bodies might be joined together for ever; and the gods granted her prayer–see Ovid, *Met.* iv], and so far natural and *generically* human; but inasmuch as it transgressed the *specifically* human law of marriage (see the preceding canto), there was an element of brutishness in it. *Bestialità* is used by Dante in many different senses; but always as opposed to the specifically human element in man. In general terms that specifically human element is reason, and therefore *bestialità* (like the French *bêtise*) is sometimes used for "stupidity" or "want of intelligence," as, for example, in *Conv.* iv. 14. Here it implies simply a neglect of the spe-

cifically human regulations of a relation which is not specifically
human in itself.

9. Thoas and Euneos, the sons of Hypsipyle; for the incident, *cf.*
Canto xxii, and see Statius, *Theb.* iv and v.

10. Lethe, the river of forgetfulness; see Canto xxviii.

11. Arnaut Daniel, a distinguished Provençal poet, flourished *ca.*
1180–1200. Among his patrons was Richard Cœur-de-Lion. He was
a master of the so-called *trobar clus*, or obscure style of poetry,
which revelled, besides, in difficult rhymes and other complicated
devices. As such, he was very naturally "caviare to the general"; and
the lines in which Dante deals with the popular preference for
Guiraut de Bornelh [*he of Limoges; ca.* 1175–*ca.* 1220; called by his
contemporaries "master of the troubadours"] are easier for us to
understand than his own evident bias in favour of Arnaut. For the
best modern criticism not only places Guiraut well above Arnaut
(whose fame is at a very low ebb), but is almost unanimous in set-
ting him at the head of all the troubadours; his only rival, if rival he
have, being Bernart de Ventadorn (whom Dante never mentions).
—The meaning here is, not that Arnaut wrote better love songs and
better prose romances than anyone else (for it is practically certain
that he wrote no prose at all), but that he surpassed every writer in
France, not only the troubadours of the South, but also the authors
of the prose romances in the north [in *De Vulg. El.* i. 10, Dante
speaks of prose works as the special province of the *langue d'oil,* or
Northern French].—For Arnaut, *cf. De Vulg. El.* ii; and for Guiraut,
ib. i and ii.

ÇANTO XXVII

Night had already fallen on the foot of the mountain when the angel of the circle greeted the Poets and pronounced the blessing on the pure in heart. When summoned to cross the flame Dante recalls with horror the sight he had ere now witnessed of men burned to death; and remains deaf to all Virgil's appeals, till the utterance of Beatrice's name at last overcomes his reluctance; whereat Virgil, for reasons of his own, smiles as we smile at a child that knows not what he seeks. Then Virgil, Dante and Statius enter the awful burning, Dante comforted by Virgil's discourse of Beatrice and by the welcome and blessing of the angel at the further side. Meanwhile the shadow of night has been creeping up the mountain, and before they have ascended many of the steps which they are now climbing, it swallows the Poet's shadow, and he is bereft of power further to ascend. Each of the pilgrims makes a stair his couch, and Dante, like a goat between two shepherds, sees the great stars shine brighter than their wont, as he drops into such a sleep as sees the things that are to be. Towards daybreak he has a vision of Leah, the type of the active life, singing of herself and her sister Rachel, the type of the contemplative life. Now nigh to his immediate goal, he awakes with the morning, and Virgil tells him that he is at last to gather that fruit of liberty which he has so long been seeking; and when he has mounted eagerly to the summit of the stair his guide informs him that his function is now discharged, for they have reached the goal of Purgatory. Dante has recovered from the dire effects of the fall of man; his will is free, unwarped and sound; he has no further need of direction or directive institutions; he has reached the goal of all imperial and ecclesiastical organization and is king and bishop of himself.

AS WHEN he shoots forth his first beams there where his Creator shed his blood, while Ebro falls beneath the lofty Scales,

and Ganges' waves by noonday heat are scorched, so stood the sun;[1] wherefore the day was passing away when God's glad angel[2] appeared to us.

351

Outside the flames on the bank he was standing and singing "*Beati mundo corde*"[3] in a voice more piercing far than ours.

Then: "No farther may ye go, O hallowed souls, if first the fire bite not; enter therein and to the singing beyond be not deaf,"

he said to us when we were nigh to him; wherefore I became when I heard him, such as one who is laid in the grave.

I bent forward over my clasped hands, gazing at the fire, and vividly imagining human bodies once seen burnt.

The kindly escorts turned them toward me, and Virgil said to me: "My son, here may be torment but not death.

Remember thee, remember thee, . . . and if on Geryon[4] I guided thee safely, what shall I do now nearer to God?

Of a surety believe, that if within the womb of these flames thou didst abide full a thousand years, they could not make thee bald of one hair;

and if perchance thou thinkest that I beguile thee, get thee toward them, and get credence with thy hands on the hem of thy garments.

Put away now, put away all fear; turn thee hither, and onward come securely." And I, yet rooted, and with accusing conscience.

When he saw me stand yet rooted and stubborn, troubled a little he said: "Now look, my son, 'twixt Beatrice and thee is this wall."

As at Thisbe's name Pyramus opened his eyes at the point of death, and gazed at her, when the mulberry became red,[5]

so, my stubbornness being softened, I turned me to my wise Leader on hearing the name which ever springs up in my mind.

Whereupon he shook his head, and said: "What? do we desire to stay this side?" then smiled as one does to a child that is won by an apple.[6]

Then he entered into the fire in front of me, praying Statius that he would come behind, who for a long way before had separated us.

When I was within, I would have flung me into molten glass to cool me, so immeasurable there was the burning.

My sweet Father, to encourage me, went on discoursing ever of Beatrice, saying: "Already I seem to behold her eyes."

A voice guided us, which was singing on the other side, and we, intent only on it, came forth, there where the ascent began.

"*Venite benedicti patris mei*,"[7] rang forth from within a light which was there, so bright that it vanquished me, and look upon it I could not.

"The sun is sinking," it added, "and the evening cometh; stay ye not but mend your pace while the west grows not dark."

Straight the way mounted through the rock, toward such a quarter, that in front of me I stayed the rays of sun who already was low.

And of few steps made we assay, when I and my sages perceived that the sun had set behind us, because of the shadow which had vanished.

And ere the horizon in all its stupendous range had become of one hue, and night held all her dominion,

each of us made a bed of a step; for the law of the mount took from us the power, rather than the desire, to ascend.

As goats that have been agile and wanton upon the heights ere they are fed, grow tame while ruminating,

silent in the shade, when the sun is hot, guarded by the shepherd who has leaned upon his staff, and, leaning, minds them;

and like the shepherd who lodges in the open, holds silent vigil by night longside his flock, watching lest a wild beast scatter it;

such were we then all three, I as a goat and they as shepherds, bounded by the high rock on this side and on that.

Little of the outside could there be seen, but through that little I saw the stars brighter and bigger than their wont.

As I was thus ruminating, and thus gazing at them, sleep fell on me, sleep which oft doth know the news ere the fact come to pass.[8]

In the hour, methinks, when Cytherea,[9] who seemeth ever burning with fire of love, first beamed from the east on the mount, meseemed to behold in a dream, a lady, young and fair, going along a plain gathering flowers; and singing she said:

"Know, whoso asketh my name, that I am Leah, and go moving my fair hands around to make me a garland.

To please me at the glass here I deck me; but Rachel my sister ne'er stirs from her mirror, and sitteth all day.

She is fain to behold her fair eyes, as I to deck me with my hands: her, contemplation; me, action, doth satisfy."[10]

And now, at the brightness ere dayspring born, which rises the gratefuller to wayfarers as on their return they lodge less far from home,

the shades of night were fleeing on every side, and my sleep with them; wherefore I arose, seeing the great Masters already risen.

"That sweet fruit[11] whereof the care of mortals goeth in search on so many boughs, this day shall give thy hungerings peace."

Words such as these did Virgil use to me, and never have there been gifts that were equal in sweetness to these.

So greatly did desire upon desire come over me to be above, that at every step after I felt my pinions grow for the flight.

When the stairway was all sped beneath us, and we were upon the topmost step, on me did Virgil fix his eyes,

and said: "Son, the temporal fire and the eternal, hast thou seen, and art come to a place where I, of myself, discern no further.

Here have I brought thee with wit and with art; now take thy pleasure for guide; forth art thou from the steep ways, forth art from the narrow.

Behold there the sun that shineth on thy brow; behold the tender grass, the flowers, and the shrubs, which the ground here of itself alone brings forth.

While the glad fair eyes are coming, which weeping made me come to thee, thou canst sit thee down and canst go among them.

No more expect my word, nor my sign. Free, upright, and whole, is thy will, and 'twere a fault not to act according to its prompting; wherefore I do crown and mitre thee over thyself."[12]

It was sunrise at Jerusalem, midnight in Spain (where Libra, the sign opposite to Aries, would be on the meridian) and noon in India: it was, therefore, sunset at the base of the Mount of Purgatory. But there was still an interval before sunset at the height the poets had reached (*cf.* Canto xvii).—See diagram on p. 241.

2. As this angel corresponds to the angels that welcome and direct Dante at the end of his journey through each of the other circles, we must suppose that he struck the last P from Dante's brow with his wing. It is vain, therefore, to seek for any personal confession in Dante's statement that he had to pass through the flame. The same is true of Statius, for whose final liberation the souls of Purgatory had already sung their hymn of glory to God. The fact seems to be that this flame, in addition to being the instrument of purification on the seventh circle, does duty for the wall of fire, which, according to some representations, surrounds the Garden of Eden.

3. "Blessed are the pure in heart: for they shall see God" (*Matt.* v. 8).

4. See *Inf.* xvii.

5. While Thisbe was waiting for her lover, Pyramus, near a mulberry-tree, a lioness came up from which she fled, dropping a garment in her haste. This beast stained with blood, having just devoured an ox. When Pyramus came up and saw it on the ground, he thought that Thisbe was dead and stabbed himself. Thisbe returned just in time to see her lover die and then slew herself too; whereupon the colour of the mulberries changed from white to red. Dante knew the story from Ovid, *Met.* iv. See Canto xxxiii, and *cf. De Mon.* ii. 9.

6. In mentioning Beatrice, Virgil is appealing to a higher motive than any he has yet urged; but he knows that Dante takes the reference on a lower plane. As yet Dante knows nothing of the celestial Beatrice, and it is an earthly emotion, however pure, that responds to Virgil's heavenly appeal. Hence a kind of half pathetic amusement on Virgil's part, on seeing the eagerness with which Dante responds, not to the higher plea he urged, but to the lower plea he suggested.

7. The words to be spoken to the righteous at the Last Judgment: "Then shall the King say unto them on his right hand, Come, ye blessed of my Father, inherit the kingdom prepared for you from the foundation of the world" (*Matt.* xxv. 34).

8. *Cf. Inf.* xxvi and *Purg.* ix.

9. Venus is often called Cytherea by Virgil, from the island Cythera, near which she rose from the sea and where she was worshipped with special veneration. For the position of the planet Venus in Pisces (the constellation preceding Aries or dawn), see Canto i, *note 2.*

10. This third and last vision of Dante's, in which Leah and Rachel, the Old Testament types of the Active and Contemplative Life (*Gen.* xxix) appear to him, is a forecast of the positions Matilda and Beatrice will occupy in the Earthly Paradise. [It should be noted that Mr. Gardner, whose view is shared by others, holds that Ma-

tilda's "counterpart, as Rachel to Leah, is not Beatrice, as some-times supposed, but St. Bernard, in the closing cantos of the *Paradiso*."] In the New Testament the types are represented by Martha and Mary; see *Conv.* iv. 17: "Verily, it is to be known that we can have in this life two happinesses by following two different roads, both good and excellent, which lead to them; the one is the Active Life and the other is the Contemplative Life, which (although by the Active Life one may attain, as has been said, to a good state of happiness) leads us to supreme happiness, even as the philosopher proves in the tenth book of the Ethics; and Christ affirms it with his own lips in the gospel of Luke, speaking to Martha, when replying to her: 'Martha, Martha, thou art anxious and troubled about many things: Verily, one thing alone is needful,' meaning, that which thou hast in hand; and he adds: 'Mary has chosen the better part, which shall not be taken from her.' And Mary, according to that which is previously written in the gospel, sitting at the feet of Christ, showed no care for the service of the house, but listened only to the words of the Saviour. For if we will explain this in the moral sense, our Lord wished to show thereby that the Contemplative Life was supremely good, although the Active Life might be good; this is evident to him who will give his mind to the words of the gospel." See, too, *Conv.* iv. 2.

11. The *fruit* is the *summum bonum*, peace with God, as opposed to the many false ideals of men on earth. *Cf. Par.* xi and *Conv.* iv. 12.

12. Note that Virgil's mission is over when he has brought Dante to the Earthly Paradise, which is the immediate goal of the souls in Purgatory. Some difficulty has been found in the last lines of the canto, because it is said that Virgil cannot make Dante bishop as well as king of himself; but we learn from the *De Mon.* iii. 5, that in Dante's opinion man would not have needed the Church, as an organized institution, any more than the Empire, had he not fallen from the state of innocence. Accordingly, when he recovers that state he is absolved from the spiritual as well as from the temporal rule. The institutions of the Empire and the Church are, of course, to be distinguished from the human and divine reason, or Philosophy and Revelation, of which they ought to be guardians and exponents. The concluding chapter of the *De Mon.* shows us very clearly the distinction between the essential means of temporal and spiritual blessedness (human reason as developed by the philosophers, and Revelation as declared by the writers of Scripture) on the one hand, and the external institutions or regimens on the other, founded to check the perversity which perpetually drives mankind out of the true path thus indicated.

ÇANTO XXVIII

Dante enters the Garden of Eden from the west, facing the rising sun, and meeting a sweet breeze laden with the odours of Paradise and full of the song of birds to which the leaves of the divine forest murmur a pedal bass. On the opposing bank of a stream that flows pure under the forest shade, he perceives a lady gathering flowers and singing, as enamoured. It is Matilda, the genius of Eden; and in answer to Dante's petition she approaches the stream with downcast eyes, the song on her lips growing ever more articulate. Then, her hands still busy with the flowers, she flings upon him the blaze of her laughing eyes. As a responsive rapture awakes in Dante's heart, she initiates him into the frank and innocent love and joy of Eden, and proffers all further service he may desire. In answer to his question she confirms what Statius had already said as to the higher regions of the mount above the gate being unaffected by meteorological phenomena. The stream and the breeze, therefore, are not such as those on earth. The breeze is caused by the sweep of the atmospheric envelope of the earth, from east to west, with the primum mobile; and it bears with it germs from the divine forest; which may explain the seeming spontaneous generation of wondrous plants on earth. And the water of the stream does not rise from the pulsations of any mist- and rain-fed vein; but issues from a fountain which draws supplies for this and a companion stream direct from the will of God. These streams are Lethe and Eunoë, the one of which washes away all memory of sin, and the other restores the memory of all righteous doing; and for the full effect to be experienced, both alike must be tasted. So much in answer to Dante's questions. But Matilda further delights her pupil by suggesting that some confused tradition of the state of innocence lay behind the dreams of the classical poets who sang of the Golden Age; whereon he sees a smile of recognition lighten the faces of Virgil and Statius.

NOW EAGER to search within and around the divine forest dense and verdant, which to mine eyes was tempering the new day,

without waiting more I left the mountain-side, crossing

the plain with lingering step, over the ground which gives
forth fragrance on every side.

A sweet breeze, itself invariable, was striking on my
brow with no greater force than a gentle wind,

before which the branches, responsively trembling, were
all bending toward that quarter, where the holy mount
casts its first shadow;[1]

yet not so far bent aside from their erect state, that the
little birds in the tops ceased to practise their very art;

but, singing, with full gladness they welcomed the first
breezes within the leaves, which were murmuring the bur-
den to their songs;

even such as from bough to bough is gathered through
the pine wood on Chiassi's shore, when Æolus looses
Sirocco forth.[2]

Already my slow steps had carried me on so far within
the ancient wood, that I could not see whence I had
entered;

and lo, a stream took from me further passage which,
toward the left with its little waves, bent the grass which
sprang forth on its bank.

All the waters which here are purest, would seem to have
some mixture in them, compared with that, which hideth
nought;

albeit full darkly it flows beneath the everlasting shade,
which never lets sun, nor moon, beam there.

With feet I halted and with mine eyes did pass beyond
the rivulet, to gaze upon the great diversity of the tender
blossoms;

and there to me appeared, even as on a sudden something
appears which, through amazement, sets all other thought
astray,

a lady[3] solitary, who went along singing, and culling
flower after flower, wherewith all her path was painted.

"Pray, fair lady, who at love's beams dost warm thee, if
I may believe outward looks, which are wont to be a
witness of the heart,

may it please thee to draw forward," said I to her, "to-
wards this stream, so far that I may understand what thou
singest.

Thou makest me to remember, where and what Proserpine was in the time her mother lost her, and she lost the spring."[4]

As a lady who is dancing turns her round with feet close to the ground and to each other, and hardly putteth foot before foot,

she turned toward me upon the red and upon the yellow flowerets, not otherwise than a virgin that droppeth her modest eyes;

and made my prayers satisfied, drawing so near that the sweet sound reached me with its meaning.

Soon as she was there, where the grass is already bathed by the waves of the fair river, she vouchsafed to raise her eyes to me.

I do not believe that so bright a light shone forth under the eyelids of Venus, pierced by her son, against all his wont.[5]

She smiled from the right bank opposite, gathering more flowers with her hands, which the high land bears without seed.

Three paces the river kept us distant; but Hellespont, where Xerxes crossed, to this day a curb to all human pride,

endured not more hatred from Leander for its turbulent waves 'twixt Sestos and Abydos, than that did from me, because it opened not then.

"New-comers are ye," she began, "and perchance, because I am smiling in this place, chosen for nest of the human race,

some doubt doth hold you marvelling; but the psalm *Delectasti*[7] giveth light which may clear the mist from your understanding.

And thou, who art in front, and didst entreat me, say if aught else thou wouldst hear: for I came ready to all thy questioning till thou be satisfied."

"The water," said I, "and the music of the forest, are combating within me a new belief in a thing which I have heard contrary to this."[8]

Wherefore she: "I will tell from what cause that arises which makes thee marvel, and I will purge away the mist that offends thee.

The highest Good, who himself alone doth please, made man good and for goodness, and gave this place to him as an earnest of eternal peace.

Through his default, small time he sojourned here; through his default, for tears and sweat he exchanged honest laughter and sweet play.

In order that the storms, which the exhalations of the water and of the earth cause below it, and which follow so far as they can after the heat,

should do no hurt to man, this mount rose thus far towards heaven, and stands clear of them from where it is locked.[9]

Now since the whole of the air revolves in a circle with the primal motion, unless its circuit is broken in some direction,

such motion strikes on this eminence, which is all free in the pure air, and makes the wood to sound because it is dense;[10]

and the smitten plant has such power that with its virtue it impregnates the air, and that in its revolution then scatters it abroad;

and the other land, according as it is worthy of itself and of its climate, conceives and brings forth divers trees of divers virtues.

Were this understood, it would not then seem a marvel yonder when some plant takes root there without manifest seed.[11]

And thou must know that the holy plain where thou art, is full of every seed, and bears fruit in it which yonder is not plucked.

The water which thou seest wells not from a spring that is fed by moisture which cold condenses, like a river that gains and loses volume,[12]

but issues from a fount, constant and sure, which regains by God's will, so much as it pours forth freely on either side.[13]

On this side it descends with a virtue which takes from men the memory of sin;[14] on the other it restores the memory of every good deed.

On this side Lethe, as on the other Eunoë 'tis called, and works not except first it is tasted on this side and on that.[15]

This exceedeth all other savours; and albeit thy thirst may be full sated, even tho' I reveal no more to thee,

I will give thee yet a corollary as a grace; nor do I think that my words will be less precious to thee if they extend beyond my promise to thee.

They who in olden times sang of the golden age[16] and its happy state, perchance dreamed in Parnassus of this place.

Here the root of man's race was innocent; here spring is everlasting, and every kind of fruit; this is the nectar whereof each one tells."

Then did I turn me right back to my poets, and saw that with smiles they had heard the last interpretation; then to the fair Lady I turned my face.

1. Towards the west.

2. The mournful notes heard in the pine-forest of Ravenna, on the Adriatic shore [Chiassi, near Ravenna = the Classis of the Romans, who used it as a naval station and harbour; in Christian times a fortress was built there], when Æolus, king of the winds (*Æn.* i), lets loose the sirocco, or south-east wind. See Byron's *Don Juan*, iv.

3. This is Matilda (see Canto xxxiii), in all probability to be taken as the type of the Active Life. Historically, it is safest to identify her with Matelda, the *Grancontessa* of Tuscany (1046–1115), the supporter of Pope Gregory VII, the friend and bounteous benefactor of the Holy See and Church. Other attempts at identification have been made, some of them, notably Göschel's and Preger's, being of great ingenuity; but here, as so often, we shall do best in following the early commentators.

4. While gathering flowers in a lovely meadow, Proserpina was carried off by Pluto (*cf. Inf.* ix), in the presence of her mother and companions. A reference to Ovid, *Met.* v and to *Par.* xxx will show that *spring* means the "spring flowers" that fell from her tunic, when Pluto bore her off in his car.

5. When she became enamoured of Adonis. See Ovid, *Met.* x: *Namque pharetratus dum dat puer oscula matri, Inscius exstanti destrinxit arundine pectus.*

6. When Xerxes, King of Persia (485–465 B.C.) crossed the Hellespont (the modern Dardanelles) over a bridge of boats, to invade Greece, he had with him a host of a million soldiers; on his return, in a fishing boat, he was accompanied by a few men only [Orosius, whom Dante probably follows, points a similar moral—ii]. The same strait separated Leander from his mistress Hero; in order to see her, he swam across it many times and was eventually drowned (see Ovid, *Heroid*, xviii, xix).

7. *Delectasti me, Domine, in factura tua.* . . . "For thou, Lord, hast made me glad through thy work: I will triumph in the works of thy hands" (*Ps.* xcii. 4).

8. See Canto xxi.

9. From the Gate of Purgatory (see Canto ix).

10. "The air also flows in a circle, because it is drawn along with the circulation of the whole" (Aristotle).—"And thus that air which exceeds the greatest altitude of the mountains flows round, but the air which is contained within the altitude of the mountains is impeded from this flow by the immoveable parts of the earth" (Thomas Aquinas).

11. Here Dante gives a sort of supernatural-rationalistic explanation of what was in his day an accepted fact. "And the same holds with plants also, since some are produced by seed, others spontaneously by nature" (Aristotle).

12. For the formation of rain on earth, *cf.* Canto v.

13. See *Genesis* ii: "These are the generations of the heavens and of the earth when they were created, in the day that the Lord God made the earth and the heavens. And every plant of the field before it was in the earth, and every herb of the field before it grew: for the Lord God had not caused it to rain upon the earth, and there was not a man to till the ground. But there went up a mist from the earth, and watered the whole face of the ground. . . . And a river went out of Eden to water the garden; and from thence it was parted, and became into four heads. . . ." *Cf.* Canto xxxiii, *note* 17.

14. For Lethe, see *Inf.* xxxiv and *Purg.* i.

15. It would be natural to understand this passage as asserting that the drinking of Lethe produced no effect until Eunoë had been also drunk; but we see from Canto xxxiii that this is not the case. We are therefore compelled to interpret the passage more subtly. It appears, then, that the true function of the twofold stream is to sift out evil and sinful memories from the sources of joy and gratitude with which they are often inseparably mixed up on earth. For instance, when some unkindness or neglect of our own has been the cause of revealing to us the beauty and generosity of another's character; or when the shock consequent upon some error or sin that we have committed has roused within us the powers of resistance and aspiration, or brought us into contact with some strong and helpful soul, it appears that the immediate effect of drinking Lethe is not to separate out the good and bad, but to engulf in the forgetfulness of all evil, into which it throws the soul, the memory of all incidental good that was connected with it. See Canto xxxiii, *note* 14.

16. For the Golden Age, see Canto xxii, *note* 18.

ÇANTO XXIX

As she chants a blessing on those whose sins are forgiven, Matilda takes her way along one bank of the stream, while Dante keeps pace with her on the other; till the air, kindling with splendour and laden with sweet strains of song, fills Dante at once with the rapture of the Earthly Paradise and a sense of indignation against the act of sin which had bereft him and mankind of such delights—delights which all the waters of Helicon can scarce enable him to set in verse. Dante is pacing eastward, with the stream on his left hand flowing towards him, and on the other side of the stream a divine pageant approaches him; the details of which, together with words of song, are gradually disentangled by eye and ear. But when he turns to Virgil for enlightenment, his faithful teacher can no longer instruct him; these are things beyond the reach of his art. Seven lights leave the air painted with seven great rainbow streamers of colour stretching away as far as the eye can reach, throwing their glory over the heaven and glowing upon the stream. They represent the sevenfold gifts of the spirit, and beneath their glory tread four and twenty elders, crowned with lilies, representing the books of the Old Testament, chanting blessings on the Virgin. They are followed by the four Gospel beasts as described by Ezekiel and John, enclosing between them the triumphal chariot of the Church, resting on the two wheels of the contemplative and active life, drawn by a griffin whose twofold nature represents the two natures in one person of Christ. The sun itself has not so glorious a chariot. By the right wheel the three theological virtues dance, and by the left the four cardinal virtues. Then come two elders, then four, then one, crowned with roses, representing the remaining books of the New Testament. When Dante is just opposite the car, a peal of thunder arrests the whole procession.

AT THE END of her words, singing like an enamoured lady, she continued: *"Beati, quorum tecta sunt peccata."*[1]

And, as nymphs who used to wend alone through the woodland shades, one desiring to see, another to flee the sun,

363

she then advanced against the stream, walking on the bank, and I abreast of her, little step answering with little step.

Not a hundred were her steps with mine, when both banks alike made a bend in such wise that I turned me to the east.

Nor yet was our way thus very far, when the lady turned her full round to me, saying, "Brother mine, look and hearken."

And lo, a sudden brightness flooded on all sides the great forest, such that it set me in doubt if 'twere lightning.

But since lightning ceases even as it cometh, and that enduring, brighter and brighter shone, in my mind I said: "What thing is this?"

And a sweet melody ran through the luminous air; wherefore righteous zeal made me reprove Eve's daring,

who, there where heaven and earth obeyed, a woman alone and but then formed, did not bear to remain under any veil,[2]

under which, if she had been devout, I should have tasted those ineffable joys ere this, and for a longer time.

While I was going amid so many first-fruits of the eternal pleasance, all enrapt and still yearning for more joys,

the air in front of us under the green boughs, became even as a flaming fire to us, and the sweet sound was heard as a chant.

O holy, holy, Virgins, if e'er for you I have endured fastings, cold, or vigils, occasion spurs me to crave my reward.

Now 'tis meet that Helicon for me stream forth and Urania aid me with her choir to set in verse things hard to conceive.[3]

A little farther on, a delusive semblance of seven trees of gold[4] was caused by the long space that was yet between us and them;

but when I had drawn so nigh to them that the general similitude of things,[5] which deceives the senses, lost not by distance any of its features,

the faculty[6] which prepares material for reason distinguished them as candlesticks,[4] even as they were, and in the words of the chant, "Hosannah."[7]

Above, the fair pageant was flaming forth, brighter far than the moon in clear midnight sky in her mid month.

Full of wonderment I turned me to the good Virgil, and he answered me with a face not less charged with amazement.

Then I turned my countenance back to the sublime things, which moved towards us so slowly, that they would be vanquished by new-wedded brides.

The lady cried to me: "Wherefore art thou so ardent only for the vision of these bright lights, and heedest not that which comes after them?"

Then I beheld people, clad in white, following as after their leaders; and whiteness so pure here never was with us.

Bright shone the water on my left flank, and reflected to me my left side, if I gazed therein, even as a mirror.

When I was so placed on my bank that the river alone kept me distant, to see better I gave halt to my steps,

and I saw the flames advance, leaving the air behind them painted, and of trailing pennants they had the semblance;

so that the air above remained streaked with seven bands, all in those colours whereof the sun makes his bow, and Delia her girdle.

These banners streamed to the rearward far beyond my sight, and as I might judge, the outermost were ten paces apart.[8]

Beneath so fair a sky, as I describe, came four and twenty elders, two by two, crowned with flower-de-luce.[9]

All were singing: "Blessed thou among the daughters of Adam, and blessed to all eternity be thy beauties."[10]

When the flowers and the other tender herbs opposite to me on the other bank, were free from those chosen people,

even as star follows star in the heavens, four creatures came after them, each one crowned with green leaves.

Every one was plumed with six wings, the plumes full of eyes; and the eyes of Argus, were they living, would be such.

To describe their form, reader, I spill no more rhymes; for other charges bind me so, that herein I cannot be lavish.

But read Ezekiel who depicts them as he saw them coming from the cold region, with whirlwind, with cloud, and with fire;

and as thou shalt find them in his pages, such were they here, save that in the pinions John is with me, and differs from him.[11]

The space within the four of them contained a car triumphal, upon two wheels,[12] which came drawn at the neck of a griffin.

And he stretched upwards one wing and the other, between the middle and the three and three bands, so that he did hurt to none by cleaving.[13]

So high they rose that they were not seen; his members had he of gold, so far as he was a bird, and the others white mingled with vermilion.[14]

Not only Africanus, nor in sooth, Augustus, e'er rejoiced Rome with a car so fair,[15] but that of the sun would be poor beside it,

that of the sun, which straying was consumed at the devout prayer of the earth, when Jove was mysteriously just.[16]

Three ladies came dancing in a round by the right wheel; one so red that hardly would she be noted in the fire;

the next was as if her flesh and bone had been made of emerald; the third seemed new-fallen snow;

and now seemed they led by the white, now by the red, and from the song of her the others took measure slow and quick.[17]

By the left wheel, four clad in purple, made festival, following the lead of one of them, who had three eyes in her head.[18]

After all the group described, I saw two aged men, unlike in raiment, but like in bearing, and venerable and grave:

one showed him to be of the familiars of that highest Hippocrates whom nature made for the creatures she holds most dear;

the other showed the contrary care, with a sword glittering and sharp, such that on this side the stream it made me afeard.[19]

Then saw I four[20] of lowly semblance; and behind all an old man solitary, coming in a trance, with visage keen.[21]

And these seven were arrayed as the first company; but of lilies around their heads no garland had they,

Rather of roses and of other red flowers; one who viewed from short distance would have sworn that all were aflame above the eyes.[22]

And when the car was opposite to me, a thunder clap was heard; and those worthy folk seemed to have their further march forbidden, and halted there with the first ensigns.

1. "Blessed is he whose transgression is forgiven, whose sin is covered" (*Ps.* xxxii. 1).

2. *Cf. Par.* xix, *note* 2.

3. With this invocation to the Muses, *cf. Inf.* ii and xxxii; *Purg.* i; *Par.* i, ii and xviii.—Helicon was in reality a *mountain* in Bœotia, sacred to the Muses (from which *sprang* two fountains associated with them—Aganippe and Hippocrene). Urania—the Muse of astronomy and heavenly things.

4. "And being turned, I saw seven golden candlesticks . . . and the seven candlesticks . . . are the seven churches" (*Rev.* i. 12, 20) . . . "and there were seven lamps burning before the throne, which are the seven Spirits of God" (*Rev.* iv. 5). Dante seems to have amalgamated these two passages for the purpose of his allegory. See, too, *Conv.* iv. 21: "By the Theological way it is possible to say that, when the supreme Deity, that is God, sees his creature prepared to receive his good gift, so freely he imparts it to his creature in proportion as it is prepared to receive it. And because these gifts proceed from ineffable Love, and the Divine Love is appropriate to the Holy Spirit, therefore it is that they are called the gifts of the Holy Spirit, which, even as the Prophet Isaiah distinguishes them [*Vulgate*, xi], are seven, namely, Wisdom, Understanding, Counsel, Might, Knowledge, Pity and the Fear of the Lord."

5. The "proper" objects of the senses are those which are perceived by one sense only, as colour by the sight, sound by the hearing, savour by the taste; and in these, according to Aristotle, the senses cannot be deceived. "But the common objects are motion, rest, number, shape, size; for such things are not the proper objects of any sense, but are common to all," and with respect to them the senses may err.

6. Probably the apprehensive faculty (see Canto xviii, *note* 1.—Mr. Butler quotes *Hamlet*, i: "A beast that wants discourse of reason."

7. "Hosanna," the word with which the Jews hailed Jesus on his entry into Jerusalem (*Matt.* xxi. 9; *Mark* xi. 9; *John* xii. 13); here used by the twenty-four elders preceding Christ's chariot.

8. The seven bands or pennons trailing behind the candlesticks may be taken as the seven sacraments, or, perhaps, better, as the working

of the seven gifts. The colours of the rainbow and of the moon's halo [Diana was born on the island of Delos] may have been suggested by *Rev.* iv. 3: "... and there was a rainbow about the throne in sight like unto an emerald "–The *paces* probably indicate the ten commandments.

9. These elders represent the twenty-four books of the Old Testament (the twelve minor prophets count as one book, 1 and 2 Kings as one, so with Samuel, Chronicles and Ezra-Nehemiah). Their voices and their white garments (emblematical of Faith; see *Hebrews* xi) were referred to above; and the whole conception of them is derived from *Rev.* iv. 4: "And round about the throne were four and twenty seats; and upon the seats I saw four and twenty elders sitting, clothed in white raiment; and they had on their heads crowns of gold." The crowns of "flower-de-luce" suggest the purity of their faith and teaching.

10. "Blessed art thou among women"—the words of the angel and of Elizabeth to Mary (*Luke* i. 28, 42); here addressed either to Mary or to Beatrice.

11. See the description of these four beasts in *Ezek.* i. 4–14 and *Rev.* iv. 6–9. The faces of the man, lion, ox (or calf) and eagle represent Matthew, Mark, Luke, and John, respectively. The green leaves indicate Hope ("Lord Jesus Christ, which is our hope" 1 *Tim.* i. 1). According to Pietro di Dante the beast's six wings are the six laws—natural, Mosaic, prophetic, evangelical, Apostolic and canonical; [in *Ezekiel* we read that "everyone had four wings"; while John says that "the four beasts had each of them six wings about him"]. The eyes indicate the knowledge of things past and future [for Argus, with the hundred eyes, see Canto xxxii, *note* 12].

12. The two wheels have been explained in many different ways, the interpretation adopted in the *Argument* being one of the most satisfactory. According to others, they indicate the Old and the New Testaments; the orders of the Dominicans and Franciscans, etc.

13. "Looking to *Pss.* xxvi and lvii and comparing verses 5 and 7 of the former with 1 and 11 of the latter, it seems that we must understand them [the wings] as denoting—the one mercy, the other truth or justice. Then their position with regard to the bands will be made intelligible by a reference to *Ps.* xxxvi. 10: 'O stretch forth thy mercy over those that know thee [*scientia*], and thy justice over them that are of a right heart [*consilium*]' " (Butler).

14. "My beloved is white and ruddy, the chiefest among ten thousand. His head is as the most fine gold ..." (*Song of Solomon*, v. 10, 11).

15. The cars used by these and all victorious Roman generals in their "triumphs."

16. "For Phaëton see *Inf.* xvii, *note* 8.

17. Faith (white), Hope (green) and Charity (red); *cf.* Canto viii. The song of Charity leads the measure because, according to

1 *Cor.* xxiii. 13: ". . . now abideth faith, hope, charity, these three; but the greatest of these is charity."

18. For the moral or cardinal virtues, see Canto i, *note* 3.—Even in the *Convito* (iv. 17), where Dante follows Aristotle (in whose system Prudence is an intellectual virtue), he feels constrained to say: "By many, Prudence, that is Wisdom, is well asserted to be a moral virtue; but Aristotle numbers that amongst the intellectual virtues, although it is the guide of the moral, and points out the way by which they are formed, and without which they cannot be." The three eyes of Prudence have reference to the past, present and future, and the purple garb of the four virtues to the Empire (*cf.* Canto xxxii, *note* 11).

19. These two are Luke (considered as author of the *Acts*) and Paul. Paul describes Luke (in *Col.* iv. 14) as "the beloved physician"; he is therefore regarded as a spiritual Hippocrates (this being the name of a famous Greek physician). The *creatures* of course = mankind. The explanation of Paul's sword is to be found either in his own words (*Eph.* vi. 17): ". . . the sword of the Spirit, which is the word of God"; or in the circumstance that he was always represented with one (in reference to his martyrdom by sword).

20. James, Peter, John and Jude—the authors of the four catholic epistles.

21. John, considered as author of *Revelation*—a series of visions, concerning things that must shortly come to pass; hence he is represented as *in a trance* and *with vision keen*.

22. We saw that the *flower-de-luce* was emblematical of the purity of the old Testament; now the charity of the New Testament is indicated by the *rose* and *other red flowers*.

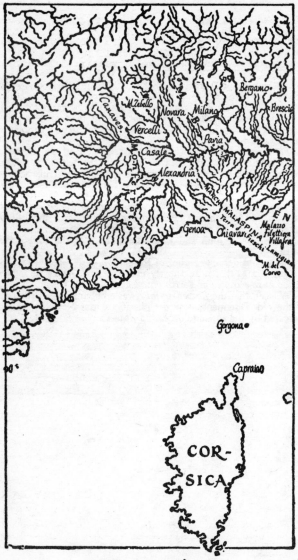

UPPER ITALY IN DANTE'S TIME

CENTRAL ITALY IN DANTE'S TIME

ÇANTO XXX

When the car arrests itself, all the elders who had preceded it, turn and face round to it; and when one of them invokes the bride of Lebanon, blessed spirits rise up around it, as men shall rise at the last day. Flowers are flung in a cloud from their hands as they utter blessings, culled from Christian and Gentile scriptures; and a form clad in the colours of the three theological virtues rises like the sun in their midst. Dante without further testimony from his eyes, recognizes the tokens of the ancient flame, and like a terrified child turns round to ask comfort and support from Virgil. But Virgil has gone, and not even the joys of the Earthly Paradise can prevent Dante's cheeks, though cleansed by the mountain dew, from darkening again with tears. But the sense of outward loss when bereft of Virgil is soon swallowed up in the sense of inward loss caused by his own faithlessness and sin; for Beatrice sternly recalls him to face his own insulted and outraged ideal. Bereft of Virgil's support when he looks around, encountering his own image in the stream when he looks down, like a child before an angered mother, Dante feels his heart at first frozen by reproaches, then melted by the pleading intercession of the angels. But Beatrice is still unbending; and turning to the angelic presences she rehearses the promise of Dante's youth and the unworthiness of his manhood, the gracious and fleeting beauty of his early vows, the pursuit of false good to which he then surrendered himself, her own unavailing pleadings with him, and his fall, so deep that naught save the vision of the region of the lost, won for him by her prayers and tears, could avail to save him. The deep fate of God were broken should he taste of the higher joys, access to which she had won for him, without paying some scot of penitential tears.

WHEN THE WAIN of the first heaven which setting nor rising never knew, nor veil of other mist than of sin,

and which made there each one aware of his duty, even as the lower wain guides him who turns the helm to come into port,[1]

had stopped still, the people of ʌruth, who had first come

between the griffin and it,[2] turned them to the car as to their peace;

and one of them as if sent from heaven "*Veni sponsa de Libano*"[3] did shout thrice in song, and all the others after him.

As the saints at the last trump shall rise ready each one from his tomb, with re-clad voice singing Halleluiah,

such on the divine chariot rose up a hundred *ad vocem tanti senis*, ministers and messengers of life eternal.[4]

All were saying: "*Benedictus qui venis*";[5] and, strewing flowers above and around, "*Manibus o date lilia plenis.*"[6]

Ere now have I seen, at dawn of day, the eastern part all rosy red, and the rest of heaven adorned with fair clear sky,

and the face of the sun rise shadowed, so that by the tempering of the mists the eye long time endured him:

so within a cloud of flowers, which rose from the angelic hands and fell down again within and without,

olive-crowned over a white veil, a lady appeared to me, clad, under a green mantle, with hue of living flame.[7]

And my spirit, that now so long a time had passed, since, trembling in her presence, it had been broken down with awe,

without having further knowledge by mine eyes through hidden virtue which went out from her, felt the mighty power of ancient love.

Soon as on my sight the lofty virtue smote, which already had pierced me ere I was out of my boyhood,

I turned me to the left with the trust with which the little child runs to his mother when he is frightened or when he is afflicted,

to say to Virgil: "Less than a drachm of blood is left in me that trembleth not; I recognize the tokens of the ancient flame."[8]

But Virgil had left us bereft of himself, Virgil sweetest Father, Virgil to whom for my weal I gave me up;

nor did all that our ancient mother lost,[9] avail to keep my dew-washed cheeks[10] from turning dark again with tears.

"Dante,[11] for that Virgil goeth away, weep not yet, weep not yet, for thou must weep for other sword."

Even as an admiral, who at stern and at bow, comes to

see the folk that man the other ships, and heartens them to brave deeds,

so on the left side of the car, when I turned me at sound of my name, which of necessity here is recorded,[11]

I saw the lady, who first appeared to me veiled beneath the angelic festival, directing her eyes to me on this side the stream.

Albeit the veil which fell from her head, crowned with Minerva's leaves, did not let her appear manifest,

queenlike, in bearing yet stern, she continued, like one who speaks and holdeth back the hottest words till the last:

"Look at me well; verily am I, verily am I Beatrice. How didst thou deign to draw nigh the mount? knewest thou not that here man is happy?"

Mine eyes drooped down to the clear fount; but beholding me therein, I drew them back to the grass, so great a shame weighed down my brow.

So doth the mother seem stern to her child, as she seemed to me; for the savour of harsh pity tasteth of bitterness.

She was silent, and straightway the angels sang: *In te, Domine, speravi*"; but beyond "*pedes meos*" they passed not.[12]

As the snow amid the living rafters along Italia's back is frozen under blast and stress of Slavonian winds,

then melted trickles down through itself, if but the land that loseth shade do breathe, so that it seems fire melting the candle,[13]

so without tears or sighs was I before the song of those who ever accord their notes after the melodies of the eternal spheres.[14]

But when I heard in their sweet harmonies their compassion on me, more than if they had said "Lady, why dost thou so shame him?"

The ice which had closed about my heart became breath and water, and with anguish through mouth and eyes issued from my breast.

She, standing yet fixed on the said side of the car, then turned her words[15] to the pitying angels thus:

"Ye watch in the everlasting day, so that nor night nor

sleep stealeth from you one step which the world may take along its ways;

wherefore my answer is with greater care, that he who yon side doth weep may understand me, so that sin and sorrow be of one measure.

Not only by operation of the mighty spheres that direct each seed to some end, according as the stars are its companions,[16]

but by the bounty of graces divine, which have for their rain vapours so high that our eyes reach not nigh them,[17]

this man was such in his new life[18] potentially, that every good talent would have made wondrous increase in him.

But so much the more rank and wild the ground becomes with evil seed and untilled, the more it hath of good strength of soil.

Some time I sustained him with my countenance; showing my youthful eyes to him I led him with me turned to the right goal.[19]

So soon as I was on the threshold of my second age, and I changed life, he forsook me, and gave him to others.[20]

When I was risen from flesh to spirit, and beauty and virtue were increased within me, I was less precious and less pleasing to him;

and he did turn his steps by a way not true, pursuing false visions of good, that pay back no promise entire.[21]

Nor did it avail me to gain inspirations, with which in dream and otherwise, I called him back; so little recked he of them.[22]

so low sank he, that all means for his salvation were already short, save showing him the lost people.

For this I visited the portal of the dead, and to him who has guided him up hither, weeping my prayers were borne.[23]

God's high decree would be broken, if Lethe were passed, and such viands were tasted, without some scot of penitence that may shed tears."

1. The "wain of the first heaven" are the seven candlesticks, which are the spiritual guides of the righteous; even as the seven stars of the Septentrio or Ursa Minor direct the mariner making for port.
2. The twenty-four elders.

3. The elder representing the books of Solomon sang aloud three times the words of the *Song of Solomon* (iv. 8): "Come with me from Lebanon, my spouse, with me from Lebanon."

4. These are identical with the angels mentioned later: *ad vocem tanti senis,* "at the voice of so great an elder."

5. "Blessed art thou that comest." See *Matt.* xxi. 9, *Mark* xi. 9, *Luke* xix. 38, *John* xii. 13; and *cf.* the preceding canto, *note* 7.

6. "Oh, with full hands give lilies" (*Æn.* vi).

7. This is Beatrice. Note the colours of Faith, Hope and Charity. In the *Vita Nuova* [the whole of which should be read in conjunction with the present and the following canto; see, too, Gardner, pp. 8, 9, 13–15, 45–53], Beatrice appears in red and white, but never in green. The olive was sacred to Minerva, the Goddess of Wisdom.

8. The appearance of Beatrice has the same effect on Dante now as in the days of the *Vita Nuova* (§ ii, xi, xiv and xxiv).—*so long a time:* ten years—1290–1300; see *note* 20. Dante first met Beatrice when he was in his ninth year, she being also eight years old, but some months younger (*Vita Nuova,* § ii). The last phrase is a translation of Virgil's *Agnosco veteris vestigia flammæ* (*Æn.* iv).

9. The beauties of the Earthly Paradise.

10. See Canto i.

11. The only instance in which Dante's name occurs in the *Commedia* (for in *Par.* xxvi *da te* is almost certainly the correct reading). In the *Vita Nuova, Conv.* and *De Mon.* he does not name himself, either; and in the *De Vulg. El.* he goes out of his way to call himself *amicus Cini* or *alius Florentinus.* The explanation of this circumstance (which would pass unnoticed with almost any other author, but which is curious in the case of so personal and subjective a writer as Dante) is to be found in the *Conv.* (i. 2), where we learn that "it appears to be unlawful for anyone to speak of himself"; and that "one does not permit any rhetorician to speak of himself without a necessary cause." In his epistles, which are personal communications, not posing as literature (though they have since achieved literary fame), Dante does not follow this rule.

12. See *Ps.* xxxi. 1–8: "In thee, O Lord, do I put my trust . . . thou hast set my feet in a large room."

13. These lines describe the snow on the ridges of the Apennines, first congealed, when the winds blow from the north; and then dissolved, at the time of the warm and gentle breezes that come from Africa ("where twice a year, at noon, the sun touches the zenith of each point; so that the shadow of an opaque body, in a vertical position, falls at its base and appears nowhere."—Antonelli).

14. See *Par.* i.

15. *Sustanzie* in the original. See Canto xviii, *note* 5; and *cf. Par.* vii.

16. *Cf. Inf.* xv and *Purg.* xvi.

17. *Cf. Par.* xx and xxxii.

18. The use of the phrase *vita nuova* in this line is relied on by those who understand Dante's work which bears this title simply as a record of his "Early Life"· but it is better to reverse the argument,

PURGATORIO

and take this verse to mean: "but in the new life into which love led him, had such power," etc. For though there are many cases in which *nova età* means "early life," none has been produced in which *nova vita* has that meaning, and Dante's elder contemporary, Dante da Majano, whose language evidently had a considerable influence upon Dante Alighieri, uses the phrase (in the poem which begins *Giovane donna dentro al cor mi siede*) in such a way as to leave no room for ambiguity: *Gli spirti inamorati cui diletta Questa lor nova vita* ("the enamoured spirits, whom this new life of theirs delights").

19. For sixteen years, from 1274, the year in which Dante first met Beatrice, till 1290, the year of her death.

20. Beatrice was twenty-five years old when she died—a period that covers the first of Dante's four ages. "The first is called Adolescence, that is the growth of life. . . . Of the first no one doubts, but each wise man agrees that it lasts even to the twenty-fifth year; and up to that time our soul waits for the increase and the embellishment of the body" (*Conv.* iv. 24).

21. These lines refer to the period of Dante's life (1290–1300) which has already been touched on in connection with Forese Donati (see Canto xxiii). The first words (as in the following canto) have a very personal ring, and would seem to refer not so much to the *donna gentile* of the *Vita Nuova*, § xxxvi (whether allegorically or literally, and whether, in the latter capacity, she be Gemma Donati or another), as to those other, less creditable, infidelities to Beatrice's memory, of which our poet was undoubtedly guilty at this time, and to which several of his minor poems and *Purg.* xxiii bear witness. On the other hand they possibly allude to Dante's temporary indifference to religion, due to his philosophical studies during this period; and may therefore be connected with the *donna gentile* of the *Vita Nuova*, who is, in the *Conv.* ii. 13, identified with Philosophy.

22. *in dream.* A vision of this kind, and apparently the last, is described in the *Vita Nuova*, § xl, where Dante tells how his "heart began painfully to repent of the desire by which it had so basely let itself be possessed during so many days, contrary to the constancy of reason. And then, this evil desire being quite gone from me, all my thoughts turned again unto their excellent Beatrice. And I say most truly that from that hour I thought constantly of her with the whole humbled and ashamed heart; the which became often manifest in sighs, that had among them the name of that most gracious creature, and how she departed from us."

23. See *Inf.* ii.

CANTO XXXI

Turning direct to Dante, Beatrice receives his broken confession of how he fell away so soon as her countenance was hidden from him. Whereon she shows him how that very loss of her bodily presence, which he urges as the cause of his defection, should have taught him the emptiness of all earthly and mortal beauty, weaned his heart from earth and given it to her in heaven. Like a chidden child, dumb with shame, confessing and repenting, Dante stands; but Beatrice will not suffer him to take refuge in childish pleas or excuses, and in the very terms whereby she summons him to look on her, reminds him that he has reached man's estate, and should long have put away childish things. Whereon, in yet deeper shame, he wrenches up his downcast face to look on her, and sees her surpassing her former self more now that erst she surpassed all others. The passion of his penitence and his hatred of all those things which had enticed him away from her so vanquish him that he falls senseless to the ground. Dante comes to himself neck-deep in the stream, into which he plunges his head, of which he drinks, and which he crosses, by Matilda's ministration. After which he is drawn into the dance of the four star-nymphs who promise to lead him to the light of Beatrice's eyes; into which their three sisters, Faith, Hope and Charity will strengthen him to gaze. They keep their word; but Dante's passionate reminiscences and longings are awed by the august impersonation of Revelation, whom he has found where he looked only for the Florentine maiden he had lost on earth. The divine and human nature of Christ are flashed alternately from the reflection in her eyes though ever combined in the mysterious Being himself, while the three nymphs implore Beatrice to turn their light upon her faithful pilgrim and unveil to him the beauty of her smile. Never was poet who could utter in words that spendour that now bursts upon him.

"O THOU THAT art yon side the sacred stream," her speech directing with the point towards me, which even with the edge had seemed sharp to me,

she began again, continuing without delay, "say, say, if
378

this is true; to such accusation thy confession must be joined."

My virtue was so confounded that the voice stirred and was spent ere it was free from its organs.

Short time she forbore, then said: "What thinkest thou? Answer me, for the sad memories in thee are not yet destroyed by the water."[1]

Confusion and fear, together mingled, drove forth from my mouth a "Yea" such that to understand it the eyes were needed.

As a cross-bow breaks, when shot at too great tension, both its string and bow, and with less force the bolt hits the mark,

so burst I under this heavy charge, pouring forth a torrent of tears and sighs, and my voice died away in its passage.

Wherefore she to me: "Within thy desires of me which led thee to love the good[2] beyond which is nought that may be aspired to,

what pits didst find athwart thy path, or what claims that thou needs must strip thee of the hope of passing onward?

And what allurements or what advantages were displayed to thee in the aspect of the others,[2] that thou must needs wander before them?"

After the heaving of a bitter sigh, scarce had I voice that answered, and my lips with labour gave it form.

Weeping I said: "Present things with their false pleasure turned away my steps soon as your face was hidden."

And she: "If thou wert silent, or if thou hadst denied what thou confessest, not less noted were thy fault; by such a judge 'tis known.

But when self-accusation of sin bursts from the cheeks in our Court, the grindstone is turned back against the edge.[3]

Howbeit in order that now thou mayst bear shame for thy transgression, and that other time hearing the Sirens thou be of stouter heart,

put away the seed of weeping, and hearken; so shalt thou hear how my buried flesh should have moved thee towards a contrary goal.

Ne'er did nature and art present to thee pleasure so great as the fair members wherein I was enclosed, and are scattered to dust;

and if the highest pleasure thus failed thee by my death, what mortal thing ought then to have drawn thee to desire it?

Truly oughtest thou, at the first arrow of deceitful things, to rise up after me who was such no longer.

Young damsel or other vain thing with so brief enjoyment, should not have weighed down thy wings to await more shots.[4]

The young bird waits two or three, but before the eyes of the full-fledged in vain the net is spread or arrow shot."[5]

As children, dumb with shame, stand listening with eyes to earth, self-confessing, and repentant,

such stood I. And she said: "Since through hearing thou art grieving, lift up thy beard and more grief shalt thou receive by looking."

With less resistance is uprooted the sturdy oak, whether by wind of ours, or that which blows from Iarbas' land,[6]

Than at her command I lifted up my chin; and when by the beard she asked for my face, well I knew the venom of the argument.

And when my face was stretched forth, my sight perceived those primal creatures[7] resting from their strewing,

and mine eyes, as yet hardly steadfast, saw Beatrice turned towards the beast, which is one sole person in two natures.

Under her veil and beyond the stream, to me she seemed to surpass more her ancient self, than she surpassed the others here when she was with us.

The nettle of repentance here so did sting me, that of all other things, that which turned me most to love of it became most hateful to me

so much remorse gnawed at my heart that I fell vanquished, and what I then became, she knoweth who gave me the cause.

Then when my heart restored to me the sense of outward things, the lady whom I had found alone I saw above me; and she said: "Hold me! Hold me!"

She had drawn me into the river up to my neck, and, pulling me after her, went along over the water light as a shuttle.

When I was nigh unto the blessed bank *"Asperges me"*[8] so sweetly I heard that I cannot remember it much less describe it.

The fair lady opened her arms, clasped my head, and dipped me where I must needs swallow of the water;

then drew me forth, and led me bathed within the dance of the four fair ones, and each did cover me with her arm.

"Here we are nymphs and in heaven are stars;[9] ere Beatrice descended to the world we were ordained to her for her handmaids.[10]

We will lead thee to her eyes; but the three on the other side who deeper gaze, will sharpen thine eyes to the joyous light that is within."

Thus singing they began; and then did lead me with them up to the breast of the griffin, where Beatrice stood turned towards us.

They said: "Look that thou spare not thine eyes; we have placed thee before the emeralds[11] whence Love once drew his shafts at thee."[12]

A thousand desires hotter than flame held mine eyes bound to the shining eyes, which remained ever fixed upon the griffin.

As the sun in a mirror, not otherwise the twofold beast was beaming within them, now with the attributes of one, now of the other nature.

Think, reader, if I marvelled within me when I saw the thing itself remain motionless, and in its image it was changing.[13]

While my soul, filled with wonderment and glad, was tasting of that food which, satisfying of itself, causes thirst of itself,[14]

the other three, showing them to be of the chiefest order in their bearing, drew forward, dancing to their angelic roundelay.

"Turn, Beatrice, turn thy holy eyes," was their song, "to thy faithful one, who to see thee hath moved so many steps.

Of thy grace do us the grace that thou unveil thy mouth to him, that he may discern the second beauty which thou hidest."[15]

O glory of living eternal, who that so pale hath grown beneath the shade of Parnassus, or hath drunk at its well,

that would not seem to have mind encumbered, on trying to render thee as thou appearedst, when in the free air thou didst disclose thee, where heaven in its harmony shadows thee forth?

1. The water of Lethe (see Canto xxviii and later in the present canto).
2. *good* = God; *others* [goods] = worldly ideals.
3. Confession, by softening the Divine wrath, blunts the edge of the sword of Justice. *Cf.* Canto viii, and the first interpretation given in *note* 3.
4. It seems best not to attempt to identify the *young damsel.*
5. *Cf. Prov.* i. 17, in the Vulgate.
6. *wind of ours*—the wind blows from the north of Europe (the continent in which Italy is); the south wind comes from Africa, called "Iarbas' land" from the Libyan king of that name, one of Dido's suitors (see *Æn.* iv).
7. The angels; *cf. Inf.* vii and *Purg.* xi.
8. "Purge me with hyssop, and I shall be clean: wash me, and I shall be whiter than snow" (*Ps.* li. 7).
9. See Canto i, *note* 3
10. It is quite natural for those who argue that Beatrice is a purely allegorical character to insist on this passage as implying her preexistence in heaven, before her incarnation as an earthly maiden. The passage, however, does not necessarily imply this, for it is only carrying a little further the familiar language employed by Dante in the *Vita Nuova*, § xxvi, the sonnet; *Conv.* iv. 28; *Purg.* xx and xxi; *Par.* xxx—all indicating that the soul comes from heaven. From the assertion that the ascent to heaven at death is a *return*, it is but a very small step to describe the birth as a *descent* to the world.
11. The eyes of Beatrice are called "emeralds," not with reference to their colour, but because of their brightness (*shining eyes*).
12. *Cf. Vita Nuova* § xxi, the first line of the sonnet: "My lady carries love within her eyes." This idea occurs elsewhere in Dante's poems and is a commonplace with his predecessors and contemporaries.
13. This passage is to be taken in a purely allegorical sense. "We may read in Revelation now the divine and now the human attributes of Christ; but the human mind is incapable of combining them. As we contemplate Revelation we may see now one and now the other, but not both at once."

14. *Cf.* the words of Wisdom in *Eccles.* xxiv. 21: "They that eat me shall yet be hungry, and they that drink me shall yet be thirsty."

15. See the canzone in the third book of the *Convito*, which runs as follows: "Her aspect shows delight of Paradise, Seen in her eyes and in her smiling face; Love brought them there as to his dwelling-place." From Dante's commentary to the words *Dico negli occhi e nel suo dolce riso* (*ib.* 8), it seems probable that the *second beauty* to which the theological virtues are now leading Dante, is the *smile* of Beatrice; the cardinal virtues having guided him to her *eyes*

CANTO XXXII

The eager gaze with which Dante quenches his ten years' thirst, is for a moment blinded by the glory on which he looks. When he recovers his full powers of vision he perceives the procession deploying north, toward the noonday sun; and he and Statius take their places by the right wheel of the chariot; and pass on, to the accompaniment of angelic song, through the forest, till Beatrice descends. They approach the tree of the knowledge of good and evil, which represents the principle of obedience, and therefore of the Empire, whereas the car from which Beatrice has descended represents the Church; the ideal relations between which two powers are represented by the reverence of the griffin for the tree, the binding of the pole of the chariot to it, and the spring beauty that at once falls on it. Here slumber falls upon the Poet, from which he wakes bewildered, like the apostles after the transfiguration, to find Beatrice bereft of all her glorious escort save the seven nymphs, bearing in their hands the seven tapers. Here, in this deserted Earthly Paradise, which would be thronged with inhabitants had Church and State been true to their mission, Dante beholds an allegorical portrayal of the perverse relations between the two, and of the disasters and corruptions of the Church, of her persecutions, of the heresies that threatened her, of the yet more fatal favour of Christian emperors, of the great schism of Islam, of the foul corruption of the Court of Rome, and the Babylonian captivity of Avignon.

SO FIXED and intent were my eyes on satisfying their ten years' thirst,[1] that all my other senses were quenched;

and they on either side had a wall of unconcern, so the holy smile drew them to itself in the toils of old;

when perforce my face was turned toward my left by those goddesses, because I heard from them a: "Too fixedly."[2]

And that condition of the sight, which is in eyes but just smitten by the sun, made me remain a while without vision;

but after my sight re-formed itself to the lesser (I mean

the lesser in respect to the greater object of sense where-
from perforce I turned me away)

I saw the glorious host had wheeled upon the right flank,
and was returning with the sun and with the seven flames
in its face.

As under its shields a troop turns about to retreat, and
wheels round with the standard ere it can wholly change
front,

that soldierly of the heavenly realm, which was in the
van, passed all by us ere the car turned its pole.

Then to the wheels the ladies returned, and the griffin
moved the hallowed burden, so that thereby no plume of it
was ruffled.[3]

The fair lady who drew me across the ford, and Statius,
and I, were following the wheel which made its orbit with
the lesser arc.[4]

So pacing the lofty forest, empty through the fault of
her who gave credence to the serpent, a melody of angels
gave measure to our steps.

Haply in three flights so much space an arrow shot forth
had covered, as we had advanced when Beatrice descended.

I heard all murmur[5] "Adam!" Then did they surround
a tree despoiled of flowers,[6] and of other foliage, in every
bough.

Its crown of foliage, which more expands the loftier it is,
would be marvelled at for its height by Indians in their
woods.[7]

"Blessed art thou, griffin, that with thy beak dost rend
naught from this tree sweet to taste, since ill writhes the
belly therefrom."

Thus round about the sturdy tree the others cried: and
the beast of two natures: "Thus[8] is preserved the seed of
all righteousness."

And having turned to the pole which he had drawn, he
dragged it to the foot of the widowed bough; and to it left
bound that which came from it.[9]

As trees of our land when the great light falls down
mingled with that which beams behind the celestial carp,[10]

burgeon forth, and each then is decked anew with its

colour ere the sun yokes his steeds beneath another con-
stellation,

opening out into a hue, less than of roses and more than
of violets,[11] the tree renewed itself, which before had its
boughs so naked.

I understood it not, nor here is sung, the hymn which
then that people sang, nor did I endure its melody out-
right.

If I could portray how the pitiless eyes did slumber
hearing of Syrinx, the eyes whose longer vigil cost so
dear,[12]

as a painter who paints from a model, I would depict
how I feel asleep; be he who he may that can rightly image
drowsiness.

Wherefore I pass on to when I awoke, and I say that a
bright light rent the veil of my sleep, and a call: "Arise,
what doest thou?"

As to behold some flowerets of the apple tree, which
makes the angels greedy for its fruit, and makes perpetual
marriage feast in heaven,

Peter and John and James were brought, and, being
overcome, came to themselves at the word by which
greater slumbers had been broken,

and saw their band diminished by Moses, as well as by
Elias, and their Master's raiment changed,[13]

even so I came to myself, and saw that pitying one bend-
ing o'er me, who before was guide to my steps along the
stream.

And all perplexed I said: "Where is Beatrice!" and she:
"Behold her sitting beneath the new foliage upon its root.[14]

Behold the company that encircleth her; the others are
mounting up after the griffin with sweeter and profounder
song."

And if her words extended farther I know not, because
now before mine eyes was she, who had shut me off from
heeding aught else.

Alone sat she upon the bare earth, left there as guard-
ian of the chariot, which I had seen the beast of two forms
make fast.[14]

The seven nymphs in a ring made of them a fence about

her, with those lights in their hands which are secure from north winds and from south.

"Here[15] shalt thou be short time a forester, and with me everlastingly shalt be a citizen of that Rome whereof Christ is a Roman.

Therefore to profit the world that liveth ill, fix now thine eyes upon the car, and look that thou write what thou seest, when returned yonder."

Thus Beatrice; and I, who was all obedient at the feet of her commands, gave mind and eyes whither she willed.

Ne'er did fire from dense cloud descend, with motion so swift, when it falls from that confine which is most remote,

as I saw Jove's bird swoop down through the tree, rending its bark, likewise its flowers and its new leaves;

and he smote the car with all his might; whereat it reeled like a vessel in a storm, beaten by the waves, now to starboard, now to larboard.[16]

Then saw I a she-fox, that seemed fasting from all good food, leap into the body of the triumphal vehicle.

But, rebuking her for foul sins, my lady put her to flight, as swift as the fleshless bones did bear.[17]

Then, from thence whence he first had come, I saw the eagle descend down into the body of the car, and leave it feathered with his plumage.

And as a voice comes from a heart that sorroweth, such voice came from heaven, and thus it spake: "O my little bark, how ill art thou laden!"[18]

Then it seemed to me that the earth opened 'twixt the two wheels, and I saw a dragon come forth that fixed his tail up through the car;

and like a wasp, that draws back her sting, drawing to him his spiteful tail he wrenched out part of the bottom and went his vagrant way.[19]

That which remained—even as teeming land with grass,—with those plumes, haply offered with sincere and kind intent,

did again cover itself, and both wheels and the pole were covered again by them, such time that a sigh keeps the mouth open longer.[20]

Thus transformed, the sacred edifice put forth heads above its parts, three over the pole, and one at each corner.

The first were horned like an ox, but the four had one single horn at the forehead; such monster never yet was seen.[21]

Seated upon it, secure as a fortress on a steep hill, a shameless harlot appeared to me, with eyes quick around.

And, as though she should not be taken from him, a giant I saw erect at her side, and from time to time each kissed the other;

but, because her lustful and vagrant eye she turned upon me, that fierce paramour did scourge her from head to feet.

Then filled with jealousy and cruel with rage, he loosed the monster, and dragged it so far through the wood, that of this alone he made a screen between me and the harlot and the strange beast.[22]

1. *Cf.* Canto xxx, *notes* 19 and 20.
2. "[Thou art gazing on Beatrice] too fixedly."
3. These lines perhaps mean that Christ guides His Church, not by force or external means, but with the spirit only.
4. The right wheel; for the whole procession had turned to the right.
5. *murmur* = "reproachfully murmur." See *Rom.* v. 12 "Wherefore, as by one man sin entered into the world, and death by sin; and so death passed upon all men, for that all have sinned."
6. For this tree, *see Gen.* ii. 9, and *cf* Canto xxii *note* 14.
7. *Cf.* the following canto.—It seems probable that Dante's conception of the height of trees in India was derived from Virgil, *Georg.* ii.
8. "Thus"—namely, by not allowing the spiritual and secular powers to encroach on each other.
9. According to legend, the cross was made of wood taken from the tree of the knowledge of good and evil.
10. In spring, when the sun is in Aries (the sign following Pisces—here called "the celestial carp").
11. The purple of Empire (*cf.* Canto xxix).
12. The "all-seeing" Argus (*cf.* Canto. xxix) was set by Juno to watch over Io, whom she had, in a fit of jealousy, changed into a cow for yielding to Jupiter. The goddess selected Argus because he was able to keep awake longer than others (*longer vigil*), resting some of his eyes while the others were watching. The monster was lulled to sleep (and then slain) by Mercury, while listening to the god's recital of the story of the nymph Syrinx (who, when pursued by Pan, was at her prayer changed into a reed; see Ovid, *Met.* i).

13. The Transfiguration; see *Matt.* xvii. 1–8: "And after six days Jesus taketh Peter, James and John his brother, and bringeth them up into an high mountain apart, and was transfigured before them: and his face did shine as the sun, and his raiment was white as the light, and, behold, there appeared unto them Moses and Elias talking with him. Then answered Peter and said unto Jesus, Lord, it is good for us to be here: if thou wilt, let us make here three tabernacles; one for thee, and one for Moses, and one for Elias. While he yet spake, behold, a bright cloud overshadowed them; and behold a voice out of the cloud, which said, This is my beloved Son, in whom I am well pleased; hear ye him. And when the disciples heard it, they fell on their face, and were sore afraid. And Jesus came and touched them, and said, Arise, and be not afraid. And when they had lifted up their eyes, they saw no man, save Jesus only." Jesus is called "the apple tree" according to the allegory of the *Song of Solomon* ii. 3 ("As the apple tree among the trees of the wood, so is my beloved among the sons").

14. Divine Wisdom is seated at the root of the tree (Rome, the seat of the Empire); and in the shadow of "the new foliage," which blossomed forth when the Church (whose seat is at Rome, too) was united to the Empire, she is left to guard the interests of that Church (the *chariot*).

15. Mr. Butler holds that *here* "signifies 'in this world,' denoted by the Earthly Paradise"; and he quotes (from the *De Mon.* iii. 15): *beatitudinem . . . hujus vitæ, quæ . . . per terrestrem Paradisum figuratur.*

16. The ten persecutions of the Christian Church, instigated by the Emperors, from Nero to Diocletian (64–314). For the eagle, *cf. Ezek.* xvii. 3; and see *Par.* xviii-xx.

17. The heresies which threatened the early Church, but which were eventually suppressed by the writings of the Fathers and more violent measures. With the fox, *cf.* Lam. v. 18.

18. This second descent of the eagle indicates the "donation of Constantine"; see *Par.* xx, *note* 6.

19. The dragon, in all probability, represents the great schism wrought by Mohammed (who figures among the "sowers of discord" in *Inf.* xxviii). Though Dante's dragon was undoubtedly suggested by the dragon of *Rev.* xii. 3, it is not necessary to assume that the two beasts have the same symbolical meaning (The Biblical monster was in the Middle Ages identified with Satan.)

20. According to Mr. Butler, the fresh feathers signify "the further gifts of territory made by Pippin and Charles."

21. It seems best to take these seven horned heads (which were evidently suggested by *Rev.* xvii. 3) as the seven capital sins.

22. The harlot (see *Rev.* xvii and *cf. Inf.* xix) represents the Papal Court in its corrupt condition under Boniface VIII and Clement V. The giant is the French dynasty, notorious for its intrigues with the Popes; the king specially referred to being undoubtedly Philip the Fair. He it was whose bitter feud with Boniface, after pseudo-alli-

THE DIVINE COMEDY

ances for political ends, was crowned by the Pope's death (*cf.* Canto xx, *note* 16); and, again, it was with Philip's connivance that Clement V transferred the Papal See to Avignon (*cf. Inf.* xix, *notes* 7 and 8.— The second last stanza is very difficult. It is perhaps safest to take Dante as occupying here the position he represents throughout the entire poem—that of the typical Christian.

CANTO XXXIII

*The seven virtues in alternate strains now proclaim, with tears, that
the forces of the world have found their hour; and Beatrice declares
that though her glory will for a time be withdrawn from them, it
is but for a season. Then she signs to Matilda, to Dante and to Statius
to follow her; but after only a few steps, graciously summons Dante
to her side, bids him drop all diffidence, interprets the things he has
just seen, and hints at the political Messiah who shall restore the due
relations of Church and State and purify them both. But her com-
ment is far darker than the text. So at least she knows it will seem
to Dante's dull and over-crusted mind; wherefore the stamp has
been impressed upon his eye rather than on his unreceptive intel-
lect. Dante gently expostulates with her for uttering herself only in
inextricable enigmas. She answers that she does so to show him how
inadequate has been the training of the teaching he has lately fol-
lowed; but he, who, since he drank of Lethe, has forgotten all the
interval between his loss of Beatrice upon earth and his finding of
her again in Eden, answers that he cannot mind him of ever having
wandered from her or being in need of any other school than that
of her wisdom; upon which she reminds him that this forgetfulness
of ever having left her is a sign that it was tainted with evil; for only
the memory of what is so tainted is washed away by Lethe. Finally
she promises that henceforth she will vex him no more by veiled
discourse, but will speak with the naked simplicity that his un-
trained powers demand. The sun is now in high heaven, and they
reach a fountain whence two streams flow, and seem loth to part
from each other. Dante has forgotten all that Matilda told him about
them, not so much that Lethe has washed away the thought, for
surely it was untainted by any evil, as that before Eunoë is tasted
and secures every good impression from being obliterated, such all-
absorbing experiences as have but now been Dante's, may obliterate
from the memory even the most beautiful thoughts that have pre-
ceded them. Henceforth, however, all fair memories of good, what-
soever their relative significance, shall be secured against oblivion
and shall take their perfect place in the perfect whole; for Dante,
followed by Statius, drinks of the stream of Eunoë; and thence with
life fresh as the leaves of spring he issues, inly equipped and cleansed
for his further journey to the stars.*

"*DEUS, venerunt gentes*":[1] now three, now four, alternately and weeping, a sweet psalmody the ladies began;

and Beatrice sighing and compassionate was hearkening to them so altered, that little more did Mary change at the cross.

But when the other virgins gave place to her to speak, uprisen erect on her feet, she answered in hue of fire:

"*Modicum, et non videbitis me, et iterum*, my beloved sisters, *modicum, et vos videbitis me*."[2]

Then she placed them all seven in front of her, and, merely by her nod, motioned behind her, me and the Lady and the Sage who had stayed.

Thus she went on, and I believe not that her tenth step was put on the ground, when with her eyes mine eyes she smote;

and with tranquil mien did say to me: "Come more quickly so that if I speak with thee, thou be well placed to listen to me."

Soon as I was with her, as 'twas my duty to be, she said . to me: "Brother, wherefore coming now with me, venturest thou not to ask of me?"

As to those, who in presence of their betters are too lowly in speech so that they bring not their voice whole to the lips,

it happened to me and without full utterance I began: "My Lady, my need you know, and that which is good for it."

And she to me: "From fear and from shame I would that now thou unbind thee, so that thou speak no more like one that is dreaming.

Know that the vessel which the serpent broke, was, and is not;[3] but let him whose fault it is, believe that God's vengeance fears no sops.[4]

Not for all time shall be without heir[5] the eagle that left the plumage on the car, whereby it became a monster and then a prey;[6]

For of a surety I see, and therefore do tell it, stars already nigh, secure from all impediment and from all hindrance, that shall bring us times

wherein a five hundred ten and five, sent by God, shall slay the thief, with that giant who sins with her.[7]

And perchance my prophecy, obscure as Themis and Sphinx, doth less persuade thee, because after their fashion it darkens thy mind;

but soon the facts shall be the Naiades that will solve this hard riddle without loss of flocks or of corn.[8]

Note thou; and even as these words from me are borne, so do thou signify them to those who live that life which is a race unto death;

and bear in mind when thou writest them, not to conceal how thou hast seen the tree which now twice hath been despoiled here.[9]

Whoso robs that or that doth rend, with blasphemy in act offendeth God, who alone for his service did create it holy.

For eating of that, in torment and in desire, five thousand years and more the first soul did yearn for him who punished the bite in himself.[10]

Thy wit sleepeth if it judge not that tree to be for special cause thus lofty and thus transposed at the top.[11]

And if thy idle thoughts had not been Elsan waters about thy mind, and their pleasantness a Pyramus to the mulberry,

by so many circumstances alone thou wouldst recognize in the tree morally, God's justice in the ban.

But because I see thy mind turned to stone and, stone-like, such in hue that the light of my word dazes thee,[12]

I also will that thou bear it away within thee, and if not written at least outlined, for the reason that the pilgrim's staff is brought back wreathed with palm."[13]

And I: "Even as wax under the seal, that the imprinted figure changeth not, my brain is now stamped by you.

But why doth your longed-for word soar so far beyond my sight, that the more it straineth the more it loses it?"

"That thou mayst know," she said, "that School which thou hast followed, and see how its teaching can keep pace with my word;

and mayst see your way so far distant from the divine way, as the heaven which highest speeds is removed from earth."

Wherefore I answered her: "I remember not that I e'er

estranged me from you, nor have I conscience thereof that gnaws me."

"And if thou canst not remember it," smiling she answered, "now bethink thee how thou didst drink of Lethe this very day;

and if from smoke fire is argued, this forgetfulness clearly proves fault in thy desire otherwhere intent.[14]

But now my words shall be naked, so far as shall be meet to discover them to thy rude vision."

Both more refulgent, and with slower steps, the sun was holding the meridian circle, which varies hither and thither as positions vary,[15]

when did halt, even as he halts who goes for escort before folk, if he finds aught that is strange or the traces thereof,

those seven ladies at the margin of a pale shadow, such as beneath green leaves and dark boughs, the Alp casts over its cool streams.[16]

In front of them I seemed to behold Euphrates and Tigris welling up from one spring, and parting like friends that linger.[17]

"O light, O glory of human kind, what water is this that here pours forth from one source, and self from self doth wend away?"

At such prayer was said to me: "Pray Matilda that she tell it thee"; and here made answer, as he doth who frees him from blame,

the fair Lady: "This and other things have been told him by me,[18] and sure am I that Lethe's water hid them not from him."

And Beatrice: "Haply a greater care that oft bereaves of memory hath dimmed his mind's eyes.

But behold Eunoë, which there flows on; lead him to it, and as thou art wont, requicken his fainting virtue."

As a gentle soul that maketh no excuse, but makes her will of the will of another, soon as it is disclosed by outward sign,

so the fair Lady, after I was taken by her, set forth, and to Statius with queenly mien did say: "Come with him."

If, reader I had greater space for writing, I would sing,

at least in part, of the sweet draught which never would have sated me;

but forasmuch as all the pages ordained for this second canticle are filled, the curb of art no further lets me go.

I came back from the most holy waves, born again, even as new trees renewed with new foliage, pure and ready to mount to the stars.

1. *Ps.* lxxix, beginning: "O God, the heathen are come into thine inheritance; thy holy temple have they defiled; they have laid Jerusalem on heaps."

2. Christ's words to his disciples: "A little while, and ye shall not see me; and again, a little while, and ye shall see me, because I go to the Father" (*John* xvi. 16).

3. See the preceding canto. Dante applies to the Church (corrupted as it was in his time) the words used by John in *Rev.* xvii. 8: "The beast thou sawest was, and is not."

4. "In the olden time in Florence, if an assassin could contrive to eat a sop of bread and wine at the grave of the murdered man, within nine days after the murder, he was free from the vengeance of the family; and to prevent this they kept watch at the tomb. There is no evading the vengeance of God in this way. Such is the interpretation of this passage by all the old commentators" (Longfellow).

5. *without heir.* In the *Conv.* iv. 3, Dante speaks of Frederick II (d. 1250) as "the last Emperor of the Romans (I say 'last' with respect to the present time, notwithstanding that Rudolf, and Adolphus, and Albert were elected after his death and from his descendants)."

6. See the preceding canto.

7. Another of the so-called *Greyhound passages* (cf. *Inf.* i, *note* 14, and see Canto xx, *note* 1) The numbers are generally explained as DVX = leader (on the analogy of the numbers in *Rev.* xiii. 18, which indicate Nero); but surmises as to who that leader might be (whether Can Grande, or Henry of Luxemburg, or another) are entirely futile.

8. When Œdipus had solved the famous riddle of the Sphinx, Themis (renowned for her oracle) was so enraged that she sent a wild beast to work havoc among the herds and fields of the Thebans. See Ovid, *Met.* vii.—The Naiads had nothing to do with the solving of riddles; Dante followed a corrupt reading of the passage in Ovid, where Heinsius' emendation of *Laiades* (for *Naiades*) is now almost universally adopted [*Laiades* = Œdipus, the son of Laius].

9. First by Adam, then by the giant: for the wood of the chariot-pole came from the tree (see the preceding canto), and the chariot was dragged away by the giant (*ib*).

10. Dante follows the chronology of Eusebius, according to which Adam was on earth for 930 years, and in Limbo for 4302 years, making 5232 years in all. Cf. *Par.* vii and xxvi.

11. See the preceding canto. The height probably indicates the vast

extent and might of the Empire; while the widening towards the summit may be compared with Canto xxii, and taken to denote the inviolability of the Empire, as desired by God.

12. The Elsa is a Tuscan river, whose water has, in certain portions of its course, the property of turning objects to stone; and the hues of the mulberry (pure white changed to guilty red) are explained in Canto xxvii, *note* 5.

13. *for the reason*, namely, to show that thou hast beer in the Earthly Paradise. Cf. *Vita Nuova*, § xl: "They are called Palmers who go beyond the seas eastward, whence often they bring palm-branches."

14. Great stress is very naturally laid upon this passage by Witte and his followers, who maintained that Dante's sin consisted, primarily at any rate, not in moral but in philosophical aberrations. They understand Beatrice to reproach Dante with having followed Philosophy instead of Religion, and, on his declaring that he had no recollection of any such thing, to answer that it is because he has drunk of Lethe and forgotten all evil actions. But the passage cannot really be cited to support this view. The school that Dante has followed just before coming to Beatrice, and which has so imperfectly prepared him to understand her, is the school of Virgil (see Canto xxi). And it is impossible to suppose that Beatrice reproaches Dante for having followed Virgil, who was her own emissary. He was the initial instrument of Dante's salvation from his error, not the seducer who led him into it.

We must apparently suppose that when Dante drank of Lethe, he forgot his fall and all the steps that led to his recovery from it, which required for their understanding a conscious reference to it. Therefore, when Beatrice speaks of the inadequacy (not the perversity) of the training he has had as yet, he misunderstands the reference as an implication that he had wandered from her to some other school. Beatrice takes him up on his own ground, and replies that, for the matter of that, so he did desert her, and guiltily too, else he would not have forgotten it.

When Dante has further drunk of Eunoë, he will remember all the incidental good of Virgil's faithful love and guidance; but it will no longer be painfully associated with his own sin, and that sin he will remember again, but as an external thing that does not now belong to his own personality. It will dwell in his mind merely as the outward occasion of the love manifested and the blessings secured to him. Cf. *Par.* ix; and see Canto xxviii, *note* 17.

15. See the diagram on p. 216.

16. At the edge of the forest, whose shadow resembled the shadow cast by the trees at the foot of the Alps on to the streams below.

17. Dante was probably thinking not of *Gen.* ii. 14, but of Boethius' verses (*De Cons. Phil* v. metr. i): *Tigris et Euphrates uno se fonte resolvunt, Et mox abjunctis dissociantur aquis.*

18. See Canto xxviii.

PARADISO

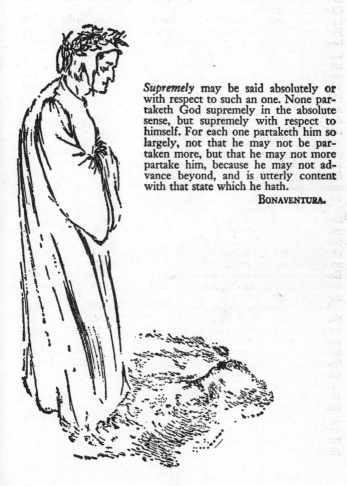

Supremely may be said absolutely **or** with respect to such an one. None partaketh God supremely in the absolute sense, but supremely with respect to himself. For each one partaketh him so largely, not that he may not be partaken more, but that he may not more partake him, because he may not advance beyond, and is utterly content with that state which he hath.

BONAVENTURA.

Note on Dante's Paradise

THE COSMOGRAPHY of the *Comedy* is much simpler and easier of comprehension than is usually supposed, but it is not within the scope of this work to enter into its details. The geographical side of it is sufficiently touched upon in the notes to Canto xxvii; and the general principles of its astronomy are developed, with a lucidity that cannot be surpassed, by Dante himself in Chapters 3 and 4 of Book ii of the *Convivio*. An excellent popular exposition of the whole system will be found in Witte's *Essays on Dante*[1] (Essay iv. Dante's Cosmography); and the account of the *Ptolemaic System* in any book of astronomy or cyclopædia will give an adequate general exposition of it.

The general principle by which we may pass from modern conceptions of astronomy to those which we find in the *Comedy* may be arrived at thus: We still speak of the heavenly bodies rising and setting, and revolving from East to West, although we believe that the appearances so described are really caused by the daily revolution of the earth round her axis from West to East. If we carry through the same principle of describing what we see, instead of what we believe, we shall substitute for all the other movements which we believe the earth to make, descriptions of movements in the heavenly bodies which would produce the same effect; and we shall then be speaking the language of Greek and medieval astronomy, which corresponds immediately with the actual appearances. Thus, for the annual motion of the earth round the sun from West to East we shall substitute an annual motion of the sun round the earth. We shall continue to speak of the planets revolving round the centre of the system from West to East, as we do now; but the apparent complications in their movements due to the fact that while they are perpetually changing their position *we* too are revolving round the centre and so perpetually changing our point of view, we shall account for by supposing that *they* engraft upon their primary movement round the centre a second-

[1] Essays on Dante. By Dr. Karl Witte, &C.

ary backward and forward movement in a circle, which now delays and now accelerates their progress from West to East. This is what the ancient and medieval astronomers did. They supposed, therefore, that each planet (besides partaking the daily movement of the heavens) had two motions, one on a greater sphere, or cycle, revolving round the earth as its centre, and another on a smaller sphere, or epicycle, revolving round a point on the equator of the greater sphere. In the case of the exterior planets, Mars, Jupiter and Saturn, the cycle corresponds to the planet's own movement round the sun, and the epicycle to ours. In the case of the inferior planets, Mercury and Venus, this must be reversed. Lastly, the slow top-like movement by which the direction of the earth's axis changes with respect to the fixed stars, causing what is known as the "precession of the equinoxes," will be described as a slow movement of all the fixed stars with respect to the pole of the daily revolution of the heavens. Thus it will be seen that the fundamental geometrical problems of ancient and modern astronomy are identical, and consist in resolving apparently complicated and irregular movements into a combination of simple and regular ones; and, accordingly, the solutions found by the ancient astronomers hold perfectly good, as far as they go, to the present day, and are incorporated in modern astronomy.

It is important thus to form a clear conception of the universe as it presented itself to Dante if we wish to enter into full imaginative sympathy with him, and to reach a point of view from which we can understand how the spiritual and material worlds stood related in his conception, and the associations with which the phenomena of nature blended in his mind, and also to appreciate the scientific value of his observations.

But for the direct appreciation of the *Paradise*, little is needed in the first instance beyond a clear conception of the succession of the several heavenly bodies through which Dante ascends, and the moral and spiritual associations which they carry.

If the reader will take any diagram of the solar system as conceived in our day, and simply exchange the places of the sun and the earth (placing the earth, with her satellite the moon, in the centre of the diagram, and placing the sun where he finds the earth marked), he will have the order in which Dante, travelling upwards from the earth, reaches 1 the Moon, 2 Mercury, 3 Venus, 4 the Sun, 5 Mars, 6 Jupiter, 7 Saturn, 8 the constellation of Gemini, 9 the invisible vault beyond the Stars, 10 the Essential Heaven of Light and Love.

The accompanying table will show the general scheme of the poem. Dante's number scheme is always based on *three* subdivided into *seven*, raised, by additions of a character differing from the rest, to *nine*, and by a last addition on an entirely different place to *ten*.

In the infra-solar heavens, Dante meets souls whom some earthy weakness or stain has so far shorn of what once were their spiritual possibilities, that though the quality of their joy is entirely pure and unalloyed, it is of lesser intensity than it might have been had they been altogether true. Perhaps we may trace, specifically, want of unshaken *faith*, and the partial substitution of earthy for heavenly *hope* and of earthy for heavenly *love* in those three heavens. It was believed that the conical shadow cast through space by the earth, reached as far as the sphere of Venus. The symbolic significance of this does not need further insisting upon.

The sun, the great *luminary*, is connected with *prudence*, the leader of the moral or cardinal virtues (see *Purg.* xxix), taken in its widest sense; and the other cardinal virtues follow; indicating that the tone and colour of the spiritual fruition of the souls is influenced by the incidence of the moral warfare by which it was earned.

Subtle analogies and hints throughout suggest the astrological appropriateness of the several planets as the places of manifestation of the several groups of souls.

In the constellation of Gemini all the souls are gathered together and are once more manifested to the Poet though he only holds converse with members of the one supreme group to which the Apostles and our First Father belong.

In like manner the Angels are manifested in the ninth heaven or *Primum Mobile*.

But none of these nine heavens is the true abode of any spirit. They are but the symbolically appropriate meeting places appointed for Dante and the several groups of spirits. God and all blessed spirits, whether men or angels, dwell where all space is *here* and all time is *now* in the Empyrean Heaven, which the Poet's vision finally reaches and where it ends.

	Empyrean		10 Wherein dwell God, *His angels*, and His Redeemed	Heaven of Light and Love, beyond space and time, wherein Spirits *abide*
	ix. Primum mobile		9 Angels	Heavens of space, wherein spirits *are manifested* to the poet on his pilgrimage
	viii. Stellar Heaven		8 Souls	
The Seven Planetary Heavens	III. Supra-solar	vii. Saturn	7 Temperance	
		vi. Jupiter	6 Justice	
		v. Mars	5 Fortitude	
	II. Solar	iv. Sun	4 Prudence	
	I. Infra-solar	iii. Venus	3 Earthly love	
		ii. Mercury	2 Ambition	
		i. Moon	1 Inconstancy	

ÇANTO I

Subject matter and invocation. The sun is in the equinoctial point. It is midday at Purgatory and midnight at Jerusalem, when Dante sees Beatrice gazing at the sun and instinctively imitates her gesture, looking away from her and straight at the sun. The light glows as though God had made a second sun, and Dante now turns once more to Beatrice who is gazing heavenward. As he looks his human nature is transmuted to the quality of heaven and he knows not whether he is still in the flesh or no. They pass through the sphere of fire and hear the harmonies of heaven, but Dante is bewildered because he knows not that they have left the earth, and when enlightened by Beatrice he is still perplexed to know how he can rise, counter to gravitation. Beatrice, pitying the delirium of his earthly mind, explains to him the law of universal (material and spiritual) gravitation. All things seek their true place, and in the orderly movement thereto, and rest therein, consists the likeness of the universe to God. Man's place is God, and to rise to him is therefore natural to man. It is departing from him that (like fire darting downwards) is the anomaly that needs to be explained.

THE ALL-MOVER'S glory penetrates through the universe, and regloweth in one region more, and less in another.[1]

In that heaven which most receiveth of his light, have I been; and have seen things which whoso descendeth from up there hath not knowledge nor power to re-tell:

because, as it draweth nigh to its desire, our intellect sinketh so deep, that memory cannot go back upon the track.

Nathless, whatever of the holy realm I had the power to treasure in my memory, shall now be matter of my song.

O good Apollo,[2] for the crowning task, make me a so-fashioned vessel of thy worth, as thou demandest for the grant of thy beloved laurel.

Up till here one peak of Parnassus[3] hath sufficed me; but

now, with both the two, needs must I enter this last wrestling-ground.

Into my bosom enter thou, and so breathe as when thou drewest Marsyas from out what sheathed his limbs.[4]

O divine Virtue, if thou dost so far lend thyself to me, that I make manifest the shadow of the blessed realm imprinted on my brain,

thou shalt see me come to thy chosen tree and crown me, then, with the leaves of which the matter and thou shalt make me worthy.

So few times, Father, is there gathered of it, for triumph or of Cæsar or of poet,—fault and shame of human wills,—

that the Peneian frond[5] should bring forth gladness in the joyous Delphic deity, when it sets any athirst for itself.

A mighty flame followeth a tiny spark; perchance, after me, shall prayer with better voices be so offered that Cirrha[6] may respond.

The lantern of the universe riseth unto mortals through divers straits; but from that which joineth four circles in three crosses[7]

he issueth with more propitious course, and united with a more propitious star, and doth temper and stamp the mundane wax more after his own mood.

Almost this strait had made morning[8] on that side and evening on this; and there that hemisphere all was aglow, and the other region darkling;

when I beheld Beatrice turned on her left side and gazing on the sun. Never did eagle so fix himself thereon.

And even as the second ray doth ever issue from the first, and rise back upward, (like as a pilgrim whose will is to return);

so from her gesture, poured through the eyes into my imagination, did mine own take shape; and I fixed mine eyes upon the sun, transcending our wont.[9]

Much is granted there which is not granted here to our powers, in virtue of the place made as proper to the human race.[10]

I not long endured him, nor yet so little but that I saw him sparkle all around, like iron issuing molten from the furnace.

And, of a sudden, meseemed that day was added unto day, as though he who hath the power, had adorned heaven with a second sun.[11]

Beatrice was standing with her eyes all fixed upon the eternal wheels,[12] and I fixed my sight, removed from there above, on her.

Gazing on her such I became within, as was Glaucus,[13] tasting of the grass that made him the sea-fellow of the other gods.

To pass beyond humanity may not be told in words, wherefore let the example satisfy him for whom grace reserveth the experience.

If I was only that of me which thou didst new-create,[14] O Love who rulest heaven, thou knowest, who with thy light didst lift me up.

When the wheel which thou, by being longed for, makest eternal,[15] drew unto itself my mind with the harmony which thou dost temper and distinguish,

so much of heaven then seemed to me enkindled with the sun's flame, that rain nor river ever made a lake so wide distended.[16]

The newness of the sound[17] and the great light kindled in me a longing for their cause, ne'er felt before so keenly.

Whence she who saw me even as I saw myself, to still my agitated mind, opened her lips, e'er I mine to ask;

and she began: "Thou thyself makest thyself dense with false imagining, and so thou seest not what thou wouldst see, if thou hadst cast it[18] off.

Thou art not upon earth, as thou believest; but lightning, fleeing its proper site,[19] ne'er darted as dost thou who are returning thither."

If I was stripped of my first perplexity by the brief smile-enwrapped discourse, I was the more enmeshed within another;

and I said: "Content already and at rest from a great marvelling, now am I in amaze how I transcend these lightsome bodies."[20]

Whereon she, after a sigh of pity, turned her eyes toward me with that look a mother casts on her delirious child;

and began: "All things whatsoever observe a mutual order; and this is the form that maketh the universe like unto God.

Herein the exalted creatures[21] trace the impress of the Eternal Worth, which is the goal whereto was made the norm now spoken of.

In the order of which I speak all things incline, by diverse lots, more near and less unto their principle;

wherefore they move to diverse ports o'er the great sea of being, and each one with instinct given it to bear it on.[22]

This beareth the fire toward the moon; this is the mover in the hearts of things that die; this doth draw the earth together and unite it.

Nor only the creatures that lack intelligence doth this bow shoot,[23] but those that have both intellect and love.

The Providence that doth assort all this, doth with its light make ever still the heaven wherein whirleth that one that hath the greatest speed;[24]

and thither now, as to the appointed site, the power of that bowstring beareth us which directeth to a joyful mark whatso it doth discharge.

True is it, that as the form often accordeth not with the intention of the art, because that the material is dull to answer;

so from this course sometimes departeth the creature that hath power, thus thrust, to swerve to-ward some other part,

(even as fire may be seen to dart down from the cloud) if its first rush be wrenched aside to earth by false seeming pleasure.[25]

Thou shouldst no more wonder, if I deem aright, at thine uprising, than at a river dropping down from a lofty mountain to the base.

Marvel were it in thee if, bereft of all impediment, thou hadst settled down below; even as were stillness on the earth in a living flame." Thereon toward Heaven she turned back her gaze.

1. God, as the unmoved source of movement, is the central conception of the Aristotelian theology. Wallace, 39, 46.
God *penetrates* into the essential nature of a thing, and is *reflected*

("regloweth"), more or less, in its concrete being. *Epist. ad Can. Grand.*, § 23; *Conv.* iii. 14.

2. Apollo = the Sun = God. *Conv.* iii. 12, and *passim*.

3. *one peak.* Hitherto the inspiration of the Muses has sufficed (*cf. Inf.* ii and *Purg.* i), but now the diviner aid of "Apollo" must be invoked as well. It is not easy to trace the origin of Dante's (erroneous) belief that one peak of Parnassus was sacred to the Muses as distinct from Apollo.

4. Compare *Purg.* i. The underlying motive seems to be an appeal to the deities to proclaim their glory through their willing instrument as zealously as they vindicated their honour against presumptuous rivals. Marsyas was flayed by Apollo for his presumption in challenging him to a contest in playing the pipe. Hence the allusion to the "sheath of his limbs."

5. Daphne, the daughter of Peneus, loved by Apollo, was changed into a laurel.

6. *Cirrha.* Apollo's peak of Parnassus.

7. The circles of the Equator, the Zodiac and the Equinoctial colure, make each a cross with the circle of the horizon. At the equinox, at sunrise, they all meet the horizon and make their crosses with it at the same spot.

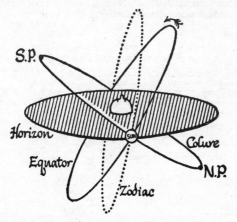

8. *had made, viz.,* when he rose. It was now noonday.

9. The point of analogy appears to consist simply in the derivative character of Dante's act.

10. The Earthly Paradise or Garden of Eden (*Purg.* xxviii).

11. Owing to their rapid approach to the sun. Cf. also *Purg.* xxvii.

12. *Wheel* or *wheels*, here and throughout the *Paradiso* used for the revolving heavens.

13. Ovid tells the tale of the fisherman Glaucus tasting the grass that

had revivified the fish he had caught, and thereon being seized with yearning for the deep, into which he plunged and became a sea god.

14. Cf. 2 *Corinthians* xii. 2. The Soul is enbreathed by God when the animal body is perfected (*Purg.* xxv), and is therefore that part of a man which is to be regarded as a new creation by God, not generated by nature. Cf. Canto iii, *note* 8, and Wallace, 56, *note* 3.

15. It is by inspiring the universe with love and longing (not by any physical means, for he is immaterial) that God, according to Aristotle, causes the never-ending cosmic movements. Wallace, 39.

16. Because they were passing through the "sphere of fire" which girt the "sphere of air" as with a second atmosphere.

17. The conception that the seven planetary heavens, like the seven strings of a lyre, uttered divine harmonies as they moved, is expressly rejected by Aristotle. This is one of the few instances in which Dante departs from his authority.

18. *it* = the *false imaginings*, the fixed idea which prevented his comprehending what was before his eyes.

19. Cf. Canto xxiii.

20. *air*, which Aristotle regarded as relatively, and *fire* which he regarded as absolutely light.

21. *exalted creatures* = angels [and men?].

22. God is the goal as well as the source of all. The orderly trend of all things to their true places is therefore their guide to God. But all things do not reach God in the same sense and in the same measure.

23. Cf. Canto xxix.

24. The Empyrean, which is not spatial at all, does not move and "hath not poles." It girds with light and love the *primum mobile*, the utmost and swiftest of the material heavens. Cf. *Cantos*. xxii, xxvii, xxx. Also *Conv.* ii. 4.

25. "As the medium in which an artist works sometimes appears to resist the impulse and direction which he would give it, so beings endowed with free will ('the creature that hath power . . . to swerve aside') may resist the impulse towards himself impressed upon them by God, if they allow themselves to be seduced by false delight."

ÇANTO II

Warning and promise to the reader, who shall see stranger tilth than when Jason sowed the dragon's teeth. They reach the moon and inconceivably penetrate into her substance without cleaving it, even as deity penetrated into humanity in Christ; which mystery shall in heaven be seen as axiomatic truth. Dante, dimly aware of the inadequacy of his science, questions Beatrice as to the dark patches on the moon which he had thought were due to rarity of substance. She explains that if such rarity pierced right through the moon in the dark parts, the sun would shine through them when eclipsed; and if not, the dense matter behind the rare would cast back the sun's light; and describes to him an experiment by which he may satisfy himself that in that case the light reflected from the dense matter at the surface and from that in the interior of the moon would be equally bright. She then explains that Dante has gone wrong and accepted a scientifically inadequate explanation, because he has not understood that all heavenly phenomena are direct utterances of God and of his Angels. The undivided power of God, differentiated through the various heavenly bodies and agencies, shines in the diverse quality and brightness of the fixed stars, of the planets and of the parts of the moon, as the vital principle manifests itself diversely in the several members of the body, and as joy beams through the pupil of the eye.

O YE WHO in your little skiff longing to hear, have followed on my keel that singeth on its way,

turn to revisit your own shores; commit you not to the open sea; for perchance, losing me, ye would be left astray.

The water which I take was never coursed before; Minerva bloweth, Apollo guideth me, and the nine Muses point me to the Bears.

Ye other few, who timely have lift up your necks for bread of angels whereby life is here sustained but wherefrom none cometh away sated,[1]

ye may indeed commit your vessel to the deep keeping my furrow, in advance of the water that is falling back to the level.

The glorious ones who fared to Colchis not so marvelled as shall ye, when Jason turned ox-plough-man in their sight.

The thirst, born with us and ne'er failing, for the god-like realm bore us swift almost as ye see the heaven.

Beatrice was gazing upward, and I on her; and perchance in such space as an arrow stays and flies and is discharged from the nocking point,

I saw me arrived where a wondrous thing drew my sight to it; and therefore she from whom my doing might not be hidden

turning to me as much in joy as beauty, "Direct thy mind to God in gratitude," she said, "who hath united us with the first star."

Meseemed a cloud enveloped us, shining, dense, firm and polished, like diamond smitten by the sun.

Within itself the eternal pearl received us, as water doth receive a ray of light, though still itself uncleft.

If I was body,[2]—and if here we conceive not how one dimension could support another, which must be, if body into body creep,—

The more should longing enkindle us to see that Essence wherein we behold how our own nature and God unified themselves.

There what we hold by faith shall be beheld, not demonstrated, but self-known in fashion of the initial truth which man believeth.[3]

I answered: "Lady, devoutly as I most may, do I thank him who hath removed me from the mortal world.

But tell me what those dusky marks upon this body, which down there on earth make folk to tell the tale of Cain?"[4]

She smiled a little, and then: "And if," she said, "the opinion of mortals goeth wrong, where the key of sense doth not unlock,

truly the shafts of wonder should no longer pierce thee; since even when the senses give the lead thou see'st reason hath wings too short.

But tell me what thou, of thyself, thinkest concerning it?" And I: "That which to us appeareth diverse in this

410

high region, I hold to be produced by bodies rare and dense."[5]

And she: "Verily, thou shalt see thy thought plunged deep in falsity, if well thou hearken to the argument which I shall make against it.

The eighth sphere revealeth many lights to you, the which in quality, as eke in quantity, may be observed of diverse countenance.

If rare and dense alone produced this thing, one only virtue, more or less or equally distributed, were in them all.

Diverse virtues must needs be fruits of formal principles, the which, save only one, would have no leave to be, upon thy reasoning.[6]

Again, were rarity cause of that duskiness whereof thou makest question, either in some certain part, right through, thus stinted of its matter

were this planet; or, like as a body doth dispose the fat and lean, would it alternate pages in its volume.

Were the first true, 'twould be revealed in the eclipses of the sun, by the light shining through it, as it doth when hurled on aught else rare.[7]

This is not; wherefore we have to see what of the other case, and if it chance that I make vain this also, thy thought will be refuted.

If it be that this rare matter goeth not throughout, needs must there be a limit, from which its contrary doth intercept its passing on;

and thence that other's ray were so cast back, as colour doth return from glass which hideth lead behind it.

Now thou wilt urge that the ray here is darkened rather than in other parts, because here it is recast from further back.

From this plea experiment may disentangle thee, (if thou wilt make the proof) which ever is the spring of the rivers of your arts.

Three mirrors thou shalt take, and set two equally remote from thee; and let the third further removed strike on thine eyes between the other two.

Turning to them, have a light set behind thy back, enkindling the three mirrors, and, backsmitten by them all, coming again to thee.

Whereas in size the more distant show shall not have so great stretch, yet thou there shalt see it needs must shine as brightly as the others.[8]

Now,—as at the stroke of the warm rays the substrate of the snow is stripped both of the colour and of the coldness which it had,—

thee, so left stripped in thine intellect, would I inform with light so living, it shall tremble as thou lookest on it.[9]

Within the heaven of the divine peace whirleth a body, in whose virtue lieth the being of all that it containeth.[10]

The heaven next following, which hath so many things to show, parteth this being amid diverse essences,[11] which it distinguisheth and doth contain;

the other circling bodies by various differentiatings, dispose the distinct powers they have within themselves, unto their end and to their fertilizings.

These organs of the universe go, as thou seest now, from grade to grade; for from above do they receive, and downward do they work.[12]

Now mark well how I thread this pass to the truth for which thou longest, that thou thereafter mayest know to keep the ford alone.[13]

The movement and the virtue of the sacred wheelings, as the hammer's art from the smith,[14] must needs be an effluence from the blessed movers;

and the heaven which so many lights make beautiful, from the deep mind[15] which rolleth it, taketh the image and thereof maketh the seal.

And as the soul within your dust, through members differing and conformed to divers powers, doth diffuse itself,

so doth the Intelligence deploy its goodness, multiplied through the stars, revolving still on its own unity.

Diverse virtue maketh diverse alloy with the precious body which it quickeneth, wherein, as life in you, it is up-bound.

By cause of the glad nature whence it floweth, the mingled virtue shineth through the body, as gladness doth through living pupil.

412

Thence cometh what seems different 'twixt light and light, and not from dense and rare; this is the formal principle that produceth, conformably to its own excellence, the turbid and the clear."

1. Contrast Canto xxiv, *note* 1.
2. Compare Canto i.
3. See Canto vi, *note* 4.
4. "The common folk tell the tale how Cain may be seen in the moon, going with a bundle of thorns to sacrifice." Benvenuto. Compare *Inf.* xx.
5. See *Conv.* ii. 14, where this explanation, based on Averroës (but inverting him), is given.
6. "The heaven of the fixed stars reveals a diversity in the luminous substance of its many heavenly bodies. The heaven of the moon reveals a diversity in the luminous substance of its one heavenly body. The problem of the eighth and of the first heaven is therefore essentially identical, and we must seek a solution applicable to both the heavens. Your proposed solution, if applied to the fixed stars, would make their difference merely quantitative, whereas it is admitted to be qualitative also, for the influences of the fixed stars differ one from another in kind."
7. "If we account for the dullness of some parts of the moon by saying that there her substance is rare right through, from side to side, that means that some of the sun's rays are not cast back at all but escape at the far side. Now if some of the sun's rays could pierce right through the moon when he is in front of her, they would do so when he is behind her (*i.e.*, in a solar eclipse) which we know they do not."
8. "If, on the contrary, the sun's rays encounter a dense stratum be-

Figure to Canto II

fore they pierce right through, they will be reflected back from that dense stratum within the moon just as they are from the dense surface of her other portions. You will then have the effect of several reflecting surfaces (*i.e.*, mirrors), at various distances, throwing back the same light. Construct a model of this by placing two mirrors before you (representing bright parts of the moon) with a third mirror, between them, further back (representing the supposed dense stratum in the interior substance of the moon where the dark patches are), and have a light (representing the sun) set behind you. You will find that the middle reflection is indeed *smaller* than the other two but not *duller*, as by your hypothesis it should be." See Fig. on p. 413.

Brightness is truly the ratio of the amount of light reaching the eye to the apparent size of the object, and since both of these diminish in proportion to the square of the distance, the brightness remains constant. But this statement neglects absorption by the medium; and, moreover, the moon is not a mirror, in which we see the sun, but is more like a piece of paper on which a lamp is shining; and the brightness of such a surface is affected by its distance from the source of light, though not by its distance from the spectator.

9. "Your mind is now a blank. All your ideas on the subject are gone, and nothing is left but the potential receptacle of ideas (your mind); just as when the sun shines on the snow, all its qualities disappear and nothing is left except that (whatever it is) that underlies the qualities, and is potentially susceptible of having them impressed again upon it."

10. *Cf.* Canto i, and *note* 24. The being of everything that exists is implicitly contained in the *primum mobile*.

11. *diverse essences*, according to the translation = the fixed stars. But the Italian may mean "distinct *from* it" (not "distinguished *by* it"), and may refer to the lower spheres and the planets.

12. Compare *Epist. ad C.G.* § 21.

13. A difficulty seems to be caused by Dante's habit of sometimes explicitly recognizing, and sometimes practically ignoring, the distinction between the heavens or heavenly bodies and their guiding and influencing Angels. There is no confusion in his own mind; but the connection between the Angels and the heavens is so close that it is often unnecessary to dwell upon the distinction, which distinction, however, is always there. It has been ignored up to this point in the present canto. Now we find the "differentiatings" of the Divine Power recognized as divers angelic virtues which are respectively *connected* with the divers heavenly bodies, so that the moving heaven is an "alloy," or union of the heavenly substance and the angelic influence. Again, the "mingled virtue" itself that shines through the heavenly body is the personality of the Angel mingled with the creating and inspiring power of God. *Cf.* Canto. xxi.

14. The hammer takes its direction, etc., from the mind of the smith, and stamps that mind upon the iron. So the heavens.

15. God, or the cherub that guides the stellar sphere.

ÇANTO III

As Dante is about to speak he sees the faint outlines of human features and taking them for reflections looks behind him but sees nothing. Beatrice smiles at his taking the most real existences he has ever yet beheld for mere semblances, tells him why they are there and bids him address them. Dante learns from Piccarda that each soul in heaven rejoices in the whole order of which it is part, and therefore desires no higher place than is assigned to it, for such desire would violate the law of love, and therefore the harmony of heaven, and with it the joy of the unduly aspiring soul itself. He further learns Piccarda's history and that of Constance. After which the souls disappear and Dante's eyes return to Beatrice.

THAT SUN which first warmed my bosom with love had thus unveiled for me, by proof and refutation, fair truth's sweet aspect;

and I, to confess me corrected and assured, in measure as was meet, sloped up my head to speak.

But there appeared to me a sight which so straitly held me to itself, to look upon it, that I bethought me not of my confession.

In such guise as, from glasses transparent and polished, or from waters clear and tranquil, not so deep that the bottom is darkened,

come back the notes of our faces, so faint that a pearl on a white brow cometh not slowlier upon our pupils;

so did I behold many a countenance, eager to speak, wherefore I fell into the counter error of that which kindled love between the man and fountain.[1]

No sooner was I aware of them, than, thinking them reflected images, I turned round my eyes to see of whom they were;

and I saw naught, and turned them forward again straight on the light of my sweet guide, whose sacred eyes glowed as she smiled.

"Wonder not that I smile," she said, "in presence of thy

child-like thought, since it trusts not its foot upon the truth,

but turneth thee after its wont, to vacancy. True substances[2] are they which thou beholdest, relegated here for failure of their vows.

Wherefore speak with them, and listen and believe; for the true light which satisfieth them, suffereth them not to turn their feet aside from it."

And I to the shade who seemed most to long for converse turned me and began, as one whom too great longing doth confound:

"O well-created spirit, who in the rays of eternal life dost feel the sweetness which, save tasted, may ne'er be understood;

it were acceptable to me, wouldst thou content me with thy name and with your lot."[3] Whereat she, eager and with smiling eyes:

"Our love doth no more bar the gate to a just wish, than doth that love which would have all its court like to itself.

In the world I was a virgin sister; and if thy memory be rightly searched, my greater beauty will not hide me from thee,

but thou wilt know me again for Piccarda,[4] who, placed here with these other blessed ones, am blessed in the sphere that moveth slowest.[5]

Our affections, which are aflame only in the pleasure of the Holy Spirit, rejoice to be informed after his order.[6]

And this lot, which seemeth so far down, therefore is given us because our vows were slighted, and on some certain side were not filled in."

Whereon I to her: "In your wondrous aspects a divine somewhat regloweth that doth transmute you from conceits of former times.

Wherefore I lagged in calling thee to mind; now what thou tellest me giveth such help that more articulately I retrace thee.

But tell me, ye whose blessedness is here, do you desire a more lofty place, to see more, or to make yourselves more dear?"

With those other shades first she smiled a little, then answered me so joyous that she seemed to burn in love's first flame:

"Brother, the quality of love stilleth our will, and maketh us long only for what we have, and giveth us no other thirst.[7]

Did we desire to be more aloft, our longings were discordant from his will who here assorteth us,

and for that, thou wilt see, there is no room within these circles, if of necessity we have our being here in love, and if thou think again what is love's nature.

Nay, 'tis the essence of this blessed being to hold ourselves within the divine will, whereby our own wills are themselves made one.

So that our being thus, from threshold unto threshold throughout the realm, is a joy to all the realm as to the king, who draweth our wills to what he willeth;

and his will is our peace; it is that sea to which all moves that it createth and that nature maketh."[8]

Clear was it then to me how everywhere in heaven is Paradise, e'en though the grace of the chief Good doth not rain there after one only fashion.

But even as it chanceth, should one food sate us while for another the appetite remaineth, that returning thanks for that, we ask for this;

so with gesture and with word did I, to learn from her what was that web through which she had not drawn the shuttle to the end.

"Perfected life and high desert enheaveneth a lady more aloft," she[9] said, "by whose rule down in your world there are who clothe and veil themselves,

that they, even till death, may wake and sleep with that Spouse who accepteth every vow that love hath made conform with his good pleasure.[10]

From the world, to follow her, I fled while yet a girl, and in her habit I enclosed myself, and promised the way of her company.

Thereafter men more used to ill than good[11] tore me away from the sweet cloister; and God doth know what my life then became.

And this other splendour who revealeth herself to thee

417

on my right side, and who kindleth herself with all the light of our sphere,

doth understand of her that which I tell of me. She was a sister, and from her head was taken in like manner the shadow of the sacred veil.

Yet, turned back as she was into the world, against her pleasure and against good usage, from her heart's veil never was she loosened.

This is the light of the great Constance, who, from the second blast of Suabia, conceived the third and final might."[12]

Thus did she speak to me, and then began to sing *Ave Maria*, and vanished as she sang, like to a heavy thing through the deep water.

My sight, which followed her far as it might, when it had lost her turned to the target of a greater longing,

and bent itself all upon Beatrice; but she so flashed upon my look, that at the first my sight endured it not; and this made me the slower with my questioning.

1. Narcissus took his own reflection for an actual being. Dante took the actual beings he now saw for reflections.
2. A *substance* is anything that exists in itself, *e.g.*, a man, a tree, a sword. It is opposed to *accident*, that which exists only as an experience or an attribute of some "substance,"*e.g.*, love, greenness, brightness. Compare *Vita Nuova*, § 25.
3. *thy* name, and *your* lot (*i.e.*, the lot thou sharest with thy companions).
4. Piccarda was the daughter of Simone Donati, and the sister of Dante's friend Forese (see *Purg.* xxiii) and of the celebrated Corso (*cf.* Gardner i, "Blacks and Whites," and Villani, vii). Dante's wife Gemma was the daughter of Manetto Donati, and she too had a brother Forese (Dante's brother-in-law therefore). This has often given rise to confusion.
5. Slowest in the daily revolution from East to West, because nearest to the centre of the Earth and of the whole celestial rotation; but swiftest in the sense that its *proper motion* (from West to East) has a shorter period than that of any other sphere.
6. Rejoice to have their *form*, or essential being, in conformity to the divine order, which is itself the *form* of the universe. *Cf.* Canto i, and also vii, *note* 16.
7. For this and six following stanzas *cf.* Canto vi.
8. "*That it createth*, out of nothing, as angels and rational souls, *and that nature maketh*, that is produceth by generating" (Benvenuto). *Cf.* Canto. vii.

9. Clara (1194–1253), the friend and disciple of Francis of Assisi.

10. Note the qualification. Not all vows are accepted. See Canto v.

11. Her brother Corso, especially, who compelled her to marry Rossellino della Tosa, a man of violent and factious character with whom at the time he sought alliance.

12. Frederick Barbarossa, his son Henry VI and his grandson Frederick II, are the three "blasts of Suabia." Constance was the heiress of the Norman house of Tancred which had conquered Sicily and Southern Italy from the Saracens in the eleventh century, and so of the crown of "the two Sicilies" (Naples and Sicily). See Villani, iv and v, and *Introduction*.

ÇANTO IV

Piccarda has left Dante entangled in two perplexities. Why are the nuns shorn of what had else been the full measure of their glory because they were torn against their will from the cloister? And if the inconstant moon is the abode of such as have left their vows unfulfilled, was Plato right after all in saying that men's souls come down from the planets connatural with them, and return thereto? This latter speculation might lead to dangerous heresy, and Beatrice hastens to explain that the souls who come to meet Dante in the several spheres all have their permanent abiding place with God and the Angels in the Empyrean. Their meeting places with Dante are but symbolical of their spiritual state. But Plato may have had in mind the divine influences that, through the agency of the planets, act upon men's dispositions and produce good or ill effects which should be credited to them rather than to the human will. And indeed it was a confused perception of these divine influences that led men into idolatry. The other difficulty is removed by a distinction between what we wish to do and what, under pressure, we consent to do; for if we consent we cannot plead violence in excuse, although we have done what we did not wish to do. More questions are started in Dante's mind, for only in the all-embracing truth of God can the human mind find that restful possession which its nature promises it. Short of that each newly acquired truth leads on to further questions. Beatrice, who had sighed at Dante's previous bewildered questions, smiles approval now, for he asks her a question as to vows which has some spiritual import.

BETWEEN TWO foods, distant and appetizing in like measure, death by starvation would ensue ere a free man put either to his teeth.

So would a lamb stand still between two cravings of fierce wolves, in equipoise of dread; so would a dog stand still between two hinds.

Wherefore, if I held my peace I blame me not, (thrust in like measure either way by my perplexities) since 'twas necessity, nor yet commend me.

420

I held my peace, but my desire was painted on my face, and my questioning with it, in warmer colours far than if set out by speech.

And Beatrice took the part that Daniel took when he lifted Nebuchadnezzar out of the wrath that had made him unjustly cruel,[1]

and she said: "Yea, but I see how this desire and that so draweth thee, that thy eagerness entangleth its own self, and therefore breathes not forth.

Thou arguest: *If the right will endureth, by what justice can another's violence sheer me the measure of desert?*

And further matter of perplexity is given thee by the semblance of the souls returning to the stars, as Plato's doctrine hath it.[2]

These are the questions which weigh equally upon thy will; and therefore I will first treat that which hath the most of gall.[3]

He of the Seraphim who most doth sink himself in God, Moses, Samuel, and that John whichso thou choose to take, not Mary's self,

in any other heaven hold their seats than these spirits who but now appeared to thee, nor have they to their being more nor fewer years.

But all make beauteous the first circle, and share sweet life, with difference, by feeling more and less the eternal breath.

They have here revealed themselves, not that this sphere is given them, but to make sign of the celestial one that hath the least ascent.

Needs must such speech address your faculty, which only from the sense-reported thing doth apprehend, what it then proceedeth to make fit matter for the intellect.[4]

And therefore doth the Scripture condescend to your capacity, assigning foot and hand to God, with other meaning:[5]

and Holy Church doth represent to you with human aspect Gabriel and Michael, and him too who made Tobit sound again.[6]

That which Timæus argueth of the souls is not the like

of what may here be seen, for seemingly he thinketh as he saith.[7]

He saith the soul returneth to its star, believing it cleft thence when nature gave it as a form.[8]

Although perchance his meaning is of other guise than the word soundeth, and may have a not-to-be-derided purport.

If he meaneth that the honour and the blame of their influence return unto these wheels, perchance his bow smiteth a certain truth.

This principle misunderstood erst wrenched aside the whole world almost, so that it rushed astray to call upon the names of Jove and Mercury and Mars.[9]

The other perplexity which troubleth thee hath less poison, because its malice could not lead thee away from me elsewhere.

For our justice to appear unjust in mortal eyes is argument of faith, and not of heretic iniquity.[10]

But since your wit hath power to pierce unto this truth, e'en as thou wishest I will satisfy thee.

If *violence* is when he who suffereth doth naught contribute to what forceth him, then these souls had not the excuse of it:

for if the will willeth not, it cannot be crushed, but doth as nature doeth in the flame, though violence wrench it aside a thousand times.[11]

For should it bend itself, or much or little, it doth abet the force; and so did these, since they had power to return to the sacred place.

If their will had remained intact, like that which held Lawrence upon the grid, and made Mucius stern against his own right hand,[12]

it would have thrust them back upon the path whence they were drawn, so soon as they were loose; but such sound will is all too rare.

Now by these words, if thou hast gleaned them as thou should'st, the argument which would have troubled thee more times than this, is rendered void.

But now across thy path another strait confronts thine

eyes, through which ere thou should'st win thy way alone, thou should'st be weary.

I have set it in thy mind for sure, that no blessed soul may lie because hard by the Primal Truth it ever doth abide;[13]

and then thou mightest hear from Piccarda[14] that her devotion to the veil Constance still held, so that here she seemeth me to contradict.

Many a time ere now, my brother, hath it come to pass that to flee peril things were done, against the grain, that were unmeet to do;

so did Alcmæon, moved by his father's prayer, slay his own mother,[15] and not to sacrifice his filial piety became an impious son.

At this point, I would have thee think, violence receiveth mixture from the will, and they so work that the offences may not plead excuse.

The absolute will consenteth not to the ill, but yet consenteth in so far as it doth fear, should it draw back, to fall into a worse annoy.

Wherefore, when Piccarda expresseth this, she meaneth it of the absolute will, and I of the other; so that we both speak truth together."[16]

Such the rippling of the sacred stream which issued from the Spring whence all truth down-floweth; and being such, it set at peace one and the other longing.

"O love of the primal Lover, O divine one," said I then, "whose speech o'erfloweth me and warmeth, so that more and more it quickeneth me,

my love hath no such depth as to suffice to render grace for grace; but may he who seeth it, and hath the power, answer thereto.

Now do I see that never can our intellect be sated, unless that Truth shine on it, beyond which no truth hath range.

Therein it resteth as a wild beast in his den so soon as it hath reached it; and reach it may; else were all longing futile.

Wherefore there springeth, like a shoot, questioning[17] at the foot of truth; which is a thing that trusteth us towards the summit, on from ridge to ridge.

This doth invite me and giveth me assurance, with reverence, lady, to make question to thee as to another truth which is dark to me.

I would know if man can satisfy you so for broken vows, with other goods, as not to weigh too short upon your balance."

Beatrice looked on me with eyes filled so divine with sparks of love, that my vanquished power turned away, and I became as lost with eyes downcast.

1. Daniel divined the dream Nebuchadnezzar had dreamed as well as the interpretation of it (*Daniel* ii). So Beatrice knew what problems were exercising Dante's mind as well as what were the solutions.

2. In the *Timæus* which was accessible to Dante in the Latin paraphrase of Chalcidius. Dante's direct knowledge of Plato was doubtless confined to this one dialogue. The doctrine ascribed to Plato, implicitly here and explicitly in *Conv.* ii. 14 and iv. 21 (compare *Eclogue* ii), goes somewhat beyond the warrant of the text either in the Greek or Latin.

3. Plato's doctrine (as understood by Dante) is poisonous because it ascribes to the admitted influences of the heavenly bodies such a pre-potency as would be fatal to the free will, and therefore to mortality. *Cf. Purg.* xvi and xviii. *Epist.* viii.

4. According to the psychology of Aristotle and the Schoolmen, the Intellect works upon images. etc., which are retained in the mind after the sense impressions that produced them have vanished. Thus the *imaginative* faculties receive from the faculties of *sense* the impressions which they then present to the *intellect* for it to work upon. Wallace, 53.

5. "And even the *literal* sense is not the figure itself, but the thing figured. For when Scripture names the arm of God, the *literal* sense is not that God hath any such corporeal member, but hath that which is signified by the said member, to wit operative power" (Thomas Aquinas).

6. Raphael. See *Tobit.* xi. 2–17. Note that the Vulgate calls the father, as well as the son, Tobias.

7. The controversy still rages as to how far Plato is to be taken literally and how far Aristotle's matter-of-fact interpretation (and refutation) of his utterances is justified. Thomas Aquinas says: "Now certain say that those poets and philosophers, and especially Plato, did not mean what the superficial sound of their words implies, but chose to hide their wisdom under certain fables and enigmatical phrases, and that Aristotle was often wont to raise objections, not to their meaning, which was sound, but to their words; lest any should be led into error by this way of speaking; and so saith Simplicius in his comment. But Alexander would have it that Plato and the other ancient philosophers meant what their words seem externally to imply; and that Aristotle strove to argue not

only against their words, but against their meaning. But we need not greatly concern ourselves as to which of these is true; for the study of philosophy is not directed to ascertaining what men have believed, but how the truth of things standeth." Simplicius (6th century) and Alexander of Aphrodisias (2nd and 3rd centuries) are the two greatest of the Greek commentators on Aristotle.

It is interesting to note that even Beatrice hesitates between the two schools of interpretation.

8. The soul is the *form*, or essential and constituent principle, of man.

9. This passage is important as throwing light on Dante's constant assumption that the heathen deities, though in one sense "false and lying" (*Inf.* i), yet stand for some truly divine reality. We see here that idolatry springs from a misconception of the divine influences of which the heavenly bodies are the instruments. Its essential content therefore is real and divine, its form is false and impious. Compare Canto viii and *Conv.* ii. 5 and 6.

10. A difficult and much controverted passage. It is taken in the translation to mean: "The apparent return of the souls to the stars might easily betray you unawares into heresy; but the apparent injustice of heaven, however it may exercise your faith, will not lead you into any positive error. You will simply be left in suspense till I explain." *Argument of faith* would then mean "the subject matter on which faith exercises itself." No explanation is quite satisfactory.

11. The whole psychology of free and enforced action is Aristotelian. The definition of enforced action is taken direct from a passage in the *Ethics*. Wallace, 63.

12. Lawrence († A.. 258) and Mucius Scævola were alike tried by fire. Note the parallel between sacred and profane history habitual with Dante.

13. *Cf.* Canto iii.

14. *Cf.* Canto iii.

15. Eriphyle, bribed by the celebrated necklace of Harmonia, persuaded her husband Amphiaräus to join the expedition of the Seven against Thebes, in which he knew he would perish. He commanded their son Alcmæon to avenge him. Compare *Inf.* xx and *Purg.* xii.

16. *Cf. Purg.* xxi.

17. This means a *question* or a *difficulty*, not a "doubt." A concrete sense is here applied, "a natural impulse." The word *natura* sometimes simply means "a thing." Compare Canto i.

CANTO V

Beatrice, rejoicing in Dante's progress, explains the supreme gift of Free Will, shared by angels and men and by no other creature. Hence may be deduced the supreme significance of vows, wherein this Free Will, by its own act, sacrifices itself. Wherefore there can be nothing so august as to form a fitting substitute, nor any use of the once consecrated thing so hallowed as to excuse the breaking of the vow. And yet Holy Church grants dispensations. The explanation lies in the distinction between the content of the vow (the specific thing consecrated) and the act of vowing. The vow must in every case be kept, but he who has made it, may, under due authority, sometimes substitute for the specific content of the vow some other, worth half as much again; which last condition precludes any substitute for the complete self-dedication of monastic vows. And he who makes a vow such as God cannot sanction, has in that act already done evil; to keep such a vow is only to deepen his guilt; and, kept or broken, it brings his religion into contempt. Dante's further questioning is cut short by their ascent to Mercury, which grows brighter at their presence. Here, in the star that scarce asserts itself, but is lost to mortals in the sun's rays, are the once ambitious souls, that now rejoice in the access of fresh objects of love. They approach Dante, and one of them, with lofty gratulations, offers himself as the vehicle of divine enlightenment. Dante questions him as to his history and the place assigned to him in heaven; whereon the spirit (Justinian) so glows with joy that his outward form is lost in light.

"IF I FLAME on thee in the warmth of love, beyond the measure witnessed upon earth, and so vanquish the power of thine eyes,

marvel not; for this proceedeth from perfect vision, which, as it apprehendeth, so doth advance its foot in the apprehended good.

Well do I note how in thine intellect already doth reglow the eternal light, which only seen doth ever kindle love;

and if aught else seduce your love, naught is it save some

vestige of this light, ill understood, that shineth through therein.

Thou wouldst know whether with other service reckoning may be paid for broken vow, so great as to secure the soul from process."

So Beatrice began this chant, and, as one who interrupteth not his speech, continued thus the sacred progress:

"The greatest gift God of his largess made at the creation, and the most conformed to his own excellence, and which he most prizeth,

was the will's liberty, wherewith creatures intelligent,[1] both all and only, were and are endowed.

Now will appear to thee (if thence thou draw due inference) the high worth of the vow, if so made that God consent when thou consentest;[2]

for in establishing the compact between God and man, the victim is made from out this treasure, such as I pronounce it, and made by its own act.

What may be rendered, then, as restoration? If thou think to make good use of that which thou hadst consecrated, thou wouldst do good works from evil gains.[3]

Thou art now assured as to the greater point; but since Holy Church granteth herein dispensations, which seemeth counter to the truth I have unfolded to thee,

it behoves thee still to sit a while at table, because the stubborn food which thou hast taken demandeth further aid for thy digestion.

Open thy mind to that which I unfold to thee, and fix it there within; for to have understood without retaining maketh not knowledge.

Two things pertain to the essence of this sacrifice: first, that whereof it is composed, and then the compact's self.

This last can ne'er be cancelled save by being kept; and concerning this it is that the discourse above is so precise;

therefore it was imperative upon the Hebrews to offer sacrifice in any case, though the thing offered might sometimes be changed, as thou shouldst know.[4]

The other thing, which hath been unfolded to thee as the matter, may in sooth be such that there is no offence if it be interchanged with other matter.

But let none shift the load upon his shoulder at his own judgment, without the turn both of the white and of the yellow key[5]

and let him hold all changing to be folly, unless the thing remitted be contained in that assumed in four to six proportion.

Wherefore what thing soe'er weigheth so heavy in virtue of its worth as to turn every scale, can never be made good by any other outlay.

Let mortals never take the vow in sport; be loyal, and in doing this not squint-eyed; like as was Jephthah in his firstling vow;

whom it had more become to say: *I did amiss,* than keep it and do worse; and in like folly mayst thou track the great chief of the Greeks,

wherefore Iphigenia wept that her face was fair, and made simple and sage to weep for her, hearing of such a rite.[6]

Ye Christians, be more sedate in moving, not like a feather unto every wind; nor think that every water cleanseth you.

Ye have the Old and the New Testament and the shepherd of the Church to guide you; let this suffice you, unto your salvation.

If sorry greed proclaim aught else to you, be men, not senseless sheep, lest the Jew in your midst should scoff at you.

Do not ye as the lamb who leaves his mother's milk, silly and wanton, fighting with himself for his disport."[7]

Thus Beatrice to me, as I write; then turned her all in longing to that part where the world quickeneth most.[8]

Her ceasing and her transmuted semblance enjoined silence on my eager wit, which already had new questionings before it.

And even as an arrow which smiteth the targe ere the cord be still, so fled we to the second realm.

There I beheld my Lady so glad, when to the light of this heaven she committed her, that the planet's self became the brighter for it.

And if the star was changed and laughed, what then did I, who of my very nature am subjected unto change through every guise!

As in a fish-pool still and clear, the fishes draw to aught that so droppeth from without as to make them deem it somewhat they may feed on,

so did I see more than a thousand splendours draw towards us, and in each one was heard:

Lo! one who shall increase our loves.[9]

And as each one came up to us, the shade appeared full filled with joy, by the bright glow that issued forth of it.

Think, reader, if what I now begin proceeded not, how thou would'st feel an anguished dearth of knowing more,

and by thyself thou shalt perceive how it was in my longing to hear from these concerning their estate, soon as they were revealed unto my eyes.

"O happy-born,[10] to whom grace concedeth to look upon the Thrones of the eternal triumph ere thou abandonest thy time of warfare,[11]

by the light that rangeth through all heaven are we enkindled; and therefore if thou desire to draw light from us, sate thee at thine own will."

Thus by one of those devout spirits was said to me, and by Beatrice: "Speak, speak securely, and believe as thou would'st deities."

"Verily, I see how thou dost nestle in thine own light, and that thou dost draw it through thine eyes, because they sparkle as thou smilest;[12]

But I know nor who thou art, nor why, O worthy soul, thou art graded in this sphere, which veileth it to mortals in another's rays."[13]

This I said, turned towards the light which first had spoken to me; whereat it glowed far brighter yet than what it was before.

Like as the sun which hideth him by excess of light when the heat hath gnawed away the tempering of the thick vapours,

so by access of joy the sacred figure hid him in his own rays, and thus enclosed, answered me in such fashion as chanteth the following chant.

1. Angels and men.

2. *Cf.* Canto iii.

3. "To apply to some *other* good purpose what has been vowed, would only be like giving the proceeds of oppression or plunder in charity."

4. Regulations as to substitution or "redemption" are found in *Exodus* xiii. 13, xxxiv. 20, and *Numbers* xviii. 15–18. But the subject is most fully treated in the last chapter of *Leviticus*.

5. In popular estimate, "the silver key of knowledge and the golden key of authority." But Aquinas says more accurately: "for either of these [*i.e.*, to decide that the penitent is fit to be absolved, and actually to absolve him] a certain power of authority is needed; and so we distinguish between two keys, one pertaining to the judgment as to the fitness of him to be absolved, the other pertaining to the absolution itself." *Cf. Purg.* ix.

6. Both Jephthah (*Judges* xi) and Agamemnon sacrificed their daughters.

7. "If ignorant and unauthorized 'pardoners' and others tempt you to light-hearted vows and offer you easy terms of remission, do not be so senseless as to be misled by them. The blessing of the Christian dispensation is turned into a curse by such as do the like, and the very Jews have a right to make a mock of them." *Cf.* Canto xxix.

8. The Equator is the swiftest part of the heaven (*Conv.* ii. 4). The equinoctial point is the germinal point of the Universe (*Par.* x). The sun is the source of all mortal life (*Par.* xxii). Dante's words may apply to any of the three; but since, at the date of the Vision, the sun is at the equinoctial point, they all coincide.

9. *Cf. Purg.* xv.

10. *Cf.* Cantos viii (*note* 3), and ix (*note* 9).

11. The Church on earth is *militant;* only in heaven *triumphant*.

12. The last reference to the features of a blessed spirit, as discerned by Dante, in any of the revolving spheres.

13. Mercury is so near the sun as to be seldom visible.

ÇANTO VI

Note that Justinian, the Lawgiver, is the spokesman of the Roman Empire, whereby is indicated that the true significance of the empire lies in its imposing and fostering the arts of peace. Justinian tells how Constantine removed the seat of Empire east from Rome to Byzantium, reversing the progress of Æneas who went from Troy to Rome, and how he, Justinian, came to the throne two hundred years later. He was a believer in the divine but not in the human nature of Christ, till converted by Agapetus to the truth which he now sees as clearly as logicians see the axiomatic law of contradictories. After his conversion God inspired him with the project of codifying the Roman Law, and he resigned the conduct of war to Belisarius. He goes on to rebuke the Guelf and Ghibelline factions by showing the august nature of the Roman Empire. In his exposition we note that the key of self-sacrifice is at once struck in the name of Pallas, the Etruscan-Greek volunteer who died for the Trojan cause, and is maintained till it leads up to the great struggles with Carthage and the East, and against internal factiousness; the founding of the Empire under Julius and Augustus and the establishment of universal peace; the great act of Redemption for which all was a preparation, and the subsequent fall of Jerusalem; and the Empire's championship of the Church which had been born under its protection. It is equally wicked, therefore, to think of opposing the Empire or of turning it to factious purposes. The story of Rome has been told in the star adorned by those souls whose virtuous deeds had in them some taint of worldly ambition or anxiety for good repute, but who are now free from all envious desire to have a greater reward, and rejoice rather in the harmony of which their estate is part. Here too is the lowly Romeo who was so disinterested but so sensitive concerning his reputation.

"AFTER CONSTANTINE had wheeled back the eagle, counter to the course of heaven which it had followed in train of the ancient wight who took Lavinia, a hundred and a hundred years and more the bird of God

431

abode on Europe's limit, neighbouring the mountains whence he first had issued;

and there he governed the world beneath the shadow of his sacred wings from hand to hand till by succeeding change he came to mine.[1]

Cæsar I was, and am Justinian[2] who, by will of the Primal Love which now I feel, withdrew from out the Laws excess and inefficiency;

and ere I fixed my mind upon the work, one nature, and no more, I held to be in Christ, and with such faith was I content;

but the blessed Agapetus, who was high pastor, to the faith without alloy directed me by his discourse.[3]

Him I believed, and now the content of his faith I see as clear as thou dost see that every contradiction is both false and true.[4]

So soon as with the Church I moved my feet, God of his grace it pleased to inspire me with the high task, and all to it I gave me;

and to my Belisarius[5] committed arms; to whom heaven's right-hand was so conjoined it was a signal I should rest me from them.

Now here already is my answer's close to thy first question;[6] but its conditions force me to go on to some addition.

That thou mayst see with how good right against the sacred standard doth proceed both he who doth annex it to himself and he who doth oppose him to it,[7]

see how great virtue hath made it worthy of reverence, beginning from the hour when Pallas died to give it sway.

Thou knowest that it made its sojourn in Alba for three hundred years and more, until the close, when three with three yet fought for it.

And thou knowest what it wrought from the Sabine women's wrong unto Lucretia's woe, through seven kings, conquering around the neighbour folk.

Thou knowest what it wrought, borne by the chosen Romans against Brennus, against Pyrrhus and against the rest, princes and governments;

whence Torquatus and Quinctius, named from his neglected locks, the Decii and the Fabii, drew the fame which I rejoice in thus embalming.

It cast down the pride of the Arabs that followed Hannibal across the Alpine rocks, whence, Po, thou glidest.

Under it, Scipio and Pompey triumphed, yet in their youth, and bitter did it seem unto those hills beneath which thou wast born.

Then, nigh the time when all heaven willed to bring the world to its own serene mood, Cæsar, at Rome's behest, laid hold of it;

and what it wrought from Var to Rhine knoweth Isère and Arar, knoweth Seine and every valley by which Rhone is filled.

What it then wrought when he issued forth of Ravenna, and sprang the Rubicon, was of such flight that neither tongue nor pen might follow it.

Towards Spain it wheeled the host, then towards Durazzo, and so smote Pharsalia that to hot Nile was felt the woe.

Antandros and Simois, whence it first came, it saw once more, and saw the spot where Hector lieth couched; and then (alas for Ptolemy!) ruffled itself again;

thereafter swooped in lighting upon Juba, then wheeled towards your west, where it heard the Pompeian trumpet.

For what it wrought with the succeeding marshal Brutus and Cassius howl in hell; and Modena and Perugia it made doleful.

Yet doth wail for it the wretched Cleopatra, who, as she fled before it, caught from the viper sudden and black death.

With him it coursed unto the Red Sea shore, with him it set the world in so deep peace that Janus saw his temple barred upon him.

But what the ensign that doth make me speak had done before, what it was yet to do throughout the mortal realm subject unto it,

becometh small and dusky to behold, if it be looked upon in the third Cæsar's hand with clear eye and pure heart;

for the living justice that inspireth me, granted it, in his hand of whom I speak, the glory of wreaking vengeance for his wrath.[8]

Now find a marvel in the double thing I tell thee! Thereafter, under Titus, to wreak vengeance on the vengeance on the ancient sin it rushed.[9]

And when the Lombard tooth bit into Holy Church, under its wings did Charlemagne victorious succour her.

Now mayst thou judge of such as I accused but now, and of their sins, which are the cause of all your ills.

The one opposeth to the public standard the yellow lilies, and the other doth annex it to a faction,[10] so that 'tis hard to see which most offendeth.

Ply, ply the Ghibellines their arts under some other standard; for this he ever followeth ill who cleaveth justice from it;

and let not that new Charles down beat it with his Guelfs, but let him fear talons that have ripped its fell from mightier lion.[11]

Many a time ere now have children wailed for father's fault, and let him not suppose God will change arms for those his lilies.[12]

This little star adorneth her with good spirits who were active that honour and that fame might come to them;

and when hereon desire, thus swerving, leaneth, needs must the rays of the true love mount upward with less life.

But in the commeasuring of our rewards to our desert is part of our joy, because we see them neither less nor more.

Whereby the living justice so sweeteneth our affection that it may ne'er be warped to any malice.

Divers voices upon earth make sweet harmony, and so the divers seats in our life render sweet harmony amongst these wheels.

And within the present pearl shineth the light of Romeo, whose beauteous and great work was so ill answered.

But the Provençals who wrought against him have not the laugh; wherefore he taketh an ill path who maketh of another's good work his own loss.

Four daughters, and each one a queen, had Raymond Berengar; and this was wrought for him by Romeo, a lowly and an alien man;

then words uttered askance moved him to demand ac‑
count of this just man, who gave him five and seven for
every ten;

then took his way in poverty and age; and might the
world know the heart he had within him, begging his life
by crust and crust, much as it praiseth, it would praise him
more."[13]

1. Constantine reigned A.D. 306–337. Justinian A.D. 527–565. Constan‑
tinople is relatively near to the site of ancient Troy. Æneas *took*
Lavinia with her father's consent, though she was already betrothed
to Turnus, King of the Latins.
2. His personality remains. His office is his no longer. *Cf. Purg.* xix.
3. The Monophysites accepted the divine nature of Christ only, not
the human. The Empress Theodora persistently favoured them, and
Justinian tolerated them till Agapetus, who was Pope A.D. 535–536,
when on an embassy at Constantinople, induced him to depose An‑
thimus, Bishop of Constantinople, on the ground of his being a
Monophysite, whereon the other heads of the sect were likewise
excommunicated.
4. *Cf.* Canto ii. It is a cardinal point of Dante's belief that in the per‑
fect state all *effort* both of will and intellect shall cease, while their
activity reaches its highest point. Even truths that now seem para‑
doxical shall be seen as axioms, and the facts that now seem perplex‑
ing or distressing shall be felt as axiomatically right and beautiful.
But unfathomed depths of the Divine Nature and Will shall ever
remain, adored but uncomprehended. *Cf.* Cantos xix and xxi.
Both in this passage and in Canto ii the union of the divine and
human natures in Christ is the point which Dante declares will be
as clear to souls in bliss as "the initial truth which man believeth,"
or is as clear to Justinian as that "every contradiction is both false
and true." Now "the initial truth which man believeth" is not a
generic term for axiomatic truth, but a specific reference to the
"law of contradictories" on which the whole system of Aristotelian
logic is build up. It asserts that the propositions: *This is so* and *this
is not so* cannot both be true in the same sense and at the same
time. Cf. Wallace, § 30. And it follows immediately from this funda‑
mental axiom, that of the two propositions "all A's are B's" and
"some A's are not B's," or of the two propositions "no A's are B's"
and "some A's are B's," one must be true and the other false. They
cannot both be true or both false in the same sense at the same time.
For example, if the proposition "some A's are not B's" be true, the
proposition "all A's are B's" is false; for if not, take one of the A's
that is not a B; now since all A's are B's, that particular A is a B;
therefore that particular A both is and is not a B, which is impos‑
sible, *therefore*, &c. Propositions so related are called contradic‑
tories, and therefore every "contradiction" or "pair of contradic‑
tories" is "both false and true" axiomatically.

5. Belisarius (*ca.* 505-565), by his campaigns against the Ostrogoths, went far towards restoring the authority of the Empire in Italy. He subsequently fell into disfavour, and an exaggerated tradition represents him in beggary as the type of fallen greatness.

6. The question implied in Canto v.

7. Compare with this passage (twenty-two stanzas) *Conv.* iv and the whole of Bk. ii of the *De Monarchia*. Compare also Virgil *Georgics*, ii, and *Æneid*, vi; and perhaps we should add the *Epistle to the Hebrews*, chap. xi. For Dante's attitude towards Guelfism and Ghibellinism generally, see Gardner i. 4, and Villani *Introduction*, § 6.

N.B. In the following summary the italicized words directly connect the narrative with the text of the canto.

Virgil, by a gracious fiction, represents the Trojan Æneas when he landed, fate-driven, on the shores of Italy, and was involved in war with Turnus, king of the Latins, as seeking and gaining the alliance of the Greek Evander, who had established a kingdom on the seven hills, afterwards to be the site of Rome. Evander's only son and heir, *Pallas*, led the band of volunteers and was slain by Turnus, but avenged by Æneas. The kingdom of the latter was founded, however, not on the seven hills, but at Lavinium, whence it was transferred by his son Ascanius to *Alba* Longa where it remained for *more than* 300 *years*, till, in the reign of Tullus Hostilius (670-638 B.C.), Alba fell under Rome, on the defeat of the *three* Alban champions, the Curatii, by the survivor of the *three* Roman champions, the Horatii; for meanwhile the Alban outcast, Romulus, had founded a camp of refuge on the Palatine (one of the seven hills), and had provided the desperadoes, who gathered there, with wives, by seizing the *Sabine women* who had come to attend the public games. Under *him and his six successors* Rome gradually extended her power, till the outrage offered to *Lucretia* by Sextus, the son of the last king, so roused the indignation of the people that the monarchy was swept away (510 B.C.).

The long period of the Republic, up to the beginning of Cæsar's campaigns in Gaul (58 B.C.) is passed over rapidly by Dante, without notice of constitutional and social struggles; but the main aspects of the outward history are dealt with by rapid and effective strokes. During this period Rome established her supremacy over the other Latin tribes, repelled invasions of Italy, both by civilized and barbarous peoples, and extended her dominion by counter invasions. Lucius *Quinctius* Cincinnatus (from cincinnus = a *curl*), called from the plough to the dictatorship, conquered the Æquians (458 B.C.); against Brennus (390 B.C., etc.) and his Gauls, one of the *Fabii*, and Titus Manlius *Torquatus* (as well as others, notably Camillus) distinguished themselves. The *Decii*,—father, son and grandson,—died self-devoted deaths in serving against the Latins (340 B.C.), the Samnites (295 B.C.) and the Greek invader Pyrrhus (280 B.C.); while the greatest of all the Fabii, Quintus *Fabius* Maximus (*Cunctator*), saved Rome from *Hannibal who crossed the*

Alps and victoriously invaded Italy in 218 B.C., in which same year *Scipio* Africanus (the Elder), *a boy of seventeen*, won military fame by saving his father's life at the defeat of Ticinus. It was he who subsequently organized the counter invasion of Africa which compelled Hannibal to withdraw from Italy. *Cf.* Canto xxvii [Note the anachronism by which Dante calls the northern Africans *Arabs*.]

By a great leap Dante now brings us to the achievements of *Pompey*, the great conqueror of the eastern kings and queller of the faction of Marius. He celebrated a triumph *when not yet twenty-five* (81 B.C.). After a passing reference to the mythical exploits of the great Romans in reducing Fiesole *which overhangs Florence*, and which was the refuge of Catiline (Villani), we find ourselves following the career of *Cæsar* preparatory to the founding of the Roman Empire. Reference is to the campaigns in *Gaul* (58–50 B.C.); to Cæsar's crossing the Rubicon (49 B.C.) between Ravenna and Rimini, thereby leaving his province, without orders from the Senate, and so formally beginning the civil war. In the same year he overcame formidable opposition in *Spain*, and next year unsuccessfully besieged Pompey in *Dyrrhachium*, and then utterly defeated him at *Pharsalia* in Thessaly. Pompey escaped to *Egypt*, where he was treacherously slain by Ptolemy. Cæsar crossed the Hellespont and, says Lucan, visited the Troad. He took Egypt from *Ptolemy* and gave it to Cleopatra, subdued *Juba*, king of Numidia who had protected his opponents after Pharsalia and then returned to Spain (45 B.C.) where *Pompey's sons* had raised an army. After the murder of Cæsar his nephew Augustus defeated Marc Antony at *Modena* (43 B.C.); then, with Antony as his ally, defeated his uncle's assassins, *Brutus* and *Cassius* (*cf. Inf.* xxxiv) at Philippi (42 B.C.), and afterwards Antony's brother Lucius at *Perugia* (41 B.C.). In 31 B.C. at Actium he finally defeated his rival Marc Antony, who soon afterwards committed suicide, and his example was followed by his paramour *Cleopatra*, who died by the tooth of a *viper*. This made Augustus master of the whole Roman Empire to the *remotest ends of Egypt*, and the *temple of Janus*, the gates of which were always open in war-time, was, for the third time only in the history of Rome, *closed* in sign of universal peace. Heaven "had brought the world to its own serene mood," and all was ready for the *birth of Christ*, who was *crucified* under Tiberius, the successor of Augustus, whereby the sin of human nature at the fall was avenged. Jerusalem fell, under Titus, whereby the sin of slaying Christ was avenged on the Jews.

The epilogue of the defence of the Church by Charlemagne against the Lombard king Desiderius, whom he dethroned in A.D. 774, produces a disjointed effect upon the modern reader, but would seem natural enough to Dante and his contemporaries (see *Argument*).

8. Compare *De Monarchia*, ii.

9. See next canto.

10. The Guelfs oppose the French arms and influence to the Empire.

The Ghibellines take the name of the Empire in vain for factious purposes.

11. Carlo Zoppo (= Charles the Lame), of Anjou, titular King of Jerusalem (see Canto xix), and actual King of Naples and head of the Guelfs of Italy. Dante is never weary of expressing his contempt for him. Many a mightier lion than Cripple Charles had had his fell torn off his back by the Imperial Eagle.

12. A forecast perhaps of some miseries that actually fell on the descendants of Charles, and of others which Dante vainly anticipated. Compare Canto ix.

13. (Last five stanzas.) See Villani, vi.

Raymond Berengar IV of Provence (reigned 1209–1245), to the distinguished from his contemporary and opponent Raymond VII of Toulouse (reigned 1222–1249), was notorious for his liberality and his patronage of poets and other men of genius. His daughter, Margaret, married Louis IX of France (St. Louis). Eleanor married Henry III of England. Sancha married Henry's brother, Richard of Cornwall; and Beatrice, his youngest daughter, whom he made his heiress, married Charles of Anjou after her father's death. Raymond's able and upright chamberlain, Romeo of Villeneuve (1170–1250), is also an historical character; but his name, Romeo, is the current term for one who has made a pilgrimage to Rome, or a pilgrim generally (see *Vita Nuova*, xli). Hence arose the romantic legend recorded by Villani, and here followed by Dante. "There came to his [Raymond Berengar's] court a certain Romeo, who was returning from St. James', and hearing the goodness of Count Raymond abode in his court, and was so wise and valorous, and came so much into favour with the Count, that he made him master and steward of all that he had. . . . Four daughters had the Count and no male child. By prudence and care the good Romeo first married the eldest for him to the good King Louis of France by giving money with her, saying to the count, 'Leave it to me, and do not grudge the cost, for if thou marriest the first well thou wilt marry all the others the better for the sake of her kinship and at less cost.' And so it came to pass; for straightway the King of England, to be of kin to the King of France, took the second with little money; afterward his carnal brother, being the king elect of the Romans, after the same manner took the third; the fourth being still to marry the good Romeo said, 'for this one I desire that thou should'st have a brave man for thy son, who may be thine heir,'—and so he did, Finding Charles, Count of Anjou, brother of King Louis of France, he said, 'Give her to him for he is like to be the best man in the world,' prophesying of him: and this was done. And it came to pass afterwards through envy, which destroys all good, that the barons of Provence accused the good Romeo that he had managed the Count's treasure ill, and they called upon him to give an account. The worthy Romeo said, 'Count, I have served thee long while, and raised thy estate from small to great, and for this, through the false counsel of thy people, thou art little grateful. I came to thy

court a poor pilgrim, and I have lived virtuously here; give me back
my mule, my staff, and my scrip, as I came here, and I renounce thy
service.' The Count would not that he should depart; but, for
nought that he could do would he remain; and, as he came so he
departed, and no one knew whence he came or whither he went.
But many held that he was a sainted soul."

ÇANTO VII

In significant connection with the Empire comes the treatment of the Redemption, the chief theological discourse in the Paradiso. Justinian and the other spirits vanish with hymns of triumph. Dante would fain ask a question, but when he raises his head to speak, he is overcome by awe, and bends it down again. Beatrice reads his thoughts, and bids him give good heed to her discourse. After man's fall, the Word of God united to himself in his own person the once pure now contaminated human nature. That human nature bore on the cross the just penalty of its sin, but that divine Person suffered by the same act the supremest outrage. At the act of justice God rejoiced and heaven opened. At the outrage the Jews exulted and the earth trembled; and vengeance fell upon Jerusalem. But why this method of redemption? Only those who love can understand the answer. God's love ungrudgingly reveals itself, and whatever it creates without intermediary is immortal, free, and god-like. Such was man till made unlike God by sin, and so disfranchised only to be reinstated by a free pardon, or by full atonement. But man cannot humble himself below what he is entitled to, as much as he had striven to exalt himself above it; and therefore he cannot make atonement. So God must reinstate man; and since "all the ways of the Lord are mercy and truth," God proceedeth both by the way of mercy, and by the way of truth or justice, since by the incarnation man was made capable of reinstating himself. Beatrice further explains that the elements and their compounds are made not direct by God, but by angels, who also draw the life of animal and plant out of compound matter that has the potentiality of such life in it; whereas first matter, the angels, and the heavens are direct creations of God; and so were the bodies of Adam and Eve, which were therefore immortal, save for sin; as are therefore the bodies of the redeemed who are restored to all the privileges of unfallen man.

"HOSANNAH! Holy God of Sabaoth! making lustrous by thy brightness from above the blessed fires of these kingdoms!"

So, revolving to its own note, I saw that being sing, on whom the twin lights double one another:[1]

and it and the others entered on their dance, and like most rapid sparks, veiled them from me by sudden distance.

I, hesitating, said, "Speak to her, speak to her," within myself, "speak to her," I said, "to my lady who slaketh my thirst with the sweet drops";

but that reverence which all o'ermastereth me, though but by Be or Ice,[2] again down-bowed me, as a man who slumbers.[3]

Short time Beatrice left me thus; and began, casting the ray upon me of a smile such as would make one blessed though in the flame:

"According to my thought that cannot err, how just vengeance justly was avenged, hath set thee pondering;[4]

but I will speedily release thy mind; and do thou hearken, for my words shall make thee gift of an august pronouncement.

Because he not endured for his own good a rein upon the power that wills,[5] that man who ne'er was born, as he condemned himself, condemned his total offspring;

wherefore the human race lay sick down there for many an age, in great error, till it pleased the Word of God to descend

where he joined that nature which had gone astray from its Creator to himself, in person, by sole act of his eternal Love.[6]

Now turn thy sight to what I now discourse: This nature, so united to its Maker, as it was when created was unalloyed and good;

but by its own self had it been exiled from Paradise, because it swerved from the way of truth, and from its proper life.

As for the penalty, then, inflicted by the cross,—if it be measured by the Nature taken on, never did any other bite as justly;[7]

and, in like manner, ne'er was any so outrageous if we look to the Person who endured it, in whom this nature was contracted.

So from one act issued effects apart; God and the Jews

rejoiced in one same death; thereat shuddered the earth and heaven opened.

No more, now, should it seem hard saying to thee that just vengeance was afterward avenged by a just court.

But now I see thy mind from thought to thought entangled in a knot, from which, with great desire, it release awaiteth.

Thou sayest, *Yea, what I hear I understand; but why God willed for our redemption this only mode, is hidden from me.*

This decree, my brother, is buried from the eyes of every one whose wit is not matured within love's flame.

But since this target much is aimed at, and discerned but little, I will declare why such mode was more worthy.

The divine excellence, which spurns all envy from it, burning within itself shooteth such sparkles out as to display the eternal beauties.[8]

That which distilleth from it without mean,[9] thereafter hath no end; because its imprint may not be removed when it hath stamped the seal.

That which down raineth from it without mean, is all free,[10] because not subject to the power of changing things.

It is more close conformed to it, therefore more pleasing to it; for the sacred glow that rayeth over everything, in that most like itself is the most living.

All these points of vantage hath the human creature, and should one fail, needs must it fall from its nobility.

Sin only is the thing that doth disfranchise it,[11] and maketh it unlike to the highest good, so that its light the less doth brighten it;

and to its dignity it ne'er may come again, except it fill again where fault hath made a void, against the ill delight setting just penalty.

Your nature, when it sinned in its totality in its first seed, from these dignities, even as from Paradise, was parted;

nor might they be recovered, if thou look right keenly, by any way save passing one or the other of these fords:

either that God, of his sole courtesy, should have remitted; or that man should of himself have given satisfaction for his folly.

Fix now thine eye within the abyss of the eternal counsel, as close attached as e'er thou mayest to my discourse.

Man had not power, within his own boundaries, ever to render satisfaction; since he might not go in humbleness by after-obedience so deep down

as in disobedience he had framed to exalt himself on high; and this the cause why from the power to render satisfaction by himself man was shut off.

Wherefore needs must God with his own ways reinstate man in his unmaimed life, I mean with one way or with both the two.[12]

But because the doer's deed is the more gracious the more it doth present us of the heart's goodness whence it issued,

the divine Goodness which doth stamp the world, deigned to proceed on all his ways to lift you up again;

nor between the last night and the first day was, nor shall be, so lofty and august a progress made on one or on the other;

for more generous was God in giving of himself to make man able to uplift himself again, than had he only of himself granted remission;

and all other modes fell short of justice, except the Son of God had humbled him to become flesh.[13]

Now, to fulfil for thee every desire, I go back to explain a certain passage, that thou may'st there discern e'en as do I.

Thou sayest: *I see the water, I see the fire, the air, the earth, and all their combinations meet their dissolution and endure but little;*

and yet these things were creatures, so that if that which I have said to thee be true, they ought to be secure against corruption.[14]

The Angels, brother, and the unsullied country in which thou art, may be declared to be created, even as they are, in their entire being;[15]

but the elements which thou hast named and all the things compounded of them, have by created virtue been informed.

Created was the matter which they hold, created was the informing virtue in these stars which sweep around them.

The life of every brute and of the plants is drawn from

compounds having potency, by the ray and movement of the sacred lights.[16]

But your life is breathed without mean by the supreme beneficence who maketh it enamoured of itself, so that thereafter it doth ever long for it.[17]

And hence[18] thou further may'st infer your resurrection, if thou think again how was the making of the human flesh then when the first parents both of them were formed."

1. Justinian, on whom the glory of Lawgiver and the glory of Emperor combine their lights, each one making the other its twin.

2. He is awed by anything that is so much as a fragment of Beatrice's name.

3. Cf. Canto iii.

4. See Canto vi.

5. Cf. Canto xxvi, note 11.

6. Note the reference to the Three Persons of the Trinity in *Word, Creator, Love*. The like references abound throughout the poem. Further, *cf.* Canto xxxiii.

7. Cf. *De Monarchia*, ii. This doctrine of Dante's that human nature, in its totality, was *judicially executed* on the Cross seems to be peculiar to himself.

8. The connection is close, though not obvious. Beatrice goes back to the creation in order to explain the state from which man fell; and begins by declaring that the Divine Goodness was moved to utter itself in creation by an impulse of love, and had no jealous reserve in communicating its own august attributes. *Cf.* Canto xxix, note 2.

9. For the distinction between mediate and immediate creation, see *note* 16.

10. True freedom consists in being subject only to the eternal truth of things, not to the dominion of changing appearances. *Cf. Purg.* xvi. But there is a difficulty here, for amongst the primal group of direct creations are the material heavens and the *first matter*, or undifferentiated material potentiality, which is the possibility of everything but the actuality of nothing. *Cf.* Canto xxix. The heavens can only be called free in the sense that they follow out their nature unimpeded, not in the higher sense of having free choice. *Cf.* Canto v. And the *first matter* can scarcely claim freedom in any sense, nor exemption from the dominion of changing things. Still less has it any special conformity of nature to the Divine. No solution of this difficulty suggests itself. It would appear as though Dante had not the full range of "direct creations" under his view at the moment, and was thinking only of angels and men, and possibly the material heavens.

11. It is in this long section of the discourse that the influence (direct or indirect) of Anselm's *Cur Deus homo* is most conspicuous.

Anselm teaches that actually (though not in intention) Adam's disobedience was an injury to himself, not at all to God, and that what was demanded, therefore, was not a propitiation or a ransom, but a restoration; which must be brought about by man giving what he did not owe in measure equal to that in which he had seized what he did not own, which is impossible, since he owes everything and owns nothing. Hence the being who alone owns that which he does not owe must become the being who alone stands in need of making such an unowed offering, *i.e.*, God must become man. See the *Cur Deus homo* passim, and (to avoid misconception) especially Bk. i. cap. 15.

12. *Cf. Psalm* xxv. 10.

13. It will appear from a comparison of the *De Monarchia*, ii, that Beatrice means "God determined to be merciful, but did better than remit the fault, for he made man capable of redeeming it. And he determined to be just, and therefore he assumed the whole of human nature into one person (his own) in order that it might collectively pay the penalty of its sin."

14. See earlier in this canto. "Why, then, do these creations of God (the elements and things compounded of them) perish?"

15. Not only in their essential or ideal quality, but in their whole concrete being, just as they are. *Cf.* Canto i, *note* 1.

16. The *first matter* is *informed* (*i.e.*, so combined with a "form" or ideal and essential principle as to pass from the possibility of being *anything* to the actuality of being *something*) not direct by God, but by created powers, *i.e.*, angels or heavenly influences. The transforming and vivifying power of the sun (and in lesser degree the moon) was supposed to have its analogies in equally real but less obvious influences of the other heavenly bodies, especially the planets. It is these heavenly influences collectively that draw the "soul" or *life* of plant (nutritive and reproductive) or animal (sensitive and locomotive) from the stage of potentiality in the germinal material into that of actuality in the living thing itself.

17. *Cf. Purg.* xxv. In *Conv.* iii. 6, another and less orthodox doctrine seems to be taught.

18. *Hence, i.e.,* "from the distinctions now drawn"; for the bodies both of Adam and Eve were made immediately by God, and when the work of redemption is finally consummated (after the last judgment) man's body will be restored to the dignity which it lost only by sin. The argument is Anselm's. He meets the obvious objection that it does not cover the case of the "resurrection unto wrath," by urging that if the saved rejoice both in body and soul, it is but fitting that the lost should suffer in both.

ÇANTO VIII

The planet Venus and ancient idolatry. All angels, heavens and blessed spirits, from the Seraphim nearest God outwards, are twined in one concerted cosmic dance; this dance the spirits in Venus leave to minister to Dante, singing Hosannah as they come; and one of them declares their kinship of movement and of love with the celestial Beings to whom he had once addressed his love hymn. Dante, with Beatrice's sanction, asks who the spirit is, and he with a flash of joy reveals himself as Dante's friend, Carlo Martello, once heir to the lordship of Provence and the kingdom of Naples, and actual king of Hungary, though Sicily had revolted from his house in consequence of that ill government against which his brother, Robert of Naples, mean offspring of a generous sire, would do well to take warning. Dante's joy in meeting his friend is increased by the knowledge that it is seen as clearly by that friend as by himself, and further, by the thought that it is in God that it is thus discerned. He asks him how it is that degenerate children can spring from noble parents. Carlo explains that for every natural attribute of any being there is provision of a corresponding good, and that since God is perfect and has made his ministers perfect for their offices, it follows that there is a fit place for everything and every one, for which place it is designed and at which it is aimed. The social relations of man demand diversity of gift, which diversity is provided for by the action of the heavens on human natures, but without regard to descent, so that natural heredity is overruled by celestial influences. Whereas we in assigning a man's place to him give heed only to hereditary position or such-like irrelevancies instead of studying his natural gift. Hence general confusion and incompetency.

THE WORLD was wont to think in its peril that the fair Cyprian rayed down mad love, rolled in the third epicycle;

   wherefore not only to her did they do honour of sacrifice and votive cry, those ancient folk in the ancient error,

   but Dione did they honour, and Cupid, the one as her

446

mother, the other as her son, and told how he had sat in Dido's lap;[1]

and from her from whom I take my start, they took the name of the star which courts the sun, now from the nape, now from the brow.

I had no sense of rising into her, but my Lady gave me full faith that I was there, because I saw her grow more beautiful.

And as we see a spark within a flame, and as a voice within a voice may be distinguished, if one stayeth firm, and the other cometh and goeth;

so in that light itself I perceived other torches moving in a circle more and less swift, after the measure, I suppose, of their eternal vision.

From a chill cloud there ne'er descended blasts, or visible or no, so rapidly as not to seem hindered and lagging[2]

to whoso should have seen those lights divine advance towards us, quitting the circling that hath its first beginning in the exalted Seraphim.

And within those who most in front appeared, *Hosannah* sounded in such wise that never since have I been free from longing to re-hear it.

Then one drew himself more nigh to us, and alone began: "All we are ready at thy will, that thou mayst have thy joy of us.

We roll with those celestial Princes in one circle and in one circling and in one thirst, to whom thou from the world didst sometime say:

Ye who by understanding give the third heaven motion, and so full of love are we that, to pleasure thee, a space of quiet shall be no less sweet to us."[3]

When mine eyes had been raised in reverence to my Lady, and she had satisfied them with herself and given them assurance,

they turned them back to the light which so largely had made proffer of itself, and, "Say who ye be," was my word, with great affection stamped.

Ah! how I saw it wax in quantity and kind at the new joy which, when I spoke, was added to its joys!

Thus changed, it[4] said to me: "The world held me below

but little space; had it been more much ill shall be that had not been.

My joy holdeth me concealed from thee, raying around me, and hideth me like to a creature swathed in its own silk.[5]

Much didst thou love me, and thou hadst good cause; for had I stayed below I had shown thee a further growth of love than the mere leaves.

That left bank which is bathed by Rhone after it hath mingled with Sorgue, me for its timely lord awaited;

so did that corner of Ausonia, down from where Tronto and Verde[6] discharge into the sea, citied by Bari, Gaeta and Catona.

Upon my brow already glowed the crown of the land the Danube watereth after it hath left its German banks;

and fair Trinacria which darkeneth between Pachynus and Pelorus, o'er the gulf tormented most by Eurus,

(not for Typheus, but for sulphur that ariseth there) would yet have looked to have its kings, sprung through me from Charles and Rudolf,

had not ill lordship, which doth ever cut the heart of subject peoples, moved Palermo to shriek out: *Die! die!*

And had my brother seen it in good time, he would already flee the greedy poverty of Catalonia, lest it should work him ill;

and of a truth provision needs be made by him or by another, lest on his bark already laden heavier load be laid.

His nature,—mean descendant from a generous forebear,—were in need of soldiery who should not give their care to storing in the chest."

"Sire, in that I believe the lofty joy which thy discourse poureth into me, there where every good hath end and hath beginning

is seen by thee even as I see it, 'tis more grateful to me; and this too I hold dear, that thou discernest it looking on God.[7]

Thou hast rejoiced me, now enlighten me; for in speaking thou hast moved me to question how from sweet seed may come forth bitter."

448

Thus I to him; and he to me: "If I can show a certain truth to thee, thou wilt get before thine eyes the thing thou askest just as thou hast it now behind thy back.

The Good which doth revolve and satisfy the whole realm thou art climbing, maketh its providence become a virtuous power in these great bodies;[8]

and not only is provision made for the diverse-natured creatures, by the mind that is perfection in itself, but for their weal too, co-related with them.[9]

Wherefore whate'er this bow dischargeth doth alight disposed to a provided end, even as a thing directed to its mark.

Were this not so, the heaven thou art traversing would so bring its effects to being, that they would be not works of art, but ruins;

and this may not be, if the intellects which move these stars be not defective, and defective, too, that primal one which failed to perfect them.

Wouldst thou that this truth be more illuminated?" And I: "Not so, for I see 'tis impossible that nature, in the needful, should fall short."

Whence he again: "Now, say, would it be worse for man on earth were he no citizen?" "Yea," I replied, "and here I ask no reason."

"And may that be, except men live below diversely and with diverse offices? No, if your master[10] write the truth for you."

Up to this point he came deduction-wise; then the conclusion: "Therefore must needs the roots of your effects be diverse;

wherefore is one born Solon and one Xerxes, one Melchizedek,[11] and one the man who, soaring through the welkin, lost his son.[12]

That which in circling hath its nature,[13] and is the seal upon the mortal wax, plieth aright its art, but maketh not distinction between one or other tenement.

Wherefore it cometh that Esau severeth himself in seed from Jacob, and Quirinus cometh of so base father that he is assigned to Mars.

The begotten nature would ever take a course like its
begetters, did not divine provision overrule.

Now that which was behind thee is before; but that thou
mayst know that I delight in thee, I will have a corollary
wrap thee round.

Ever doth nature, if she find fortune unharmonious with
herself, like any other seed out of its proper region, make
an ill essay.

And if the world down there took heed to the founda-
tion nature layeth, and followed it, it would have satis-
faction in its folk.

But ye wrench to a religious order him born to gird the
sword, and make a king of him who should be for dis-
course; wherefore your track runneth abroad the road."

1. See Canto iv, and *note* 9; and also "Note on Dante's Paradise,"
p. 399.
2. Visible and invisible blasts = lightning and wind. "And it also
appears that lightnings are winds kindled or enflamed by the swift-
ness of their motion." And again "Because a hot exhalation, when it
mounts up, strikes a cold and moist region, and it comes to pass that
it is cast earthwards and chilled with a certain coldness, and a
downward direction is given to it" (Averroës).
3. When Dante wrote the ode here referred to (*Conv.* ii, Canzone)
he believed, with Brunetto Latini, that the angels who presided over
the Heaven of Venus belonged to the order of *Thrones*. See *Conv.*
ii, 6. He afterwards followed "Dionysius" in assigning them to the
order of *Principalities*. See Canto xxviii. *Princes* may be equivalent
to "Principalities" and so imply the correction, but since both terms
are generic (see *Conv.* ii. 6) this need not be so. In Canto ix, still
in the planet Venus, there is a reference to *Thrones* so specific that
one would take it to indicate Dante's continued belief in the special
connection between *Thrones* and the planet Venus, were it not that
in the planet Mercury there is a similar specific reference to
Thrones. The apparent confusion is not easy to remove. For a sug-
gested solution see Canto xxviii, *note* 12.
4. On Charles Martel, see Canto ix, *note* 1. See also maps on pp.
452, 453, 454.
5. The illustration of a silk-worm in its cocoon corresponds closely
to representations, in early Italian art, of souls surrounded by a
yellow glory.
6. From this, together with *Purg.* iii, it has been inferred that the R.
Garigliano was formerly known as the Verde.
7. The distinction is subtle but real. "I rejoice that you see it (which
you do, in God), and I rejoice that it is in God (and not otherwise)
that you see it."

8. Cf. Canto ii, *note* 11.
9. Cf. Cantos i and xxix.
10. Aristotle. See Wallace 68–70.
11. Lawgiver, soldier, priest. Melchizedek is the priest *par excellence*, because he offered "bread and wine." See *Gen.* xiv. 18.
12. Dædalus, the typical mechanician. See *Inf.* xvii.
13. The heavens.

To Cantos VIII and XIX

452

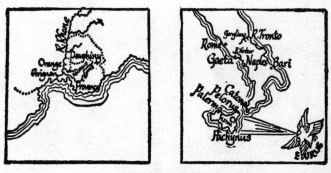

To Canto VIII

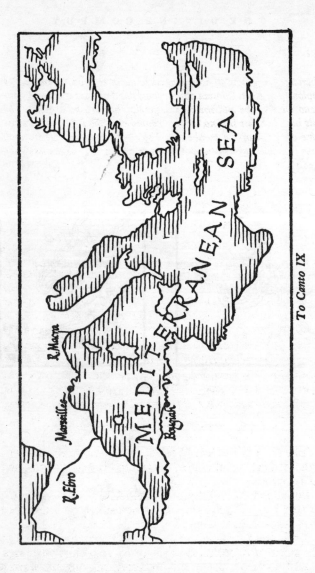

R. Efiro

Marseille

R. Macra

Boujiur

MEDITERRANEAN SEA

To Canto IX

ÇANTO IX

Charles, after a note of warning, turns again to God, whom we so impiously neglect. Cunizza approaches; she describes the site of Romano whence she and the tyrant Ezzelin, her brother, sprang. She tells how her past sins no longer trouble her. She speaks of the fair fame on earth of the troubadour Folco, and laments that no such fame is now sought by her countrymen of Venetia; whose woes she predicts and whose crimes she denounces; and then seeming no longer to heed Dante drops again into her place in the cosmic dance. Folco now flashes brighter in Dante's sight, and at his entreaty diverts his voice from its place in the universal song (which, like the universal dance, takes its note from the Seraphim) to minister to his special need. He indicates his birthplace of Marseilles. He tells of his amorous youth but shows how in heaven there is no repentance, because the sin is only seen or remembered as the occasion of the act of God by which the fallen one was uplifted again into his true element: and it is on this divine power and grace that the soul's whole thought and love are centred. He points out to Dante the light of Rahab, speaks of this heaven as just within the range of the cone of the earth's shadow, thereby indicating that the place of these souls in heaven is, in part, determined by the earthly sin that is now no longer in their minds; refers to Rahab's help given to Joshua in conquering the Holy Land, and denounces the Pope for his indifference to its recovery. It is devil-planted Florence that corrupts the world, both shepherd and flock, by her florins. But vengeance shall not lag.

WHEN THY CHARLES,[1] fair Clemence, had enlightened me, he told me of the frauds his seed was destined to encounter;

but added: "Hold thy peace, and let the years revolve"; so that I can say naught, save that wailing well-deserved shall track your wrongs.

And already the life of that sacred light had turned to the sun that filleth it, as to the good ample for all things.

Ah! souls deceived, ah! creatures impious, who from

455

such good wry-twist your hearts, squaring your temples unto vanity!

And lo, another of those splendours drew him towards me, and signified his will to pleasure me, by brightening outwardly.

Beatrice's eyes, fixed on me as before, of dear assent to my desire assured me.

"Nay! make swift counterpoise unto my will," I said, "thou blessed spirit, and give proof that I can cast reflection upon thee of what I think."[2]

Whereat the light which was new to me, from out its depth, wherein it first was singing, went on as one rejoicing to do well:

"In that region of the depraved Italian land which sitteth 'twixt Rialto and the springs of Brenta and Piave,

riseth a hill, lifted to no great height, whence erst came down a firebrand that made a dire assault upon the country.[3]

Out of one root spring I with it; Cunizza was I called, and here I glow because the light of this star overcame me.

But joyously I grant myself indulgence for the occasion of my lot, nor doth it grieve me, which would seem, mayhap, hard saying to your common herd.[4]

Of this shining and dear gem of our heaven, which most doth neighbour me, great fame remaineth, and ere it shall perish

this centenary year shall be five times repeated. See if a man should make himself excel, so that the first life leave another after!

And of this thinketh not the present crowd that Tagliamento and Adige enclose; the which, though smitten, yet repenteth not.

But soon shall come to pass that Padua at the pool shall change the water that doth bathe Vicenza, because the folk are stubborn against duty.[5]

And where Sile meets Cagnano, one holdeth sway and goeth with uplifted head to catch whom even now the net is being woven.[6]

A wail shall yet arise from Feltro for the trespass of its

impious pastor,[7] which shall be so foul that for the like
none ever entered Malta.[8]

Too ample were the charger which should receive Fer-
rara's blood, and weary who should weigh it ounce by
ounce,

which this obliging priest shall give to prove himself a
partisan; and such-like gifts shall suit the country's way
of life.

Aloft are mirrors,—ye name them Thrones,[9]—whence
God in judgment shineth upon us so that these words ap-
prove themselves to us."

Here she was silent, and to me her semblance was of one
who turneth him to other heeding, judging as by the wheel
whereto she gave herself, like as she was before.[10]

The other joy, noted already to me as a thing illustrious,
shone in my sight like a fine ruby that the sun should strike.

By joy up there brightness is won, just as a smile on
earth; but down below darkeneth the shade externally as
the mind saddeneth.

"God seeth all, and into him thy seeing sinketh," said I,
"blessed spirit, so that no wish may steal itself from thee.

Then wherefore doth thy voice, which gladdeneth
Heaven ceaselessly,—together with the singing of those
Flames devout, which make themselves a cowl with the
six wings,—[11]

not satisfy my longings? Not till now had I awaited thy
demand, were I in thee even as thou art in me."

"The greatest valley in which water stretcheth," then
began his words, "forth from that sea which garlandeth
the earth,

betwixt opposing shores, against the sun, goeth so far
that it meridian maketh of what was first horizon.[12]

Of this valley was I a shoresman, midway 'twixt the Ebro
and the Macra, which, with short course, parteth the
Genoese and Tuscan.

Almost alike for sunset and for sunrise the site of
Bougiah and of the place I spring from, which with its
blood once made the harbour warm.[13]

Folco[14] they called me to whom my name was known,
and this heaven is stamped by me, as I was stamped by it;

for Belus' daughter,[15] wronging alike Sichæus and Creüsa, did not more burn than I, so long as it consorted with my locks;

nor yet the Rhodopeian maid who was deluded by Demophoön,[16] neither Alcides when he had shut Iole in his heart.[17]

Yet here we not repent, but smile; not at the sin, which cometh not again to mind, but at the Worth that ordered and provided.

Here gaze we on the Art that beautifieth its so great effect, and here discern the Good which bringeth back the world below unto the world above.

But that thou mayst bear away full satisfied all the desires born within this sphere, needs must I yet proceed.

Thou wouldst know who is within that light which here by me so sparkleth as the sun's ray in pure water.

Now know that there within hath Rahab peace; and when she joined our order, it stamped itself with her in the highest grade.

By this heaven,—touched by the shadow's point which your world casteth,—ere other soul was she uptaken from Christ's triumph.

And soothly it beseemed to leave her as a trophy, in some heaven, of the lofty victory which was achieved with the one and the other palm;

because she favoured Joshua's first glory in the Holy Land, which little toucheth the Papal memory.[18]

Thy city,—of his planting who first turned his shoulders on his Maker, and from whose envy hath such wailing sprung,—

maketh and spreadeth that accursed flower which hath set sheep and lambs astray, for it hath turned the shepherd to a wolf.

Therefore it is the Gospel and great Doctors are deserted, and only the Decretals are so studied, as may be seen upon their margins.[19]

Thereon the Pope and Cardinals are intent; ne'er wend their thoughts to Nazareth, where Gabriel spread his wings.

But Vatican, and the other parts elect of Rome, the

cemetery of the soldiery that followed Peter, shall soon
be freed from the adultery."

1. Charles of Anjou, brother of St. Louis, conquered Naples and
Sicily from Manfred, son of Frederick II, and became Charles I.
Towards the end of his life his misgovernment of Sicily caused the
massacre known as the "Sicilian Vespers" (1282) and the loss of
Sicily (Canto viii and Villani vii). His son Charles II (see Canto vi,
and *note* 11. Dante nowhere else allows him the generosity ascribed
to him in Canto viii) was the father of a numerous family, including
Dante's friend, Charles Martel, who died before his father (1295);
and Robert. Charles married Clemence, daughter of the Emperor
Rudolph; hence the allusion in Canto viii. He visited Florence in
the last year of his life, and it was probably then that Dante formed
his acquaintance. On his death his son, Caroberto, became heir to
the throne of Naples; but his uncle Robert (known as Robert the
Wise), supported by Charles II's will, ousted him from the suces-
sion. This was in 1309. At the date of the vision, therefore, Robert
could not yet have been abusing his powers as king; but according
to Charles, he was already preparing to do so by cultivating the
Spanish friendships he had formed when a hostage in Spain, and
so laying the train for oppression of the much enduring Apulia by
the instrumentality of Spanish favourites. As to Clemence there has
been much discussion. It would be natural to suppose that she is
Charles's wife. It was her son Caroberto that Robert of Naples had
excluded from the succession to Naples and Provence; and to her
and her son, therefore, the *your wrongs* would naturally apply. But
the date of her death is given in recent commentaries as 1301, long
before the time at which these words were written; and evidence
has now been produced to show that she really died in 1295, as in-
deed several of the early commentators declare; and in that case she
had been dead some years before the assumed date of the vision,
1300. This would make the direct address to her difficult, and the
implied communication well-nigh impossible. And yet the only
alternative seems still more difficult to accept, namely, that the
Clemence addressed was Charles's daughter who married Louis X,
le Hutin (*cf.* Villani, ix), and was living in 1328. This Clemence was
in no special way wronged by the proceedings of Robert, nor is it
easily conceivable that Dante in speaking of a father to a daughter
would call him "thy Charles." The reader must take his choice be-
tween these two impossibilities. As to the woes that are said to be
approaching, we note that since no conspicuous disaster had over-
taken Robert, Dante has to fall back upon general forebodings of
evil.

2. By answering before I ask.

3. The hideous tyrant Ezzelino da Romano (*Cf. Inf.* xii); whose
mother dreamed she gave birth to a firebrand that consumed the
whole district.

4. Her amours with Sordello were specially notorious. In 1265 (when

she was about 67 years old) she executed a deed of manumission, conferring formal freedom on a number of slaves (who probably had already secured the reality) in the house of Dante's friends the Cavalcanti. It is therefore possible that Dante was in possession of private sources of information as to penitence in closing years, an edifying end, grateful dependents who prayed for the departed soul, etc. No such knowledge, however, except that she had a certain reputation for humanity, has reached the world at large, and the scandalized protest which Dante anticipated and defied has not failed to make itself heard!

5. A much discussed passage, which probably refers to the defeats inflicted on the Paduans at Vicenza by Can Grande of Verona (see Villani, ix) in and about 1314. "Paduan blood shall dye the Bacchiglione red because of Paduan resistance to the Empire."

6. Riccardo da Cammino, Lord of Treviso. He was murdered in 1312. He was the son of the "Good Gherard" (*Purg.* xvi and *Conv.* iv. 14), and the husband of Judge Nino's daughter Giovanna (*Purg.* viii).

7. Alessandro Novello, Bishop of Feltre, 1298–1320. In 1314 he surrendered certain Ghibelline refugees from Ferrara to Pino della Tosa, King Robert's vicar there, who executed them.

8. A papal prison on lake Bolsena, or perhaps in Viterbo.

9. Cf. Cantos viii (*note 3*) and xxviii (*note 12*). "For they are called *Thrones* by whom God doth exercise his judgments" (Gregory, quoted by Aquinas).

10. Cf. Canto viii.

11. Cf. Canto viii. *Argument. Cf. Isaiah* vi. 2.

12. At Gibraltar, where the Mediterranean flows out of the ocean, the sun (according to Dante's geography) is on the horizon when it is noonday on the Levant. Thus the stretch of the sea makes zenith at its end of what is horizon at its beginning; *i.e.*, it extends over a quadrant. See map on p. 454.

13. When Cæsar's fleet won a victory over the Pompeians in 49 B.C. *Cf. Purg.* xviii.

14. Folco of Marseilles was a Troubadour (fl. 1180–1195), and afterwards a Cistercian monk. As bishop of Toulouse (1205–1231) he took a leading part in the infamous Albigensian Crusades.

15. Dido, whose love for Æneas wronged the memory of her husband Sichæus and of his wife Creüsa.

16. Phyllis, beloved of Demophoön the son of Theseus and Phedra, was the daughter of the Tracian king Sithon, and hence is called Rhodopeian, after the mountain Rhodope in Thrace. According to Ovid, Demophoön ultimately returned to keep his plighted faith, but Phyllis had already slain herself in despair at his protracted absence.

17. Iole was the last love of Hercules (Alcides). On hearing of this attachment, Dejanira, the wife of Hercules, sent him the fatal shirt of Nessus, thus causing his death. Nessus the Centaur had offered an insult to Dejanira as he was bearing her across a stream, and

Hercules shot him. As he expired he told Dejanira that the garment, steeped in his blood, would have the power of winning back the affections of Hercules if ever they wandered from her. It is this vengeance of the Centaur which is referred to by Dante in *Inf.* xii.
18. Rebukes the slackness of the Pope in face of the capture of Acre by the Saracens in 1291, after which the Christians had no foothold in the Holy Land. *Cf.* Villani vii.
19. *Cf.* Canto xii. There was money to be got out of studying Ecclesiastical Law. *Cf. Conv.* i. 9.

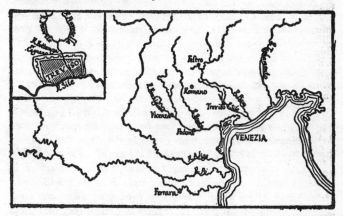

ÇANTO X

God as self-existent contemplating himself as manifested, in that love which in either aspect he breathes forth, made all objects of intelligence or sense with that order which speaks of him to all beholders. Let the reader, then, look upon the equinoctial point, which so clearly displays that art of God which he himself ever contemplates, in love. Let him reflect how the influences of the sun and planets—the seasons and other alternations—would be effective over a smaller part of the earth if the inclination of the ecliptic were less, and would be too violent in their contrasts if it were greater. If the reader will not give himself time to work out these and other such hints, weary listlessness instead of enjoyment will be the fruit of his study, for the author cannot pause to elaborate them for him. The sun is in the spring equinoctial point and Dante is with him. Standing out against the sun by their very brightness are spirits rejoicng in the vision of the relation of the Father to the Son and to the Holy Spirit. Beatrice calls on Dante to thank the sun of the angels; and he thereon so concentrates his thought on God as to forget Beatrice; in pleasure whereat she smiles so beauteously as to shatter the undivided unity of his mind; which thus broken up distributes itself amongst the wondrous objects that claim it. Twelve spirits surround Dante and Beatrice, as with a crown, and thrice circle them, uttering music that may not be conceived on earth; then pause, while one of them, Thomas Aquinas, declares that since the divine grace has kindled in Dante such true love as must ever increase itself by the mere act of loving, and has revealed to him that heavenly bliss to which he who has once known it must ever return, it follows that every blessed soul must freely love to do him pleasure; whereon he tells him who are the other flames; whereon the wheel of lights again begins to revolve with ineffable music.

GAZING upon his Son with the Love which the one and the other eternally breathes forth, the primal and ineffable Worth,[1]

made whatsoever circleth through mind or space with so

great order that whoso looketh on it may not be without some taste of him.

Then, reader, raise with me thy sight to the exalted wheels, directed to that part where the one movement smiteth on the other;[2]

and amorously there begin to gaze upon that Master's art, who within himself so loveth it, that never doth he part his eye from it.

See how thence offbrancheth the oblique circle that beareth the planets, to satisfy the world that calleth on them;

and were their pathway not inclined, much virtue in the heaven were in vain, and dead were almost every potency on earth;

and if, from the straight course, or more or less remote were the departure, much were lacking to the cosmic order below and eke above.

Now stay thee, reader, on thy bench, back thinking on this foretaste, wouldst thou have good joyance ere that thou be weary.

I have set before thee; now feed thou thyself, for that matter whereof I have made me scribe, now wresteth to itself my total care.

The greatest minister of Nature, who with the worth of heaven stampeth the world, and with his light measureth the time for us,

united with that part now called to mind, was circling on the spirals whereon he doth present him ever earlier.[3]

And I was with him; but of my ascent I was no more aware than is a man, ere his first thought, aware that it is coming.

'Tis Beatrice who leadeth thus from good to better, so instantly that her act doth not expatiate through time.

How shining in itself must that needs be which in the sun, whereinto I had entered, itself revealeth not by hue, but light!

Though I should summon genius, art, tradition, ne'er could I so express it as to make it imaged; but it may be believed—and let men long to see it.

And if our fantasies are low for such an exaltation, it is

no marvel, for never was there eye that could transcend the sun.

Such, there, was the fourth household of the exalted Father who ever satisfieth it, showing how he doth breathe, and how beget.

And Beatrice began: "Give thanks, give thanks to the sun of the Angels, who of his grace hath to this sun of sense exalted thee."

Never was heart of mortal so disposed unto devotion, and so keen to give itself to God with all its will,

as to those words was I; and so wholly was my love committed unto him, it eclipsed Beatrice in oblivion.

Her it displeased not; but she so smiled thereat, the splendour of her laughing eyes parted my erst united mind amongst things multiform

Then saw I many a glow, living and conquering, make of us a centre, and of themselves a crown; sweeter in voice than shining in appearance.

Thus girt we sometimes see Latona's daughter, when the air is so impregnated as to retain the thread that makes her zone.

In the court of heaven, whence I have returned, are many gems so dear and beauteous that from that realm they may not be withdrawn,

and the song of these lights was of such; he who doth not so wing himself that he may fly up there, must look for news thence from the dumb.

When, so singing, those burning suns had circled round us thrice, like stars neighbouring the fixed poles,

they seemed as ladies, not from the dance released, but pausing, silent, listening till they catch the notes renewed.

And within one I heard begin: "Since the ray of grace,—whereat true love is kindled, and then doth grow, by loving,

multifold—doth so glow in thee as to conduct thee up upon that stairway, which, save to reascend, no one descendeth,

whoso refused his vial's wine to quench thy thirst, were no more free than water that should flow not to the sea.

Thou wouldst know with what plants this garland is en-

flowered, which amorously doth circle round the beaute
ous lady who strengtheneth thee for heaven.

I was of the lambs of the sacred flock that Dominic lead-
eth upon the way where is good fattening if there be no
straying.

This, who most neighboureth me upon the right, brother
and master was to me, and he was Albert of Cologne, I
Thomas of Aquino.[4]

If in like manner thou wouldst be assured of all the rest,
take way with thy sight after my words, circling above
along the blessed wreath.

This next flaming issueth from the smile of Gratian,[5]
who gave such aid to the one and the other forum, as is
acceptable in Paradise.

The other who doth next adorn our choir, was that
Peter who, with the poor widow, offered his treasure unto
Holy Church.[6]

The fifth light,[7] which amongst us is most fair, doth
breathe from such a love that all the world down there
thirsteth to know the news of it;

within there is the lofty mind, to which a wisdom so pro-
found was granted, that, if the truth be true,[8] no second
ever rose to such full vision.

Next look upon that taper's light, which, in the flesh
below, saw deepest into the angelic nature and its min-
istry.[9]

In the next little light laugheth that pleader for the
Christian times, with whose discourse Augustine fortified
him.[10]

Now if thou drawest thy mind's eye from light to light,
following my praises, already for the eighth thou art a-
thirst.

In seeing every good therein rejoiceth the sainted soul,[11]
which unmasketh the deceitful world to whoso giveth it
good hearing.

The body whence it was chased forth, lieth down below
in Cieldauro,[12] and itself from martyrdom and exile came
unto this peace.

See flaming next the glowing breath of Isidor, of Bede,

and of Richard,[13] who, in contemplating, was more than man.

The one from which thy glance returneth unto me, is the light of a spirit who, in weighty thoughts, him seemed went all too slowly to his death;

it is the light eternal of Sigier who, lecturing in the *Vicus Straminis*, syllogized truths that brought him into hate."[14]

Then as the horologue, that calleth us, what hour the spouse of God[15] riseth to sing her matins to her spouse that he may love her,

wherein one part drawing and thrusting other, giveth a chiming sound of so sweet note, that the well-ordered spirit with love swelleth;

so did I see the glorious wheel revolve and render voice to voice in harmony and sweetness that may not be known except where joy maketh itself eternal.

1. Note the special frequency of reference to the Trinity in this and the next following cantos. Also the emphasis laid on the procession of the Holy Ghost *from the Son* as well as from the Father. The *filioque* controversy was one of the chief sources of the alienation between the East and West, which, after widening for centuries, resulted at last in the great schism of 1054 by which the Greek and Latin Churches were severed.

2. At the first point of Aries and at the first point of Libra the Equator and the Zodiac cross on the heavenly sphere. The daily movement of the Sun (and all other heavenly bodies) is parallel to the Equator, and his annual movement is along the Zodiac ("the oblique circle that beareth the planets"), so that the daily and the annual movements smite one upon the other at these two points.

3. From midwinter to midsummer the Sun rises every day a little earlier and a little further North than the day before, and from midsummer to midwinter a little later and a little further South. Thus he always travels on a spiral, up or down. It is in the middle of his up-spiral that he encounters the Spring equinoctial point. This passage then indicates the *Spring equinox* with perfect precision.

4. Albertus Magnus (1193–1280) and Thomas Aquinas (*ca.* 1225–1274) "christianized Aristotle," *i.e.*, made Aristotle's works the philosophical basis of Christian doctrine, as well as the store-house of profane learning, thus putting an end to the dislike of the Aristotelian learning which the elder theologians had felt when it was introduced in the twelfth century. From Thomas Aquinas (Doctor Angelicus), and especially his *Summa*, Dante drew much of his theological learning. Albertus Magnus (Doctor Universalis) taught in Cologne and Paris, and Thomas was his beloved pupil.

5. Gratian (fl. *ca.* 1150) brought ecclesiastical and civil law into relation with each other. His *Decretum* was the first systematic treatise on Canon Law.

6. Peter Lombard (*ca.* 1100–1160) collected and discussed the pronouncements of the Christian Fathers in his four books of *Sentences*, dealing respectively with God, the creation, the Redemption, and the Sacraments and Last Things. In the preface he compares himself to the poor widow of *Luke* xxi. 1–4. His work became the text-book of theological teaching, and Bonaventura, Aquinas, and other wrote commentaries on it.

7. Solomon. 1 *Kings* iii. 12. "There is a dispute amongst certain holy men and theologians whether he [Solomon] be damned or saved" (Petrus Alighieri).

8. As sure as Scripture.

9. Dionysius the Areopagite. See *Acts* xvii. 34. (*Cf.* Canto xxviii.) The works on the *Celestial Hierarchy*, etc., that went under his name are now supposed to date from the 5th or 6th century.

10. Probably Paulus Orosius (early 5th century), whose *Historia adversus Paganos* was an apologetic treatise written in connection with Augustine's *De Civitate Dei* to disarm the Pagan contention that Christianity had ruined the Roman Empire.

11. Boethius (*ca.* 475–525), whose penetrating influence on Dante is to be traced everywhere. *Cf. Conv.* ii. 13, and many other passages. When in prison, in Pavia, condemned to death by Theodoric, he wrote the *Consolation of Philosophy*, a book of noble Pagan morality and religion, maintaining that even in this world, and as judged by human reason, the life of the virtuous man is to be preferred before that of the vicious, and the ways of God to man may be justified. Thus he supplemented the exclusive reliance of Christian writers on the compensations of a future life, and on revealed, as distinct from philosophical truth. The medieval consciousness, uncritical as usual, but with a correct enough instinct, laid hold of this welcome supplement without perceiving its essentially Pagan presentation, and so found room for Boethius amongst the Christian teachers. The process was facilitated by the fact that Boethius moved in Christian circles, had, in his youth, written certain theological tracts in defence of Christian orthodoxy against Eutychian and other heresies (dealing with the questions at issue from the philosophical point of view), and appears never to have separated himself from the Christian communion, though his spiritual life was fed entirely from Pagan sources. The authenticity of his theological treatises, though raised above all reasonable doubt, is still occasionally disputed.

Special prominence is given in the last book of the *Consolation of Philosophy* to the problem of the reconciliation of God's foreknowledge with man's free will. Boethius treats it very fully and with great beauty. In substance the answer is that God's knowledge of the future no more determines it than does his knowledge of the past, and that indeed the distinction between fore-knowledge and after-knowledge does not apply to God at all, since he is not subject to the condition of time. The distinction between *divine* and *human* knowledge absorbs the lesser distinction between *fore-* and *after-* knowledge, and if we are to inquire into the relations in question at all, it must be by trying to form some conception of the higher plane of the divine knowledge in general, not by tormenting ourselves as to the specific implications of God's *fore-*knowledge. It is in this connection that Boethius gives the definition of eternity that became classical: "Whatsoever, therefore, comprehendeth and possesseth the whole plenitude of unlimited life at once, to which nought of the future is wanting, and from which nought of the past hath flowed away, this may rightly be deemed eternal." *Cf.* Canto xxii. *Argument* and *note* 5 together with the other passages there referred to.

12. Cieldauro (Golden Ceiling) is a name of St. Peter's church in Pavia.

13. Isidore of Seville (*ca.* 560–636), the author of a great Cyclopedia. Bede the Venerable (*ca.* 673–735). Richard of St. Victor (d. 1173) wrote a treatise entitled *De Contemplatione. Cf. Epist. ad Can. Grand.,* § 28. See further, Canto xii, *note* 25.

14. Sigier of Brabant (d. probably about 1283), a professor in the University of Paris, where the *Rue du Fouarre* ran "close to the river, in the region which is still known as the *Quartier Latin*, and was the centre of the Arts Schools at Paris" (Toynbee). He took a leading part in the disputes between the mendicant orders and the University, and it is noteworthy that Thomas Aquinas himself was one of his chief opponents. He met his death (apparently by an assassin's dagger) at the Papal court at Orvieto, but exactly when does not appear.

15. Spouse of God = the Church.

ϚΑΝΤΟ XI

Contrast between earth and heaven. Thomas, reading Dante's thoughts, renews his discourse in order to remove certain difficulties. Providence raised up Francis and Dominic to succour the Church. From Assisi Francis rose sun-like, even as the sun in which Doctor and Poet are now discoursing rises to mortals from Ganges or elsewhere according to the place of their abode. His marriage with poverty. The founding and confirming of his order. He preaches to the Soldan, receives the stigmata, and dies commending his bride to his disciples. If he was such, what must Dominic have been, seeing that he was worthy to be his colleague. But almost all his followers are degenerate.

INSENSATE care of mortals! Oh how false the arguments which make thee downward beat thy wings!

One was following after law, and one aphorisms,[1] one was pursuing priesthood, and one dominion by violence or by quibbles,

and another plunder, and another civil business, and one, tangled in the pleasures of the flesh, was moiling, and one abandoned him to ease;

the whilst, from all these things released, with Beatrice up in heaven thus gloriously was I received.

When each had come again to that point of the circle whereat he was before, he stayed him, as the taper in its stand.

And within that light which first had spoken to me I heard smiling begin, as it grew brighter:

"Even as I glow with its ray, so, gazing into the Eternal Light, I apprehend whence thou dost take occasion for thy thoughts.

Thou questionest and wouldst fain discern, in such open and dispread discourse as may be level to thine understanding, my utterance

wherein I said but now: *Where is good fattening,* and

wherein I said: *No second ever rose;* and here we need to make precise distinction.[3]

The providence which governeth the world,—with counsel wherein every creature's gaze must stay, defeated, e'er it reach the bottom,—

in order that the spouse of him, who with loud cries espoused her with the blessed blood, might go toward her delight,

secure within herself and faithfuller to him, two Princes did ordain on her behalf, who on this side and that should be for guides.

The one was all seraphic in his ardour, the other by his wisdom was on earth a splendour of cherubic light.[4]

Of one will I discourse, because of both the two he speaketh who doth either praise, which so he will; for to one end their works.

Between Tupino and the stream[5] that drops from the hill chosen by the blessed Ubaldo,[6] a fertile slope hangs from a lofty mount,

wherefrom Perugia feeleth cold and heat through Porta Sole,[7] and behind it waileth Nocera, for the heavy yoke, and Gualdo.[8]

From this slope, where most it breaks the steepness of decline, was born into the world a sun, even as is this some whiles from Ganges.

Wherefore who speaketh of that place, let him not say *Assisi,*[9] 'twere to speak short, but *Orient,* would he name it right

Not yet was he far distant from his rising when he began to make the earth to feel from his great power a certain strengthening;

for in his youth[10] for such a lady did he rush into war against his father,[11] to whom, as unto death, not one unbars the gate of his good pleasure;

and in the spiritual court that had rule over him, and in his father's presence he was united to her, and then from day to day loved her more strongly.

She, reft of her first husband,[12] a thousand and a hundred years and more, despised, obscure, even till him stood without invitation.

And nought availed her the report that she was found unterrified together with Amyclas,[13] when sounded that man's voice, who struck all the world with terror;

and nought availed her to have been so constant and undaunted, that she, when Mary stayed below, mounted the cross with Christ.[14]

But, lest I should proceed too covertly, Francis and Poverty as these two lovers now accept in speech outspread.

Their harmony and joyous semblance, made love and wonder and tender looks the cause of sacred thoughts;

so that the venerable Bernard first cast off his sandals and ran to follow so great peace, and as he ran him thought him all too slow.

Oh wealth unrecognized, oh fertile good! Unsandals him Egidius, unsandals him Sylvester, following the spouse, so doth the bride delight.

Thence took his way, this father and this master, together with his lady, and with the household already binding on the humble cord;[15]

nor abjectness of heart weighed down his brow, that he was Pietro Bernadone's son, nor that he seemed so marvellous despised.

But royally his stern intent to Innocent revealed he, and from him had the first[16] imprint upon his Order.

When the poor folk increased, after his track whose marvellous life were better sung in heaven's glory,[17]

then was the holy will of this chief shepherd circled with a second[16] crown by Honorius at the eternal inspiration.

And when, in thirst of martyrdom, in the proud presence of the Soldan, he preached Christ and his followers;

and because he found the folk too crude against conversion,—not to stay in vain,—returned to gather fruit from the Italian herbage;

then on the harsh rock[18] between Tiber and Arno, from Christ did he receive that final[16] imprint which his limbs two years carried.

When it pleased him who for such good ordained him, to draw him up to his reward which he had earned in making himself lowly.

to his brethren; as to his right heirs, his dearest lady he commended, and bade that they should love her faithfully;

and from her bosom the illustrious soul willed to depart, turning to its own realm, and for its body would no other bier.[19]

Think now what he was, who was a worthy colleague[20] to maintain the bark of Peter in deep sea towards the right sign!

And such was our patriarch; wherefore who followeth him as he commandeth, thou must perceive, loadeth him with good wares.

But his flock hath grown so greedy for new viands, it may not be but that through divers glades it strayeth;

and the more his sheep distant and wandering depart from him, the emptier of milk they return foldwards.

There are of them, indeed, who fear the loss and cleave close to the shepherd, but they are so few that little cloth doth furnish forth their cowls.

Now if my words have not been faint, if thy listening hath been attent, if thou call back to mind what I have said,

in part thy will must now be satisfied, for thou shalt see the plant from which they whittle, and thou shalt see the rebuke[21] that is intended in: *Where is good fattening if there be no straying.*"

1. *Aphorisms.* The name of a celebrated work of Hippocrates (460–357 B.C.). Hence equivalent to *medicine.*
2. See Canto x.
3. *Cf.* Canto xiii. To "distinguish" is a technical term of logic. It consists in showing that the inference is not correct though the premises are true, because there is a difference between the sense in which a word is used in the true premise and the sense in which alone it would justify the false conclusion. If an argument is refuted by denying one of the premises the process is called *interemption* = "destruction." *Cf. De Monarchia,* iii. 4.
4. The Seraphs, in popular estimate, are symbolical of love and the Cherubs of knowledge. Hence Francis (1182–1226), known as the Seraphic Father, and Dominic (1170–1221) are respectively akin to them. But see Canto xxviii, *note* 13.
5. The Chiascio.
6. Ubaldo (bishop of Gubbio, d. 1160) selected this hill for his hermitage, but (according to Scartazzini) was never able to carry out his intention of retiring to it. Hence the term *chosen.*
7. *Porta Sole,* the eastern gate of Perugia.

8. They were under the Angevin dynasty so hated by Dante. *Cf,* Canto vi, *note* 11. But others (with less probability) interpret *heavy yoke* as referring to the barren eastern slope of Monte Subasio.

9. Dante uses *Ascesi,* an old form of Assisi, which may be translated "I have ascended." A play upon the word, in connection with *Orient,* is found by some commentators. The comparison of Francis to the rising Sun is ancient and widespread. "Glowing as the light-bearer and as the morning star, yea, even as the rising Sun, illuminating, cleansing and fertilizing the world like some new luminary, was Francis seen to arise," says the Prologue of one of the earliest Lives.

10. He was about twenty-four when he began to woo Poverty.

11. In the early biographies of Francis (including the *Fioretti* or popular stories of him) with which every reader of Dante should be familiar, we are told how he fell in love with Poverty; how his father indignantly sought to reclaim him; how he appealed to the Bishop, stripped himself naked before him, giving to his earthly father Pietro Bernadone that which was his, and dedicating himself to his heavenly father, and thus publicly espousing Poverty; how Bernard, the nobleman of Assisi, was converted by overhearing his devotions; how Egidius whose thoughts were already turning from the world flung himself at the feet of Francis and implored him to receive him as a companion; how Sylvester, the priest, tried to cheat him over some stones he had from him with which to repair a church and was overcome by his unworldly generosity; how he rejoiced in all suffering and humiliation; how he loved and rejoiced in all God's creatures; how two successive Popes sanctioned his Order (1210 (?) and 1223); how he preached to the Soldan in Egypt; and finally, how he received the stigmata or impress of the nails and the lance as a testimony to his oneness of spirit with Christ (b. 1182, d. 1226).

12. Jesus Christ.

13. Lucan tells how Cæsar found the fisherman, Amyclas, lying on a bed of seaweed, undismayed when he roused him to demand his services, and unmoved by the revolutions of the times, secure in his poverty.

14. Nearly all the MSS. read *pianse* (wept) for *salse* (rose) and the best modern editions for the most part follow them. Dr. Moore, however (rightly as we think), adheres to the reading we have adopted. It is supported not only by internal evidence, but by some of the old commentators and by the analogy of the ancient prayer for Poverty ascribed to St. Francis, in which are the words "when thy very mother, *because the cross was so high* . . . could not come at thee, Lady Poverty, embraced thee more closely," etc.

15. The rope girdle worn by the Franciscans.

16. Note the *first, second, final.*

17. An enigmatical phrase, since it is in heaven that the song of praise is being sung. *Cf.* Canto xii.

18. Alvernia.

19. "And when he had blessed the brothers he had them take off his tunic, and place him naked on the ground" (Old Biography).

20. St. Thomas now passes to his own founder, Dominic, and rebukes the degenerate Dominicans. Cf. Canto xii, *note* 20.

21. Another reading of the original is *coreggier*, which would mean *the Dominican* (that is, one girt with the leather thong), and would refer either to the speaker (St. Thomas) himself or to any Dominican who might reprove his order in this way.

ÇANTO XII

A second circle of lights encloses the first and—with music whereof our sweetest strains are but as the reflection—the two, like the parallels of a double rainbow, circle Dante and Beatrice, first moving and then at rest. Like the needle of the compass to the north star so Dante is swept round to one of the new-come lights at the sound of its voice. It is Bonaventura, the Franciscan, who undertakes the enconium of Dominic, just as Thomas, the Dominican, had pronounced that of Francis. Dominic's zeal for true learning and against heresy. If he was such, what must his colleague have been? But his disciples are ruined by the extremes of the strict and lax schools of observance. Bonaventura names himself and the other lights that circle with him.

SOON AS the blessed flame had taken up the final word to speak, began the sacred millstone to revolve,[1]

and in its rolling had not turned full round ere a second, circling, embraced it and struck motion to its motion and song to its song;

song which so far surpasseth our Muses, our Sirens, in those sweet tubes, as the first splendour that which it back throweth.[2]

As sweep o'er the thin mist two bows, parallel and like in colour, when Juno maketh behest to her handmaiden,

the one without born from the one within—in fashion of the speech of that wandering nymph whom love consumed as the sun doth the vapours,—

making folk here on earth foreknow, in virtue of the compact that God made with Noah, that the world never shall be drowned again;[3]

so of those sempiternal roses revolved around us the two garlands, and so the outmost answered to the other.[4]

Soon as the dance and high great festival,—alike of song and flashing light with light, gladsome and benign,—

accordant at a point of time and act of will had stilled

them, like to the eyes which at the pleasure that moveth them must needs be closed and lifted in accord,

from out the heart of one of the new lights there moved a voice which made me seem the needle to the star in turning me to where it was;

and it began:[5] "the love which maketh me beautiful draweth me to discourse of the other chief, on whose account such fair utterance is made to us concerning mine.[6]

Meet is it that wherever is the one the other be led in, that, as they warred together, so may their glory shine in union.

Christ's army, which it cost so dear to re-equip, was following the standard, laggard, fearsome and thin-ranked;

when the Emperor who ever reigneth took counsel for his soldiery that was in peril, of his grace only, not that it was worthy;

and, as hath been said, came to the succour of his spouse with two champions, at whose doing, at whose saying, the straggling squadron gathered itself again.

To-wards that part where sweet Zephyr riseth to open the new leaves, wherewith Europe seeth herself reclad,

not far off from the smiting of the waves, behind the which, because of their long stretch, the sun sometimes hideth himself from all,

the fortune-favoured Calahorra[7] sitteth under protection of the mighty shield, whereon submits the lion, and subdueth.[8]

Therewithin was born the amorous frere of the Christian faith, the sacred athlete, benignant to his own and cruel to his foes;[9]

and, so soon as created, his mind was so replete with living virtue, that in his mother's womb he made her prophetess.[10]

When the espousals were complete at the sacred font, betwixt him and the faith, where they gave dower of mutual salvation,[11]

the lady who for him gave the assent saw in her sleep the marvellous fruit destined to issue from him and from his heirs;

and that he might in very construing be what he was,[12]

a spirit from up here moved them to call him by the posses-
sive adjective of him whose he all was.

Dominic was he named; and I speak of him as of the
husbandman whom Christ chose for his orchard, to bring
aid to it.

Well did he show himself a messenger and a familiar of
Christ, for the first love made manifest in him was to the
first counsel that Christ gave.[13]

Many a time, silent and awake, was he found on the
floor, by her who nursed him, as who should say, *It was
for this I came.*

Oh father his, Felice[14] in good sooth! Oh mother his,
Giovanna[15] in good sooth, if the word means, translated,
what they say!

Not for the world for whose sake now men toil after
him of Ostia and Thaddeus,[16] but for love of the true
manna,

in short season he became a mighty teacher, such that
he set him to go round the vineyard, which soon turneth
gray if the vine-dresser be to blame;

and from the seat which erst was more benign to the just
poor—not in itself, but in him who sitteth on it, and de-
generateth—[17]

not to dispense or two or three for six, not for the for-
tune of the next vacancy, not for the tithes belonging to
God's poor,[18]

he made demand; but for leave against the erring world
to fight for that seed wherefrom these four and twenty
plants ensheaf thee.

Then with teaching and with will together, with the
apostolic office he moved forth,[19] like a torrent that a deep
vein out-presseth,

and his rush smote amongst the stumps of heresy most
livingly where the resistances were grossest.

From him then diverse streamlets sprung, whereby the
Catholic orchard is so watered that its shrubs have the
fuller life.

If such was the one wheel of the chariot[20] wherein Holy
Church defended her, and won in open field her civil
strife,

clear enough should be to thee the excellence of that other, concerning whom, ere my coming, Thomas was so courteous.

But the track which the highest part of its circumference took hath been so abandoned, that there now is mould where once was crust.

His household, who marched straight with feet in his footprints, hath turned so round, that the toe striketh on the heel's imprint;

and soon shall sight be had of the harvest of the ill-culture, when the tare shall wail that the chest is reft from it.[21]

I well allow that whoso should search leaf after leaf through our volume, might yet find a page where he might read: *I am as I was wont;*

but not from Casale, nor from Acquasparta shall he be, whence come such to our Scripture that the one shirketh, the other draweth it yet tighter.[22]

I am the life of Bonaventura of Bagnoregio, who in the great offices did ever place behind the left-hand care.[23]

Illuminato and Augustine[24] are here, who were of the first unshod poor brethren, that with the cord made themselves friends to God.

Hugh of St. Victor[25] is here with them, and Pietro Mangiadore, and Pietro Ispano,[26] who giveth light below in twelve booklets;

Nathan the prophet, the metropolitan Chrysostom, and Anselm, and that Donatus[27] who deigned to set his hand to the first art;

Rabanus[28] is here, and there shineth at my side the Calabrian abbot Joachim,[29] dowed with prophetic spirit.

To emulous speech of so great paladin moved me the enkindled courtesy of brother Thomas and his well-judged discourse, and moved this company with me."

1. The horizontal sweep of a millstone is contrasted with the vertical motion of a wheel in *Conv.* iii. 5. The Apostles are frequently represented in art as working the Divine mill, and it may be under the influence of this association, as well as the direct fascination of the sight of a mill at work, that Dante compares the circling of these lights of the Church to the sweep of a millstone.

2. The reference is general. "Every song and every note produced

in the throat or in the tubes of musical instruments is but a faint
reflection of the heavenly music."

3. This passage is often cited to illustrate Dante's love of packing
one simile within another. The two circles of lights were like a
double rainbow (Juno's handmaid = Iris = Rainbow), and one
rainbow is like the echo of another, and the nymph Echo was con-
sumed by love as vapours are consumed by the Sun. Note the char-
acteristic combination of Pagan mythology and Hebrew legend.
Cf. *Gen.* ix. 8-17.

4. The Italian presents a difficulty; *ultima* = the "last" (counting
from outside inwards), being used for *intima* = the "inmost."

5. The speaker is Bonaventura (1221-1274), known as the Seraphic
Doctor. He became General of the Franciscans in 1256.

6. *Cf.* balance of this canto, and *notes* 20-26.

7. Calahorra, in Spain, not far from the Gulf of Gascony.

8. The royal arms of Castile bear a castle in the first and third quar-
ters, and a lion in the second and fourth. Thus on one side of the
shield the lion is subdued by the castle, and on the other subdues it.

9. Of Dominic (1170-1221) comparatively little is known, but it
presents a striking parallel and contrast to Francis. Dominic was a
man of learning, and Francis was unlettered. Dominic's concern was
for soundness of the faith, and Francis was given to deeds of love.
Dominic's most characteristic work was the attempted conversion of
the Albigensian heretics, and the stimulating of theological study at
the universities, that of Francis tending the lepers of Italy. Dominic
embraced poverty as a pledge of Apostolic zeal, and Francis for pure
love of her; that is to say, from a sense that the more we *have* the
less we can *be*, and a passionate joy in coming into naked contact
with God and nature.

For the rest, Dominic did *not* found the Inquisition; he did *not*
take any considerable part in the persecution of the Albigenses
(though he was united in close friendship with Folco, who did.
Cf. Canto ix, *note* 14); he did *not* introduce the use of the Rosary,
and he did *not* utter the well-known rebuke of the pomp and
luxury of the Papal legates, but listened to it as his superior
Didacus delivered it. Very little of his biography, as usually told,
is left after this; but that little shows him as a man of boundless
love and compassion. When a student, he sold his books in a season
of famine to give to the poor; he once offered to sell himself to
redeem a captive; and his "frequent and special prayer" to God
was for the gift of true charity.

10. "His mother when pregnant dreamed that she had in her womb
a dog-whelp, with a torch in his mouth, whereby to set the world
aflame when he should come into light" (*Brev. Rom.*).

11. "For the lady who held him at his baptism dreamed that Dominic
himself had a most bright star on his brow, which illuminated all
the world" (Benvenuto).

12. *Dominicus* (the possessive adjective of *Dominus*)="pertaining
to the Lord."

13. The counsel of poverty (*Matt.* xix. 21, whence the phrase "counsels of perfection"). Thomas Aquinas, while distinguishing between the *precepts* and the *counsels* of Christ, says that the latter may all be reduced to three—Poverty, Continence and Obedience. The "first" counsel, then, is Poverty.

14. *Felice* = favoured by fortune.

15. *Giovanna* is translated by Jerome "grace of the Lord." It is curious that Bonventura in heaven is still dependent on Jerome for his Hebrew (*cf.* Canto xi, but also iv, *note* 7).

16. Henry of Susa, who became Cardinal Bishop of Ostia in 1261, was a commentator on the Decretals. *Cf.* Canto ix, *note* 19. Traddeus was a celebrated writer on medical subjects, who died in 1303. He was the author of the Italian translation of Aristotle's *Ethics*, which Dante cites as a warning (*Conv.* i. 10). The meaning is, of course, that Dominic studied not to qualify for a lucrative profession, but to come at the truth. *Cf.* Canto xi.

17. A marked case of severing the ideal Papacy from the actual Popes. The Papacy, *in itself* is as benign to the poor as ever; but the degenerate Pope (Boniface VIII) makes it manifest itself in other fashion.

18. His application was not for leave to plunder on condition of paying a third or a half of the plunder to pious purposes, nor a petition for the first fat appointment that should fall vacant, or for leave to apply the tithes to his own purposes. The *erring world* = the heretics, notably the Albigenses, against whom Dominic's efforts were mainly directed.

19. He obtained the sanction of his order from Honorius III in 1216.

20. The panegyric on Francis is pronounced by a Dominican, and that on Dominic by a Franciscan (whereas the denunciation of the unworthy Dominicans and Franciscans is in each case pronounced by one of themselves). Thus Dante foreshadowed what afterwards became a general usage, *viz.*, for a Dominican to read mass in a Franciscan convent on their founder's day (Oct. 4), and a Franciscan to do the like for a Dominican convent on their founder's day (Aug. 4).

21. *Cf. Matt.* xiii. 30.

22. From the moment of the death of Francis disputes as to the lax or strict observance of the rule devastated the Order. They have left their trace on all the earliest biographies. In Dante's time Ubertino of Cassale (1259–1338) was one of the leaders of the "Spirituals," or party of the strict observance. Matteo d'Acquasparta, who was elected General of the Order in 1287, and who was sent to Florence in 1300 and again in 1301 by Boniface VIII (see Gardner, i, "the Jubilee," etc., and Villani, viii, § 40, 43, 49) as pacificator, introduced relaxations into the discipline of the Order. Dante here makes Bonaventura (who was General from 1256 to 1274, and who, as a matter of fact, pursued a conciliatory policy) plead for the *via media*, against both extremes. In Dante's own time there had been an elabo-

rate appeal to Clement V to settle the affairs of the Order, which resulted in the issuing of the Bull *Exivi de Paradiso.*

23. *Left-hand care* =temporal affairs. There is a story of Bonaventura, on a certain visitation, spending hours with a young Franciscan, answering his questions and removing his difficulties. His companions urged him to leave him and continue his journey. "Shall I disobey my master?" he answered. He took his title of *minister* seriously.

24. Illuminato (who accompanied Francis to the Holy Land) and Augustine, joined the Order in 1210. Possibly placed here to vindicate the significance of a man's life as teaching; though they were not (as Benvenuto says) unlettered men.

25. *St. Victor* was an abbey in Paris, which became the centre of the old-fashioned and conservative learning as distinguished from the Aristotelian and scholastic learning. Hugo (*ca.* 1097-1141) was one of its greatest lights. He was the teacher of Richard, and of Peter Lombard. *Cf.* Canto x.

26. Peter "the devourer" of books (d. 1179) was the author of the *Historia Scholastica,* a paraphrase of the Scriptures, a French translation of which was very widely known in the Middle Ages. He became Chancellor of the University of Paris in 1164. Petrus Hispanus, afterwards Pope John XXI, was the author of a little cram book of logic, which retained its popularity deep into the Renaissance period. It is from it that the well-known Memoria Technica verses, *Barbara Celarent,* etc., are derived; though whether he invented them or not is a matter of dispute.

27. John Chrysostom, or Golden Mouth (*ca.* 344-407), Archbishop of Constantinople, renowned for his fearless eloquence, denounced the vices of the court, and was persecuted and exiled by the Empress Eudoxia in consequence. No doubt his collocation with Nathan, who denounced David's sin (2 *Sam.* xii), is designed. Anselm (1033-1109), Archbishop of Canterbury, is known as the second father of scholasticism, Scotus Erigena (9th century) being the first. Both alike endeavoured to show that the contents of natural reason and of revealed truth coincide. Donatus (*fl.* middle of 4th century) was the author of the grammar in current use, though the far more elaborate work of Priscian (*fl.* 500) was always recognized as the typical grammar. Priscian is mentioned in *Inf.* xv.

28. Rabanus Maurus (*ca.* 766-856), Bishop of Mayence. He compiled, amongst other works, a cyclopedia *De universo* in twenty-two books. In the unsettled state of theology at the time, and in his zeal for orthodoxy, he came nigh himself to falling unawares into heresies concerning Predestination.

29. Joachim (*ca.* 1130-1202) was the reputed author of many prophecies. He was also the first preacher of the doctrine that the dispensation of the Father (Old Testament) and of the Son (New Testament, and the Church as an institution) would be followed by the dispensation of the Holy Spirit, the period of perfection and freedom, without the necessity of disciplinary institutions. This was

the "Everlasting Gospel"—a dispensation, not a book. Joachim was
a Cistercian, not a Franciscan; but the Franciscan "Spirituals" were
much influenced by him, and one of them, Gerardus by name, wrote
a book entitled *Introduction to the Everlasting Gospel*. "Joachism"
henceforth became a feature of the extreme Spiritual movement
among the Franciscans, and as such was opposed by Bonaventura.
Cf. Canto x, *note* 14.

ÇANTO XIII

The four and twenty brightest stars of heaven, ranged in two crowns, will give a feeble image of the two circles that swept round Dante and his guide. They sing of the Three Persons in the one nature of God and of the two natures in the one Person of Christ. Then they pause again, and Thomas once more speaks. He reads Dante's perplexity: "Did not both Adam and Christ possess all human knowledge in perfection? How then can it be that none ever rose to equal Solomon's wisdom?" Behold the answer: All mortal and immortal things are but a reflection of the divine Idea—i.e., of the loving self-utterance of the Divine Power—which remains one in itself while it is broken into countless manifestations. But the imprinting influences of heaven and the imprinted matter of earth are not always in equally propitious habit, and hence individual diversities of excellence. But matter was perfectly disposed and the heaven was in supreme excellence of power when Adam was created and when the Virgin conceived. Therefore Dante's initial supposition is true. But there is no contradiction; for Solomon desired not astronomical, nor logical, nor metaphysical, nor geometrical, but regal wisdom. Of all who ever rose to kingly rule (which Adam and Christ did not) none had such wisdom as Solomon. Let Dante take warning from this discussion and observe extremest caution in making unqualified deductions however obvious they may appear; for when once we are committed our own vanity prevents us from retreating and we had better not have thought about a problem than so thought as to fortify ourselves against the truth. Philosophy and Theology alike furnish sad examples. And seeming-obvious moral judgments may be as hasty and false as intellectual ones.

LET HIM imagine, who would grasp rightly what I now beheld (and let him hold the image while I speak, like a firm rock),

fifteen of those stars that, in sundry regions, quicken the heaven with such brightness as to pierce all the knitted air,

let him imagine that wain for which the bosom of our

heaven sufficeth night and day, so that it faileth not to the wain-pole's sweep,

let him imagine the mouth of that horn which starteth from the axle round which the primal circling goeth,

all to have made of themselves two signs in heaven, such as Minos' daughter made when she felt the chill of death;[2]

and one to have its rays within the other, and both the two to turn them in such fashion that one should take the lead, and the other follow;

and he shall have as though the shade of the real constellation and the twofold dance which circled round the point whereat I was;

for it as far transcendeth our use as doth transcend the movement of Chiana the motion of that heaven which all the rest surpasseth.[2]

There did they sing, not Bacchus, and not Pæan, but three Persons in the divine nature, and it and the human nature in one Person.

The song and wheeling had fulfilled their measure, and to us turned their heed those sacred torches, rejoicing as they passed from charge to charge.

Then 'mid the harmonious divinities silence was broken by the light wherein the wondrous life of the poor man of God had been rehearsed to me,

which said: "Since the one sheaf is thrashed, and its seed stored already, to beat out the other sweet love inviteth me.[3]

Thou holdest that into the breast wherefrom the rib was drawn to form the beauteous cheek for whose palate all the world doth pay,

and into that which, thrust by the lance, made satisfaction both for past and future, such as to turn the scale against all trespass,

such light as human nature may receive was all infused by that same Worth which made the one and the other.

And so thou wonderest at what I said above, when I declared the good enclosed in the fifth light ne'er to have had a second.

Now ope thine eyes to what I answer thee, and thou

shalt see what thou believest and what I say, strike on the truth as centre in the circle.

That which dieth not, and that which can die, is nought save the reglow[4] of that Idea which our Sire, in Loving, doth beget;

for that living Light which so outgoeth from its Source that it departeth not therefrom, nor from the Love that maketh three with them,[5]

doth, of its goodness, focus its own raying, as though reflected, in nine existences, eternally abiding one.

Thence it descendeth to the remotest potencies, down, from act to act, becoming such as maketh now mere brief contingencies;

by which contingencies I understand the generated things which are produced from seed, or seedless, by the moving heaven.

The wax of these, and that which mouldeth it, standeth not in one mode, and therefore, 'neath the ideal stamp, is more and less transparent;[6]

whence cometh, that one same tree in kind better and worse doth fruit; and ye are born with diverse genius.

Were the wax exactly moulded, and were the heaven in its supremest virtue, the light of the signet would be all apparent;

but nature ever furnisheth it faulty, doing as doth the artist who hath the knack of the art and a trembling hand.

Wherefore if the warm Love, if the clear Vision, of the primal Power dispose and stamp, entire perfection is acquired there.[7]

Thus was the clay[8] made worthy once of the full animal perfection; and thus the Virgin was impregnated.

Wherefore I sanction thine opinion that human nature never was, nor shall be, such as in those two persons.

Now, should I proceed no further, 'how then was he without a peer?' were the beginning of thy words.

But, that what now appeareth not may be apparent, think who he was, and what the cause which moved him—when he was bidden: 'Choose,'—to make demand.[9]

I have not spoken so but that thou mayst perceive he
485

was a king, who chose such wit that as a king he might be adequate;

not to know the number in which exist the mover spirits here above, nor if a necessary and a contingent premise can ever give a necessary conclusion;

nor whether we must grant a *primum motum;* nor whether in a semi-circle can be constructed a triangle that shall have no right angle.[10]

Wherefore, (if this and all that I have said thou note) that insight without peer whereon the arrow of my intention smiteth, is regal prudence.

And if to *rose* thou turn discerning eyes, thou shalt see that it hath respect only to kings, the which are many and the good ones few.

Thus qualified do thou accept my saying; and so it may consist with what thou holdest of the first father and of our delight.

And let this ever be lead to thy feet, to make thee move slow, like a weary man; both to the yea and nay thou seest not;

for he is right low down amongst the fools who maketh affirmation or negation without distinction between case and case;[11]

wherefore it chanceth many times swift-formed opinion leaneth the wrong way, and then conceit bindeth the intellect.

Far worse than vainly doth he leave the shore, since he returneth not as he puts forth, who fisheth for the truth and hath not the art;

and of this to the world are open proofs, Parmenides, Melissus, Bryson,[12] and the host who still were going, but they knew not whither.

So did Sabellius and Arius,[13] and those fools who were as swords unto the Scripture, in making the straight countenances crooked.[14]

Let not folk yet be too secure in judgment, as who should count the ears upon the field ere they be ripe;

for I have seen first all the winter through the thorn display itself hard and forbidding and then upon its summit bear the rose;

and I have seen ere now a ship fare straight and swift over the sea through her entire course, and perish at the last, entering the harbour mouth.

Let not Dame Bertha or Squire Martin[15] think, if they perceive one steal and one make offering, they therefore see them as in the divine counsel; for the one yet may rise and the other fall."

1. The seven bright stars of the Great Bear (which in our latitude never sets), the two brightest of the Little Bear (to which constellation the pole-star belongs), and fifteen others, not specified, make up the twenty-four required; and the reader is to imagine them all arranged in a double Ariadne's crown.

2. The Chiana in Dante's time made its sluggish way southward to the Tiber through pestiferous swamps. It is taken as the type of the slowest motion, as the whirling of the *primum mobile* is of the swiftest.

3. *Cf.* Cantos x and xi.

4. Dante is careful in his use of *splendor* to signify *reflected* light (see Canto i, *note* 1). All created things, then, are reflections of the Word, or Idea, of God. *Reflection* and *refraction* are not clearly differentiated; and created things are spoken of as the points on which the rays of God are focussed, though the conception of the mirror is still retained. The "nine existences" we take to be the nine heavens, which, as immediate creations of God, are not subject to change. But as the divine light descends upon and vivifies the remoter and duller potentialities of the *materia prima*, successively realizing their possibilities, the result is contingent and short-lived. Compare with the whole passage, Cantos i, ii, vii and xxix; and note that in the present passage and the lines that follow, the veiled dualism, which may constantly be traced in Dante's conception of the universe, becomes particularly prominent. The *prima materia*, though explicitly declared in Cantos vii and xxix, to be the direct creation of God, is here and elsewhere treated as something external, on which his power acts and which answers only imperfectly to it. *Cf. De Monarchia*, ii. 2, *Conv.* iii. 12, and *Purg.* xxviii.

5. The Son emanating from the Father without separation from him or from the Holy Ghost.

6. "The better disposed the material the more completely it lets the ideal shine through it, when under the impress of the seal."

7. The original is ambiguous. The translation (which is grammatically somewhat hazardous) takes it to mean that if both the wax is prepared and the stamp impressed immediately by the Deity, a perfect result will ensue.

8. The clay out of which Adam was made.

9. See 1 *Kings* iii. 5–15.

10. No disrespect is intended to the branches of study here referred to. Solomon asked for practical, not philosophical or scien-

tific, wisdom. The explanation, however, apart from its subtlety, is unsatisfactory; since the supreme position of Solomon amongst the sages and doctors of the Church hardly lends itself to it. *Cf. Conv.* ii. 6. The problem of the *contingent premise* may be stated thus: It is a general principle that no limitation that occurs in either of the premises can be escaped in the conclusion. Thus, if either of the premises is negative you cannot get a positive conclusion; if either of them is particular you cannot get a general conclusion; if either is contingent you cannot get a necessary conclusion. For instance, from "The man on whom the lot falls *must* be sacrified," and "The lot *may* fall on you," you can infer: "therefore you *may* be sacrified," but not "therefore you *must* be sacrified." Ingenious attempts to get a necessary conclusion out of a necessary and a contingent premise are exposed by the logicians, *e. g.*, "Anyone who may run from the foe must be a coward; some of these troops may run from the foe, therefore some of them must be cowards." The fallacy lies in the ambiguous use of "may run from the foe." In the first instance it means, "is, *as a matter of fact, capable of running away*"; in the second, "*may, for anything I know, run away.*" So that the two propositions do not hang together, and the conclusion is invalid. *Cf.* Cantos i, *note* 1, and xxiv, *note* 11.

See Euclid iii. Euclid's *Elements* were in Dante's time, as in our own, the accepted text-book of Geometry. *Cf. De Monarchia*, i. 1.

11. *Cf.* Canto xi, *note* 3.

12. *De Monarchia*, iii. They were known to Dante only through Aristotle's refutations.

13. Sabellius (d. *ca.* 265) confounded the persons of the Father and the Son; Arius (d. 336) divided their substance.

14. Some take the allusion to be to the distorted reflections from the blade of a sword, others to hacking by sword-strokes.

15. For "Martin," as equivalent to "such an one," compare *Conv.* i. 8 and iii. 11. And for "Bertha," *De Vulgari Eloquentia*, ii. 6.

ÇANTO XIV

*As vibrations pass outward and inward in a vessel filled with water,
when disturbed by a blow, so the speech of the blessed spirits passed
from Thomas in the circumference to Beatrice in the centre, and
then back from her to the circumference. Dante has now become
accustomed to the spirit world freed from those limitations of cor-
poreal sense-organs of which he is himself still conscious, and the
perplexity is diffusing itself within him, though not yet precipitated
into definite thought, as to how it can be that the resurrection of the
body shall not reimpose limitations and weariness upon the now
emancipated souls, making the very glory of heaven painful. Or will
that glory be then tempered? Beatrice requests an answer for this
yet unspoken and even unthought demand; and when all have sung
a hymn of praise, Solomon tells how human nature includes body
and soul, and therefore the disembodied soul is less complete than
the whole person when the soul shall be reclad with the glorified
body. When more complete it will be more pleasing to God, and
will so receive more of his grace (above its merit, though not given
without relation thereto), and will thus see him more adequately
and therefore love him more warmly and therein have greater joy,
expressed in more dazzling brightness. But the organs of sense will
be incapable of pain or weariness; no excess of delight will be be-
yond their joyous grasp. The souls quiver in response to the refer-
ence to the resurrection. A third circle shows itself, first in dubious
faintness then with a sudden flash, at the very moment when Dante
and his guide pass into the rea-glowing Mars. A cross gleams white
athwart the red planet, whereon Christ flashes in such fashion as
tongue may not tell. Souls in light move and pass upon the limbs of
the cross, uttering divine melody and singing hymns of victory but
half comprehended by Dante, yet more entrancing than aught that
he had hitherto experienced; experienced hitherto, but he had not
yet looked upon the beloved eyes of his guide in this fifth heaven,
and therefore he must not be taken, by implication, to place the
heavenly song above the ever-deepening beauty of Beatrice's eyes*

FROM CENTRE to circumference and again from circumference to centre vibrates the water in a rounded vessel according as 'tis smitten from without or from within.

Into my mind this thought dropped sudden, just as the glorious life of Thomas held its peace,

because of the resemblance that sprang from his discourse, and then from Beatrice's, whom to begin thus after him it pleased:

"This man hath need, and telleth it you not, neither with voice, nor as yet with his thought, to track another truth unto its root.

Tell if the light wherewith your being blossometh, eternally will cleave to you as now,

and if it doth remain, tell how, when ye grow visible again, it may not grieve your vision."

As by access of gladness thrust and drawn, at once all they who circle in the dance uplift their voice and gladden their gestures,

so at the eager and devoted prayer the sacred circles showed new joy in their revolving and their wondrous note.

Whoso lamenteth that we here must die to live up yonder seeth not here the refreshment of the eternal shower.

That One and Two and Three who ever liveth and reigneth ever in Three and Two and One, not circumscribed, but all circumscribing,

three times was hymned by each one of those spirits with such melody as were a fit reward to any merit.

And I heard in the divinest light of the smaller circle an unassuming voice,[1] perchance such as the Angel's unto Mary,

answering: "As long as the festival of Paradise shall be, so long our love shall cast round us the rays of such a garment.

Its brightness shall keep pace with our ardour, our ardour with our vision, and that shall be as great as it hath grace beyond its proper worth.

Whenas the garment of the glorified and sainted flesh

shall be resumed, our person shall be more acceptable by being all complete.[2]

Whereby shall grow that which the highest Good giveth to us of unearned light, light which enableth us him to see;

wherefore the vision must needs wax, and wax the ardour which is kindled by it, and wax the ray which goeth forth from it.[3]

But like the coal which giveth forth the flame, and by its living glow o'ercometh it, so that its own appearance is maintained,

so shall this glow which doth already swathe us, be conquered in appearance by the flesh which yet and yet the earth o'ercovereth;

nor shall such light have power to baffle us, for the organs of the body shall be strong to all that may delight us."

So swift and eager to cry *Amen*, meseemed, was the one and the other chorus, that verily they showed desire for their dead bodies;

not only, as I take it, for themselves, but for their mothers and their fathers and the others who were dear, ere they became eternal flames.[4]

And lo! around, of lustre equable, upsprings a shining beyond what was there, in fashion of a brightening horizon.

And as, at the first rise of evening, new things-to-see begin to show in heaven, so that the sight doth, yet doth not, seem real;

I there began to perceive new-come existences making a circle out beyond the other two circumferences.

Oh very sparkling of the Holy Breath! how sudden and how glowing it became before my eyes, which, vanquished, might not bear it![5]

But Beatrice showed herself to me so beauteous and smiling, it must be left amongst those sights that followed not my memory.

Therefrom my eyes regained their power to uplift them, and I saw me transported, only with my Lady, to more exalted weal.

Surely did I perceive that I was more uplifted by the enkindled smile of the star which seemed to me more ruddy than his wont.

With all the heart, and in that tongue which is one unto all, to God I made burnt sacrifice such as befitted this new-given grace;

and not yet from my bosom was drawn out the ardour of the sacrifice before I knew the prayer had been accepted and propitious;

for with such shining, and so ruddy, within two rays, splendours appeared to me, that I exclaimed: "O God! who thus dost glorify them!"

As, pricked out with less and greater lights, between the poles of the universe the Milky Way so gleameth white as to set very sages questioning,[6]

so did those rays, star-decked, make in the depth of Mars the venerable sign which crossing quadrant lines make in a circle.

Here my memory doth outrun my wit, for that cross so flashed forth Christ I may not find example worthy.

But whoso taketh his cross and followeth Christ shall yet forgive me what I leave unsaid, when he shall see Christ lighten in that glow.

From horn to horn, from summit unto base, were moving lights that sparkled mightily in meeting one another and in passing.

So we see here, straight, twisted, swift, or slow, changing appearance, long or short, the motes of bodies

moving through the ray which doth sometimes streak the shade, which folk with skill and art contrive for their defence.

And as viol and harp tuned in harmony of many cords, make sweet chiming to one by whom the notes are not apprehended,

so from the lights that there appeared to me was gathered on the cross a strain that rapt me albeit I followed not the hymn.

Well I discerned it was of lofty praise, for there came to me "Rise thou up and conquer," as to who understandeth not, but heareth.

And so was I enamoured there, that up till then there had been naught that me had bound with so sweet chains.

Perchance my saying may appear too bold, as slighting the delight of those fair eyes, gazing in which my longing hath repose.

But he who doth advise him how the living signets of all beauty have ever more effect in higher region, and that I there had not yet turned to them,

may find excuse from my own accusation, brought that I may excuse it; and may see that I speak truth; for the sacred joy is not excluded here, which as it mounteth groweth more unalloyed.

1. Solomon. Cf. Canto x.
2. Cf. Inf. vi. Aquinas says: "The soul without the body hath not the perfection of its nature."
3. Cf. Canto xxviii.
4. Bernard writes on the resurrection of the body in his treatise On Loving God. It is his consistent doctrine that the blessedness of heaven is found in the complete absorption of the soul in God, self-consciousness being, as it were, replaced not by unconsciousness but by God-consciousness. "But if, as is not denied, they [the disembodied spirits of the blessed] would fain have received their bodies again, or at any rate desire and hope to receive them, it is clear beyond question that they are not yet utterly transmuted from themselves, since it is admitted that there is still somewhat proper to themselves toward which, though it be but a little, their thought is deflected. Therefore, until death be swallowed up in victory, and the perennial light so invade the boundaries of darkness and take possession of them on every side that the celestial glory shine forth even in the very bodies, the souls cannot utterly empty themselves and pass over into God, since they are even yet bound to their bodies, if not by life and sense, yet by natural affection, because of which they have neither the will nor the power to be consummated without them. And so, before the restoration of the bodies there cannot be that lapse of the souls [into God] which is their perfect and supreme state. Nor is it any marvel if the body, now of glory, seems to confer somewhat upon the spirit, since even in its infirmity and mortality it of a surety was of no small avail to it. Oh how true did he speak who said that all things work together for the good of them that love God! To the soul that loveth God, its body availeth in its infirmity, availeth in its death, availeth in its resurrection; first for the fruit of penitence, second for repose, third for consummation. And rightly doth the soul not will to be made perfect without that which it feeleth hath in every state served it in good things."

5. This makes it clear that this third circle specially represents the Holy Spirit, and so completes the symbol of the Trinity. *Cf.* Canto xxxiii.

In its dimness at first and brightness afterwards, there may be a reference to the difficulty that has always been experienced in finding an adequate *philosophical* basis for the doctrine of the Third Person of the Trinity corresponding to the clearness of the distinction between the conceptions of God in his essence (Father) and God as manifested (Son); whereas to the more strictly *theological* speculation, or rather to the religious experience, the doctrine of the Holy Spirit (God regarded not as the Creator or the Redeemer, but as the Inspirer) has always had a special vividness. *Cf.* Canto xii, *note* 29.

6. *Cf.* Conv. ii. 15, a passage interesting on many grounds.

ÇANTO XV

*The souls of the warriors of God upon the cross of Mars cease their
hymn, that Dante may converse with one of their number, who
shoots like a falling star from his place and, approaching Dante with
such joy as Anchises showed to Æneas in the Elysian Fields, greets
him as his offspring and as the recipient of unique grace, the twice-
received (now and at his death) of heaven. Dante, giving heed to
him and (now first in this higher sphere) looking on Beatrice, is
smitten with twofold marvel. The spirit, after rapturous words be-
yond the scope of the Poet's comprehension, gives thanks to God,
tells Dante how eager yet how sweet has been his longing for his
arrival, foreread in the heavens; confirms his thought that the spirits
see all things in God, as the true mathematician sees all numbers in
the conception of unity; but bids him none the less speak out his
questions, though already known to him, in God, with their ap-
pointed answers. Dante, unlike the souls in glory, has no utterance
adequate to show forth his thanks. The spirit, in answer to his ques-
tion, reveals himself as his great-great-grandfather, the father of
Alighieri from whom the Poet's family name is derived. He describes
the ancient Florence, confined within the walls to which the Badia
was adjacent, and dwells upon the simple ways of her citizens. In
such a city was he born, baptized and married. Thence he followed
Conrad in his crusade, was knighted, was slain, and arose to the
peace of heaven.*

THE BENIGN WILL—wherein distilleth ever the
love that hath the right perfume, as doth, in the grudging
will, cupidity—

imposed silence on that sweet lyre and stilled the sacred
strings, which the right hand of heaven looseneth and
stretcheth.

How shall those beings unto righteous prayers be deaf,
who, to excite in me the will to make my prayer to them,
agreed in silence?

Right is it he should grieve without a limit, who, for the

495

love of what endureth not, eternally doth strip him of this love.

As through the tranquil and pure skies darteth, from time to time, a sudden flame setting a-moving eyes that erst were steady,

seeming a star that changeth place, save that from where it kindleth no star is lost, and that itself endureth but a little;

such from the horn that stretcheth to the right unto that cross's foot, darted a star of the constellation that is there a-glow;

nor did the gem depart from off its riband, but coursed along the radial line, like fire burning behind alabaster.

With such-like tenderness Anchises' shade proffered itself, if our greatest Muse deserveth credit, when in Elysium he perceived his son.[1]

"Oh blood of mine! oh grace of God poured o'er thee! to whom, was ever twice, as unto thee, heaven's gate thrown open?"

So spake that light; wherefore I gave my heed to him. Then I turned back my sight unto my Lady, and on this side and that I was bemazed;

for in her eyes was blazing such a smile, I thought with mine I had touched the bottom both of my grace and of my Paradise.

Then—joyous both to hearing and to sight—the spirit added things to his beginning I understood not, so profound his speech;

neither of choice hid he himself from me, but of necessity, for above the target of mortals his thought took its place.

And when the bow of ardent love was so tempered that his discourse descended towards the target of our intellect;

the first I understood was, "Blessed be thou, thou Three and One, who art so greatly courteous in my seed."

And followed on: "A dear long-cherished hunger, drawn from the reading of the mighty volume wherein not changeth ever white nor black,

thou hast assuaged, my son, within this light, wherein I

speak to thee; thanks unto her who for the lofty flight clad thee with wings.

Thou deemest that to me thy thought hath way e'en from the primal Thought, as ray forth from the monad, rightly known, the pentad and the hexad;

and therefore, who I be, or why I seem to thee more gladsome than another in this festive throng thou makest not demand.

Rightly thou deemest; for less and great in this life gaze on the mirror[2] whereon, or ere thou thinkest, thou dost outspread thy thought.

But that the sacred love, wherein I watch with sight unintermitted, and which setteth me athirst with a sweet longing, may be fulfilled the better,

secure and bold and joyous let thy voice sound forth the will, sound forth the longing, whereto my answer already is decreed."

I turned to Beatrice, and she heard ere that I spoke, and granted me a signal that made the wings of my desire increase.

Then I thus began: "Love and intelligence, soon as the prime equality appeared to you, became of equal poise to each of you,

because the sun which lightened you and warmed with heat and brightness hath such equality that illustrations all fall short of it.

But unto mortals, will and instrument, for reason manifest to you, unequally are feathered in their wings.[3]

Wherefore I, a mortal, feel the stress of this unequalness, and therefore only with my heart give thanks for the paternal greeting.

But I may and do entreat thee, living topaz, who dost be-gem this precious jewel, that thou assuage me with thy name."

"Oh leaf of mine, in whom I took delight, only expecting thee, I was thy taproot," such opening in his answer made he me.

Then said: "He from whom thy kindred hath its name, and who a hundred years and more[4] hath circled round the Mount on the first terrace, was son to me, and thy grandfather's father; meet it is, that with thy works thou shouldst abate his long-stretched toil for him.

Florence, within the ancient circling wherefrom she still receiveth tierce and nones,[5] abode in peace, sober and chaste.

There was no chain or coronet, nor dames decked out, nor girdle that should set folk more agaze than she who wore it.

As yet the daughter's birth struck not the father with dismay; for wedding day and dowry evaded not the measure on this side and on that.[6]

There were no mansions empty of the household;[7] Sardanapalus[8] had not yet arrived to show what may be done within the chamber.

Not yet was Montemalo overpassed by your Uccellatoio,[9] which, as it hath been passed in the uprising, shall be in the fall.

Bellincion Berti[10] have I seen no girt with bone and leather, and his dame come from her mirror with unpainted face;

I have seen him of the Nerlo, and him of the Vecchio, content with the skin jerkin and nought over it, and their dames at the spindle and the flax.

O happy they, each one of them secure of her burial place, and none yet deserted in her couch because of France.[11]

The one kept watch in minding of the cradle, and soothing spake that speech which first delighteth fathers and mothers;

another, as she drew its locks from the distaff, would tell her household about the Trojans, and Fiesole, and Rome.[12]

Then a Cianghella, or a Lapo Salterello,[13] would have been as great a marvel as now would Cincinnatus or Cornelia.

To so reposeful and so fair a life among the citizens, to so faithful cityhood, to so sweet abode,

Mary—with deep wailings summoned[14]—gave me; and, in your ancient Baptistery, at once a Christian I became and Cacciaguida.

Moronto was my brother and Eliseo;[15] my wife came to me from Po valley, and from her was thy surname derived.

Then followed I the Emperor Conrad,[16] who girt me with his knighthood, so much by valiant work did I advance me in his grace.

In his train I marched against the infamy of that Law[17] whose people doth usurp, shame to the pastors, what is yours by right.

There by that foul folk was I unswathed of the deceitful world, whose love befouleth many a soul, and came from martyrdom unto this peace."

1. For the meeting of Anchises and Æneas, see *Æneid*, vi. For family tree, see p. 625.
2. God.
3. God who is the supreme "equality," *i.e.*, in whom all things realize their absolute proportion and perfection (*cf.* Canto xxxiii), fills the blessed spirits with love and insight in equal measure, so that their utterance is the perfect expression of their emotion, but we mortals find our wills out-flying our power of utterance.
4. Dante has fallen into a slight error. There is documentary evidence that this Alighieri was living in 1201.
5. An allusion to the Badia, from the belfry of which the canonical hours were sounded. Tierce was at nine o'clock, nones at twelve. *Conv.* iii. 6.
6. The bride's age too little, her dowry too much.
7. The families being decayed, or in exile.
8. Sardanapalus, king of Nineveh, is taken as the general type of luxury.
9. Montemalo, or Montemario, was the first point at which the traveller on the road from Viterbo came in sight of Rome, and the Uccellatojo is the first place at which the traveller along the *old* road from Bologna comes in sight of Florence.
10. Bellincion Berti was the father of the "good Gualdrada" (*Inf.* xvi). See Villani, v. 37.
11. None was in fear lest she should die in exile. The reference to France is obscure; perhaps it alludes to the frequency of travel in France, in Dante's time, for business or other purposes.
12. Compare the early chapters of Villani.
13. Cianghella della Tosa, a notorious shrew, married an Imolese Benvenuto da Imola, declares he could tell us many tales of her. Lapo Salterello, took an active part in the patriotic task of resisting the encroachments of Bonifacc (see Gardner, i. 4, "the Jubilee," etc.), but appears to have been a worthless person. He was one of Dante's fellow exiles. *Cf.* Canto xvii.

14. The Virgin Mary was invoked by women in labour, as the virgin goddess Diana had been in Pagan times. *Cf. Purg.* xx.

15. The name Eliseo may be taken as an indication, but not as a proof, of the connection of the Alighieri with the noble family of the Elisei, asserted by Boccaccio. Compare Canto xvi and Gardner, i. 2.

16. Conrad III (reigned 1137–1152) joined Bernard's crusade in 1147.

17. *Law* here as elsewhere = "Religion." See *Conv.* ii. 9.

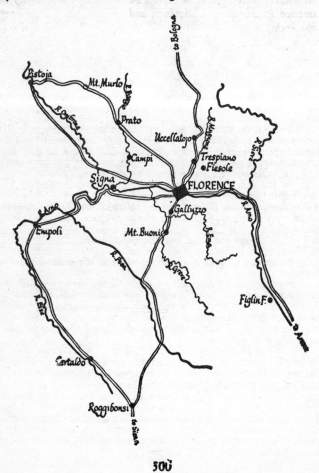

ÇANTO XVI

*In profound reverence for his ancestor, and not without a sense
of his own derived dignity, Dante addresses the spirit with the
ceremonious plural ye, said to have originated in Rome, though
no longer in use there; and hereon Beatrice (only moderately in-
terested in Florentine antiquities, and so standing a little apart,
but keenly alert to all that may affect the moral or spiritual weal
of her charge) checks his rising vanity with a warning smile.
Dante, full of such lofty joy as would on earth strain the mind
to bursting, questions Cacciaguida as to ancient Florence, whereon
he, in the speech of an earlier day, tells the date of his birth and
the place where his forebears dwelt, declining, in enigmatical
terms, to say more of them. The population of military age was
then but a fifth of what it had since become, and the narrow
limits of the territory of Florence kept the blood of her citizens
pure. Would that it were so yet! But lust of power, the con-
fusion resulting from Papal ambition, and the fatal quarrel be-
tween the Buondelmonti and Amidei, have ruined all, and have
given unwieldly bulk to Florence while polluting her blood. Then
follows a dirge on the great families of ancient Florence, intro-
duced by tragic reflections on the tide-like instability of all
earthly things. Many of these families are mentioned by name,
others are indicated by their characteristics or their blazon. Count
Hugo ennobled the six families that bear his coat of arms, with
various differences, though Giano della Bella had since joined the
people. The Gualterotti and Importuni were already in Florence,
but the Buondelmonti were not yet—would that they had never
been!—their neighbours. The Amidei and their associates were
held in honour. Alas that Buondelmonte broke his marriage word
with them, and gave rise to all the internal strife of Florence.
How much ill had been avoided if God had plunged him into the
Ema as he rode into Florence. But it was fated that she should make
her sacrifice to that torso of Mars, at whose feet he was slain.*

AH PUNY blood-nobility of ours! If thou makest folk glory in thee here below, where our affections sicken,

it shall be marvel to me never more; for there, where appetite is unwarped, I mean in heaven, I gloried me therein.

Yet verily thou art a mantle that soon shrinketh, so that, if day by day there be nought added, time goeth round with the shears.[1]

With that *ye* that Rome was first to allow wherein her household doth least persevere, my words began again;[2]

whereon Beatrice, who was a little sundered from us, smiled, and seemed to me like her who coughed at the first trespass writ of Guinivere.[3]

I began: "Ye are my father, ye give me full boldness to speak, ye so uplift me, that I am more than I.

By so many streams my mind is filled with gladness, it giveth itself joy that it can bear it and yet not be rent.

Tell me, then, dear stock from which I spring, what was your ancestry, and what the years recorded in your boyhood.

Tell me of the sheepfold of St. John,[4] how great it then was, and who were the folk worthy of loftiest seats in it."

As a coal quickeneth into flame at the wind's breathing, so did I see that light glow forth at my caressing words;

and even as to my sight it grew more beauteous, so with a voice more sweet and gentle, but not in this our modern dialect,[5]

he said: "From the day on which *Ave* was uttered, to the birth wherein my mother, now sainted, unburdened her of me with whom she was laden,

five hundred, fifty, and thirty times[6] did this flame return to his own Lion[7] to rekindle him beneath his feet.

My forebears and myself were born in the spot where he who runneth in your annual games doth first encounter the last sesto.[8]

About my ancestors let it suffice so much to hear; of who they were and whence they hither came silence were comelier than discourse.[9]

At that time all who were there, between Mars and the

Baptist,[10] capable of arms, were but the fifth of the now living ones.

But the citizenship, contaminated now from Campi, from Certaldo and from Fighine, saw itself pure down to the humblest artisan.

Oh, how much better were it for these folk of whom I speak to be your neighbours,[11] and to have your boundary at Galluzzo and at Trespiano,

than to have them within, and bear the stench of the hind of Aguglion, and of him of Signa,[12] who still for jobbery hath his eye alert!

Had the race, which goeth most degenerate on earth, not been to Cæsar as a stepmother, but, as a mother to her son, benign,

one who is now a Florentine and changeth coin and wares, had been dispatched to Simifonte, where his own grandfather went round a-begging.[13]

Still would Montemurlo[14] pertain unto the Conti, still were the Cerchi in Acone[15] parish, and perchance in Valdigreve were still the Buondelmonti.[16]

Ever was mingling of persons the source of the city's woes, as piled on food is of the body's.

And a blind bull falleth more presently than a blind lamb, and many a time cutteth one sword better and more than five.

If thou regard Luni and Urbisaglia,[17] how they have perished, and how are following them Chiusi and Sinigaglia;[18]

it shall not seem a novel or hard thing to hear how families undo themselves, since even cities have their term.

Your affairs all have their death, even as have ye; but in such an one as long endureth, it escapeth note because your lives are short.

And as the rolling of the lunar heaven covereth and layeth bare the shores incessantly, so fortune doth to Florence;

wherefore it should appear no wondrous thing which I shall tell of the exalted Florentines whose fame lieth concealed by time.

I have seen the Ughi, seen the Catellini, Filippi, Greci,

Ormanni, and Alberichi, illustrious citizens, already in decline;[19]

I have seen, even as great as ancient, with him of the Sannella, him of the Arca, and Sołdanieri and Ardinghi and Bostichi.

Over the gate[20] which is now laden with new felony of so great weight, that soon 'twill be the wrecking of the bark,

were the Ravignani, whence descendeth the County Guy, and whoso since hath taken lofty Bellincione's name.

The Della Pressa knew already how to govern, and Galigaio in his mansion already had the hilt and pummel gilt.[21]

Great already were the Vair column,[22] Sacchetti, Giuochi, Fifanti, and Barucci; and Galli, and they who blush red for the bushel.[23]

The stock whence the Calfucci sprang was great already,[24] and already drawn to curule office were Sizii and Arrigucci.

Oh, how great have I seen those now undone by their pride! And the balls of gold adorned Florence in all her mighty feats.[25]

So did their fathers who, whene'er your church is vacant, stand guzzling in consistory.[26]

The outrageous tribe that playeth dragon after whoso fleeth, and to whoso showeth tooth—or purse—is quiet as a lamb,[27]

was coming up already, but from humble folk, so that it pleased not Ubertin Donato when his father-in-law made him their relative.[28]

Already Caponsacco had come down from Fiesole into the market-place; and good citizens already were Giuda and Infangato.

I will tell a thing incredible but true: the little circuit was entered by a gate named after them of Pera.[29]

Each one who beareth aught of the fair arms of the great baron whose name and worth the festival of Thomas keepeth living,

from him derived knighthood and privilege;[30] though he who fringeth it around hath joined him now unto the people.[31]

Already there were Gaulterotti and Importuni; and still were Borgo a more quiet spot, if from new neighbours they were still afasting.[32]

The house from which your wailing sprang, because of the just anger which hath slain you and placed a term upon your joyous life,[33]

was honoured, it and its associates.[34] Oh Buondelmonte, how ill didst thou flee its nuptials at the prompting of another!

Joyous had many been who now are sad, had God committed thee unto the Ema the first time that thou camest to the city.

But to that mutilated stone which guardeth the bridge 'twas meet that Florence should give a victim in her last time of peace.[35]

With these folk, and with others with them, did I see Florence in such full repose, she had not cause for wailing;

with these folk I saw her people so glorious and so just, ne'er was the lily on the shaft reversed,[36] nor yet by faction dyed vermilion."[37]

1. Dante deals with the subject of nobility in the *De Monarchia*, ii, and in *Conv.* iv.
2. The legend ran that when Cæsar united in himself all the high offices of state, he was addressed as a plurality of individuals, "ye"; but as a matter of fact in Dante's time the Romans adhered to the old-fashioned thou. "Nay, they would not address either Pope or Emperor save as *thou*" (Benvenuto).
3. "At these words which the queen spake to him [Lancelot] it came to pass that the lady of Malehaut coughed, of a set purpose, and uplifted her head which she had bowed down." Romance of Lancelot. See Toynbee under *Galeotto*.
4. Florence, the patron saint of which was St. John Baptist.
5. Does not imply that Cacciaguida spoke throughout in Latin as he had begun (Canto xv), but that he spoke in the ancient Florentine dialect of his day. Dante was well aware of the rapidity with which spoken dialects, not yet fixed by a standard literature, vary. See *De Vulgari Eloquentia*, i. 9.
6. Some MSS. and editions read *three* for *thirty;* and the question is also raised whether the period of Mars is to be calculated at the rough approximation of two years (*cf. Conv.* ii. 15, where the half revolution is given at "about a year"), or at the nearer approximation of 687 days, which was known in Dante's age. Two of the four combinations which might thus arise are excluded by the date of

Conrad's crusade 1147. (*Cf.* Canto xv.) Two years multiplied by 553 would give A.D. 1106 as the year of Cacciaguida's birth, and 687 days multiplied by 580 would give the year 1091. The former date would make Cacciaguida forty-one when he went on crusade, which seems more appropriate than fifty-six; but the reading that gives the latter has the better authority.

7. *His own Lion.* Apparently the kinship between Leo and Mars is to be found in the attribute of courage, not in any specific astrological belief of the time.

8. The annual race was run along the *Corso,* and the Sesto of St. Peter was the last that the racers entered. Just as you come to it you pass the house of the Elisei on your right. (*Cf.* Canto xv, *note* 15.) It is a place of ancient families. On the Quarters and Sesti of Ancient Florence, see Villani, iii. 2.

9. The reader may make what he can of this ambiguous utterance. The commentators throw no fresh light on it.

10. The Baptistery lay at the north of the ancient Florence, and the statue of Mars (at the head of the Ponte Vecchio on the north side) was practically its southern boundary. On this statue of Mars compare *Inf.* xiii. Further, see Villani, i. 42; iii. 1; v. 38. The associations with this torso of Mars are so vivid and pervading that every student of Dante should make himself thoroughly acquainted with them. See further *note* 35.

11. *neighbours,* not fellow-citizens.

12. Baldo d'Aguglione and Fazio de' Mori Ubaldini da Signa, both of them lawyers, and both of them deserters from the White to the Black faction in 1302. Baldo was a prior in 1298 and in 1311, in which last year he drew up the decree recalling many of the exiles, but expressly including Dante. (Gardner, i. 6, "Letters and Fresh Sentence.") In 1299 he had been convicted of cutting an inconvenient entry out of the public records of the courts of justice. *Cf Purg.* xii. Fazio held several high offices from 1310 onwards. He was a bitter opponent of the Whites and also of Henry VII.

13. Simifonti was a fortress in Valdelsa, captured in 1202. See Villani, v. 30. The specific allusion is obscure. Does it refer to a descendant of the traitor mentioned by Villani? or to some event more closely connected with papal intrigues and aggressions? The clear reference to the Roman priesthood points to the latter interpretation. (*Cf. Purg.* xvi.)

14. *Montemurlo,* between Prato and Pistoia, was sold by the Conti Guidi to the Florentines in 1254, as they themselves felt unequal to the task of defending it against the Pistoians. Its acquisition, therefore, marks a step in the aggressive expansion of Florence.

15. *Acone* was probably in the Val di Sieve. Well if the Cerchi (leaders of the Whites) had stayed there! *Cf. note* 20.

16. This is the climax. The implication is that in that case all the intestine conflicts of Florence would have been averted. *Cf. note* 32.

17. *Luni* or Luna, "now destroyed," Villani, i. 50. It was on the

Macra, the northern boundary of Tuscany, and was celebrated in legendary lore.

Urbisaglia a decayed city of the March of Ancona.

18. *Chiusi*, the ancient Clusium, was in the pestilent Val di Chiana (*cf.* Canto xiii, *note* 2). Hence probably its decline. Like Sinigallia (on the sea shore, north of Ancona) it had escaped the complete desolation which Dante anticipated for it.

19. Information concerning many of these and the following families will be found up and down the pages of Villani, especially iv. 10–13; and the sites of their houses, as identified by Carbone, are given (with the exception of the Chiarmontesi, the Gangalandi, the Uccellini and the Gherardeschi) in the accompanying map, which also follows Carbone. The alternative site of the house of the Alighieri is taken from Witte.

20. The gate of St. Peter, the abode in Dante's time of the Cerchi. *Cf. note* 15. (Gardner, i. 4, "Blacks and Whites.") Further, *cf.* Canto xv, *note* 10.

21. Insignia of knighthood.

22. The Pigli whose arms are barred with vair (= ermine).

23. The Chiarmontesi, a Guelf family who dwelt in the quarter of St. Peter, but the site of whose houses has not been further identified. One of the family, in Dante's time, had falsified the measure by which in his public capacity he issued salt to tne Florentines. *Cf. Purg.* xii.

24. The Donati, of whom the Calfucci were a branch.

25. The Uberti, once the dominating family in Florence (see Villani, v. 9, and many other passages). Their characteristic pride survived in the great Farinata. (*Cf. Inf.* x.) The *golden balls* were the device of the Lamberti, of whom was Mosca. *Inf.* xxviii.

26. The Visdomini, who, with the Della Tosa, "were patrons and defenders of the bishopric." Villani, iv. 10. Hence Dante's taunt that they fed fat on the sequestrated revenues when the See was vacant.

27. The Ademari, between whom and Dante there was an implacable hostility.

28. Ubertino Donati had married a daughter of Bellincion Berti, and, says Cacciaguida, objected to another of Bellincion's daughters being given in marriage to one of the Ademari. *Cf.* Gardner, i. 3; last paragraph.

29. "Who would believe that the della Pera were an ancient family? But I say to thee that they are so ancient that a gate of the first circle of the city was called after them" (Ottimo Comento).

30. Hugh of Brandenbourg, Imperial Vicar of Tuscany, died on St. Thomas' Day, 1006, "and whilst the said Hugh was living, he made in Florence many knights of the family of the Giandonati, of the Pulci, of the Nerli, of the Counts of Gangalandi, and of the family Della Bella, which all, for love of him, retained and bore his arms; barry, white and red, with divers charges." Villani, iv. 2; where the

whole story of Hugh is given. To these families the Ciuffagni are added in iv. 13.

31. Giano della Bella, the great democratic leader, the prime mover of the "Ordinances of Justice." *Cf.* Gardner, i. 4; Villani, *Introduction* § 5, and book viii. § 1, 8, &c. The della Bella had a border of gold on their coat of arms.

32. The reference is to the Buondelmonti, whose houses will be seen to neighbour those of the Gualterotti and the Importuni.

33. The Amidei. See *note 35.*

34. *Associates,* the Uccellini and Gherardini. In the democratic legislation against the Magnates (who systematically defied the civic law and recognized no authority save that of the Family Council), members of a family who had ceased to act with it were regarded as no longer belonging to it, and members of another family who had joined its Tower-club, that it is say, its association for the maintenance of a tower for military purposes, were regarded as its "consorts," or associates, forming one *consorteria* with it, and therefore legally identified with it.

35. Buondelmonte was betrothed to a maiden of the Amidei; but a lady of the Donati, introducing him to her beautiful daughter, persuaded him to break faith with his bride. Her friends and relatives held a council of war and debated whether to slay him or be content with some lesser chastisement. Then "Mosca de' Lamberti said the evil word: 'Thing done hath an end'; to wit, that he should be slain; and so it was done." He was slain at the foot of the statue of Mars. Villani vi. 38.

36. By the triumphant foe.

37. The old standard of Florence bore white lilies on a red field. It was maintained by the Ghibellines. In 1251 the Guelfs adopted a red lily on a white field. (See Villani, vi. 43.)

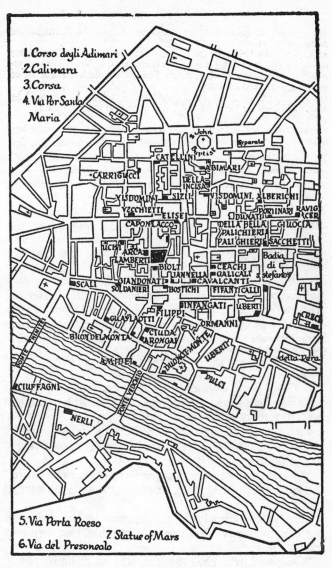

1. Corso degli Adimari
2. Calimara
3. Corsa
4. Via Por Santa
   Maria

s. John Bpti.sK

Reparata

CATELLINI

ABIMARI

CARRIGUCCI

DELLA
INCISA

VISDOMINI   SIZII   VISDOMINI. ALBERICHI

YZCCHIETII

ELISE

ODUNATII

PORTINARI RAVIG

CER

CAPONLACCO

DELLA BELLA   GIUOCIA
PALICHIERIA

UCHI   ARCA

PALI GHIERI   SACCHETTI

LAMBERTI   BIOLI

Badia
di
stefano's

JANNELLA

CEACHI
GALICALI

GIANDONATI

CAVALCANTI

SCALI   SOLDANIER   BOSTICHI   FIFANTI CALLI

INFANGATI   UBERTI

CREC
H

FILIPPI

GLA. LAOTTI

ORMANNI

BRON DELMONTA

CIUDA
ARONGA

DUOMI. MONTE

UBERTI

della Vera

AMIDEI

DULCI

CIUFFAGNI

NERLI

5. Via Porta Roeso
7. Statue of Mars
6. Via del Presoncalo

509

ÇANTO XVII

As Phaëton came to Clymene to have his doubts resolved, so, en-
couraged by Beatrice, did Dante turn to Cacciaguida to learn from
him the meaning of all the dark hints as to his future lot which he
had heard in the three realms. Cacciaguida, not in oracular am-
biguities but in plain speech, tells how contingency is but relative to
material and human limitations (though free will is an absolute real-
ity), and therefore he already sees, as a harmonious part of the
blessed whole, the future that as a fragment of Dante's experience
shall be so bitter. Florence shall accuse him of that treachery of
which herself is guilty, and shall do it as at the instigation of the
Pope. Slandered, exiled, and in penury, he must go his way, in evil
company, till he isolates himself from all, and is justified in so doing
by the event. His first refuge shall be in the court of the Scaliger
who will anticipate all his requests by granting them, and with
whom he shall find the now youthful hero who shall give proof of
his worth before Henry VII's mission, and shall at last do deeds
which even they who see them shall not credit. He further bids
Dante not envy the wrong-doers, whose downfall he shall long out-
live, and in answer to the timid suggestions of prudence urges him
to reveal to the world the whole content of his vision.

AS CAME to Clymene, to have assurance as to that
which he had heard uttered against himself, he who still
maketh fathers grudging to their sons;[1]

such was I; and such was I felt both by Beatrice and by
the sacred lamp which had already, for my sake, changed
its position.

Wherefore my Lady: "Let forth the heat of thy desire,"
she said, "that it may issue, struck aright with the internal
stamp;

not that our knowledge may increase by thy discourse,
but that thou mayst learn to tell thy thirst, that men may
mingle for thee."

"Dear turf, wherein I root me, who art so high uplifted

that even as earthly minds perceive that two obtuse angles
may not find room in one triangle,

so thou dost see contingent things, or ere themselves
exist, gazing upon the point whereto all times are present;[2]

whilst I was companioned by Virgil along the mount
which cureth souls, and down-going through the world
defunct,

heavy words were said to me anent my future life; albeit
I feel me squarely set against the blows of fortune;[3]

wherefore my will were well content to hear what the
disaster drawing nigh to me; for the arrow seen before
cometh less rudely."

So spake I unto that same light which had before ad-
dressed me, and, as Beatrice willed, was my wish confessed.

In no dark sayings, such as limed the foolish folk of old,
before the Lamb of God who taketh sins away, was slain,

but in clear words, and with precise discourse, answered
that love paternal, hidden and revealed by his own smile:

"Contingency, which beyond the sheet of your material
stretcheth not, is all limned in the eternal aspect;

albeit it deriveth not necessity from this, no more than
doth the ship that droppeth down the stream from the
sight wherein she doth reflect herself.[4]

Thence,[5] as cometh to the ear sweet harmony from an
organ, cometh to my sight the time that is in store for thee.

As Hippolytus was severed from Athens by machina-
tion of his cruel and perfidious stepmother,[6] so must thou
needs sever thee from Florence.

So it is willed, so already plotted, and so shall be accom-
plished soon, by him who pondereth upon it in the place
where Christ, day in day out, is put to sale.[7]

The blame shall cleave unto the injured side in fame, as
is the wont; but vengeance shall bear witness to the truth
which doth dispense it.

Thou shalt abandon everything beloved most dearly;
this is the arrow which the bow of exile shall first shoot.

Thou shalt make trial of how salt doth taste another's
bread, and how hard the path to descend and mount upon
another's stair.

And that which most shall weigh thy shoulders down,

shall be the vicious and ill company with which thou shalt fall down into this vale,

for all ungrateful, all mad and impious shall they become against thee; but, soon after, their temples and not thine shall redden for it.[8]

Of their brutishness their progress shall make proof, so that it shall be for thy fair fame to have made a party for thyself.

Thy first refuge and first hostelry shall be the courtesy of the great Lombard, who on the ladder beareth the sacred bird,[9]

for he shall cast so benign regard on thee that of doing and demanding, that shall be first betwixt you two, which betwixt others most doth lag.

With him shalt thou see the one who so at his birth stamped by this strong star, that notable shall be his deeds.

Not yet have folk taken due note of him, because of his young age, for only nine years have these wheels rolled round him.[10]

But ere the Gascon have deceived the lofty Henry, sparkles of his virtue shall appear in carelessness of silver and of toils.[11]

His deeds munificent shall yet be known so that concerning them his very foes shall not be able to keep silent tongues.

Look to him and to his benefits; by him shall many folk be changed, altering state, the wealthy and the beggars;

and thou shalt bear it written in thy mind of him, but shalt not tell it";—and he told me things past the belief even of who shall see them.

Then he added: "Son, these are the notes on what hath been said to thee; behold the snares that behind but few circlings are hidden.

Yet would I not have thee envious of thy neighbours, since thy life shall be prolonged far beyond falling of the penalty upon their perfidies."

When by his silence the sacred soul showed he had finished setting of the woof across the warp I had held out in readiness to him,

I began, as he who longeth in doubt for counsel from one who seeth and willeth straight, and loveth:

"Well do I see, my father, how time cometh spurring toward me to give me such a buffet as is heaviest to whoso most abandoneth himself;

wherefore with foresight it were well to arm me, that if the dearest place be reft from me, I lose not all the rest by reason of my songs.

Down in the world endlessly bitter, and along the mount from whose fair summit my Lady's eyes uplifted me,

and after, through the heaven from light to light, I have learnt that which if I tell again, will have strong-bitter flavour unto many;

and if to truth I am a shrinking friend, I fear to lose life amongst those who shall call this time ancient."

The light wherein was smiling my treasure which I there had found, first coruscated as at the sun's rays doth a golden mirror;

then answered: "Conscience darkened, or by its own or by another's shame, will in truth feel thy utterance grating.

But none the less, every lie set aside, make thy entire vision manifest, and let them scratch wherever is the scab;

for if thy voice be grievous at first taste, yet vital nutriment shall it leave thereafter when digested.

This cry of thine shall do as doth the wind, which smiteth most upon the loftiest summits; and this shall be no little argument of honour.

Therefore have been displayed to thee, in these wheels, upon the mount, and in the dolorous vale, only souls known to fame;

for the soul of him who heareth resteth not nor fixeth faith by an example which hath its root unknown and hidden, nor other unconspicuous argument."

1. Phaëton. The fatal consequences of his father giving him leave to drive the chariot of the Sun still act as a warning to fathers. What he "had heard uttered against himself" was that he was not really Apollo's son.

2. *Cf.* Cantos vi. ii and xxix.

3. *Cf. Inf.* x, xv, xxiv; and *Purg.* xi, and more vaguely *Purg* viii and xxiv.

4. See Canto x, *note* 11.

5. "Thence" = from the "eternal aspect" mentioned above.
6. Phædra accused Hippolytus of the sin of which she herself was really guilty. So Florence.
7. Gardner, i. 4, "The Jubilee," etc.
8. Apparently implying that Dante had broken with the Whites before the "affair of Lastra." Gardner, i. 5, "Benedict xi"; and Villani, viii. 72.
9. Bartolomeo della Scala, Lord of Verona, brother of Can Grande. Gardner, i, 5; "Verona," etc. His arms were an eagle on a ladder (scala).
10. Can Grande. Cf. Inf. i.
11. Clement V encouraged Henry VII's expedition to Italy, but he was not loyal to him. See Canto xxx, and note 7. Also Gardner, i. 6.

ÇANTO XVIII

Dante, pondering Cacciaguida's revelation, is roused from his reverie by the consoling words and by the beauty of Beatrice who directs him once again to the spirit of his ancestor; who names to him some of the warrior saints that shoot, as he speaks, along the cross; and who then himself joins in their hymn. Dante turns again to Beatrice and sees, by her yet greater beauty, that they have risen into a higher heaven. Then as he looks again upon the star he sees that the white glowing Jupiter has replaced the ruddy Mars. The spirits here form themselves into successive letters and spell out the opening words of the book of Wisdom "Love righteousness ye that be judges of the earth." Then other spirits gather upon the crest of the last letter, twine round its limbs and insensibly form it into an eagle, the symbol of Roman law and justice. From this star, then, proceeds our justice. Oh that the divine mind whence it draws its power would once more, in wrath, cleanse the mercenary temple which pollutes its rays! Oh that the chivalry of heaven would pray for the misled world! As for the Pope who makes a traffic of his awful power to grant or withhold Communion, let him think of Peter and Paul! But he will plead that John Baptist, whose image is stamped upon the golden florins, has absorbed all his thoughts.

ALREADY WAS that blessed mirror rejoicing only in his own discourse, and I was tasting mine, tempering with the sweet the bitter;

and that Lady, who was leading me to God, said: "Change thy thought; think that I am nigh to him who every wrong unloadeth."

I turned me to the lovesome sound of my comfort, and what love I then beheld within the sacred eyes, I here attempt not;

not because merely I distrust my speech, but for my memory which may not re-ascend so far above itself unless another guide it.

So much anent this point may I re-tell, that as I gazed upon her my affection was freed from every other longing, whilst the eternal joy which rayed direct on Beatrice was satisfying me with its derived aspect from the fair face.

O'ercoming me with the light of a smile, she said[1] to me: "Turn thee, and hearken, for not only in my eyes is Paradise."

As here sometimes we read the affection in the countenance, if it be so great that all the mind is taken up by it,

so in the flaming of the sacred glow to which I turned me, I recognized the will in him yet further somewhat to discourse with me.

He began: "In this fifth range of the tree which liveth from the summit, and ever beareth fruit, and never sheddeth leaf,

are spirits blessed, who below, ere they came unto heaven, were of a great name, so that every Muse would be enriched by them.

Wherefore gaze upon the horns of the cross; he whom I shall name shall there do the act which in a cloud its swift flame doth."

I saw a light drawn along the cross at the naming of Joshua, as it was done; nor was the word known to me ere the fact.

And at the name of the lofty Maccabee I saw another move, wheeling, and gladness was the lash unto the top.

Thus for Charlemagne and for Orlando two more were followed by my keen regard, as the eye followeth its falcon flying.

Then drew my sight along that cross William and Rinoardo and the duke Godfrey, and Robert Guiscard.[2]

Thereon amongst the other lights, moving and mingling, the soul which had discoursed to me showed me his artist quality among heaven's singers.

I turned to my right side to see in Beatrice my duty, whether by speech or gesture indicated,

and I saw her eyes so clear, so joyous, that her semblance surpassed all former usage and the last.

And as by feeling more delight in doing well, man from day to day perceiveth that his virtue gaineth ground;

so did I perceive that my circling round together with

516

the heaven had increased its arc,[3] seeing this miracle yet more adorned.

And such change as cometh in short passage of time over a fair dame, when her countenance unburdeneth shame's burden,

was presented to my eyes, when I turned me, because of the white glow of the temperate sixth star[4] which had received me into it.

I saw in that torch of Jove the sparkling of the love which was therein signalling to my eyes our speech.

And as birds, risen from the bank, as though rejoicing together o'er their pasture, make themselves now a round, now a long, flock,

so within the lights the sacred creatures flying sang, and in their shapings made themselves now D, now I, now L.

First singing to their note they moved, then as they made themselves one of these signs, a little space would stay and hold their peace.

O goddess Pegasæan,[5] who givest glory unto genius, and renderest it long life, as with thy aid doth it to cities and to realms,

make me bright with thyself, that I may throw into relief their figures as I have them in conception; let thy might show in these brief verses.

They displayed them then in five times seven vowels and consonants, and I took note of the members, even as they appeared in utterance to me.

Diligite justitiam, were the first verb and substantive of all the picturing; *qui judicatis terram* were the last.[6]

Then ordered in the M[7] of the fifth word they stayed, so that Jove seemed silver in that place, pricked out with gold;

and I saw descending other lights where was the M's peak, and there still them; singing, I take it, the good that moveth them unto himself.

Then, as at the smiting of burnt brands there rise innumerable sparks, wherefrom the foolish ones use to draw augury,[8]

meseemed there rose thence more than thousand lights, and mounted some much, some little, even as the sun which kindleth them, ordained them;

and when each one had stilled it in its place, an eagle's head and neck I saw presented by that pricked-out fire.

He who there painteth hath not one to guide him, but he himself doth guide, and from him cometh to the mind that power which is form unto the nests;[9]

the other blessedness,[10] which at first seemed content to twine the M with lilies, by a slight motion followed the imprint.

O sweet star, what quality and magnitude of gems made plain to me that our justice is the effect of the heaven thou dost engem!

Wherefore I pray the mind wherein thy motion and thy power hath beginning, to look upon the place whence issueth the smoke that vitiates thy ray;

so that once more the wrath be kindled against the buying and the selling in the temple which made its walls of miracles and martyrdoms.[11]

O soldiery of heaven, whom I look upon, pray for them who have all gone astray on earth, following the ill example.

Erst 'twas the wont to make war with swords; now it is made by withholding, now here, now there, the bread the tender father bars from none;

but thou, who but to cancel,[12] dost record, reflect that Peter and Paul who died for the vineyard thou layest waste, are living yet.

Though thou indeed mayst urge: "I have so fixed my longing on him who lived a solitary, and by tripping steps was drawn to martyrdom, that I know not the fisherman nor Paul."

1. A disputed passage. We take it: "I was, all satisfied, gazing upon the reflection of the light of God which shone from Beatrice's face. But she said, smiling," etc.

2. William of Orange, like Rinoardo and Orlando, is a hero of romance, whereas Godfrey de Bouillon (d. 1100), conqueror of Jerusalem, and Robert Guiscard (d. 1085) of the house of Tancred (cf. Canto iii, note 12), are entirely historical.

3. Because they had ascended higher.

4. Jupiter is temperate or equable, between cold Saturn and hot Mars. Cf. Canto xxii.

5. Pegasus, the winged horse, struck out the fountain Hippocrene

from the earth with his hoof, which fountain was sacred to the Muses. Hence the Muse is "goddess of the spring of Pegasus."

6. *Wisdom of Solomon*, i. 1 (see *Argument*).

7. Note that M is the central letter of the Latin and Italian alphabet, which has no W. An M of the old fashion (ᛖ) may with a little ingenuity be transformed into the body and wings of a bird, the head gathering above the centre.

8. The method being to ask, "How many lambs, florins, or what not, shall I get?" then strike a brand and count the sparks for answer.

9. Dante is describing the work of God, whom no one can instruct (*Isaiah* xl. 13, 14; *Job* xxxviii. 4 *sqq.*), and from whom all knowledge comes into every mind. But why *nests?* Are the nests the heavens, nestling one within another? Or is the instinct of birds selected as the symbol of all intelligence save the divine?

10. The spirits that had formed neither the limbs of the M nor the head, but had twined round the former, now moulded themselves into the eagle's body and wings.

11. The papal court. *Cf. Purg.* xvi and *De Mon.*, bk. i.

12. The cancelling of excommunication being a source of revenue.

ÇANTO XIX

The just Kings, who compose the eagle of Jupiter, speak as one per-
son, just as many brands give out one warmth, so indicating that the
work of all righteous governors is one and the same, the voice of all
of them being the one voice of justice. In the heaven of justice, there
rises in Dante's mind a passion of hope that he may find the solution
of the problem, which so long has tortured him, as to the exclusion
of the virtuous heathen from heaven, so contrary in seeming to
God's justice. The divine eagle first responds with a burst of trium-
phant joy, then tells how God's wisdom is in excess of all that the
whole creation expresses; and since Lucifer himself, the highest of
created things, could not see all (and fell because he would not wait
for the full measure of light God would have given him), it follows
far more that lesser minds cannot so see but that God sees unutter-
ably deeper. Wherefore our sight must needs be lost in the depths
of divine justice, which God's eye alone can pierce. But our very
idea of justice is from God, and this thought must quiet Dante's pro-
test as to the exclusion of the virtuous heathen. Who is he that he
should judge? There were matter enough for the human mind to
boggle at, had we not the authority of Scripture for our guidance
and did we not know that the Will of God is itself the perfect
standard of goodness and of justice, not to be called to account
by any other standard. As the little stork (the symbol of obedient
docility) looks up, when fed, to the parent bird that wheels over
the nest, so Dante gazes on the eagle; which sings a hymn as far
above our understanding as God's judgments are; and then, while
reasserting without qualification that belief in Christ is the sole
means of access to heaven, yet declares that many heathen will be
far nearer Christ on the judgment day than many who call upon
his name; whereon follows a long denunciation, in detail, of con-
temporary Christian monarchs.

WITH OUTSTRETCHED wings appeared before
me the fair image which those enwoven souls, rejoicing in
their sweet fruition, made.

Each one appeared as a ruby whereon the sun's ray should burn, enkindled so as to re-cast it on mine eyes.

And that which I must now retrace, nor ever voice conveyed, nor ink did write, nor ere by fantasy was comprehended;

for I saw and eke I heard the beak discourse and utter in its voice both *I* and *Mine*, when in conception it was *We* and *Our*.

And it began: "In that I was just and duteous am I here exalted to this glory which suffereth not itself to be surpassed by longing;

and upon earth have I left a memory, so fashioned that there the evil folk commend it, though they follow not the tale."

So do we feel one glow from many coals as from those many loves there issued forth one only sound out of that image.

Whereon straightway I: "O perpetual flowers of the eternal gladness, ye who make all your odours seem to me but one,

solve, as ye breathe, the great fast which long hath held me hungering, because on earth I found no food for it.

Well do I know that if the divine justice maketh any other realm of heaven its mirror, yours apprehendeth it without a veil.

Ye know how eager I prepare me to hearken; ye know what is that question which hath been to me a fast of so long date."[1]

As the falcon issuing from the hood shaketh head and clappeth wings, showing his will and making himself beauteous,

such did I see that ensign which was woven of the praises of divine grace, with songs such as be known to whoso up there rejoiceth.

Then it began: "He who rolled the compass round the limit of the universe, and within it marked out so much both hidden and revealed,

could not so stamp his worth on all the universe but that his word remained in infinite excess.

And this is certified by that first proud being, who was

the summit of all creation, because he would not wait for light, falling unripe;[2]

and hence it is apparent that each lesser nature is a receptacle too scant for that good which hath not end, and itself measureth with itself.

Wherefore our[3] sight, which needs must be one of the rays of that mind whereby all things are filled,

cannot of its nature have so great power but that its principle should discern far beyond that which unto it appeareth.

Wherefore in the eternal justice such sight as your world doth receive, like the eye in the ocean, is absorbed;

for, albeit it can see the bottom by the shore, in the open sea it seeth it not, and none the less 'tis there, but the depth it hath concealeth it.

There is no light unless from that serene which never is disturbed, else it is darkness or shadow of the flesh or else its poison.[4]

Enough is opened to thee now the labyrinth which hid from thee the living justice of which thou hast made question so incessantly;

for thou didst say: 'A man is born upon the bank of Indus and there is none to tell of Christ, nor none to read, nor none to write;

and all his volitions and his deeds are good so far as human reason seeth, sinless in life or in discourse.

He dieth unbaptized and without faith; where is that justice which condemneth him? where is his fault, in that he not believes?'

Now who art thou who wouldst sit upon the seat to judge at a thousand miles away with the short sight that carries but a span?

Truly to him who goeth subtly to work with me, were not the Scripture over you, there were marvellous ground for questioning.

O animals of earth, minds gross! the primal Will, good in itself, never departed from its own self which is the highest good.

All is just which doth harmonize with it; no created good draweth it to itself,[5] but it by raying forth giveth rise to it."

As right above her nest the stork sweepeth when she hath fed her brood, and as the one which she hath fed looketh up to her;

so did (and so did I uplift my brow) the blessed image, which plied its wings driven by so many counsels.

Wheeling it sang, and said: "As are my notes to thee who understandest them not, such is the eternal judgment to you mortals."

When those glowing flames of the Holy Spirit were stilled, yet in the ensign which gained the Romans reverence from all the world,

it began again: "To this realm ne'er rose one who believed not in Christ, neither before nor after he was nailed unto the tree.

But see, many cry Christ, Christ, who at the judgment shall be far less near to him than such as know not Christ;

and such Christians the Ethiop shall condemn when the two colleges shall dispart, the one for ever rich, the other stripped.

What may the Persians[6] say unto your kings when they shall see that volume opened wherein are their dispraises ail recorded?

There shall be seen amidst the deeds of Albert[7] that one which soon shall move its wing to make the realm of Prague a desert.[8]

There shall be seen the woe which he is bringing on the Seine by making false the coinage,[9] who by the wild boar's stroke shall die.

There shall be seen the pride which maketh athirst and doth the Scot and Englishman so madden they may not abide within their proper bound.

The lechery shall be seen and life effeminate of him of Spain, and him of Bohemia, who knew not ever worthiness, nor willed it.

For the cripple of Jerusalem shall be seen marked with an I, his excellence, whereas an M shall mark the countercharge.[10]

The avarice and baseness shall be seen of him who hath in ward the Isle of Fire where Anchises ended his long life:[11]

and to give to understand how great his paltriness, his record shall be kept in stunted letters which shall note much in little space.[12]

And plain to all shall be revealed the foul deeds of his uncle and his brother[13] which have made so choice a family, and two crowns, cuckold.

And he of Portugal and he of Norway there shall be known, and he of Rascia, who in ill hour saw the coin of Venice.[14]

O happy Hungary,[15] if she suffereth herself to be mauled no more! And happy Navarre, were she to arm herself with the mount that fringeth her![16]

And all should hold that 'tis in pledge of this that Nicosia and Famagosta already wail and shriek by reason of their beast, who doth not part him from beside the others."

1. The same problem is referred to in the *De Monarchia*, ii. 8, as one which the human reason cannot solve unaided, but to the solution of which it can rise by the aid of faith. There is no indication in the *De Monarchia* of the mental anguish which throbs through the appeal in this present passage.

2. Both Lucifer and Adam and Eve sinned not by desiring knowledge that was to be permanently withheld, but by desiring it before the appointed time. "He therefore [the devil] desired something which he had not, and which he ought not to have desired at that time; just as Eve desired to be like the deities before God desired that she should" (Anselm).

3. *our.* Cf. Cantos xx and xxi. Another reading is *your* (vostra), which seems more germane to the immediate object of the appeal. But *our* effects the transition from "the summit of all creation" to the mind of earthly man, and beautifully associates the spirits in heaven with those on earth in dependence upon God.

4. *darkness, shadow* of ignorance, *poison* of vice.

5. The context and the comparison of *De Monarchia*, ii. 2, sufficiently explain this passage. Conformity with the will of God is the ultimate test of justice.

6. *Persians*, representing all non-Christians, like the *Ethiopian* just above.

7. The following indiscriminate condemnation of contemporary monarchs is far from being justified in all its details by history. Compare with this passage the parallel in *Purg.* vii. The accompanying tables, which might be united into one connected whole, will serve to identify the monarchs referred to.

8. The translation personifies Albert's invasion of Bohemia in 1304, but the Italian may equally well be translated: "set the pen (*viz.*, of the Recording Angel) in motion." On Albert. cf *Purg.* vi.

9. **Philip the Fair.** Compare *Purg.* vii and xx, and numerous references to his relations with Clement in the *Comedy* and in the *Epistles*. He debased the coinage to one third of its value, in order to meet the expenses of his Flemish campaigns in 1302. This is one of several passages in which we see the horror of tampering with the coinage entertained by Dante, the citizen of the greatest commercial city of Europe. As the symbol of greed the *Florin* was the "accursed flower" (of Canto ix), but as the foundation of all commercial relations it was worthy of such reverence that he who tampered with it was to be ranked with him who falsified the very personality of human beings, the ultimate basis of human intercourse. See *Inf.* xxix. (Compare the story told in Villani, vi. 53.)

10. *Cf.* Canto ix, *note* 1. One good quality to a thousand bad ones.

11. Anchises died at Drepanum in Sicily (the Isle of *fire*, because of Mount Etna). On Frederick, compare *Purg.* iii and *De Vulgari Eloquentia*, i. 12. There was a tradition in Boccaccio's time that Dante had originally intended to dedicate the *Purgatorio* to him, but modern scholars treat it with contempt. If Dante ever really entertained such a purpose, his changed estimate of Frederick was probably caused by the latter's slackness in espousing the imperial cause in opposition to his hereditary foe, Robert of Naples, the head of the Italian Guelfs.

12. The space allotted to the record of so paltry a man being limited, contracted words must be used if room is to be found for all his bad qualities and deeds.

13. James of the Balearic Isles and James of Aragon.

14. Orosius of Rascia issued counterfeit Venetian coins. See map on p. 454.

15. In 1300 Andrew was king of Hungary. He was succeeded by Caroberto (1310-1342), the son of Dante's friend Carlo Martello whom his uncle Robert had ousted from the Neapolitan succession. (*Cf.* Canto ix, *note* 1.) Hungary had suffered from the evils of a disputed succession and of terrible wars. Happy if she had now seen the end of them!

16. Navarre was the separate kingdom of Joanna, wife of Philip the Fair. Happy if she maintained the barrier of the Pyrenees between herself and her great neighbour! The fate of Cyprus under the French dynasty of Lusignan may warn her of her fate should she fall under France.

ÇANTO XX

As when the one light of the sun disappears, the heaven is straight-
way rekindled by many stars, so when the one voice of the eagle
ceased the many beings that composed it, shining yet more brightly,
burst into an angelic chime of many notes, which was followed by a
murmuring as of falling waters, gathering once more in the neck of
the eagle into a single voice. The eagle declares that the six lights
which forms its pupil and eyebrow are the greatest of all, and goes
on to enumerate them, using, in most cases, rich and pregnant cir-
cumlocution, but expressly naming Ripheus the Trojan, that there
may be no room to misconceive a statement so incredible as that he
(as well as Trajan, the heathen emperor, already indicated by a para-
phrase not to be misunderstood) is in heaven. Then once more the
eagle bursts into rapturous song, and when it pauses, Dante, though
he knows that the spirits read his inmost thoughts as we on earth see
colour through a sheet of glass, yet can not restrain the utterance of
his amazement at the presence of these two heathen; whereon the
eagle declares that both of them died in the true faith, Ripheus in
Christ to come and Trajan in Christ come; and so explains the former
case as to suggest that revelations may have been vouchsafed to other
righteous Pagans. So little do men fathom the divine counsels! Nay,
the redeemed souls, as they look on God, know not yet who shall be
the saved; and in this very limitation of their knowledge they re-
joice, for it is a point of conscious contact with the will of God.
Thus, as the souls of Trajan and Ripheus glint responsive to the
eagle's discourse, Dante receives sweet solace partly from the
thought that he knows not, after all, how many of the supposed
heathen are in truth saved, and partly from the spectacle of the
souls in bliss rejoicing in the limitations of their knowledge no less
than in its conquests.

WHEN HE who doth illumine all the world descendeth
so from our hemisphere that day on every side is done
away,

the heaven which before is kindled by him only, now

straightway maketh itself reappear by many lights wherein the one regloweth.[1]

And this act of heaven came to my mind when the ensign of the world and of its leaders within its blessed beak was silent;

because all those living lights, far brightlier shining, began songs which from my memory must slip and fall.

O sweet love, smile-bemantled, how glowing didst thou seem in those flute holes breathed on only by sacred ponderings![2]

When the dear and shining stones, whereby I saw the sixth heaven gemmed, had imposed silence on the angelic chimes,

meseemed to hear the murmuring of a river which droppeth clear from rock to rock and showeth the abundance of its source.

And as the sound taketh its form in the lute-neck, or at the opening of the pipes the wind that entereth,

so, delay of expectation done away, that murmuring of the eagle rose up through its neck as it were hollow;

there it became a voice and issued thence, out from its beak, in form of words, such as the heart awaited, whereon I wrote them.

"That part in me which seeth and which doth endure the sun in mortal eagles," it began to me, "must now fixedly be gazed upon,

for of the fires wherefromout I make my figure, those with which the eye sparkleth in my head, of all their ranks are chief.

He who shineth midmost, as the pupil, was the singer of the Holy Spirit who bore the ark from city unto city;

now knoweth he the merit of his song, in so far as 'twas the effect of his own counsel,[3] by the remuneration like unto it.

Of the five who make the eyebrow's arch, he who doth neighbour closest on the beak consoled the widow for her son;[4]

now knoweth he how dear it costs Christ not to follow, by his experience of this sweet life and of the opposite.

And he who followeth on the circumference whereof I

tell, upon the upper arch, death did delay by his true penitence;[5]

now knoweth he that the eternal judgment is not transmuted when a worthy prayer giveth unto to-morrow upon earth what was to-day's.

The next who followeth, with the laws and me, with good intention that bore evil fruit, to give place to the pastor, made himself a Greek;

now knoweth he that the ill deduced from his good deed hurteth not him though the world be destroyed thereby.[6]

And him thou seest on the down-sloping arch was William, whom that land deploreth which weepeth for that Charles and Frederick live;

now knoweth he how heaven is enamoured of the righteous king, and by the semblance of his glow he maketh it yet seen.[7]

Who would believe, down in the erring world, the Trojan Ripheus[8] in this circle to be the fifth of the holy lights?

now knoweth he right much of the divine grace that the world hath no power to see, albeit his sight discerneth not the bottom."

Like to the lark who soareth in the air, first singing and then silent, content with the last sweetness that doth sate her,

so seemed to me the image of the imprint of the eternal pleasure, by longing for whom each thing becometh what it is.[9]

And albeit there I was to my questioning like glass unto the colour which it clothes, yet would it not endure to bide its time in silence;[10]

but from my mouth: "What things[11] are these?" it thrust by force of its own weight, whereat I saw great glee of coruscation.

Then straightway, with its eye more kindled, the blessed ensign answered me, that it might not hold me in suspense of wonder:

"I see that thou believest these things because I tell them thee, but the how thou seest not; so that, although believed, yet are they hidden.

Thou art as he who doth apprehend the thing by name,

but may not see its quidity unless another bring it forth to light.

The kingdom of heaven suffereth violence from warm love and living hope which conquereth the divine will;

not in fashion wherein man subdueth man, but conquereth it because it willeth to be conquered, and, conquered, with its own benignity doth conquer.

The first life of the eyebrow and the fifth set thee a-marvelling, because thou seest the region of the angels painted with them.

From their bodies they issued not, as thou supposest, Gentiles, but Christians in established faith, in the feet that —to the one—should suffer, and—to the other—had already suffered.[12]

For the one from hell,—where none returneth ever to right will, came back unto its bones, and this was the reward of living hope;[13]

the living hope which put might into the prayers made unto God to raise him up, that his will might have power to be moved.[14]

The glorious soul, whereof is the discourse, returning to the flesh where it abode short space, believed in him who had the power to aid it;

and believing kindled into so great flame of very love, that at the second death it was worthy to come unto this mirth.

The other, by that grace which welleth from so deep a fountain that never creature thrust eye down to its first wave,

set all his love below on righteousness, wherefore from grace to grace God opened his eye to our redemption yet to come;[15]

whereat he believed therein, and thenceforth endured not the mire of paganism, and reproved the folk perverse concerning it.

Those three dames[16] stood as baptism for him, whom thou didst see at the right wheel, more than a thousand years before baptizing.

O predestination, how far withdrawn is thy root from such vision as sees not the first cause entire!

And ye mortals, hold yourselves straitly back from judging; for we who see God, know not as yet all the elect;

and sweet to us is such defect because our good in this good is refined, that what God willeth we too will."

So by this divine image to clear my curtailed vision was given me sweet medicine.

And as on a good singer a good harpist maketh the quivering of the chord attend, wherein the song gaineth more pleasantness,

so whilst he spake I mind me that I saw the two blessed lights, just as the beating of the eyes concordeth, making their flames to quiver to the words.

1. It was the general belief that the light of all the stars was reflected from the Sun.
2. A much disputed passage. It is taken in the translation to mean, "As the flute is played on by the breath of the musician, so these spirits were played upon by their own holy thoughts, wherein that same divine love which clad them with the smiling brightness of joy, breathed upon them."
3. Contains by implication Dante's doctrine of inspiration. The human instrument of the Divine Spirit has a genuine part to play.
4. Cf. Purg. i.
5. 2 Kings xx. 1–11.
6. The donation of Constantine, called by Bryce "the most stupendous of all mediæval forgeries," set forth how Constantine, when cured of his leprosy by Pope Sylvester, resolved to transfer his capital to Constantinople ("made himself a Greek") in order to leave to the Pope and his successors the sovereignty over Italy. Dante, while accepting the supposed fact, regarded it as one of the most disastrous events of history. (Cf. Inf. xix and Purg. xxxii.) He warmly maintained that the donation was invalid, since the Emperor could not alienate, nor the Pope receive, temporal power. (De Monarchia, iii. 10, etc. Cf. Gardner, iii. 1, under "Book iii."
7. William the Good (1166–1189) was the last king of the house of Tancred who reigned over the "Two Sicilies." See Cantos iii (note 12) and ix (note 1); and Tables i and iv on pp. 621, 624. The kingdom of Naples, under Charles II, and the kingdom of Sicily, under Frederick, bewail him.
8. Ripheus. Virgil calls him "the one man amongst the Trojans most just and observant of the right." Æneid, ii.
9. The imprint of the eternal pleasure probably means justice. By longing for God everything becomes its true self.
10. it = "my questioning."
11. Quidity = the "what-ness" of a thing, as quality is the "what-like-ness" of it. "You know the name of a thing, but know not what the thing is."

22. Ripheus had faith in the crucified feet that were to be, Trajan in the crucified feet that had been.

13. Repentance or change of will, in hell, was so inconceivable, that even when the divine prerogative overrode the decree, it was thought of as acting not to change the will in hell, but to bring back the soul to the body, that the will might be changed on earth.

14. Thomas Aquinas repeatedly refers to the story of Gregory and Trajan. He says: "Damascenus [d. before 754] . . . tells how Gregory, when pouring out prayer for Trajan, heard a voice borne to him from heaven: *I have heard thy voice and I grant pardon to Trajan;* to which fact, . . . the whole East and West is witness." In discussing prayer and predestination, he declares that prayer cannot alter the divine will, but may be the appointed instrument for its accomplishment; and declares that "though Trajan was in the place of the reprobate, yet he was not reprobate himself in the absolute sense, since he was predestined to be saved by Gregory's prayers." Gregory himself [Pope, 590–606] is emphatic on the futility of prayer for the damned. "The saints pray not for the unbelieving and impious defunct, because they shrink from the merit of their prayers, for those whom they already know to be damned to eternal punishment, being annulled before that countenance of the righteous Judge."

15. The principle implied in this passage opens the door through which Cato enters heaven. *Cf. Purg.* i. There is a remarkable passage in which Aquinas says: "A man may prepare himself by what is contained in natural reason for receiving faith. Wherefore it is said that if anyone born in barbarous nations do what lieth in him, God will reveal to him that which is necessary for salvation, either by inspiration or by sending a teacher." Perhaps Dante's own mind dwelt increasingly on this conception. The tradition which told how Paul wept over Virgil's tomb at Naples may have been taken as specific evidence that Virgil was not one of the heathen thus saved.

16. Faith, Hope and Charity. See *Purg.* xxix.

ÇANTO XXI

Beatrice and Dante have risen to Saturn, now in the constellation of Leo, and there Beatrice smiles not (lest her beauty should shatter Dante's mortal senses as Jove's undisguised presence burned Semele to ashes) but bids him gaze upon that which shall be revealed to him. The joy it gives him to obey her behests is compensation even for the withdrawal of his eyes from her countenance, whereon they feasted; and he sees the golden Jacob's ladder stretch up from Saturn; while a throng of splendours descends, as though all heaven had been emptied, and splashes in light upon a certain step of the ladder. Dante addresses the light that arrests itself nearest to him, first with silent thought, then, when Beatrice gives him leave, with open speech; and asks why he more than others has approached him, and why the harmony of heaven is no longer heard. The spirit answers that Dante's senses are not yet sufficiently inured to bear the divine music in this higher sphere; and that he has approached to welcome him not because he has greater love than others, but because the divine love, to which all eagerly respond, has assigned that office to him. Dante though satisfied by the answer within its limits, yet pushes his demand further and asks why God assigned this office just to his interlocutor and no other. Hereon the spirit whirls and glows, rapt into such immediate and intense communion with God as to see his very essence, and yet declares that neither he nor the highest of the Seraphim sees the answer to this question, which lies unfathomably deep in the being of God. Let Dante warn the world, with its smoke-dimmed faculties, not to presume henceforth to attempt a problem which even in heaven is insoluble. Appalled by this reply, Dante now bashfully requests to know who it is that has thus checked his presumptuous enquiry, and he learns that it is Peter Damiani, who called himself Peter the Sinner, and who had dwelt in the now degenerate convent of Fonte Avellana, and in that of S. Maria in Pomposa. In connection with his reception, shortly before his death, of the Cardinal's hat he denounces the pomp and obesity of the Church dignitaries, whereupon there comes whirling down a throng of flames that group themselves round him and raise a cry which so stuns Dante that he understands not what it says.

ALREADY WERE mine eyes fixed on my Lady's countenance again, and my mind with them, from all other intent removed;

and she smiled not, but: "Were I to smile," she began, "thou wouldst be such as was Semele, when she turned to ashes;

for my beauty, which, along the steps of the eternal palace kindleth more, as thou hast seen, the higher the ascent,

were it not tempered, so doth glow as that thy mortal power, at its flash, would be like foliage that the thunder shattereth.

We have arisen to the seventh splendour, which, underneath the bosom of the glowing Lion, downrayeth now mingling with its power.

Fix thy mind after thine eyes, and make of them mirrors to the figure which in this mirror shall be shown unto thee."

Whoso should know what was the pasture of my sight in the blessed aspect when I changed me to another care,

would recognize how much it was my joy to be obedient to my heavenly guide, weighing the one against the other side.[1]

Within the crystal which doth bear the name, circling the world, of its illustrious leader, beneath whom every wickedness lay dead,[2]

coloured like gold which doth re-cast the ray, I saw a ladder erected upward so far that my sight might not follow it.

I saw, moreover, descend upon the steps so many splendours that methought every light which shineth in the heaven had been thence poured down.

And as, after their nature's way, the daws at the beginning of the day set out in company to warm their chilled feathers;

then some go off without return, others come again to whence they started, and others make a wheeling sojourn;

such fashion, meseemed, was in that sparkling which came in company, soon as it smote upon a certain step,

and the one[3] which abode nighest to us became so bright that in my thought I said: "I do perceive the love which thou art signalling unto me.

But she from whom I wait the how and when of speech and silence, pauses, and therefore I, counter to my desire, do well not to demand."

Whereat she, who saw my silence in his sight who seeth all, said to me: "Loose thy warm desire."

And I began: "My merit maketh me not worthy of thy response, but for her sake who granteth me to make request,

O blessed life, who abidest hidden in thy gladness, make known to me the cause which so nigh to me hath placed thee;

and say, wherefore in this wheel the sweet symphony of Paradise keepeth silence, which below throughout the others soundeth so devoutly."

"Thou hast the hearing, as the sight, of mortals," he answered me; "wherefore here is no song for that same reason for which Beatrice hath not smiled.

Down by the steps of the sacred ladder I so far descended only to do thee joyance with speech and with the light which mantleth me;

nor was it greater love that made me swifter; for more and so much love up there doth burn, as the flashing maketh plain to thee;

but the deep love which holdeth us prompt servants of the counsel which governeth the world, maketh assignment here as thou observest."

"Yea, I perceive, O sacred lamp," said I, "how free love in this court sufficeth to make follow the eternal providence;

but this it is, which seemeth me hard to discern: Wherefore thou alone amongst thy consorts wast predestined to this office."

Nor had I come to the last word, ere the light made his mid point a centre, and whirled himself like to a swift millstone.

Then answered the love that was therein: "The divine light doth focus it on me, piercing into that wherein I am embowelled;[4]

the power whereof, conjoined unto my sight, uplifteth

534

me above myself so far that I perceive the supreme essence[5] whence it is milked.

Thence cometh the joy wherewith I flame; for to my sight, even as it is clear, the brightness of the flame do I equate.[6]

But that soul in heaven which is most illuminated, that Seraph who hath his eye most fixed on God, had given no satisfaction to thy question;

because so far within the abyss of the eternal statute lieth the thing thou askest, that from all created vision it is cut off.

And to the mortal world, when thou returnest, take this report, that it presume not more to move its feet to-ward so great a goal.

The mind which shineth here, on earth doth smoke, and therefore think how it should have power there below, which it hath not even though heaven take it to itself."

Such limits did his words impose on me, I left the question, and restrained me to demanding humbly who himself was.

"'Twixt the two shores of Italy crags arise, and not far distant from thy fatherland, so high the thunders sound far lower down,

and make a hump whose name is Catria, 'neath which a hermitage is consecrate, which erst was given only unto prayer."[7]

So he began to me again the third discourse, and then continuing, said: "There in God's service I became so rooted

that only with olive-juice viands[8] I lightly traversed heat and cold, satisfied in thoughts contemplative.

That cloister erst bore ample fruit unto these heavens, and is now become so futile, that ere long needs must it be revealed.

I, Peter of Damian, was in that same place; and I, Peter the Sinner, was in the house of Our Lady on the Adriatic shore.[9]

Little of mortal life was left to me when I was called and drawn unto the hat[10] which doth but change from bad receptacle to worse.

Cephas came, and the great vessel of the Holy Spirit came,[11] lean and unshod, taking their food from every hostelry.

Now the modern pastors must needs be buttressed on this side and on that, and have one to lead them on, so heavy are they, and one to hoist behind.

With their mantles they o'erspread their palfreys, so that two beasts travel beneath one hide; O patience, that so much endureth!"

At this voice I saw more flames from step to step descend and whirl, and every whirl made them more beauteous.

Around this one they came and stayed themselves and raised a cry of so deep sound that here it may not find similitude; nor did I understand it, so vanquished me the thunder.

1. The joy of contemplation against that of obedience.

2. Saturn reigned in the age of gold, which is identified by the classical poets with the age of absolute simplicity and temperance.

3. This is the spirit of Peter Damiani (d. 1072). The poverty of his parents induced them to expose him as an infant; but he was rescued, and after much hardship was educated by his brother Damian, in gratitude to whom he took the surname of "Damian's Peter." He was made Cardinal Bishop of Ostia in 1058. He is best known for his unsparing castigation of the corrupt morals of the monks of his day.

4. "The light in the centre of which I dwell."

5. God.

6. Cf. Canto xiv.

7. The monastery of Fonte Avellana upon the Apennines.

8. Lenten fare, cooked with olive oil, not lard or butter.

9. A vexed passage. The reading of the original is doubtful. If we read fui="I was," the two Peters are to be identified. If we read fu,="he was," they are to be distinguished. Reading fu, we must identify Peter the Sinner with Peter degli Onesti who founded the church of Santa Maria del Porto, near Ravenna, in accomplishment of a vow, about A.D. 1096. He lived in a little house adjoining the church till his death in 1119. His tomb may still be seen in the church, and he is described upon it as Petrus Peccans. The meaning would then be: "I, Damian's Peter, was in Fonte Avellana, whereas Petrus Peccans dwelt by Santa Maria del Porto, and is another man." In this case Dante intended the lines expressly to guard against the confusion between the two Peters. But the passage so read seems somewhat frigid.

Now Peter Damiani also was in the constant habit of calling himself *Petrus Peccator*. It seems extremely improbable that Dante was ignorant of this; and if he knew it, he certainly would not have used this designation expressly to distinguish Peter Damiani from another Peter. The best editors, then, are probably right in reading *fui*, and identifying the Pietro Damiani and the Pietro Peccator. But this does not end the difficulty. Did Dante confound the Pietro degli Onesti, buried in Santa Maria del Porto, with Peter Damiani, and did he mean to say: "I went by the name of Peter Damiani in Fonte Avellana, but by the name of Petrus Peccator in the hermitage of Santa Maria del Porto?" This seems extremely improbable. Dante can hardly have confounded the two Peters. Moreover, Peter Damiani used the signature *Petrus Peccator* when he was in Fonte Avellana as well as elsewhere, and we may be sure that Dante would not have gone out of his way to make so precise a statement about the different appellations for the same man in different places when he could not have ascertained it to be true. There is a third hypothesis suggested by a passage in the *Breviarium Romanum*, which, after recording Peter Damiani's reception into Fonte Avellana, says that not long afterwards "he was sent by his abbot on a mission to the monastery of Pomposa, and afterwards to the convent of St. Vincent of Petra Pertusa," both of which he reformed. Now this monastery of Pomposa," which is situated on a small island at the mouth of the Po, near Commachio" (Toynbee), was a convent of Santa Maria, and is so described by Peter Damiani himself. Moreover, it has recently been shown that Peter Damiani spent two years there. Probably, therefore, the reference is to this monastery rather than to the hermitage of Santa Maria del Porto. But even then there remains a great difficulty of translation. One of the suggestions made is grammatically admissible, but poetically worse than impossible. "I dwelt there, Peter Damiani also known as Petrus Peccator. I once visited the monastery of Pomposa." On the other hand, the translation offered in the text supposes so awkward a construction that it may well be open to doubt. Fortunately (if we accept the reading *fui* and take the monastery to be Pomposa) the sense, if not the construing, is clear.

10. The cardinal's hat.

11. Peter (*John* i. 42) and Paul (*Acts* ix. 15).

CANTO XXII

Beatrice soothes and reassures Dante in his terror, and tells him of the divine vengeance, invoked in the cry he has heard. She bids him look again upon the lights of Saturn; and the brightest amongst them then advances to him, encourages him to trust in the affection of the spirits that surround him, and answers his question without awaiting its utterance. He is Benedict, of Monte Cassino fame, and he is surrounded by other contemplative saints. Encouraged by his words to fling all restraint aside, Dante asks if he may see him in his undisguised form of glory; and he replies that this lofty desire shall be fulfilled in the Empyrean where all desires have their perfect fulfilment, because there is no temporal succession there but eternal fulness. Contemplation alone can lead to this timeless and spaceless life, whence the Jacob's ladder, that Dante's human eye cannot follow to its summit, is planted upon the star of abstinence and contemplation, and reaches to the heaven which Jacob saw it touch. But now none mounts this ladder, for all the monastic orders are degenerate. Yet God has ere now wrought greater wonders than the renewal of their spirit would be. Therefore there is yet hope. Hereon Benedict returns to his company, and they all are swept whirling back to the highest heaven, while Beatrice by her glance raises Dante instantaneously into his natal sign of Gemini, to the influences of which the Poet now appeals for aid in his recording task. Beatrice bids him, as he draws near to the final glory, and ere he meets the triumphant hosts in this eighth sphere, to strengthen and rejoice his heart by gathering together his heavenly experiences up to this point and realizing how far he has left earth behind. He looks down through all the seven spheres, sees the clear side of the moon and all the related movements and positions of the heavenly bodies, sees the little earth for which we fight so fiercely stretched out before him so that he can trace the rivers right down from the watersheds to the seashore. Then he turns again to Beatrice's eyes.

OPPRESSED with stupor to my guide I turned, as
doth a little child who hath recourse ever where most he
hath his confidence:

and she, like a mother who succoureth quick her pale
and gasping child, with her own voice which still disposeth him aright,

said to me: "Knowest thou not thou art in heaven? and
knowest thou not heaven is all holy, and that which here
is done cometh of righteous zeal?

How the song had transmuted thee, and I in smiling,
now mayst thou think since the cry hath so moved thee;

wherein, hadst thou understood their prayers, already
would be known to thee the vengeance which thou shalt
see ere that thou die.

The sword from here above cleaveth not in haste nor
tardy, save to his deeming who in longing or in fear awaiteth it.

But turn thee now to others; for many illustrious spirits
shalt thou see, if thou again dost lead thy look accordant
to my speaking."

As was her pleasure directed I mine eyes, and saw an
hundred spherelets, which together were made more beauteous by their mutual rays.

I stood as one repressing in himself the prick of his desire, who doth not frame to ask, so feareth he to exceed.

And the greatest and most shining of these pearls[1] came
forward to make my will content concerning him.

Then there within I heard: "Didst thou see, as I, the
love which burneth amongst us, thy thoughts had been
expressed;[2]

but, lest thou by waiting lag from the lofty goal, I will
make answer only to the thought of which thou art thus
circumspect.

That mount, upon whose slope Cassino lieth, was erst
thronged on its summit by the folk deceived and ill-disposed.[3]

And I am he who first bore up there his name, who
brought to earth that truth which doth lift us so high;

and so great grace shone o'er me, that I drew the places
round about back from the impious cult which did seduce
the world.

These other flames were all contemplatives kindled by

that warmth which giveth birth to the holy flowers and fruits.

Here is Maccarius, here is Romoaldus,[4] here are my brothers who within the cloisters stayed their feet and kept sound their heart."

And I to him: "The love thou showest, speaking with me, and the propitious semblance which I perceive and note in all your glows,

hath so outstretched my confidence as the sun doth the rose when it openeth to its utmost power;

wherefore, I pray thee, and do thou, father, give me assurance whether I may receive so great grace as to behold thee with uncovered image."

Whereat he: "Brother, thy high desire shall be fulfilled in the last sphere, where all the rest have their fulfilment, and mine too.

There perfect, ripe, and whole is each desire; in it alone is every part there where it ever was,

for it is not in space, nor hath it poles; and our ladder even to it goeth, wherefore it thus doth steal it from thy sight.[5]

Right up to there the patriarch Jacob saw it stretch its upper part, when it was seen by him so with angels laden.

But to ascend it now none severeth his feet from earth, and my rule abideth there for wasting of the parchments.[6]

The walls which were wont to be a house of prayer, have become dens, and the hoods are sacks full of foul meal.

But heavy usury is not exacted so counter to God's pleasure as that fruit[7] which doth so madden the monks' hearts.

For what the Church holdeth in her keeping, all pertaineth to the folk that make petition in God's name; not unto kindred, or other filthier thing.

The flesh of mortals is so blandishing[8] that down on earth good beginning sufficeth not for all the space from the upspringing of the oak to acorn-bearing.

Peter began his gathering without gold or silver, and I mine with prayers and fast, and Francis his in humbleness.

And if thou scan the beginning of each one, and scan

again whither it hath gone astray, thou shalt see the white turned dusky.

But Jordan back returning, and the sea fleeing when God willed, are more wondrous sights than were the rescue here."

So spake he to me, and then gathered him to his assembly; and the assembly drew close; then like a whirlwind was all gathered upward.

The sweet Lady thrust me after them, only with a sign, up by that ladder, so did her power overcome my nature;

nor ever here below, where we mount and descend by nature's law, was so swift motion as might compare unto my wing.

O reader, by my hopes of turning back to that devout triumph, for the which I many a time bewail my sins, and smite upon my breast,

thou hadst not drawn back and plunged thy finger in the flame in so short space as that wherein I saw the sign that followeth the Bull, and was within it.

O stars of glory, O light impregnated with mighty power, from which I recognize all, whatsoe'er it be, my genius;

with you was rising, and hiding him with you, he who is father of each mortal life, when I first felt the air of Tuscany;[9]

and then when grace was bestowed on me to enter the lofty wheel that rolleth you, your region was assigned to me.

To you devoutly now my soul doth breathe, to gain the power for the hard passage that doth draw her to it.

"Thou art so nigh to the supreme weal," began Beatrice, "that thou shouldst have thine eyes clear and keen.

And therefore, ere thou further wend thereinto, look down and see how great a universe I have already put beneath thy feet;

so that thy heart, rejoicing to its utmost, may be presented to the throng triumphant which cometh glad through this sphered ether."

With my sight I turned back through all and every of

the seven spheres, and saw this globe such that I smiled at its sorry semblance;

and that counsel I approve as best which holdeth it for least; and he whose thoughts are turned elsewhither may be called truly upright.

I saw the daughter of Latona kindled without that shade which erst gave me cause to deem her rare and dense.[10]

The aspect of thy son, Hyperion,[11] I there endured, and saw how Maia and Dione[12] move about and near him.

Next appeared to me the tempering of Jove[13] between his father and his son; and there was clear to me the varying they make in their position.[14]

And all the seven were displayed to me, how great they are and swift, and how distant each from other in repair.

The thrashing-floor which maketh us wax so fierce,[15] as I rolled with the eternal Twins, was all revealed to me from ridge to river-mouth;[16] then to the beauteous eyes mine eyes again I turned.

1. Benedict (480–543), the founder of the Benedictines, is frequently represented in paintings as the type of monastic discipline.

2. "You would not have held back, timidly repressing your questions."

3. Monte Cassino "is situated on the spur of Monte Cairo, a few miles from Aquino, in the north of Campania, almost exactly halfway between Rome and Naples." It was "crowned by a temple of Apollo, and a grove sacred to Venus" (Toynbee).

4. Probably Macarius the Egyptian (301–391), one of the monks of the Saitic desert, a disciple of Anthony.

Romualdus "saw in a vision a ladder stretching from earth to heaven after the similitude of the patriarch Jacob; whereon men in white vesture ascended and descended; whereby he perceived that the monks of Camaldoli, of whose institution he was the author, were wondrously set forth. Finally, when he had lived 120 years, and during 100 of them had served God in the utmost austerity of life, he took his way to him in the year of salvation 1027" (*Breviarium Romanum*). He was of the Ravennese family of Onesti. Camaldoli is in the Casentino district, and is the hermitage referred to in *Purg.* v.

5. *i.e.*, "Therein is no temporal succession, but eternal co-existence, and therefore completeness." (*Cf.* Cantos xxix and xxx, *Argument.*)

6. My "Rule" serves no purpose except to spoil the parchments on which it is written.

7. *Interest* is regarded as the "increase" of the capital. Hence Dante speaks of it by implication as "fruit," and says that the illicit increase

or gain of usury is not so hateful to God as those illicit gains in frenzied greed for which the monks rob the poor, whose guardians they are, and enrich their relatives, or even their paramours.

8. The Italian *blanda* is variously taken as "seducing" or as "easily seduced."

9. This fixes Dante's birthday as somewhere between May 18th and June 17th (both inclusive), the time during which the sun was in Gemini.

10. *Cf.* Canto ii. Dante conceived that the other side of the moon, which is always turned away from us and toward the higher heavens, had no dark patches.

11. Apollo = the sun.

12. *Maia* and *Dione*, somewhat strangely put for the son of Maia (Mercury) and the daughter of Dione (Venus).

13. The temperate Jove between the hot Mars and the chill Saturn. *Cf.* Canto xviii.

14. The nature of their orbits.

15. A thrashing-floor was a round flat area. Hence the comparison.

16. Not to be understood as implying that the whole inhabited area of the earth was visible to him. *Cf.* Canto xxvii, *Argument*, note 10, and *Map* (p. 601).

CANTO XXIII

Beatrice turns towards Cancer, the region of the summer Solstice, from Gemini where the Poet and his guide are placed; and her intent look wakes the eagerness of expectancy in him. Ere long he sees heaven lighted by the approach of the triumphant hosts of Christ, the whole harvest of the heavenly husbandry; and outshining all is Christ, whose person pierces the swathings of his glory with blinding light; whereupon, as lightning dilating in the womb of a cloud bursts forth, having no space within, so Dante's mind bursts its own limits and loses itself. . . . Beatrice recalls him as from a forgotten dream, and his sight strengthened by the vision of Christ, is now able to endure her smile. What he then saw he needs must leave untold, albeit what he is forcing himself, line by line, to record proclaims that he yields to no shrinking desire to spare himself. At Beatrice's bidding he mans himself again to look upon the garden of Christ, the Virgin rose and the Apostolic lilies; but Christ himself, in tenderness to the pilgrim's powers, has withdrawn above and shines down upon his chosen ones, himself unseen. Gabriel descends and crowns the virgin who then rises through the Primum Mobile far out of sight, while the saints reach up tenderly after her with their flames. Oh, what wealth of glory is in these sainted souls who on earth chose and spread the true riches that wax not old. There Peter triumphs in the victory of Christ, with the ancient and the modern assembly for whom his key has unlocked heaven.

AS THE BIRD amidst the loved foliage who hath brooded on the nest of her sweet offspring through the night which hideth things from us,

who, to look upon their longed-for aspect and to find the food wherewith to feed them, wherein her heavy toils are pleasant to her,

foreruns the time, upon the open spray, and with glowing love awaiteth the sun, fixedly gazing for the dawn to rise;

so was my Lady standing, erect and eager, turned toward the region beneath which the sun showeth least speed;

so that, as I looked on her in her suspense and longing, I became like him who, desiring, would fain have other than he hath, and payeth him with hope.

But short the space 'twixt one and the other *when*, of fixing my attent I mean, and of seeing the heaven grow brilliant more and more.

And Beatrice said: "Behold the hosts of Christ's triumph, and all the fruit gathered by the circling of these spheres."[1]

Meseemed her countenance was all a-glow, and her eyes so full of gladness, that I must needs pass it unconstrued by.

As in the calm full moons Trivia smileth amongst the eternal nymphs who paint the heaven in each recess,

I saw, thousands of lamps surmounting, one sun which all and each enkindled, as doth our own the things we see above;[2]

and through the living light outglowed the shining substance so bright upon my vision that it endured it not.

O Beatrice, sweet guide and dear! She said to me: "That which o'ercometh thee is power against which nought hath defence.

Therein is the wisdom and the might[3] which oped the pathways betwixt heaven and earth, for which there erst had been so long desire."

Even as fire is unbarred from the cloud, because it so dilateth that it hath not space within, and counter to its nature dasheth down to earth,

so my mind, grown greater 'mid these feasts, forth issued from itself, and what it then became knoweth not to recall. . . .

"Open thine eyes and look on what I am; thou hast seen things by which thou art made mighty to sustain my smile."

I was as one who cometh to himself from a forgotten vision, and doth strive in vain to bring it back unto his mind,

when I heard this proffer, worthy of so great gratitude,

as never to be blotted from the book that doth record the past.

If now there were to sound all of those tongues which Polyhymnia with her sisters made richest with their sweetest milk,

it would not mount, in aiding me, unto the thousandth of the truth, hymning the sacred smile, and how deep-clear it made the sacred aspect.[4]

And therefore, figuring Paradise, needs must the sacred poem make a leap, as who should find his pathway intercepted.

But whoso thinketh of the weighty theme and of the mortal shoulder which hath charged itself therewith, will think no blame if under it it trembleth.

It is no voyage for a little bark, that which my daring keel cleaveth as it goeth, nor for a helmsman who doth spare himself.

"Wherefore doth my face so enamour thee that thou turnest thee not to the fair garden which flowereth beneath the rays of Christ?

There is the Rose wherein the Word Divine made itself flesh; there are the Lilies at whose odour the good path was taken."

So Beatrice: and I, who to her counsels was all eager, again surrendered me to the conflict of the feeble brows.

As under the sun's ray, which issueth pure through a broken cloud, ere now mine eyes have seen a meadow full of flowers, when themselves covered by the shade;

so beheld I many a throng of splendours, glowed on from above by ardent rays, beholding not the source whence came the glowings.

O benign power which dost so imprint them! thou hadst thyself uplifted to yield place there for mine eyes that lacked in power.

The name of the beauteous flower which I ever invoke, morning and evening, drew all my mind together to look upon the greatest flame.

And when on both mine eyes had been depicted the quality and greatness of the living star which conquereth up there, e'en as down here it conquered, from within the heaven descended a torch circle-formed, in fashion of a crown, and girt her and wheeled round her.

Whatever melody soundeth sweetest here below, and most doth draw the soul unto itself, would seem a rent cloud thundering,

compared unto the sound of that lyre whereby was crowned the beauteous sapphire by which the brightest heaven is ensapphired.

"I am the angelic love who circles the lofty gladness that doth breathe from out the womb which was the hostelry of our desire;

and I will circle, Lady of heaven, until thou followest thy son, and dost make yet more divine the supreme sphere in that thou enterest it."[5]

Thus the circling melody impressed itself, and all the other lights made sound the name of Mary.

The royal mantel of all the swathings of the universe which most doth burn and most is quickened in the breath and in the ways of God,[6]

above us had its inner shore so distant that its appearance, there where I was, not yet appeared to me.

Therefore mine eyes had not power to follow the crowned flame as she ascended after her own offspring.

And as the infant who toward his mother stretcheth up his arms when he hath had the milk, because his mind flameth forth even into outward gesture;

so each one of these glowings up-stretched with its flame, so that the deep love which they had for Mary was made plain to me.

Then they stayed there within my sight, singing O Queen of heaven so sweetly that ne'er hath parted from me the delight.

Oh how great the wealth crammed in those most rich chests, which here on earth were goodly acres for the seeding!

Here they have life and joy even in that treasure which was earned in weeping in the exile of Babylon, where gold was scorned.[7]

Here triumphs under the lofty Son of God and Mary, in

his victory, together with the ancient and new council, he who doth hold the keys of so great glory.

1. Dante has seen in the seven planetary spheres the different classes and grades of blessedness representing the "many mansions." Now in the heaven of the stars he sees in varied groups the whole fruit of creation and history gathered together, as typifying the "one home." The "circling of these spheres" signifies the whole cosmic evolution, and the working of the spirit of God upon man. *Cf.* Canto xiii, *note* 4.

2. See Canto xx, *note* 1.

3. *Cf.* 1 *Corinthians* i. 24.

4. Another well-supported reading of the Italian has a second *il* before *facea*. The meaning would then be, "and how bright the sacred aspect made it," *i.e.*, "the countenance of Christ, on which she had looked, made Beatrice's smile ineffably beauteous."

5. The Empyrean.

6. The *primum mobile*.

7. The Babylonian exile is a favourite symbol of the life upon Earth, wherein we are "strangers and pilgrims." *Cf. Purg.* xiii.

ÇANTÓ XXÍV

Beatrice appeals to the saints in the starry heaven to give Dante to drink from the heavenly table to which they have been summoned. The divine grace which gives him a foretaste of their feast is their warrant, his immeasurable longing is his claim, and their unbroken enjoyment of that knowledge which he desires makes it easy for them to give. The saints respond joyously to her appeal and in groups of circling lights reveal their varying measures of ecstasy. Peter comes out from the brightest group in answer to Beatrice's prayer. She addresses him as the representative of that Faith by which he himself once walked upon the sea, and to which heaven owes all its citizens; and urges him to test Dante as to Faith. Dante prepares himself, as for examination, and Peter questions him. Dante founds his confession upon the definition in the Epistle to the Hebrews. Faith is the substance or foundation upon which hope is reared, and the basis of the argument by which the reality of unseen things is established. His own faith is unquestioning. It is based on Scripture which is authenticated by miracle. And if one should question the miracles he must face the yet greater miracle of the spread of Christianity without miracle. Peter further demands to hear the positive content of Dante's faith and the specific warrant for it. Dante declares his faith in God, defined first in Aristotelian phrase as the unmoved mover whom the heaven loves and longs for, and then as three Persons in one Essence. For the first belief proofs are drawn from the Physics and Metaphysics as well as from Scripture, for the second from Scripture alone. All else is secondary. Peter signifies his delight in Dante's confession by circling him thrice.

"O FELLOWSHIP elect to the great supper of the blessed Lamb, who feedeth you in such fashion that your desire ever is fulfilled;[1]

if by the grace of God this man foretasteth of that which falleth from your table ere death prescribe the time to him,

give heed to his unmeasured yearning and bedew him somewhat: ye drink ever of the fountain whence floweth that on which his thought is fixed."

549

Thus Beatrice: and those glad souls made themselves spheres upon fixed poles, outflaming mightily like unto comets.

And even as wheels in harmony of clock-work so turn that the first, to whoso noteth it, seemeth still, and the last to fly,

so did these carols[2] with their differing whirl, or swift or slow, make me deem of their riches.

From the one I noted of most beauty, I saw issue a so blissful flame it left none there of greater brightness;

and thrice round Beatrice did it sweep with so divine a song, my fantasy repeateth it not to me;

wherefore my pen leapeth, and I write it not; for such folds our imagination, not only our speech, is too vivid colouring.[3]

"O holy sister mine, who thus dost pray to us devoutly, by thy glowing love, thou dost unloosen me from this fair sphere."

The breath that thus discoursed, as I have written down, was turned unto my Lady by that blessed flame so soon as it had stayed.

And she: "O light eternal of that great man to whom our Lord gave up the keys he brought down of this wondrous joy,

test this man here on the points both light and grave, as it doth please thee, anent the faith whereby thou once didst walk upon the sea.

Whether he loveth well and well hopeth and believeth is not hidden from thee, for thou hast thy vision there where everything is seen depicted.

But since this realm hath made its citizens by the true faith, 'tis well that, for the glorifying of it, it should chance him to speak thereof."

Even as the bachelor armeth himself and speaketh not until the master setteth forth the question, to sanction it, but not determine it:[4]

so did I arm myself with every reason whilst she was speaking, that I might be ready for such examiner and such profession.

"Good Christian, speak, and manifest thyself; what thing

is faith?" Whereat I lifted up my brow upon that light whence breathed forth this word;

then turned me to Beatrice, and she made eager indication to me that I should pour the water forth from my inward fountain.

"May the grace that granteth me to confess me," I began, "to the veteran fore-fighter, make my thought find expression!"

And I followed on: "As wrote for us, O father, the veracious pen of thy dear brother,[5] who, with thee, set Rome on the good track;

faith is the substance of things hoped for, and argument of things which are not seen; and this I take to be its quiddity."[6]

Then heard I: "Rightly dost thou deem, if well thou understandest wherefore he placed it amongst the substances, and then amongst the arguments."[7]

And I thereon: "The deep things which grant me here the largess to appear before me, are from the eyes of them below so hidden

that their existence is there only in belief, whereon is built the lofty hope; and so of *substance* it embraceth the intention;[8]

and from this belief needs must we syllogize without further sight; therefore it includes the intention of *argument*."

Then heard I: "If all that is acquired down below by teaching were so understood, there were no room left for the wit of sophist."

Thus was breathed forth from that enkindled love; then did it add: "Right well hath now been traversed this coin's alloy and weight;

but tell me if thou hast it in thy purse." Whereupon I: "Yea, so bright and round I have it that for me is no *perhaps* in its impression."

Then issued from the deep light that was glowing there: "This dear gem on which all virtue is up-built,

whence came it to thee?" And I: "The ample shower of the Holy Spirit which is poured over the old and over the new parchments, is syllogism that hath brought it to so sharp conclusion for me, that, compared to it, all demonstration seemeth blunt to me."

Then heard I: "That old and that new proposition which bringeth thee to such conclusion,[9] wherefore dost hold it for divine discourse?"

And I: "The proof which doth unfold the truth to me lieth in the works that followed, for which nature ne'er heated iron yet, nor hammered anvil."

The answer came to me: "Say, who assureth thee that these works were? The very script that would attest itself, no other, sweareth it to thee."

"If the world turned to Christianity," I said, "without miracles, this one is such that the others are not the hundredth of it;

for thou didst enter poor and hungry upon the battle-field to sow the good plant which was erst a vine, but now has grown a thorn."

This ended, the high holy court made *God we praise* ring through the spheres, in melody such as up there is sung.

And that baron who so from branch to branch, examining, had drawn me now, that we were nigh unto the utmost leaves,

began again: "The grace which holdeth amorous converse with thy mind hath oped thy mouth till now as it behoved to open;

so that I sanction that which forth emerged; but now behoveth thee to utter what it is thou dost believe, and whence it offered it to thy believing."

"O holy father, thou spirit who now seest that which of old thou didst so believe that thou didst overcome more youthful feet drawing anigh the sepulchre,"[10]

I began, "thou wouldst have me here make plain the form of my eager belief, and dost also ask the cause of it;

whereto I answer: I believe in one God, sole and eternal, who moveth all the heaven, himself unmoved, with love and with desire.

And for such belief I have not only proofs physic and

metaphysic,[11] but it is given me likewise by the truth
which hence doth rain

through Moses, through the Prophets and through the
Psalms, through the Gospel and through you who wrote
when the glowing Spirit had made you fosterers.[12]

And I believe in three eternal Persons, and I believe them
one Essence, so One and so Trine as to comport at once
with *are* and *is*..

With the profound divine state whereof I speak, my
mind is stamped more times than once by evangelic teach-
ing.[13]

This the beginning is; this is the spark which then dilates
into a living flame, and like a star in heaven shineth in me."

Like as the master who heareth what doth please him,
and thereupon embraceth the servant, rejoicing at the
news, so soon as he is silent;

so, blessing me as it sang, three times circled me, so soon
as I was silent, the apostolic light at whose command I had
discoursed; so did I please him in my utterance.

1. Contrast Canto ii, *note* 1.
2. *Carol*, in old English, as in Italian, signifies a group of dancers.
3. Giotto's vivid colouring went with a love of large surfaces,
whence his treatment of drapery, "cumbrous, from the exceeding
simplicity of the terminal lines"; whereas the Byzantines, both in
the earlier period of pale colouring and in the "solemn and deep"
system of the later 12th and 13th centuries, used to "break up their
draperies by a large number of minute folds." (After Ruskin.)
Dante regards human speech and even human imagination as too
aggressive and undiscriminating for the delicate folds of the pic-
tures he fain would paint.
4. Graduation is a religious experience analogous to confirmation.
Note the place of the authors of school text-books amongst the great
religious teachers in Canto xii. These lines have been much dis-
cussed. The translation takes them as meaning that by propounding
the question the master sanctions the discussion without determin-
ing the conclusion.
5. St. Paul; for the anonymous *Epistle to the Hebrews*, from which
the definition is taken (ix. 1), was attributed to him. The Catholic
Church has always maintained that faith is an *intellectual* virtue;
hence the rationalistic colouring of this canto, from which the
Protestant reader will miss much that comes under his conception
of faith(based on the really Pauline Epistles to the *Galatians* and
Romans), and which he will find elsewhere in the *Comedy*, but
not here.

6. *Quiddity*, see Canto xx, *note* 11.

7. The usual meaning of *substance* in the scholastic philosophy is something which exists in itself. (See Canto iii, *note* 2.) Hence an objection to the definition in *Hebrews* noticed by Aquinas: "No quality is a substance; but faith is a quality. . . . therefore it is not a substance." Dante meets the difficulty by taking *substance* in its other sense, as that which "stands under."

8. *Intention*. A difficult word because of the variety of its technical uses. Cf. *Purg.* xviii, *note* 1. Here it is nearly equivalent to "meaning." Faith includes "what is meant by *substance*," and also "what is meant by *argument*.

9. *Proposition*, as applied to the Old and the New Testament carries on the logical terminology given several lines above.

10. See *John* xx. 3–6. Dante has fallen into a confusion between "first entering" and "first approaching" the sepulchre.

11. Cf. Canto i, *notes* 1 and 15. See Wallace, § 39, 46.

12. *Made you fosterers, i.e.*, "made you the foster fathers of the faithful." But the more usual rendering takes *almi* simply as "beautiful" or "holy."

13. The schoolmen found the scriptural references to the Trinity chiefly in the Old Testament, in the plural form of the Hebrew word for "God," in the use of the plural in *Gen.* i. 26; in the threefold cry in *Isaiah* vi. 3, etc. The chief passages from the New Testament are the formula of baptism in *Matt.* xxviii. 19; the text of the three "heavenly witnesses" in 1 *John* v. 7 (Vulgate and A.V.); and the threefold formula in *Romans* xi. 36, after citing which, with some others, Petrus Lombardus adds: "but since almost every syllable of the New Testament agrees in suggesting this truth of the ineffable Unity and Trinity, let us dispense with gathering testimonies on this latter."

ÇANTO XXV

It was the Faith that gained Dante the high privilege of the apostolic benediction. Therefore if his poem should ever melt the heart of the Florentines he will take the poet's crown at that same font whereat he was received into the Faith. St. James now joins St. Peter. When we read of the three chosen disciples to whom Jesus reveals more than to the others we are to take Peter as representing faith, James hope, and John love; and therefore Beatrice urges James to test Dante as to Hope. James questions him. Beatrice herself declares on his behalf that he possesses in fullest measure the virtue of hope, and that it is on that very ground that he has been allowed to anticipate death in his vision of divine things. As to the nature of Hope and its source he shall answer for himself. Dante defines hope with exclusive reference to the future life, and derives it from Scripture. James, whose own hope, which followed him even to death, is now swallowed up in victory, still loves the virtue he once practised, and demands to hear the content of Dante's hope, and its source. Dante declares that Isaiah and John tell him of the double garments of the blessed, and that this symbol indicates to him the resurrection of the body as well as the immortality of the soul as the substantive content of his hope. A light as bright as the sun now joins Peter and James, and is declared by Beatrice to be the Apostle John. Dante strains his sight to see John's body, but is blinded by the glory, and is told that his body is dust, and awaits the general resurrection; Jesus and Mary alone of human beings having arisen with their bodies to heaven. Then of a sudden the harmony is stilled, and the blinded Dante turns in vain to look upon Beatrice.

SHOULD IT E'ER come to pass that the sacred poem to which both heaven and earth so have set hand, that it hath made me lean through many a year,[1]

should overcome the cruelty which doth bar me forth from the fair sheepfold wherein I used to sleep, a lamb, foe to the wolves which war upon it;

with changed voice now, and with changed fleece[2] shall

I return, a poet, and at the font of my baptism shall I assume the chaplet;

because into the Faith which maketh souls known of God, 'twas there I entered; and afterward Peter, for its sake, circled thus my brow.

Thereafter moved a light toward us from out that sphere whence issued forth the first fruits of his vicars left by Christ.[3]

And my Lady, full of gladness, said to me, "Look! look! behold the Baron for whose sake, down below, they seek Galicia."[4]

As when a dove taketh his place near his companion, and one poureth out his love for the other, circling round murmuring,

so did I see one great chieftain glorious received by the other, praising the food which there above doth feast them.

But when the greeting was fulfilled, silent before me each one fixed himself, so kindled that it subdued my countenance.

Smiling then Beatrice said: "Illustrious life, by whom the generosity of our court was chronicled,[5]

make hope be sounded in this height; thou knowest that all those times thou figurest it when Jesus gave more light unto the three."[6]

"Uplift thy head, and see thou reassure thee, for whatso cometh from the mortal world up hither, behoves it ripen in our rays."

Such exhortation from the second flame came to me; whereat I lifted up mine eyes unto the mountains, which had before down-bowed them with excess of weight.

"Since of his grace our Emperor willeth that ere thy death thou be confronted with his Counts in his most secret hall;

that, having seen the truth of this court, thou mayst thereby strengthen in thyself and mo' the hope that upon earth enamoureth folk of good;

say what thing it is, and how thy mind is therewith enflowered, and say whence unto thee it cometh", so followed on the second light.

And that tender one who guided the feathers of my wings to so lofty flight, thus foreran me in answer:

"Church militant hath not a child richer in hope, as is written in the sun who o'errayeth all our host;

therefore was it granted him to come from Egypt to Jerusalem, to look on her, e'er the prescribed limit of his soldiery.[7]

Those two other points—asked not that thou mayst learn, but that he may bear back word how much this virtue is held in pleasure by thee.—[8]

to him I leave; for they will not be hard, nor boastful matter, to him; so let him thereto answer, and may the grace of God concede this to him."

As the pupil who followeth the teacher, eager and glad, in that wherein he is expert, in order that his excellence may be revealed;

"Hope," said I, "is a certain expectation of future glory, the product of divine grace and precedent merit.[9]

From many stars cometh this light to me; but he first distilled it into my heart who was the supreme singer of the supreme leader.

Let them hope in thee,[10] in his divine song he saith, *who know thy name;* and who knoweth it not, having my faith?

Thou then didst drop it on me with his dropping, in thine Epistle,[11] so that I am full and pour again your shower upon others."

Whilst I was speaking, within the living bosom of that flame trembled a flash sudden and dense like unto lightning.

Then breathed forth: "The love whence I am still a-flame to-ward that virtue which followed me even to the palm and issuing from the field,[12]

willeth that I breathe on thee who dost delight thee in her; and further, 'tis my pleasure that thou tell the thing which hope doth promise thee."

And I: "The new and the ancient scriptures set down the symbol, which again doth point me to the thing itself. Of the souls which God hath made his friends

Isaiah saith that each one shall be clad with double garb in its own land, and its own land is this sweet life.

And more worked out by far, doth thy brother, where he treateth of the white robes, set forth this revelation to us."[13]

And, close upon the ending of these words, first rang above us, *Let them hope in thee*, whereunto all the carols answered;

then, from amongst themselves, a light flashed out, in fashion such that if the Crab contained a crystal like it winter would have a month of one unbroken day.[14]

And as doth rise and go her way and enter on the dance a joyous virgin, only to do honour to the bride, and not for any failing,[15]

so did I see the illumined splendour join the other two, who were wheeling round in such guise as their burning love befitted.

There it launched itself into their music and their words; and my Lady held her look upon them just like a bride, silent and unmoving.

"This is he who lay upon the breast of our Pelican, and this was he chosen from upon the cross for the great office."[16]

My Lady thus; but no more after than before her words moved she her eyes from their fixed intent.

As who doth gaze and strain to see the sun eclipsed a space, who by looking grows bereft of sight;

so did I to this last flame till a word came: "Wherefore dost dazzle thee to see that which hath here no place?

Earth in the earth my body is, and there it shall be, with the rest, until our number equalleth the eternal purpose.[17]

With the two robes in the blessed cloister are the two lights alone which rose; and this thou shalt take back into your world."[18]

At this voice the flamed circle stilled itself, together with the sweet interlacing made by the sound of the three-fold breath,

as, to avert or weariness or peril, the oars till now smitten upon the water, all pause at a whistle's sound.

Ah! how was I stirred in my mind, turning to look on Beatrice, for that I might not see her, albeit I was nigh to her and in the world of bliss!

1. For first three stanzas, *cf. Ecloga*, i, and the *Ecloga responsiva of* Johannes del Virgilio, and Gardner, iii.

2. *fleece;* keeping up the metaphor of the lamb and the sheepfold.

3. Peter.

4. James, of the "Peter, James and John," referred to in the Gospels, is James son of Zebedee, and is identified with the James said, by tradition, to have preached the Gospel in Spain, whose most celebrated shrine was at Compostela in Galicia. *Cf. Vita Nuova*, xli. But the James associated with Peter and John as a "pillar" of the Church in *Gal.* ii. 9. is "James the Lord's brother" (*Gal.* i. 19) mentioned in *Acts* xv. 13 and elsewhere. It is to him, and not to the son of Zebedee that the *Epistle of James* has usually been assigned. But Dante forgets or ignores the distinction.

5. *James* i. 5.

6. *i.e.*, admitted Peter, James and John to more intimate knowledge and familiarity than was extended to the other disciples. *Cf. Conv.* ii. 1. The occasion specially referred to are the Transfiguration, the raising of the daughter of Jairus, and the agony of Gethsemane.

7. The Exodus from Egypt had a manifold significance. Amongst other things it was the symbol of the liberation of the soul from the bondage of the flesh; as the entry into the Promised Land and the City of God was the symbol of the heavenly life. *Cf. Purg.* ii, *Epist. ad Can. Grand.*, § 7, and the cruder statement in *Conv.* ii. 1.

8. *Cf.* Cantos xvii and xxiv.

9. It is to be noted that the theological virtue of *Hope*, as understood by the Catholic Church, is not a general hopefulness of disposition, but the specific hope of the bliss of heaven. Dante's definition is closely copied from Peter Lombard's "Hope is the certain expectation of future bliss, coming from the grace of God and from preceding merits."

10. *Psalm* ix. 10. In the *Vulgate*, ix. 11, where the reading is *sperent* = "let them hope."

11. *James* i. 12. "With his dropping" = "in combination with his (David's) teaching."

12. Martyrdom and death.

13. "*Isaiah* (lxi. 7, 10); in describing the gathering of the redeemed, declares that they shall *possess double things*, to wit *robes*, as your brother-apostle John in describing the same scene (*Revelation*, vii. 9), makes yet clearer. Scripture tells us, then, in symbolical language, that we shall have *two robes*, and this symbol, in its turn, assures me that we shall have joy of *body* as well as joy of *soul*. The content of my hope, then, is the unbroken immortality of the soul and the resurrection to immortality of the body." (*Cf.* Canto xiv, *note* 4.) The fanciful and indirect character of this scriptural support for the belief in the resurrection of the body is the more remarkable when we consider that 1 *Cor.* xv. would have furnished Dante with a perfectly explicit statement. Thomas Aquinas, as one would expect, makes frequent use of this chapter.

14. "The light was as bright as the sun, so that if it had been in the

Crab during the month of midwinter (parts of December and January) where the sun is in the opposite sign of Capricorn, one or the other always being above the horizon, there would be no night."

15. Not *performing* with any self-conscious desire for admiration, but simply throwing herself into the festivities in honour of the bride.

16. The pelican, supposed to feed her young with her own blood, is a frequent symbol of Christ. Further, see *John* xiii. 23; xix. 25-27.

17. *Cf. John* xxi, 22, 23.

18. Christ and the Virgin (*cf.* Canto xxiii) alone ascended to heaven with the two robes (*i.e.*, in the body as well as the spirit). Note that according to the conception prevalent in the Middle Ages, Enoch and Elijah, who were also taken up bodily from the earth, were not in heaven, but in the Earthly Paradise. Perhaps the present passage may be taken as indirect evidence that Dante too accepted the tradition

CANTO XXVI

The Apostle John reassures Dante as to his lost sight, which Beatrice will restore to him as Ananias restored his to Paul; and invites him to discourse meanwhile of Love; and first to tell him what is the supreme object on which his soul's affection is fixed. Dante, resignedly awaiting Beatrice's succour, declares that he is still burning in that same flame which she brought into his heart, and that God is the beginning and end of that and of all his other loves. Moved by the Apostle to declare more at large the justification of his love Dante answers that, since good as good must be loved, to know God is of necessity to love him, and goes on to declares how Aristotle and the Scriptures have made this truth level to his capacity. When questioned as to other reasons for loving God Dante perceives that he is expected to supplement his account of the supreme love of God, as good in himself, by a statement of the accessory gratitude to God as good to us, and enumerates the creation of the world, his own creation, the redemption and the hope of heaven. He adds that all creatures share his love in proportion as they share the good which is supreme in the Creator. A hymn of praise is raised, and Dante's sight is restored to him; whereon he is bewildered by Beatrice's greater beauty and then by the presence of a fourth flame, weberin he learns the soul of Adam to abide. Overwhelmed at first, then moved to eagerness that will not brook delay, by finding himself face to face with the human being who has had such unique exprerience and who holds the answer to questions that have so long tantalized the world, Dante reads the answering affection of the first father in the swaying undulations of the light that clothes him and receives the answer to his unspoken questions, as to chronology, the language of Eden, the length of the period of innocence and the nature of the sin that cost the world so dear.

WHILST I WAS in suspense concerning my quenched sight, I was made heedful by a breath that issued from the glowing flame which quenched it,

saying: "Until thou hast again the sense of sight thou

hast consumed on me, 'tis well thou compensate it by discourse.

Begin then, and declare whereon thy mind is focussed; and assure thee that thy sight within thee is confounded, not destroyed;

because the lady who through this divine region doth conduct thee hath in her look the power that was in Ananis' hand."[1]

I said: "At her good pleasure, soon or late, let succour come to the eyes which were the gates when she did enter with the fire wherewith I ever burn.

The good which satisfieth this court is Alpha and Omega of all the scripture which love readeth to me with light or heavy stress."

That same voice which had removed my terror at the sudden dazzlement, set my concern again upon discourse,

and said: "Yea, through a closer sieve thou needs must strain; needs must thou tell me what it was that aimed thy bow at such a targe."

And I: "By philosophic arguments and by authority which down-cometh hence, such love must needs stamp itself on me;

for good, as good, so far as understood, kindleth love, and so much more by how much more of excellence it graspeth in itself.[2]

Therefore to the Essence which hath such privilege that whatsoever good be found outside of it is nought else save a light of its own ray,

more than to any other must the mind needs move, in love, of whoso doth discern the truth whereon this proof is founded.[3]

And this same truth is made level to my intellect by him who doth reveal to me the primal love of all the eternal beings.[4]

It is made level to me by the voice of that veracious author who saith to Moses speaking of himself: *I will cause thee to see all worth*.[5]

It is made level to me by thee also, where thou openest the lofty proclamation which doth herald upon earth the secrets of this place above all other declaration."[6]

And I heard: "As urged by human intellect and by authorities concordant with it, of thy loves keep for God the sovereign one.

But tell me yet if thou feel other cords draw thee towards him, so that thou utter forth with how many teeth this love doth grip thee."

Not hidden was the sacred purpose of Christ's eagle,[7] but rather I perceived whither he willed to lead on my profession.

Wherefore I began again: "All those toothgrips which have power to make the heart turn unto God co-work upon my love;

for the being of the world and my own being, the death that he sustained that I might live, and that which each believer hopeth, as do I,

together with the aforesaid living consciousness, have drawn me from the sea of the perverted and placed me on the shore of the right love.

The leaves wherewith all the garden of the eternal Gardener is leafed, I love in measure of the good that hath been proffered to them from him."

Soon as I held my peace a sweetest song rang through the Heaven, and my Lady with the rest cried: "Holy, Holy, Holy!"

And as at a keen light one wakeneth from slumber by reason of the vessel spirit which runneth to meet the glow that pierceth tunic after tunic,[8]

and he thus awakened confoundeth what he seeth, so undiscerning his sudden vigil until reflection cometh to its succour;

so from mine eyes did Beatrice dissipate every scale with the ray of hers that might cast their glow more than a thousand miles;

whence better than before I saw thereafter, and as one stupefied, made question as to a fourth light which I perceived with us.

And my Lady: "Within those rays holdeth amorous converse with its maker the first soul that the first Power e'er created."

As the spray which bendeth down its head as the wind

passeth over, and doth then uplift itself by its own power which doth raise it up,

did I, whilst she was speaking, all bemazed; and then was reassured by a desire to speak, wherewith I was a-burning;

and I began: "O fruit, who wast alone produced mature, O ancient father who hast both daughter and daughter-in-law in every bride;

devoutly as I may do I implore thee that thou speak to me; thou seest my will, and to hear thee the sooner I not utter it."

Sometimes an animal swayeth beneath a covering so that its impulse must needs be apparent, since what envelopeth it followeth its movements;

and in like manner that first soul made appear through its covering with what elation it advanced to do me pleasure.

And from it breathed: "Though not set forth to me by thee, I better do discern thy will than thou the thing which is most certain to thee,

because I see it in the veracious Mirror which doth make himself reflector of all other things, and nought doth make itself reflector unto him.[9]

Thou wouldst know how long the time since God placed me in the uplifted garden wherein she there prepared thee for so long a stair,[10]

and how long the delight endured unto my eyes, and the true cause of the great indignation, and the idiom which I used and which myself composed.

Now know, my son, that not the tasting of the tree was in itself the cause of so great exile, but only the transgressing of the mark.[11]

From that place[12] whence thy Lady dispatched Virgil, four thousand three hundred and two revolutions of the sun went out my longing for this gathering;

and I beheld him course through all the lights of his path nine hundred times and thirty whilst I abode on earth.

The tongue I spoke was all quenched long ere the work that ne'er might be completed was undertaken by the folk of Nimrod;[13]

for never yet did product of the reason maintain itself

for ever, because of human preference which doth change in sequence with the heaven.[14]

That man should speak is nature's doing; but thus or thus nature permitteth to you as best seemeth you.

Ere I descended to the infernal anguish, *J*[15] was the name on earth of that supreme good whence cometh the gladness that doth swathe me;

El[16] was he called thereafter; and this is fitting, for the use of mortals is as the leaf upon the branch which goeth and another followeth.

On the mount which most doth rise from out the wave was I, with life pure and disgraced, from the first hour to that which followeth, when the sun changeth quadrant, next on the sixth hour."[17]

1. *Acts* ix. 10–18.

2. *Cf.* Cantos xxviii and xiv, and see *note* 4 in this canto.

3. "Whosoever perceives that God is the supreme good (the truth on which rests the proof that he is the supreme object of love) cannot fail to love him supremely."

4. This is clearly *Aristotle*, who teaches that God is the supreme object towards whom the heavens yearn (Wallace, 39 and 46). The extension of this idea from the heavens to the Angels or Deities is not remote from Aristotle's spirit, and is entirely germane to Dante's conception of it. (*Cf. Conv.* ii. 5; and also Canto ii, *note* 13.) The principle of *good kindling love* underlies all Aristotle's philosophy; but perhaps Dante had specially in mind the passage in the *Metaphysics* where Aristotle says that what moves other things, though itself unmoved, is "the object of longing" or "the object of intellectual apprehension;" and adds that "the principles of these two are identical." Albertus (with whom Thomas substantially agrees) interprets them as meaning *appetibile bonum* and *intelligibile bonum*, "that which asserts itself as good to our desire" and "that which asserts itself as good to our intellect." He goes on to explain that the former may be delusive and may be resisted, but the latter "provoketh our longing without let and without intermediary; because there is no need that it should first announce itself as good through the sense in order to stir the appetite; nor is there any clog to it on the part of the receiving intellect, since the thing loved is good in itself and ... winneth the undivided longing of him upon whom it is poured."

5. *Exodus* xxxiii. 19. The Vulgate reads, "*ego ostendam omne bonum tibi.*"

6. Probably the reference is to *Rev.* i. 8. Others understand 1 *John* iv. 16; but it seems impossible to take these lines as anything but an express description of the *Apocalypse.*

7. *Christ's eagle. Cf. Rev.* iv. 7. See also *Purg.* xxix.

8. The various coats of the eye.

9. Both the construing and the interpretation of this passage have given rise to much dispute. The translation here given takes it to mean that everything is perfectly reflected in God, and therefore he who looks on God sees everything perfectly. But no single thing and no single truth (nor even the sum of them all, *cf.* xix) is a complete and perfect reflection of God. Therefore he who sees anything, or everything, apart from God, cannot see it in its completeness. Hence he who looks on God sees the most secret and complex thing more perfectly than he can grasp even the most axiomatic truth in detachment. *Cf.* Canto xxxiii; also Cantos ii and vi.

10. The Earthly Paradise or Garden of Eden, where Beatrice met Dante.

11. Speculations were frequent as to whether the eating of the fruit was to be taken literally, or whether it was a mere veil under which some more heinous offence was really indicated. These lines are intended to brush aside such speculations, and to explain that no breach of a direct command of God can be regarded as trivial. Compare Anselm: "Wert thou to find thyself in the presence of God, and were one to say to thee, *Look this way,* and God counterwise, *I would by no means have thee look that way,* search thou in thy heart what there is amongst all things that are, for which thou shouldst cast that glance, counter to the will of God." Anselm's interlocutor declares that he would not do it to save the whole creation, no, nor to save many creations, did such exist.

12. Limbo. *Cf. Inf.* ii and iv.

13. Contrast *De Vulgari Eloquentia,* i. 6.

14. *I.e.,* human pleasure, choice, or preference, varies under the changing influence of the heavenly bodies.

15. To be pronounced *jah. Cf. Psalm* lxviii. 4. (*Psalm* lxvii. 5, in the Vulgate, which reads *Dominus nomen illi.* But Jerome had noted the Hebrew reading here and elsewhere, and had passed the name *Jah* into the current of Christian tradition.) There are many proper names and some other words compounded with the divine name in this form, such as *Hallejulah.*

16. *El,* signifying "the Mighty," is, according to Hebrew lexicographers "the most ancient and general name" for Deity. It frequently occurs in various books of the Bible. But the more common designation is *Elohim,* probably not to be connected etymologically with *El.*

17. The life in Paradise, therefore, only endured six hours, or something over.

CANTO XXVII

The Poet's ear and eye drink for a space of the glory of Paradise and afterwards, amid deep silence, first the light of Peter glows red with indignation, as he denounced the doings of Pope Boniface VIII; then all heaven is suffused with the same glow and Beatrice's cheek flushes as at a tale of shame, while Peter pursues his denunciation, including Clement the Gascon and John of Cahors in its sweep and then promises redress and bids Dante bear the news to earth. The triumphant spirits, like flashes of flame, rain upwards into the higher heaven, and Beatrice bids Dante look down upon the earth. Dante is in Gemini and the Sun in Aries, with Taurus between, and therefore the half of the earth illuminated by the sun does not correspond with the half that the Seer commands. He sees the earth as we see the moon when she is past the full. The illuminated portion stretches from far west of Gibraltar to the shore of the Levant; and the darkened portion stretches further east. Turning back with renewed longing to Beatrice Dante sees her yet more beautiful and rises with her to the Primum Mobile. Beatrice expounds to him how time and space take their source and measure from this sphere, and have no relevancy to aught that lies beyond it. It is girt (how, God only understandeth) not by space but by the Divine light and love. Then, with deep yearning, Beatrice turns her thoughts back to the besotted world wherein faith and innocence find refuge only in the hearts and lives of infants, and where humanity blackens from its birth. And all this not because of any inherent degeneracy but because there is none to rule. But ere the hundredth of a day by which the Julian exceeds the Solar year shall by its accumulations have made January cease to be a Winter month! the course shall be reversed.

ALL PARADISE took up the strain, "To the Father, to the Son, to the Holy Spirit, glory!" so that the sweet song intoxicated me.

Meseemed I was beholding a smile of the universe; wherefore my intoxication entered both by hearing and by sight.

O joy! O gladness unspeakable! O life compact of love and peace! O wealth secure that hath no longing!

Before my eyes the four torches stood enkindled, and the one which had first approached me began to grow more living;

and such became in semblance as would Jupiter if he and Mars were birds and should exchange their plumage.[1]

The providence which there assigneth function and office had imposed silence on the blessed choir on every side,

when I heard: "If I transform my hue, marvel thou not; for, as I speak, thou shalt see all of these transform it too.

He who usurpeth upon earth my place, my place, my place, which in the presence of the Son of God is vacant,[2]

hath made my burial-ground a conduit for that blood and filth, whereby the apostate one who fell from here above, is soothed down there below."

With that colour which painteth a cloud at even or at morn by the opposing sun, did I then see all heaven o'erfused;

and as a modest dame who remaineth sure of herself, yet at another's fault, though only hearing it, feeleth all timid,

so Beatrice changed her semblance; and such, I take it, was the eclipse in heaven when the supreme Might suffered.

Then his discourse proceeded, with voice so far transmuted from itself, that his semblance had not altered more:

"The spouse of Christ was not reared upon my blood, and that of Linus and of Cletus, that she might then be used for gain of gold;

but 'twas for gain of this glad life that Sixtus and Pius, Calixtus and Urban shed their blood after many a tear.[3]

It was not our purpose that on the right hand of our successors one part of the Christian folk should sit, and one part on the other;[4]

nor that the keys given in grant to me should become the ensign on a standard waging war on the baptized;[5]

nor that I should become the head upon the seal to sold and lying privileges, whereat I often blush and shoot forth flames.

In garb of pastors ravening wolves are seen from here above in all the pastures. Succour of God! oh wherefore liest thou prone?

Cahorsines and Gascons[6] make ready to drink our blood. Oh fair beginning, to what vile ending must thou fall!

But the lofty Providence,[7] which with Scipio defended the glory of the world for Rome, will soon bring succour, as I deem.

And thou, my son, who, for thy mortal weight, shalt return below once more, open thy mouth and hide thou not the thing which I not hide."

As our atmosphere raineth down in flakes the frozen vapours when the horn of the heavenly Goat is touched by the sun;[8]

so did I see the ether adorn itself and rain upward the flakes of the triumphal flashes, which had made sojourn there with us.

My sight was following their semblance, and followed till the medium, by excess, deprived it of the power to pierce more far.[9]

Whereat the Lady, who saw me now absolved from straining upward, said to me: "Down plunge thy sight and see how thou hast rolled."

From the hour at which I had before looked down, I saw that I had moved through the whole arc which the first Climate makes from middle unto end;[10]

so that I saw beyond Cadiz the mad way which Ulysses took, and on this side, hard by, the shore whereon Europa made herself a sweet burden.[11]

And further had the site of this thrashing-floor been unfolded to me, save that the sun was in advance beneath my feet, served by a Sign and more from me.

My enamoured mind, which held amorous converse ever with my Lady, burned more than ever to bring back my eyes to her;

and whatsoever food nature or art e'er made, to catch the eyes and so possess the mind, be it in human flesh, be it in pictures,

if all united, would seem nought towards the divine delight which glowed upon me when that I turned me to her smiling face.

And the power of which that look made largess to me, from the fair nest of Leda[12] plucked me forth, and into the swiftest heaven thrust me.

Its parts most living and exalted are so uniform that I know not to tell which Beatrice chose for my position.

But she, who saw my longing, smiling began—so glad that God seemed joying in her counterance—

"The nature of the universe which stilleth the centre and moveth all the rest around, hence doth begin as from its starting point.[13]

And this heaven hath no other *where* than the divine mind wherein is kindled the love which rolleth it and the power which it sheddeth.

Light and love grasp it in one circle, as doth it the others, and this engirdment he only who doth gird it understandeth.

Its movement by no other is marked out; but by it all the rest are measured, as ten by half and fifth.

And how Time in this same vessel hath its roots, and in the rest its leaves, may now be manifest to thee.

O greed, who so dost abase mortals below thee, that not one hath power to draw his eyes forth from thy waves!

'Tis true the will in men hath vigour yet; but the continuous drench turneth true plum fruits into cankered rubers.

Faith and innocence are found only in little children; then each of them fleeth away before the cheeks are covered.

Many a still lisping child observeth fast, who after, when his tongue is free, devoureth every food in every month;

and many a lisping child loveth and hearkeneth to his mother, who after, when his speech is full, longeth to see her buried.

So blackeneth at the first aspect the white skin of his fair daughter who bringeth morn and leaveth evening.[14]

And thou, lest thou make marvel at it, reflect that there is none to govern upon earth, wherefore the human household so strayeth from the path.

But, ere that January be all unwintered by that hundredth part neglected upon earth,[15] so shall these upper circles roar

that the fated season so long awaited shall turn round the poops where are the prows, so that the fleet shall have straight course; and true fruit shall follow on the flower."

1. Changed from white to red.

2. The charge of usurpation and the declaration that the Papacy is vacant doubtless bear a specific reference to the measures which Boniface took to force his predecessor Celestine V (*cf. Inf.* iii) to resign. See Villani, viii. 5. But Dante does not consistently regard Boniface as a no-pope. *Cf. Purg.* xx.

3. A selection of the Popes of the first three centuries.

4. Refers to the Papal hostility to the adherents of the Empire.

5. Perhaps a specific reference to the struggle of Boniface with the Colonna family. *Cf. Inf.* xxvii. Villani, viii. 23.

6. Clement V (1305–1314) was a Gascon, and John XXII (1316–1334) a native of Cahors.

7. *Cf.* Canto vi, *note* 7, and *Conv.* iv. 5.

8. The Sun is in Capricorn in parts of December and January.

9. Contrast Cantos xxx and xxxi.

10. *Cf.* Canto xxii. The *Climates* are latitudinal divisions which may be applied equally to the heavens and the earth. There is some difference of usage amongst the medieval geographers, but it seems probable that Dante regarded the Twins, in which he was situated, as lying on the upper confines of the first climate. The passage, therefore, seems to mean simply, "I had revolved, with the first climate, through a whole quadrant."

11. It was now sunset on the coast of Phœnicia, where Jupiter, in the form of a bull, took Europa on his shoulders. From this we must calculate back to the position indicated at the close of Canto xxii. It should be borne in mind that according to Dante's geography Jerusalem was the centre of the inhabited globe; the mouths of the Ganges were the extreme to the east, 90° distant from Jerusalem; and Gibraltar the extreme to the west, also 90° from Jerusalem; Rome being midway between Jerusalem and Gibraltar. The maps on p. 601 will complete the explanation.

12. The twins, Castor and Pollux, children of Leda, whom Jupiter wooed in the form of a swan.

13. "The *natural property* in virtue of which," etc. *Cf.* Canto iv, *note* 17.

14. A difficult and disputed passage. *Who* can only mean "the Sun"; and since he is the "father of each mortal life" (Canto xxii), and since man is "begotten by man and by the sun" (*Cf. De Monarchia*, i. 9), we are perhaps right in taking his "fair daughter" to be *Humanity*.

15. The Julian calendar (which we rectified in 1752) makes the

year 11 m. 14 sec. (very roughly one hundredth of a day) too long. In Dante's time, therefore, January began, by calendar, a little later in the real year every season; and thus, in the course of ages, it would begin so late that winter would really be over before we came to New Year's Day by calendar. The substitution of an immense period for a short one is parallel to our "not a thousand miles hence."

ÇANTO XXVIII

After Beatrice's discourse Dante, gazing upon her eyes, is suddenly aware of the reflection in them of a thing which was not in his sight or thought, and on turning to see what it may be he perceives a point of intensest light with nine concentric circles wheeling around it; swift and bright in proportion to their nearness to the point. Beatrice, quoting Aristotle's praise concerning God, declares that Heaven and all Nature hang upon that point, and bids Dante note the burning love that quickens the movement of the inmost circle. Thereon Dante at once perceives that the nine circles represent the Intelligences or angelic orders connected with the nine revolving heavens, but cannot see why the outmost, swiftest, widest sweeping and most divine heaven should correspond with the inmost and smallest angelic circle. Beatrice explains that the divine substance of the heavens being uniform that heaven which is materially greatest has in it the most of excellence; but it is the excellence, not the size, that is essential. In like manner swiftness and brightness are the measure of the excellence of the angelic circles, and therefore the inmost of them which is swiftest and brightest represents those intelligences that love and know most; and the spiritual correspondence is complete between the two diverse spatial presentations. Thus the relativity of space-conceptions is suggested. God may be conceived as the spaceless centre of the universe just as well as the all-embracer. Dante, now enlightened, sees the circles shoot out countless sparks that follow them in their whirling; and hears them all sing Hosanna; while Beatrice further explains how the swift joy of the angels is proportioned to their sight, their sight to their merit, won by grace and by exercise of will; whereas love is not the foundation but the inevitable consequence of knowledge. She has explained the three hierarchies and nine orders of the Angels, as Dionysius (enlightened by his own intense passion of contemplation, and instructed by Paul who had been rapt to heaven) had set them forth. Gregory, having departed from the scheme of Dionysius, smiled at his own error when he beheld this heaven.

573

WHEN, COUNTER to the present life of wretched mortals the truth had been revealed by her who doth emparadise my mind;

as in the mirror a taper's flame, kindled behind a man, is seen of him or ere itself be in his sight or thought,

and he turneth back to see whether the glass speak truth to him, and seeth it accordant with it as song-words to their measure;

so doth my memory recall it chanced to me, gazing upon the beauteous eyes whence love had made the noose to capture me;

and when I turned, and mine own were smitten by what appeareth in that volume whene'er upon its circling the eye is rightly fixed,[1]

a point[2] I saw which rayed forth light so keen, needs must the vision that it flameth on be closed because of its strong poignancy;

and whatever star from here appeareth smallest, were seen a moon neighboured with it, as star with star is neighboured.

Perhaps as close as the halo seemeth to gird the luminary that doth paint it, whenso the vapour which supporteth it is thickest,[3]

at such interval around the point there wheeled a circle of fire so rapidly it had surpassed the motion which doth swiftest gird the universe;

and this was by a second girt around, that by a third, and the third by a fourth, by a fifth the fourth, then by a sixth the fifth.

Thereafter followed the seventh, already in its stretch so far outspread that were the messenger of Juno[4] made complete, it were too strait to hold it.

And so the eighth and ninth; and each one moved slower according as in number it was more remote from unity;

and that one had the clearest flame, from which the pure spark was least distant; because, I take it, it sinketh deepest into the truth thereof.[5]

My Lady, who beheld me in toil of deep suspense, said: "From that point doth hang heaven and all nature.[6]

Look on that circle which is most conjoint thereto, and

know its movement is so swift by reason of the enkindled
love whereby 'tis pierced."

And I to her: "Were the universe disposed in the order
I behold in these wheelings, then were I satisfied with what
is set before me.

But in the universe of sense we may see the circlings
more divine as from the centre they are more removed.

Wherefore, if it behoveth my desire to find its goal in
this wondrous and angelic temple which hath only love
and light for boundary,[7]

needs must I further hear wherefore the copy and the
pattern go not in one fashion; for, for myself, I gaze on it
in vain."

"And if for such a knot thy fingers are not able, no mar-
vel is it; so hard hath it become by never being tried."

So my Lady; and then said: "Take that which I shall tell
thee, wouldst thou be satisfied, and ply thy wit around it.

The corporeal circles are ample or strait according to the
more or less of the virtue which spreadeth over all their
parts.

Greater excellence hath purpose to work greater weal;
and greater weal is comprehended in the greater body if
that the parts be equally consummate.

Therefore the one which sweepeth with it all the rest of
the universe, correspondeth to the circle that most loveth
and most knoweth.[8]

Wherefore, if thou draw thy measure round the virtue,
not the semblance of the substances which appear to thee
in circles,[9]

thou wilt see a wondrous congruence of greater unto
more and smaller unto less in every heaven to its intelli-
gence."

As the hemisphere of air becometh shining and serene
when Boreas bloweth from his gentler cheek,[10]

whereby is purged and is resolved the film which erst
obscured it, so that the heaven laugheth with the beauties
of its every district;

so did I, when my Lady had made provision to me of her
clear-shining answer; and like a star in heaven the truth was
seen.

And when her words stayed, no otherwise doth iron shoot forth sparkles, when it boileth, than did the circles sparkle.

And every spark followed their blaze; and their numbers were such as ran to thousands beyond the duplication of the chessboard.[11]

From choir to choir I heard Hosanna sung to that fixed point which holdeth and shall ever hold them to the *where*, in which they have been ever;

and she who saw the questioning thoughts within my mind, said: "The first circles have revealed to thee the Seraphs and the Cherubs.

So swift they follow their withies that they may liken them unto the point as most they may; and they may in measure as they are sublime in vision.

Those other loves which course around them are named Thrones of the divine aspect, because they brought to its completion the first ternary.[12]

And thou shouldst know that all have their delight in measure as their sight sinketh more deep into the truth wherein every intellect is stilled.

Hence may be seen how the being blessed is founded on the act that seeth, not that which loveth, which after followeth;[13]

and the measure of sight is the merit which grace begetteth and the righteous will; and thus from rank to rank the progress goeth.

The second ternary which thus flowereth in this eternal spring which nightly Aries doth not despoil,[14]

unceasingly unwintereth[15] Hosanna with three melodies which sound in the three orders of gladness, whereof it is three-plied.

In that hierarchy are the three divinities, first Dominations, and then Virtues; the third order is of Powers.

Then in the two last-save-one up-leapings, Principalities and Archangels whirl; the last consisteth all of Angelic sports.

These orders all gaze upward, and downward have such conquering might that toward God all are drawn and all draw.

And Dionysius with such yearning set himself to contemplate these orders that he named them and distinguished them as I.

But Gregory afterward departed rrom him,[16] wherefore so soon as he opened his eye in this heaven he smiled at his own self.

And if so hidden truth was uttered forth by mortal upon earth, I would not have thee marvel; for he who saw it here above revealed it to him, with much beside of truth about these circles."[17]

1. *Mine own* = "eyes." "The heavens declare the glory of God," *Psalm* xix. 1; and whoso looketh at them aright perceives that glory.
2. "And it has been shown that this Being [the Divine Being] hath not magnitude, but is without parts and indivisible" (Aristotle).
3. *Cf.* Canto x.
4. *Iris* = the rainbow. *Cf.* Canto xii.
5. *thereof, i.e.,* of the pure spark.
6. "Now from such a principle heaven and earth depend" (Aristotle). Wallace, 39, *note* 1.
7. "It is not contained in space." *Cf.* Canto xxx.
8. The Seraphs, who "see more of the First Cause than any other angelic nature" (*Conv.* ii. 6) and therefore must needs love more. *Cf.* Canto xxvi.
9. "If thou consider the intensive quantity and not the extensive. For extensive quantity is corporeal and apparent, whereas intensive quantity is spiritual and unapparent" (Benvenuto).
10. North-east, the sky-clearing wind, as opposed to north-west, the sky-clouding wind. The usage of the Latin writers (*e.g.*, Boethius and Virgil) leaves no room to doubt that this is the meaning.
11. If one grain of corn were reckoned for the first square of a chess-board, two for the second, four for the third, etc., it may be seen by a calculation which a logarithmic table will make extremely easy, that the total will be about 18½ million million million.
12. By what logic are they called "Thrones" *because* they close the first ternary? Apparently because *Seraphs* with their wings, and *Cherubs* with their eyes, emphasize the up-going to God and insight into his being; and a complete reflection of the relations between the first hierarchy and the Deity would not be given in the nomenclature unless the *Thrones* were added to signify the superincumbent power of God manifesting itself through and in the Angels, as well as his glory drawing them to himself. Perhaps this may explain why Dante treats utterances of gladness in God as directly connected with the *Seraphim* (*cf.* Cantos viii and ix) and confidence in the manifestations of God's power as connected with

the *Thrones* (*cf.* Cantos v and ix), without reference to the sphere in which the words are spoken.

13. The conception here formulated pervades the whole poem. *Cf.* Cantos xiv and xxix; and *note* 8 of this canto. It is interesting to compare with this view the following passage from Aquinas: "Knowledge existeth in measure as the things known are in him who knoweth, but love in measure as the lover is united to the loved. Now the higher abide after a more noble fashion in themselves than in those below them; but the lower in a more noble fashion in those above them than in themselves. And therefore the knowledge of what is beneath us excelleth the love thereof; but the love of what is above us, and especially of God, excelleth the knowledge of the same." Observe, however, that there is no inconsistency between this doctrine and the teaching of Dante; for Dante maintains that knowledge is the condition of love, rather than love the condition of knowledge, not that knowledge is itself intrinsically superior to love, an idea which he was evidently far from holding. See the final vision in Canto xxxiii.

14. From the autumn Equinox all through the winter till the spring Equinox the sign of Aries is visible in the sky at nightfall. The line therefore means "where there is no autumn nor winter."

15. *unwintereth.* A use of the word bold almost to audacity. In the Troubadour poetry the birds are said to "unwinter" themselves, that is to say, to put off winter in their spring songs, and so to "unwinter Hosanna" is used for "to sing Hosanna in the eternal spring of heaven."

16. Gregory (Pope, 590–604) has an arrangement that differs from that of Dionysius only in the interchange of Virtues and Principalities. Probably he was unacquainted with the works attributed to Dionysius, since they first gained currency in the West through the translations of Scotus Erigena in the 9th century. The arrangement which Dante had followed in *Conv.* ii. 6 is identical with that of Brunetto Latini, and is ultimately derived from Isidore of Seville.

17. *St. Paul. Cf. Acts* xvii. 34, and 2 *Cor.* xii. 2–4.

CANTO XXIX

Beatrice gazes for a moment upon that point of light wherein every where is here and every when is now, and therein reads the questions Dante would fain have her answer. It was not to acquire any good for himself, but that his reflected light might itself have the joy of conscious existence, that God, in his timeless eternity, uttered himself as love in created beings, themselves capable of loving. It is vain to ask what God was doing before the creation, for Time has no relevance except within the range of creation; nor was the first creation itself successive, or temporal at all; for pure form or act (the angels) pure matter or potentiality (the materia prima) *and inseparably united act and potentiality (the material heavens) issued into simultaneous being. Jerome was wrong (as Scripture and reason testify) in thinking that the angels were created long before the heavens over which it is the office of certain of them to preside. Dante now knows where the angels were created (in God's eternity) and when (contemporaneously with Time and with the Heavens) and how (all loving); but has yet to learn how soon certain fell (ere one might count twenty) and why (because of Satan's pride), and how the less presumptuous ones recognized the source of their swift and wide range of understanding, and so received grace (the acceptance of which was itself a merit), and were confirmed. This instruction were enough, did not the prevalence of erroneous teaching (honest and dishonest) make it needful to add that the angels, ever rejoicing in the direct contemplation of God, see all things always, and therefore exercise no changing stress of attention, and therefore need no power of memory, since their thought never having lost immediate hold of aught needs not to recall aught. Beatrice goes on to denounce the vain and flippant teaching by which the faithful are deluded, and especially the unauthorized pardonings; and finally, returning to the subject of the angels, explains that though in number they surpass the power of human language or conception, yet each has his own specific quality of insight and of resultant love. Such is the wonder of the divine love which breaks itself upon such countless mirrors, yet remains ever one.*

WHEN BOTH the two children of Latona, covered by
the Ram and by the Scales, make the horizon their girdle
at one same moment,

as long as from the point when the zenith balanceth the
scale, till one and the other from that belt unbalanceth it-
self, changing its hemisphere,[1]

so long, with a smile traced on her countenance, did
Beatrice hold her peace, gazing fixedly on the point which
had o'ermastered me;

then she began: "I tell, not ask, that which thou fain
wouldst hear; for I have seen it where every *where* and
every *when* is focussed.

Not to have gain of any good unto himself, which may
not be, but that his splendour might, as it glowed, declare,
I am.

In his eternity beyond time, beyond all other compre-
hension, as was his pleasure, the eternal love revealed him
in new loves.[2]

Nor did he lie, as slumbering, before; for nor before nor
after[3] was the process of God's outflowing over these
waters.

Form and matter, united[4] and in purity, issued into be-
ing which had no flaw, as from a three-stringed bow three
arrows;

and as in glass, in amber, or in crystal, a ray so gloweth
that from its coming to its pervading all, there is no in-
terval;[5]

so the threefold effect of its Lord rayed out all at once
into its being, without distinction of beginning.

Co-created was order and co-woven with the sub-
stances; and those were the summit in the universe wherein
pure act was produced.[6]

Pure potentiality[7] held the lowest place; in the midst
power twisted such a withy with act as shall ne'er be un-
withied.[8]

Jerome wrote to you of a long stretch of ages wherein
the Angels were created ere aught else of the universe was
made;

but the truth I tell is writ[9] on many a page of the writers of the Holy Spirit, and thou shalt be aware of it if well thou look;

and also reason seeth it some little, which would not grant that the movers should so long abide without their perfecting.[10]

Now dost thou know where and when these Loves were chosen and how, so that three flames are quenched already in thy longing.

Nor should one, counting, come so soon to twenty as did a part of the Angels disturb the substrate of your elements.[11]

The rest abode and began this art which thou perceivest, with so great delight that from circling round they ne'er depart.

The beginning of the fall was the accursed pride of him whom thou didst see constrained by all the weights of the universe.[12]

Those whom thou seest here were modest to acknowledge themselves derived from that same Excellence which made them swift to so great understanding;

wherefore their vision was exalted with grace illuminating and with their merit, so that they have their will full and established.

And I would not have thee doubt, but be assured that 'tis a merit to receive the grace by laying the affection open to it.

Now, as concerns this consistory much mayst thou contemplate (if my words have been upgathered) with no other aid.

But since on earth in your school 'tis said in lectures that the angelic nature is such as understandeth and remembereth and willeth,[13]

I will speak on, that thou mayst see in purity the truth that down there is confounded by the equivocations of such like discourse.

These substances, since first they gathered joy from the face of God, have never turned their vision from it wherefrom nought is concealed;

wherefore their sight is never intercepted by a fresh object, and so behoveth not to call aught back to memory because thought hath been cleft.

Wherefore they dream, down there, though sleeping not; thinking or thinking not, they speak the truth; but more in one than other is the fault and shame.

Ye below tread not on one path when ye philosophize, so far doth love of show, and the thought it begets transport you.

Yet even this with lesser indignation is endured here above than when divine Scripture is thrust behind or wrenched aside.

They think not how great the cost of blood to sow it in the world, and how he pleaseth who humbly keepeth by its side.

Each one straineth his wit to make a show and plieth his inventions; and these are handled by the preachers, and the Gospel left in silence.

One saith the moon drew herself back when Christ suffered, and interposed herself that the sun's light spread not itself below;

and others, that the light concealed itself of its own self; wherefore that same eclipse responded to the Spaniards and the Indians as to the Jews.

Florence hath not so many Lapos and Bindos as the fables of such fashion that yearly are proclaimed from the pulpit on this side and on that;

so that the sheep, who know not aught, return from their pasture fed with wind, and not to see their loss doth not excuse them.

Christ said not to his first assembly: *Go and preach trifles to the world;*—but gave to them the true foundation;

that, and that only, sounded on their lips; wherefore for their battle to kindle faith they made both shield and lance out of the Gospel.

Now they go forth with jests and with grimaces to preach, and if loud laughter rise, the hood inflates and no more is required.

But such a bird[14] is nestling in the hood-tail that if the crowd should see it, they would see what pardon they are trusting in;

wherefore such folly hath increased on earth that with-out proof of any testimony the folk would jump with any promise.

Whereby Antonio fatteneth his swine, and others too, more swinish far than they, paying with money that hath no imprint.[15]

But since we have digressed enough, turn back thine eyes now to the true path, so that our journey may contract with our time.

This nature[16] ranketh so wide in number that ne'er was speech nor thought of mortal that advanced so far:

and if thou look at that which is revealed by Daniel, thou shalt see that in his thousands determinate number is lost to sight.[17]

The primal light which doth o'erray it all, is received by it in so many ways as are the splendours wherewithal it paireth.

Wherefore, since affection followeth on the act that doth conceive, the sweetness of love in diverse fashion boil-eth or is warm in them.

See now the height and breadth of the eternal worth, since it hath made itself so many mirrors wherein it break-eth, remaining in itself one as before."

1. The Moon (Diana), when at the full, rises just as the Sun (Apollo) sets, or sets as he rises.

2. Dante is careful in the use of *splendour* for reflected, not direct light. (*Epist. ad Can. Grand.*, § 20-23, and *Conv.* iii. 14.) Therefore we must not understand this passage as declaring the manifestation of his own glory to be God's motive in creation, but rather the conferring of conscious being, the sense of existence, upon his creatures. "In order that his creatures (*i.e.*, his reflected glory, his *splendour*) might be able to say: *I am.*" This is in conformity with what Aquinas and others say as to love as God's motive in creation. Cf. Canto vii, *note* 8.

3. If we might read, with some MSS., *preceded* for *proceeded* the meaning would be much easier: "Since there is no *before* nor *after* save with reference to creation (because Time itself is a creation), the question is equivalent to: *What was God doing before there was any before?*" But the authority for *proceeded* is too strong to be neglected. The translation and argument explain the sense in which we take it.

4. *united* in the material heavens; and in their several *purity* in the Angels and the *materia prima*.

5. It was a received point in the Aristotelian physics that light oo`

cupies no time in diffusing itself through a translucent medium or substance. Beatrice, then, declares that the creation of the Angels, of the *prima materia*, of the physical heavens [and also time and space] was instantaneous. The successional creation recorded in *Genesis* was a subsequent process of evolution which took place in time, and through the instrumentality of the Angels.

6. The Angels. *Act* or *actuality* is opposed to *potentiality*. Man's intellect is "possible" or "potential," that is to say, we know potentially much that we do not know actually, and (in another but allied sense) are potentially thinking and feeling many things that we are not actually thinking and feeling; whereas the whole potentialities of an angel's existence are continuously actualized. (*Cf. De Monarchia*, i. 3.)

7. The *materia prima*.

8. The material heavens; not humanity. (*Cf.* Canto vii.)

9. Perhaps *Ecclesiaticus* xviii. 1, where the *Vulgate* reads, "He who liveth eternally created all things at once (*simul*)." It was also argued from *Gen.* i, 1, *"in the. beginning"* that there had been no long-previous creation.

10. *Without their perfecting, i.e.*, as organs without a function, not being able to perform that for which they were created. On the relation of those Angels who specially presided over the revolving heavens and the other Angels in the Orders to which they respectively pertained, see *Conv.* ii. 5.

11. Here Dante avoids the vexed question as to whether some angels fell from each of the Orders. In *Conv.* ii. 6, he had expressly declared that some, perhaps a tenth, of each Order fell. *The substrate of your elements* is usually (and perhaps rightly) taken to] mean "that one of your elements that underlies the rest," *i.e.*, Earth. Cf. *Inf.* xxxiv. But if we take this passage on its own merits it seems better to understand the *substrate* of the elements to mean the *prima materia* (*cf.* Cantos ii and vii); the elaboration of the elements being the subsequent work of the Angels and the heavens.

12. See *Inf.* xxxiv.

13. These are the precise powers which Dante believed the disembodied human soul actually to possess before assuming its provisional aerial body. (See *Purg.* xxv.) As far as *intelligence* and *will* are concerned, the assertion is equally true of the Angels, but not so as to *memory*. (See below.)

14. Devils are called *birds* in *Inf.* xxii and xxxiv, as here. Angels are called birds in the *Purgatorio* (ii and viii), but not in the *Paradiso*.

15. The pigs which infested Florence and its neighbourhood, and which belonged to a neighbouring monastry or monasteries, were under the patronage of St. Anthony (251–356), whose symbol is a pig. It had been well had they been the worst things fed on the proceeds of the fraudulent gains of the religious!

16. *i.e.*, the Angels.

17. *"Daniel* vii. 10 is not intended to give the number of the Angels, but to express that they are more numerous than man can conceive."

ÇANTO XXX

When it is dawn with us and noon six thousand miles to the East of us, and the shadow of the earth cast by the sun is level with the plane of our horizon, the stars one by one disappear. And in like manner the angelic rings that seemed to enclose the all-enclosing divine point gradually disappeared; whereon Dante turned to Beatrice and saw her of such transcendent beauty that like every artist who has reached the extreme limit of his skill he must leave this excess unchronicled. Beatrice tells him that they have now issued forth from the heaven that compasses all space into the heaven of light, love, joy, which is not a thing of space, and where he shall behold the angels, and shall see the elect in the forms they will wear after the resurrection. A blinding flash of light enwraps the Poet, and his sight then becomes such that naught can vanquish it; whereon he sees (first in symbolic form, as by the stream of Time; then in their true shapes, as gathering round the circle of Eternity) the things of heaven. The light of God, striking upon the Primum Mobile, is reflected up upon the ranks of the blest, to whom it gives power to look upon God himself. Dante, in this region, where far and near have no relevancy, gazes upon the saints and Beatrice bids him rejoice in their number; and then directs his sight to one of the few places yet vacant. It is appointed for the emperor Henry who shall strive to set Italy straight, but shall be thwarted by the blinding greed of the Italians and the hypocrisy of Pope Clement, whose fearful fate Beatrice proclaims.

PERCHANCE six thousand miles away from us blazeth the noon, and this world already slopeth its shadow as to a level couch,

when the midst of heaven deep above us, beginneth to grow such that here and there a star loseth power to shine down to this floor;

and as the brightest handmaid of the Sun advanceth, so doth the heaven close up sight after sight even till the most fair.

Not otherwise the triumph which ever sporteth round

the point which vanquished me, seeming embraced by that which it embraceth,

little by little quenched itself from my sight; wherefore my seeing nought, and love, constrained me to turn with mine eyes to Beatrice.

If that which up till here is said of her were all compressed into one act of praise 'twould be too slight to serve this present turn.

The beauty I beheld transcendeth measure, not only past our reach, but surely I believe that only he who made it enjoyeth it complete.

At this pass I yield me vanquished more than e'er yet was overborne by his theme's thrust comic or tragic poet.

For as the Sun in sight that most trembleth, so the remembrance of the sweet smile sheareth my memory of its very self.

From the first day when in this life I saw her face, until this sight, my song hath ne'er been cut off from the track;

but now needs must my tracking cease from following her beauty further forth in poesy, as at his utmost reach must every artist.

Such as I leave her for a mightier proclamation than of my trumpet, which draweth its arduous subject to a close,

with alert leader's voice and gesture, did she again begin: "We have issued forth from the greatest body into the heaven which is pure light,

light intellectual full-charged with love, love of true good full-charged with gladness, gladness which transcendeth every sweetness.

Here shalt thou see the one and the other soldiery of Paradise,[1] and the one in those aspects which thou shalt see at the last judgment."

As a sudden flash of lightning which so shattereth the visual spirits as to rob the eye of power to realize e'en strongest objects;

so there shone around me a living light, leaving me swathed in such a web of its glow that naught appeared to me.

"Ever doth the love which stilleth heaven, receive into

itself with such like salutation, duly to fit the taper for its flame."

So soon as these brief words came into me I felt me to surmount my proper power;

and kindled me with such new-given sight that there is no such brightness unalloyed that mine eyes might not hold their own with it.

And I saw a light, in river form, glow tawny betwixt banks painted with marvellous spring.

From out this river issued living sparks, and dropped on every side into the blossoms, like rubies set in gold.

Then as inebriated with the odours they plunged themselves again into the marvellous swirl, and as one entered issued forth another.

"The lofty wish that now doth burn and press thee to have more knowledge of the things thou seest, pleaseth me more the more it swelleth.

But of this water needs thou first must drink, ere so great thirst in thee be slaked." So spoke mine eyes' sun unto me;

then added: "The river and the topaz-gems that enter and go forth, and the smiling of the grasses are the shadowy prefaces of their reality.

Not that such things are harsh as in themselves; but on thy side is the defect, in that thy sight not yet exalteth it so high."[2]

Never doth child so sudden rush with face turned to the milk, if he awake far later than his wont,

as then did I, to make yet better mirrors of mine eyes, down bending to the wave which floweth that we may better us.

And no sooner drank of it mine eye-lids' rim than into roundness seemed to change its length.

Then—as folk under masks seem other than before, if they do off the semblance not their own wherein they hid them,—

so changed before me into ampler joyance the flowers and the sparks, so that I saw both the two courts of heaven manifested.

O splendour[3] of God whereby I saw the lofty triumph

of the truthful realm, give me the power to tell how I beheld it.

A light there is up yonder which maketh the Creator visible unto the creature, who only in beholding him hath its own peace;

and it so far outstretcheth circle-wise that its circumference would be too loose a girdle for the sun.

All its appearance is composed of rays reflected from the top of the First Moved, which draweth thence its life and potency.

And as a hill-side reflect itself in water at its foot, as if to look upon its own adornment when it is rich in grasses and in flowers,

so, mounting o'er the light, around, around, casting reflection in more than thousand ranks I saw all that of us hath won return up yonder.[4]

And if the lowest step gathereth so large a light within itself, what then the amplitude of the rose's outmost petals?

My sight in the breath and height lost itself not, but grasped the scope and nature of that joyance.

Near and far addeth not nor subtracteth there, for where God governeth without medium the law of nature hath no relevance.[5]

Within the yellow of the eternal rose, which doth expand, rank upon rank, and reeketh perfume of praise unto the Sun that maketh spring for ever,

me—as who doth hold his peace yet fain would speak—Beatrice drew, and said: "Behold how great the white-robed concourse!

See how large our city sweepeth! See our thrones so filled that but few folk are now awaited there.

On that great seat where thou dost fix thine eyes, for the crown's sake already placed above it, ere at this wedding feast thyself do sup,

shall sit the soul (on earth 't will be imperial), of the lofty Henry[6] who shall come to straighten Italy ere she be ready for it.

The blind greed which bewitcheth you hath made you like the little child who dieth of hunger and chaseth off his nurse;

and he who then presideth in the court of things divine shall be such an one as, openly and covertly, shall not tread the same path with him.[7]

But short space thereafter shall he be endured[8] of God in the sacred office; for he shall be thrust down where Simon Magus is for his desert, and lower down shall force him of Anagna."[9]

1. The redeemed and the Angels. The former as though reclad with the body.

2. Cf. Canto xxxiii, and *Argument. Harsh*, literally unmellowed, and therefore "repellent to the senses"; here "repellent to the mind"; not to be assimilated by it without jar.

3. Bearing in mind Dante's careful use of the word *splendour* (*cf.* Canto xxix, *note* 2), and following the descriptions of this canto closely, we may conclude that the perpetual reflection of the light of God cast back from the *primum mobile* upon the eyes of the saints, ministers to their perpetual power of looking direct into the light itself. Nearly the same phrase is used in Canto xiv for internal light, or power of vision.

4. All the redeemed that had regained their native heaven.

5. It had been maintained by Democritus, but was denied by Aristotle, that were it not for the medium, even the smallest things could be seen at any distance whatsoever. This is one of the many instances in which Dante gives a spiritual turn to the physical speculations of the Greeks.

6. See Gardner i, and the account of Henry's expedition in Villani.

7. The translation should be taken as meaning that Clement, while outwardly favouring Henry, would secretly oppose him; which agrees with Canto xvii, and is a not inaccurate description of Clement's conduct. *Cf. Epist.* v. § 10. But the Italian, like the translation, will also bear the meaning "who will work against him (Henry) openly and covertly," and this interpretation is preferred by many scholars, perhaps as bringing a more concrete charge against Clement, and so leading up better to the *thereafter* of the next stanza.

8. Henry died in August, 1313, Clement in April, 1314.

9. *Cf. Inf.* xix.

ÇANTO XXXI

The redeemed are seen, rank above rank, as the petals of the divine rose; and the angels flying between them and God minister peace and ardour to them, for passion is here peaceful and peace passionate. Nor does this angelic multitude intercept the piercing light of God nor the piercing sight of the redeemed. The realm, whose joy no longer needs the stimulus supplied by the fear of losing it or the effort to retain it, centres its look and love on the triune God. Oh! that he would look down on the storm-tossed earth; from the most evil quarter of which Dante coming to that region is smitten dumb by the contrast. Mutely gazing, as the pilgrim at the shrine of his pilgrimage, thinking to tell again what he has seen, Dante after a time turns to question Beatrice, but finds her gone. Bernard, the type of contemplation, or immediate vision, has come at Beatrice's request, to bring Dante to the goal of his desire, by directing his eyes to that actual vision of divine things in their true forms for which her patient instructions have prepared him. And he first directs his sight to Beatrice herself in her place of glory. To her he pours out his gratitude, while imploring her further protection and praying that he may live and die worthy of her love; whereon she smiles upon him and then turns to God in whom alone is true and abiding union of human souls. Dante now learns who his guide is and gazes with awe-struck wonder on the features of the saint who had seen God while yet on earth; then, at his prompting, he looks above and sees the glory of Mary like the glory of the dawn, flaming amongst countless angels—each one having his own specific beauty of light and gesture—and gladdening all the saints.

IN FORM, then, of a white rose displayed itself to me that sacred soldiery which in his blood Christ made his spouse;

but the other, which as it flieth seeth and doth sing his glory who enamoureth it, and the excellence which hath made it what it is,

like to a swarm of bees which doth one while plunge into

the flowers and another while wend back to where its toil is turned to sweetness,

ever descended into the great flower adorned with so many leaves, and reascended thence to where its love doth ceaseless make sojourn.

They had their faces all of living flame, and wings of gold, and the rest so white that never snow reacheth such limit.

When they descended into the flower, from rank to rank they proffered of the peace and of the ardour[1] which they acquired as they fanned their sides,

nor did the interposing of so great a flying multitude, betwixt the flower and that which was above, impede the vision nor the splendour;

for the divine light so penetrateth through the universe, in measure of its worthiness, that nought hath power to oppose it.

This realm, secure and gladsome,[2] thronged with ancient folk and new, had look and love all turned unto one mark.

O threefold light, which in a single star, glinting upon their sight doth so content them, look down upon our storm!

If the Barbarians coming from such region as every day is spanned by Helice,[3] wheeling with her son towards whom she yearneth,[4]

on seeing Rome and her mighty works—what time the Lateran transcended mortal things—were stupefied;[5]

what then of me, who to the divine from the human, to the eternal from time had passed, and from Florence to a people just and sane,

with what stupor must I needs be filled! verily, what with it and what with joy, my will was to hear nought and to be dumb myself.

As the pilgrim who doth draw fresh life in the temple of his vow as he gazeth, and already hopeth to tell again how it be placed,

so, traversing the living light, I led mine eyes along the ranks, now up, now down, and now round circling.

I saw countenances suasive of love, adorned by another's

light and their own smile, and gestures graced with every dignity.

The general form of Paradise my glance had already taken in, in its entirety, and on no part as yet had my sight paused;

and I turned me with rekindled will to question my Lady concerning things whereanent my mind was in suspense.

One thing I purposed, and another answered me; I thought to see Beatrice, and I saw an elder clad like the folk in glory.

His eyes and cheeks were overpoured with benign gladness, in kindly gesture as befits a tender father.

And: "Where is she?" all sudden I exclaimed; whereunto he: "To bring thy desire to its goal Beatrice moved me from my place;[6]

and if thou look up to the circle third from the highest rank, thou shalt re-behold her, on the throne her merits have assigned to her."

Without answering I lifted up mine eyes and saw her, making to herself a crown as she reflected from her the eternal rays.

From that region which thundereth most high, no mortal eye is so far distant, though plunged most deep within the sea,

as there from Beatrice was my sight; but that wrought not upon me, for her image descended not to me mingled with any medium.[7]

"O Lady, in whom my hope hath vigour, and who for my salvation didst endure to leave in Hell thy footprints;

of all the things which I have seen I recognize the grace and might, by thy power and by thine excellence.

Thou hast drawn me from a slave to liberty by all those paths, by all those methods by which thou hadst the power so to do.

Preserve thy munificence[8] in me, so that my soul which thou hast made sound, may unloose it from the body, pleasing unto thee.

So did I pray; and she, so distant as she seemed, smiled and looked on me, then turned her to the eternal fountain.

And the holy elder said: "That thou mayest consummate thy journey perfectly—whereto prayer and holy love dispatched me,—

fly with thine eyes throughout this garden; for gazing on it will equip thy glance better to mount through the divine ray.

And the Queen of heaven for whom I am all burning with love, will grant us every grace, because I am her faithful Bernard."[9]

As is he who perchance from Croatia cometh to look on our Veronica[10] and because of ancient fame is sated not,

but saith in thought, so long as it be shown; "My Lord Jesus Christ, true God, and was this, then, the fashion of thy semblance?"

such was I, gazing upon the living love of him who in this world by contemplation tasted of that peace.[11]

"Son of grace! this joyous being," he began, "will not become known to thee by holding thine eyes only here down at the base;

but look upon the circles even to the remotest, until thou seest enthroned the Queen to whom this realm is subject and devoted."

I lifted up mine eyes, and as at morn the oriental regions of the horizon overcome that where the sun declineth,

so, as from the valley rising to the mountain; with mine eyes I saw a region at the boundary surpass all the remaining ridge in light.

And as with us that place where we await the chariot pole that Phaëton guided ill,[12] is most aglow, and on this side and on that the light is shorn away;

so was that pacific oriflamme[13] quickened in the midst, on either side in equal measure tempering its flame.

And at that mid point, with out-stretched wings, I saw more than a thousand Angels making festival, each one distinct in glow and art.[14]

I saw there, smiling to their sports and to their songs, a beauty which was gladness in the eyes of all the other saints.

And had I equal wealth in speech as in conception, yet

dared I not attempt the smallest part of her delightsomeness.

Bernard, when he saw mine eyes fixed and eager towards the glowing source of his own glow, turned his eyes to her, with so much love that he made mine more ardent to regaze.

1. *Peace and ardour.* The collocation is significant. (See *Argument.*)
2. *Secure and gladsome.* (See *Argument,* and *cf.* Canto xxvii.)
3. Helice was turned into a bear by Juno's jealousy, and then transformed by Jupiter to the heavens, as the constellation of the Great Bear; her son (Orcas) being changed into Boötes.
4. The brightest star in Boötes is Arcturus, to which the bow of the bear's tail points. If we are to take Dante as describing the region over which Arcturus never sets, we should have to go as far north as 70° latitude, but his notions of northern geography may have been vague; he means to indicate barbarians coming from the far north.
5. Obviously the Lateran stands for Rome—the part for the whole, but many commentators seek for a special significance in the selection of this particular palace to represent the whole city. The ambiguity of *transcended mortal things* and the natural association of the Lateran (which in Dante's time was the Papal palace) with the Church, have led some scholars to explain the passage as a reference to pilgrims from the far north coming to Rome in the days when the Church minded spiritual things. But this is obviously a mistake. The Lateran was (and is) currently believed to have been an imperial palace from the days of Nero until Constantine presented it to Pope Sylvester; and the passage doubtless refers to the amazement felt by the rude barbarians at the stupendous edifices of Rome, at the period "when the imperial seat surpassed in magnificence all the works of man."
6. This and the following nine stanzas. "Blessed is he who loves thee and his friend in thee, and his enemy for thy sake; for he alone never loses any dear one to whom all are dear in him who is never lost" (Augustine). True union consists not in an exclusively appropriating possession of the dear one, but in the divine fruition of the union. *Cf.* Canto xxxiii; also *Purg.* xix. For the rest, note how Beatrice's human personality drops its allegorical veil and shines in its simple purity in this closing scene.
7. *Cf.* Canto xxx.
8. *Magnificence* in medieval writings is often to be interpreted by the use of *magnificentia* in the Latin Aristotle. It is the translation of μεγαλοπρέπεια which means *munificence, i.e.,* liberality or generosity, but on a grand scale. A man may be liberal with small means, but not munificent. See the table in Wallace, 40, where *vulgarity* is to be taken as *vulgar ostentation.*
9. Bernard's devotion to the Virgin Mary is expressed in his four

594

homilies, *"De laudibus Virginis matris,"* and his nine sermons for the feasts of her *Purification, Assumption, Nativity*, etc., as well as incidentally in other works. It is noteworthy that he opposed the celebration of her Immaculate Conception. His contemporary, Peter Cellensis, says of him: "He was the most intimate fosterling of Our Lady, to whom he dedicated not only one monastery, but the monasteries of the whole Cistercian order."

10. St. Veronica lent her kerchief to Christ to wipe his brow as he was bearing the cross, and when he returned it, it bore the impress of his features. It was exhibited at Rome annually at the New Year and at Easter. *Cf. Vita Nuova*, xli.

11. St. Bernard was the type of contemplation, and the question was even raised whether he had not seen God "essentially" (*per essentiam*) while yet living.

12. The point at which the sun is about to rise.

13. The Oriflamme (*aurea flamma*) was the standard given by the Angel Gabriel to the ancient kings of France, representing a flame on a golden ground. No one who fought under it could be conquered. The golden glow of heaven is the invincible ensign not of war but peace.

14. According to medieval angelology, each angel constituted in itself a distinct species. (*Cf.* Canto xxix.)

ÇANTO XXXII

Beginning with Mary, Bernard indicates to Dante the great distinctions of heaven. Cleaving the rose downwards into two halves run the lines that part those who looked forward to Christ about to come from those who looked back upon him after he had come. Mary who had faith in Christ before he was conceived ranks as a Hebrew, and John Baptist who, when still in the womb, greeted him and afterwards proclaimed him as already come, ranks as a Christian. The two aspects of the faith embrace equal numbers of saints, the one tale being already full and the other near upon it. Midway across the cleaving lines runs the circle that divides the infants who died ere they had exercised free choice, and who were saved by the faith and the due observances of their parents, from those whose own acts of faith or merit have contributed to their salvation. The children are ranked in accordance with the abysmal but just and orderly judgments of God in the assignment of primal endowment. Dante then gazes in transport upon the face of Mary and sees the rejoicing Gabriel exult before her. He looks upon other great denizens of heaven, and is then bidden to turn again in prayer to Mary that after this so great preparation he may receive from her the final grace to enable him to lift his eyes right upon the Primal Love.

WITH HIS LOVE fixed on his Delight, that contemplating saint took the free office of the teacher on him, and began these sacred words:

"The wound which Mary closed and anointed, she who is so beauteous at her feet opened and thrust.

In the order which the third rank maketh sitteth below her, Rachael with Beatrice, even as thou seest.

Sarah, Rebecca, Judith, and her from whom, third in descent, the singer came who for grief at his sin cried out *have pity on me!*

these mayst thou see from rank to rank descending;[1] even as I, naming their proper names, go down the rose petal by petal.[2]

And down from the seventh onward, even as thereto,
follow Hebrew dames, disparting all the flower's locks;

because, accordant with the way faith looked to Christ,
these are the partition-wall whereat the sacred steps are
parted.

On this side, wherein the flower is mature in all its petals,
are seated who believe in Christ to come.

On the other side, where they are broke by empty seats,
abide in semi-circles such as had their sight turned to-
wards Christ come.

And as on the one side the glorious seat of the Lady of
heaven and the other seats below it make so great partition,

so, over against her, doth the seat of that great John who
ever holy endured the desert and the martyr death and
thereafter Hell for two years' space;[3]

and beneath him the making of such severance hath been
assigned to Francis, Benedict and Augustine, and others
down to here from circle unto circle.

Now marvel at the deep divine provision; for either as-
pect of the faith, in equal measure shall fill full this garden.

And know that, downward from the rank which in mid
line cleaveth the two divisions, in virtue of no merit of
their own they have their seats,

but by another's, under fixed conditions; for these are
spirits all released ere they had exercised true choice.

Well mayst thou perceive it by their faces, and also their
child voices if thou look aright and if thou listen.

Now thou art perplexed, and in perplexity thou keepest
silence; but I will loose the hard knot for thee wherein thy
subtle thoughts are binding thee.

Within this kingdom's amplitude no chance point may
have place, no more than sadness may nor thirst, nor
hunger;

because established by eternal law is whatsoe'er thou
seest, so that the correspondence is exact between the ring
and finger.[4]

Wherefore this swift-sped folk to the true life is here,
not without cause, more or less excellent in mutual order.

The King through whom this realm resteth in so great

love and in so great delight that never will hath daring for aught more,

as he createth all minds in his own glad sight, doth at his pleasure with grace endow them diversely; and here let the effect suffice.[5]

And this, express and clear, is noted unto you in Holy Writ, anent those twins whose wrath was stirred within their mother's womb.[6]

Wherefore accordant to the colour of the locks[7] of such grace, needs must the lofty light enchaplet them after their worth.

Wherefore, without reward for their own ways, they are placed in different ranks, differing only in their primal keenness.[8]

Thus, in the new-born ages the parents' faith alone sufficed, with innocence, to secure salvation;

when the first ages were complete male children behoved to gather power to their innocent wings by circumcision.

But when the time of grace had come, then without perfect baptism of Christ such innocence was held back there below.[9]

Look now upon the face which is most likened unto Christ; for its brightness, and no other, hath power to fit thee to see Christ."

I saw rain down upon that face such joyance (borne on the sacred minds created for flying through that lofty region),

that all which I had seen before held me not in suspense of so great marvelling, nor showed me so great semblance of God.

And that Love which first descended to her, singing: *Hail, Mary, full of grace* now spread his wings before her.

The divine canticle was answered from every side by the blest Court, so that every face thereby gathered serenity.

"O holy Father, who for my sake acceptest being here below, leaving the sweet place wherein thou sittest by eternal lot,

what is that angel who with such delight looketh our Queen in the eyes, enamoured so he seemeth all aflame?"

So did I turn again unto his teaching who drew beauty from Mary, as from the sun the morning star.

And he to me, "Exultancy and winsomeness as much as there may be in angel or in soul, is all in him; and we would have it so,

for he it is who brought down the palm to Mary, when the Son of God willed to load him with our burden.

But come now with thine eyes even as I shall traverse in discourse, and note the great patricians of this most just and pious empire.

Those two who sit up there, most blest by being nearest to the Empress, are as two roots of this our rose.

He who neighboureth her upon the left is that Father because of whose audacious tasting the human race tasteth such bitterness.

On the right, look upon that ancient Father of Holy Church to whom Christ commended the keys of this lovesome flower.

And he who, ere he died, saw all the grievous seasons of that fair spouse who with the lance and with the nails was won,[10]

sitteth by his side; and by the other resteth that leader under whom was fed by manna the folk ungrateful, fickle and mutinous.

Over against Peter see Anna sit, so satisfied to gaze upon her daughter that she removeth not her eyes to sing Hosanna.

And o'er against the greatest of housefathers sitteth Lucy who moved thy Lady when thou wert stooping down thy brows to thy destruction.[11]

But since the time that doth entrance thee fleeth, here let us make a stop, like to the careful tailor who to the cloth he hath cutteth the garment;

and let us turn our eyes to the Primal Love, so that gazing toward him thou mayst pierce as far as may be into his shining.

But—lest perchance thou backward fall as thou dost ply thy wings, thinking to forward thee,—by prayer behoveth grace to be acquired,

grace from her who hath power to aid thee; and do thou

follow me with such affection that from my words thy heart be severed not." And he began this holy prayer.

1. See *Ruth* iv. 21, 22. "Boaz [the husband of Ruth] begat Obed, and Obed begat Jesse, and Jesse begat David." *Cf.*, further, *Psalm* li (Vulgate l) and its inscription.

2. Compare the diagram in illustration of the Rose of Paradise in Gardner.

3. The two years that elapsed between his martyrdom and the descent of Christ to Limbo. *Cf. Inf.* iv.

4. *Ring and finger* = the thing fitting and the thing to be fitted; here the grace that is given and the grace that would be appropriate.

5. *Cf. Purg.* iii.

6. See *Genesis* xxv. 22, 23; and *cf.* Canto viii.

7. *The colour of the locks* seems to mean nothing more than the complexion, tone, or quality of grace.

8. *keenness* of vision, *i.e.*, power to See God.

9. It is noteworthy that Bernard himself, in a treatise addressed to Hugo of St. Victor, shrinks from this appalling conclusion. "We must suppose that the ancient sacraments were efficacious as long as it can be shown that they were not notoriously prohibited. And after that? It is in God's hands. Not mine be it to set the limit!"

10. John the Evangelist. The allusion is not to his long life, but to the vision recorded in the *Apocalypse*, regarded as a prophecy of the future sufferings of the Church.

11. See *Inf.* ii.

To Canto XXVII

To Canto XXII

CANTO XXXIII

The final goal of divine Providence, the mysteries of the incarnation and the redemption, the contrast between earthly hope and heavenly fruition, the whole order of the spiritual universe epitomized in the Poet's journey, the crowning grace still awaiting him, the need of yet further purging away of mortal dross if he is to receive it, the high obligation that will rest upon his life hereafter, the sustaining grace that will be needed to enable him to meet it by keeping his affections true to so great a vision, and the intense sympathy with which all the saints enter into his aspiration and plead for the fulfilment of the utmost grace to him as a part of their own bliss,—all this, with the praises of the Virgin, etherialized into the very perfume of devotion, rises in Bernard's prayer to Mary. Mary answers the prayer by looking into the light of God, thereby to gain Bernard's petition for Dante; and Dante, anticipating Bernard's permission, with the passion of his longing already assuaged by the peace of now assured fruition, looks right into the deep light. Memory cannot hold the experience that then was his, though it retains the sweetness that was born of it. But as he gropes for the recovery of some fragment of his vision, he feels in the throb of an ampler joy the assurance that he is touching on the truth as he records his belief that he saw the whole essence of the universe, all beings and all their attributes and all their relations, no longer as scattered and imperfect fragments, but as one perfect whole, and that whole naught else than one single flame of love. So keen is the light of that flame that it would shrivel up the sight if it should turn aside. But that may not be, since good, which is the object of all volition, is whole and perfect in it, and only fragmentary and imperfect away from it, so that a free will cannot by its nature turn away; and the sight is ever strengthened that turns right into it. As when we look upon a picture or a script, glorious but at first imperfectly mastered by us, and as our eyes slowly adjust themselves, the details rise and assert themselves and take their places, and all the while that the impression changes and deepens the thing that we look upon changes not nor even seems to change, but only we to see it clearer, so Dante's kindling vision reads deeper and deeper into the unchanging glory of the triune Deity, till his mind fastens itself upon the contemplation of the union (in the second Person) of the circle of Deity and the featured countenance of humanity—the unconditioned self-completeness of God that reverent thought asserts and the character and features which the heart demands and which its experience proclaims,—but his powers fail to grapple with the contradiction till the reconciliation is brought home to him in a flash of exalted insight. Then the vision passes away and may not be recalled, but already all jarring protest and opposition to the divine order has given way in the seer's heart to oneness of wish and will with God, who himself is love.

"VIRGIN MOTHER, daughter of thy son, lowly and uplifted more than any creature, fixed goal of the eternal counsel,

thou art she who didst human nature so ennoble that its own Maker scorned not to become its making.[1]

In thy womb was lit again the love under whose warmth in the eternal peace this flower hath thus unfolded.

Here art thou unto us the meridian torch of love and there below with mortals art a living spring of hope.

Lady, thou art so great and hast such worth, that if there be who would have grace yet betaketh not himself to thee, his longing seeketh to fly without wings.

Thy kindliness not only succoureth whoso requesteth, but doth oftentimes freely forerun request.

In thee is tenderness, in thee is pity, in thee munificence,[2] in thee united whatever in created being is of excellence.

Now he who from the deepest pool of the universe even to here hath seen the spirit lives one after one

imploreth thee, of grace, for so much power as to be able to uplift his eyes more high towards final bliss;

and I, who never burned for my own vision more than I do for his, proffer thee all my prayers and pray they be not scant

that thou do scatter for him every cloud of his mortality with prayers of thine, so that the joy supreme may be unfolded to him.

And further do I pray thee, Queen who canst all that

thou wilt, that thou keep sound for him, after so great a vision, his affections.

Let thy protection vanquish human ferments; see Beatrice, with how many Saints, for my prayers folding hands."

Those eyes, of God beloved and venerated, fixed upon him who prayed, showed us how greatly devout prayers please her.

Then to the eternal light they bent themselves, wherein we may not ween that any creature's eye findeth its way so clear.[3]

And I, who to the goal of all my longings was drawing nigh, even as was meet the ardour of the yearning quenched within me.

Bernard gave me the sign and smiled to me that I should look on high, but I already of myself was such as he would have me;[4]

because my sight, becoming purged, now more and more was entering through the ray of the deep light which in itself is true.

Thence forward was my vision mightier than our discourse, which faileth at such sight, and faileth memory at so great outrage.

As is he who dreaming seeth, and when the dream is gone the passion stamped remaineth, and nought else cometh to the mind again;

even such am I; for almost wholly faileth me my vision, yet doth the sweetness that was born of it still drop within my heart.

So doth the snow unstamp it to the sun, so to the wind on the light leaves was lost the Sybil's wisdom.

O light supreme who so far dost uplift thee o'er mortal thoughts, re-lend unto my mind a little of what then thou didst seem,

and give my tongue such power that it may leave only a single sparkle of thy glory unto the folk to come;

for by returning to my memory somewhat, and by a little sounding in these verses, more of thy victory will be conceived.

I hold that by the keenness of the living ray which I endured I had been lost, had mine eyes turned aside from it.

And so I was the bolder, as I mind me, so long to sustain it as to unite my glance with the Worth infinite.

O grace abounding, wherein I presumed to fix my look on the eternal light so long that I consumed my sight thereon!

Within its depths I saw ingathered, bound by love in one volume, the scattered leaves of all the universe;

substance and accidents and their relations,[6] as though together fused, after such fashion that what I tell of is one simple flame.

The universal form of this complex[7] I think that I beheld, because more largely, as I say this, I feel that I rejoice.

A single moment maketh a deeper lethargy for me than twenty and five centuries have wrought on the emprise that erst threw Neptune in amaze at Argo's shadow.[8]

Thus all suspended did my mind gaze fixed, immovable, intent, ever enkindled by its gazing.

Such at that light doth man become that to turn thence to any other sight could not by possibility be ever yielded.

For the good, which is the object of the will, is therein wholly gathered, and outside it that same thing is defective which therein is perfect.

Now shall my speech fall farther short even of what I can remember than an infant's who still bathes his tongue at breast.

Not that more than a single semblance was in the living light whereon I looked, which ever is such as it was before;

but by the sight that gathered strength in me one sole appearance even as I changed worked on my gaze.

In the profound and shining being of the deep light appeared to me three circles, of three colours and one magnitude;

one by the second as Iris by Iris seemed reflected, and the third seemed a fire breathed equally from one and from the other.[9]

Oh but how scant the utterance, and how faint, to my conceit! and it, to what I saw, is such that it sufficeth not to call it little.

O Light eternal who only in thyself abidest, only thyself

dost understand, and to thyself, self-understood self-understanding, turnest love and smiling!

That circling which appeared in thee to be conceived as a reflected light, by mine eyes scanned some little,

in itself, of its own colour, seemed to be painted with our effigy, and thereat my sight was all committed to it.

As the geometer who all sets himself to measure the circle and who findeth not, think as he may, the principle he lacketh;[10]

such was I at this new-seen spectacle; I would perceive how the image consorteth with the circle, and how it settleth there;

but not for this were my proper wings, save that my mind was smitten by a flash wherein its will came to it.

To the high fantasy here power failed; but already my desire and will were rolled—even as a wheel that moveth equally—by the Love that moves the sun and the other stars.[11]

1. The Son, when he became man, was *made* in the Virgin's womb, and so by human nature.
2. *Cf.* Canto xxxi, *note* 8.
3. *Cf.* Canto iv.
4. This furnishes one of several consistent indications that in Paradise one can see that at which he is not looking. This is one of the subtle ways in which Dante indicates that all spatial and temporal terms in Paradise are merely symbolical.
5. The Cumæan Sybil wrote her oracles on leaves, which the wind then scattered in confusion. *Æneid*, iii and vi.
6. *Cf.* Canto iii, *note* 2.
7. This *knot* or *complex* = the universe.
8. When the vision broke, a single moment plunged the actual thing he saw into a deeper oblivion than five and twenty centuries had wrought over the voyage of the Argonauts. The memory of an intent gaze, of deeping vision, of absorbed volition, of a final flash of insight—the assured possession of a will and affections laid to rest by the sweetness of what came to him—the uncertain impression of the images and symbols amid which it came—all these remain: but the vision itself is utterly past recall. *Cf.* Canto i.
The Argo was the first ship,—a new thing to Neptune.
9. *Cf.* Cantos x and xii.
10. The problem loosely described as "squaring the circle" is stated by Dante with his usual accuracy. The radius and circumference of a circle being incommensurable, it is impossible to express the circumference in terms of the radius—as impossible as it is to ex-

press deity in terms of humanity. The radius being the unit, then, the circle cannot be exactly *measured*. There is no difficulty in constructing (by means of a cycloid) a square equal in area to a given circle. But *cf. Conv.* ii. 14.

11. "The whole work was undertaken, not for a speculative but for a practical end." And again: "the purpose of the whole [the *Comedy*] and of this portion [the *Paradiso*] is to remove those who are living in this life from the state of wretchedness, and to lead them to the state of blessedness." *Epist. ad Can. Grand.*, § 16 and 15.

What shall then give delight shall not be so much that our wants are put to rest nor that our bliss is gained, but that God's will shall be visibly fulfilled in us and concerning us; which also is what we implore day by day in prayer, when we say *Thy will be done, as in heaven, so on earth.*—BERNARD.

GENEALOGICAL
TABLES

Thick letters indicate names of kings, &c., in the valley (*Purgatorio VII and VIII*).

Capitals indicate those persons mentioned for illustration or contrast in connection with them.

Ordinary type indicates persons mentioned elsewhere by Dante, *except* in family or house tables.

Italics indicate persons not mentioned by Dante, *except* in family or house tables.

At many points these tables supplement, and are supplemented by, those on pages 621–634 of the Paradiso.

HOUSE OF ESTE

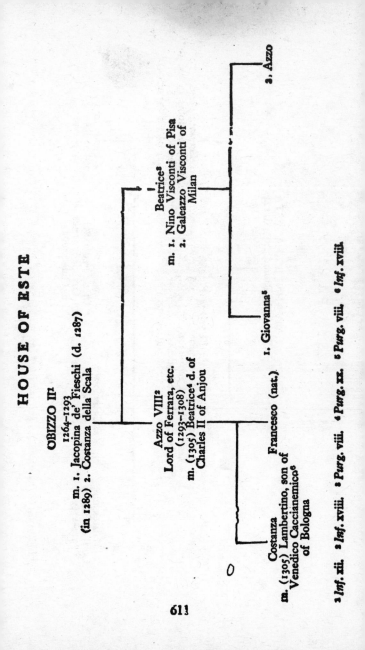

OBIZZO II[1]
1264–1293
m. 1. Jacopina de' Fieschi (d. 1287)
(in 1289) 2. Costanza della Scala

Azzo VIII[2]
Lord of Ferrara, etc.
(1293–1308)
m. (1305) Beatrice[4] d. of
Charles II of Anjou

Beatrice[3]
m. 1. Nino Visconti of Pisa
2. Galeazzo Visconti of
Milan

3, Azzo

1. Giovanna[5]

Francesco (nat.)

Costanza
m. (1305) Lambertino, son of
Venedico Caccianemico[6]
of Bologna

O

[1] Inf. xii.   [2] Inf. xviii.   [3] Purg. viii.   [4] Purg. xx.   [5] Purg. viii.   [6] Inf. xviii.

611

MALATESTA FAMILY

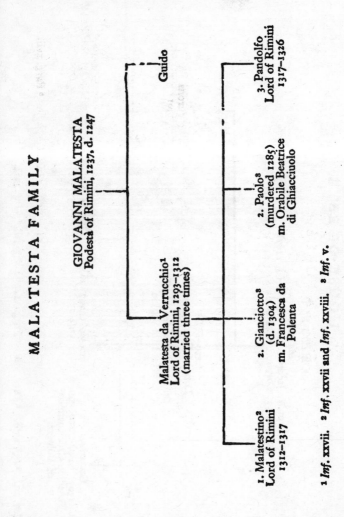

GIOVANNI MALATESTA
Podestà of Rimini, 1237, d. 1247

Guido

Malatesta da Verrucchio[1]
Lord of Rimini, 1293–1312
(married three times)

1. Malatestino[2]
Lord of Rimini
1312–1317

2. Gianciotto[3]
(d. 1304)
m. Francesca da
Polenta

2. Paolo[3]
(murdered 1285)
m. Orabile Beatrice
di Ghiacciuolo

3. Pandolfo
Lord of Rimini
1317–1326

[1] *Inf.* xxvii.   [2] *Inf.* xxvii and *Inf.* xxviii.   [3] *Inf.* v.

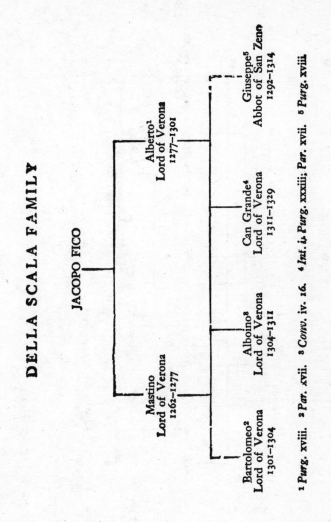

DELLA SCALA FAMILY

JACOPO FICO

Mastino
Lord of Verona
1262–1277

Alberto[1]
Lord of Verona
1277–1301

Bartolomeo[2]
Lord of Verona
1301–1304

Alboino[3]
Lord of Verona
1304–1311

Can Grande[4]
Lord of Verona
1311–1329

Giuseppe[5]
Abbot of San Zeno
1292–1314

[1] *Purg.* xviii. [2] *Par.* xvii. [3] *Conv.* iv. 16. [4] *Inf.* i.; *Purg.* xxxiii; *Par.* xvii. [5] *Purg.* xviii.

TABLE I

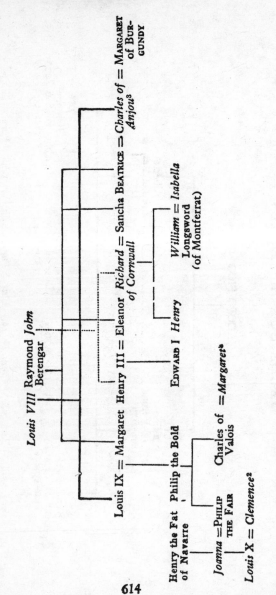

² See Table II. ³ See Table III.

TABLE II

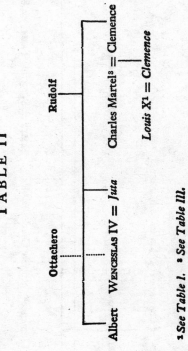

Ottachero ....

Rudolf

Albert   WENCESLAS IV = *Juta*   Charles Martel[3] = Clemence

Louis X[1] = *Clemence*

[1] *See Table 1.*   [3] *See Table III.*

TABLE III

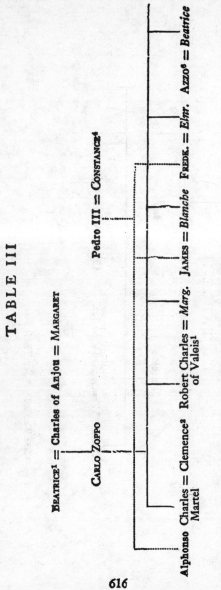

Beatrice[1] = Charles of Anjou = Margaret

Carlo Zoppo

Pedro III = Constance[4]

Alphonso   Charles = Clemence[2]   Robert   Charles = Marg.   James = Blanche   Fredk. = Elnr.   Azzo[6] = Beatrice
Martel   of Valeis[1]

[1] See Table I.   [2] See Table II.   [4] See Table IV.   [6] See Table VI.

616

TABLE IV

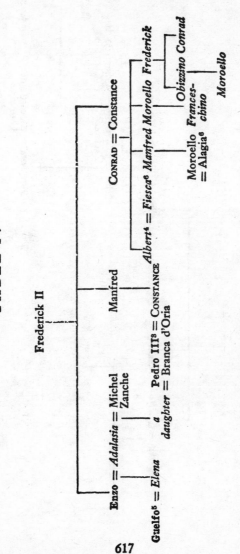

Frederick II

Enzo = *Adalasia* = Michel Zanche

a daughter = Branca d'Oria

Guelfo[5] = *Elena*

Manfred

Pedro III[3] = CONSTANCE

Albert[4] = *Fiesca*[6] *Manfred Moroello Frederick*

Moroello = *Alagia*[6]

Frances-chino

Obizzino Conrad

Moroello

CONRAD = Constance

617

See Table III. *See Table V.* *See Table VI.*

TABLE V

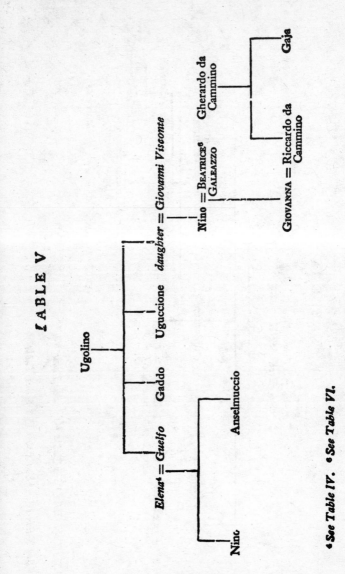

*See Table IV. *See Table VI.

TABLE VI

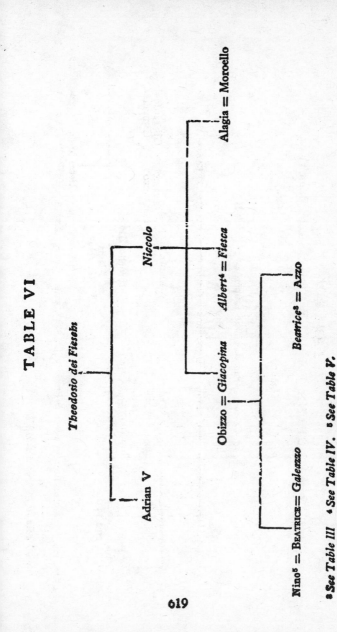

Theodosio dei Fieschi

Adrian V

Niccolo

Alagia = Moroello

Obizzo = Giacopina   Albert[4] = Fiesca

Beatrice[3] = Azzo

Nino[5] = BEATRICE = Galeazzo

[3] See Table III   [4] See Table IV.   [5] See Table V.

MALASPINA FAMILY ("Spino Secco" Branch)

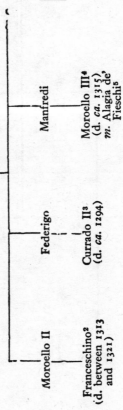

Currado I[1]
(d. *ca.* 1255)
m. Costanza, nat. d. of the Emperor Frederick II

Federigo

Manfredi

Moroello II

Franceschino[2]
(d. between 1313
and 1321)

Currado II[3]
(d. *ca.* 1294)

Moroello III[4]
(d. *ca.* 1315)
m. Alagia de'
Fieschi[5]

Alberto

[1] *Purg.* viii.   [2] Dante's host in 1306.   [3] *Purg.* viii.   [4] *Inf.* xxiv.   [5] *Purg.* xix.

Thick letters indicate persons mentioned in *Paradiso XIX*

TABLE I

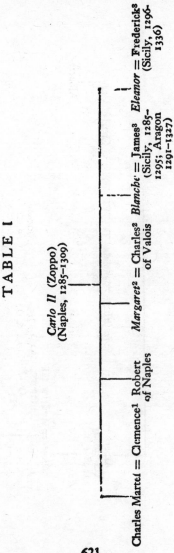

Charles Martel = Clemence[1]   Robert   *Margaret*[2] = Charles[2]   *Blanche*[1] *James*[3] *Eleanor* = **Frederick**[8]
                              of Naples   of Valois   (Sicily, 1285- (Sicily, 1296-
                                                                            1295; Aragon   1336)
        Carlo II (Zoppo)   1291-1327)
        (Naples, 1285-1309)

[1] *See Table II.* [2] *See Table III.* [8] *See Table IV.*

TABLE II

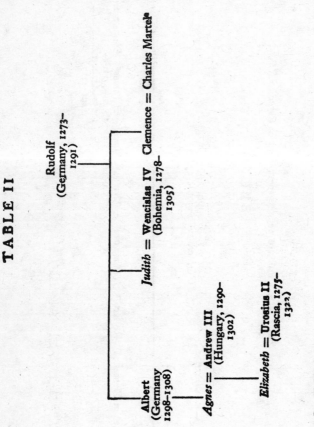

Rudolf
(Germany, 1273–1291)

Judith = Wenceslas IV
(Bohemia, 1278–1305)

Clemence = Charles Martel[1]

Albert
(Germany, 1298–1308)

Agnes = Andrew III
(Hungary, 1290–1302)

Elizabeth = Urosius II
(Rascia, 1275–1321)

[1] See Table I.

TABLE III

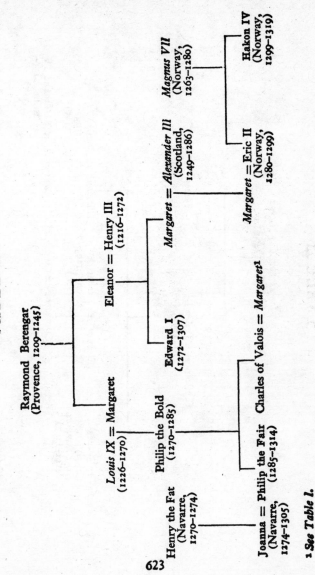

Raymond Berengar (Provence, 1209–1245)

Eleanor = Henry III (1216–1272)

Louis IX = Margaret (1226–1270)

Henry the Fat (Navarre, 1270–1274)

Philip the Bold (1270–1285)

Edward I (1272–1307)

Margaret = Alexander III (Scotland, 1249–1286)

Magnus VII (Norway, 1263–1280)

Joanna = Philip the Fair (Navarre, (1285–1314) 1274–1305)

Charles of Valois = Margaret[1]

Margaret = Eric II (Norway, 1280–1299)

Hakon IV (Norway, 1299–1319)

[1] See Table 1.

623

TABLE IV

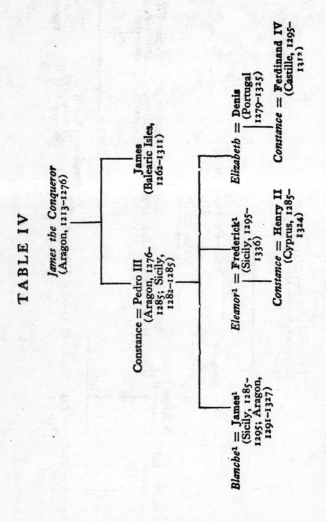

James the Conqueror
(Aragon, 1213–1276)

Constance = Pedro III
(Aragon, 1276–
1285; Sicily,
1282–1285)

James
(Balearic Isles,
1262–1311)

Blanche[1] = James[1]
(Sicily, 1285–
1295; Aragon,
1291–1327)

Eleanor[1] = Frederick[1]
(Sicily, 1295–
1336)

Elizabeth = Denis
(Portugal
1279–1325)

Constance = Henry II
(Cyprus, 1285–
1324)

Constance = Ferdinand IV
(Castille, 1295–
1312)

[1] See Table I.

624

DANTE'S DESCENT FROM CACCIAGUIDA.

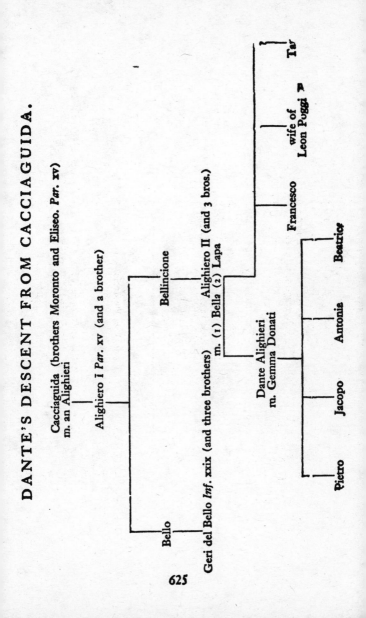